MW00804662

MORDENKAINEN PRESENTS
MONSTERS OF THE MULTIVERSE™

VANCE KELLY

CREDITS

Lead Designer: Jeremy Crawford
Art Directors: Emi Tanji, Kate Irwin

This book is a revision of content that originally appeared in the books *Volo's Guide to Monsters* (2016) and *Mordenkainen's Tome of Foes* (2018). It also includes revised options from *Princes of the Apocalypse* (2015), *Eberron: Rising from the Last War* (2019), and *Mythic Odysseys of Theros* (2020).

Original Design: Jeremy Crawford, Adam Lee, Mike Mearls, Christopher Perkins, Ben Petrisor, Sean K Reynolds, Robert J. Schwalb, Matt Sernett, Chris Sims, Nolan Whale, Steve Winter
Revision Design: Sydney Adams, Judy Bauer, Jeremy Crawford, Makenzie De Armas, Dan Dillon, Ari Levitch, Ben Petrisor, Taymoor Rehman
Editing: Judy Bauer, Michele Carter, Kim Mohan, Christopher Perkins

Graphic Designers: Trystan Falcone, Emi Tanji
Cover Illustrator: Grzegorz Rutkowski
Interior Illustrators: Dave Allsop, Tom Babbey, John-Paul Balmet, Thomas M. Baxa, Mark Behm, Eric Belisle, Michael Berube, Mike Bierek, Jared Blando, Zoltan Boros, Christopher Bradley, Alix Branwyn, Aleksi Briclot, IP Dmitry Burmak, Filip Burburan, Christopher Burdett, Sidharth Chaturvedi, Jedd Chevrier, Conceptopolis, Daarken, Nikki Dawes, Eric Deschamps, Simon Dominic, Dave Dorman, Nicholas Elias, Wayne England, Jason Felix, Justin Gerard, Justyna Gil, Lars Grant-West, Jon Hodgson, Ralph Horsley, Tyler Jacobson, Mike Jordana, Vance Kelly, Julian Kok, Michael Komarck, Daniel Landerman, Olly Lawson, Daniel Ljunggren, Valera Lutfullina, Warren Mahy, Lorenzo Mastroianni, Brynn Metheney, Aaron Miller, Francisco Miyara, Caio Monteiro, Scott Murphy, Marta Nael, Marco Nelor, Jim Nelson, Adam Paquette, PINDURSKI, Claudio Pozas, April Prime, Grzegorz Rutkowski, Marc Sasso, Chris Seaman, Ilya Shkipin, Rudy Siswanto, David Sladek, Craig J Spearing, Bryan Sola, Zack Stella, Sarah Stone, Philip Straub, Arnie Swekel, Thom Tenery, Cory Trego-Erdner, David A. Trampier, Beth Trott, Brian Valeza, Randy Vargas, Franz Vohwinkel, Anthony S. Waters, Campbell White, Richard Whitters, Eva Widermann, Sam Wood, Shawn Wood, Ben Wootten, Zuzanna Wuuyk, Min Yum

Project Engineer: Cynda Callaway
Imaging Technician: Kevin Yee
Prepress Specialist: Jefferson Dunlap

D&D STUDIO
Executive Producer: Ray Winninger
Principal Designers: Jeremy Crawford, Christopher Perkins
Design Manager: Steve Scott
Design Department: Sydney Adams, Judy Bauer, Makenzie De Armas, Dan Dillon, Amanda Hamon, Ari Levitch, Ben Petrisor, Taymoor Rehman, F. Wesley Schneider, James Wyatt
Senior Art Director: Richard Whitters
Art Department: Trystan Falcone, Kate Irwin, Emi Tanji, Shawn Wood, Trish Yochum
Senior Producer: Dan Tovar
Producers: Bill Benham, Robert Hawkey, Lea Heleotis
Director of Product Management: Liz Schuh
Product Managers: Natalie Egan, Chris Lindsay, Hilary Ross

MARKETING
Director of Global Brand Marketing: Brian Perry
Global Brand Manager: Shelly Mazzanoble
Senior Marketing Communications Manager: Greg Tito
Community Manager: Brandy Camel

ON THE COVER
The wizard Mordenkainen soars through the Astral Plane astride a ki-rin—unaware of the astral dreadnought slinking toward them—in this painting by Grzegorz Rutkowski.

620D0868000001 EN
ISBN: 978-0-7869-6787-2
First Printing: November 2021

9 8 7 6 5 4 3 2 1

Disclaimer: We asked the wizard Mordenkainen to write a humorous disclaimer for this book. We received this response: "The day I start writing frivolous disclaimers for game manuals is the day I retire from wizardry and abandon all self-respect." Mordenkainen's rival wizard Tasha apparently intercepted our request and sent us this note: "Mordenkainen lost his sense of humor somewhere between the City of Greyhawk and the Astral Plane. Keep your chins up, my dearest ones. The multiverse is filled with horrors, many of which are detailed in this book. Marshal your laughter and a few good spells. If we're going to be devoured, better to face the darkness with a smile."

Contents

USING THIS BOOK

The multiverse of DUNGEONS & DRAGONS brims with peril, and many of the greatest dangers are monsters. A companion to the *Monster Manual*, this book collects monsters from many different planes of existence, each creature ready to imperil D&D heroes of different levels. The book also includes game statistics for nonplayer characters, who may assist or oppose the heroes, and an array of fantastical races for players to consider for their characters.

The monsters and fantastical races in the following chapters are accompanied by the occasional comments of the mighty wizard Mordenkainen, one of the most learned mages of the D&D world of Greyhawk. The archmage Tasha, Mordenkainen's friendly rival, interjects as well.

All together, the monsters, nonplayer characters, and fantastical races herein provide a host of new friends and foes to populate your D&D worlds.

WHAT YOU'LL FIND WITHIN

Chapter 1, "Fantastical Races," presents over 30 race options for player characters, complementing the options in the *Player's Handbook* and other D&D books. These races debuted elsewhere and appear all together for the first time here, each of them revised to fit into the current state of the game.

Chapter 2, "Bestiary," contains over 250 monsters and NPCs, each one represented by a stat block and story text. When you're preparing to run an adventure as the DM, consider sprinkling these creatures into your games, mixing them with the monsters and NPCs from the *Monster Manual*. The creatures in this chapter fit seamlessly with the ones you use from other D&D books.

Appendix, "Monster Lists," makes it easy for you to find the right stat blocks for your adventures. This appendix lists the book's monsters and NPCs by creature type, challenge rating, and environment.

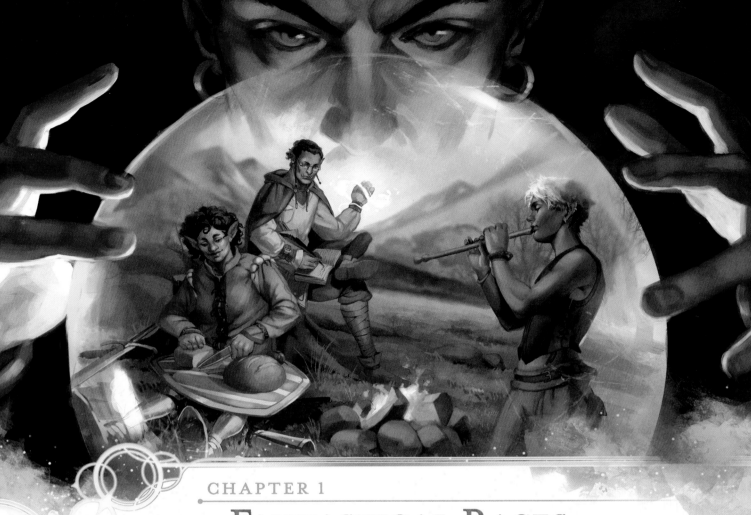

CHAPTER 1
FANTASTICAL RACES

GATHERING TOGETHER FANTASTICAL RACES from throughout the D&D multiverse, this chapter offers the following races for player characters, supplementing the race options in the *Player's Handbook*:

Aarakocra	Firbolg	Harengon	Shadar-kai
Aasimar	Genasi, Air	Hobgoblin	Shifter
Bugbear	Genasi, Earth	Kenku	Tabaxi
Centaur	Genasi, Fire	Kobold	Tortle
Changeling	Genasi, Water	Lizardfolk	Triton
Deep Gnome	Githyanki	Minotaur	Yuan-ti
Duergar	Githzerai	Orc	
Eladrin	Goblin	Satyr	
Fairy	Goliath	Sea Elf	

Many of these races are based on creatures that appear in the *Monster Manual* or the bestiary of this book. Consult with your DM to see whether an option here is appropriate for your campaign.

If you do use a race in this chapter, first read the "Creating Your Character" section below.

CREATING YOUR CHARACTER

At 1st level, you choose whether your character is a member of the human race or of a fantastical race. If you select a fantastical race in this chapter, follow these additional rules during character creation.

ABILITY SCORE INCREASES

When determining your character's ability scores, increase one score by 2 and increase a different score by 1, or increase three different scores by 1. Follow this rule regardless of the method you use to determine the scores, such as rolling or point buy. The "Quick Build" section for your character's class offers suggestions on which scores to increase. You can follow those suggestions or ignore them, but you can't raise any of your scores above 20.

LANGUAGES

Your character can speak, read, and write Common and one other language that you and your DM agree is appropriate for the character. The *Player's Handbook* offers a list of languages to choose from. The DM is free to modify that list for a campaign.

CREATURE TYPE

Every creature in D&D, including each player character, has a special tag in the rules that identifies the type of creature they are. Most player characters are of the Humanoid type. A race in this chapter tells you what your character's creature type is.

Here's a list of the game's creature types in alphabetical order: Aberration, Beast, Celestial, Construct, Dragon, Elemental, Fey, Fiend, Giant, Humanoid, Monstrosity, Ooze, Plant, Undead. These types don't have rules themselves, but some rules in the game affect creatures of certain types in different ways. For example, the *cure wounds* spell doesn't work on a Construct or an Undead.

LIFE SPAN

The typical life span of a player character in the D&D multiverse is about a century, assuming the character doesn't meet a violent end on an adventure. Members of some races, such as dwarves and elves, can live for centuries. If typical members of a race in this book can live longer than a century, that fact is mentioned in the race's description.

HEIGHT AND WEIGHT

Player characters, regardless of race, typically fall into the same ranges of height and weight that humans have in our world. If you'd like to determine your character's height or weight randomly, consult the Random Height and Weight table in the *Player's Handbook*, and choose the row in the table that best represents the build you imagine for your character.

AARAKOCRA

A winged people who originated on the Elemental Plane of Air, aarakocra soar through the sky wherever they wander. The first aarakocra served the Wind Dukes of Aaqa—mighty beings of air—and were imbued with a measure of their masters' power over winds. Their descendants still command echoes of that power.

From below, aarakocra look like large birds and thus are sometimes called birdfolk. Only when they roost on a branch or walk across the ground is their Humanoid nature clear. Standing upright, aarakocra are typically about 5 feet tall, and they have long, narrow legs that taper to sharp talons. Feathers cover their bodies—usually red, orange, yellow, brown, or gray. Their heads are also avian, often resembling those of parrots or eagles.

AARAKOCRA TRAITS

As an aarakocra, you have the following racial traits.

Creature Type. You are a Humanoid.

Size. Your size is Medium.

Speed. Your walking speed is 30 feet.

Flight. Because of your wings, you have a flying speed equal to your walking speed. You can't use this flying speed if you're wearing medium or heavy armor.

Talons. You have talons that you can use to make unarmed strikes. When you hit with them, the strike deals 1d6 + your Strength modifier slashing damage, instead of the bludgeoning damage normal for an unarmed strike.

Wind Caller. Starting at 3rd level, you can cast the *gust of wind* spell with this trait, without requiring a material component. Once you cast the spell with this trait, you can't do so again until you finish a long rest. You can also cast the spell using any spell slots you have of 2nd level or higher.

Intelligence, Wisdom, or Charisma is your spellcasting ability for it when you cast *gust of wind* with this trait (choose when you select this race).

Aasimar

Whether descended from a celestial being or infused with heavenly power, aasimar are mortals who carry a spark of the Upper Planes within their souls. They can fan that spark to bring light, ease wounds, and unleash the fury of the heavens.

Aasimar can arise among any population of mortals. They resemble their parents, but they live for up to 160 years and often have features that hint at their celestial heritage. These often begin subtle and become more obvious when the aasimar gains the ability to reveal their full celestial nature. The Aasimar Celestial Features table has examples you can choose or use as inspiration to create your own.

Aasimar Celestial Features

d6	Celestial Feature
1	A dusting of metallic, white, or charcoal freckles
2	Metallic, luminous, or dark eyes
3	Starkly colored hair
4	An unusual hue tinting your shadow
5	A ghostly halo crowning your head
6	Rainbows gleaming on your skin

Aasimar Traits

As an aasimar, you have the following racial traits.

Creature Type. You are a Humanoid.

Size. You are Medium or Small. You choose the size when you select this race.

Speed. Your walking speed is 30 feet.

Celestial Resistance. You have resistance to necrotic damage and radiant damage.

Darkvision. You can see in dim light within 60 feet of you as if it were bright light and in darkness as if it were dim light. You discern colors in that darkness only as shades of gray.

Healing Hands. As an action, you can touch a creature and roll a number of d4s equal to your proficiency bonus. The creature regains a number of hit points equal to the total rolled. Once you use this trait, you can't use it again until you finish a long rest.

Light Bearer. You know the *light* cantrip. Charisma is your spellcasting ability for it.

Celestial Revelation. When you reach 3rd level, choose one of the revelation options below. Thereafter, you can use a bonus action to unleash the celestial energy within yourself, gaining the benefits of that revelation. Your transformation lasts for 1 minute or until you end it as a bonus action. Once you transform using your revelation below, you can't use it again until you finish a long rest:

Necrotic Shroud. Your eyes briefly become pools of darkness, and ghostly, flightless wings sprout from your back temporarily. Creatures other than your allies within 10 feet of you that can see you must succeed on a Charisma saving throw (DC 8 + your proficiency bonus + your Charisma modifier) or become frightened of you until the end of your next turn. Until the transformation ends, once on each of your turns, you can deal extra necrotic damage to one target when you deal damage to it with an attack or a spell. The extra damage equals your proficiency bonus.

Radiant Consumption. Searing light temporarily radiates from your eyes and mouth. For the duration, you shed bright light in a 10-foot radius and dim light for an additional 10 feet, and at the end of each of your turns, each creature within 10 feet of you takes radiant damage equal to your proficiency bonus. Until the transformation ends, once on each of your turns, you can deal extra radiant damage to one target when you deal damage to it with an attack or a spell. The extra damage equals your proficiency bonus.

Radiant Soul. Two luminous, spectral wings sprout from your back temporarily. Until the transformation ends, you have a flying speed equal to your walking speed, and once on each of your turns, you can deal extra radiant damage to one target when you deal damage to it with an attack or a spell. The extra damage equals your proficiency bonus.

Bugbear

Neither bugs nor bears, bugbears are the hulking cousins of goblins and hobgoblins. With roots in the Feywild, early bugbears resided in hidden places, in hard-to-reach and shadowed spaces. Long ago and from out of the corner of your eye, they came to the Material Plane, urged to spread throughout the multiverse by the conquering god Maglubiyet. Centuries later, they still bear a fey gift for lurking just out of sight, and many of them have sneaked away from that god's influence.

They are long of limb and covered in coarse hair, with wedge-shaped ears and pointed teeth. Despite their formidable build, bugbears are quiet skulkers, thanks to a fey magic that allows them to hide in spaces seemingly too small for them.

Bugbear Traits

As a bugbear, you have the following racial traits.

Creature Type. You are a Humanoid. You are also considered a goblinoid for any prerequisite or effect that requires you to be a goblinoid.

Size. Your size is Medium.

Speed. Your walking speed is 30 feet.

Darkvision. You can see in dim light within 60 feet of you as if it were bright light and in darkness as if it were dim light. You discern colors in that darkness only as shades of gray.

Fey Ancestry. You have advantage on saving throws you make to avoid or end the charmed condition on yourself.

Long-Limbed. When you make a melee attack on your turn, your reach for it is 5 feet greater than normal.

Powerful Build. You count as one size larger when determining your carrying capacity and the weight you can push, drag, or lift.

Sneaky. You are proficient in the Stealth skill. In addition, without squeezing, you can move through and stop in a space large enough for a Small creature.

Surprise Attack. If you hit a creature with an attack roll, the creature takes an extra 2d6 damage if it hasn't taken a turn yet in the current combat.

FILIP BURBURAN

Centaur

Centaurs gallop throughout the multiverse and trace their origins to many different realms. The centaurs presented here hail from the Feywild and mystically resonate with the natural world. From the waist up, they resemble elves, displaying all the elf varieties of skin tone. From the waist down, they have the bodies of horses.

Centaur Traits

As a centaur, you have the following racial traits.

Creature Type. You are a Fey.

Size. Your size is Medium.

Speed. Your walking speed is 40 feet.

Charge. If you move at least 30 feet straight toward a target and then hit it with a melee weapon attack on the same turn, you can immediately follow that attack with a bonus action, making one attack against the target with your hooves.

Equine Build. You count as one size larger when determining your carrying capacity and the weight you can push or drag.

In addition, any climb that requires hands and feet is especially difficult for you because of your equine legs. When you make such a climb, each foot of movement costs you 4 extra feet instead of the normal 1 extra foot.

Hooves. You have hooves that you can use to make unarmed strikes. When you hit with them, the strike deals 1d6 + your Strength modifier bludgeoning damage, instead of the bludgeoning damage normal for an unarmed strike.

Natural Affinity. Your fey connection to nature gives you an intuitive connection to the natural world and the animals within it. You therefore have proficiency in one of the following skills of your choice: Animal Handling, Medicine, Nature, or Survival.

Changeling

With ever-changing appearances, changelings reside in many societies undetected. Each changeling can supernaturally adopt any face they like. For some changelings, a new face is only a disguise. For other changelings, a new face may reveal an aspect of their soul.

The first changelings in the multiverse appeared in the Feywild, and the wondrous, mutable essence of that plane lingers in changelings today—even in those changelings who have never set foot in the fey realm. Each changeling decides how to use their shape-shifting ability, channeling either the peril or the joy of the Feywild. Sometimes they adopt new forms for the sake of mischief or malice, and other times they don a new identity to right wrongs or delight the downtrodden.

In their true form, changelings appear faded, their features almost devoid of detail. It is rare to see a changeling in that form, for a typical changeling changes their shape the way others might change clothes. A casual shape—one created on the spur of the moment, with no depth or history—is called a mask. A mask can be used to express a mood or to serve a specific purpose and then might never be used again. However, many changelings develop identities that have more depth, crafting whole personas complete with histories and beliefs. A changeling adventurer might have personas for many situations, including negotiation, investigation, and combat.

Personas can be shared by multiple changelings; a community might be home to three healer changelings, with whoever is on duty adopting the persona of Andrea, the gentle physician. Personas can even be passed down through a family, allowing a younger changeling to take advantage of contacts established by the persona's previous users.

Changeling Traits

As a changeling, you have the following racial traits.

Creature Type. You are a Fey.

Size. You are Medium or Small. You choose the size when you select this race.

Speed. Your walking speed is 30 feet.

Changeling Instincts. Thanks to your connection to the fey realm, you gain proficiency with two of the following skills of your choice: Deception, Insight, Intimidation, Performance, or Persuasion.

Shapechanger. As an action, you can change your appearance and your voice. You determine the specifics of the changes, including your coloration, hair length, and sex. You can also adjust your height and weight and can change your size between Medium and Small. You can make yourself appear as a member of another race, though none of your game statistics change. You can't duplicate the appearance of an individual you've never seen, and you must adopt a form that has the same basic arrangement of limbs that you have. Your clothing and equipment aren't changed by this trait.

You stay in the new form until you use an action to revert to your true form or until you die.

DEEP GNOME

Deep gnomes, or svirfneblin, are natives of the Underdark and are suffused with that subterranean realm's magic. They can supernaturally camouflage themselves, and their svirfneblin magic renders them difficult to locate. These abilities have enabled them to survive for generations among the perils of the Underdark.

Like other gnomes, deep gnomes can live for centuries, up to 500 years.

DEEP GNOME TRAITS

As a deep gnome, you have the following racial traits.

Creature Type. You are a Humanoid. You are also considered a gnome for any prerequisite or effect that requires you to be a gnome.

Size. You are Small.

Speed. Your walking speed is 30 feet.

Darkvision. You can see in dim light within 120 feet of you as if it were bright light and in darkness as if it were dim light. You discern colors in that darkness only as shades of gray.

Gift of the Svirfneblin. Starting at 3rd level, you can cast the *disguise self* spell with this trait. Starting at 5th level, you can also cast the *nondetection* spell with it, without requiring a material component. Once you cast either of these spells with this trait, you can't cast that spell with it again until you finish a long rest. You can also cast these spells using spell slots you have of the appropriate level.

Intelligence, Wisdom, or Charisma is your spellcasting ability for these spells when you cast them with this trait (choose when you select this race).

Gnomish Magic Resistance. You have advantage on Intelligence, Wisdom, and Charisma saving throws against spells.

Svirfneblin Camouflage. When you make a Dexterity (Stealth) check, you can make the check with advantage. You can use this trait a number of times equal to your proficiency bonus, and you regain all expended uses when you finish a long rest.

DUERGAR

Duergar are dwarves whose ancestors were transformed by centuries living in the deepest places of the Underdark. That chthonic realm is saturated with strange magical energy, and over generations, early duergar absorbed traces of it. They were further altered when mind flayers and other Aberrations invaded and performed horrific experiments on them. Fueled by Underdark magic, those experiments left early duergar with psionic powers, which have been passed down to their descendants. In time, they liberated themselves from their aberrant tyrants and forged a new life for themselves in the Underdark and beyond.

Like other dwarves, duergar typically have a life span of 350 years.

DUERGAR TRAITS

As a duergar, you have the following racial traits.

Creature Type. You are a Humanoid. You are also considered a dwarf for any prerequisite or effect that requires you to be a dwarf.

Size. You are Medium.

Speed. Your walking speed is 30 feet.

Darkvision. You can see in dim light within 120 feet of you as if it were bright light and in darkness as if it were dim light. You discern colors in that darkness only as shades of gray.

Duergar Magic. Starting at 3rd level, you can cast the *enlarge/reduce* spell on yourself with this trait, without requiring a material component. Starting at 5th level, you can also cast the *invisibility* spell on yourself with this trait, without requiring a material component. Once you cast either of these spells with this trait, you can't cast that spell with it again until you finish a long rest. You can also cast these spells using spell slots you have of the appropriate level.

Intelligence, Wisdom, or Charisma is your spellcasting ability for these spells when you cast them with this trait (choose when you select this race).

Dwarven Resilience. You have advantage on saving throws you make to avoid or end the poisoned condition on yourself. You also have resistance to poison damage.

Psionic Fortitude. You have advantage on saving throws you make to avoid or end the charmed or stunned condition on yourself.

Eladrin

Eladrin are elves of the Feywild, a realm of perilous beauty and boundless magic. Using that magic, eladrin can step from one place to another in the blink of an eye, and each eladrin resonates with emotions captured in the Feywild in the form of seasons—affinities that affect the eladrin's mood and appearance. An eladrin's season can change, though some remain in one season forever. Choose your season or roll on the Eladrin Seasons table. Your Trance trait lets you change your season.

Like other elves, eladrin can live to be over 750 years old.

Eladrin Seasons

d4	Season
1	**Autumn:** peace and goodwill, when summer's harvest is shared with all
2	**Winter:** contemplation and dolor, when the vibrant energy of the world slumbers
3	**Spring:** cheerfulness and celebration, marked by merriment and hope as winter's sorrow passes
4	**Summer:** boldness and aggression, a time of unfettered energy and calls to action

Eladrin Traits

As an eladrin, you have the following racial traits.

Creature Type. You are a Humanoid. You are also considered an elf for any prerequisite or effect that requires you to be an elf.

Size. You are Medium.

Speed. Your walking speed is 30 feet.

Darkvision. You can see in dim light within 60 feet of you as if it were bright light and in darkness as if it were dim light. You discern colors in that darkness only as shades of gray.

Fey Ancestry. You have advantage on saving throws you make to avoid or end the charmed condition on yourself.

Fey Step. As a bonus action, you can magically teleport up to 30 feet to an unoccupied space you can see. You can use this trait a number of times equal to your proficiency bonus, and you regain all expended uses when you finish a long rest.

When you reach 3rd level, your Fey Step gains an additional effect based on your season; if the effect requires a saving throw, the DC equals 8 + your proficiency bonus + your Intelligence, Wisdom, or Charisma modifier (choose when you select this race):

Autumn. Immediately after you use your Fey Step, up to two creatures of your choice that you can see within 10 feet of you must succeed on a Wisdom saving throw or be charmed by you for 1 minute, or until you or your companions deal any damage to the creatures.

Winter. When you use your Fey Step, one creature of your choice that you can see within 5 feet of you before you teleport must succeed on a Wisdom saving throw or be frightened of you until the end of your next turn.

Spring. When you use your Fey Step, you can touch one willing creature within 5 feet of you. That creature then teleports instead of you, appearing in an unoccupied space of your choice that you can see within 30 feet of you.

Summer. Immediately after you use your Fey Step, each creature of your choice that you can see within 5 feet of you takes fire damage equal to your proficiency bonus.

Keen Senses. You have proficiency in the Perception skill.

Trance. You don't need to sleep, and magic can't put you to sleep. You can finish a long rest in 4 hours if you spend those hours in a trancelike meditation, during which you retain consciousness.

Whenever you finish this trance, you can change your season, and you can gain two proficiencies that you don't have, each one with a weapon or a tool of your choice selected from the *Player's Handbook*. You mystically acquire these proficiencies by drawing them from shared elven memory, and you retain them until you finish your next long rest.

Fairy

The Feywild is home to many fantastic peoples, including fairies. Fairies are a wee folk, but not nearly as much so as their pixie and sprite friends. The first fairies spoke Elvish, Goblin, or Sylvan, and encounters with human visitors prompted many of them to learn Common as well.

Infused with the magic of the Feywild, most fairies look like Small elves with insectile wings, but each fairy has a special physical characteristic that sets the fairy apart. For your fairy, roll on the Fey Characteristics table or choose an option from it. You're also free to come up with your own characteristic if none of the suggestions below fit your character.

Fey Characteristics

d8	Characteristic
1	Your wings are like those of a bird.
2	You have shimmering, multicolored skin.
3	You have exceptionally large ears.
4	A glittering mist constantly surrounds you.
5	You have a small spectral horn on your forehead, like a little unicorn horn.
6	Your legs are insectile.
7	You smell like fresh brownies.
8	A noticeable, harmless chill surrounds you.

Fairy Traits

As a fairy, you have the following racial traits.

Creature Type. You are a Fey.

Size. You are Small.

Speed. Your walking speed is 30 feet.

Fairy Magic. You know the *druidcraft* cantrip. Starting at 3rd level, you can cast the *faerie fire* spell with this trait. Starting at 5th level, you can also cast the *enlarge/reduce* spell with this trait. Once you cast *faerie fire* or *enlarge/reduce* with this trait, you can't cast that spell with it again until you finish a long rest. You can also cast either of those spells using any spell slots you have of the appropriate level.

Intelligence, Wisdom, or Charisma is your spellcasting ability for these spells when you cast them with this trait (choose when you select this race).

Flight. Because of your wings, you have a flying speed equal to your walking speed. You can't use this flying speed if you're wearing medium or heavy armor.

FIRBOLG

Distant cousins of giants, the first firbolgs wandered the primeval forests of the multiverse, and the magic of those forests entwined itself with the firbolgs' souls. Centuries later, that magic still thrums inside a firbolg, even one who has never lived under the boughs of a great forest.

A firbolg's magic is an obscuring sort, which allowed their ancestors to pass through a forest without disturbing it. So deep is the connection between a firbolg and the wild places of the world that they can communicate with flora and fauna.

Firbolgs can live up to 500 years.

FIRBOLG TRAITS

As a firbolg, you have the following racial traits.

Creature Type. You are a Humanoid.

Size. You are Medium.

Speed. Your walking speed is 30 feet.

Firbolg Magic. You can cast the *detect magic* and *disguise self* spells with this trait. When you use this version of *disguise self*, you can seem up to 3 feet shorter or taller. Once you cast either of these spells with this trait, you can't cast that spell with it again until you finish a long rest. You can also cast these spells using any spell slots you have.

Intelligence, Wisdom, or Charisma is your spellcasting ability for these spells when you cast them with this trait (choose when you select this race).

Hidden Step. As a bonus action, you can magically turn invisible until the start of your next turn or until you attack, make a damage roll, or force someone to make a saving throw. You can use this trait a number of times equal to your proficiency bonus, and you regain all expended uses when you finish a long rest.

Powerful Build. You count as one size larger when determining your carrying capacity and the weight you can push, drag, or lift.

Speech of Beast and Leaf. You have the ability to communicate in a limited manner with Beasts, Plants, and vegetation. They can understand the meaning of your words, though you have no special ability to understand them in return. You have advantage on all Charisma checks you make to influence them.

> As a child, I learned that playing hide-and-seek with disappearing firbolgs is fun but futile.
>
> TASHA

LEFT TO RIGHT: EARTH GENASI, WATER GENASI, FIRE GENASI, AND AIR GENASI

GENASI

Tracing their ancestry to the genies of the Elemental Planes, each genasi can tap into the power of one of the elements. Air, earth, fire, and water—these are the four pillars of the Material Plane and the four types of genasi. Some genasi are direct descendants of a genie, while others were born to non-genasi parents who lived near a place suffused by a genie's magic.

A typical genasi has a life span of 120 years.

AIR GENASI TRAITS

Air genasi are descended from djinn, the genies of the Elemental Plane of Air. Embodying many of the airy traits of their otherworldly ancestors, air genasi can draw upon their connection to the winds.

Air genasi's skin tones include many shades of blue, along with the full range of human skin tones, with bluish or ashen casts. Sometimes their skin is marked by lines that seem like cracks with bluish-white energy spilling out. An air genasi's hair might blow in a phantom wind or be made entirely of clouds or vapor.

As an air genasi, you have the following traits.

Creature Type. You are a Humanoid.

Size. You are Medium or Small. You choose the size when you select this race.

Speed. Your walking speed is 35 feet.

Darkvision. You can see in dim light within 60 feet of you as if it were bright light and in darkness as if it were dim light. You discern colors in that darkness only as shades of gray.

Unending Breath. You can hold your breath indefinitely while you're not incapacitated.

Lightning Resistance. You have resistance to lightning damage.

Mingle with the Wind. You know the *shocking grasp* cantrip. Starting at 3rd level, you can cast the *feather fall* spell with this trait, without requiring a material component. Starting at 5th level, you can also cast the *levitate* spell with this trait, without requiring a material component. Once you cast *feather fall* or *levitate* with this trait, you can't cast that spell with it again until you finish a long rest. You can also cast either of those spells using any spell slots you have of the appropriate level.

Intelligence, Wisdom, or Charisma is your spellcasting ability for these spells when you cast them with this trait (choose when you select this race).

Earth Genasi Traits

Tracing their ancestry to dao, the genies of the Elemental Plane of Earth, earth genasi inherit dao's steadfast strength and control over earth.

An earth genasi's skin can be the colors of stone and earth or a human skin tone with glittering sparkles like gem dust. Some earth genasi have lines marking their skin like cracks, either showing glimmering gemlike veins or a dim, yellowish glow. Earth genasi hair can appear carved of stone or crystal or resemble strands of spun metal.

As an earth genasi, you have the following traits.

Creature Type. You are a Humanoid.

Size. You are Medium or Small. You choose the size when you select this race.

Speed. Your walking speed is 30 feet.

Darkvision. You can see in dim light within 60 feet of you as if it were bright light and in darkness as if it were dim light. You discern colors in that darkness only as shades of gray.

Earth Walk. You can move across difficult terrain without expending extra movement if you are using your walking speed on the ground or a floor.

Merge with Stone. You know the *blade ward* cantrip. You can cast it as normal, and you can also cast it as a bonus action a number of times equal to your proficiency bonus, regaining all expended uses when you finish a long rest.

Starting at 5th level, you can cast the *pass without trace* spell with this trait, without requiring a material component. Once you cast that spell with this trait, you can't do so again until you finish a long rest. You can also cast it using any spell slots you have of 2nd level or higher.

Intelligence, Wisdom, or Charisma is your spellcasting ability for these spells when you cast them with this trait (choose when you select this race).

Fire Genasi Traits

Descended from efreet, the genies of the Elemental Plane of Fire, fire genasi channel the flamboyant and often destructive nature of flame. They show their heritage in their skin tones, which can range from deep charcoal to shades of red and orange. Some bear skin tones common to humanity but with fiery marks, such as slowly swirling lights under their skin that resemble embers or glowing red lines tracing over their bodies like cracks. Fire genasi hair can resemble threads of fire or sooty smoke.

As a fire genasi, you have the following traits.

Creature Type. You are a Humanoid.

Size. You are Medium or Small. You choose the size when you select this race.

Speed. Your walking speed is 30 feet.

Darkvision. You can see in dim light within 60 feet of you as if it were bright light, and in darkness as if it were dim light. You discern colors in that darkness only as shades of gray.

Fire Resistance. You have resistance to fire damage.

Reach to the Blaze. You know the *produce flame* cantrip. Starting at 3rd level, you can cast the *burning hands* spell with this trait. Starting at 5th level, you can also cast the *flame blade* spell with this trait, without requiring a material component. Once you cast *burning hands* or *flame blade* with this trait, you can't cast that spell with it again until you finish a long rest. You can also cast either of those spells using any spell slots you have of the appropriate level.

Intelligence, Wisdom, or Charisma is your spellcasting ability for these spells when you cast them with this trait (choose when you select this race).

Water Genasi Traits

Water genasi descend from marids, aquatic genies from the Elemental Plane of Water. Water genasi are perfectly suited to life underwater and carry the power of the waves inside themselves.

Their skin is often shades of blue or green, sometimes a blend of the two. If they have a human skin tone, there is a glistening texture that catches the light, like water droplets or nearly invisible fish scales. Their hair can resemble seaweed, waving as if in a current, or it can even be like water itself.

As a water genasi, you have the following traits.

Creature Type. You are a Humanoid.

Size. You are Medium or Small. You choose the size when you select this race.

Speed. Your walking speed is 30 feet, and you have a swimming speed equal to your walking speed.

Acid Resistance. You have resistance to acid damage.

Amphibious. You can breathe air and water.

Call to the Wave. You know the *acid splash* cantrip. Starting at 3rd level, you can cast the *create or destroy water* spell with this trait. Starting at 5th level, you can also cast the *water walk* spell with this trait, without requiring a material component. Once you cast *create or destroy water* or *water walk* with this trait, you can't cast that spell with it again until you finish a long rest. You can also cast either of those spells using any spell slots you have of the appropriate level.

Intelligence, Wisdom, or Charisma is your spellcasting ability for these spells when you cast them with this trait (choose when you select this race).

Darkvision. You can see in dim light within 60 feet of you as if it were bright light, and in darkness as if it were dim light. You discern colors in that darkness only as shades of gray.

Githyanki

Once members of a people who escaped servitude to mind flayers, githyanki split from their cousins, githzerai, and fled to the Astral Plane. In that timeless, silvery realm, githyanki honed their psionic powers and built a great city called Tu'narath. They have since spread throughout the multiverse, starting in outposts outside the Astral Plane, called creches, where time passes and their children can reach adulthood.

A lanky people with skin tones of yellows, greens, and browns, githyanki complement their physical prowess with psionic might, instilled in them by mind flayers and cultivated over eons in the Astral Plane. Now all githyanki can use their psychic bond with that plane to access splinters of knowledge left behind by beings who travel, live, and die among the silver astral clouds.

Githyanki who reside in the Astral Plane can live indefinitely.

Githyanki Traits

As a githyanki, you have the following racial traits.

Creature Type. You are a Humanoid.

Size. You are Medium.

Speed. Your walking speed is 30 feet.

Astral Knowledge. You can mystically access a reservoir of experiences of entities connected to the Astral Plane. Whenever you finish a long rest, you gain proficiency in one skill of your choice and with one weapon or tool of your choice, selected from the *Player's Handbook*, as you momentarily project your consciousness into the Astral Plane. These proficiencies last until the end of your next long rest.

Githyanki Psionics. You know the *mage hand* cantrip, and the hand is invisible when you cast the cantrip with this trait.

Starting at 3rd level, you can cast the *jump* spell with this trait. Starting at 5th level, you can also cast the *misty step* spell with it. Once you cast *jump* or *misty step* with this trait, you can't cast that spell with it again until you finish a long rest. You can also cast either of those spells using any spell slots you have of the appropriate level.

Intelligence, Wisdom, or Charisma is your spellcasting ability for these spells when you cast them with this trait (choose when you select this race). None of these spells require spell components when you cast them with this trait.

Psychic Resilience. You have resistance to psychic damage.

Githzerai

Githzerai migrated to the Everchanging Chaos of Limbo after the ancient schism that split their ancestors from their cousins, githyanki. Limbo is a roiling maelstrom of matter and energy, collapsing and reforming without purpose or direction, until a creature exerts deliberate will to stabilize it. Through their potent psionic power, githzerai carved a home for themselves amid the chaos. As the ages passed, githzerai explorers ranged out to other planes and worlds of the multiverse.

Githzerai are generally slender, with speckled skin in shades of yellow, green, or brown. Eons of cultivating their mental powers within the endless chaos of Limbo have imbued githzerai with the ability to shape psionic energy to protect themselves and probe minds.

Githzerai Traits

As a githzerai, you have the following racial traits.

Creature Type. You are a Humanoid.

Size. You are Medium.

Speed. Your walking speed is 30 feet.

Githzerai Psionics. You know the *mage hand* cantrip, and the hand is invisible when you cast the cantrip with this trait.

Starting at 3rd level, you can cast the *shield* spell with this trait. Starting at 5th level, you can also cast the *detect thoughts* spell with it. Once you cast *shield* or *detect thoughts* with this trait, you can't cast that spell with it again until you finish a long rest. You can also cast either of those spells using any spell slots you have of the appropriate level.

Intelligence, Wisdom, or Charisma is your spellcasting ability for these spells when you cast them with this trait (choose when you select this race). None of these spells require spell components when you cast them with this trait.

Mental Discipline. Your innate psychic defenses grant you advantage on saving throws you make to avoid or end the charmed and frightened conditions on yourself.

Psychic Resilience. You have resistance to psychic damage.

SCOTT MURPHY

Goblin

A subterranean folk, goblins can be found in every corner of the multiverse, often beside their bugbear and hobgoblin kin. Long before the god Maglubiyet conquered them, early goblins served in the court of the Queen of Air and Darkness, one of the Feywild's archfey. Goblins thrived in her dangerous domain thanks to a special boon from her—a supernatural knack for finding the weak spots in foes larger than themselves and for getting out of trouble. Goblins brought this fey boon with them to worlds across the Material Plane, even if they don't remember the fey realm they inhabited before Maglubiyet's rise. Now many goblins pursue their own destinies, escaping the plots of both archfey and gods.

Goblin Traits

As a goblin, you have the following racial traits.

Creature Type. You are a Humanoid. You are also considered a goblinoid for any prerequisite or effect that requires you to be a goblinoid.

Size. You are Small.

Speed. Your walking speed is 30 feet.

Darkvision. You can see in dim light within 60 feet of you as if it were bright light and in darkness as if it were dim light. You discern colors in that darkness only as shades of gray.

Fey Ancestry. You have advantage on saving throws you make to avoid or end the charmed condition on yourself.

Fury of the Small. When you damage a creature with an attack or a spell and the creature's size is larger than yours, you can cause the attack or spell to deal extra damage to the creature. The extra damage equals your proficiency bonus.

You can use this trait a number of times equal to your proficiency bonus, regaining all expended uses when you finish a long rest, and you can use it no more than once per turn.

Nimble Escape. You can take the Disengage or Hide action as a bonus action on each of your turns.

MIKE JORDANA

ERIC BELISLE, JON HODGSON

GOLIATH

The first goliaths lived on the highest mountain peaks—far above the tree line, where the air is thin and frigid winds howl. Distantly related to giants and infused with the supernatural essence of their ancestors' mountainous home, goliaths stand between 7 and 8 feet tall and have a wide array of skin tones resembling different types of stone.

GOLIATH TRAITS

As a goliath, you have the following racial traits.

Creature Type. You are a Humanoid.

Size. You are Medium.

Speed. Your walking speed is 30 feet.

Little Giant. You have proficiency in the Athletics skill, and you count as one size larger when determining your carrying capacity and the weight you can push, drag, or lift.

Mountain Born. You have resistance to cold damage. You also naturally acclimate to high altitudes, even if you've never been to one. This includes elevations above 20,000 feet.

Stone's Endurance. You can supernaturally draw on unyielding stone to shrug off harm. When you take damage, you can use your reaction to roll a d12. Add your Constitution modifier to the number rolled and reduce the damage by that total.

You can use this trait a number of times equal to your proficiency bonus, and you regain all expended uses when you finish a long rest.

HARENGON

Harengons originated in the Feywild, where they spoke Sylvan and embodied the spirit of freedom and travel. In time, these rabbitfolk hopped into other worlds, bringing the fey realm's exuberance with them and learning new languages as they went.

Harengons are bipedal, with the characteristic long feet of the rabbits they resemble and fur in a variety of colors. They share the keen senses and powerful legs of leporine creatures and are full of energy, like a wound-up spring. Harengons are blessed with a little fey luck, and they often find themselves a few fortunate feet away from dangers during adventures.

Here and gone. Fey puns are a menace!
— *Mordenkainen*

HARENGON TRAITS

As a harengon, you have the following racial traits.

Creature Type. You are a Humanoid.

Size. You are Medium or Small. You choose the size when you select this race.

Speed. Your walking speed is 30 feet.

Hare-Trigger. You can add your proficiency bonus to your initiative rolls.

Leporine Senses. You have proficiency in the Perception skill.

Lucky Footwork. When you fail a Dexterity saving throw, you can use your reaction to roll a d4 and add it to the save, potentially turning the failure into a success. You can't use this reaction if you're prone or your speed is 0.

Rabbit Hop. As a bonus action, you can jump a number of feet equal to five times your proficiency bonus, without provoking opportunity attacks. You can use this trait only if your speed is greater than 0. You can use it a number of times equal to your proficiency bonus, and you regain all expended uses when you finish a long rest.

HOBGOBLIN

Hobgoblins trace their origins to the ancient courts of the Feywild, where they first appeared with their goblin and bugbear kin. Many of them were driven from the Feywild by the conquering god Maglubiyet, who marshaled them as soldiers, but the fey realm left its mark; wherever they are in the multiverse, they continue to channel an aspect of the Feywild's rule of reciprocity, which creates a mystical bond between the giver and the receiver of a gift.

On some worlds, such bonds lead hobgoblins to form communities with deep ties to one another. In Eberron and the Forgotten Realms, vast hobgoblin legions have emerged, with ranks of devoted soldiers famed for their unity.

Hobgoblins are generally taller than their goblin cousins but not quite as big as bugbears. They have curved, pointed ears and noses that turn bright red or blue during displays of emotion.

HOBGOBLIN TRAITS

As a hobgoblin, you have the following racial traits.

Creature Type. You are a Humanoid. You are also considered a goblinoid for any prerequisite or effect that requires you to be a goblinoid.

Size. You are Medium.

Speed. Your walking speed is 30 feet.

Darkvision. You can see in dim light within 60 feet of you as if it were bright light and in darkness as if it were dim light. You discern colors in that darkness only as shades of gray.

Fey Ancestry. You have advantage on saving throws you make to avoid or end the charmed condition on yourself.

Fey Gift. You can use this trait to take the Help action as a bonus action, and you can do so a number of times equal to your proficiency bonus. You regain all expended uses when you finish a long rest.

Starting at 3rd level, choose one of the options below each time you take the Help action with this trait:

Hospitality. You and the creature you help each gain a number of temporary hit points equal to 1d6 plus your proficiency bonus.

Passage. You and the creature you help each increase your walking speeds by 10 feet until the start of your next turn.

Spite. Until the start of your next turn, the first time the creature you help hits a target with an attack roll, that target has disadvantage on the next attack roll it makes within the next minute.

Fortune from the Many. If you miss with an attack roll or fail an ability check or a saving throw, you can draw on your bonds of reciprocity to gain a bonus to the roll equal to the number of allies you can see within 30 feet of you (maximum bonus of +3). You can use this trait a number of times equal to your proficiency bonus, and you regain all expended uses when you finish a long rest.

I have long envied the agility of kenku memory. My memory palace is splendid and vast, yet a kenku's memory is a gleaming edifice that puts my palace to shame.

— *Mordenkainen*

Kenku

Feathered folk who resemble ravens, kenku are blessed with keen observation and supernaturally accurate memories. None of them can remember the origin of the first kenku, however, and they often joke that there are as many kenku origin stories as there are kenku. Some of them paint their genesis as a curse, being a flightless bird people doomed to mimic other people's creations. Other kenku recite cryptic but beautiful poems about their advent being a blessed event in which they were sent into the multiverse to observe and catalog its many wonders.

Whatever their true origin, kenku are most often found in the Shadowfell and the Material Plane, and they tend to have the coloration typical of ravens.

Kenku Traits

As a kenku, you have the following racial traits.

Creature Type. You are a Humanoid.

Size. Your size is Medium or Small. You choose the size when you select this race.

Speed. Your walking speed is 30 feet.

Expert Duplication. When you copy writing or craftwork produced by yourself or someone else, you have advantage on any ability checks you make to produce an exact duplicate.

Kenku Recall. Thanks to your supernaturally good memory, you have proficiency in two skills of your choice.

Moreover, when you make an ability check using any skill in which you have proficiency, you can give yourself advantage on the check before rolling the d20. You can give yourself advantage in this way a number of times equal to your proficiency bonus, and you regain all expended uses when you finish a long rest.

Mimicry. You can accurately mimic sounds you have heard, including voices. A creature that hears the sounds you make can tell they are imitations only with a successful Wisdom (Insight) check against a DC of 8 + your proficiency bonus + your Charisma modifier.

KOBOLD

Some of the smallest draconic creatures in the multiverse, kobolds display their draconic ancestry in the glint of their scales and in their roars. Legends tell of the first kobolds emerging from the Underdark near the lairs of the earliest dragons. In some lands, kobolds serve chromatic or metallic dragons—even worshiping them as divine beings. In other places, kobolds know too well how dangerous those dragons can be and help others defend against draconic destruction.

Whatever their relationship to dragons, kobold scales tend to be rust colored, although the occasional kobold sports a scale color more akin to that of a chromatic or a metallic dragon. A kobold's cry can express a range of emotion: anger, resolve, elation, fear, and more. Regardless of the emotion expressed, their cry resonates with draconic power.

KOBOLD TRAITS

As a kobold, you have the following racial traits.

Creature Type. You are a Humanoid.

Size. You are Small.

Speed. Your walking speed is 30 feet.

Darkvision. You can see in dim light within 60 feet of you as if it were bright light, and in darkness as if it were dim light. You discern colors in that darkness only as shades of gray.

Draconic Cry. As a bonus action, you let out a cry at your enemies within 10 feet of you. Until the start of your next turn, you and your allies have advantage on attack rolls against any of those enemies who could hear you. You can use this trait a number of times equal to your proficiency bonus, and you regain all expended uses when you finish a long rest.

Kobold Legacy. Kobolds' connection to dragons can manifest in unpredictable ways in an individual kobold. Choose one of the following legacy options for your kobold:

Craftiness. You have proficiency in one of the following skills of your choice: Arcana, Investigation, Medicine, Sleight of Hand, or Survival.

Defiance. You have advantage on saving throws to avoid or end the frightened condition on yourself.

Draconic Sorcery. You know one cantrip of your choice from the sorcerer spell list. Intelligence, Wisdom, or Charisma is your spellcasting ability for that cantrip (choose when you select this race).

LIZARDFOLK

The saurian lizardfolk are thought by some sages to be distant cousins of dragonborn and kobolds. Despite their resemblance to those other scaled folk, however, lizardfolk are their own people and have lived on the worlds of the Material Plane since the worlds' creation. Gifted by the gods with remarkable physical defenses and a mystical connection to the natural world, lizardfolk can survive with just their wits in situations that would be deadly for other folk. Because of that fact, many lizardfolk myths state that their people were placed by the gods in the Material Plane to guard its natural wonders.

Lizardfolk have colorful scales and exhibit a wide array of scale patterns. Their individual facial features are as varied as those of lizards.

LIZARDFOLK TRAITS

As a lizardfolk, you have the following racial traits.

Creature Type. You are a Humanoid.

Size. You are Medium.

Speed. Your walking speed is 30 feet, and you have a swimming speed equal to your walking speed.

Bite. You have a fanged maw that you can use to make unarmed strikes. When you hit with it, the strike deals 1d6 + your Strength modifier slashing damage, instead of the bludgeoning damage normal for an unarmed strike.

Hold Breath. You can hold your breath for up to 15 minutes at a time.

Hungry Jaws. You can throw yourself into a feeding frenzy. As a bonus action, you can make a special attack with your Bite. If the attack hits, it deals its normal damage, and you gain temporary hit points equal to your proficiency bonus. You can use this trait a number of times equal to your proficiency bonus, and you regain all expended uses when you finish a long rest.

Natural Armor. You have tough, scaly skin. When you aren't wearing armor, your base AC is 13 + your Dexterity modifier. You can use your natural armor to determine your AC if the armor you wear would leave you with a lower AC. A shield's benefits apply as normal while you use your natural armor.

Nature's Intuition. Thanks to your mystical connection to nature, you gain proficiency with two of the following skills of your choice: Animal Handling, Medicine, Nature, Perception, Stealth, or Survival.

MINOTAUR

Minotaurs are barrel-chested humanoids with heads resembling those of bulls. Blessed with a supernaturally strong sense of direction, minotaurs make great navigators. Some sages believe minotaurs were first created by the Lady of Pain to patrol the magical mazes that she uses to trap her foes.

Minotaur horns range in size from about 1 foot long to easily three times that length. Minotaurs often carve their horns to sharpen their edges, etch symbols of power into them, or sheathe them in bronze to prevent them from shattering during battle.

Thick hair extends down minotaurs' necks and powerful backs, and some have long patches of hair on their chins and cheeks. Their legs end in heavy, cloven hooves, and they have long, tufted tails.

MINOTAUR TRAITS

As a minotaur, you have the following racial traits.

Creature Type. You are a Humanoid.

Size. You are Medium.

Speed. Your walking speed is 30 feet.

Horns. You have horns that you can use to make unarmed strikes. When you hit with them, the strike deals 1d6 + your Strength modifier piercing damage, instead of the bludgeoning damage normal for an unarmed strike.

Goring Rush. Immediately after you take the Dash action on your turn and move at least 20 feet, you can make one melee attack with your Horns as a bonus action.

Hammering Horns. Immediately after you hit a creature with a melee attack as part of the Attack action on your turn, you can use a bonus action to attempt to push that target with your horns. The target must be within 5 feet of you and no more than one size larger than you. Unless it succeeds on a Strength saving throw against a DC equal to 8 + your proficiency bonus + your Strength modifier, you push it up to 10 feet away from you.

Labyrinthine Recall. You always know which direction is north, and you have advantage on any Wisdom (Survival) check you make to navigate or track.

Orc

Orcs trace their creation to the one-eyed god Gruumsh, an unstoppable warrior and powerful leader. The divine qualities of Gruumsh resonate within orcs, granting them a reflection of his toughness and tenacity that can't be matched, and the god equipped his children to be able to live above or below ground.

On some worlds, such as Eberron, orcs were among the first defenders of the natural order from the encroachments of Fiends and other extraplanar threats. Gruumsh's blessings have made orcs tireless guardians and mighty allies wherever they are found, even when they turn their devotion to other gods.

Orc Traits

As an orc, you have the following racial traits.

Creature Type. You are a Humanoid.

Size. You are Medium.

Speed. Your walking speed is 30 feet.

Adrenaline Rush. You can take the Dash action as a bonus action. You can use this trait a number of times equal to your proficiency bonus, and you regain all expended uses when you finish a long rest.

Whenever you use this trait, you gain a number of temporary hit points equal to your proficiency bonus.

Darkvision. You can see in dim light within 60 feet of you as if it were bright light, and in darkness as if it were dim light. You discern colors in that darkness only as shades of gray.

Powerful Build. You count as one size larger when determining your carrying capacity and the weight you can push, drag, or lift.

Relentless Endurance. When you are reduced to 0 hit points but not killed outright, you can drop to 1 hit point instead. Once you use this trait, you can't do so again until you finish a long rest.

MIKE JORDANA

Satyr

Originating in the Feywild—a realm of pure emotion—satyrs thrive on the energy of merriment. They resemble elves but have goatlike legs, cloven hooves, and ram or goat horns. The magic of the fey realm has given them an innate ability to perform, to delight, and to resist magical intrusion. While they're usually found in the Feywild, satyrs do wander to other planes of existence, most often to the Material Plane. There they seek to bring a bit of their home plane's splendor to other worlds.

Satyr Traits

As a satyr, you have the following racial traits.

Creature Type. You are a Fey.

Size. You are Medium.

Speed. Your walking speed is 35 feet.

Ram. You can use your head and horns to make unarmed strikes. When you hit with them, the strike deals 1d6 + your Strength modifier bludgeoning damage, instead of the bludgeoning damage normal for an unarmed strike.

Magic Resistance. You have advantage on saving throws against spells.

Mirthful Leaps. Whenever you make a long jump or a high jump, you can roll a d8 and add the number rolled to the number of feet you cover, even when making a standing jump. This extra distance costs movement as normal.

Reveler. As an embodiment of revelry, you have proficiency in the Performance and Persuasion skills, and you have proficiency with one musical instrument of your choice.

Sea Elf

Sea elves fell in love with the wild beauty of the ocean in the earliest days of the multiverse. While other elves traveled from realm to realm, sea elves navigated the currents and explored the waters of many worlds. Today these elves can be found wherever oceans exist, as well as in the Elemental Plane of Water.

Like other elves, sea elves can live to be over 750 years old.

Sea Elf Traits

As a sea elf, you have the following racial traits.

Creature Type. You are a Humanoid. You are also considered an elf for any prerequisite or effect that requires you to be an elf.

Size. You are Medium.

Speed. Your walking speed is 30 feet, and you have a swimming speed equal to your walking speed.

Child of the Sea. You can breathe air and water, and you have resistance to cold damage.

Elves of Many Realms

Created by the god Corellon, the first elves were Fey beings who cavorted on various planes of existence, changing their physical forms at will. Outside the glory of Arvandor, their favorite place was the Feywild—a realm of unbridled passion. It was to that place of splendors that elves fled after they were exiled from Corellon's presence for plotting with their god's rival, Lolth. And it was there that they transformed from Fey creatures into Humanoids and lost their ability to shape-shift at will. Afterward, they often wept as they realized what they had lost, their sorrow made even deeper by the Feywild's influence. But in the Feywild, they also discovered the potential joys of being people of fixed forms, and they rediscovered hope once they renounced Lolth's treachery.

Most elves eventually spread from the Feywild to other worlds, as wanderlust and curiosity drove them to the far reaches of the multiverse. In those other worlds, elves developed the physical forms now associated with them. Because of their original mutable nature, each group of elves mystically took on characteristics of the environment with which they bonded, whether forests (wood elves), fey crossings in the Material Plane (high elves), the Underdark (drow), the Shadowfell (shadar-kai), the Feywild (eladrin), or oceans (sea elves).

In some places, Corellon has passed from elves' memory, but the god's blood flows within them still, even if they know nothing of its source. That blood is what causes them to evolve after spending centuries connected to a particular environment, so it is only a matter of time before other kinds of elves emerge.

Darkvision. You can see in dim light within 60 feet of you as if it were bright light, and in darkness as if it were dim light. You discern colors in that darkness only as shades of gray.

Fey Ancestry. You have advantage on saving throws you make to avoid or end the charmed condition on yourself.

Friend of the Sea. Aquatic animals have an extraordinary affinity with your people. You can communicate simple ideas to any Beast that has a swimming speed. It can understand your words, though you have no special ability to understand it in return.

Keen Senses. You have proficiency in the Perception skill.

Trance. You don't need to sleep, and magic can't put you to sleep. You can finish a long rest in 4 hours if you spend those hours in a trancelike meditation, during which you retain consciousness.

Whenever you finish this trance, you can gain two proficiencies that you don't have, each one with a weapon or a tool of your choice selected from the *Player's Handbook*. You mystically acquire these proficiencies by drawing them from shared elven memory, and you retain them until you finish your next long rest.

SHADAR-KAI

Shadar-kai are the elves of the Shadowfell, originally drawn to that dread realm by the Raven Queen. Over the centuries, some of them have continued to serve her, while others have ventured into the Material Plane to forge their own destinies.

Once shadar-kai were Fey like the rest of their elven kin; now they exist in a state between life and death, thanks to being transformed by the Shadowfell's grim energy.

Shadar-kai have ashen skin tones, and while they're in the Shadowfell, they also become wizened, reflecting the somber nature of that gloomy plane.

Like other elves, shadar-kai can live to be over 750 years old.

SHADAR-KAI TRAITS

As a shadar-kai, you have the following racial traits.

Creature Type. You are a Humanoid. You are also considered an elf for any prerequisite or effect that requires you to be an elf.

Size. You are Medium.

Speed. Your walking speed is 30 feet.

Blessing of the Raven Queen. As a bonus action, you can magically teleport up to 30 feet to an unoccupied space you can see. You can use this trait a number of times equal to your proficiency bonus, and you regain all expended uses when you finish a long rest.

Starting at 3rd level, you also gain resistance to all damage when you teleport using this trait. The resistance lasts until the start of your next turn. During that time, you appear ghostly and translucent.

Darkvision. You can see in dim light within 60 feet of you as if it were bright light, and in darkness as if it were dim light. You discern colors in that darkness only as shades of gray.

Fey Ancestry. You have advantage on saving throws you make to avoid or end the charmed condition on yourself.

Keen Senses. You have proficiency in the Perception skill.

Necrotic Resistance. You have resistance to necrotic damage.

Trance. You don't need to sleep, and magic can't put you to sleep. You can finish a long rest in 4 hours if you spend those hours in a trancelike meditation, during which you retain consciousness.

Whenever you finish this trance, you can gain two proficiencies that you don't have, each one with a weapon or a tool of your choice selected from the *Player's Handbook*. You mystically acquire these proficiencies by drawing them from shared elven memory, and you retain them until you finish your next long rest.

d6	Ancestor	Suggested Shifting Option
1	Werebear	Beasthide
2	Wereboar	Beasthide
3	Wererat	Swiftstride
4	Weretiger	Swiftstride
5	Werewolf (wolflike)	Longtooth
6	Werewolf (doglike)	Wildhunt

SHIFTER TRAITS

As a shifter, you have the following racial traits.

Creature Type. You are a Humanoid.

Size. You are Medium.

Speed. Your walking speed is 30 feet.

Bestial Instincts. Channeling the beast within, you have proficiency in one of the following skills of your choice: Acrobatics, Athletics, Intimidation, or Survival.

Darkvision. You can see in dim light within 60 feet of you as if it were bright light, and in darkness as if it were dim light. You discern colors in that darkness only as shades of gray.

Shifting. As a bonus action, you can assume a more bestial appearance. This transformation lasts for 1 minute, until you die, or until you revert to your normal appearance as a bonus action. When you shift, you gain temporary hit points equal to 2 × your proficiency bonus. You can shift a number of times equal to your proficiency bonus, and you regain all expended uses when you finish a long rest.

Whenever you shift, you gain an additional benefit based on one of the following options (choose when you select this race):

Beasthide. You gain 1d6 additional temporary hit points. While shifted, you have a +1 bonus to your Armor Class.

Longtooth. When you shift and as a bonus action on your other turns while shifted, you can use your elongated fangs to make an unarmed strike. If you hit with your fangs, you can deal piercing damage equal to 1d6 + your Strength modifier, instead of the bludgeoning damage normal for an unarmed strike.

Swiftstride. While shifted, your walking speed increases by 10 feet. Additionally, you can move up to 10 feet as a reaction when a creature ends its turn within 5 feet of you. This reactive movement doesn't provoke opportunity attacks.

Wildhunt. While shifted, you have advantage on Wisdom checks, and no creature within 30 feet of you can make an attack roll with advantage against you unless you're incapacitated.

SHIFTER

Shifters are sometimes called weretouched, as they are descendants of people who contracted full or partial lycanthropy. Humanoids with a bestial aspect, shifters can't fully change shape, but they can temporarily enhance their animalistic features by entering a state they call shifting.

Shifters are similar to humans in height and build but are typically more lithe and flexible. Their facial features have a bestial cast, often with large eyes and pointed ears; most shifters also have prominent canine teeth. They grow fur-like hair on nearly every part of their bodies. While a shifter's appearance might remind an onlooker of an animal, they remain clearly identifiable as shifters even when at their most feral.

Most shifters resemble a particular kind of lycanthrope. You can choose the kind of lycanthrope in your past, or you can determine it randomly by rolling on the Lycanthrope Ancestor table. The table also provides a suggestion for the Shifting option you might have as a result of your ancestry.

I once met the Cat Lord. His eyes pierced me, and his grace beguiled me. And never have I seen fur so luxurious! I have no great love of cats, but he ... he made me reconsider.

—Mordenkainen

Tabaxi

Created by the Cat Lord—a divine being of the Upper Planes—to blend the qualities of humanoids and cats, tabaxi are a varied people in both attitude and appearance. In some lands, tabaxi live like the cats they resemble, naturally curious and at home in playful environments. In other places, tabaxi live as other folk do, not exhibiting the feline behavior the Cat Lord intended.

Tabaxi's appearance is as varied as their attitudes. Some tabaxi have features or patterning in their fur like tigers, jaguars, or other big cats, while others have appearances more like a house cat. Still others have unique patterns or might style their fur to their preferences—or might even be hairless!

Tabaxi Traits

As a tabaxi, you have the following racial traits.

Creature Type. You are a Humanoid.

Size. You are Medium or Small. You choose the size when you select this race.

Speed. Your walking speed is 30 feet, and you have a climbing speed equal to your walking speed.

Cat's Claws. You can use your claws to make unarmed strikes. When you hit with them, the strike deals 1d6 + your Strength modifier slashing damage, instead of the bludgeoning damage normal for an unarmed strike.

Cat's Talent. You have proficiency in the Perception and Stealth skills.

Darkvision. You can see in dim light within 60 feet of you as if it were bright light, and in darkness as if it were dim light. You discern colors in that darkness only as shades of gray.

Feline Agility. Your reflexes and agility allow you to move with a burst of speed. When you move on your turn in combat, you can double your speed until the end of the turn. Once you use this trait, you can't use it again until you move 0 feet on one of your turns.

TORTLE

Tortles have a saying: "We wear our homes on our backs." These turtle folk live on many worlds, most often journeying up and down coasts, along waterways, and across the sea. Tortles don't have a unified story of how they were created, but they all have a sense of being mystically connected to the natural world. Carrying their shelter on their backs gives tortles a special feeling of security wherever they go, for even if they visit a far, unknown country, they have a place to lay their heads.

Tortles exhibit the same range of coloration and patterns found among turtles, and many tortles enjoy adorning their shells in distinctive ways.

TORTLE TRAITS

As a tortle, you have the following racial traits.

Creature Type. You are a Humanoid.

Size. You are Medium or Small. You choose the size when you select this race.

Speed. Your walking speed is 30 feet.

Claws. You have claws that you can use to make unarmed strikes. When you hit with them, the strike deals 1d6 + your Strength modifier slashing damage, instead of the bludgeoning damage normal for an unarmed strike.

Hold Breath. You can hold your breath for up to 1 hour.

Natural Armor. Your shell provides you a base AC of 17 (your Dexterity modifier doesn't affect this number). You can't wear light, medium, or heavy armor, but if you are using a shield, you can apply the shield's bonus as normal.

Nature's Intuition. Thanks to your mystical connection to nature, you gain proficiency with one of the following skills of your choice: Animal Handling, Medicine, Nature, Perception, Stealth, or Survival.

Shell Defense. You can withdraw into your shell as an action. Until you emerge, you gain a +4 bonus to your AC, and you have advantage on Strength and Constitution saving throws. While in your shell, you are prone, your speed is 0 and can't increase, you have disadvantage on Dexterity saving throws, you can't take reactions, and the only action you can take is a bonus action to emerge from your shell.

> *Once you discover that all oceans connect to the Elemental Plane of Water and that the Elemental Planes connect to all worlds, you begin to grasp the interconnectedness of the multiverse. Dive to the bottom of any sea, and you may later surface under an alien sky.*
>
> —Mordenkainen

TRITON

Originally from the Elemental Plane of Water, many tritons entered the Material Plane centuries ago in response to the growing threat of evil elementals. Those tritons spread across the worlds' oceans, protecting the surface from terrors in the deep. Over time, triton have extended their stewardship over the sea floor to the ocean's surface.

Tritons have webbed hands and feet, small fins on their calves, and coloration that favors blues and greens.

TRITON TRAITS

As a triton, you have the following racial traits.

Creature Type. You are a Humanoid.

Size. You are Medium.

Speed. Your walking speed is 30 feet, and you have a swimming speed equal to your walking speed.

Amphibious. You can breathe air and water.

Control Air and Water. You can cast *fog cloud* with this trait. Starting at 3rd level, you can cast the *gust of wind* spell with this trait. Starting at 5th level, you can also cast the *water walk* spell with it. Once you cast any of these spells with this trait, you can't cast that spell with it again until you finish a long rest. You can also cast these spells using any spell slots you have of the appropriate level.

Intelligence, Wisdom, or Charisma is your spellcasting ability for these spells when you cast them with this trait (choose when you select this race).

Darkvision. You can see in dim light within 60 feet of you as if it were bright light and in darkness as if it were dim light. You discern colors in that darkness only as shades of gray.

Emissary of the Sea. You can communicate simple ideas to any Beast, Elemental, or Monstrosity that has a swimming speed. It can understand your words, though you have no special ability to understand it in return.

Guardian of the Depths. Adapted to the frigid ocean depths, you have resistance to cold damage.

Yuan-ti

Yuan-ti were originally humans who transformed themselves into serpent folk through ancient rituals. Most yuan-ti were corrupted into monsters by those rites, but some yuan-ti instead became a new people who mix characteristics of humans and snakes.

Blessed with resistance to magical and poisonous effects by the rituals that created them, each of these yuan-ti manifests their serpentine heritage in a variety of ways: a forked tongue, snake eyes, a snakelike nose, or some other ophidian characteristic. However a yuan-ti looks, they have the power to pursue great good or evil in the multiverse.

Yuan-ti Traits

As a yuan-ti, you have the following racial traits.

Creature Type. You are a Humanoid.

Size. You are Medium or Small. You choose the size when you select this race.

Speed. Your walking speed is 30 feet.

Darkvision. You can see in dim light within 60 feet of you as if it were bright light, and in darkness as if it were dim light. You discern colors in that darkness only as shades of gray.

Magic Resistance. You have advantage on saving throws against spells.

Poison Resilience. You have advantage on saving throws you make to avoid or end the poisoned condition on yourself. You also have resistance to poison damage.

Serpentine Spellcasting. You know the *poison spray* cantrip. You can cast *animal friendship* an unlimited number of times with this trait, but you can target only snakes with it. Starting at 3rd level, you can also cast *suggestion* with this trait. Once you cast it, you can't do so again until you finish a long rest. You can also cast it using any spell slots you have of 2nd level or higher.

Intelligence, Wisdom, or Charisma is your spellcasting ability for these spells when you cast them with this trait (choose when you select this race).

CHAPTER 2

BESTIARY

THIS BESTIARY PROVIDES GAME STATISTICS and lore for more than 250 monsters, which are suitable for any D&D campaign. The chapter includes old favorites from past editions of the game as well as creatures created for the current edition.

This chapter is a companion to the *Monster Manual* and adopts a similar presentation. If you are unfamiliar with the monster stat block format, read the introduction of the *Monster Manual* before proceeding further. It explains stat block terminology and gives rules for various monster traits—information that isn't repeated here.

The creatures in this bestiary are organized alphabetically. A few are gathered under a group heading; for example, the "Dinosaurs" section contains stat blocks for various dinosaurs.

Herein you will find some weapons that deal unusual damage types and spellcasting that functions in atypical ways. Such an exception is a special feature of a monster and represents how it uses the weapon or casts its spells; the exception has no effect on how a weapon or a spell functions for someone else.

Finally, if a stat block contains the name of a class in the monster's name or in parentheses under the name, the monster is considered a member of that class for the purpose of meeting prerequisites for magic items.

My friend Mordenkainen constantly fights monsters and makes notes about them. I love notes as much as the next wizard, but fighting gets old. Why not sit down and have a drink with the monster? I've learned the most delicious secrets from my monstrous drinking companions. The other monsters? I disintegrated them.

TASHA

Abishais

Each abishai was once a mortal who somehow won Tiamat's favor before death and, as a reward, found its soul transformed into a draconic devil to serve at her pleasure in the Nine Hells. Each type of abishai is associated with one of Tiamat's five dragon heads: black, blue, green, red, and white.

Tiamat deploys abishais as her agents, sending them forth to represent her interests in the Hells and across the multiverse. Some have simple tasks, such as delivering a message to cultists. Others have greater responsibilities, such as leading large groups, assassinating targets, and serving in armies. In all cases, abishais are fanatically loyal to Tiamat, ready to lay down their lives if needed.

Abishais stand outside the normal hierarchy of the Nine Hells, having their own chain of command and ultimately answering to Tiamat (and Asmodeus, when he chooses to use them). Other archdevils can command abishais to work for them, but most archdevils do so rarely, since it is never clear whether an abishai follows Tiamat's orders or Asmodeus's. There is inherent risk in countermanding an order given by Tiamat, but interfering with Asmodeus's plans invites certain destruction.

Black Abishai

Expert assassins and infiltrators, black abishais can weave shadows to mask their presence, allowing them to reach a location where they can deliver a fatal strike to their targets.

Black Abishai

Medium Fiend (Devil), Typically Lawful Evil

Armor Class 15 (natural armor)
Hit Points 58 (9d8 + 18)
Speed 30 ft., fly 40 ft.

STR	DEX	CON	INT	WIS	CHA
14 (+2)	17 (+3)	14 (+2)	13 (+1)	16 (+3)	11 (+0)

Saving Throws Dex +6, Wis +6
Skills Perception +6, Stealth +6
Damage Resistances cold; bludgeoning, piercing, and slashing from nonmagical attacks that aren't silvered
Damage Immunities acid, fire, poison
Condition Immunities poisoned
Senses darkvision 120 ft., passive Perception 16
Languages Draconic, Infernal, telepathy 120 ft.
Challenge 7 (2,900 XP)   **Proficiency Bonus** +3

Devil's Sight. Magical darkness doesn't impede the abishai's darkvision.

Magic Resistance. The abishai has advantage on saving throws against spells and other magical effects.

Actions

Multiattack. The abishai makes one Bite attack and two Scimitar attacks.

Bite. *Melee Weapon Attack:* +6 to hit, reach 5 ft., one target. *Hit:* 8 (1d10 + 3) piercing damage plus 9 (2d8) acid damage.

Scimitar. *Melee Weapon Attack:* +6 to hit, reach 5 ft., one target. *Hit:* 6 (1d6 + 3) force damage.

Creeping Darkness (Recharge 6). The abishai casts *darkness* at a point within 120 feet of it, requiring no spell components or concentration. Wisdom is its spellcasting ability for this spell. While the spell persists, the abishai can move the area of darkness up to 60 feet as a bonus action.

Bonus Actions

Shadow Stealth. While in dim light or darkness, the abishai takes the Hide action.

BLUE ABISHAI

Seekers of forgotten lore and lost relics, blue abishais are the most cunning and learned of their kind. Their research into occult subjects gleaned from tomes plundered from across the multiverse enables them to become accomplished spellcasters. They use their magic to devastate Tiamat's enemies.

GREEN ABISHAI

Green abishais are adept at discovering secrets and other sensitive information, while their diplomatic skills and their magic ensure they can manipulate even the shrewdest opponents.

RED ABISHAI

Red abishais have no equals among the abishais when it comes to leadership ability and raw power. Red abishais lead other devils into battle or take charge of troublesome cults to ensure that they continue to carry out Tiamat's commands. A red abishai cuts a fearsome figure, and that sight can be inspiring to the abishai's allies, filling them with a fanatical willingness to fight.

WHITE ABISHAI

White abishais fight with a reckless fury, making them ideally suited for bolstering the ranks of Tiamat's armies. White abishais fight without fear, becoming whirlwinds of destruction on the battlefield.

BLUE ABISHAI
Medium Fiend (Devil, Wizard), Typically Lawful Evil

Armor Class 19 (natural armor)
Hit Points 202 (27d8 + 81)
Speed 30 ft., fly 50 ft.

STR	DEX	CON	INT	WIS	CHA
15 (+2)	14 (+2)	17 (+3)	22 (+6)	23 (+6)	18 (+4)

Saving Throws Int +12, Wis +12
Skills Arcana +12
Damage Resistances cold; bludgeoning, piercing, and slashing from nonmagical attacks that aren't silvered
Damage Immunities fire, lightning, poison
Condition Immunities poisoned
Senses darkvision 120 ft., passive Perception 16
Languages Draconic, Infernal, telepathy 120 ft.
Challenge 17 (18,000 XP)   **Proficiency Bonus** +6

Devil's Sight. Magical darkness doesn't impede the abishai's darkvision.

Magic Resistance. The abishai has advantage on saving throws against spells and other magical effects.

ACTIONS

Multiattack. The abishai makes three Bite or Lightning Strike attacks.

Bite. *Melee Weapon Attack:* +8 to hit, reach 5 ft., one target. *Hit:* 13 (2d10 + 2) piercing damage plus 14 (4d6) lightning damage.

Lightning Strike. *Ranged Spell Attack:* +12 to hit, range 120 ft., one target. *Hit:* 36 (8d8) lightning damage.

Spellcasting. The abishai casts one of the following spells, using Intelligence as the spellcasting ability (spell save DC 20):

At will: *disguise self, mage hand, minor illusion*
2/day each: *charm person, dispel magic, greater invisibility, wall of force*

BONUS ACTIONS

Teleport. The abishai teleports, along with any equipment it is wearing or carrying, up to 30 feet to an unoccupied space that it can see.

Green Abishai

Medium Fiend (Devil), Typically Lawful Evil

Armor Class 18 (natural armor)
Hit Points 195 (26d8 + 78)
Speed 30 ft., fly 40 ft.

STR	DEX	CON	INT	WIS	CHA
12 (+1)	17 (+3)	16 (+3)	17 (+3)	12 (+1)	19 (+4)

Saving Throws Int +8, Cha +9
Skills Deception +9, Insight +6, Perception +6, Persuasion +9
Damage Resistances cold; bludgeoning, piercing, and slashing from nonmagical attacks that aren't silvered
Damage Immunities fire, poison
Condition Immunities poisoned
Senses darkvision 120 ft., passive Perception 16
Languages Draconic, Infernal, telepathy 120 ft.
Challenge 15 (13,000 XP)   **Proficiency Bonus** +5

Devil's Sight. Magical darkness doesn't impede the abishai's darkvision.

Magic Resistance. The abishai has advantage on saving throws against spells and other magical effects.

Actions

Multiattack. The abishai makes two Fiendish Claw attacks, or it makes one Fiendish Claw attack and uses Spellcasting.

Fiendish Claw. *Melee Weapon Attack:* +8 to hit, reach 5 ft., one target. *Hit:* 12 (2d8 + 3) force damage. If the target is a creature, it must succeed on a DC 16 Constitution saving throw or take 16 (3d10) poison damage and become poisoned for 1 minute. The poisoned target can repeat the saving throw at the end of each of its turns, ending the effect on itself on a success.

Spellcasting. The abishai casts one of the following spells, requiring no material components and using Charisma as the spellcasting ability (spell save DC 17):

At will: *alter self, major image*
3/day each: *charm person, detect thoughts, fear*
1/day each: *confusion, dominate person, mass suggestion*

Red Abishai

Medium Fiend (Devil), Typically Lawful Evil

Armor Class 22 (natural armor)
Hit Points 289 (34d8 + 136)
Speed 30 ft., fly 50 ft.

STR	DEX	CON	INT	WIS	CHA
23 (+6)	16 (+3)	19 (+4)	14 (+2)	15 (+2)	19 (+4)

Saving Throws Str +12, Con +10, Wis +8
Skills Intimidation +10, Perception +8
Damage Resistances cold; bludgeoning, piercing, and slashing from nonmagical attacks that aren't silvered
Damage Immunities fire, poison
Condition Immunities frightened, poisoned
Senses darkvision 120 ft., passive Perception 18
Languages Draconic, Infernal, telepathy 120 ft.
Challenge 19 (22,000 XP)   **Proficiency Bonus** +6

Devil's Sight. Magical darkness doesn't impede the abishai's darkvision.

Magic Resistance. The abishai has advantage on saving throws against spells and other magical effects.

Actions

Multiattack. The abishai makes one Bite attack and one Claw attack, and it can use Frightful Presence or Incite Fanaticism.

Bite. *Melee Weapon Attack:* +12 to hit, reach 5 ft., one target. *Hit:* 22 (3d10 + 6) piercing damage plus 38 (7d10) fire damage.

Claw. *Melee Weapon Attack:* +12 to hit, reach 5 ft., one target. *Hit:* 17 (2d10 + 6) force damage plus 11 (2d10) fire damage.

Frightful Presence. Each creature of the abishai's choice that is within 120 feet and aware of the abishai must succeed on a DC 18 Wisdom saving throw or become frightened of it for 1 minute. A creature can repeat the saving throw at the end of each of its turns, ending the effect on itself on a success. If a creature's saving throw is successful or the effect ends for it, the creature is immune to the abishai's Frightful Presence for the next 24 hours.

Incite Fanaticism. The abishai chooses up to four other creatures within 60 feet of it that can see it. Until the start of the abishai's next turn, each of those creatures makes attack rolls with advantage and can't be frightened.

Power of the Dragon Queen. The abishai targets one Dragon it can see within 120 feet of it. The Dragon must make a DC 18 Charisma saving throw. A chromatic dragon makes this save with disadvantage. On a successful save, the target is immune to the abishai's Power of the Dragon Queen for 1 hour. On a failed save, the target is charmed by the abishai for 1 hour. While charmed in this way, the target regards the abishai as a trusted friend to be heeded and protected. This effect ends if the abishai or its companions deal damage to the target.

White Abishai

Red Abishai

Green Abishai

White Abishai

Medium Fiend (Devil), Typically Lawful Evil

Armor Class 15 (natural armor)
Hit Points 68 (8d8 + 32)
Speed 30 ft., fly 40 ft.

STR	DEX	CON	INT	WIS	CHA
16 (+3)	11 (+0)	18 (+4)	11 (+0)	12 (+1)	13 (+1)

Saving Throws Str +6, Con +7
Damage Resistances bludgeoning, piercing, and slashing from nonmagical attacks that aren't silvered
Damage Immunities cold, fire, poison
Condition Immunities poisoned
Senses darkvision 120 ft., passive Perception 11
Languages Draconic, Infernal, telepathy 120 ft.
Challenge 6 (2,300 XP)　　　　**Proficiency Bonus** +3

Devil's Sight. Magical darkness doesn't impede the abishai's darkvision.

Magic Resistance. The abishai has advantage on saving throws against spells and other magical effects.

Reckless. At the start of its turn, the abishai can gain advantage on all melee weapon attack rolls during that turn, but attack rolls against it have advantage until the start of its next turn.

Actions

Multiattack. The abishai makes one Bite attack, one Claw attack, and one Longsword attack.

Bite. *Melee Weapon Attack:* +6 to hit, reach 5 ft., one target. *Hit:* 5 (1d4 + 3) piercing damage plus 3 (1d6) cold damage.

Claw. *Melee Weapon Attack:* +6 to hit, reach 5 ft., one target. *Hit:* 8 (1d10 + 3) slashing damage.

Longsword. *Melee Weapon Attack:* +6 to hit, reach 5 ft., one target. *Hit:* 7 (1d8 + 3) force damage, or 8 (1d10 + 3) force damage if used with two hands.

Reactions

Vicious Reprisal. In response to taking damage, the abishai makes one Bite attack against a random creature within 5 feet of it. If no creature is within reach, the abishai moves up to half its speed toward an enemy it can see, without provoking opportunity attacks.

Alhoon

Mind flayers that pursue arcane magic are exiled as deviants, and for them no everlasting communion with an elder brain (appears in this book) is possible. The road to lichdom offers an alternative way to escape the permanency of death, but that path is long and fraught with barriers. Alhoons are mind flayers who have used a shortcut to attain a lich-like state.

Elder brains forbid mind flayers from pursuing magic power aside from psionics, but it isn't an interdiction they must often enforce. Illithids brook no masters but members of their own kind, so it isn't in their nature to bow to any god or otherworldly patron. However, wizardry remains a temptation. In the pages of a spellbook, an illithid sees a system to acquire authority. Through the writings of the wizard who penned it, the illithid perceives the workings of a highly intelligent mind. Most mind flayers who find a spellbook react with abhorrence or indifference, but for some, a spellbook is a gateway to a new way of thinking.

For a time, the study of such forbidden texts can be hidden from other illithids and even from an elder brain. Yet eventually, mind flayer arcanists determined to pursue wizardry must flee the colony for their own safety. Once they taste freedom from the colony, some prize their privacy, others seek to commune with similar minds, and still others seek to dominate a colony by elevating themselves to the position of leadership normally held by an elder brain. Regardless, all such arcanists face the same stark fact: when they die, they will not join the host of minds in the elder brain—deviant minds are never accepted as part of the collective. For them, death means oblivion.

Lichdom offers salvation and the prospect of being able to pursue knowledge indefinitely. Yet learning the secret of achieving lichdom requires an arcane spellcaster to be at the apex of power—a significant challenge for mind flayers, given the scarcity of available mentors and training.

Confronting this reality, a group of nine mind flayer arcanists used their arcane magic and psionics to weave a new truth. These nine called themselves the Alhoon, and those who follow in their footsteps are referred to by the same name.

Collaborative Undeath

To become alhoons, mind flayer arcanists must cooperate in the creation of a *periapt of mind trapping*, a fist-sized container made of silver, emerald, and amethyst. The process requires at least three mind flayer arcanists and the sacrifice of an equal number of souls from living victims in a three-day-long ritual of spellcasting and psionic communion. Upon its completion, free-willed undeath is conferred on the mind flayers, turning them into alhoons.

Initially, an alhoon can be difficult to distinguish from a normal mind flayer. The most obvious difference is the lack of a mind flayer's ever-present mucus coating. Without that protection, an alhoon's skin becomes dry and cracked, and its eyes might appear shriveled and sunken. Both of these clues are easily missed by someone who hasn't seen a mind flayer. However, in short order, an alhoon's flesh withers away and its empty eye sockets gleam with cold pinpricks of light like those of other liches.

Unlike a true lich's phylactery, the *periapt of mind trapping* doesn't restore the alhoons to undeath if they are destroyed. Instead, a destroyed alhoon's mind is transferred to the periapt, where it remains in communion with any other trapped alhoon minds, as well as the souls of those sacrificed.

The undeath conferred by a *periapt of mind trapping* lasts only so long as the life of the living victim selected. Thus an alhoon who sacrificed a 200-year-old elf looks forward to a much longer existence than one that sacrificed a 35-year-old person. Alhoons can extend their existence by repeating the ritual with new victims, effectively resetting the clocks for themselves.

Destroying a *periapt of mind trapping* consigns those trapped within it to oblivion, and thus alhoons often work together to create elaborate protections for their periapt and their preferred ritual site. Sometimes a single alhoon is entrusted with the *periapt of mind trapping*, but this is a dangerous proposition. Anyone who holds the periapt gains advantage on attacks, saving throws, and checks against the alhoons associated with its creation, and those alhoons in turn suffer disadvantage on attacks, saving throws, and checks against the holder. In addition, the holder can telepathically communicate with any sacrificed soul trapped within, and alhoons within the periapt can speak telepathically with the holder. A creature carrying the periapt can't prevent communication from alhoons but can silence trapped souls.

ALHOON

Medium Undead (Mind Flayer, Wizard), Typically Neutral Evil

Armor Class 15 (natural armor)
Hit Points 150 (20d8 + 60)
Speed 30 ft., fly 15 ft. (hover)

STR	DEX	CON	INT	WIS	CHA
11 (+0)	12 (+1)	16 (+3)	19 (+4)	17 (+3)	17 (+3)

Saving Throws Con +7, Int +8, Wis +7, Cha +7
Skills Arcana +8, Deception +7, History +8, Insight +7, Perception +7, Stealth +5
Damage Resistances cold, lightning, necrotic
Damage Immunities poison
Condition Immunities charmed, exhaustion, frightened, paralyzed, poisoned
Senses truesight 120 ft., passive Perception 17
Languages Deep Speech, Undercommon, telepathy 120 ft.
Challenge 10 (5,900 XP)   **Proficiency Bonus** +4

Magic Resistance. The alhoon has advantage on saving throws against spells and other magical effects.

Turn Resistance. The alhoon has advantage on saving throws against any effect that turns Undead.

ACTIONS

Multiattack. The alhoon makes two Chilling Grasp or Arcane Bolt attacks.

Chilling Grasp. *Melee Spell Attack:* +8 to hit, reach 5 ft., one target. *Hit:* 14 (4d6) cold damage, and the alhoon regains 14 hit points.

Arcane Bolt. *Ranged Spell Attack:* +8 to hit, range 120 ft., one target. *Hit:* 28 (8d6) force damage.

Mind Blast (Recharge 5–6). The alhoon magically emits psychic energy in a 60-foot cone. Each creature in that area must succeed on a DC 16 Intelligence saving throw or take 22 (4d8 + 4) psychic damage and be stunned for 1 minute. A target can repeat the saving throw at the end of each of its turns, ending the effect on itself on a success.

Spellcasting. The alhoon casts one of the following spells, requiring no material components and using Intelligence as the spellcasting ability (spell save DC 16):

At will: *dancing lights, detect magic, detect thoughts, disguise self, mage hand, prestidigitation*
1/day each: *dominate monster, globe of invulnerability, invisibility, modify memory, plane shift (self only), wall of force*

REACTIONS

Negate Spell (3/Day). The alhoon targets one creature it can see within 60 feet of it that is casting a spell. If the spell is 3rd level or lower, the spell fails, but any spell slots or charges are not wasted.

There are many reasons to avoid the way of the lich. An impermanent solution is paradoxical. Take alhoons. They require souls to keep from shriveling. I fail to see the appeal.

—Mordenkainen

Alkilith

An alkilith is easily mistaken for some kind of foul fungal growth that appears on doorways, windows, and other portals. These dripping infestations conceal the demonic nature of the alkilith, making what should be a dire warning appear strange but otherwise innocuous. Wherever alkiliths take root, they weaken the fabric of reality, creating a portal through which even nastier demons can invade.

The appearance of an alkilith in the world heralds a great wrongness and an imminent catastrophe. An alkilith searches for an aperture such as a window or a door around which it can take root, stretching its body around the opening and anchoring itself with a sticky secretion. If left undisturbed, the opening becomes attuned to the Abyss and eventually becomes a portal to that plane (see "Planar Portals" in the *Dungeon Master's Guide*).

Alkiliths spring from cast-off bits of the hideous, shuddering body of Juiblex (appears in this book). They gradually become self-aware and seek to find their way onto the Material Plane. Since most cultists consider them too risky to summon—they can, after all, create portals to the Abyss—alkiliths must find other escape routes out of their native plane.

Alkilith
Medium Fiend (Demon), Typically Chaotic Evil

Armor Class 17 (natural armor)
Hit Points 168 (16d8 + 96)
Speed 40 ft., climb 40 ft.

STR	DEX	CON	INT	WIS	CHA
12 (+1)	19 (+4)	22 (+6)	6 (−2)	11 (+0)	7 (−2)

Saving Throws Dex +8, Con +10
Skills Stealth +8
Damage Resistances acid, cold, fire, lightning; bludgeoning, piercing, and slashing from nonmagical attacks
Damage Immunities poison
Condition Immunities charmed, frightened, poisoned
Senses darkvision 120 ft., passive Perception 10
Languages understands Abyssal but can't speak
Challenge 11 (7,200 XP)   **Proficiency Bonus** +4

Abyssal Rift. If the alkilith surrounds a door, window, or similar opening continuously for 6d6 days, the opening becomes a permanent portal to a random layer of the Abyss.

Amorphous. The alkilith can move through a space as narrow as 1 inch wide without squeezing.

False Appearance. If the alkilith is motionless at the start of combat, it has advantage on its initiative roll. Moreover, if a creature hasn't observed the alkilith move or act, that creature must succeed on a DC 18 Intelligence (Investigation) check to discern that the alkilith isn't ordinary slime or fungus.

Foment Confusion. Any creature that isn't a demon that starts its turn within 30 feet of the alkilith must succeed on a DC 18 Wisdom saving throw, or it hears a faint buzzing in its head for a moment and has disadvantage on its next attack roll, saving throw, or ability check.

If the saving throw against Foment Confusion fails by 5 or more, the creature is instead subjected to the *confusion* spell for 1 minute (no concentration required by the alkilith). While under the effect of that *confusion*, the creature is immune to Foment Confusion.

Magic Resistance. The alkilith has advantage on saving throws against spells and other magical effects.

Spider Climb. The alkilith can climb difficult surfaces, such as upside down on ceilings, without making an ability check.

Unusual Nature. The alkilith doesn't require air, food, drink, or sleep.

Actions

Multiattack. The alkilith makes three Tentacle attacks.

Tentacle. *Melee Weapon Attack:* +8 to hit, reach 15 ft., one target. *Hit:* 18 (4d6 + 4) acid damage.

CLAUDIO POZAS

INSIDIOUS LORE

An allip might attempt to share its lore to escape its curse and enter the afterlife. It can transfer knowledge from its mind by guiding another creature to write down what it knows. This process takes days or possibly weeks. An allip can accomplish this task by lurking in the study or workplace of a scholar. If the allip remains hidden, its victim is gradually overcome by frantic energy. A scholar, driven by sudden insights to work night and day, produces reams of text with little memory of exactly what the documents contain. If the allip succeeds, it passes from the world—and its terrible secret hides somewhere in the scholar's text, waiting to be discovered by its next victim.

ALLIP

ALLIP

When a creature uncovers a secret that a powerful being has protected with a mighty curse, the result is often the creation of an allip. Secrets protected in this manner range in scope from a demon lord's true name to the hidden truths of the cosmic order. The creature acquires the secret, but the curse annihilates its body and leaves behind a spectral being composed of fragments from the victim's psyche and overwhelming psychic agony.

Every allip is wracked with a horrifying insight that torments what remains of its mind. In the presence of other creatures, an allip seeks to relieve this burden by sharing its secret. The creature can impart only a shard of the knowledge that doomed it, but that piece is enough to wrack the recipient with temporary mental anguish and violent compulsions. The survivors of an allip's attack are sometimes left with a compulsion to learn more about what spawned this monstrosity. Strange phrases echo through their minds, and weird visions occupy their dreams. The sense that some colossal truth sits just outside their recall plagues them for days, months, and sometimes years after their fateful encounter.

ALLIP
Medium Undead, Typically Neutral Evil

Armor Class 13
Hit Points 40 (9d8)
Speed 0 ft., fly 40 ft. (hover)

STR	DEX	CON	INT	WIS	CHA
6 (−2)	17 (+3)	10 (+0)	17 (+3)	15 (+2)	16 (+3)

Saving Throws Int +6, Wis +5
Skills Perception +5, Stealth +6
Damage Resistances acid, fire, lightning, thunder; bludgeoning, piercing, and slashing from nonmagical attacks
Damage Immunities cold, necrotic, poison
Condition Immunities charmed, exhaustion, frightened, grappled, paralyzed, petrified, poisoned, prone, restrained
Senses darkvision 60 ft., passive Perception 15
Languages the languages it knew in life
Challenge 5 (1,800 XP)   **Proficiency Bonus** +3

Incorporeal Movement. The allip can move through other creatures and objects as if they were difficult terrain. It takes 5 (1d10) force damage if it ends its turn inside an object.

Unusual Nature. The allip doesn't require air, food, drink, or sleep.

ACTIONS

Maddening Touch. *Melee Spell Attack:* +6 to hit, reach 5 ft., one target. *Hit:* 17 (4d6 + 3) psychic damage.

Howling Babble (Recharge 6). Each creature within 30 feet of the allip that can hear it must make a DC 14 Wisdom saving throw. On a failed save, a target takes 12 (2d8 + 3) psychic damage, and it is stunned until the end of its next turn. On a successful save, it takes half as much damage and isn't stunned. Constructs and Undead are immune to this effect.

Whispers of Compulsion. The allip chooses up to three creatures it can see within 60 feet of it. Each target must succeed on a DC 14 Wisdom saving throw, or it takes 12 (2d8 + 3) psychic damage and must use its reaction to make a melee weapon attack against one creature of the allip's choice that the allip can see. Constructs and Undead are immune to this effect.

AMNIZU

Amnizus lead infernal legions into battle and command guardians at the gateways to the Hells. Amnizus are arrogant, bullying, and ruthless, but they're also highly intelligent tacticians and unfailingly loyal—qualities the hellish archdukes value.

Some amnizus perform the critical task of watching over the River Styx from fortresses along the river's blighted banks, where it flows through Dis and Stygia. They collect the souls arriving in the form of lemures (see the *Monster Manual*). Lemures have no personalities or memories; they're driven only by the desire to commit evil. The amnizus that patrol here drill the rules of the Nine Hells into the new arrivals' minds and marshal them into legions.

VARIANT: DEVIL SUMMONING

Some amnizus have an action that allows them to summon other devils:

Summon Devil (1/Day). The amnizu summons 2d4 **bearded devils** or 1d4 **barbed devils** (both appear in the *Monster Manual*). A summoned devil appears in an unoccupied space within 60 feet of the amnizu, acts as an ally of the amnizu, and can't summon other devils. It remains for 1 minute, until the amnizu dies, or until its summoner dismisses it as an action.

AMNIZU
Medium Fiend (Devil), Typically Lawful Evil

Armor Class 21 (natural armor)
Hit Points 202 (27d8 + 81)
Speed 30 ft., fly 40 ft.

STR	DEX	CON	INT	WIS	CHA
11 (+0)	13 (+1)	16 (+3)	20 (+5)	12 (+1)	18 (+4)

Saving Throws Dex +7, Con +9, Wis +7, Cha +10
Skills Perception +7
Damage Resistances cold; bludgeoning, piercing, and slashing from nonmagical attacks that aren't silvered
Damage Immunities fire, poison
Condition Immunities charmed, poisoned
Senses darkvision 120 ft., passive Perception 17
Languages Common, Infernal, telepathy 1,000 ft.
Challenge 18 (20,000 XP)   **Proficiency Bonus** +6

Devil's Sight. Magical darkness doesn't impede the amnizu's darkvision.

Magic Resistance. The amnizu has advantage on saving throws against spells and other magical effects.

ACTIONS

Multiattack. The amnizu uses Blinding Rot or Forgetfulness, if available. It also makes two Taskmaster Whip attacks.

Taskmaster Whip. *Melee Weapon Attack:* +11 to hit, reach 10 ft., one target. *Hit:* 9 (1d8 + 5) slashing damage plus 16 (3d10) force damage.

Blinding Rot. The amnizu targets one or two creatures that it can see within 60 feet of it. Each target must succeed on a DC 19 Wisdom saving throw or take 26 (4d12) necrotic damage and be blinded until the start of the amnizu's next turn.

Forgetfulness (Recharge 6). The amnizu targets one creature it can see within 60 feet of it. That creature must succeed on a DC 18 Intelligence saving throw or take 26 (4d12) psychic damage and become stunned for 1 minute. A stunned creature repeats the saving throw at the end of each of its turns, ending the effect on itself on a success. If the target is stunned for the full minute, it forgets everything it sensed, experienced, and learned during the last 5 hours.

Spellcasting. The amnizu casts one of the following spells, requiring no material components and using Intelligence as the spellcasting ability (spell save DC 19):

At will: *command*
3/day: *dominate monster*
1/day: *feeblemind*

REACTIONS

Instinctive Charm. When a creature within 60 feet of the amnizu makes an attack roll against it, and another creature is within the attack's range, the attacker must make a DC 19 Wisdom saving throw. On a failed save, the attacker must target the creature that is closest to it, not including the amnizu or itself. If multiple creatures are closest, the attacker chooses which one to target. If the saving throw is successful, the attacker is immune to the amnizu's Instinctive Charm for 24 hours.

ANNIS HAG

Annis hags lair in mountains or hills. These hunch-backed and hump-shouldered hags are the largest and most physically imposing of their kind, standing eight feet tall. They can easily tear a fully grown person apart, but they love hunting the young, pre-ferring their flesh above all others.

Annis hags leave tokens of their cruelty at the edges of forests and other areas they claim to pro-voke fear and distrust in nearby villages and set-tlements. To an annis hag, nothing is sweeter than making a once-vibrant community paralyzed with terror, so folk never venture out at night, strangers are met with suspicion and anger, and parents warn their children: "Be good, or the annis will get you."

When an annis feels especially cruel, the hag adopts the appearance of a kindly elder, approaches a child in a remote place, and gives them an *iron to-ken* (described below), through which the child can magically confide in the hag. Over time, "Granny" or "Grampy" convinces the child that it's okay to do bad deeds—starting with breaking things or wan-dering without permission, then graduating to push-ing someone down the stairs or setting a house on fire. Eventually, the child's terrified family and com-munity face painful decisions of what to do about the seemingly remorseless child.

Much as annis hags befriend children in order to corrupt them, they may adopt a group of ogres, trolls, or other creatures (ogres and trolls appear in the *Monster Manual*), ruling them through brute strength, insults, and superstition.

IRON TOKEN

An annis hag can pull out one of their iron teeth or nails and spend 1 minute shaping and polishing it into the form of a coin, a ring, or a tiny mirror. Thereafter, any creature that holds this *iron token* can have a whispered conversation with the hag, provided the creature and the hag are within 10 miles of each other. When the hag speaks through the token, the holder can hear the hag's whisper but not any other sounds at the hag's location. Similarly, the hag can hear the holder of the token but not the noise around it.

A hag can have up to three *iron tokens* active at one time. As an action, the hag can discern the direction and approximate distance to those active tokens. The hag can deactivate any of those tokens at any distance (no action required), whereupon the token retains its current form but loses its magic.

HAG COVENS

An annis hag that is part of a coven (see the "Hag Covens" sidebar in the *Monster Manual*) has a chal-lenge rating of 8 (3,900 XP).

ANNIS HAG
Large Fey, Typically Chaotic Evil

Armor Class 17 (natural armor)
Hit Points 90 (12d10 + 24)
Speed 40 ft.

STR	DEX	CON	INT	WIS	CHA
21 (+5)	12 (+1)	14 (+2)	13 (+1)	14 (+2)	15 (+2)

Saving Throws Con +5
Skills Deception +5, Perception +5
Damage Resistances cold
Senses darkvision 60 ft., passive Perception 15
Languages Common, Giant, Sylvan
Challenge 6 (2,300 XP)   **Proficiency Bonus** +3

ACTIONS

Multiattack. The annis makes one Bite attack and two Claw attacks.

Bite. *Melee Weapon Attack:* +8 to hit, reach 5 ft., one target. *Hit:* 15 (3d6 + 5) piercing damage.

Claw. *Melee Weapon Attack:* +8 to hit, reach 5 ft., one target. *Hit:* 15 (3d6 + 5) slashing damage.

Crushing Hug. *Melee Weapon Attack:* +8 to hit, reach 5 ft., one target. *Hit:* 36 (9d6 + 5) bludgeoning damage, and the target is grappled (escape DC 15) if it is a Large or smaller creature. Un-til the grapple ends, the target takes 36 (9d6 + 5) bludgeon-ing damage at the start of each of the hag's turns. The hag can't make attacks while grappling a creature in this way.

Spellcasting. The hag casts one of the following spells, using Charisma as the spellcasting ability (spell save DC 13):

3/day each: *disguise self* (including the form of a Medium Hu-manoid), *fog cloud*

ARCHDRUID

Archdruids watch over the natural wonders of their domains. They seldom interact with folk away from their druid groves and shrines, unless there is a great threat to the natural order or to a nearby community. An archdruid typically has one or more pupils who are druids (see the *Monster Manual*), and the archdruid's lair is usually guarded by loyal Beasts and Fey creatures.

When an archdruid uses their Change Shape action, you may choose the creature they turn into, abiding by the action's restrictions. Or you may roll on the Archdruid Favored Shapes table to determine the form the archdruid adopts. These creatures appear in the *Monster Manual*, unless otherwise noted.

ARCHDRUID FAVORED SHAPES

d8	Favored Shape
1	Air elemental
2	Earth elemental
3	Fire elemental
4	Giant crocodile
5	Mammoth
6	Flail snail (appears in this book)
7	Triceratops
8	Water elemental

ARCHDRUID

Medium Humanoid (Druid), Any Alignment

Armor Class 14 (hide armor)
Hit Points 154 (28d8 + 28)
Speed 30 ft.

STR	DEX	CON	INT	WIS	CHA
14 (+2)	14 (+2)	12 (+1)	12 (+1)	20 (+5)	11 (+0)

Saving Throws Int +5, Wis +9
Skills Medicine +9, Nature +5, Perception +9
Senses passive Perception 19
Languages Druidic plus any two languages
Challenge 12 (8,400 XP)   **Proficiency Bonus** +4

ACTIONS

Multiattack. The archdruid makes three Staff or Wildfire attacks. It can replace one attack with a use of Spellcasting.

Staff. *Melee Weapon Attack:* +6 to hit, reach 5 ft., one target. *Hit:* 5 (1d6 + 2) bludgeoning damage plus 21 (6d6) poison damage.

Wildfire. *Ranged Spell Attack:* +9 to hit, range 120 ft., one target. *Hit:* 26 (6d6 + 5) fire damage, and the target is blinded until the start of the druid's next turn.

Spellcasting. The archdruid casts one of the following spells, using Wisdom as the spellcasting ability (spell save DC 17):

At will: *beast sense, entangle, speak with animals*
3/day each: *animal messenger, dominate beast, faerie fire, tree stride*
1/day each: *commune with nature* (as an action), *mass cure wounds*

BONUS ACTIONS

Change Shape (2/Day). The archdruid magically transforms into a Beast or an Elemental with a challenge rating of 6 or less and can remain in that form for up to 9 hours. The archdruid can choose whether its equipment falls to the ground, melds with its new form, or is worn by the new form. The archdruid reverts to its true form if it dies or falls unconscious. The archdruid can revert to its true form using a bonus action.

While in a new form, the archdruid's stat block is replaced by the stat block of that form, except the archdruid keeps its current hit points, its hit point maximum, this bonus action, its languages and ability to speak, and its Spellcasting action.

The new form's attacks count as magical for the purpose of overcoming resistances and immunity to nonmagical attacks.

ARCHER

Archers defend castles, hunt wild game on the fringes of civilization, serve as artillery in military units, and occasionally make good coin as brigands or caravan guards.

Some renowned archers and groups of archers are known for the special fletching of their arrows. You may roll on the Archer Fletching table to determine the distinctive fletching used by an individual archer or a group of them.

ARCHER FLETCHING

d12	Fletching
1	Feathers from an owlbear's mane
2	Cockatrice feathers
3	Axe beak feathers
4	Planetar feathers
5	Couatl feathers
6	Pegasus feathers
7	Griffon feathers
8	Vrock feathers
9	Peryton feathers
10	Dryad leaf vanes
11	Drake scale vanes
12	Stirge wing vanes

ARCHER
Medium Humanoid, Any Alignment

Armor Class 16 (studded leather)
Hit Points 75 (10d8 + 30)
Speed 30 ft.

STR	DEX	CON	INT	WIS	CHA
11 (+0)	18 (+4)	16 (+3)	11 (+0)	13 (+1)	10 (+0)

Skills Acrobatics +6, Perception +5
Senses passive Perception 15
Languages any one language (usually Common)
Challenge 3 (700 XP)   **Proficiency Bonus** +2

ACTIONS

Multiattack. The archer makes two Shortsword or Longbow attacks.

Shortsword. *Melee Weapon Attack:* +6 to hit, reach 5 ft., one target. *Hit:* 7 (1d6 + 4) piercing damage.

Longbow. *Ranged Weapon Attack:* +6 to hit, range 150/600 ft., one target. *Hit:* 8 (1d8 + 4) piercing damage.

BONUS ACTIONS

Archer's Eye (3/Day). Immediately after making an attack roll or a damage roll with a ranged weapon, the archer can roll a d10 and add the number rolled to the total.

Armanite

Great herds of armanites race across the blasted fields of the Abyss, bent on slaughter and death, driven by unrestrained bloodlust. Whether they're controlled by more powerful demons or charging into battle for the sake of it, armanites use their claws and hooves, as well as their long, whiplike tails, to tear apart foes.

In the armies of demon lords, armanites perform the role of heavy cavalry, leading the charge and tearing into their enemies' flanks. Armanites fight all the time—even battling each other if they can't find another enemy. They make ideal shock troops, utterly ruthless and bold to the point of stupidity.

Part of what makes armanites so fearsome is the number of weapons they have at their disposal. They possess dense hooves, claws that end in curling talons, and long tails whose serrated ridges can flense the flesh from a victim, and they use them all to carve through their foes. When they're up against tough formations, they can call on their innate magic to loose bolts of lightning and blow holes in enemy ranks.

ARMANITE

Large Fiend (Demon), Typically Chaotic Evil

Armor Class 16 (natural armor)
Hit Points 94 (9d10 + 45)
Speed 60 ft.

STR	DEX	CON	INT	WIS	CHA
21 (+5)	18 (+4)	21 (+5)	8 (−1)	12 (+1)	13 (+1)

Damage Resistances cold, fire, lightning
Damage Immunities poison
Condition Immunities poisoned
Senses darkvision 120 ft., passive Perception 11
Languages Abyssal, telepathy 120 ft.
Challenge 7 (2,900 XP)　　　　**Proficiency Bonus** +3

Magic Resistance. The armanite has advantage on saving throws against spells and other magical effects.

ACTIONS

Multiattack. The armanite makes one Claw attack, one Hooves attack, and one Serrated Tail attack.

Claw. Melee Weapon Attack: +8 to hit, reach 5 ft., one target. *Hit:* 10 (2d4 + 5) slashing damage plus 9 (2d8) lightning damage.

Hooves. Melee Weapon Attack: +8 to hit, reach 5 ft., one target. *Hit:* 12 (2d6 + 5) bludgeoning damage. If the target is a Large or smaller creature, it must succeed on a DC 16 Strength saving throw or be knocked prone.

Serrated Tail. Melee Weapon Attack: +8 to hit, reach 10 ft., one target. *Hit:* 16 (2d10 + 5) slashing damage.

Lightning Lance (Recharge 5–6). The armanite looses a bolt of lightning in a line that is 60 feet long and 10 feet wide. Each creature in the line must make a DC 15 Dexterity saving throw, taking 36 (8d8) lightning damage on a failed save, or half as much damage on a successful one.

Astral Dreadnought

Enormous and terrifying, astral dreadnoughts haunt the silvery void of the Astral Plane, causing planar travelers to shudder at the very thought of them. Dreadnoughts have been gliding through the astral mists since the dawn of the multiverse, trying to devour all other creatures they encounter.

Covered from head to tail in layers of thick, spiked plates, a dreadnought has two gnarled limbs that end in magic-enhanced pincer claws. Constellations appear to swirl in the depths of its single eye, and its serpentine tail trails off into the silvery void. Anything it swallows is deposited in a unique demiplane—an enclosed space that contains eons worth of detritus, as well as the remains of travelers. The place has gravity and breathable air, and organic matter decays there. When the dreadnought dies, its demiplane vanishes, and its contents are released into the Astral Plane.

Astral Dreadnought

Gargantuan Monstrosity (Titan), Unaligned

Armor Class 20 (natural armor)
Hit Points 297 (17d20 + 119)
Speed 15 ft., fly 80 ft. (hover)

STR	DEX	CON	INT	WIS	CHA
28 (+9)	7 (−2)	25 (+7)	5 (−3)	14 (+2)	18 (+4)

Saving Throws Dex +5, Wis +9
Skills Perception +9
Damage Resistances bludgeoning, piercing, and slashing from nonmagical attacks
Condition Immunities charmed, exhaustion, frightened, paralyzed, petrified, poisoned, prone, stunned
Senses darkvision 120 ft., passive Perception 19
Languages —
Challenge 21 (33,000 XP)   **Proficiency Bonus** +7

Antimagic Cone. The dreadnought's eye creates an area of antimagic, as in the *antimagic field* spell, in a 150-foot cone. At the start of each of its turns, it decides which way the cone faces. The cone doesn't function while the eye is closed or while the dreadnought is blinded.

Astral Entity. The dreadnought can't leave the Astral Plane, nor can it be banished or otherwise transported out of that plane.

Demiplanar Donjon. Anything the dreadnought swallows is transported to a demiplane that can be entered by no other means except a *wish* spell or the dreadnought's Bite and Donjon Visit. A creature can leave the demiplane only by using magic that enables planar travel, such as the *plane shift* spell. The demiplane resembles a stone cave roughly 1,000 feet in diameter with a ceiling 100 feet high. Like a stomach, it contains the remains of past meals. The dreadnought can't be harmed from within the demiplane. If the dreadnought dies, the demiplane disappears, and everything inside it appears around the dreadnought's corpse. The demiplane is otherwise indestructible.

Legendary Resistance (3/Day). If the dreadnought fails a saving throw, it can choose to succeed instead.

Sever Silver Cord. If the dreadnought scores a critical hit against a creature traveling by means of the *astral projection* spell, the dreadnought can cut the target's silver cord instead of dealing damage.

Unusual Nature. The dreadnought doesn't require air, food, drink, or sleep.

Actions

Multiattack. The dreadnought makes one Bite attack and two Claw attacks.

Bite. *Melee Weapon Attack:* +16 to hit, reach 10 ft., one target. *Hit:* 36 (5d10 + 9) force damage. If the target is a Huge or smaller creature and this damage reduces it to 0 hit points or it is incapacitated, the dreadnought swallows it. The swallowed target, along with everything it is wearing and carrying, appears in an unoccupied space on the floor of the Demiplanar Donjon.

Claw. *Melee Weapon Attack:* +16 to hit, reach 20 ft., one target. *Hit:* 19 (3d6 + 9) force damage.

Legendary Actions

The dreadnought can take 3 legendary actions, choosing from the options below. Only one legendary option can be used at a time and only at the end of another creature's turn. The dreadnought regains spent legendary actions at the start of its turn.

Claw. The dreadnought makes one Claw attack.
Donjon Visit (Costs 2 Actions). One Huge or smaller creature that the dreadnought can see within 60 feet of it must succeed on a DC 19 Charisma saving throw or be teleported to an unoccupied space on the floor of the Demiplanar Donjon. At the end of the target's next turn, it reappears in the space it left or in the nearest unoccupied space if that space is occupied.
Psychic Projection (Costs 3 Actions). Each creature within 60 feet of the dreadnought must make a DC 19 Wisdom saving throw, taking 26 (4d10 + 4) psychic damage on a failed save, or half as much damage on a successful one.

I'm unimpressed by most children. They are a blend of their ancestors but often more disappointing. You'd think two of the most beautiful, bloodthirsty beings of the Lower Planes would create a creature of greater potential. Instead, the ghastly babau fails to match the fiendish splendor of its parents.

—Mordenkainen

Babau

Medium Fiend (Demon), Typically Chaotic Evil

Armor Class 16 (natural armor)
Hit Points 82 (11d8 + 33)
Speed 40 ft.

STR	DEX	CON	INT	WIS	CHA
19 (+4)	16 (+3)	16 (+3)	11 (+0)	12 (+1)	13 (+1)

Skills Perception +5, Stealth +5
Damage Resistances cold, fire, lightning; bludgeoning, piercing, and slashing from nonmagical attacks
Damage Immunities poison
Condition Immunities poisoned
Senses darkvision 120 ft., passive Perception 15
Languages Abyssal
Challenge 4 (1,100 XP) **Proficiency Bonus** +2

Actions

Multiattack. The babau makes two Claw attacks. It can replace one attack with a use of Spellcasting or Weakening Gaze.

Claw. *Melee Weapon Attack:* +6 to hit, reach 5 ft., one target. *Hit:* 6 (1d4 + 4) slashing damage plus 2 (1d4) acid damage.

Spellcasting. The babau casts one of the following spells, requiring no material components and using Wisdom as the spellcasting ability (spell save DC 11):

At will: *darkness, dispel magic, fear, heat metal, levitate*

Weakening Gaze. The babau targets one creature that it can see within 20 feet of it. The target must make a DC 13 Constitution saving throw. On a failed save, the target deals only half damage with weapon attacks that use Strength for 1 minute. The target can repeat the saving throw at the end of each of its turns, ending the effect on itself on a success.

Babau

Demons and devils clash endlessly for control of the Lower Planes. One of these battles pitted the legions of the archdevil Glasya against the screaming hordes of the demon lord Graz'zt (appears in this book). It is said that when Glasya wounded Graz'zt with her sword, the first babaus arose where his blood struck the ground. Their sudden appearance helped rout Glasya and secured Graz'zt's place as one of the preeminent demon lords of the Abyss.

A babau demon has the cunning of a devil and the bloodthirstiness of a demon. It has leathery skin pulled tight over its gaunt frame and a curved horn protruding from the back of its elongated skull. A babau's baleful glare can weaken a creature, and its talons gleam with acidic slime.

BAEL

With the Blood War between devils and demons raging for eons and no end in sight, opportunities abound for ambitious archdevils to win fame, glory, and power in the ongoing struggle. Duke Bael, one of Mammon's most important vassals, has won fame and acclaim for his victories. Charged with leading sixty-six companies of barbed devils (see the *Monster Manual*), Bael has proven to be a tactical genius, earning esteem for himself and his master as a result of victory after victory over the abyssal host. Mammon relies on Bael to safeguard his holdings because of Bael's battle acumen. During a time when so many other archdevils have lost their positions, Mammon has never been ousted, which is a testament to Bael's skill on the battlefield.

For his accomplishments, Bael has been granted the title of Bronze General. His accolades notwithstanding, he has had a difficult time navigating the quagmire of infernal politics. His critics call him naive, though never to his face. His primary interest has always been leading soldiers in battle, so he finds it frustrating to have his ambitions of ascending to a higher rank constantly stymied by politically shrewd rivals.

Bael prefers to make servants out of his adversaries, and mortals bound to his service earn their wretched place by falling victim to his superior stratagems. Bael gladly spares the lives of those he defeats—if they pledge their souls and service to him. Demons are an exception; although he is willing to corrupt almost any other foes, he always destroys demons he defeats.

Bael also welcomes mortals into his service if they can provide him with an advantage in his politicking. He recruits savvy individuals and relies on them to represent his interests at Mammon's court, which leaves him free to pursue his battle lust.

Despite his lack of interest in affairs outside battle, or perhaps because of it, Bael has gained a small following of cultists. Those who worship at his altar call him the King of Hell, and the most deluded believe that he is the lord of all devils. In arcane circles, certain writings, such as the dreaded *Book of Fire*, say that Bael revealed the *invisibility* spell to the world, though some scholars of magic hotly refute such claims. Bael is sometimes depicted as a toad, a cat, a human, or some combination of these forms.

BAEL

Large Fiend (Devil), Lawful Evil

Armor Class 18 (plate)
Hit Points 189 (18d10 + 90)
Speed 30 ft.

STR	DEX	CON	INT	WIS	CHA
24 (+7)	17 (+3)	20 (+5)	21 (+5)	24 (+7)	24 (+7)

Saving Throws Dex +9, Con +11, Int +11, Cha +13
Skills Intimidation +13, Perception +13, Persuasion +13
Damage Resistances cold; bludgeoning, piercing, and slashing from nonmagical attacks that aren't silvered
Damage Immunities fire, poison
Condition Immunities charmed, exhaustion, frightened, poisoned
Senses truesight 120 ft., passive Perception 23
Languages all, telepathy 120 ft.
Challenge 19 (22,000 XP)   **Proficiency Bonus** +6

Dread. Any creature, other than a devil, that starts its turn within 10 feet of Bael must succeed on a DC 22 Wisdom saving throw or be frightened of him until the start of its next turn. A creature succeeds on this saving throw automatically if Bael wishes it or if he is incapacitated.

Legendary Resistance (3/Day). If Bael fails a saving throw, he can choose to succeed instead.

Magic Resistance. Bael have advantage on saving throws against spells and other magical effects.

Regeneration. Bael regains 20 hit points at the start of his turn. If he takes cold or radiant damage, this trait doesn't function at the start of his next turn. Bael dies only if he starts his turn with 0 hit points and doesn't regenerate.

ACTIONS

Multiattack. Bael makes two Hellish Morningstar attacks.

Hellish Morningstar. *Melee Weapon Attack:* +13 to hit, reach 20 ft., one target. *Hit:* 16 (2d8 + 7) force damage plus 9 (2d8) necrotic damage.

Infernal Command. Each of Bael's allies within 60 feet of him can't be charmed or frightened until the end of his next turn.

Spellcasting. Bael casts one of the following spells, requiring no material components and using Charisma as the spellcasting ability (spell save DC 21):

At will: *alter self* (can become Medium), *charm person, detect magic, invisibility, major image*
3/day each: *dispel magic, fly, suggestion, wall of fire*
1/day: *dominate monster*

Teleport. Bael teleports, along with any equipment he is wearing or carrying, up to 120 feet to an unoccupied space he can see.

LEGENDARY ACTIONS

Bael can take 3 legendary actions, choosing from the options below. Only one legendary action option can be used at a time and only at the end of another creature's turn. Bael regains spent legendary actions at the start of his turn.

Fiendish Magic. Bael uses Spellcasting or Teleport.
Infernal Command. Bael uses Infernal Command.
Attack (Costs 2 Actions). Bael makes one Hellish Morningstar attack.

BALHANNOTH

Native to the Shadowfell, the vicious, predatory balhannoth alters reality in its lair to make the place appear inviting to travelers. A limited form of telepathy enables a balhannoth to identify images of places where its prey expects their needs and desires to be met, such as an inn or a temple offering healing. It then warps reality around itself, hiding itself and remaking its environment to resemble such a place. The imitation is imperfect, but it's good enough to fool greedy or desperate creatures. Once its prey enters the trap, it snatches the targets and teleports away to feed on their fear and despair.

Dungeon builders and Underdark tyrants sometimes venture into the Shadowfell to capture balhannoths for use as guardians.

A BALHANNOTH'S LAIR

In the Shadowfell, balhannoths make their lairs near places inhabited by creatures they hunt. They typically haunt well-traveled roads and paths, snatching people who come along. A balhannoth used as a guardian in the Underdark might lair in caves near Underdark passages and guard the ways in and out of its keepers' enclave.

LAIR ACTIONS

On initiative count 20 (losing initiative ties), a balhannoth can take one of the following lair actions; the balhannoth can't take the same lair action two rounds in a row:

Teleport. The balhannoth targets one creature within 500 feet of it. The target must succeed on a DC 16 Wisdom saving throw, or the target, along with whatever it is wearing and carrying, teleports to an unoccupied space of the balhannoth's choice within 60 feet of it.

Vanish. The balhannoth targets one creature within 500 feet of it. The target must succeed on a DC 16 Wisdom saving throw, or the balhannoth becomes invisible to that creature for 1 minute. This effect ends if the balhannoth attacks the target.

Warp Terrain. The balhannoth warps reality around it in an area up to 500 feet square. After 10 minutes, the terrain in the area reshapes to assume the appearance of a location sought by one Humanoid whose desires the balhannoth has sensed (see Regional Effects below). The transformation affects nonliving material only and can't create anything with moving parts or magical properties. Any object created in this area is, upon

close inspection, revealed as a fake. Books are filled with empty pages, golden items are obvious counterfeits, and so on. The transformation lasts until the balhannoth dies or takes this lair action again.

REGIONAL EFFECTS

A region containing a balhannoth's lair becomes warped by the creature's unnatural presence, which creates one or more of the following effects:

Sense Desires. The balhannoth can sense the strongest desires of any Humanoid within 1 mile of it and learns whether those desires involve a place: a safe location to rest, such as a temple, a home, or somewhere else.

Supernatural Lure. Creatures within 1 mile of the balhannoth's lair experience the sensation of being close to whatever they desire most. The sensation grows stronger the closer the creatures come to the balhannoth's lair.

If the balhannoth dies, these effects end immediately.

BALHANNOTH
Large Aberration, Typically Chaotic Evil

Armor Class 17 (natural armor)
Hit Points 114 (12d10 + 48)
Speed 25 ft., climb 25 ft.

STR	DEX	CON	INT	WIS	CHA
17 (+3)	8 (−1)	18 (+4)	6 (−2)	15 (+2)	8 (−1)

Saving Throws Con +8
Skills Perception +6
Condition Immunities blinded
Senses blindsight 500 ft. (blind beyond this radius), passive Perception 16
Languages understands Deep Speech, telepathy 1 mile
Challenge 11 (7,200 XP)   **Proficiency Bonus** +4

Legendary Resistance (2/Day). If the balhannoth fails a saving throw, it can choose to succeed instead.

ACTIONS

Multiattack. The balhannoth makes one Bite attack and two Tentacle attacks.

Bite. *Melee Weapon Attack:* +7 to hit, reach 5 ft., one target. *Hit:* 19 (3d10 + 3) piercing damage.

Tentacle. *Melee Weapon Attack:* +7 to hit, reach 10 ft., one target. *Hit:* 10 (2d6 + 3) bludgeoning damage, and the target is grappled (escape DC 15) and is moved up to 5 feet toward the balhannoth. Until this grapple ends, the target is restrained, and the balhannoth can't use this tentacle against other targets. The balhannoth has four tentacles.

LEGENDARY ACTIONS

The balhannoth can take 3 legendary actions, choosing from the options below. Only one legendary action can be used at a time and only at the end of another creature's turn. The balhannoth regains spent legendary actions at the start of its turn.

Bite. The balhannoth makes one Bite attack against one creature it has grappled.

Teleport. The balhannoth teleports, along with any equipment it is wearing or carrying and any creatures it has grappled, up to 60 feet to an unoccupied space it can see.

Vanish. The balhannoth magically becomes invisible for up to 10 minutes or until immediately after it makes an attack roll.

BRYNN METHENEY

Banderhobb

A banderhobb is a hybrid of shadow and flesh. Through vile magic, these components take on an enormous and horrific upright shape resembling a bipedal toad. In this form, a banderhobb temporarily serves its creator as a thug, a thief, and a kidnapper that swallows the unwary.

Hags have devised a ritual for creating banderhobbs—a hag who knows the ritual might be willing to teach it for the right price. Some other wicked Fey and powerful Fiends also know of the process, as do a few mortal mages.

During its brief existence, a banderhobb attempts to carry out its creator's bidding. It accomplishes its mission with no concern for the harm it suffers or causes. Its only desire is to serve and succeed. A banderhobb that is assigned to track down a target is particularly dangerous when it is provided with a lock of hair, a personal belonging, or another object connected to the target. Possession of such an item allows it to sense the creature's location from as far as a mile away.

A banderhobb fulfills its duties until its existence ends. When it expires, usually several days after its birth, it leaves behind only tarry goo and wisps of shadow. Legends tell of an ominous tower in the Shadowfell where the shadows sometimes reform and banderhobbs roam.

Banderhobb

Large Monstrosity, Typically Neutral Evil

Armor Class 15 (natural armor)
Hit Points 84 (8d10 + 40)
Speed 30 ft.

STR	DEX	CON	INT	WIS	CHA
20 (+5)	12 (+1)	20 (+5)	11 (+0)	14 (+2)	8 (−1)

Skills Athletics +8, Stealth +7
Condition Immunities charmed, frightened
Senses darkvision 120 ft., passive Perception 12
Languages understands Common and the languages of its creator but can't speak
Challenge 5 (1,800 XP)   **Proficiency Bonus** +3

Resonant Connection. If the banderhobb has even a tiny piece of a creature or an object in its possession, such as a lock of hair or a splinter of wood, it knows the most direct route to that creature or object if it is within 1 mile of the banderhobb.

Actions

Multiattack. The banderhobb makes one Bite attack and one Tongue attack. It can replace one attack with a use of Shadow Step.

Bite. *Melee Weapon Attack:* +8 to hit, reach 5 ft., one target. *Hit:* 15 (3d6 + 5) piercing damage, and the target is grappled (escape DC 16) if it is a Large or smaller creature. Until this grapple ends, the target is restrained, and the banderhobb can't use its Bite attack or Tongue attack on another target.

Tongue. *Melee Weapon Attack:* +8 to hit, reach 15 ft., one creature. *Hit:* 10 (3d6) necrotic damage, and the target must make a DC 16 Strength saving throw. On a failed save, the target is pulled to a space within 5 feet of the banderhobb.

Shadow Step. The banderhobb teleports up to 30 feet to an unoccupied space of dim light or darkness that it can see.

Swallow. *Melee Weapon Attack:* +8 to hit, reach 5 ft., one Medium or smaller creature grappled by the banderhobb. *Hit:* 15 (3d6 + 5) piercing damage. The creature is also swallowed, and the grapple ends. The swallowed creature is blinded and restrained, it has total cover against attacks and other effects outside the banderhobb, and it takes 10 (3d6) necrotic damage at the start of each of the banderhobb's turns. A creature reduced to 0 hit points in this way stops taking the necrotic damage and becomes stable.

The banderhobb can have only one creature swallowed at a time. While the banderhobb isn't incapacitated, it can regurgitate the creature at any time (no action required) in a space within 5 feet of it. The creature exits prone. If the banderhobb dies, it likewise regurgitates a swallowed creature.

Bonus Actions

Shadow Stealth. While in dim light or darkness, the banderhobb takes the Hide action.

BAPHOMET

Civilization is weakness and brutality is strength in the credo of Baphomet, the Horned King and the Prince of Beasts. He is worshiped by those who want to break the confines of civility and unleash their bestial natures, for Baphomet envisions a world without restraint, where creatures live out their most bloodthirsty desires.

Cults devoted to Baphomet use mazes and complex knots as their emblems. They create secret places to indulge themselves, including labyrinths of the sort their master favors. Bloodstained crowns and weapons of iron and brass decorate their profane altars.

Over time, a cultist of Baphomet becomes tainted by his influence, gaining bloodshot eyes and coarse, thickening hair. Small horns eventually sprout from the cultist's forehead. In time, a devoted cultist might transform entirely into a minotaur, which is considered the greatest gift of the Prince of Beasts.

Baphomet appears as a fearsome, 20-foot-tall minotaur with six iron horns. A fiendish light burns in his red eyes. Although he is filled with bestial blood lust, there lies within him a cruel and cunning intellect devoted to subverting all civilization.

Baphomet wields a great glaive called Heartcleaver. He also charges his enemies and gores them with his horns, trampling his foes into the earth and rending them with his teeth like a beast.

BAPHOMET'S LAIR

Baphomet's lair is his palace, the Lyktion, which is on the layer of the Abyss called the Endless Maze. Nestled within the twisting passages of the plane-wide labyrinth, the Lyktion is immaculately maintained and surrounded by a moat constructed in the fashion of a three-dimensional maze. The palace is a towering structure whose interior is as labyrinthine as the plane on which it stands; it is populated by minotaurs, goristros, and quasits, all of which appear in the *Monster Manual*.

LAIR ACTIONS

On initiative count 20 (losing initiative ties), Baphomet can take one of the following lair actions; he can't take the same lair action two rounds in a row:

Illusory Room. Baphomet casts *mirage arcane*, affecting a room within the lair that is no larger in any dimension than 100 feet. The effect ends on the next initiative count 20. Charisma is Baphomet's spellcasting ability for this spell.

Reverse Gravity. Baphomet chooses a room within the lair that is no larger in any dimension than 100 feet. Until the next initiative count 20, gravity is reversed within that room. Any creatures or objects in the room when this happens fall in the direction of the new pull of gravity, unless they have some means of remaining aloft. Baphomet can ignore the gravity reversal if he's in the room, although he likes to use this action to land on a ceiling to attack targets flying near it.

Seal the Way. Baphomet seals one doorway or other entryway within the lair. The opening must be unoccupied. It is filled with solid stone for 1 minute or until Baphomet takes this lair action again.

REGIONAL EFFECTS

The region containing Baphomet's lair is warped by his magic, creating one or more of the following effects:

Beguiling Realm. Within 6 miles of the lair, all Charisma (Persuasion) and Charisma (Performance) checks have disadvantage, and all Charisma (Deception) and Charisma (Intimidation) checks have advantage.

Hedge Mazes. Plant life within 1 mile of the lair grows thick and forms walls of trees, hedges, and other flora in the form of small mazes.

Panicked Beasts. Beasts within 1 mile of the lair become frightened and disoriented, as though constantly under threat of being hunted, and might lash out or panic even when no visible threat is nearby.

If Baphomet dies, these effects fade over the course of 1d10 days.

CULTISTS OF BAPHOMET

Baphomet grants his cultists special abilities. All his devotees gain the Labyrinthine Recall trait below. He grants his rank-and-file followers the Unerring Tracker trait, and cult leaders gain the Incite the Hunters trait.

Labyrinthine Recall. This creature can perfectly recall any path it has traveled.

Unerring Tracker. As a bonus action, this creature magically creates a psychic link with one creature it can see. For the next hour, as a bonus action this creature learns the current distance and direction to the target if it is on the same plane of existence. The link ends if this creature is incapacitated or if it uses this ability on a different target.

Incite the Hunters (Recharges after a Short or Long Rest). As an action, this creature allows each ally within 30 feet of it that has the Unerring Tracker trait to make one weapon attack as a reaction against the target of that ally's Unerring Tracker.

BAPHOMET
Huge Fiend (Demon), Chaotic Evil

Armor Class 22 (natural armor)
Hit Points 319 (22d12 + 176)
Speed 40 ft.

STR	DEX	CON	INT	WIS	CHA
30 (+10)	14 (+2)	26 (+8)	18 (+4)	24 (+7)	16 (+3)

Saving Throws Dex +9, Con +15, Wis +14
Skills Intimidation +17, Perception +14
Damage Resistances cold, fire, lightning
Damage Immunities poison; bludgeoning, piercing, and slashing that is nonmagical
Condition Immunities charmed, exhaustion, frightened, poisoned
Senses truesight 120 ft., passive Perception 24
Languages all, telepathy 120 ft.
Challenge 23 (50,000 XP)   **Proficiency Bonus** +7

Labyrinthine Recall. Baphomet can perfectly recall any path he has traveled, and he is immune to the *maze* spell.

Legendary Resistance (3/Day). If Baphomet fails a saving throw, he can choose to succeed instead.

Magic Resistance. Baphomet has advantage on saving throws against spells and other magical effects.

ACTIONS

Multiattack. Baphomet makes one Bite attack, one Gore attack, and one Heartcleaver attack. He also uses Frightful Presence.

Bite. *Melee Weapon Attack:* +17 to hit, reach 10 ft., one target. *Hit:* 19 (2d8 + 10) piercing damage.

Gore. *Melee Weapon Attack:* +17 to hit, reach 10 ft., one target. *Hit:* 17 (2d6 + 10) piercing damage. If Baphomet moved at least 10 feet straight toward the target immediately before the hit, the target takes an extra 16 (3d10) piercing damage. If the target is a creature, it must succeed on a DC 25 Strength saving throw or be pushed up to 10 feet away and knocked prone.

Heartcleaver. *Melee Weapon Attack:* +17 to hit, reach 15 ft., one target. *Hit:* 21 (2d10 + 10) force damage.

Frightful Presence. Each creature of Baphomet's choice within 120 feet of him and aware of him must succeed on a DC 18 Wisdom saving throw or become frightened for 1 minute. A frightened creature can repeat the saving throw at the end of each of its turns, ending the effect on itself on a success. These later saves have disadvantage if Baphomet is within line of sight of the creature.

If a creature succeeds on any of these saves or the effect ends on it, the creature is immune to Baphomet's Frightful Presence for the next 24 hours.

Spellcasting. Baphomet casts one of the following spells, requiring no material components and using Charisma as the spellcasting ability (spell save DC 18):

3/day each: *dispel magic, dominate beast, maze, wall of stone*
1/day: *teleport*

LEGENDARY ACTIONS

Baphomet can take 3 legendary actions, choosing from the options below. Only one legendary action option can be used at a time and only at the end of another creature's turn. Baphomet regains spent legendary actions at the start of his turn.

Heartcleaver Attack. Baphomet makes one Heartcleaver attack.
Charge (Costs 2 Actions). Baphomet moves up to his speed without provoking opportunity attacks, then makes a Gore attack.

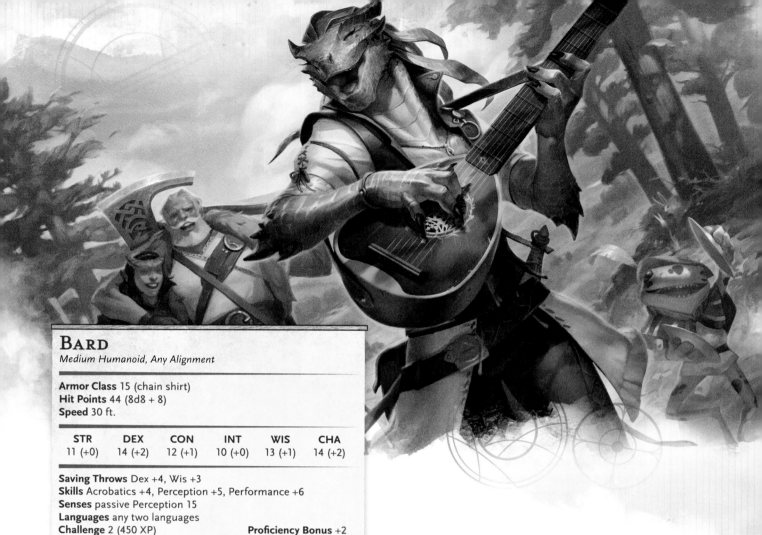

Bard

Medium Humanoid, Any Alignment

Armor Class 15 (chain shirt)
Hit Points 44 (8d8 + 8)
Speed 30 ft.

STR	DEX	CON	INT	WIS	CHA
11 (+0)	14 (+2)	12 (+1)	10 (+0)	13 (+1)	14 (+2)

Saving Throws Dex +4, Wis +3
Skills Acrobatics +4, Perception +5, Performance +6
Senses passive Perception 15
Languages any two languages
Challenge 2 (450 XP)   **Proficiency Bonus** +2

Actions

Multiattack. The bard makes two Shortsword or Shortbow attacks. It can replace one attack with a use of Spellcasting.

Shortsword. *Melee Weapon Attack:* +4 to hit, reach 5 ft., one target. *Hit:* 5 (1d6 + 2) piercing damage.

Shortbow. *Ranged Weapon Attack:* +4 to hit, range 80/320 ft., one target. *Hit:* 5 (1d6 + 2) piercing damage.

Cacophony (Recharge 4–6). Each creature in a 15-foot cube originating from the bard must make a DC 12 Constitution saving throw. On a failed save, a creature takes 9 (2d8) thunder damage and is pushed up to 10 feet away from the bard. On a successful save, a creature takes half as much damage and isn't pushed.

Spellcasting. The bard casts one of the following spells, using Charisma as the spellcasting ability (spell save DC 12):

At will: *dancing lights*, *mage hand*, *prestidigitation*
1/day each: *charm person*, *invisibility*, *sleep*

Bonus Actions

Taunt (2/Day). The bard targets one creature within 30 feet of it. If the target can hear the bard, the target must succeed on a DC 12 Charisma saving throw or have disadvantage on ability checks, attack rolls, and saving throws until the start of the bard's next turn.

Bard

Bards are gifted poets, storytellers, and entertainers who travel far and wide. They're commonly found in taverns or in the company of jolly bands of adventurers, rough-and-tumble mercenaries, and wealthy patrons.

Each bard is a master of at least one type of performance. You may choose a bard's main type, or you may roll on the Bard Performance Types table to determine it.

Bard Performance Types

d10	Performance Type
1	Poetry
2	Singing
3	Bagpipe
4	Flute
5	Dancing
6	Drum
7	Lute
8	Puppetry
9	Mime
10	Acting

BARGHEST

Long ago, the god Maglubiyet—conqueror and then lord of early goblinoids—bargained with the General of Gehenna for aid. The General provided yugoloths, which then died in service to Maglubiyet. Yet when the time came to honor his part of the compact, Maglubiyet reneged on the deal. In vengeance, the General of Gehenna created the soul-devouring barghests to devour goblinoid souls.

The mission of every barghest, implanted in it by the General of Gehenna, is to consume souls. It eats these souls by devouring the bodies of those it kills, preferring goblinoids.

A barghest hungers for the day when it can complete its mission, return to Gehenna, and serve the General directly in his yugoloth legions, but it doesn't kill goblinoids indiscriminately. By devouring the souls of goblinoid leaders and other powerful individuals, a barghest earns elevated status in the afterlife. Barghests typically keep their true nature secret, preying on the occasional lone goblin when the opportunity arises, until they reach adulthood and are capable of seeking out stronger prey.

A barghest avoids contact with large, open fires. Any conflagration larger than its body acts as a gateway to Gehenna and banishes it to that plane, where it is likely to be slain or enslaved by a yugoloth for its failure.

BARGHEST

Large Fiend, Typically Neutral Evil

Armor Class 17 (natural armor)
Hit Points 60 (8d10 + 16)
Speed 60 ft. (30 ft. in goblin form)

STR	DEX	CON	INT	WIS	CHA
19 (+4)	15 (+2)	14 (+2)	13 (+1)	12 (+1)	14 (+2)

Skills Deception +4, Intimidation +4, Perception +5, Stealth +4
Damage Resistances cold, lightning; bludgeoning, piercing, and slashing from nonmagical attacks
Damage Immunities acid, poison
Condition Immunities poisoned
Senses blindsight 60 ft., darkvision 60 ft., passive Perception 15
Languages Abyssal, Common, Goblin, Infernal, telepathy 60 ft.
Challenge 4 (1,100 XP)   **Proficiency Bonus** +2

Fire Banishment. When the barghest starts its turn engulfed in flames that are at least 10 feet high or wide, it must succeed on a DC 15 Charisma saving throw or be instantly banished to Gehenna.

Soul Feeding. The barghest can feed on the corpse of a Fey or Humanoid it killed within the past 10 minutes. This feeding takes at least 1 minute, and it destroys the corpse. The victim's soul is trapped in the barghest for 24 hours, after which time it is digested and the person is incapable of being revived. If the barghest dies before the soul is digested, the soul is released. While a soul is trapped in the barghest, any magic that tries to restore the soul to life has a 50 percent chance of failing and being wasted.

ACTIONS

Multiattack. The barghest makes one Bite attack and one Claw attack.

Bite. *Melee Weapon Attack:* +6 to hit, reach 5 ft., one target. *Hit:* 13 (2d8 + 4) piercing damage.

Claw. *Melee Weapon Attack:* +6 to hit, reach 5 ft., one target. *Hit:* 8 (1d8 + 4) slashing damage.

Spellcasting. The barghest casts one of the following spells, requiring no material components and using Charisma as the spellcasting ability (spell save DC 12):

At will: *levitate, minor illusion, pass without trace*
1/day each: *charm person, dimension door, suggestion*

BONUS ACTIONS

Change Shape. The barghest transforms into a Small goblin or back into its true form. Other than its size and speed, its statistics are the same in each form. Any equipment it is wearing or carrying isn't transformed. The barghest reverts to its true form if it dies.

BERBALANG

Berbalangs creep across the petrified remains of dead gods adrift on the Astral Plane. Obsessed with gathering secrets, both from the gods they inhabit and from the bones of dead creatures, they call forth the spirits of the dead and force them to divulge what they learned in life.

Berbalangs prefer to speak only to dead things, and specifically only to the spirits they call forth in the hope of learning secrets. They record their stories on the bones that once belonged to these creatures, thus preserving the information they gain.

Pursuit of knowledge drives everything berbalangs do. Although they mostly learn their secrets from the dead, they aren't above spying on the living to take knowledge from them as well. A berbalang can create a spectral duplicate of itself and send the duplicate out to gather information on other planes by watching places where the gods and their servants gather. When a berbalang is perceiving its environment through its duplicate, its actual body is unconscious and can't protect itself. Thus, a berbalang typically uses its duplicate for only a short time before returning its consciousness to its body.

The knowledge that berbalangs accumulate makes them great sources of information for powerful people traveling the planes. Berbalangs ignore petitioners, however, unless they come bearing a choice secret or the bones of a particularly interesting creature. Some githyanki have been able to strike deals with the creatures, using berbalangs to spy on their enemies and to watch over their crèches on the Material Plane.

BERBALANG
Medium Aberration, Typically Neutral Evil

Armor Class 14 (natural armor)
Hit Points 49 (14d8 − 14)
Speed 30 ft., fly 40 ft.

STR	DEX	CON	INT	WIS	CHA
9 (−1)	16 (+3)	9 (−1)	17 (+3)	11 (+0)	10 (+0)

Saving Throws Dex +5, Int +5
Skills Arcana +5, History +5, Insight +2, Perception +2, Religion +5
Senses truesight 120 ft., passive Perception 12
Languages all
Challenge 2 (450 XP)   **Proficiency Bonus** +2

ACTIONS

Multiattack. The berbalang makes one Bite attack and one Claw attack.

Bite. *Melee Weapon Attack:* +5 to hit, reach 5 ft., one target. *Hit:* 8 (1d10 + 3) piercing damage plus 4 (1d8) psychic damage.

Claw. *Melee Weapon Attack:* +5 to hit, reach 5 ft., one target. *Hit:* 8 (2d4 + 3) slashing damage.

Spellcasting. The berbalang casts one of the following spells, requiring no material components and using Intelligence as the spellcasting ability:

At will: *speak with dead*
1/day: *plane shift* (self only)

BONUS ACTIONS

Spectral Duplicate (Recharges after a Short or Long Rest). The berbalang creates one spectral duplicate of itself in an unoccupied space it can see within 60 feet of it. While the duplicate exists, the berbalang is unconscious. A berbalang can have only one duplicate at a time. The duplicate disappears when it or the berbalang drops to 0 hit points or when the berbalang dismisses it (no action required).

The duplicate has the same statistics and knowledge as the berbalang, and everything experienced by the duplicate is known by the berbalang. All damage dealt by the duplicate's attacks is psychic damage.

BHEUR HAG

Bheur hags live in wintry lands, favoring snowy mountains. These hags become more active during winter, using their ice and weather magic to make life miserable for nearby settlements.

A bheur hag's skin has the bluish hue of a person who has frozen to death. The hag's hair is white, and the hag is emaciated, with pale eyes surrounded by bruise-colored flesh. A bheur hag carries a twisted gray wooden staff that can be ridden like a flying broom and that augments the hag's magic.

Bheur hags are attracted to selfish actions inspired by deadly cold, such as murdering a traveler for a winter coat or chopping down a dryad's grove for firewood. These actions are especially sweet to a bheur if they are unwarranted, such as a greedy merchant hoarding excess food for the winter while others starve. Bheurs use their ability to manipulate weather to batter villages with freezing cold, hoping to instill a despair that turns folk against each other.

In combat, a bheur hag also strives to inspire horror. When near a recently slain foe, the hag may forgo an attack to feed on the corpse. The sight of this butchery is enough to terrify most witnesses.

HAG COVENS

A bheur hag that is part of a coven (see the "Hag Covens" sidebar in the *Monster Manual*) has a challenge rating of 9 (5,000 XP).

BHEUR HAG
Medium Fey, Typically Chaotic Evil

Armor Class 17 (natural armor)
Hit Points 91 (14d8 + 28)
Speed 30 ft., fly 50 ft. (hover, Graystaff Magic)

STR	DEX	CON	INT	WIS	CHA
13 (+1)	16 (+3)	14 (+2)	12 (+1)	13 (+1)	16 (+3)

Saving Throws Wis +4
Skills Nature +4, Perception +4, Stealth +6, Survival +4
Damage Immunities cold
Senses darkvision 60 ft., passive Perception 14
Languages Auran, Common, Giant
Challenge 7 (2,900 XP)   **Proficiency Bonus** +3

Control Weather (1/Day). The hag can cast the *control weather* spell, requiring no material components and using Charisma as the spellcasting ability.

Graystaff Magic. The hag carries a *graystaff*, a magic staff. The hag can use its flying speed only while astride the staff. If the staff is lost or destroyed, the hag must craft another, which takes a year and a day. Only a bheur hag can use a *graystaff*.

Ice Walk. The hag can move across and climb icy surfaces without needing to make an ability check, and difficult terrain composed of ice or snow doesn't cost the hag extra moment.

ACTIONS

Multiattack. The hag makes two Slam or Frost Shard attacks.

Slam. *Melee Weapon Attack:* +4 to hit, reach 5 ft., one target. *Hit:* 10 (2d8 + 1) bludgeoning damage plus 18 (4d8) cold damage.

Frost Shard. *Ranged Spell Attack:* +6 to hit, range 60 ft., one target. *Hit:* 30 (6d8 + 3) cold damage, and the target's speed is reduced by 10 feet until the start of the hag's next turn.

Horrific Feast. The hag feeds on the corpse of one enemy within reach that died within the past minute. Each creature of the hag's choice that is within 60 feet and able to see the feeding must succeed on a DC 15 Wisdom saving throw or be frightened of the hag for 1 minute. While frightened in this way, a creature is incapacitated, can't understand what others say, can't read, and speaks only in gibberish. A creature can repeat the saving throw at the end of each of its turns, ending the effect on itself on a success. If a creature's saving throw is successful or the effect ends for it, the creature is immune to the hag's Horrific Feast for the next 24 hours.

Spellcasting. While holding or riding the *graystaff*, the hag casts one of the following spells, requiring no material components and using Charisma as the spellcasting ability (spell save DC 14):

At will: *hold person*
1/day each: *cone of cold*, *ice storm*, *wall of ice*

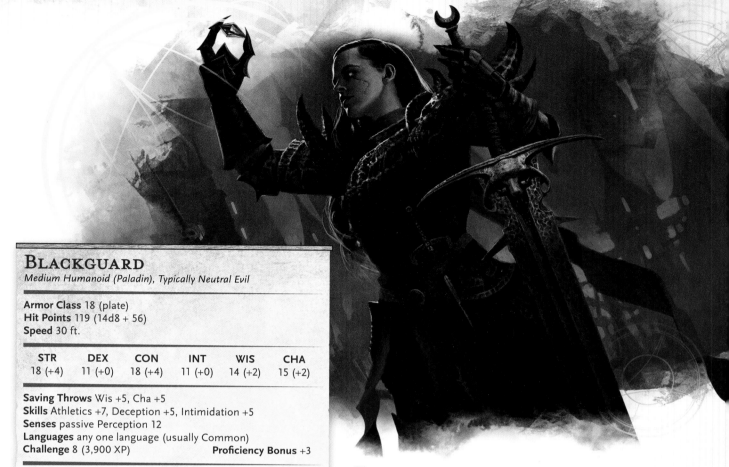

BLACKGUARD

Medium Humanoid (Paladin), Typically Neutral Evil

Armor Class 18 (plate)
Hit Points 119 (14d8 + 56)
Speed 30 ft.

STR	DEX	CON	INT	WIS	CHA
18 (+4)	11 (+0)	18 (+4)	11 (+0)	14 (+2)	15 (+2)

Saving Throws Wis +5, Cha +5
Skills Athletics +7, Deception +5, Intimidation +5
Senses passive Perception 12
Languages any one language (usually Common)
Challenge 8 (3,900 XP)   **Proficiency Bonus** +3

ACTIONS

Multiattack. The blackguard makes three attacks, using Glaive, Shortbow, or both.

Glaive. *Melee Weapon Attack:* +7 to hit, reach 10 ft., one target. *Hit:* 9 (1d10 + 4) slashing damage plus 9 (2d8) necrotic damage.

Shortbow. *Ranged Weapon Attack:* +3 to hit, range 80/320 ft., one target. *Hit:* 5 (1d6 + 2) piercing damage.

Dreadful Aspect (Recharges after a Short or Long Rest). Each enemy within 30 feet of the blackguard must succeed on a DC 13 Wisdom saving throw or be frightened of the blackguard for 1 minute. If a frightened target ends its turn more than 30 feet away from the blackguard, the target can repeat the saving throw, ending the effect on itself on a success.

Spellcasting. The blackguard casts one of the following spells, using Charisma as the spellcasting ability (spell save DC 13):

2/day each: *command, dispel magic, find steed*

BONUS ACTIONS

Smite. Immediately after the blackguard hits a target with an attack roll, the blackguard can force that target to make a DC 13 Constitution saving throw. On a failed save, the target suffers one of the following effects of the blackguard's choice:

Blind. The target is blinded for 1 minute. The blinded target can repeat the save at the end of each of its turns, ending the effect on itself on a success.

Shove. The target is pushed up to 10 feet away and knocked prone.

BLACKGUARD

Blackguards are paladins who broke their sacred oaths and now indulge their own villainous ambitions. They consort with Fiends and Undead, and they reject many of the goodly things from their former lives.

Blackguards often adorn their armor and weapons with dread accoutrements or are marked by eerie phenomena. You may choose a blackguard's accoutrement or roll on the Blackguard Accoutrements table to determine it.

BLACKGUARD ACCOUTREMENTS

d8	Accoutrement
1	Armor etched with stylized depictions of gruesome battles
2	Helm wrought in the shape of a demonic boar
3	Helm wrought to resemble a death mask
4	Cloak decorated with bloody handprints
5	Curls of inky smoke seeping from armor at the joints
6	Dozens of flies buzzing about the blackguard
7	Severed hand hanging from a chain around the blackguard's neck
8	Glaive adorned with a length of cloth bearing the words "I choose violence"

LORENZO MASTROIANNI

Bodak

A bodak is the undying remains of someone who revered Orcus (appears in this book). Devoid of life and soul, it exists only to cause death.

A worshiper of Orcus can take ritual vows while carving the demon lord's symbol on their chest over the heart. Orcus's power flays body, mind, and soul, leaving behind a sentient husk that consumes life energy near it. Most bodaks come into being in this way, then are unleashed to spread death in Orcus's name.

Bodaks are extensions of Orcus's will outside the Abyss, serving the demon prince's aims and other minions. Orcus can recall anything a bodak sees or hears. If he so chooses, he can speak through a bodak to address his enemies and followers directly.

A bodak retains vague impressions of its past life. It seeks out its former allies and enemies alike to destroy them, as its warped soul seeks to erase anything connected to its former life. Minions of Orcus are the one exception to this compulsion; a bodak recognizes them as kindred souls and spares them from its wrath. Anyone who knew the individual before its transformation into a bodak can recognize mannerisms or other subtle clues to its original identity.

BODAK
Medium Undead, Typically Chaotic Evil

Armor Class 15 (natural armor)
Hit Points 58 (9d8 + 18)
Speed 30 ft.

STR	DEX	CON	INT	WIS	CHA
15 (+2)	16 (+3)	15 (+2)	7 (−2)	12 (+1)	12 (+1)

Skills Perception +4, Stealth +6
Damage Resistances cold, fire; bludgeoning, piercing, and slashing from nonmagical attacks
Damage Immunities necrotic, poison
Condition Immunities charmed, frightened, poisoned
Senses darkvision 120 ft., passive Perception 14
Languages Abyssal, the languages it knew in life
Challenge 6 (2,300 XP)   **Proficiency Bonus** +3

Death Gaze. When a creature that can see the bodak's eyes starts its turn within 30 feet of the bodak, the bodak can force it to make a DC 13 Constitution saving throw if the bodak isn't incapacitated and can see the creature. If the saving throw fails by 5 or more, the creature is reduced to 0 hit points unless it is immune to the frightened condition. Otherwise, a creature takes 16 (3d10) psychic damage on a failed save.

Unless surprised, a creature can avert its eyes to avoid the saving throw at the start of its turn. If the creature does so, it has disadvantage on attack rolls against the bodak until the start of its next turn. If the creature looks at the bodak in the meantime, that creature must immediately make the saving throw.

Sunlight Hypersensitivity. The bodak takes 5 radiant damage when it starts its turn in sunlight. While in sunlight, it has disadvantage on attack rolls and ability checks.

Unusual Nature. The bodak doesn't require air, food, drink, or sleep.

ACTIONS

Fist. *Melee Weapon Attack:* +5 to hit, reach 5 ft., one target. *Hit:* 4 (1d4 + 2) bludgeoning damage plus 9 (2d8) necrotic damage.

Withering Gaze. One creature that the bodak can see within 60 feet of it must make a DC 13 Constitution saving throw, taking 22 (4d10) necrotic damage on a failed save, or half as much damage on a successful one.

BONUS ACTIONS

Aura of Annihilation. The bodak activates or deactivates this deathly aura. While active, the aura deals 5 necrotic damage to any creature that ends its turn within 30 feet of the bodak. Undead and Fiends ignore this effect.

RICHARD WHITTERS

BOGGLE
Small Fey, Typically Chaotic Neutral

Armor Class 14
Hit Points 18 (4d6 + 4)
Speed 30 ft., climb 30 ft.

STR	DEX	CON	INT	WIS	CHA
8 (−1)	18 (+4)	13 (+1)	6 (−2)	12 (+1)	7 (−2)

Skills Perception +5, Sleight of Hand +6, Stealth +6
Damage Resistances fire
Senses darkvision 60 ft., passive Perception 15
Languages Sylvan
Challenge 1/8 (25 XP)   **Proficiency Bonus** +2

ACTIONS

Pummel. *Melee Weapon Attack:* +1 to hit, reach 5 ft., one target. *Hit:* 2 (1d6 − 1) bludgeoning damage.

Oil Puddle. The boggle creates a puddle of nonflammable oil. The puddle is 1 inch deep and covers the ground in the boggle's space. The puddle is difficult terrain for all creatures except boggles and lasts for 1 hour. The oil has one of the following additional effects of the boggle's choice:

Slippery Oil. Any non-boggle creature that enters the puddle or starts its turn there must succeed on a DC 11 Dexterity saving throw or fall prone.

Sticky Oil. Any non-boggle creature that enters the puddle or starts its turn there must succeed on a DC 11 Strength saving throw or be restrained. On its turn, a creature can use an action to try to extricate itself, ending the effect and moving into the nearest unoccupied space of its choice with a successful DC 11 Strength check.

BONUS ACTIONS

Boggle Oil. The boggle excretes nonflammable oil from its pores, giving itself one of the following benefits of its choice until it uses this bonus action again:

Slippery Oil. The boggle has advantage on Dexterity (Acrobatics) checks made to escape bonds and end grapples, and it can move through openings large enough for a Tiny creature without squeezing.

Sticky Oil. The boggle has advantage on Strength (Athletics) checks made to grapple and any ability check made to maintain a hold on another creature, a surface, or an object. The boggle can also climb difficult surfaces, including upside down on ceilings, without needing to make an ability check.

Dimensional Rift. The boggle creates an invisible and immobile rift within an opening or frame it can see within 5 feet of it, provided that the space is no bigger than 10 feet on any side. The dimensional rift bridges the distance between that space and a point within 30 feet of it that the boggle can see or specify by distance and direction (such as "30 feet straight up"). While next to the rift, the boggle can see through it and is considered to be next to the destination as well, and anything the boggle puts through the rift (including a portion of its body) emerges at the destination. Only the boggle can use the rift, and it lasts until the end of the boggle's next turn.

BOGGLE

Boggles are the little bogeys of fairy tales. They lurk in the fringes of the Feywild and are also found on the Material Plane, where they hide under beds and in closets, waiting to frighten and bedevil folk with their mischief.

Boggles are born out of feelings of loneliness. They materialize when a sapient being feels isolated or abandoned near a place where the Feywild touches the world. For example, a forsaken child might unintentionally conjure a boggle and see them as a sort of imaginary friend. A boggle might also appear in the attic of a lonely widower's house or in a hermit's cave.

Boggles engage in petty pranks to amuse themselves, using the oil they excrete to cause trouble. A boggle also isn't above breaking dishes, hiding tools, startling cows to decrease their milk, or hiding a baby in an attic. Although a boggle's antics might cause distress and unintentional harm, mischief—not mayhem—is usually the intent. If threatened, a boggle flees rather than stand and fight.

A boggle can create magical openings to travel short distances or to pilfer items that would otherwise be beyond its reach. To create such a rift in space, a boggle must be adjacent to a space defined by a frame, such as an open window or a doorway, a gap between the bars of a cage, or the opening between the feet of a bed and the floor. The rift is invisible and disappears after a few seconds—just enough time for the boggle to step, reach, or attack through it.

SHAWN WOOD

BONECLAW

A wizard who tries to become a lich but fails might become a boneclaw instead. These hideous, cackling monsters share a few of liches' attributes, but while liches are immortal masters of the arcane, boneclaws are thralls to evil, hatred, and pain.

The most important part of the transformation ritual occurs when the soul of the aspiring lich migrates to a prepared phylactery. If the wizard is too physically or magically weak to compel the soul into its new home, the soul instead seeks out a master—a person within a few miles who has a hate-filled heart. The soul bonds to that person and becomes enslaved to its new master's wishes. The boneclaw forms near its master, sometimes appearing before that individual to receive orders and other times simply seeking to fulfill its master's desires.

A boneclaw can serve only an evil creature. If its master finds redemption or sincerely turns away from the path of evil, the boneclaw is destroyed. Otherwise, a boneclaw can't be destroyed while its master lives. No matter what happens to the boneclaw's body, it re-forms within hours.

In service to its master, a boneclaw delights in causing horrific pain. It lurks like a spider in shadowy recesses, waiting for victims to approach within reach of its long, bony limbs. Once speared, a creature is pulled into the darkness to be sliced apart.

BONECLAW
Large Undead, Typically Chaotic Evil

Armor Class 16 (natural armor)
Hit Points 150 (20d10 + 40)
Speed 40 ft.

STR	DEX	CON	INT	WIS	CHA
19 (+4)	16 (+3)	15 (+2)	13 (+1)	15 (+2)	9 (−1)

Saving Throws Dex +7, Con +6, Wis +6
Skills Perception +6, Stealth +7
Damage Resistances cold, necrotic
Condition Immunities charmed, exhaustion, frightened, paralyzed, poisoned
Senses darkvision 60 ft., passive Perception 16
Languages Common plus one language spoken by its master
Challenge 12 (8,400 XP)   **Proficiency Bonus** +4

Rejuvenation. While its master lives, a destroyed boneclaw gains a new body in 1d10 hours, with all its hit points. The new body appears within 1 mile of the boneclaw's master.

Unusual Nature. The boneclaw doesn't require air, food, drink, or sleep.

ACTIONS

Multiattack. The boneclaw makes two Piercing Claw attacks.

Piercing Claw. *Melee Weapon Attack:* +8 to hit, reach 15 ft., one target. *Hit:* 20 (3d10 + 4) piercing damage plus 11 (2d10) necrotic damage. If the target is a creature, the boneclaw can pull the target up to 10 feet toward itself, and the target is grappled (escape DC 14). The boneclaw has two claws. While a claw grapples a target, the claw can attack only that target.

Shadow Jump (Recharge 5–6). If the boneclaw is in dim light or darkness, each creature of the boneclaw's choice within 15 feet of it must succeed on a DC 14 Constitution saving throw or take 34 (5d12 + 2) necrotic damage.

The boneclaw then teleports up to 60 feet to an unoccupied space it can see. It can bring one creature it's grappling, teleporting that creature to an unoccupied space it can see within 5 feet of its destination. The destination spaces of this teleportation must be in dim light or darkness.

BONUS ACTIONS

Shadow Stealth. While in dim light or darkness, the boneclaw takes the Hide action.

REACTIONS

Deadly Reach. In response to a creature entering a space within 15 feet of it, the boneclaw makes one Piercing Claw attack against that creature.

Bulezau

Diseased manifestations of animalistic rage, bulezaus embody the violence of nature. Across the Abyss, these demons lurk in deep canyons and lofty crags, and many find a place in the ranks of demon lords' armies, serving as foot soldiers in the Abyss's endless warring.

Bulezaus crave violence. Their eagerness to kill and willingness to die make them common members of many demon lords' entourages. When not being corralled by larger and tougher demons, bulezaus gather into scrabbling mobs, wrestling and fighting among themselves until a better target comes along or until a stronger demon bullies them into subservience.

Disfiguring ailments plague bulezaus: crusted eyes, maggots wriggling in open sores, and a reek of rotten meat that follows them wherever they go.

Bulezau

Medium Fiend (Demon), Typically Chaotic Evil

Armor Class 14 (natural armor)
Hit Points 52 (7d8 + 21)
Speed 40 ft.

STR	DEX	CON	INT	WIS	CHA
15 (+2)	14 (+2)	17 (+3)	8 (−1)	9 (−1)	6 (−2)

Damage Resistances cold, fire, lightning
Damage Immunities poison
Condition Immunities charmed, frightened, poisoned
Senses darkvision 120 ft., passive Perception 9
Languages Abyssal, telepathy 60 ft.
Challenge 3 (700 XP)   **Proficiency Bonus** +2

Rotting Presence. When any creature that isn't a demon starts its turn within 30 feet of the bulezau, that creature must succeed on a DC 13 Constitution saving throw or take 3 (1d6) necrotic damage.

Standing Leap. The bulezau's long jump is up to 20 feet and its high jump is up to 10 feet, with or without a running start.

Sure-Footed. The bulezau has advantage on Strength and Dexterity saving throws made against effects that would knock it prone.

Actions

Barbed Tail. *Melee Weapon Attack:* +4 to hit, reach 5 ft., one target. *Hit:* 8 (1d12 + 2) piercing damage plus 4 (1d8) necrotic damage. If the target is a creature, it must succeed on a DC 13 Constitution saving throw against disease or become poisoned until the disease ends. While poisoned in this way, the target sports festering boils, coughs up flies, and sheds rotting skin, and the target must repeat the saving throw after every 24 hours that elapse. On a successful save, the disease ends. On a failed save, the target's hit point maximum is reduced by 4 (1d8). The target dies if its hit point maximum is reduced to 0.

Some ask why the bulezau, for all its rage and violence, has the head of a goat. I always respond, have you met a goat? They're stubborn, they're vicious, and they rarely go down without bashing you several times in the shins.

You might say, that's awfully specific. I say, don't pry.

TASHA

Cadaver Collector

The ancient war machines known as cadaver collectors lumber aimlessly across the blasted plains of Acheron until they are called upon by a necromancer to bolster the ranks of a conquering army on the Material Plane. These fearsome Constructs obey their summoners until they are dismissed back to Acheron, but if a summoner comes to a bad end, a cadaver collector might wander the Material Plane for centuries, collecting corpses while searching for a way to return home.

Cadaver collectors respond to a summons from a mortal only when they are called to the scene of a great battle—either where one is in progress, where one is imminent, or where one once took place. They encase themselves in the armor and weapons of fallen warriors and impale the corpses of those warriors on the lances and other weapons embedded in their salvaged armor.

Corpses that accumulate on a cadaver collector's shell aren't just grisly battle trophies. A cadaver collector can summon the spirits of these cadavers to battle against its enemies. Although these specters are individually weak, a cadaver collector can call up an almost endless supply of them, if given enough time.

Cadaver Collector

Large Construct, Typically Lawful Evil

Armor Class 17 (natural armor)
Hit Points 189 (18d10 + 90)
Speed 30 ft.

STR	DEX	CON	INT	WIS	CHA
21 (+5)	14 (+2)	20 (+5)	5 (–3)	11 (+0)	8 (–1)

Damage Immunities necrotic, poison, psychic; bludgeoning, piercing, and slashing from nonmagical attacks that aren't adamantine
Condition Immunities charmed, exhaustion, frightened, paralyzed, petrified, poisoned
Senses darkvision 60 ft., passive Perception 10
Languages understands all languages but can't speak
Challenge 14 (11,500 XP)   **Proficiency Bonus** +5

Magic Resistance. The collector has advantage on saving throws against spells and other magical effects.

Unusual Nature. The collector doesn't require air, food, drink, or sleep.

Actions

Multiattack. The collector makes two Slam attacks.

Slam. *Melee Weapon Attack:* +10 to hit, reach 5 ft., one target. *Hit:* 18 (3d8 + 5) bludgeoning damage plus 16 (3d10) necrotic damage.

Paralyzing Breath (Recharge 5–6). The collector releases paralyzing gas in a 30-foot cone. Each creature in that area must succeed on a DC 18 Constitution saving throw or be paralyzed for 1 minute. A paralyzed creature repeats the saving throw at the end of each of its turns, ending the effect on itself with a success.

Bonus Actions

Summon Specters (Recharges after a Short or Long Rest). The collector calls up the enslaved spirits of those it has slain; 1d4 **specters** (without Sunlight Sensitivity; see the *Monster Manual*) arise in unoccupied spaces within 15 feet of it. The specters act right after the collector on the same initiative count and fight until they're destroyed. They disappear when the collector is destroyed.

TOM BABBEY

Canoloth

A type of yugoloth, canoloths are fiendish trackers and guardians employed by evil powers. They prefer to enter into contracts to guard valuable treasures and important locations. They always do exactly as asked—never any more, never any less.

With senses sharp enough to pinpoint the locations of nearby invisible creatures, canoloths respond unfailingly to any threat to their charges. Furthermore, they emit a magical distortion field that prevents creatures close to them from teleporting.

Canoloths confront intruders with swift and terrible force, projecting long, spiny tongues to grab their foes and drag them close. What happens next depends on the contract. Unless instructed to kill, a canoloth merely holds on to its prisoner, but if given the order to do so, it tears its prey limb from limb.

> Canoloths are glorified guard dogs. If you must engage one, just find out exactly what it's been assigned to do. I've often found I can waltz right past them by taking advantage of a relevant loophole.
>
> —Mordenkainen

Canoloth

Medium Fiend (Yugoloth), Typically Neutral Evil

Armor Class 16 (natural armor)
Hit Points 120 (16d8 + 48)
Speed 50 ft.

STR	DEX	CON	INT	WIS	CHA
18 (+4)	10 (+0)	17 (+3)	5 (−3)	17 (+3)	12 (+1)

Skills Investigation +3, Perception +9
Damage Resistances cold, fire, lightning; bludgeoning, piercing, and slashing from nonmagical attacks
Damage Immunities acid, poison
Condition Immunities poisoned
Senses truesight 120 ft., passive Perception 19
Languages Abyssal, Infernal, telepathy 60 ft.
Challenge 8 (3,900 XP)   **Proficiency Bonus** +3

Dimensional Lock. Other creatures can't teleport to or from a space within 60 feet of the canoloth. Any attempt to do so is wasted.

Magic Resistance. The canoloth has advantage on saving throws against spells and other magical effects.

Uncanny Senses. The canoloth can't be surprised unless it's incapacitated.

Actions

Multiattack. The canoloth makes one Bite or Tongue attack and one Claw attack.

Bite. *Melee Weapon Attack:* +7 to hit, reach 5 ft., one target. *Hit:* 7 (1d6 + 4) piercing damage plus 18 (4d8) force damage.

Claw. *Melee Weapon Attack:* +7 to hit, reach 5 ft., one target. *Hit:* 7 (1d6 + 4) slashing damage plus 9 (2d8) force damage.

Tongue. *Melee Weapon Attack:* +7 to hit, reach 30 ft., one target. *Hit:* 10 (1d12 + 4) piercing damage plus 7 (2d6) acid damage. If the target is Medium or smaller, it is grappled (escape DC 15), pulled up to 30 feet toward the canoloth, and restrained until the grapple ends. The canoloth can grapple one target at a time with its tongue.

Catoblepas

The catoblepas is as loathsome as the vile swamplands in which it lives, a conglomeration of bloated buffalo, dinosaur, warthog, and hippopotamus parts. Despite its ungainly physiology, a catoblepas resembles a natural animal in its behavior, ambling through its marshy home, munching choice vegetation, eating the occasional bit of carrion, and wallowing in mire. A catoblepas might be found with the one mate it chooses for life and, on occasion, with a calf. A catoblepas attacks anyone that moves too close, especially if guarding its young.

A catoblepas's stink, like the stench of death mixed with swamp gas and skunk musk, gives it away as being much more ghastly than its appearance suggests. When it is on the attack, a catoblepas reveals the extent of its horrific nature. The creature's serpentine neck has trouble lifting its head, but one glare from its bloodshot eyes can rot flesh. At the end of its tail is a club that can rattle body and soul if it strikes true, leaving a victim unable to act while the catoblepas feasts on its body.

Blighted Territory

A catoblepas's nature as a creature of disease and decay brings out similar characteristics in the creature's swampy habitat. Such a wetland becomes gloomy, tangled, and more fetid than it was before. Beneficial qualities of the environment, such as healing herbs and clean water, become degraded, and swamp gases take on a hint of the catoblepas's foulness. Animals in the area are more aggressive and liable to be diseased. Degenerate creatures are likely to take up residence near a catoblepas's territory, as are those seeking to avoid notice.

Catoblepases in Folklore

Ordinary folk rarely see a catoblepas, but the creature has such a feared reputation that stories about it are ingrained in the popular culture. Any rumor of a catoblepas taking up residence nearby is taken to be a bad omen, even if the rumor is proven false. In some lands, the silhouette of a catoblepas, with its tail extended over its body and its head held low, is a baleful heraldic figure signifying death or doom.

Sages say that gods of pestilence and rot created catoblepases as embodiments of their influence, while other stories link them to misfortune. Some such tales claim that swamp-dwelling hags tend catoblepases like cattle, drinking the monsters' milk and using them as guardians or pets. Other legends say that those of impure heart can tame a catoblepas and whisper of malevolent warlocks and wicked knights who ride them into battle.

Catoblepas
Large Monstrosity, Unaligned

Armor Class 14 (natural armor)
Hit Points 84 (8d10 + 40)
Speed 30 ft.

STR	DEX	CON	INT	WIS	CHA
19 (+4)	12 (+1)	21 (+5)	3 (−4)	14 (+2)	8 (−1)

Skills Perception +5
Senses darkvision 60 ft., passive Perception 15
Languages —
Challenge 5 (1,800 XP)   **Proficiency Bonus** +3

Stench. Any creature other than a catoblepas that starts its turn within 10 feet of the catoblepas must succeed on a DC 16 Constitution saving throw or be poisoned until the start of the creature's next turn. On a successful saving throw, the creature is immune to the Stench of any catoblepas for 1 hour.

Actions

Tail. *Melee Weapon Attack:* +7 to hit, reach 10 ft., one target. *Hit:* 21 (5d6 + 4) bludgeoning damage, and the target must succeed on a DC 16 Constitution saving throw or be stunned until the start of the catoblepas's next turn.

Death Ray (Recharge 5–6). The catoblepas targets one creature it can see within 30 feet of it. The target must make a DC 16 Constitution saving throw, taking 36 (8d8) necrotic damage on a failed save, or half as much damage on a successful one. If the saving throw fails by 5 or more, the target instead takes 64 necrotic damage. The target dies if reduced to 0 hit points by this ray.

RICHARD WHITTERS

AUROCHS

CATTLE

Many kinds of cattle roam the multiverse, some of them domesticated and others feral. In many cultures, cattle are almost like family to the folk who tend to them.

AUROCHS

An aurochs is a large, fierce bovine with jutting horns. In many lands, herds of aurochs roam free, while elsewhere orcs and humans train them from an early age to carry riders into combat.

AUROCHS
Large Beast (Cattle), Unaligned

Armor Class 11 (natural armor)
Hit Points 38 (4d10 + 16)
Speed 50 ft.

STR	DEX	CON	INT	WIS	CHA
20 (+5)	10 (+0)	19 (+4)	2 (−4)	12 (+1)	5 (−3)

Senses passive Perception 11
Languages —
Challenge 2 (450 XP)   **Proficiency Bonus** +2

ACTIONS

Gore. *Melee Weapon Attack:* +7 to hit, reach 5 ft., one target. *Hit:* 14 (2d8 + 5) piercing damage. If the aurochs moved at least 20 feet straight toward the target immediately before the hit, the target takes an extra 9 (2d8) piercing damage, and the target must succeed on a DC 15 Strength saving throw or be knocked prone if it is a creature.

DEEP ROTHÉ

Deep rothé are Underdark cattle that communicate with one another using the *dancing lights* spell. Some scholars speculate that rothé came originally from the Feywild and brought the ability to cast the spell with them. Other sages attribute the ability to the centuries rothé have spent in the Underdark, where ambient magic slowly transforms everything.

DEEP ROTHÉ
Medium Beast (Cattle), Unaligned

Armor Class 10
Hit Points 13 (2d8 + 4)
Speed 30 ft.

STR	DEX	CON	INT	WIS	CHA
18 (+4)	10 (+0)	14 (+2)	2 (−4)	10 (+0)	4 (−3)

Senses darkvision 60 ft., passive Perception 10
Languages —
Challenge 1/4 (50 XP)   **Proficiency Bonus** +2

Beast of Burden. The rothé is considered to be one size larger for the purpose of determining its carrying capacity.

ACTIONS

Gore. *Melee Weapon Attack:* +6 to hit, reach 5 ft., one target. *Hit:* 7 (1d6 + 4) piercing damage. If the rothé moved at least 20 feet straight toward the target immediately before the hit, the target takes an extra 7 (2d6) piercing damage.

Dancing Lights. The rothé casts *dancing lights*, requiring no spell components and using Wisdom as the spellcasting ability.

DEEP ROTHÉ

Ox

Oxen are domesticated cattle bred for milk and meat production and for hauling. Many cultures incorporate the ox into their labor and diets.

Stench Kow

Stench kows are misshapen bison native to the Lower Planes. These orange and green creatures defend themselves by exuding a miasma so hideous as to be toxic. Some mischievous and malevolent wizards have summoned stench kows to the Material Plane, disguised the creatures as oxen, and let the infernal bison loose on unsuspecting villages.

Ox

Large Beast (Cattle), Unaligned

Armor Class 10
Hit Points 15 (2d10 + 4)
Speed 30 ft.

STR	DEX	CON	INT	WIS	CHA
18 (+4)	10 (+0)	14 (+2)	2 (−4)	10 (+0)	4 (−3)

Senses passive Perception 10
Languages —
Challenge 1/4 (50 XP)   **Proficiency Bonus** +2

Beast of Burden. The ox is considered to be one size larger for the purpose of determining its carrying capacity.

Actions

Gore. *Melee Weapon Attack:* +6 to hit, reach 5 ft., one target. *Hit:* 7 (1d6 + 4) piercing damage. If the ox moved at least 20 feet straight toward the target immediately before the hit, the target takes an extra 7 (2d6) piercing damage.

Stench Kow

Large Fiend (Cattle), Unaligned

Armor Class 10
Hit Points 15 (2d10 + 4)
Speed 30 ft.

STR	DEX	CON	INT	WIS	CHA
18 (+4)	10 (+0)	14 (+2)	2 (−4)	10 (+0)	4 (−3)

Damage Resistances cold, fire, poison
Senses darkvision 60 ft., passive Perception 10
Languages —
Challenge 1/2 (50 XP)   **Proficiency Bonus** +2

Stench. Any creature other than a stench kow that starts its turn within 5 feet of the stench kow must succeed on a DC 12 Constitution saving throw or be poisoned until the start of the creature's next turn. On a successful saving throw, the creature is immune to the Stench of all stench kows for 1 hour.

Actions

Gore. *Melee Weapon Attack:* +6 to hit, reach 5 ft., one target. *Hit:* 7 (1d6 + 4) piercing damage. If the stench kow moved at least 20 feet straight toward the target immediately before the hit, the target takes an extra 7 (2d6) piercing damage.

SAM WOOD

Cave Fisher

A cave fisher is a subterranean arachnid with a long snout that houses spinnerets, enabling the creature to produce sticky filaments, much like the strands of a spider's webbing, which the creature uses to snag prey.

A cave fisher usually hunts small animals and is particularly fond of bats, so it stretches a filament over an opening that such prey might travel through. It then climbs to a hiding spot and adheres itself to the surface to rest and wait. When prey blunders into the filament, the cave fisher reels in its meal. A group of cave fishers might work together to cover a large area with filaments, but as soon as one captures potential food, every cave fisher in the area competes for the prize. If a victim escapes from the initial ambush, a cave fisher can reclaim its prey by shooting a filament out to capture it again.

Scarce food might draw a group of cave fishers up to the surface, into a shadowy canyon or a gloomy forest that features both native animal prey and creatures such as explorers or travelers occasionally moving through the area.

Valuable Parts

Nearly every part of a cave fisher is useful after the creature has been dispatched. Cave fisher filaments can be woven into rope that is thin, tough, and nearly invisible. The creature's shell is used in the manufacture of tools, armor, and jewelry. Its blood is alcoholic and tastes like strong liquor. Several dwarven spirits include cave fisher blood, and some dwarves, especially berserkers, drink the blood straight. Cave fisher meat is edible, tasting much like crab cooked in strong wine.

While some folk hunt cave fishers to kill them to harvest their filaments, shells, and blood, others capture cave fisher eggs and rear the hatchlings, which can be trained to guard passages or serve as beasts of war. Cave fishers have a natural aversion to fire, since their blood is flammable. As such, Underdark denizens often use the threat of fire when training them.

SHAWN WOOD

Cave Fisher
Medium Monstrosity, Unaligned

Armor Class 16 (natural armor)
Hit Points 58 (9d8 + 18)
Speed 20 ft., climb 20 ft.

STR	DEX	CON	INT	WIS	CHA
16 (+3)	13 (+1)	14 (+2)	3 (−4)	10 (+0)	3 (−4)

Skills Perception +2, Stealth +5
Senses blindsight 60 ft., passive Perception 12
Languages —
Challenge 3 (700 XP)　　　　**Proficiency Bonus** +2

Flammable Blood. If the cave fisher drops to half its hit points or fewer, it gains vulnerability to fire damage.

Spider Climb. The cave fisher can climb difficult surfaces, including upside down on ceilings, without needing to make an ability check.

Actions

Multiattack. The cave fisher makes two Claw attacks.

Claw. *Melee Weapon Attack:* +5 to hit, reach 5 ft., one target. *Hit:* 10 (2d6 + 3) slashing damage.

Retract Filament. One Large or smaller creature grappled by the cave fisher's Adhesive Filament must make a DC 13 Strength saving throw. On a failed save, the target is pulled into an unoccupied space within 5 feet of the cave fisher, and the cave fisher makes one Claw attack against it. Anyone else who was attached to the filament is released. Until the grapple ends on the target, the cave fisher can't use Adhesive Filament.

Bonus Actions

Adhesive Filament. The cave fisher extends a sticky filament up to 60 feet, and the filament adheres to anything that touches it. A creature the filament adheres to is grappled by the cave fisher (escape DC 13), and ability checks made to escape this grapple have disadvantage. The filament can be attacked (AC 15; 5 hit points; immunity to poison and psychic damage). A weapon that fails to sever it becomes stuck to it, requiring an action and a successful DC 13 Strength check to pull free. Destroying the filament deals no damage to the cave fisher. The filament crumbles away if the cave fisher takes this bonus action again.

Bountiful and overrated. You can't spit in this realm without hitting one. I have witnessed the birth, death, and unlife of more champions than I dare recount. Few are worth remembering.

—Mordenkainen

Champion

Champions are mighty warriors who have honed their fighting skills in wars or gladiatorial pits. To soldiers and other people who fight for a living, champions are as influential as nobles, and their presence is courted as a sign of status among rulers.

A typical champion bears a coat of arms, heraldry that is associated with the champion far and wide. You may create a coat of arms for a champion or roll on the Champion's Coats of Arms table to determine it.

Champion's Coats of Arms

d12	Coat of Arms
1	Three lit candles on a purple field
2	Sea serpent coiled around a trident on a blue field
3	Hunting horn banded in gold on a gray field
4	Raised fist grasping an anchor on a quartered field of blue and white
5	Turtle with crenelated tower on its shell on a white field
6	Dragon skull supported on either side by dragon wings on a red field
7	Yellow chicken foot on a black field
8	Lightning bolt splitting a galley in two on a blue field
9	Two crouching displacer beasts facing each other on a yellow field
10	Knotted brambles on a green field
11	Red owlbear with a silver crown on a checkered field of black and white
12	Black anvil cracked down the middle on an orange field

Champion
Medium Humanoid, Any Alignment

Armor Class 18 (plate)
Hit Points 143 (22d8 + 44)
Speed 30 ft.

STR	DEX	CON	INT	WIS	CHA
20 (+5)	15 (+2)	14 (+2)	10 (+0)	14 (+2)	12 (+1)

Saving Throws Str +9, Con +6
Skills Athletics +9, Intimidation +5, Perception +6
Senses passive Perception 16
Languages any one language (usually Common)
Challenge 9 (5,000 XP)   **Proficiency Bonus** +4

Indomitable (2/Day). The champion rerolls a failed saving throw.

Actions

Multiattack. The champion makes three Greatsword or Shortbow attacks.

Greatsword. *Melee Weapon Attack:* +9 to hit, reach 5 ft., one target. *Hit:* 12 (2d6 + 5) slashing damage, plus 7 (2d6) slashing damage if the champion has more than half of its total hit points remaining.

Shortbow. *Ranged Weapon Attack:* +6 to hit, range 80/320 ft., one target. *Hit:* 5 (1d6 + 2) piercing damage, plus 7 (2d6) piercing damage if the champion has more than half of its total hit points remaining.

Bonus Actions

Second Wind (Recharges after a Short or Long Rest). The champion regains 20 hit points.

CHITINE

Dedicated to Lolth, chitines are multiarmed bipeds with arachnid qualities. Most live in colonies in the Underdark and fight the enemies of the Demon Queen of Spiders. Long ago, the cult of Lolth first subjected elf prisoners to horrible rituals that transformed them into creatures with both elven and spider traits, which their creators dubbed chitines. The intention was to create servile warriors dedicated first to the cult and then, only by association with it, to Lolth. The goddess found this arrangement unacceptable.

As punishment, the Spider Queen twisted her worshipers' rituals. The process usually transformed subjects into the spindly creatures her devotees expected, but occasionally, an elf changed into a choldrith (appears in this book): an arachnid Monstrosity able to command and create more chitines on its own. These choldriths soon led the chitines to rebel and abandon their creators, founding free colonies elsewhere in the Underdark. On occasion, though, colonies can be found in remote, gloomy areas of the surface world, warring against Lolth's enemies.

The cult of Lolth still creates chitines as the need arises. Outside the presence of a choldrith, chitines make good workers, and they can be useful if the cult finds an independent chitine colony and want to infiltrate it. If the creation process yields a choldrith, though, the cult destroys the creature.

As servants of Lolth, chitines love spiders. They rear spiders and similar arachnids, such as cave fishers (also in this book). Chitine colonies erect shrines to Lolth that serve as beacons, attracting spiders and other beings that serve her. Anywhere chitines set up a colony quickly becomes a web-shrouded, gloomy, and treacherous place.

Chitines resemble spiders, but they behave more like social insects such as ants. They are divided into worker and warrior castes; choldriths, when present, occupy the top levels of a colony's hierarchy. Each chitine has a social position that comes with duties related to that rank, and all are expected to sacrifice themselves to protect the colony's choldriths. Every chitine has spinnerets and slowly produces webbing that is used to build floors, walls, structures, objects, and traps that benefit the colony. A warrior might be responsible for crafting web armor (which is as tough as hide or leather), while a group of workers might be tasked to dig pit traps and cover them with fragile webbing disguised with loose dirt to appear as a solid surface.

CHITINE
Small Monstrosity, Typically Chaotic Evil

Armor Class 14 (hide armor)
Hit Points 18 (4d6 + 4)
Speed 30 ft., climb 30 ft.

STR	DEX	CON	INT	WIS	CHA
10 (+0)	14 (+2)	12 (+1)	10 (+0)	10 (+0)	7 (−2)

Skills Athletics +4, Stealth +4
Senses darkvision 60 ft., passive Perception 10
Languages Undercommon
Challenge 1/2 (100 XP)　　　　**Proficiency Bonus** +2

Fey Ancestry. The chitine has advantage on saving throws against being charmed, and magic can't put the chitine to sleep.

Sunlight Sensitivity. While in sunlight, the chitine has disadvantage on attack rolls, as well as on Wisdom (Perception) checks that rely on sight.

Web Sense. While in contact with a web, the chitine knows the exact location of any other creature in contact with the same web.

Web Walker. The chitine ignores movement restrictions caused by webbing.

ACTIONS

Multiattack. The chitine makes three Dagger attacks.

Dagger. *Melee or Ranged Weapon Attack:* +4 to hit, reach 5 ft. or range 20/60 ft., one target. *Hit:* 4 (1d4 + 2) piercing damage.

SHAWN WOOD

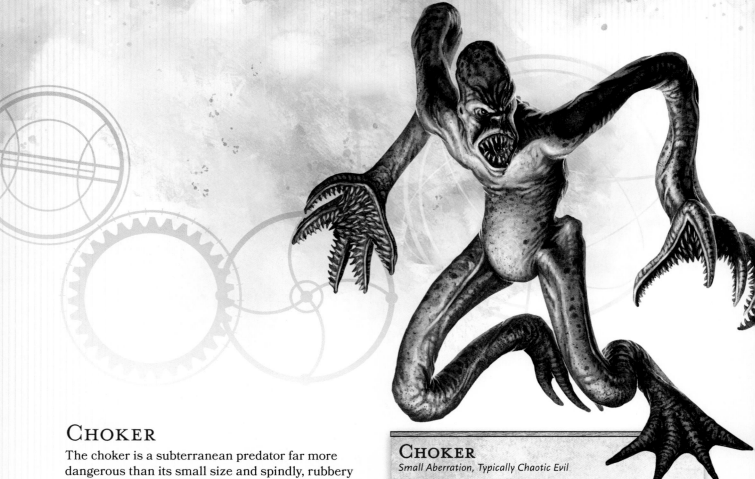

Choker

The choker is a subterranean predator far more dangerous than its small size and spindly, rubbery limbs would suggest.

Chokers have cartilage rather than a bony skeleton. This flexible internal structure enables them to easily slip into narrow fissures and niches in the walls of their cavern homes. They lurk in these spots, silent and unseen, waiting for prey to happen by.

A choker's usual method for luring prey involves positioning the body of its latest catch just outside its hiding spot. Whenever it gets hungry, it tears off a few chunks of flesh to feed itself. In the meantime, the corpse serves to entice other curious folk—explorers from the surface world, drow, duergar, or the choker's favorite prey, goblins—to come within reach.

When a target presents itself, the choker's starfish-shaped hands dart out of its hiding spot, wrap around the victim's throat, and pin the unfortunate creature against the cavern wall. Because its arms are so long, the choker can keep its body deep inside the crevice where it hides, beyond the reach of most normal weapons.

Chokers tend to set their ambushes alone, rather than working in concert, but where one choker is found, others are likely to be nearby. They communicate through eerie, keening howls that travel long distances through caves and tunnels but are difficult to identify or locate in a typical echo-filled cavern.

Choker
Small Aberration, Typically Chaotic Evil

Armor Class 16 (natural armor)
Hit Points 13 (3d6 + 3)
Speed 30 ft.

STR	DEX	CON	INT	WIS	CHA
16 (+3)	14 (+2)	13 (+1)	4 (–3)	12 (+1)	7 (–2)

Skills Stealth +6
Senses darkvision 60 ft., passive Perception 11
Languages Deep Speech
Challenge 1 (100 XP)   **Proficiency Bonus** +2

Aberrant Quickness (Recharges after a Short or Long Rest). The choker can take an extra action on its turn.

Boneless. The choker can move through and occupy a space as narrow as 4 inches wide without squeezing.

Spider Climb. The choker can climb difficult surfaces, including upside down on ceilings, without needing to make an ability check.

Actions

Multiattack. The choker makes two Tentacle attacks.

Tentacle. *Melee Weapon Attack:* +5 to hit, reach 10 ft., one target. *Hit:* 5 (1d4 + 3) piercing damage. If the target is a Large or smaller creature, it is grappled (escape DC 15). Until this grapple ends, the target is restrained, and the choker can't use this tentacle on another target. The choker has two tentacles. If this attack is a critical hit, the target also can't breathe or speak until the grapple ends.

CHOLDRITH

Medium Monstrosity (Cleric), Typically Chaotic Evil

Armor Class 15 (natural armor)
Hit Points 66 (12d8 + 12)
Speed 30 ft., climb 30 ft.

STR	DEX	CON	INT	WIS	CHA
12 (+1)	16 (+3)	12 (+1)	11 (+0)	14 (+2)	10 (+0)

Skills Athletics +5, Religion +2, Stealth +5
Senses darkvision 60 ft., passive Perception 12
Languages Undercommon
Challenge 3 (700 XP)   **Proficiency Bonus** +2

Fey Ancestry. The choldrith has advantage on saving throws against being charmed, and magic can't put the choldrith to sleep.

Spider Climb. The choldrith can climb difficult surfaces, including upside down on ceilings, without needing to make an ability check.

Sunlight Sensitivity. While in sunlight, the choldrith has disadvantage on attack rolls, as well as on Wisdom (Perception) checks that rely on sight.

Web Sense. While in contact with a web, the choldrith knows the exact location of any other creature in contact with the same web.

Web Walker. The choldrith ignores movement restrictions caused by webbing.

ACTIONS

Dagger. *Melee or Ranged Weapon Attack:* +5 to hit, reach 5 ft. or range 20/60 ft., one target. *Hit:* 5 (1d4 + 3) piercing damage plus 10 (3d6) poison damage.

Spellcasting. The choldrith casts one of the following spells, using Wisdom as the spellcasting ability (spell save DC 12):

At will: *guidance, thaumaturgy*
1/day each: *bane, hold person*

Web (Recharge 5–6). *Ranged Weapon Attack:* +5 to hit, range 30/60 ft., one Large or smaller creature. *Hit:* The target is restrained by webbing. As an action, the restrained target can make a DC 11 Strength check, bursting the webbing on a success. The webbing can also be attacked and destroyed (AC 10; 5 hit points; vulnerability to fire damage; immunity to bludgeoning, poison, and psychic damage).

BONUS ACTIONS

Spectral Dagger (Recharges after a Short or Long Rest). The choldrith conjures a floating, spectral dagger within 60 feet of itself. The choldrith can make a melee spell attack (+4 to hit) against one creature within 5 feet of the dagger. On a hit, the target takes 6 (1d8 + 2) force damage.

The dagger lasts for 1 minute. As a bonus action on later turns, the choldrith can move the dagger up to 20 feet and repeat the attack against one creature within 5 feet of the dagger.

CHOLDRITH

Choldriths are monstrous spiderlike creatures originally created to serve Lolth. They rule colonies of chitines (in this book) and lead them into battle in Lolth's war against her enemies.

When devotees of Lolth created the first chitines, she watched as her followers used arcane magic and demonic powers and invoked her aid for the divine spark needed to ensure the subjects' survival, expecting to see these new abominations dedicated solely to her, but the devotees performed no such ritual. As revenge for the devotees' betrayal, the Spider Queen manipulated the creation rituals so that they sometimes created choldriths instead of chitines.

At first, these devotees were unaware that the new creatures, which they dubbed choldriths, were signs of Lolth's wrath. Instead, they were pleased, because choldriths could lay eggs that birthed more chitines (and the rare choldrith) and could direct the chitines in their work. But the devotees soon realized their mistake—choldriths belonged to Lolth, body and soul. Choldriths whispered to the chitines of their adoration of the Spider Queen and their enmity against their creators, and led them in a successful revolt.

Choldriths are born with a mystical connection to Lolth, which gives them divine magic. They also make up the ruling caste of most chitine colonies. A colony can support numerous choldriths, who serve as commanders, priests, and supervisors. The choldriths continually jockey for position, although they rarely confront one another in a way that puts the colony at risk. The colony is ruled by a sovereign, who determines which colony members perform which tasks, including whether a choldrith is permitted to lay eggs. Sometimes a choldrith ruler receives a vision from Lolth that inspires the entire colony into some grand, often violent, action.

SHAWN WOOD

Clockworks

Gnomes' tinkering with magic and mechanical devices has produced many failed Constructs but also has resulted in genuine advances, such as clockworks. The methods used to craft clockworks have been shared between gnome communities over many generations.

Bronze Scout

A bronze scout seldom emerges from underground. Its telescoping eyestalks observe foes at close range while most of its segmented body remains buried. If detected, it sends electrical shocks through the ground toward pursuers while it retreats.

Iron Cobra

An iron cobra is exactly what its name implies: a metal snake with a poisonous bite. Gnomes load this clockwork with alchemical concoctions that can paralyze creatures and cloud the mind.

Oaken Bolter

No ordinary ballista, an oaken bolter is a Construct capable of striking at long distances. The bolts it launches can rend flesh, destroy armor, or drag enemies toward traps or melee-oriented clockworks—and at shorter ranges, burst with explosive force.

Stone Defender

The thick plates of stone riveted onto a stone defender give it substantial protection. Its chief role is as a bodyguard.

Individual Designs

Gnome artisans prefer unique clockworks over perfectly functioning ones that copy too much from other creations. A clockwork can be customized by adding one of the following enhancements and one potential malfunction to its stat block. You can select randomly or choose a pair of modifications that fit the temperament of the clockwork's builder.

Clockwork Enhancements

d10	Enhancement
1	**Camouflaged.** The clockwork gains proficiency in Stealth if it lacks that proficiency. While motionless, it is indistinguishable from a stopped machine.
2	**Sensors.** The range of the clockwork's darkvision increases by 60 feet, and it gains proficiency in Perception if it lacks that proficiency.
3	**Fortified.** The clockwork's AC increases by 2.
4	**Increased Speed.** The clockwork's speed increases by 10 feet.
5	**Reinforced Construction.** The clockwork has resistance to force, lightning, and thunder damage.
6	**Self-Repairing.** If the clockwork starts its turn with fewer than half its hit points but at least 1 hit point, it regains 5 hit points. If it takes lightning damage, this ability doesn't function at the start of its next turn.
7	**Sturdy Frame.** The clockwork's hit point maximum increases by an amount equal to its number of Hit Dice.
8	**Suction.** The clockwork gains a climbing speed of 30 feet.
9	**Vocal Resonator.** The clockwork gains the ability to speak rudimentary Common or Gnomish.
10	**Water Propulsion.** The clockwork gains a swimming speed of 30 feet.

Clockwork Malfunctions

d8	Malfunction
1	**Faulty Sensors.** Roll a d6 at the start of the clockwork's turn. If you roll a 1, the clockwork is blinded until the end of its turn.
2	**Flawed Targeting.** Roll a d6 at the start of the clockwork's turn. If you roll a 1, the clockwork makes attack rolls with disadvantage until the end of its turn.
3	**Ground Fault.** The clockwork has vulnerability to lightning damage.
4	**Imprinting Loop.** Roll a d6 at the start of the clockwork's turn. If you roll a 1, the clockwork mistakes one creature it can see within 30 feet for its creator. The clockwork won't willingly harm that creature for 1 minute or until that creature attacks or damages it.
5	**Limited Steering.** The clockwork must move in a straight line. It can turn up to 90 degrees before moving and again at the midpoint of its movement. It can rotate freely if it doesn't use any of its speeds on its turn.
6	**Overactive Sense of Self-Preservation.** If the clockwork has half its hit points or fewer at the start of its turn in combat, roll a d6. If you roll a 1, it retreats from combat if possible. It otherwise keeps fighting.
7	**Overheats.** Roll a d6 at the start of the clockwork's turn. If you roll a 1, the clockwork is incapacitated until the end of its turn.
8	**Rusty Gears.** The clockwork has disadvantage on initiative rolls, and its speed decreases by 10 feet.

> I've sometimes made the mistake of disavowing gnomish contraptions altogether. Yet some are downright functional. That said, I still won't entrust my well-being to a whirling kettle.
>
> —Mordenkainen

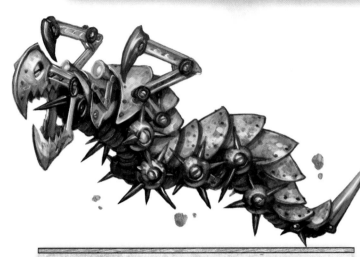

CLOCKWORK IRON COBRA
Medium Construct, Unaligned

Armor Class 13
Hit Points 91 (14d8 + 28)
Speed 30 ft.

STR	DEX	CON	INT	WIS	CHA
12 (+1)	16 (+3)	14 (+2)	3 (−4)	10 (+0)	1 (−5)

Skills Stealth +7
Damage Immunities poison
Condition Immunities charmed, exhaustion, frightened, paralyzed, petrified, poisoned
Senses darkvision 60 ft., passive Perception 10
Languages understands one language of its creator but can't speak
Challenge 4 (1,100 XP)   **Proficiency Bonus** +2

Magic Resistance. The clockwork has advantage on saving throws against spells and other magical effects.

Unusual Nature. The clockwork doesn't require air, food, drink, or sleep.

ACTIONS

Bite. *Melee Weapon Attack:* +5 to hit, reach 5 ft., one target. *Hit:* 6 (1d6 + 3) piercing damage. If the target is a creature, it must succeed on a DC 13 Constitution saving throw or suffer one random effect (roll a d6):

1–2: Confusion. On its next turn, the target must use its action to make one weapon attack against a random creature it can see within 30 feet of it, using whatever weapon it has in hand and moving beforehand if necessary to get in range. If it's holding no weapon, it makes an unarmed strike. If no creature is visible within 30 feet, it takes the Dash action, moving toward the nearest creature.

3–4: Paralysis. The target is paralyzed until the end of its next turn.

5–6: Poison. The target takes 13 (3d8) poison damage.

CLOCKWORK BRONZE SCOUT
Medium Construct, Unaligned

Armor Class 13
Hit Points 36 (8d8)
Speed 30 ft., burrow 30 ft.

STR	DEX	CON	INT	WIS	CHA
10 (+0)	16 (+3)	11 (+0)	3 (−4)	14 (+2)	1 (−5)

Skills Perception +6, Stealth +7
Damage Immunities poison
Condition Immunities charmed, exhaustion, frightened, paralyzed, petrified, poisoned
Senses darkvision 60 ft., passive Perception 16
Languages understands one language of its creator but can't speak
Challenge 1 (200 XP)   **Proficiency Bonus** +2

Earth Armor. The clockwork doesn't provoke opportunity attacks when it burrows.

Magic Resistance. The clockwork has advantage on saving throws against spells and other magical effects.

Unusual Nature. The clockwork doesn't require air, food, drink, or sleep.

ACTIONS

Bite. *Melee Weapon Attack:* +5 to hit, reach 5 ft., one target. *Hit:* 5 (1d4 + 3) piercing damage plus 3 (1d6) lightning damage.

Lightning Flare (Recharges after a Short or Long Rest). Each creature in contact with the ground within 15 feet of the clockwork must make a DC 13 Dexterity saving throw, taking 14 (4d6) lightning damage on a failed save, or half as much damage on a successful one.

CLOCKWORK OAKEN BOLTER

Medium Construct, Unaligned

Armor Class 16 (natural armor)
Hit Points 117 (18d8 + 36)
Speed 30 ft.

STR	DEX	CON	INT	WIS	CHA
12 (+1)	18 (+4)	15 (+2)	3 (−4)	10 (+0)	1 (−5)

Damage Immunities poison
Condition Immunities charmed, exhaustion, frightened, paralyzed, petrified, poisoned
Senses darkvision 60 ft., passive Perception 10
Languages understands one language of its creator but can't speak
Challenge 5 (1,800 XP)   **Proficiency Bonus** +3

Magic Resistance. The clockwork has advantage on saving throws against spells and other magical effects.

Unusual Nature. The clockwork doesn't require air, food, drink, or sleep.

ACTIONS

Multiattack. The clockwork makes two Lancing Bolt attacks or one Lancing Bolt attack and one Harpoon attack.

Lancing Bolt. *Melee or Ranged Weapon Attack:* +7 to hit, reach 5 ft. or range 100/400 ft., one target. *Hit:* 15 (2d10 + 4) piercing damage.

Harpoon. *Ranged Weapon Attack:* +7 to hit, range 50/200 ft., one target. *Hit:* 9 (1d10 + 4) piercing damage, and the target is grappled (escape DC 12). While grappled in this way, a creature's speed isn't reduced, but it can move only in directions that bring it closer to the clockwork. A creature takes 5 (1d10) slashing damage if it escapes from the grapple or if it tries and fails. The clockwork can grapple only one creature at a time with its harpoon.

Explosive Bolt (Recharge 5–6). The clockwork launches an explosive charge at a point within 120 feet. Each creature in a 20-foot-radius sphere centered on that point must make a DC 15 Dexterity saving throw, taking 17 (5d6) fire damage on a failed save, or half as much damage on a successful one.

BONUS ACTIONS

Reel In. The clockwork pulls the creature grappled by its Harpoon up to 20 feet closer.

CLOCKWORK STONE DEFENDER

Medium Construct, Unaligned

Armor Class 16 (natural armor)
Hit Points 105 (14d8 + 42)
Speed 30 ft.

STR	DEX	CON	INT	WIS	CHA
19 (+4)	10 (+0)	17 (+3)	3 (−4)	10 (+0)	1 (−5)

Damage Immunities poison
Condition Immunities charmed, exhaustion, frightened, paralyzed, petrified, poisoned
Senses darkvision 60 ft., passive Perception 10
Languages understands one language of its creator but can't speak
Challenge 4 (1,100 XP)   **Proficiency Bonus** +2

Magic Resistance. The clockwork has advantage on saving throws against spells and other magical effects.

Unusual Nature. The clockwork doesn't require air, food, drink, or sleep.

ACTIONS

Slam. *Melee Weapon Attack:* +6 to hit, reach 5 ft., one target. *Hit:* 11 (2d6 + 4) bludgeoning damage, and if the target is Large or smaller, it is knocked prone.

REACTIONS

Intercept Attack. In response to another creature within 5 feet of it being hit by an attack roll, the clockwork gives that creature a +5 bonus to its AC against that attack, potentially causing a miss. To use this ability, the clockwork must be able to see the creature and the attacker.

CLOUD GIANT SMILING ONE
Huge Giant, Typically Chaotic Neutral

Armor Class 15 (natural armor)
Hit Points 250 (20d12 + 120)
Speed 40 ft., fly 40 ft. (hover)

STR	DEX	CON	INT	WIS	CHA
26 (+8)	12 (+1)	22 (+6)	15 (+2)	16 (+3)	17 (+3)

Saving Throws Con +10, Int +6, Cha +7
Skills Deception +11, Insight +7, Perception +11,
  Sleight of Hand +9
Senses passive Perception 21
Languages Common, Giant
Challenge 11 (7,200 XP)   **Proficiency Bonus** +4

Control Weather (8th-level Spell). The giant can cast the *control weather* spell, requiring no material components and using Charisma as the spellcasting ability.

ACTIONS

Multiattack. The giant makes two Slam attacks or two Telekinetic Strike attacks.

Slam. *Melee Weapon Attack:* +12 to hit, reach 10 ft., one target. *Hit:* 21 (3d8 + 8) bludgeoning damage plus 5 (1d10) psychic damage.

Telekinetic Strike. *Ranged Spell Attack:* +7 to hit, range 240 ft., one target. *Hit:* 25 (4d10 + 3) force damage.

Change Shape. The giant magically transforms to look and feel like a Beast or a Humanoid it has seen or to return to its true form. Any equipment the giant is wearing or carrying is absorbed by the new form. Its statistics, other than its size, don't change. It reverts to its true form if it dies.

Spellcasting. The giant casts one of the following spells, requiring no material components and using Charisma as the spellcasting ability (spell save DC 15):

At will: *detect magic, fog cloud, light, minor illusion*
3/day each: *invisibility, silent image, suggestion, tongues*
1/day each: *gaseous form, major image*

BONUS ACTIONS

Cloud Step (Recharge 4–6). The giant teleports, along with any equipment it is wearing or carrying, up to 60 feet to an unoccupied space it can see.

CLOUD GIANT SMILING ONE

Smiling ones are cloud giants who honor and emulate the craftiness and deceit of the deity Memnor above all else. They are tricksters supreme who use sleight of hand, deception, misdirection, and magic in their pursuit of wealth. They also possess a flair for unpredictability and a wicked sense of humor. Smiling ones overstep all bounds of decorum with their behavior, doing and saying things that even other knavish folk consider beneath their dignity.

Smiling ones take their name from the strange two-faced masks they wear. The smiling half of the face often looks more like a smirk or a triumphant sneer than a pleasant grin. The frowning half represents the displeasure smiling ones feel about cloud giants' place in the ordning—second to storm giants. The masks serve as symbols of smiling ones' devotion and also conceal their wearers' true facial expressions.

Corpse Flower

A corpse flower can sprout atop the grave of an evil necromancer or the remains of powerful Undead creatures. Unless it is uprooted and burned while it is still a seedling, the corpse flower grows to enormous size over several weeks, then tears itself free of the earth and begins scavenging Humanoid corpses from battlefields and graveyards. Using its fibrous tentacles, it stuffs the remains into its body to sustain and repair itself. The plant has a malevolent bent and despises the living.

With or without corpses nested in its body, a corpse flower exudes a stench of decay that can overwhelm the senses of nearby creatures, causing them to become nauseated. The stench, which serves as a defense mechanism, fades 2d4 days after the corpse flower dies.

Corpse Flower
Large Plant, Typically Chaotic Evil

Armor Class 12
Hit Points 127 (15d10 + 45)
Speed 20 ft., climb 20 ft.

STR	DEX	CON	INT	WIS	CHA
14 (+2)	14 (+2)	16 (+3)	7 (−2)	15 (+2)	3 (−4)

Condition Immunities blinded, deafened, poisoned
Senses blindsight 120 ft. (blind beyond this radius), passive Perception 12
Languages —
Challenge 8 (3,900 XP)　　　　**Proficiency Bonus** +3

Corpses. When first encountered, a corpse flower contains the corpses of 1d6 + 3 Humanoids. A corpse flower can hold the remains of up to nine Humanoids. These remains have total cover against attacks and other effects outside the corpse flower. If the corpse flower dies, the corpses within it can be pulled free.

Spider Climb. The corpse flower can climb difficult surfaces, including upside down on ceilings, without needing to make an ability check.

Stench of Death. Each creature that starts its turn within 10 feet of the corpse flower or one of its zombies must make a DC 14 Constitution saving throw, unless the creature is a Construct or an Undead. On a failed save, the creature is poisoned until the start of its next turn. On a successful save, the creature is immune to the Stench of Death of all corpse flowers for 24 hours.

Actions

Multiattack. The corpse flower makes three Tentacle attacks.

Tentacle. *Melee Weapon Attack:* +5 to hit, reach 10 ft., one target. *Hit:* 9 (2d6 + 2) bludgeoning damage plus 10 (3d6) poison damage.

Harvest the Dead. The corpse flower swallows one unsecured Humanoid corpse within 10 feet of it, along with any equipment the corpse is wearing or carrying.

Bonus Actions

Digest. The corpse flower digests one corpse in its body and instantly regains 11 (2d10) hit points. Nothing of the digested corpse remains. Any equipment on the corpse is expelled from the corpse flower in its space.

Reanimate. The corpse flower animates one corpse in its body, turning it into a **zombie** (see the *Monster Manual*). The zombie appears in an unoccupied space within 5 feet of the corpse flower and acts immediately after it in the initiative order. The zombie acts as an ally of the corpse flower but isn't under its control, and the flower's stench clings to it (see Stench of Death).

SHAWN WOOD

CRANIUM RATS

Mind flayers create cranium rats by bombarding rats with psionic energy. Cranium rats are somewhat smarter than ordinary rats and behave as such. If enough cranium rats come together to form a swarm, they merge their minds into a single intelligence with the accumulated memories of all the swarm's constituents. The rats become smarter as a result, and retain their heightened intelligence for as long as the swarm persists. The swarm also awakens latent psionic abilities implanted within each cranium rat by its mind flayer creators, bestowing upon the swarm psionic powers.

A single cranium rat uses its natural telepathy to communicate hunger, fear, and other base emotions. A swarm of cranium rats communicating telepathically "speaks" as one creature, often referring to itself using the collective pronouns "we" and "us."

Some mind flayer colonies use cranium rats as spies. The rats invade communities and act as eyes and ears for the colony's elder brain (appears in this book), transmitting their thoughts when they swarm and are within range of the elder brain's telepathy.

CRANIUM RAT

Tiny Aberration, Unaligned

Armor Class 12
Hit Points 2 (1d4)
Speed 30 ft.

STR	DEX	CON	INT	WIS	CHA
2 (−4)	14 (+2)	10 (+0)	4 (−3)	11 (+0)	8 (−1)

Senses darkvision 30 ft., passive Perception 10
Languages telepathy 30 ft.
Challenge 0 (10 XP)   **Proficiency Bonus** +2

Telepathic Shroud. The cranium rat is immune to any effect that would sense its emotions or read its thoughts, as well as to all divination spells.

ACTIONS

Bite. *Melee Weapon Attack:* +4 to hit, reach 5 ft., one target. *Hit:* 1 piercing damage.

BONUS ACTIONS

Illumination. The cranium rat sheds dim light from its exposed brain in a 5-foot radius or extinguishes the light.

SWARM OF CRANIUM RATS

Medium Swarm of Tiny Aberrations, Typically Lawful Evil

Armor Class 12
Hit Points 76 (17d8)
Speed 30 ft.

STR	DEX	CON	INT	WIS	CHA
9 (−1)	14 (+2)	10 (+0)	15 (+2)	11 (+0)	14 (+2)

Damage Resistances bludgeoning, piercing, slashing
Condition Immunities charmed, frightened, grappled, paralyzed, petrified, prone, restrained, stunned
Senses darkvision 30 ft., passive Perception 10
Languages telepathy 30 ft.
Challenge 5 (1,800 XP)   **Proficiency Bonus** +3

Swarm. The swarm can occupy another creature's space and vice versa, and the swarm can move through any opening large enough for a Tiny rat. The swarm can't regain hit points or gain temporary hit points.

Telepathic Shroud. The swarm is immune to any effect that would sense its emotions or read its thoughts, as well as to all divination spells.

ACTIONS

Bites. *Melee Weapon Attack:* +5 to hit, reach 0 ft., one target in the swarm's space. *Hit:* 14 (4d6) piercing damage, or 7 (2d6) piercing damage if the swarm has half of its hit points or fewer, plus 22 (5d8) psychic damage.

Spellcasting (Psionics). As long as it has more than half of its hit points remaining, the swarm casts one of the following spells, requiring no spell components and using Intelligence as the spellcasting ability (spell save DC 13):

At will: *command, comprehend languages, detect thoughts*
1/day each: *confusion, dominate monster*

BONUS ACTIONS

Illumination. The swarm sheds dim light from its brains in a 5-foot radius, increases the illumination to bright light in a 5- to 20-foot radius (and dim light for an additional number of feet equal to the chosen radius), or extinguishes the light.

DARKLINGS

Ancient legends speak of a seelie fey who betrayed the Summer Queen. In the Summer Queens' wrath, she cursed every member of his house. The seelie fey's true name has been stricken from history, but the stories call him Dubh Catha ("Dark Crow" in Common), and other Fey refer to the house's descendants as dubh sith—"darklings." Darklings dwell in secluded caverns and chambers beneath the towns of other species. From such enclaves, they quietly ply their trade as thieves and assassins.

DARKLING

The Summer Queen's curse causes a darkling's body to absorb light, which wizens the creature, much like the effect of rapid aging. For this reason, darklings cover their entire bodies with clothing when exposure to light is a risk. The light darklings absorb over the course of their lives explodes outward when they die, incinerating the creatures and much of their possessions.

DARKLING ELDER

A wise and respected darkling can undergo a ritual to become an elder. Other elders mark the suppliant with glowing tattoos, channeling away some of the darkling's absorbed light. If the ritual succeeds, the darkling grows into a taller, elf-like form. The darkling perishes if the ritual fails.

DARKLING

Small Fey, Typically Chaotic Neutral

Armor Class 14 (leather armor)
Hit Points 13 (3d6 + 3)
Speed 30 ft.

STR	DEX	CON	INT	WIS	CHA
9 (−1)	16 (+3)	12 (+1)	10 (+0)	12 (+1)	10 (+0)

Skills Acrobatics +5, Deception +2, Perception +5, Stealth +7
Senses blindsight 30 ft., darkvision 120 ft., passive Perception 15
Languages Elvish, Sylvan
Challenge 1/2 (100 XP)   **Proficiency Bonus** +2

Death Flash. When the darkling dies, nonmagical light flashes out from it in a 10-foot radius as its body and possessions, other than metal or magic objects, burn to ash. Any creature in that area must succeed on a DC 10 Constitution saving throw or be blinded until the end of its next turn.

Light Sensitivity. While in bright light, the darkling has disadvantage on attack rolls, as well as on Wisdom (Perception) checks that rely on sight.

ACTIONS

Dagger. *Melee or Ranged Weapon Attack:* +5 to hit, reach 5 ft. or range 20/60 ft., one target. *Hit:* 5 (1d4 + 3) piercing damage plus 7 (2d6) necrotic damage.

DARKLING ELDER

Medium Fey, Typically Chaotic Neutral

Armor Class 15 (studded leather armor)
Hit Points 27 (5d8 + 5)
Speed 30 ft.

STR	DEX	CON	INT	WIS	CHA
13 (+1)	17 (+3)	12 (+1)	10 (+0)	14 (+2)	13 (+1)

Skills Acrobatics +5, Deception +3, Perception +6, Stealth +7
Senses blindsight 30 ft., darkvision 120 ft., passive Perception 16
Languages Elvish, Sylvan
Challenge 2 (450 XP)   **Proficiency Bonus** +2

Death Burn. When the darkling elder dies, magical light flashes out from it in a 10-foot radius as its body and possessions, other than metal or magic objects, burn to ash. Any creature in that area must make a DC 11 Constitution saving throw. On a failed save, the creature takes 7 (2d6) radiant damage and is blinded until the end of its next turn. On a successful save, the creature takes half as much damage and isn't blinded.

ACTIONS

Multiattack. The darkling elder makes two Scimitar attacks.

Scimitar. *Melee Weapon Attack:* +5 to hit, reach 5 ft., one target. *Hit:* 6 (1d6 + 3) slashing damage plus 7 (2d6) necrotic damage.

Darkness (Recharges after a Short or Long Rest). The darkling elder casts *darkness*, requiring no spell components and using Wisdom as the spellcasting ability.

D

BRIAN VALEZA

Death Kiss

A death kiss is a lesser beholder that can come into being when a true beholder has a vivid nightmare about losing blood. Its coloration and shape resemble those of the beholder that dreamed it into existence, but its hue is more muted, and instead of magical eye rays, it has ten long tentacles, each ending in a mouth full of teeth. It can speak through any of its tentacle-maws in a high-pitched, nasal voice.

Death kisses fear true beholders, which can easily kill or subdue them. Lacking the egotism of their stronger kin, a death kiss usually submits to the rule of its creator or any other beholder it encounters, but it tries to escape as soon as the beholder is preoccupied.

A death kiss consumes ingested blood, which it also uses to heal and generate electrical energy inside its body. Terrified of dying from starvation, it obsessively drains even little creatures such as rats, leaving behind a trail of bloodless corpses. When underground, it uses its tentacles as feelers, prodding and examining the environment in all directions. Above ground, it usually keeps its tentacles retracted when on the hunt, then lashes out with them to catch opponents off guard.

A death kiss lacks the combat finesse and intelligence of a true beholder. In most cases, it simply latches on to its prey with one or more of its tentacles and drains blood until the prey collapses. If it's in a superior position and its foe poses no threat, it might toy with its food, drawing out its prey's death.

A death kiss prefers to hunt alone. If it meets another of its kind, it might fight, flee, or team up, depending on its health and pride.

DEATH KISS
Large Aberration (Beholder), Typically Neutral Evil

Armor Class 15 (natural armor)
Hit Points 142 (15d10 + 60)
Speed 0 ft., fly 30 ft. (hover)

STR	DEX	CON	INT	WIS	CHA
18 (+4)	14 (+2)	18 (+4)	10 (+0)	12 (+1)	10 (+0)

Saving Throws Con +8, Wis +5
Skills Perception +5
Damage Immunities lightning
Condition Immunities prone
Senses darkvision 120 ft., passive Perception 15
Languages Deep Speech, Undercommon
Challenge 10 (5,900 XP)   **Proficiency Bonus** +4

Lightning Blood. A creature within 5 feet of the death kiss takes 5 (1d10) lightning damage whenever it hits the death kiss with a melee attack that deals piercing or slashing damage.

ACTIONS

Multiattack. The death kiss makes three Tentacle attacks. Up to three of these attacks can be replaced by Blood Drain—one replacement per tentacle grappling a creature.

Tentacle. *Melee Weapon Attack:* +8 to hit, reach 20 ft., one target. *Hit:* 11 (2d6 + 4) piercing damage, and the target is grappled (escape DC 14) if it is a Huge or smaller creature. Until this grapple ends, the target is restrained, and the death kiss can't use the same tentacle on another target. The death kiss has ten tentacles.

Blood Drain. One creature grappled by a tentacle of the death kiss must make a DC 16 Constitution saving throw. On a failed save, the target takes 22 (4d10) lightning damage, and the death kiss regains half as many hit points.

DEATHLOCKS

The forging of a pact between a warlock and a patron is no minor occasion—at least not for the warlock. The consequences of breaking that pact can be dire and, in some cases, lethal. A warlock who fails to live up to a bargain with an evil patron runs the risk of rising from the dead as a deathlock, a foul Undead driven to serve its otherworldly patron.

An powerful necromancer might also discover the wicked methods of creating a deathlock and then subjugate it, acting as the deathlock's patron.

DEATHLOCK

An overpowering urge to serve consumes the mind of a newly awakened deathlock. Any goals and ambitions it had in life that don't please its patron fall away as its master's desires become the purpose that drives it. The deathlock immediately resumes work on its patron's behalf.

Whatever the goal, it always reflects the patron's interests, ranging from small-scale concerns to matters of cosmic scope. A deathlock in the thrall of a Fiend might work to destroy a specific temple dedicated to a good god, while one that serves a Great Old One might hunt for the materials needed to call forth a horrifying entity into the world. To accomplish a difficult goal, the deathlock might be forced to serve another powerful creature or might need to gather servants of its own.

DEATHLOCK MASTERMIND

Though deathlocks exist to serve their patrons, they retain some freedom when it comes to devising tactics and carrying out plans. Powerful deathlocks recruit lesser creatures to help them carry out their missions, becoming the masterminds behind vast conspiracies and intrigues that culminate in the accomplishment of great acts of evil.

DEATHLOCK WIGHT

Deprived of much of its magic as a special punishment, a deathlock wight lingers between the warlock it was and the wretched existence of a wight.

DEATHLOCK

Medium Undead (Warlock), Typically Neutral Evil

Armor Class 12 (15 with *mage armor*)
Hit Points 36 (8d8)
Speed 30 ft.

STR	DEX	CON	INT	WIS	CHA
11 (+0)	15 (+2)	10 (+0)	14 (+2)	12 (+1)	16 (+3)

Saving Throws Int +4, Cha +5
Skills Arcana +4, History +4
Damage Resistances necrotic; bludgeoning, piercing, and slashing from nonmagical attacks that aren't silvered
Damage Immunities poison
Condition Immunities exhaustion, poisoned
Senses darkvision 60 ft., passive Perception 11
Languages the languages it knew in life
Challenge 4 (1,100 XP)   **Proficiency Bonus** +2

Turn Resistance. The deathlock has advantage on saving throws against any effect that turns Undead.

Unusual Nature. The deathlock doesn't require air, food, drink, or sleep.

ACTIONS

Multiattack. The deathlock makes two Deathly Claw or Grave Bolt attacks.

Deathly Claw. *Melee Weapon Attack:* +4 to hit, reach 5 ft., one target. *Hit:* 9 (2d6 + 2) necrotic damage.

Grave Bolt. *Ranged Spell Attack:* +5 to hit, range 120 ft., one target. *Hit:* 14 (2d10 + 3) necrotic damage.

Spellcasting. The deathlock casts one of the following spells, using Charisma as the spellcasting ability (spell save DC 13):

At will: *detect magic, disguise self, mage armor, mage hand*
1/day each: *dispel magic, hunger of Hadar, invisibility, spider climb*

DEATHLOCK MASTERMIND

Medium Undead (Warlock), Typically Neutral Evil

Armor Class 13 (16 with *mage armor*)
Hit Points 110 (20d8 + 20)
Speed 30 ft.

STR	DEX	CON	INT	WIS	CHA
11 (+0)	16 (+3)	12 (+1)	15 (+2)	12 (+1)	17 (+3)

Saving Throws Int +5, Cha +6
Skills Arcana +5, History +5, Perception +4
Damage Resistances necrotic; bludgeoning, piercing, and slashing from nonmagical attacks that aren't silvered
Damage Immunities poison
Condition Immunities exhaustion, poisoned
Senses darkvision 120 ft., passive Perception 14
Languages the languages it knew in life
Challenge 8 (3,900 XP)   **Proficiency Bonus** +3

Devil's Sight. Magical darkness doesn't impede the deathlock's darkvision.

Turn Resistance. The deathlock has advantage on saving throws against any effect that turns Undead.

Unusual Nature. The deathlock doesn't require air, food, drink, or sleep.

ACTIONS

Multiattack. The deathlock makes two Deathly Claw or Grave Bolt attacks.

Deathly Claw. *Melee Weapon Attack:* +6 to hit, reach 5 ft., one target. *Hit:* 13 (3d6 + 3) necrotic damage.

Grave Bolt. *Ranged Spell Attack:* +6 to hit, range 120 ft., one target. *Hit:* 13 (3d8) necrotic damage. If the target is Large or smaller, it must succeed on a DC 16 Strength saving throw or become restrained as shadowy tendrils wrap around it for 1 minute. A restrained target can use its action to repeat the saving throw, ending the effect on itself on a success.

Spellcasting. The deathlock casts one of the following spells, using Charisma as the spellcasting ability (spell save DC 14):

At will: *detect magic, disguise self, mage armor, minor illusion*
1/day each: *darkness, dimension door, dispel magic, fly, invisibility*

DEATHLOCK WIGHT

Medium Undead (Warlock), Typically Neutral Evil

Armor Class 12 (15 with *mage armor*)
Hit Points 37 (5d8 + 15)
Speed 30 ft.

STR	DEX	CON	INT	WIS	CHA
11 (+0)	14 (+2)	16 (+3)	12 (+1)	14 (+2)	16 (+3)

Saving Throws Wis +4
Skills Arcana +3, Perception +4
Damage Resistances necrotic; bludgeoning, piercing, and slashing from nonmagical attacks
Damage Immunities poison
Condition Immunities exhaustion, poisoned
Senses darkvision 60 ft., passive Perception 14
Languages the languages it knew in life
Challenge 3 (700 XP)   **Proficiency Bonus** +2

Sunlight Sensitivity. While in sunlight, the deathlock has disadvantage on attack rolls, as well as on Wisdom (Perception) checks that rely on sight.

Unusual Nature. The deathlock doesn't require air, food, drink, or sleep.

ACTIONS

Multiattack. The deathlock makes two Life Drain or Grave Bolt attacks.

Life Drain. *Melee Weapon Attack:* +4 to hit, reach 5 ft., one creature. *Hit:* 6 (1d8 + 2) necrotic damage. The target must succeed on a DC 13 Constitution saving throw, or its hit point maximum is reduced by an amount equal to the damage taken. This reduction lasts until the target finishes a long rest. The target dies if its hit point maximum is reduced to 0.

A Humanoid slain by this attack rises 24 hours later as a **zombie** (see the *Monster Manual*) under the deathlock's control, unless the Humanoid is restored to life or its body is destroyed. The deathlock can have no more than twelve zombies under its control at one time.

Grave Bolt. *Ranged Spell Attack:* +5 to hit, range 60 ft., one target. *Hit:* 12 (2d8 + 3) necrotic damage.

Spellcasting. The deathlock casts one of the following spells, using Charisma as the spellcasting ability (spell save DC 13):

At will: *detect magic, disguise self, mage armor*
1/day each: *fear, hold person*

DEEP SCION IN
HYBRID FORM

The training to which a deep scion is subjected rids it of empathy for those they spy on. Though a deep scion might behave as though infatuated, laugh at the joke of a friend, or appear incensed at some injustice, each of these acts is artificial to the deep scion, a means to an end. The creature believes that their true form is the shape they take when they return to the sea they think of as home. Ironically, however, a deep scion that is killed when in their piscine form is stripped of the magic that enabled them to transform, leaving behind the corpse of the person the deep scion once was.

DEEP SCION

Deep scions began life as people who were stolen from shore or saved from sinking ships and offered a terrible bargain by an undersea power: surrender, body and soul, or drown. Those who submit are subjected to an ancient ritual widespread among evil aquatic creatures. Its methods are painful and the result never certain, but when it works, the magic transforms an air-breathing person into a shapeshifter that can take on an aquatic form.

A deep scion emerges from the depths in service to their underwater master, which is likely a kraken or some other ancient being of the deep. While wearing the mind and body of the person they once were as a sort of mask, the creature is bent on fulfilling their master's desires. Sometimes a deep scion returns to their former home—unexpectedly found alive when all hope was lost. At other times the deep scion takes on a new identity. In any case, it is the deep scion's duty to infiltrate the air-breathing world and report back to their master. When set to this task, a deep scion worms their way into the life of an unsuspecting enemy as a new friend, a lover, the perfect candidate for a job, or some other role that enables the minion to carry out their master's commands.

DEEP SCION

Medium Monstrosity, Typically Chaotic Evil

Armor Class 11
Hit Points 67 (9d8 + 27)
Speed 30 ft. (20 ft. and swim 40 ft. in hybrid form)

STR	DEX	CON	INT	WIS	CHA
18 (+4)	13 (+1)	16 (+3)	10 (+0)	12 (+1)	14 (+2)

Saving Throws Wis +3, Cha +4
Skills Deception +6, Insight +3, Sleight of Hand +3, Stealth +3
Senses darkvision 120 ft., passive Perception 11
Languages Aquan, Common, thieves' cant
Challenge 3 (700 XP)   **Proficiency Bonus** +2

Amphibious (Hybrid Form Only). The deep scion can breathe air and water.

ACTIONS

Multiattack. The deep scion makes two Battleaxe attacks, or it makes one Bite attack and two Claw attacks.

Battleaxe. *Melee Weapon Attack:* +6 to hit, reach 5 ft., one target. *Hit:* 8 (1d8 + 4) slashing damage, or 9 (1d10 + 4) slashing damage if used with two hands.

Bite (Hybrid Form Only). *Melee Weapon Attack:* +6 to hit, reach 5 ft., one creature. *Hit:* 6 (1d4 + 4) piercing damage.

Claw (Hybrid Form Only). *Melee Weapon Attack:* +6 to hit, reach 5 ft., one target. *Hit:* 7 (1d6 + 4) slashing damage.

Psychic Screech (Hybrid Form Only; Recharges after a Short or Long Rest). The deep scion emits a terrible scream audible within 300 feet. Creatures within 30 feet of the deep scion must succeed on a DC 13 Wisdom saving throw or be stunned until the end of the deep scion's next turn.

In water, the psychic screech also telepathically transmits the deep scion's memories of the last 24 hours to its master, regardless of distance, so long as it and its master are in the same body of water.

BONUS ACTIONS

Change Shape. The deep scion transforms into a hybrid form (humanoid-piscine) or back into its true form, which is humanlike. Its statistics, other than its speed, are the same in each form. Any equipment it is wearing or carrying isn't transformed. The deep scion reverts to its true form if it dies.

BRYNN METHENEY

DEMOGORGON

Prince of Demons, the Sibilant Beast, and Master of the Spiraling Depths, Demogorgon is the embodiment of chaos, confusion, and destruction, seeking to corrupt all that is good and undermine order in the multiverse, to see everything dragged howling into the infinite depths of the Abyss.

The demon lord is a meld of different forms. He has a saurian lower body and clawed, webbed feet; suckered tentacles sprout from the shoulders of his great apelike torso, which is surmounted by two hideous simian heads named Aameul and Hathradiah. Their gaze brings bewilderment and confusion to any who confront them.

Similarly, the spiraling Y sign of Demogorgon's cult drives those who contemplate it for too long to delirium. As a result, all followers of the Prince of Demons break with reality sooner or later.

DEMOGORGON'S LAIR

Demogorgon makes his lair in a palace called Abysm, found on a layer of the Abyss known as the Gaping Maw. Demogorgon's lair is a place of confusion and duality; the portion of the palace that lies above water takes the form of two serpentine towers, each crowned by a skull-shaped minaret. There, Demogorgon's heads contemplate the mysteries of the arcane while arguing about how best to obliterate their rivals. The bulk of this palace extends deep underwater, in chill and darkened caverns.

LAIR ACTIONS

On initiative count 20 (losing initiative ties), Demogorgon can take one of the following lair actions; he can't take the same lair action two rounds in a row:

Darkness. Demogorgon casts the *darkness* spell four times, targeting different areas with the spell. Demogorgon doesn't need to concentrate on the spells, which end on initiative count 20 of the next round.

Illusory Duplicate. Demogorgon creates an illusory duplicate of himself, which appears in his space and lasts until initiative count 20 of the next round. On his turn, Demogorgon can move the illusory duplicate a distance equal to his walking speed (no action required). The first time a creature or an object interacts physically with Demogorgon (for example, by hitting him with an attack), there is a 50 percent chance that the illusory duplicate is affected, not Demogorgon, in which case the illusion disappears.

REGIONAL EFFECTS

The region containing Demogorgon's lair is warped by his magic, creating one or more of the following effects:

Beguiling Realm. Within 6 miles of the lair, all Charisma (Persuasion) and Charisma (Performance) checks have disadvantage, and all Charisma (Deception) and Charisma (Intimidation) checks have advantage.

Frenzied Animals. Beasts within 1 mile of the lair become frenzied and violent—even creatures that are normally docile. Within that area, any ability check involving Animal Handling has disadvantage.

Venomous Beasts. The area within 6 miles of the lair becomes overpopulated with poisonous snakes and other venomous Beasts.

If Demogorgon dies, these effects fade over the course of 1d10 days.

CULTISTS OF DEMOGORGON

Demogorgon's followers are typically lone killers driven by the whispering voice of their master. His most blessed followers gain the Two Minds of Chaos trait.

Two Minds of Chaos. This creature has advantage on all Intelligence, Wisdom, and Charisma saving throws.

Are two heads better than one? In Demogorgon's case, the two double the horror and the chaos.

—Mordenkainen

DEMOGORGON

Huge Fiend (Demon), Chaotic Evil

Armor Class 22 (natural armor)
Hit Points 464 (32d12 + 256)
Speed 50 ft., swim 50 ft.

STR	DEX	CON	INT	WIS	CHA
29 (+9)	14 (+2)	26 (+8)	20 (+5)	17 (+3)	25 (+7)

Saving Throws Dex +10, Con +16, Wis +11, Cha +15
Skills Insight +11, Perception +19
Damage Resistances cold, fire, lightning
Damage Immunities poison; bludgeoning, piercing, and slashing that is nonmagical
Condition Immunities charmed, exhaustion, frightened, poisoned
Senses truesight 120 ft., passive Perception 29
Languages all, telepathy 120 ft.
Challenge 26 (90,000 XP)   **Proficiency Bonus** +8

Legendary Resistance (3/Day). If Demogorgon fails a saving throw, he can choose to succeed instead.

Magic Resistance. Demogorgon has advantage on saving throws against spells and other magical effects.

Two Heads. Demogorgon has advantage on saving throws against being blinded, deafened, stunned, or knocked unconscious.

ACTIONS

Multiattack. Demogorgon makes two Tentacle attacks. He can replace one attack with a use of Gaze.

Tentacle. *Melee Weapon Attack:* +17 to hit, reach 10 ft., one target. *Hit:* 28 (3d12 + 9) force damage. If the target is a creature, it must succeed on a DC 23 Constitution saving throw, or its hit point maximum is reduced by an amount equal to the damage taken. This reduction lasts until the target finishes a long rest. The target dies if its hit point maximum is reduced to 0.

Gaze. Demogorgon turns his magical gaze toward one creature he can see within 120 feet of him. The target must succeed on a DC 23 Wisdom saving throw or suffer one of the following effects (choose one or roll a d6):

1–2: Beguiling Gaze. The target is stunned until the start of Demogorgon's next turn or until Demogorgon is no longer within line of sight.

3–4: Confusing Gaze. The target suffers the effect of the *confusion* spell without making a saving throw. The effect lasts until the start of Demogorgon's next turn. Demogorgon doesn't need to concentrate on the spell.

5–6: Hypnotic Gaze. The target is charmed by Demogorgon until the start of Demogorgon's next turn. Demogorgon chooses how the charmed target uses its action, reaction, and movement.

Spellcasting. Demogorgon casts one of the following spells, requiring no material components and using Charisma as the spellcasting ability (spell save DC 23):

At will: *detect magic, major image*
3/day each: *dispel magic, fear, telekinesis*
1/day each: *feeblemind, project image*

LEGENDARY ACTIONS

Demogorgon can take 2 legendary actions, choosing from the options below. Only one legendary action option can be used at a time and only at the end of another creature's turn. Demogorgon regains spent legendary actions at the start of his turn.

Gaze. Demogorgon uses Gaze and must use either Beguiling Gaze or Confusing Gaze.

Tail. *Melee Weapon Attack:* +17 to hit, reach 15 ft., one target. *Hit:* 20 (2d10 + 9) bludgeoning damage plus 11 (2d10) necrotic damage.

Cast a Spell (Costs 2 Actions). Demogorgon uses Spellcasting.

DERRO

Derro slink through the subterranean realms, seeking places that are safe from the perils of the Underdark. Equal parts fearful and vicious, bands of these dwarf-kin prey on those weaker than themselves, while giving simpering obeisance to any creatures they deem more powerful. A lone derro may seem pitiable, but a cackling, spitting, growling, howling horde of them is horrifying to behold.

Fractious in groups and individually weak, derro would have died out long ago but for two elements of their character. They are cautious and distrustful, which serves them well as they navigate the dangers of the Underdark and its societies. They also have a stronger-than-normal tendency to develop sorcerous power. Individuals who do so usually serve as leaders and are known as savants.

Grandiose fantasies and rampant fanaticism have obscured derro's true origin, even among themselves. Most dwarves don't recognize derro as kin, but the legends that derro tell about their people and the story that duergar believe share a grain of truth. According to the histories of some duergar, derro are descended from a dwarven community that was left behind when the others escaped the rule of mind flayers. These remnants were so distorted by the mind flayers' psionic power that the dwarves became Aberrations.

Derro tell their own stories of flight and survival in the Underdark, in which mind flayers aren't always the enemy. They tell of two brothers, the gods Diirinka and Diinkarazan, and of how Diirinka cleverly betrayed his sibling so that he could steal magical power from the evil they escaped. The danger the brothers are said to face in this legend varies, depending on whatever foe the savants want to lead their people against, yet the essence of the story remains the same: a lesson of survival at any price and an example of how deceitfulness and cruelty can be virtues.

ILYA SHKIPIN

DERRO
Small Aberration, Typically Chaotic Evil

Armor Class 13 (leather armor)
Hit Points 13 (3d6 + 3)
Speed 30 ft.

STR	DEX	CON	INT	WIS	CHA
10 (+0)	14 (+2)	12 (+1)	11 (+0)	5 (−3)	9 (−1)

Skills Stealth +4
Senses darkvision 120 ft., passive Perception 7
Languages Dwarvish, Undercommon
Challenge 1/4 (50 XP)   **Proficiency Bonus** +2

Magic Resistance. The derro has advantage on saving throws against spells and other magical effects.

Sunlight Sensitivity. While in sunlight, the derro has disadvantage on attack rolls, as well as on Wisdom (Perception) checks that rely on sight.

ACTIONS

Hooked Spear. *Melee Weapon Attack:* +2 to hit, reach 5 ft., one target. *Hit:* 3 (1d6) piercing damage. If the target is Medium or smaller, the derro can choose to deal no damage and knock it prone.

Light Crossbow. *Ranged Weapon Attack:* +4 to hit, range 80/320 ft., one target. *Hit:* 6 (1d8 + 2) piercing damage.

Mind flayers must be stopped. They have visited horrors on countless worlds, and entire groups of people have been mutated by illithid experiments. Such are the derro.

Whenever I've met them, I refuse to fight, no matter how violent they might be. I think of the dwarves they once were, and I must confess that even I have shed tears.

—Mordenkainen

Derro Savant

Small Aberration (Sorcerer), Typically Chaotic Evil

Armor Class 13 (leather armor)
Hit Points 36 (8d6 + 8)
Speed 30 ft.

STR	DEX	CON	INT	WIS	CHA
9 (−1)	14 (+2)	12 (+1)	11 (+0)	5 (−3)	14 (+2)

Skills Stealth +4
Senses darkvision 120 ft., passive Perception 7
Languages Dwarvish, Undercommon
Challenge 3 (700 XP) **Proficiency Bonus** +2

Magic Resistance. The derro has advantage on saving throws against spells and other magical effects.

Sunlight Sensitivity. While in sunlight, the derro has disadvantage on attack rolls, as well as on Wisdom (Perception) checks that rely on sight.

Actions

Quarterstaff. *Melee Weapon Attack:* +1 to hit, reach 5 ft., one target. *Hit:* 2 (1d6 − 1) bludgeoning damage.

Chromatic Beam. The derro launches a brilliant beam of magical energy in a 5-foot-wide line that is 60 feet long. Each creature in the line must make a DC 12 Dexterity saving throw, taking 21 (6d6) radiant damage on a failed save, or half as much damage on a successful one.

Spellcasting. The derro casts one of the following spells, using Charisma as the spellcasting ability (spell save DC 12):

At will: *mage hand, message, prestidigitation*
1/day each: *invisibility, sleep, spider climb*

Devourer

Of all the abominations unleashed by Orcus (appears in this book), devourers are among the most feared. These tall, mummy-like Undead wander the planes, consuming souls and spreading Orcus's creed of replacing all life with everlasting death.

A lesser demon that proves itself to Orcus might be granted the privilege of becoming a devourer. The Prince of Undeath transforms such a demon into an 8-foot-tall, desiccated biped with a hollowed-out ribcage, then fills the new creature with a hunger for souls. Orcus grants each new devourer the essence of a less fortunate demon to power the devourer's first foray into the planes. Most devourers remain in the Abyss or on the Astral or Ethereal Plane, pursuing Orcus's schemes and interests in those realms. When Orcus sends devourers to the Material Plane, he often sets them on a mission to create, control, and lead a plague of Undead. Skeletons, zombies, ghouls, ghasts, and shadows (all of which appear in the *Monster Manual*) are particularly attracted to the presence of a devourer.

Devourers hunt Humanoids with the intent of consuming them body and soul. After a devourer brings a target to the brink of death, it pulls the victim's body in and traps the creature within its own ribcage. As the victim tries to stave off death (usually without success), the devourer tortures its soul with telepathic noise. When the victim expires, it undergoes a horrible transformation, springing forth from the devourer's body to begin its new existence as an Undead servitor of the monster that spawned it.

Devourer
Large Undead, Typically Chaotic Evil

Armor Class 16 (natural armor)
Hit Points 189 (18d10 + 90)
Speed 30 ft.

STR	DEX	CON	INT	WIS	CHA
20 (+5)	12 (+1)	20 (+5)	13 (+1)	10 (+0)	16 (+3)

Damage Resistances cold, fire, lightning
Damage Immunities poison
Condition Immunities poisoned
Senses darkvision 120 ft., passive Perception 10
Languages Abyssal, telepathy 120 ft.
Challenge 13 (10,000 XP)   **Proficiency Bonus** +5

Unusual Nature. A devourer doesn't require air, drink, or sleep.

Actions

Multiattack. The devourer makes two Claw attacks and can use either Imprison Soul or Soul Rend, if available.

Claw. Melee Weapon Attack: +10 to hit, reach 5 ft., one target. *Hit:* 12 (2d6 + 5) slashing damage plus 21 (6d6) necrotic damage.

Imprison Soul. The devourer chooses a living Humanoid with 0 hit points that it can see within 30 feet of it. That creature is teleported inside the devourer's ribcage and imprisoned there. While imprisoned in this way, the creature is restrained and has disadvantage on death saving throws. If the creature dies while imprisoned, the devourer regains 25 hit points and immediately recharges Soul Rend. Additionally, at the start of its next turn, the devourer regurgitates the slain creature as a bonus action, and the creature becomes an Undead. If the victim had 2 or fewer Hit Dice, it becomes a **zombie**. If it had 3 to 5 Hit Dice, it becomes a **ghoul**. Otherwise, it becomes a **wight**. (All three appear in the *Monster Manual*.) A devourer can imprison only one creature at a time.

Soul Rend (Recharge 6). The devourer creates a vortex of life-draining energy in a 20-foot radius centered on itself. Each creature in that area must make a DC 18 Constitution saving throw, taking 44 (8d10) necrotic damage on a failed save, or half as much damage on a successful one.

SHAWN WOOD

DHERGOLOTH

A kind of yugoloth, dhergoloths rush into battle like whirlwinds of destruction, lashing out with the five sets of claws that extend from their squat, barrel-shaped bodies. They take contracts to put down uprisings, clear out rabble, and eliminate scouts and skirmishers, and they revel in the butchery they create, their gleeful laughter rising above their victims' screams.

Since dhergoloths are little more than brutes, employers must use caution when instructing them. They can handle simple orders that don't take a lot of time to resolve. When given anything complex to do, however, they either forget what they're told or don't listen in the first place, and then bungle the task that was set for them.

DHERGOLOTH

Medium Fiend (Yugoloth), Typically Neutral Evil

Armor Class 15 (natural armor)
Hit Points 119 (14d8 + 56)
Speed 30 ft.

STR	DEX	CON	INT	WIS	CHA
17 (+3)	10 (+0)	19 (+4)	7 (−2)	10 (+0)	9 (−1)

Saving Throws Str +6
Damage Resistances cold, fire, lightning; bludgeoning, piercing, and slashing from nonmagical attacks
Damage Immunities acid, poison
Condition Immunities poisoned
Senses blindsight 60 ft., darkvision 60 ft., passive Perception 10
Languages Abyssal, Infernal, telepathy 60 ft.
Challenge 7 (2,900 XP) **Proficiency Bonus** +3

Magic Resistance. The dhergoloth has advantage on saving throws against spells and other magical effects.

ACTIONS

Multiattack. The dhergoloth makes two Claw attacks.

Claw. *Melee Weapon Attack:* +6 to hit, reach 5 ft., one target. *Hit:* 12 (2d8 + 3) force damage.

Flailing Claws (Recharge 5–6). The dhergoloth moves up to its speed in a straight line and targets each creature within 5 feet of it during its movement. Each target must succeed on a DC 14 Dexterity saving throw or take 22 (3d12 + 3) force damage.

Spellcasting. The dhergoloth casts one of the following spells, requiring no material components and using Charisma as the spellcasting ability (spell save DC 10):

At will: *darkness, fear*

Teleport. The dhergoloth teleports, along with any equipment it is wearing or carrying, up to 60 feet to an unoccupied space it can see.

A dhergoloth's head doesn't turn along with its furiously spinning torso, and its torso can spin a different direction from its dancing legs.

I'd like to vivisect one at some point to find out how this can be.

—Mordenkainen

DINOSAURS

The *Monster Manual* has statistics for several kinds of dinosaurs. This section provides several more.

BRONTOSAURUS

This massive four-legged dinosaur is large enough that most predators leave it alone. Its deadly tail can drive away or kill smaller threats.

DEINONYCHUS

This larger cousin of the velociraptor kills by gripping its target with its claws and feeding.

DIMETRODON

This sail-backed reptile is commonly found in areas where dinosaurs live. It hunts on shores and in shallow water, filling a similar role to a crocodile.

HADROSAURUS

A hadrosaurus is a semi-quadrupedal herbivore with bony head crests. If raised from a hatchling, it can be trained to carry a rider.

QUETZALCOATLUS

This giant relative of the pteranodon has a wingspan exceeding 30 feet. Although it can walk like a quadruped, it is more comfortable in the air.

STEGOSAURUS

This heavily built dinosaur has rows of plates on its back and a flexible, spiked tail held high to strike predators. It tends to travel in herds of mixed ages.

BRONTOSAURUS

Gargantuan Beast (Dinosaur), Unaligned

Armor Class 15 (natural armor)
Hit Points 121 (9d20 + 27)
Speed 30 ft.

STR	DEX	CON	INT	WIS	CHA
21 (+5)	9 (−1)	17 (+3)	2 (−4)	10 (+0)	7 (−2)

Saving Throws Con +6
Senses passive Perception 10
Languages —
Challenge 5 (1,800 XP)   **Proficiency Bonus** +3

ACTIONS

Stomp. *Melee Weapon Attack:* +8 to hit, reach 20 ft., one target. *Hit:* 27 (5d8 + 5) bludgeoning damage, and the target must succeed on a DC 14 Strength saving throw or be knocked prone.

Tail. *Melee Weapon Attack:* +8 to hit, reach 20 ft., one target. *Hit:* 32 (6d8 + 5) bludgeoning damage

VELOCIRAPTOR

This feathered dinosaur is about the size of a large turkey. It is an aggressive predator and often hunts in packs to bring down larger prey.

DEINONYCHUS

Medium Beast (Dinosaur), Unaligned

Armor Class 13 (natural armor)
Hit Points 26 (4d8 + 8)
Speed 40 ft.

STR	DEX	CON	INT	WIS	CHA
15 (+2)	15 (+2)	14 (+2)	4 (−3)	12 (+1)	6 (−2)

Skills Perception +3
Senses passive Perception 13
Languages —
Challenge 1 (200 XP)   **Proficiency Bonus** +2

Pounce. If the deinonychus moves at least 20 feet straight toward a creature and then hits it with a Claw attack on the same turn, that target must succeed on a DC 12 Strength saving throw or be knocked prone. If the target is prone, the deinonychus can make one Bite attack against it as a bonus action.

ACTIONS

Multiattack. The deinonychus makes one Bite attack and two Claw attacks.

Bite. *Melee Weapon Attack:* +4 to hit, reach 5 ft., one target. *Hit:* 6 (1d8 + 2) piercing damage.

Claw. *Melee Weapon Attack:* +4 to hit, reach 5 ft., one target. *Hit:* 6 (1d8 + 2) slashing damage.

DIMETRODON

Medium Beast (Dinosaur), Unaligned

Armor Class 12 (natural armor)
Hit Points 19 (3d8 + 6)
Speed 30 ft., swim 20 ft.

STR	DEX	CON	INT	WIS	CHA
14 (+2)	10 (+0)	15 (+2)	2 (−4)	10 (+0)	5 (−3)

Skills Perception +2
Senses passive Perception 12
Languages —
Challenge 1/4 (50 XP)   **Proficiency Bonus** +2

ACTIONS

Bite. *Melee Weapon Attack:* +4 to hit, reach 5 ft., one target. *Hit:* 9 (2d6 + 2) piercing damage.

HADROSAURUS
Large Beast (Dinosaur), Unaligned

Armor Class 11 (natural armor)
Hit Points 19 (3d10 + 3)
Speed 40 ft.

STR	DEX	CON	INT	WIS	CHA
15 (+2)	10 (+0)	13 (+1)	2 (−4)	10 (+0)	5 (−3)

Skills Perception +2
Senses passive Perception 12
Languages —
Challenge 1/4 (50 XP)   **Proficiency Bonus** +2

ACTIONS

Tail. *Melee Weapon Attack:* +4 to hit, reach 5 ft., one target. *Hit:* 7 (1d10 + 2) bludgeoning damage.

QUETZALCOATLUS
Huge Beast (Dinosaur), Unaligned

Armor Class 13 (natural armor)
Hit Points 30 (4d12 + 4)
Speed 10 ft., fly 80 ft.

STR	DEX	CON	INT	WIS	CHA
15 (+2)	13 (+1)	13 (+1)	2 (−4)	10 (+0)	5 (−3)

Skills Perception +2
Senses passive Perception 12
Languages —
Challenge 2 (450 XP)   **Proficiency Bonus** +2

Flyby. The quetzalcoatlus doesn't provoke an opportunity attack when it flies out of an enemy's reach.

ACTIONS

Bite. *Melee Weapon Attack:* +4 to hit, reach 10 ft., one creature. *Hit:* 12 (3d6 + 2) piercing damage. If the quetzalcoatlus flew least 30 feet toward the target immediately before the hit, the target takes an extra 10 (3d6) piercing damage.

STEGOSAURUS
Huge Beast (Dinosaur), Unaligned

Armor Class 13 (natural armor)
Hit Points 76 (8d12 + 24)
Speed 40 ft.

STR	DEX	CON	INT	WIS	CHA
20 (+5)	9 (−1)	17 (+3)	2 (−4)	11 (+0)	5 (−3)

Senses passive Perception 10
Languages —
Challenge 4 (1,100 XP)   **Proficiency Bonus** +2

ACTIONS

Tail. *Melee Weapon Attack:* +7 to hit, reach 10 ft., one target. *Hit:* 26 (6d6 + 5) piercing damage.

VELOCIRAPTOR
Tiny Beast (Dinosaur), Unaligned

Armor Class 13 (natural armor)
Hit Points 10 (3d4 + 3)
Speed 30 ft.

STR	DEX	CON	INT	WIS	CHA
6 (−2)	14 (+2)	13 (+1)	4 (−3)	12 (+1)	6 (−2)

Skills Perception +3
Senses passive Perception 13
Languages —
Challenge 1/4 (50 XP)   **Proficiency Bonus** +2

Pack Tactics. The velociraptor has advantage on an attack roll against a creature if at least one of the velociraptor's allies is within 5 feet of the creature and the ally isn't incapacitated.

ACTIONS

Multiattack. The velociraptor makes one Bite attack and one Claw attack.

Bite. *Melee Weapon Attack:* +4 to hit, reach 5 ft., one creature. *Hit:* 5 (1d6 + 2) piercing damage.

Claw. *Melee Weapon Attack:* +4 to hit, reach 5 ft., one target. *Hit:* 4 (1d4 + 2) slashing damage.

DOLPHIN
Medium Beast, Unaligned

Armor Class 12 (natural armor)
Hit Points 11 (2d8 + 2)
Speed 0 ft., swim 60 ft.

STR	DEX	CON	INT	WIS	CHA
14 (+2)	13 (+1)	13 (+1)	6 (−2)	12 (+1)	7 (−2)

Skills Perception +3
Senses blindsight 60 ft., passive Perception 13
Languages —
Challenge 1/8 (25 XP) **Proficiency Bonus** +2

Hold Breath. The dolphin can hold its breath for 20 minutes.

ACTIONS

Slam. *Melee Weapon Attack:* +4 to hit, reach 5 ft., one target. *Hit:* 5 (1d6 + 2) bludgeoning damage. If the dolphin moved at least 30 feet straight toward the target immediately before the hit, the target takes an extra 3 (1d6) bludgeoning damage.

DOLPHIN DELIGHTER
Medium Fey, Typically Chaotic Good

Armor Class 14 (natural armor)
Hit Points 27 (5d8 + 5)
Speed 0 ft., swim 60 ft.

STR	DEX	CON	INT	WIS	CHA
14 (+2)	13 (+1)	13 (+1)	11 (+0)	12 (+1)	16 (+3)

Saving Throws Wis +3, Cha +5
Skills Perception +3, Performance +5
Senses blindsight 60 ft., passive Perception 13
Languages Aquan, telepathy 120 ft.
Challenge 3 (700 XP) **Proficiency Bonus** +2

Hold Breath. The dolphin can hold its breath for 20 minutes.

ACTIONS

Multiattack. The dolphin makes two Dazzling Slam attacks.

Dazzling Slam. *Melee Weapon Attack:* +4 to hit, reach 5 ft., one target. *Hit:* 5 (1d6 + 2) bludgeoning damage plus 7 (2d6) psychic damage, and the target is blinded until the start of the dolphin's next turn.

BONUS ACTIONS

Delightful Light (Recharge 5–6). The dolphin magically emanates light in a 10-foot radius for a moment. The dolphin and each creature of its choice in that light gain 11 (2d10) temporary hit points.

Fey Leap. The dolphin teleports up to 30 feet to an unoccupied space it can see. Immediately before teleporting, the dolphin can choose one creature within 5 feet of it. That creature can teleport with the dolphin, appearing in an unoccupied space within 5 feet of the dolphin's destination space.

DOLPHINS

Dolphins are clever, social marine mammals that feed on small fish and squid. An adult specimen is between 5 and 6 feet long.

DOLPHIN

Dolphins are symbols of wisdom and playfulness among the sea folk of many worlds. Found in oceans and in the Elemental Plane of Water, dolphins are befriended by druids and rangers, and many tales speak of dolphins that appeared out of nowhere to protect swimmers from sharks and other aquatic predators.

DOLPHIN DELIGHTER

In the Feywild, dolphin delighters brighten the moods of those who travel the seas of the Domains of Delight. Telepathically singing sea chanteys, these dolphins leap and teleport through the luminous waters of Faerie and the Material Plane, and they are faithful allies to any who battle the forces of gloom and brutality under the waves.

Dolphin delighters often accompany groups of sea elves, tritons, and tortles as guardians and friends.

Draegloth

A draegloth is a demon created by an elf priest of Lolth in an unholy, dangerous ritual in which it is infused with the fey essence of the creator and the fiendish essence of a glabrezu. This ritual rarely succeeds, but Lolth's faithful consider it worth the risk, as the resulting creature is gifted with innate magic and physical might. The draegloth usually serves its creator, lending its thirst for destruction to the creator's plans to triumph over rivals.

A draegloth is an ogre-sized, four-armed biped with purple skin and pale hair. Two of its arms are muscular, tipped with sharp claws; the other two are the size and shape of an elf's arms, capable of delicate movements. Although the creature is heavily muscled, it is graceful like an elf. Its bestial face features glowing red eyes, a doglike snout, and a mouth full of sharp teeth.

Among the drow noble houses of Menzoberranzan in the Forgotten Realms, a high priestess's successful creation of a draegloth is seen as a sign of Lolth's favor toward her house—and a sign of the demon lord's disregard for the family's rivals, who were not thus gifted. The creation prompts the leaders of the house to begin crafting new plans to strike at its rivals when the draegloth is fully grown. These plans use the draegloth in a significant role, because its abilities can turn the tide in a battle against a house that doesn't have a draegloth of its own.

Although draegloths plays an important part in the plans of Lolth's cult, a draegloth can't rise above the status of a favored servant to a priest in that cult. Before a draegloth is given any duties, it receives instruction in accepting the role set for it and not challenging authority. Most draegloths fiercely resent being given orders, but thanks to their training, they typically take out their frustration on their creator's enemies, rather than on their creator. A draegloth that can't suppress its ambitions might abandon its creator and strike out on its own. Whether these rebellious draegloths are part of Lolth's plan for sowing chaos is unclear.

DRAEGLOTH
Large Fiend (Demon), Typically Chaotic Evil

Armor Class 15 (natural armor)
Hit Points 123 (13d10 + 52)
Speed 30 ft.

STR	DEX	CON	INT	WIS	CHA
20 (+5)	15 (+2)	18 (+4)	13 (+1)	11 (+0)	11 (+0)

Skills Perception +3, Stealth +5
Damage Resistances cold, fire, lightning
Damage Immunities poison
Condition Immunities poisoned
Senses darkvision 120 ft., passive Perception 13
Languages Abyssal, Elvish, Undercommon
Challenge 7 (2,900 XP)   **Proficiency Bonus** +3

Fey Ancestry. The draegloth has advantage on saving throws against being charmed, and magic can't put it to sleep.

ACTIONS

Multiattack. The draegloth makes one Bite attack and two Claw attacks.

Bite. *Melee Weapon Attack:* +8 to hit, reach 5 ft., one creature. *Hit:* 16 (2d10 + 5) piercing damage.

Claw. *Melee Weapon Attack:* +8 to hit, reach 10 ft., one target. *Hit:* 16 (2d10 + 5) slashing damage.

Spellcasting. The draegloth casts one of the following spells, requiring no material components and using Charisma as the spellcasting ability (spell save DC 11):

At will: *dancing lights, darkness*
1/day each: *confusion, faerie fire*

DROW ARACHNOMANCER

Drow spellcasters who seek to devote themselves wholly to Lolth, the Spider Queen, sometimes walk the sinister path of the arachnomancer. By offering up body and soul to Lolth, they gain tremendous power and a supernatural connection to the ancient spiders of the Demonweb Pits, channeling magic from that dread place.

DROW ARACHNOMANCER

Medium Humanoid (Elf), Typically Chaotic Evil

Armor Class 15 (studded leather)
Hit Points 162 (25d8 + 50)
Speed 30 ft., climb 30 ft.

STR	DEX	CON	INT	WIS	CHA
11 (+0)	17 (+3)	14 (+2)	19 (+4)	14 (+2)	16 (+3)

Saving Throws Con +7, Int +9, Cha +8
Skills Arcana +9, Nature +9, Perception +7, Stealth +8
Damage Resistances poison
Senses blindsight 10 ft., darkvision 120 ft., passive Perception 17
Languages Elvish, Undercommon, can speak with spiders
Challenge 13 (10,000 XP)   **Proficiency Bonus** +5

Fey Ancestry. The drow has advantage on saving throws against being charmed, and magic can't put the drow to sleep.

Spider Climb. The drow can climb difficult surfaces, including upside down on ceilings, without needing to make an ability check.

Sunlight Sensitivity. While in sunlight, the drow has disadvantage on attack rolls, as well as on Wisdom (Perception) checks that rely on sight.

Web Walker. The drow ignores movement restrictions caused by webbing.

ACTIONS

Multiattack. The drow makes three attacks, using Bite, Poisonous Touch, Web, or a combination of them. One attack can be replaced by a use of Spellcasting.

Bite (Spider Form Only). Melee Weapon Attack: +8 to hit, reach 5 ft., one target. Hit: 12 (2d8 + 3) piercing damage, and the target must make a DC 15 Constitution saving throw, taking 31 (7d8) poison damage on a failed save, or half as much damage on a successful one. If the poison damage reduces the target to 0 hit points, the target is stable but poisoned for 1 hour, even after regaining hit points, and is paralyzed while poisoned in this way.

Poisonous Touch (Humanoid Form Only). Melee Weapon Attack: +8 to hit, reach 5 ft., one target. Hit: 35 (10d6) poison damage.

Web (Spider Form Only; Recharge 5–6). Ranged Weapon Attack: +8 to hit, range 30/60 ft., one target. Hit: The target is restrained by webbing. As an action, the restrained target can make a DC 15 Strength check, bursting the webbing on a success. The webbing can also be attacked and destroyed (AC 10; hp 5; vulnerability to fire damage; immunity to bludgeoning, poison, and psychic damage).

Spellcasting. The drow casts one of the following spells, requiring no material components and using Intelligence as the spellcasting ability (spell save DC 17):

At will: *dancing lights*, *mage hand*
1/day each: *darkness*, *dispel magic*, *etherealness*, *faerie fire*, *fly*, *insect plague*, *invisibility*

BONUS ACTIONS

Change Shape (Recharges after a Short or Long Rest). The drow magically transforms into a Large spider, remaining in that form for up to 1 hour, or back into its true form. Its statistics, other than its size, are the same in each form. It can speak and cast spells while in spider form. Any equipment it is wearing or carrying in Humanoid form melds into the spider form. It can't activate, use, wield, or otherwise benefit from any of its equipment. It reverts to its Humanoid form if it dies.

Drow Favored Consort

Nearly every priestess of Lolth, including the powerful drow matron mother in this book, takes an attractive drow as consort. Chosen as much for beauty as for magical might, a drow favored consort can hold their own in both conversation and combat. Combining the roles of advisor, protector, and beloved, some favored consorts are content with a supporting role, while more ambitious consorts aspire to be the power behind the throne—or even to claim the throne themselves.

Those favored consorts who prove their cunning gain the ear, and perhaps even the heart, of their priestess and are relied on to provide useful advice. No position of consort is assured for long, though; Lolth's priestesses are notoriously fickle, and a consort must often contend with rivals.

Some favored consorts work behind the scenes to undermine the evils encouraged by Lolth. Others can be found in Underdark cities free of Lolth's influence, where these powerful spellcasters apply their might toward ending her tyranny.

Drow Favored Consort

Medium Humanoid (Elf, Wizard), Any Alignment

Armor Class 15 (18 with *mage armor*)
Hit Points 240 (32d8 + 96)
Speed 30 ft.

STR	DEX	CON	INT	WIS	CHA
15 (+2)	20 (+5)	16 (+3)	18 (+4)	15 (+2)	18 (+4)

Saving Throws Dex +11, Con +9, Cha +10
Skills Acrobatics +11, Athletics +8, Perception +8, Stealth +11
Senses darkvision 120 ft., passive Perception 18
Languages Elvish, Undercommon
Challenge 18 (20,000 XP)   **Proficiency Bonus** +6

Fey Ancestry. The drow has advantage on saving throws against being charmed, and magic can't put the drow to sleep.

Sunlight Sensitivity. While in sunlight, the drow has disadvantage on attack rolls, as well as on Wisdom (Perception) checks that rely on sight.

Actions

Multiattack. The drow makes three Scimitar or Arcane Eruption attacks. The drow can replace one of the attacks with a use of Spellcasting.

Scimitar. *Melee Weapon Attack:* +11 to hit, reach 5 ft., one target. *Hit:* 8 (1d6 + 5) slashing damage plus 27 (6d8) poison damage.

Arcane Eruption. *Ranged Spell Attack:* +10 to hit, range 120 ft., one target. *Hit:* 36 (8d8) force damage, and the drow can push the target up to 10 feet away if it is a Large or smaller creature.

Spellcasting. The drow casts one of the following spells, requiring no material components and using Intelligence as the spellcasting ability (spell save DC 18):

At will: *dancing lights, mage armor, mage hand, message*
3/day each: *dimension door, fireball, invisibility*
1/day each: *darkness, faerie fire, levitate* (self only)

Reactions

Protective Shield (3/Day). When the drow or a creature within 10 feet of it is hit by an attack roll, the drow gives the target a +5 bonus to its AC until the start of the drow's next turn, which can cause the triggering attack roll to miss.

Drow House Captain

Medium Humanoid (Elf), Any Alignment

Armor Class 16 (chain mail)
Hit Points 162 (25d8 + 50)
Speed 30 ft.

STR	DEX	CON	INT	WIS	CHA
14 (+2)	19 (+4)	15 (+2)	12 (+1)	14 (+2)	13 (+1)

Saving Throws Dex +8, Con +6, Wis +6
Skills Perception +6, Stealth +8
Senses darkvision 120 ft., passive Perception 16
Languages Elvish, Undercommon
Challenge 9 (5,000 XP)   **Proficiency Bonus** +4

Fey Ancestry. The drow has advantage on saving throws against being charmed, and magic can't put the drow to sleep.

Sunlight Sensitivity. While in sunlight, the drow has disadvantage on attack rolls, as well as on Wisdom (Perception) checks that rely on sight.

Actions

Multiattack. The drow makes two Scimitar attacks and one Whip or Hand Crossbow attack.

Scimitar. *Melee Weapon Attack:* +8 to hit, reach 5 ft., one target. *Hit:* 7 (1d6 + 4) slashing damage plus 14 (4d6) poison damage.

Whip. *Melee Weapon Attack:* +8 to hit, reach 10 ft., one target. *Hit:* 6 (1d4 + 4) slashing damage.

Hand Crossbow. *Ranged Weapon Attack:* +8 to hit, range 30/120 ft., one target. *Hit:* 7 (1d6 + 4) piercing damage, and the target must succeed on a DC 13 Constitution saving throw or be poisoned for 1 hour. If the saving throw fails by 5 or more, the target is also unconscious while poisoned in this way. The target regains consciousness if it takes damage or if another creature takes an action to shake it.

Spellcasting. The drow casts one of the following spells, requiring no material components and using Charisma as the spellcasting ability (spell save DC 13):

At will: *dancing lights*
1/day each: *darkness, faerie fire, levitate* (self only)

Bonus Actions

Battle Command. Choose one creature within 30 feet of the drow that the drow can see. If the chosen creature can see or hear the drow, that creature can use its reaction to make one melee attack or to take the Dodge or Hide action.

Reactions

Parry. The drow adds 3 to its AC against one melee attack roll that would hit it. To do so, the drow must see the attacker and be wielding a melee weapon.

House captains will do anything to protect their family—whether that's their birth house or their platoon of scrappy rebels. I'd do anything for my (sometimes infuriating) mother and for my chosen family, so I admire their dedication.

TASHA

Drow House Captain

A drow house captain leads the troops of an Underdark faction, whether defending a stronghold or leading forces against enemies. These officers make extensive study of strategy and tactics to become effective leaders in battle.

Among Lolth's devotees in the city of Menzoberranzan in the Forgotten Realms, each noble house entrusts the leadership of its military forces to a house captain, who is typically the first or second son of a drow matron mother (appears in this book). Elsewhere drow house captains fight in the war against Lolth, often allying with duergar and others who also wish to rid their subterranean world of that god's malevolence.

Nikki Dawes

Drow Inquisitor

Lolth's worshipers expect treachery—the Spider Queen encourages it, after all. A certain amount of backstabbing and double-crossing can be managed, but too much can undermine an entire community. To keep some semblance of order and to root out traitors, priestesses of Lolth employ inquisitors. Inquisitors are chosen from the ranks of the priesthood, and their authority is equaled only by that of the drow matron mothers (also in this book) of the noble houses. Anyone they decide is at odds with the hierarchy faces painful interrogation and usually an excruciating death.

Variant: Demon Summoning

Some drow inquisitors have an action that allows them to summon a yochlol.

Summon Demon (1/Day). The drow attempts to magically summon a **yochlol** (see the *Monster Manual*), with a 50 percent chance of success. If the attempt fails, the drow takes 5 (1d10) psychic damage. Otherwise, the summoned demon appears in an unoccupied space within 60 feet of its summoner, acts as an ally of its summoner, and can't summon other demons. It remains for 10 minutes, until it or its summoner dies, or until its summoner dismisses it as an action.

DROW INQUISITOR
Medium Humanoid (Cleric, Elf), Typically Neutral Evil

Armor Class 16 (breastplate)
Hit Points 149 (23d8 + 46)
Speed 30 ft.

STR	DEX	CON	INT	WIS	CHA
11 (+1)	15 (+2)	14 (+2)	16 (+3)	21 (+5)	20 (+5)

Saving Throws Con +7, Wis +10, Cha +10
Skills Insight +10, Perception +10, Religion +8, Stealth +7
Condition Immunities frightened
Senses darkvision 120 ft., passive Perception 20
Languages Elvish, Undercommon
Challenge 14 (11,500 XP)   **Proficiency Bonus** +5

Discern Lie. The drow discerns when a creature in earshot speaks a lie in a language the drow knows.

Fey Ancestry. The drow has advantage on saving throws against being charmed, and magic can't put the drow to sleep.

Sunlight Sensitivity. While in sunlight, the drow has disadvantage on attack rolls, as well as on Wisdom (Perception) checks that rely on sight.

Actions

Multiattack. The drow makes three Death Lance attacks.

Death Lance. *Melee Weapon Attack:* +10 to hit, reach 5 ft., one target. *Hit:* 8 (1d6 + 5) piercing damage plus 18 (4d8) necrotic damage. The target's hit point maximum is reduced by an amount equal to the necrotic damage taken. This reduction lasts until the target finishes a long rest. The target dies if its hit point maximum is reduced to 0.

Spellcasting. The drow's casts one of the following spells, requiring no material components and using Charisma as the spellcasting ability (spell save DC 18):

At will: *dancing lights, detect magic, message, thaumaturgy*
1/day each: *clairvoyance, darkness, detect thoughts, dispel magic, faerie fire, levitate* (self only), *silence, suggestion, true seeing*

Bonus Actions

Spectral Dagger (Recharges after a Short or Long Rest). The drow conjures a floating, spectral dagger within 60 feet of itself. The drow can make a melee spell attack (+10 to hit) against one creature within 5 feet of the dagger. On a hit, the target takes 9 (1d8 + 5) force damage.

The dagger lasts for 1 minute. As a bonus action on later turns, the drow can move the dagger up to 20 feet and repeat the attack against one creature within 5 feet of the dagger.

DROW MATRON MOTHER

Among drow followers of Lolth, each noble house is led by a matron mother, an influential priestess of Lolth charged with carrying out the god's will while also advancing the interests of the family. Matron mothers embody the scheming and treachery associated with the Queen of Spiders. Each stands at the center of a vast conspiratorial web, with demons, spiders, and conscripted soldiers positioned between them and their enemies. Although matron mothers command great power, that power depends on maintaining the Spider Queen's favor, and the goddess sometimes capriciously takes back what she has given. The stat block here represents a matron mother at the height of her power.

A matron mother is almost never encountered alone. She is typically accompanied by a drow favored consort and a drow house captain, each of whom appears in this book. Other Underdark creatures might also be in the priestess's presence, providing protection or advice.

MOTHERS OF REBELLION

Some matron mothers renounce Lolth and join the war against their former goddess. Such drow could be of any alignment, and they lose the following abilities in the stat block: Lolth's Fickle Favor, Summon Servant, and Compel Demon. Even without these abilities, drow matron mothers are formidable opponents, and several of them hold positions of great influence in the Underdark armies arrayed against the followers of Lolth.

A MATRON MOTHER'S LAIR

The palace of a drow matron mother is her home and fortress. Sigils throughout the building allow the matron mother to use the following lair actions while within it.

Any temple of Lolth also functions as a matron mother's lair while she is inside it, unless she has renounced Lolth or another matron mother is present. When two or more matron mothers gather within a temple of their goddess, none of them can use it as their lair.

LAIR ACTIONS

On initiative count 20 (losing initiative ties), the drow can take one of the following lair actions when in her lair; she can't take the same lair action two rounds in a row:

Perceive Interlopers. The drow projects her mind throughout her lair, marking any potential threats against her or her retinue. Until initiative count 20

of the next round, hostile creatures within the lair can't become hidden from her and gain no benefit from the invisible condition against her.

Spectral Web. A glistening spectral spider web erupts from a point the drow can see within 120 feet of her. Each creature within 60 feet of that point must succeed a DC 19 Dexterity saving throw or be restrained for 1 minute. A creature can repeat the saving throw at the end of each of its turns, ending the effect on itself on a success.

Telekinetic Throw. The drow targets one creature she can see within 60 feet of her and attempts to expel it from her presence. The target must succeed on a DC 19 Strength saving throw or be flung 2d6 × 10 feet through the air. A creature smashed into a solid object takes 1d6 bludgeoning damage for every 10 feet moved. If released in midair, the creature takes falling damage as normal.

Drow Matron Mother

Medium Humanoid (Cleric, Elf), Typically Neutral Evil

Armor Class 17 (half plate)
Hit Points 247 (33d8 + 99)
Speed 30 ft.

STR	DEX	CON	INT	WIS	CHA
12 (+1)	18 (+4)	16 (+3)	17 (+3)	21 (+5)	22 (+6)

Saving Throws Con +9, Wis +11, Cha +12
Skills Insight +11, Perception +11, Religion +9, Stealth +10
Condition Immunities charmed, frightened, poisoned
Senses darkvision 120 ft., passive Perception 21
Languages Elvish, Undercommon
Challenge 20 (25,000 XP)   **Proficiency Bonus** +6

Fey Ancestry. The drow has advantage on saving throws against being charmed, and magic can't put the drow to sleep.

Special Equipment. The drow wields a *tentacle rod.*

Sunlight Sensitivity. While in sunlight, the drow has disadvantage on attack rolls, as well as on Wisdom (Perception) checks that rely on sight.

Actions

Multiattack. The drow makes two Demon Staff attacks or one Demon Staff attack and three Tentacle Rod attacks.

Demon Staff. *Melee Weapon Attack:* +10 to hit, reach 5 ft., one target. *Hit:* 7 (1d6 + 4) bludgeoning damage, or 8 (1d8 + 4) bludgeoning damage if used with two hands, plus 14 (4d6) psychic damage. The target must succeed on a DC 19 Wisdom saving throw or become frightened of the drow for 1 minute. The frightened target can repeat the saving throw at the end of each of its turns, ending the effect on itself on a success.

Tentacle Rod. *Melee Weapon Attack:* +9 to hit, reach 15 ft., one creature. *Hit:* 3 (1d6) bludgeoning damage. If the target is hit three times by the rod on one turn, the target must succeed on a DC 15 Constitution saving throw or suffer the following effects for 1 minute: the target's speed is halved, it has disadvantage on Dexterity saving throws, and it can't use reactions. Moreover, on each of its turns, it can take either an action or

a bonus action, but not both. At the end of each of its turns, it can repeat the saving throw, ending the effect on itself on a success.

Divine Flame (2/Day). A 10-foot-radius, 40-foot-high column of divine fire sprouts in an area up to 120 feet away from the drow. Each creature in the column must make a DC 20 Dexterity saving throw, taking 14 (4d6) fire damage and 14 (4d6) radiant damage on a failed save, or half as much damage on a successful one.

Spellcasting. The drow casts one of the following spells, requiring no material components and using Charisma as the spellcasting ability (spell save DC 20):

At will: *command, dancing lights, detect magic, thaumaturgy*
2/day each: *banishment, blade barrier, cure wounds, hold person, plane shift, silence*
1/day each: *clairvoyance, darkness, detect thoughts, dispel magic, faerie fire, gate, levitate* (self only), *suggestion*

Bonus Actions

Lolth's Fickle Favor. The drow bestows the Spider Queen's blessing on one ally she can see within 30 feet of her. The ally takes 7 (2d6) psychic damage but has advantage on the next attack roll it makes before the end of its next turn.

Summon Servant (1/Day). The drow magically summons a **glabrezu** or a **yochlol** (both appear the *Monster Manual*). The summoned creature appears in an unoccupied space within 60 feet of its summoner, acts as an ally of its summoner, and can't summon other demons. It remains for 10 minutes, until it or its summoner dies, or until its summoner dismisses it as an action.

Legendary Actions

The drow can take 3 legendary actions, choosing from the options below. Only one legendary action option can be used at a time and only at the end of another creature's turn. The drow regains spent legendary actions at the start of her turn.

Compel Demon. An allied demon within 30 feet of the drow uses its reaction to make one attack against a target of the drow's choice that she can see.
Demon Staff. The drow makes one Demon Staff attack.
Cast a Spell (Costs 2 Actions). The drow uses Spellcasting.

DROW SHADOWBLADE

Medium Humanoid (Elf), Any Alignment

Armor Class 17 (studded leather)
Hit Points 150 (20d8 + 60)
Speed 30 ft.

STR	DEX	CON	INT	WIS	CHA
14 (+2)	21 (+5)	16 (+3)	12 (+1)	14 (+2)	13 (+1)

Saving Throws Dex +9, Con +7, Wis +6
Skills Perception +6, Stealth +9
Senses darkvision 120 ft., passive Perception 16
Languages Elvish, Undercommon
Challenge 11 (7,200 XP)　　　　**Proficiency Bonus** +4

Devil's Sight. Magical darkness doesn't impede the drow's darkvision.

Fey Ancestry. The drow has advantage on saving throws against being charmed, and magic can't put the drow to sleep.

Sunlight Sensitivity. While in sunlight, the drow has disadvantage on attack rolls, as well as on Wisdom (Perception) checks that rely on sight.

ACTIONS

Multiattack. The drow makes three Shadow Sword attacks. One of the attacks can be replaced by a Hand Crossbow attack. The drow can also use Spellcasting to cast *darkness*.

Shadow Sword. *Melee or Ranged Weapon Attack:* +9 to hit, reach 5 ft. or range 30/60 ft., one target. *Hit:* 27 (7d6 + 5) necrotic damage.

Hand Crossbow. *Ranged Weapon Attack:* +9 to hit, range 30/120 ft., one target. *Hit:* 8 (1d6 + 5) piercing damage, and the target must succeed on a DC 13 Constitution saving throw or be poisoned for 1 hour. If the saving throw fails by 5 or more, the target is also unconscious while poisoned in this way. The target regains consciousness if it takes damage or if another creature takes an action to shake it.

Spellcasting. The drow casts one of the following spells, requiring no material components and using Charisma as the spellcasting ability (spell save DC 13):

At will: *dancing lights, darkness*
1/day each: *faerie fire, levitate* (self only)

BONUS ACTIONS

Shadow Step. While in dim light or darkness, the drow teleports, along with any equipment it is wearing or carrying, up to 60 feet to an unoccupied space it can see that is also in dim light or darkness. It then has advantage on the first melee attack it makes before the end of the turn.

DROW SHADOWBLADE

Drow shadowblades steal down the dim passages of the Underdark, bound on errands of mayhem. They protect enclaves and Underdark cities from enemies and track down thieves who make off with prized treasures. In the city of Menzoberranzan in the Forgotten Realms, noble houses often employ shadowblades to eliminate rivals from other houses. In communities free of Lolth's sway, they serve as spies tasked with foiling the plots of that demon lord's cult. In any role they take on, they move undetected until the moment they attack—and then they are the last thing their victims see.

A shadowblade gains their powers over shadow via a ritual in which they kill a shadow demon and mystically prevent it from re-forming in the Abyss, siphoning its essence into themselves.

VARIANT: DEMON SUMMONING

Some drow shadowblades have an action that allows them to summon a demon.

Summon Shadow Demon (1/Day). The drow attempts to magically summon a **shadow demon** (see the *Monster Manual*) with a 50 percent chance of success. If the attempt fails, the drow takes 5 (1d10) psychic damage. Otherwise, the summoned demon appears in an unoccupied space within 60 feet of its summoner, acts as an ally of its summoner, and can't summon other demons. It remains for 10 minutes, until it or its summoner dies, or until its summoner dismisses it as an action.

DUERGAR

Duergar are dwarves of the deep reaches of the Underdark and other sunless realms. Their personalities and abilities have been deeply impacted by their ancestors' captivity and torment by mind flayers; they were infused with powerful psionic abilities but also a profound gloom. In some, this strain of sorrow inspires works of grand but melancholic beauty, while in others, it manifests as rage.

Like many who dwell in the Underdark, duergar must constantly be on guard against the raids and plots of their neighbors. To this end, duergar warriors fulfill a variety of combat roles, often marrying their fury in battle with their psionic abilities or training dangerous Underdark creatures as mounts.

Denigrated by some as joyless, duergar are in fact deeply passionate in all that they do—even if that passion rarely manifests as mirth. They bring an emotional intensity to their lives, whether they're exploring neighboring tunnels, defending their homes, engaging with their families, or crafting bold new works. The bonds of friendship and kinship are strong, though navigating the inevitable outbursts of frustration and despair is not always easy. Similarly, duergar tend to be very community-minded—in the Underdark, all must cooperate to survive.

Among the duergar of the Forgotten Realms, creation is a fiercely passionate process. They tend to favor works that are sturdy and grand, but in a bare, stripped-down fashion that favors geometric forms. The strongholds they design are blocky and stark, and the weapons they forge are blatantly tools of violence. While others may decry their creations as cold and bare of ornamentation to the point of austerity, duergar see them as honoring the materials used and honest about their purpose.

D

DUERGAR DESPOT

Duergar despots replace parts of their bodies with mechanical devices that they control through their psionic abilities.

DUERGAR DESPOT

Medium Humanoid (Dwarf), Any Alignment

Armor Class 21 (natural armor)
Hit Points 119 (14d8 + 56)
Speed 25 ft.

STR	DEX	CON	INT	WIS	CHA
20 (+5)	5 (–3)	19 (+4)	15 (+2)	14 (+2)	13 (+1)

Saving Throws Con +8, Wis +6
Damage Immunities poison
Condition Immunities charmed, exhaustion, frightened, paralyzed, poisoned
Senses darkvision 120 ft., passive Perception 12
Languages Dwarvish, Undercommon
Challenge 12 (8,400 XP)   **Proficiency Bonus** +4

Magic Resistance. The duergar has advantage on saving throws against spells and other magical effects.

Psychic Engine. When the duergar suffers a critical hit or is reduced to 0 hit points, psychic energy erupts from its frame to deal 14 (4d6) psychic damage to each creature within 5 feet of it.

Sunlight Sensitivity. While in sunlight, the duergar has disadvantage on attack rolls, as well as on Wisdom (Perception) checks that rely on sight.

ACTIONS

Multiattack. The duergar makes two Iron Fist attacks and two Stomping Foot attacks. After one of the attacks, the duergar can move up to its speed without provoking opportunity attacks. It can replace one of the attacks with a use of Flame Jet.

Iron Fist. *Melee Weapon Attack:* +9 to hit, reach 5 ft., one target. *Hit:* 23 (4d8 + 5) bludgeoning damage. If the target is a Large or smaller creature, it must succeed on a DC 17 Strength saving throw or be pushed up to 30 feet away in a straight line and be knocked prone.

Stomping Foot. *Melee Weapon Attack:* +9 to hit, reach 5 ft., one target. *Hit:* 10 (1d10 + 5) bludgeoning damage, or 21 (3d10 + 5) to a prone target.

Flame Jet. The duergar spews flames in a line 100 feet long and 5 feet wide. Each creature in the line must make a DC 16 Dexterity saving throw, taking 18 (4d8) fire damage on a failed save, or half as much damage on a successful one.

Spellcasting (Psionics). The duergar casts one of the following spells, requiring no spell components and using Intelligence as the spellcasting ability (spell save DC 12):

At will: *mage hand, minor illusion*
1/day: *stinking cloud*

DUERGAR KAVALRACHNI

Kavalrachni are duergar cavalry trained to fight while riding female steeders (in this book) or other Underdark creatures as mounts.

DUERGAR KAVALRACHNI

Medium Humanoid (Dwarf), Any Alignment

Armor Class 16 (scale mail, shield)
Hit Points 26 (4d8 + 8)
Speed 25 ft.

STR	DEX	CON	INT	WIS	CHA
14 (+2)	11 (+0)	14 (+2)	11 (+0)	10 (+0)	9 (–1)

Damage Resistances poison
Senses darkvision 120 ft., passive Perception 10
Languages Dwarvish, Undercommon
Challenge 2 (450 XP)   **Proficiency Bonus** +2

Cavalry Training. When the duergar hits a target with a melee attack while mounted, the mount can use its reaction to make one melee attack against the same target.

Duergar Resilience. The duergar has advantage on saving throws against spells and the charmed, paralyzed, and poisoned conditions.

Sunlight Sensitivity. While in sunlight, the duergar has disadvantage on attack rolls, as well as on Wisdom (Perception) checks that rely on sight.

ACTIONS

Multiattack. The duergar makes two War Pick attacks.

War Pick. *Melee Weapon Attack:* +4 to hit, reach 5 ft., one target. *Hit:* 6 (1d8 + 2) piercing damage plus 5 (2d4) poison damage.

Heavy Crossbow. *Ranged Weapon Attack:* +2 to hit, range 100/400 ft., one target. *Hit:* 5 (1d10) piercing damage.

Shared Invisibility (Recharges after a Short or Long Rest). The duergar magically turns invisible for up to 1 hour or until it attacks, it forces a creature to make a saving throw, or its concentration is broken (as if concentrating on a spell). Any equipment the duergar wears or carries is invisible with it. While the invisible duergar is mounted, the mount is invisible as well. The invisibility ends early on the mount immediately after it attacks.

D

Duergar Mind Master

Wearing fearsome masks, duergar mind masters usually operate as spies, both inside and beyond a duergar stronghold. Their psionically augmented abilities enable them to see through illusions with ease and shrink down to miniature size to spy on their targets.

Duergar Soulblade

Soulblades are duergar combatants whose mastery of psionics allows them to manifest blades of psychic energy to slice apart their foes.

Duergar Mind Master
Medium Humanoid (Dwarf), Any Alignment

Armor Class 14 (leather armor)
Hit Points 39 (6d8 + 12)
Speed 25 ft.

STR	DEX	CON	INT	WIS	CHA
11 (+0)	17 (+3)	14 (+2)	15 (+2)	10 (+0)	12 (+1)

Saving Throws Wis +2
Skills Perception +2, Stealth +5
Damage Resistances poison
Senses darkvision 120 ft., truesight 30 ft., passive Perception 12
Languages Dwarvish, Undercommon
Challenge 2 (450 XP)   **Proficiency Bonus** +2

Duergar Resilience. The duergar has advantage on saving throws against spells and the charmed, paralyzed, and poisoned conditions.

Sunlight Sensitivity. While in sunlight, the duergar has disadvantage on attack rolls, as well as on Wisdom (Perception) checks that rely on sight.

Actions

Multiattack. The duergar makes two Mind-Poison Dagger attacks. It can replace one attack with a use of Mind Mastery.

Mind-Poison Dagger. *Melee Weapon Attack:* +5 to hit, reach 5 ft., one target. *Hit:* 5 (1d4 + 3) piercing damage plus 10 (3d6) psychic damage, or 1 piercing damage plus 10 (3d6) psychic damage while under the effect of Reduce.

Invisibility (Recharge 4–6). The duergar magically turns invisible for up to 1 hour or until it attacks, it forces a creature to make a saving throw, or its concentration is broken (as if concentrating on a spell). Any equipment the duergar wears or carries is invisible with it.

Mind Mastery. The duergar targets one creature it can see within 60 feet of it. The target must succeed on a DC 12 Intelligence saving throw, or the duergar causes it to use its reaction, if available, either to make one weapon attack against another creature the duergar can see or to move up to 10 feet in a direction of the duergar's choice. Creatures that can't be charmed are immune to this effect.

Bonus Actions

Reduce (Recharges after a Short or Long Rest). For 1 minute, the duergar magically decreases in size, along with anything it is wearing or carrying. While reduced, the duergar is Tiny, reduces its weapon damage to 1, and makes attack rolls, ability checks, and saving throws with disadvantage if they use Strength. It gains a +5 bonus to all Dexterity (Stealth) checks and a +5 bonus to its AC. It can also take a bonus action on each of its turns to take the Hide action.

LEFT TO RIGHT: DUERGAR SOULBLADE, WARLORD, AND XARRORN

DUERGAR SOULBLADE

Medium Humanoid (Dwarf), Any Alignment

Armor Class 14 (leather armor)
Hit Points 27 (6d8)
Speed 25 ft.

STR	DEX	CON	INT	WIS	CHA
16 (+3)	16 (+3)	10 (+0)	11 (+0)	10 (+0)	12 (+1)

Damage Resistances poison
Senses darkvision 120 ft., passive Perception 10
Languages Dwarvish, Undercommon
Challenge 1 (200 XP)   **Proficiency Bonus** +2

Duergar Resilience. The duergar has advantage on saving throws against spells and the charmed, paralyzed, and poisoned conditions.

Sunlight Sensitivity. While in sunlight, the duergar has disadvantage on attack rolls, as well as on Wisdom (Perception) checks that rely on sight.

ACTIONS

Soulblade. *Melee Spell Attack:* +5 to hit, reach 5 ft., one target. *Hit:* 10 (2d6 + 3) force damage, or 13 (3d6 + 3) force damage while under the effect of Enlarge.

Invisibility (Recharges after a Short or Long Rest). The duergar magically turns invisible for up to 1 hour or until it attacks, it forces a creature to make a saving throw, or its concentration is broken (as if concentrating on a spell). Any equipment the duergar wears or carries is invisible with it.

BONUS ACTIONS

Enlarge (Recharges after a Short or Long Rest). For 1 minute, the duergar magically increases in size, along with anything it is wearing or carrying. While enlarged, the duergar is Large, doubles its damage dice on Strength-based weapon attacks (included in the attacks), and makes Strength checks and Strength saving throws with advantage. If the duergar lacks the room to become Large, it attains the maximum size possible in the space available.

DAARKEN

> The mental power that duergar wield was given to them by illithids. But why would illithids create servants who could turn invisible or grow to ogre size?
>
> Most likely because those servants would excel at herding their masters' other minions. In retrospect, it seems arguable that duergar escaped bondage because their jailers had given them the keys.
>
> —Mordenkainen

DUERGAR STONE GUARD

Stone guards are elite troops deployed in small numbers to bolster war bands of regulars or organized into elite strike forces for specific missions.

DUERGAR STONE GUARD

Medium Humanoid (Dwarf), Any Alignment

Armor Class 18 (chain mail, shield)
Hit Points 39 (6d8 + 12)
Speed 25 ft.

STR	DEX	CON	INT	WIS	CHA
18 (+4)	11 (+0)	14 (+2)	11 (+0)	10 (+0)	9 (−1)

Damage Resistances poison
Senses darkvision 120 ft., passive Perception 10
Languages Dwarvish, Undercommon
Challenge 2 (450 XP) **Proficiency Bonus** +2

Duergar Resilience. The duergar has advantage on saving throws against spells and the charmed, paralyzed, and poisoned conditions.

Phalanx Formation. The duergar has advantage on attack rolls and Dexterity saving throws while standing within 5 feet of an ally wielding a shield.

Sunlight Sensitivity. While in sunlight, the duergar has disadvantage on attack rolls, as well as on Wisdom (Perception) checks that rely on sight.

ACTIONS

Multiattack. The duergar makes two Shortsword or Javelin attacks.

Shortsword. *Melee Weapon Attack:* +6 to hit, reach 5 ft., one target. *Hit:* 7 (1d6 + 4) piercing damage, or 11 (2d6 + 4) piercing damage while under the effect of Enlarge.

Javelin. *Melee or Ranged Weapon Attack:* +6 to hit, reach 5 ft. or range 30/120 ft., one target. *Hit:* 7 (1d6 + 4) piercing damage, or 11 (2d6 + 4) piercing damage while under the effect of Enlarge.

Invisibility (Recharges after a Short or Long Rest). The duergar magically turns invisible for up to 1 hour or until it attacks, it forces a creature to make a saving throw, or its concentration is broken (as if concentrating on a spell). Any equipment the duergar wears or carries is invisible with it.

BONUS ACTIONS

Enlarge (Recharges after a Short or Long Rest). For 1 minute, the duergar magically increases in size, along with anything it is wearing or carrying. While enlarged, the duergar is Large, doubles its damage dice on Strength-based weapon attacks (included in the attacks), and makes Strength checks and Strength saving throws with advantage. If the duergar lacks the room to become Large, it attains the maximum size possible in the space available.

MARK BEHM

D

DUERGAR WARLORD

Medium Humanoid (Dwarf), Any Alignment

Armor Class 20 (plate mail, shield)
Hit Points 75 (10d8 + 30)
Speed 25 ft.

STR	DEX	CON	INT	WIS	CHA
18 (+4)	11 (+0)	17 (+3)	12 (+1)	12 (+1)	14 (+2)

Damage Resistances poison
Senses darkvision 120 ft., passive Perception 11
Languages Dwarvish, Undercommon
Challenge 6 (2,300 XP)   **Proficiency Bonus** +3

Duergar Resilience. The duergar has advantage on saving throws against spells and the charmed, paralyzed, and poisoned conditions.

Sunlight Sensitivity. While in sunlight, the duergar has disadvantage on attack rolls, as well as on Wisdom (Perception) checks that rely on sight.

ACTIONS

Multiattack. The duergar makes three Psychic-Attuned Hammer or Javelin attacks and uses Call to Attack.

Psychic-Attuned Hammer. *Melee Weapon Attack:* +7 to hit, reach 5 ft., one target. *Hit:* 9 (1d10 + 4) bludgeoning damage, or 15 (2d10 + 4) bludgeoning damage while under the effect of Enlarge, plus 5 (1d10) psychic damage.

Javelin. *Melee or Ranged Weapon Attack:* +7 to hit, reach 5 ft. or range 30/120 ft., one target. *Hit:* 7 (1d6 + 4) piercing damage, or 11 (2d6 + 4) piercing damage while under the effect of Enlarge.

Call to Attack. Up to three allies within 120 feet of this duergar that can hear it can each use their reaction to make one weapon attack.

Invisibility (Recharge 4–6). The duergar magically turns invisible for up to 1 hour or until it attacks, it forces a creature to make a saving throw, or its concentration is broken (as if concentrating on a spell). Any equipment the duergar wears or carries is invisible with it.

BONUS ACTIONS

Enlarge (Recharges after a Short or Long Rest). For 1 minute, the duergar magically increases in size, along with anything it is wearing or carrying. While enlarged, the duergar is Large, doubles its damage dice on Strength-based weapon attacks (included in the attacks), and makes Strength checks and Strength saving throws with advantage. If the duergar lacks the room to become Large, it attains the maximum size possible in the space available.

REACTIONS

Scouring Instruction. When an ally that the duergar can see makes a d20 roll, the duergar can roll a d6, and the ally can add the number rolled to the d20 by taking 3 (1d6) psychic damage.

DUERGAR WARLORD

A warlord is cunning, inspiring, and merciless in equal parts. A skilled leader in battle, the warlord can use spikes of psionic energy to compel the warriors they command to fight harder.

DUERGAR XARRORN

Xarrorn are specialists who construct weapons using a mixture of alchemy and psionics.

DUERGAR XARRORN

Medium Humanoid (Dwarf), Any Alignment

Armor Class 18 (plate mail)
Hit Points 26 (4d8 + 8)
Speed 25 ft.

STR	DEX	CON	INT	WIS	CHA
16 (+3)	11 (+0)	14 (+2)	11 (+0)	10 (+0)	9 (−1)

Damage Resistances poison
Senses darkvision 120 ft., passive Perception 10
Languages Dwarvish, Undercommon
Challenge 2 (450 XP)   **Proficiency Bonus** +2

Duergar Resilience. The duergar has advantage on saving throws against spells and the charmed, paralyzed, and poisoned conditions.

Sunlight Sensitivity. While in sunlight, the duergar has disadvantage on attack rolls, as well as on Wisdom (Perception) checks that rely on sight.

ACTIONS

Fire Lance. *Melee Weapon Attack:* +5 to hit, reach 10 ft., one target. *Hit:* 9 (1d12 + 3) piercing damage, or 16 (2d12 + 3) piercing damage while under the effect of Enlarge, plus 3 (1d6) fire damage.

Fire Spray (Recharge 5–6). From its fire lance, the duergar shoots a 15-foot cone of fire or a line of fire 30 feet long and 5 feet wide. Each creature in that area must make a DC 12 Dexterity saving throw, taking 10 (3d6) fire damage on a failed save, or half as much damage on a successful one.

Invisibility (Recharges after a Short or Long Rest). The duergar magically turns invisible for up to 1 hour or until it attacks, it forces a creature to make a saving throw, or its concentration is broken (as if concentrating on a spell). Any equipment the duergar wears or carries is invisible with it.

BONUS ACTIONS

Enlarge (Recharges after a Short or Long Rest). For 1 minute, the duergar magically increases in size, along with anything it is wearing or carrying. While enlarged, the duergar is Large, doubles its damage dice on Strength-based weapon attacks (included in the attacks), and makes Strength checks and Strength saving throws with advantage. If the duergar lacks the room to become Large, it attains the maximum size possible in the space available.

DUERGAR CONSTRUCTS

Creative duergar engineers have built numerous war machines, including some that can be fused with a duergar. Such a duergar-machine hybrid is fueled by the duergar's psionic energy, and the duergar inside the machine can psychically channel pain into power when attacked.

These machines are deployed to assist with construction projects and war. Some duergar bravely volunteer to become hybrids, while other duergar are forced into the fusion by Underdark tyrants.

Unless incapacitated, the duergar inside a machine can extricate themselves from it over the course of a short rest, completing the process at the rest's end.

DUERGAR HAMMERER

The duergar hammerer is a digging machine and siege engine, used to dig tunnels and besiege enemy fortifications.

DUERGAR SCREAMER

A duergar screamer uses sonic energy to grind rock into dust and to hurl invaders to the ground.

DUERGAR HAMMERER
Medium Construct (Dwarf), Any Alignment

Armor Class 17 (natural armor)
Hit Points 33 (6d8 + 6)
Speed 20 ft.

STR	DEX	CON	INT	WIS	CHA
17 (+3)	7 (−2)	12 (+1)	5 (−3)	5 (−3)	5 (−3)

Damage Immunities poison
Condition Immunities charmed, exhaustion, frightened, paralyzed, petrified, poisoned
Senses darkvision 60 ft., passive Perception 7
Languages understands Dwarvish but can't speak
Challenge 2 (450 XP)   **Proficiency Bonus** +2

Siege Monster. The hammerer deals double damage to objects and structures.

ACTIONS

Multiattack. The hammerer makes one Claw attack and one Hammer attack.

Claw. *Melee Weapon Attack:* +5 to hit, reach 5 ft., one target. *Hit:* 6 (1d6 + 3) piercing damage.

Hammer. *Melee Weapon Attack:* +5 to hit, reach 5 ft., one target. *Hit:* 10 (2d6 + 3) bludgeoning damage.

REACTIONS

Engine of Pain. Immediately after a creature within 5 feet of the hammerer hits it with an attack roll, the hammerer makes a Hammer attack against that creature.

DUERGAR SCREAMER
Medium Construct (Dwarf), Any Alignment

Armor Class 15 (natural armor)
Hit Points 38 (7d8 + 7)
Speed 20 ft.

STR	DEX	CON	INT	WIS	CHA
18 (+4)	7 (−2)	12 (+1)	5 (−3)	5 (−3)	5 (−3)

Damage Immunities poison
Condition Immunities charmed, exhaustion, frightened, paralyzed, petrified, poisoned
Senses darkvision 60 ft., passive Perception 7
Languages understands Dwarvish but can't speak
Challenge 3 (700 XP)   **Proficiency Bonus** +2

ACTIONS

Multiattack. The screamer makes one Drill attack, and it uses Sonic Scream.

Drill. *Melee Weapon Attack:* +6 to hit, reach 5 ft., one target. *Hit:* 10 (1d12 + 4) piercing damage.

Sonic Scream. The screamer emits destructive energy in a 15-foot cube. Each creature in that area must succeed on a DC 11 Strength saving throw or take 7 (2d6) thunder damage and be knocked prone.

REACTIONS

Engine of Pain. Immediately after a creature within 5 feet of the screamer hits it with an attack roll, the screamer makes a Drill attack against that creature.

DYBBUK

Dybbuks are demons that terrorize mortals on the Material Plane by possessing corpses and giving them a semblance of life, after which the demons use them to engage in a range of sordid activities.

In their natural form, dybbuks appear as translucent flying jellyfish, trailing long tentacles as they move through the air. They rarely travel in this fashion, however. Instead, a dybbuk possesses a suitable corpse as a vehicle, rousing the body from death. Dybbuks delight in terrorizing other creatures by making their host bodies behave in horrifying ways—throwing up gouts of blood, excreting piles of squirming maggots, and contorting their limbs in impossible ways as they scuttle across the ground.

DYBBUK
Medium Fiend (Demon), Typically Chaotic Evil

Armor Class 14
Hit Points 37 (5d8 + 15)
Speed 0 ft., fly 40 ft. (hover)

STR	DEX	CON	INT	WIS	CHA
6 (−2)	19 (+4)	16 (+3)	16 (+3)	15 (+2)	14 (+2)

Skills Deception +6, Intimidation +4, Perception +4
Damage Resistances acid, cold, fire, lightning, thunder; bludgeoning, piercing, and slashing from nonmagical attacks
Damage Immunities poison
Condition Immunities charmed, exhaustion, frightened, grappled, paralyzed, petrified, poisoned, prone, restrained
Senses darkvision 120 ft., passive Perception 14
Languages Abyssal, Common, telepathy 120 ft.
Challenge 4 (1,100 XP)   **Proficiency Bonus** +2

Incorporeal Movement. The dybbuk can move through other creatures and objects as if they were difficult terrain. It takes 5 (1d10) force damage if it ends its turn inside an object.

Magic Resistance. The dybbuk has advantage on saving throws against spells and other magical effects.

ACTION

Tentacle. *Melee Weapon Attack:* +6 to hit, reach 5 ft., one target. *Hit:* 13 (2d8 + 4) necrotic damage. If the target is a creature, its hit point maximum is also reduced by 3 (1d6). This reduction lasts until the target finishes a short or long rest. The target dies if its hit point maximum is reduced to 0.

Possess Corpse (Recharge 6). The dybbuk disappears into an intact corpse within 5 feet of it that belonged to a Large or smaller Beast or Humanoid. The dybbuk gains 20 temporary hit points. While possessing the corpse, the dybbuk adopts the corpse's size and can't use Incorporeal Movement. Its game statistics otherwise remain the same.

The possession lasts until the temporary hit points are lost or the dybbuk ends it as a bonus action. When the possession ends, the dybbuk appears in an unoccupied space within 5 feet of the corpse.

Spellcasting. The dybbuk casts one of the following spells, requiring no material components and using Charisma as the spellcasting ability (spell save DC 12):

At will: *dimension door*
3/day: *phantasmal force*

BONUS ACTIONS

Control Corpse. While Possess Corpse is active, the dybbuk makes the corpse do something unnatural, such as vomit blood, twist its head all the way around, or cause a quadruped to move as a biped. Any Beast or Humanoid that sees this behavior must succeed on a DC 12 Wisdom saving throw or become frightened of the dybbuk for 1 minute. The frightened creature can repeat the saving throw at the end of each of its turns, ending the effect on itself on a success. A creature that succeeds on a saving throw against this ability is immune to Control Corpse for 24 hours.

AARON MILLER

Eidolon

To protect sites they deem holy, gods often rely on eidolons, ghostly spirits bound to safeguard a sacred place. Forged from the souls of those with unwavering devotion, eidolons stalk temples and vaults to ensure that no enemy defiles, damages, or plunders these sites. If an enemy sets foot inside a warded location, the eidolon plunges into a statue specially prepared to house its soul; it then animates this effigy and uses the statue to drive out the intruders.

Eidolon

Medium Undead, Any Alignment

Armor Class 9
Hit Points 63 (18d8 – 18)
Speed 0 ft., fly 40 ft. (hover)

STR	DEX	CON	INT	WIS	CHA
7 (−2)	8 (−1)	9 (−1)	14 (+2)	19 (+4)	16 (+3)

Saving Throws Wis +8
Skills Perception +8
Damage Resistances acid, fire, lightning, thunder; bludgeoning, piercing, and slashing from nonmagical attacks
Damage Immunities cold, necrotic, poison
Condition Immunities charmed, exhaustion, frightened, grappled, paralyzed, petrified, poisoned, prone, restrained
Senses darkvision 60 ft., passive Perception 18
Languages the languages it knew in life
Challenge 12 (8,400 XP)   **Proficiency Bonus** +4

Incorporeal Movement. The eidolon can move through other creatures and objects as if they were difficult terrain. It takes 5 (1d10) force damage if it ends its turn inside an object other than a sacred statue.

Sacred Animation (Recharge 5–6). When the eidolon moves into a space occupied by a sacred statue, the eidolon can disappear, causing the statue to become a creature under the eidolon's control. The eidolon uses the sacred statue's stat block in place of its own.

Turn Resistance. The eidolon has advantage on saving throws against any effect that turns Undead.

Unusual Nature. The eidolon doesn't require air, food, drink, or sleep.

Actions

Divine Dread. Each creature within 60 feet of the eidolon that can see it must succeed on a DC 15 Wisdom saving throw or be frightened of it for 1 minute. While frightened in this way, the creature must take the Dash action and move away from the eidolon by the safest available route at the start of each of its turns, unless there is nowhere for it to move, in which case the creature also becomes stunned until it can move again. A frightened target can repeat the saving throw at the end of each of its turns, ending the effect on itself on a success. If a target's saving throw is successful or the effect ends for it, the target is immune to any eidolon's Divine Dread for the next 24 hours.

Sacred Statue

Large Construct, As the Eidolon's Alignment

Armor Class 19 (natural armor)
Hit Points 95 (10d10 + 40)
Speed 25 ft.

STR	DEX	CON	INT	WIS	CHA
19 (+4)	8 (−1)	19 (+4)	14 (+2)	19 (+4)	16 (+3)

Saving Throws Wis +8
Damage Resistances acid, fire, lightning; bludgeoning, piercing, and slashing from nonmagical attacks
Damage Immunities cold, necrotic, poison
Condition Immunities charmed, exhaustion, frightened, paralyzed, petrified, poisoned
Senses darkvision 60 ft., passive Perception 14
Languages the languages the eidolon knew in life

False Appearance. If the statue is motionless at the start of combat, it has advantage on its initiative roll. Moreover, if a creature hasn't observed the statue move or act, that creature must succeed on a DC 18 Intelligence (Investigation) check to discern that the statue isn't an object.

Ghostly Inhabitant. The eidolon that enters the statue remains inside it until the statue drops to 0 hit points, the eidolon uses a bonus action to move out of the statue, or the eidolon is turned or forced out by an effect such as the *dispel evil and good* spell. When the eidolon leaves the statue, it appears in an unoccupied space within 5 feet of the statue.

Inert. Without an eidolon inside, the statue is an object.

Unusual Nature. The statue doesn't require air, food, drink, or sleep.

Actions

Multiattack. The statue makes two Slam or Rock attacks.

Slam. *Melee Weapon Attack:* +8 to hit, reach 10 ft., one target. *Hit:* 43 (6d12 + 4) bludgeoning damage.

Rock. *Ranged Weapon Attack:* +8 to hit, range 60 ft./240 ft., one target. *Hit:* 37 (6d10 + 4) bludgeoning damage.

ELADRIN

Eladrin dwell in the verdant splendor of the Feywild. They are related to the elves found on the Material Plane. But while other elves can temper their wild impulses, eladrin are ruled by emotion—and due to their magical nature, they undergo physical changes to match their changes in temperament.

Eladrin have spent centuries in the Feywild, and most of them have become Fey creatures as a result—those presented here are of the Fey variety. Some are still Humanoid, however, similar in that respect to their other elven kin.

The magic flowing through eladrin responds to their emotional state by transforming them into different seasonal aspects, with behaviors and abilities that change with their forms. Some eladrin might remain in a particular aspect for years, while others run through the emotional spectrum each week.

CHANGEABLE NATURES

Whenever one of the eladrin presented here finishes a long rest, they can associate themself with a different season, provided they aren't incapacitated. When the eladrin makes this change, they use the stat block of the new season rather than their old stat block. Any damage the eladrin sustained in their previous form applies to the new form, as do any conditions or other ongoing effects affecting them.

AUTUMN ELADRIN

Eladrin often enter the autumn season when they are overcome by feelings of goodwill. In this aspect, they defuse conflicts and alleviate suffering by using their magic to relieve any ailments that afflict the people who come to them for aid. They tolerate no violence in their presence and move quickly to settle disputes, to ensure that peace continues to reign.

AUTUMN ELADRIN
Medium Fey (Elf), Typically Chaotic Neutral

Armor Class 19 (natural armor)
Hit Points 165 (22d8 + 66)
Speed 30 ft.

STR	DEX	CON	INT	WIS	CHA
12 (+1)	16 (+3)	16 (+3)	14 (+2)	17 (+3)	18 (+4)

Skills Insight +7, Medicine +7
Damage Resistances psychic
Senses darkvision 60 ft., passive Perception 13
Languages Common, Elvish, Sylvan
Challenge 10 (5,900 XP)   **Proficiency Bonus** +4

Enchanting Presence. Any non-eladrin creature that starts its turn within 60 feet of the eladrin must make a DC 16 Wisdom saving throw. On a failed save, the creature becomes charmed by the eladrin for 1 minute. On a successful save, the creature becomes immune to any eladrin's Enchanting Presence for 24 hours.

Whenever the eladrin deals damage to the charmed creature, the charmed creature can repeat the saving throw, ending the effect on itself on a success.

Magic Resistance. The eladrin has advantage on saving throws against spells and other magical effects.

ACTIONS

Multiattack. The eladrin makes two Longsword or Longbow attacks. It can replace one attack with a use of Spellcasting.

Longsword. *Melee Weapon Attack:* +5 to hit, reach 5 ft., one target. *Hit:* 5 (1d8 + 1) slashing damage, or 6 (1d10 + 1) slashing damage if used with two hands, plus 22 (5d8) psychic damage.

Longbow. *Ranged Weapon Attack:* +7 to hit, range 150/600 ft., one target. *Hit:* 7 (1d8 + 3) piercing damage plus 22 (5d8) psychic damage.

Spellcasting. The eladrin casts one of the following spells, requiring no material components and using Charisma as the spellcasting ability (spell save DC 16):

At will: *hold person*
2/day each: *cure wounds* (as a 5th-level spell), *lesser restoration*
1/day each: *greater restoration*, *revivify*

BONUS ACTIONS

Fey Step (Recharge 4–6). The eladrin teleports, along with any equipment it is wearing or carrying, up to 30 feet to an unoccupied space it can see.

REACTIONS

Foster Peace. If a creature charmed by the eladrin hits with an attack roll while within 60 feet of the eladrin, the eladrin magically causes the attack to miss, provided the eladrin can see the attacker.

Spring Eladrin

Their hearts filled with joy, spring eladrin cavort through their sylvan realms, their songs and laughter filling the air. These playful eladrin beguile other creatures to fill them with the joy of spring. Their antics can lead other creatures into danger and make mischief for them.

Spring Eladrin
Medium Fey (Elf), Typically Chaotic Neutral

Armor Class 19 (natural armor)
Hit Points 165 (22d8 + 66)
Speed 30 ft.

STR	DEX	CON	INT	WIS	CHA
14 (+2)	16 (+3)	16 (+3)	18 (+4)	11 (+0)	18 (+4)

Skills Deception +8, Persuasion +8
Damage Resistances psychic
Senses darkvision 60 ft., passive Perception 10
Languages Common, Elvish, Sylvan
Challenge 10 (5,900 XP)   **Proficiency Bonus** +4

Joyful Presence. Any non-eladrin creature that starts its turn within 60 feet of the eladrin must make a DC 16 Wisdom saving throw. On a failed save, the creature becomes charmed by the eladrin for 1 minute. On a successful save, the creature becomes immune to any eladrin's Joyful Presence for 24 hours.

Whenever the eladrin deals damage to the charmed creature, the charmed creature can repeat the saving throw, ending the effect on itself on a success.

Magic Resistance. The eladrin has advantage on saving throws against spells and other magical effects.

Actions

Multiattack. The eladrin makes two Longsword or Longbow attacks. It can replace one attack with a use of Spellcasting.

Longsword. Melee Weapon Attack: +6 to hit, reach 5 ft., one target. Hit: 6 (1d8 + 2) slashing damage, or 7 (1d10 + 2) slashing damage if used with two hands, plus 22 (5d8) psychic damage.

Longbow. Ranged Weapon Attack: +7 to hit, range 150/600 ft., one target. Hit: 7 (1d8 + 3) piercing damage plus 22 (5d8) psychic damage.

Spellcasting. The eladrin casts one of the following spells, requiring no material components and using Charisma as the spellcasting ability (spell save DC 16):

At will: *Tasha's hideous laughter*
1/day each: *major image, suggestion*

Bonus Actions

Fey Step (Recharge 4–6). The eladrin teleports, along with any equipment it is wearing or carrying, up to 30 feet to an unoccupied space it can see.

Summer Eladrin

When angered, eladrin enter the season of summer, a burning, tempestuous state that transforms them into aggressive warriors eager to vent their wrath. Their magic responds to their fury and amplifies their fighting ability, helping them move with astonishing quickness and strike with terrible force.

Summer Eladrin
Medium Fey (Elf), Typically Chaotic Neutral

Armor Class 19 (natural armor)
Hit Points 165 (22d8 + 66)
Speed 50 ft.

STR	DEX	CON	INT	WIS	CHA
19 (+4)	21 (+5)	16 (+3)	14 (+2)	12 (+1)	18 (+4)

Skills Athletics +8, Intimidation +8
Damage Resistances fire
Senses darkvision 60 ft., passive Perception 9
Languages Common, Elvish, Sylvan
Challenge 10 (5,900 XP)   **Proficiency Bonus** +4

Fearsome Presence. Any non-eladrin creature that starts its turn within 60 feet of the eladrin must make a DC 16 Wisdom saving throw. On a failed save, the creature becomes frightened of the eladrin for 1 minute. A creature can repeat the saving throw at the end of each of its turns, ending the effect on itself on a success. If a creature's saving throw is successful or the effect ends for it, the creature is immune to any eladrin's Fearsome Presence for the next 24 hours.

Magic Resistance. The eladrin has advantage on saving throws against spells and other magical effects.

Actions

Multiattack. The eladrin makes two Longsword or Longbow attacks.

Longsword. Melee Weapon Attack: +8 to hit, reach 5 ft., one target. Hit: 13 (2d8 + 4) slashing damage, or 15 (2d10 + 4) slashing damage if used with two hands, plus 9 (2d8) fire damage.

Longbow. Ranged Weapon Attack: +9 to hit, range 150/600 ft., one target. Hit: 14 (2d8 + 5) piercing damage plus 9 (2d8) fire damage.

Bonus Actions

Fey Step (Recharge 4–6). The eladrin teleports, along with any equipment it is wearing or carrying, up to 30 feet to an unoccupied space it can see.

Reactions

Parry. The eladrin adds 3 to its AC against one melee attack that would hit it. To do so, the eladrin must see the attacker and be wielding a melee weapon.

Winter Eladrin

When sorrow distresses eladrin, they enter the winter season, becoming figures of melancholy. Frozen tears drop from their cheeks, and their palpable sadness emanates from them as icy cold.

Winter Eladrin

Medium Fey (Elf), Typically Chaotic Neutral

Armor Class 19 (natural armor)
Hit Points 165 (22d8 + 66)
Speed 30 ft.

STR	DEX	CON	INT	WIS	CHA
11 (+0)	16 (+3)	16 (+3)	18 (+4)	17 (+3)	13 (+1)

Damage Resistances cold
Senses darkvision 60 ft., passive Perception 13
Languages Common, Elvish, Sylvan
Challenge 10 (5,900 XP)   **Proficiency Bonus** +4

Magic Resistance. The eladrin has advantage on saving throws against spells and other magical effects.

Sorrowful Presence. Any non-eladrin creature that starts its turn within 60 feet of the eladrin must make a DC 13 Wisdom saving throw. On a failed save, the creature becomes charmed by the eladrin for 1 minute. While charmed in this way, the creature has disadvantage on ability checks and saving throws. The charmed creature can repeat the saving throw at the end of each of its turns, ending the effect on itself on a success. If a creature's saving throw is successful or the effect ends for it, the creature is immune to any eladrin's Sorrowful Presence for the next 24 hours.

Whenever the eladrin deals damage to the charmed creature, the charmed creature can repeat the saving throw, ending the effect on itself on a success.

Actions

Multiattack. The eladrin makes two Longsword or Longbow attacks. It can replace one attack with a use of Spellcasting.

Longsword. *Melee Weapon Attack:* +4 to hit, reach 5 ft., one target. *Hit:* 4 (1d8) slashing damage, or 5 (1d10) slashing damage if used with two hands, plus 13 (3d8) cold damage.

Longbow. *Ranged Weapon Attack:* +7 to hit, range 150/600 ft., one target. *Hit:* 7 (1d8 + 3) piercing damage plus 13 (3d8) cold damage.

Spellcasting. The eladrin casts one of the following spells, requiring no material components and using Intelligence as the spellcasting ability (spell save DC 16):

At will: *fog cloud, gust of wind, sleet storm*

Bonus Actions

Fey Step (Recharge 4–6). The eladrin teleports, along with any equipment it is wearing or carrying, up to 30 feet to an unoccupied space it can see.

Reactions

Frigid Rebuke. When the eladrin takes damage from a creature the eladrin can see within 60 feet of it, the eladrin can force that creature to make a DC 16 Constitution saving throw. On a failed save, the creature takes 11 (2d10) cold damage.

SPRING ELADRIN

SUMMER ELADRIN

WINTER ELADRIN

ERIC BELISLE

ELDER BRAIN

The ultimate expression of mind flayer domination, an elder brain sprawls within a vat of viscous brine, cared for by mind flayer minions as it touches the thoughts of creatures near and far. It scrawls upon the canvas of the creatures' minds, rewriting their thoughts and authoring their dreams.

An elder brain sustains itself by consuming the brains of other creatures. If its mind flayer servants don't bring meals directly to it, the elder brain reaches out with tendrils of thought, compelling creatures to come to it so that it can feed on them.

When a mind flayer perishes, the elder brain's servants feed its brain to their master, which then absorbs the knowledge and experience contained therein. Mind flayers conceive of this oneness with the elder brain as a sacred state akin to an afterlife.

HIVE MIND

Elder brains are so-called among non-illithids because they act as the central communication hub for an entire mind flayer colony, just as a brain does for a living body. Linked to the elder brain, the colony acts like a single organism, acting in concert as if each illithid were the digit of a hand.

An elder brain considers itself and its desires the most important things in the multiverse, and the mind flayers in its colony nothing more than extensions of its will. Each presides over its colony according to its own unique personality and storehouse of collected knowledge and experience. Some elder brains reign as tyrants, while others serve as sages, counselors, and repositories of information and lore for the mind flayers that protect and nourish them.

AN ELDER BRAIN'S LAIR

The lair of an elder brain lies deep in the heart of a mind flayer colony. The brain dwells in a dimly glowing brine pool filled with brackish water infused with its vital fluids and psionic energy.

An elder brain's ambitions are always tempered by its relative immobility. Although its telepathic senses can reach for miles, moving anywhere is always a dangerous proposition. If forced outside its brine pool, an elder brain swiftly expires, and transporting an elder brain in its pool through confining and tortuous subterranean tunnels frequently proves difficult or impossible.

LAIR ACTIONS

On initiative count 20 (losing initiative ties), an elder brain can take one of the following lair actions; the elder brain can't take the same lair action two rounds in a row:

Force Wall. The elder brain casts *wall of force*.

Psionic Anchor. The elder brain targets one creature it can sense within 120 feet of it and anchors it by sheer force of will. The target must make a DC 18 Charisma saving throw. On a failed save, its speed is reduced to 0, and it can't teleport. It can repeat the saving throw at the end of each of its turns, ending the effect on itself on a success.

Psychic Inspiration. The elder brain targets one friendly creature it can sense within 120 feet of it. The target has a flash of inspiration and gains advantage on one attack roll, ability check, or saving throw it makes before the end of its next turn.

GUARDROOM

ILLITHID QUARTERS

COMMON ROOM

CLEANSING CHAMBERS

ELDER BRAIN CHAMBER

BRAIN LIBRARY

RESTING POOL

TRANSFORMATION CHAMBER

PRISON

TADPOLE CHAMBERS

LIBRARY/DISSECTION CHAMBER

ESCAPE SHAFT

GUARDROOM

UNDERCAVERN

MIND FLAYER COLONY

50 FEET

BLANDO

REGIONAL EFFECTS

The territory within 5 miles of an elder brain is altered by the creature's psionic presence, which creates one or more of the following effects:

Paranoia. Creatures within 5 miles of an elder brain feel as if they are being followed, even when they're not.

Psychic Whispers. Any creature with which the elder brain has formed a psychic link hears faint, incomprehensible whispers in the deepest recesses of its mind. This psychic detritus consists of the elder brain's stray thoughts commingled with those of other creatures to which it is linked.

Telepathic Eavesdropping. The elder brain can overhear any telepathic conversation within 5 miles of it. The creature that initiated the telepathic conversation makes a DC 18 Wisdom saving throw when telepathic contact is first established. If the save is successful, the creature is aware that something is eavesdropping. The nature of the eavesdropper isn't revealed.

If the elder brain dies, these effects immediately end.

ELDER BRAIN

Large Aberration (Mind Flayer), Typically Lawful Evil

Armor Class 10
Hit Points 210 (20d10 + 100)
Speed 5 ft., swim 10 ft.

STR	DEX	CON	INT	WIS	CHA
15 (+2)	10 (+0)	20 (+5)	21 (+5)	19 (+4)	24 (+7)

Saving Throws Int +10, Wis +9, Cha +12
Skills Arcana +10, Deception +12, Insight +14, Intimidation +12, Persuasion +12
Senses blindsight 120 ft., passive Perception 14
Languages understands Common, Deep Speech, and Undercommon but can't speak, telepathy 5 miles
Challenge 14 (11,500 XP)   **Proficiency Bonus** +5

Creature Sense. The elder brain is aware of creatures within 5 miles of it that have an Intelligence score of 4 or higher. It knows the distance and direction to each creature, as well as each one's Intelligence score, but can't sense anything else about it. A creature protected by a *mind blank* spell, a *nondetection* spell, or similar magic can't be perceived in this manner.

Legendary Resistance (3/Day). If the elder brain fails a saving throw, it can choose to succeed instead.

Magic Resistance. The elder brain has advantage on saving throws against spells and other magical effects.

Telepathic Hub. The elder brain can use its telepathy to initiate and maintain telepathic conversations with up to ten creatures at a time. The elder brain can let those creatures telepathically hear each other while connected in this way.

ACTIONS

Tentacle. *Melee Weapon Attack:* +7 to hit, reach 30 ft., one target. *Hit:* 20 (4d8 + 2) bludgeoning damage. If the target is a Huge or smaller creature, it is grappled (escape DC 15) and takes 9 (1d8 + 5) psychic damage at the start of each of its turns until the grapple ends. The elder brain can have up to four targets grappled at a time.

Mind Blast (Recharge 5–6). Creatures of the elder brain's choice within 60 feet of it must succeed on a DC 18 Intelligence saving throw or take 32 (5d10 + 5) psychic damage and be stunned for 1 minute. A target can repeat the saving throw at the end of each of its turns, ending the effect on itself on a success.

Spellcasting (Psionics). The elder brain casts one of the following spells, requiring no spell components and using Intelligence as the spellcasting ability (spell save DC 18):

At will: *detect thoughts, levitate*
3/day: *modify memory*
1/day each: *dominate monster, plane shift* (self only)

BONUS ACTIONS

Psychic Link. The elder brain targets one incapacitated creature it senses with its Creature Sense trait and establishes a psychic link with the target. Until the link ends, the elder brain can perceive everything the target senses. The target becomes aware that something is linked to its mind once it is no longer incapacitated, and the elder brain can terminate the link at any time (no action required). The target can use an action on its turn to attempt to break the link, doing so with a successful DC 18 Charisma saving throw. On a successful save, the target takes 10 (3d6) psychic damage. The link also ends if the target and the elder brain are more than 5 miles apart. The elder brain can form psychic links with up to ten creatures at a time.

Sense Thoughts. The elder brain targets a creature with which it has a psychic link. The elder brain gains insight into the target's emotional state and foremost thoughts (including worries, loves, and hates).

LEGENDARY ACTIONS

The elder brain can take 3 legendary actions, choosing from the options below. It can take only one legendary action at a time and only at the end of another creature's turn. The elder brain regains spent legendary actions at the start of its turn.

Break Concentration. The elder brain targets one creature within 120 feet of it with which it has a psychic link. The elder brain breaks the creature's concentration on a spell it has cast. The creature also takes 2 (1d4) psychic damage per level of the spell.

Psychic Pulse. The elder brain targets one creature within 120 feet of it with which it has a psychic link. The target and enemies of the elder brain within 30 feet of target take 10 (3d6) psychic damage.

Sever Psychic Link. The elder brain targets one creature within 120 feet of it with which it has a psychic link. The elder brain ends the link, causing the creature to have disadvantage on all ability checks, attack rolls, and saving throws until the end of the creature's next turn.

Tentacle (Costs 2 Actions). The elder brain makes one Tentacle attack.

ELDER TEMPEST

Terrifying storms manifest in the bodies of elder tempests. Beings carved from clouds, wind, rain, and lightning, elder tempests assume the shape of serpents that slither through the sky. They drown the land beneath them with rain and stab the earth with lances of lightning. Punishing winds scream around them as they fly, feeding the chaos they create.

ELDER TEMPEST

Gargantuan Elemental, Typically Neutral

Armor Class 19
Hit Points 264 (16d20 + 96)
Speed 0 ft., fly 120 ft. (hover)

STR	DEX	CON	INT	WIS	CHA
23 (+6)	28 (+9)	23 (+6)	2 (−4)	21 (+5)	18 (+4)

Saving Throws Wis +12, Cha +11
Damage Resistances bludgeoning, piercing, and slashing from nonmagical attacks
Damage Immunities lightning, poison, thunder
Condition Immunities exhaustion, grappled, paralyzed, petrified, poisoned, prone, restrained, stunned
Senses darkvision 60 ft., passive Perception 15
Languages —
Challenge 23 (50,000 XP)   **Proficiency Bonus** +7

Air Form. The tempest can enter a hostile creature's space and stop there. It can move through a space as narrow as 1 inch wide without squeezing.

Flyby. The tempest doesn't provoke opportunity attacks when it flies out of an enemy's reach.

Legendary Resistance (3/Day). If the tempest fails a saving throw, it can choose to succeed instead.

Living Storm. The tempest is always at the center of a storm 1d6 + 4 miles in diameter. Heavy precipitation in the form of either rain or snow falls there, causing the area to be lightly obscured. Heavy rain also extinguishes open flames and imposes disadvantage on Wisdom (Perception) checks that rely on hearing. In addition, strong winds swirl in the area covered by the storm. The winds impose disadvantage on ranged attack rolls. They also extinguish open flames and disperse fog.

Siege Monster. The tempest deals double damage to objects and structures.

ACTIONS

Multiattack. The tempest makes two Thunderous Slam attacks.

Thunderous Slam. *Melee Weapon Attack:* +16 to hit, reach 20 ft., one target. *Hit:* 23 (4d6 + 9) thunder damage.

Lightning Storm (Recharge 6). Each creature within 120 feet of the tempest must make a DC 21 Dexterity saving throw, taking 27 (6d8) lightning damage on a failed save, or half as much damage on a successful one. If a target's saving throw fails by 5 or more, the creature is also stunned until the end of its next turn.

LEGENDARY ACTIONS

The tempest can take 3 legendary actions, choosing from the options below. Only one legendary action option can be used at a time and only at the end of another creature's turn. The tempest regains spent legendary actions at the start of its turn.

Move. The tempest moves up to its speed.
Lightning Strike (Costs 2 Actions). The tempest can cause a bolt of lightning to strike a point on the ground anywhere under its storm. Each creature within 5 feet of that point must make a DC 21 Dexterity saving throw, taking 16 (3d10) lightning damage on a failed save, or half as much damage on a successful one.
Screaming Gale (Costs 3 Actions). The tempest releases a blast of thunder and wind in a line that is 300 feet long and 20 feet wide. Objects in that area take 22 (4d10) thunder damage. Each creature there must succeed on a DC 21 Dexterity saving throw or take 22 (4d10) thunder damage and be flung up to 60 feet in a direction away from the line. If a thrown target collides with an immovable object (such as a wall or floor) or another creature, the target takes 3 (1d6) bludgeoning damage for every 10 feet it was thrown before impact. If the target collides with another creature, that other creature must succeed on a DC 19 Dexterity saving throw or take the same impact damage and be knocked prone.

AARON MILLER

ELEMENTAL MYRMIDONS

Elemental myrmidons are Elementals conjured and bound by magic into ritually created suits of plate armor. In this form, they possess no recollection of their former existence as free Elementals. They exist only to follow the commands of their creators.

AIR ELEMENTAL MYRMIDON
Medium Elemental, Typically Neutral

Armor Class 18 (plate)
Hit Points 117 (18d8 + 36)
Speed 30 ft., fly 30 ft. (hover)

STR	DEX	CON	INT	WIS	CHA
18 (+4)	14 (+2)	14 (+2)	9 (−1)	10 (+0)	10 (+0)

Damage Resistances lightning, thunder; bludgeoning, piercing, and slashing from nonmagical attacks
Damage Immunities poison
Condition Immunities paralyzed, petrified, poisoned, prone
Senses darkvision 60 ft., passive Perception 10
Languages Auran, one language of its creator's choice
Challenge 7 (2,900 XP)   **Proficiency Bonus** +3

ACTIONS

Multiattack. The myrmidon makes three Flail attacks.

Flail. *Melee Weapon Attack:* +7 to hit, reach 5 ft., one target. *Hit:* 8 (1d8 + 4) force damage.

Lightning Strike (Recharge 6). The myrmidon makes one Flail attack. On a hit, the target takes an extra 18 (4d8) lightning damage, and the target must succeed on a DC 13 Constitution saving throw or be stunned until the end of the myrmidon's next turn.

EARTH ELEMENTAL MYRMIDON
Medium Elemental, Typically Neutral

Armor Class 18 (plate)
Hit Points 127 (17d8 + 51)
Speed 30 ft.

STR	DEX	CON	INT	WIS	CHA
18 (+4)	10 (+0)	17 (+3)	8 (−1)	10 (+0)	10 (+0)

Damage Resistances bludgeoning, piercing, and slashing from nonmagical attacks
Damage Immunities poison
Condition Immunities paralyzed, petrified, poisoned, prone
Senses darkvision 60 ft., passive Perception 10
Languages Terran, one language of its creator's choice
Challenge 7 (2,900 XP)   **Proficiency Bonus** +3

ACTIONS

Multiattack. The myrmidon makes two Maul attacks.

Maul. *Melee Weapon Attack:* +7 to hit, reach 5 ft., one target. *Hit:* 11 (2d6 + 4) force damage.

Thunderous Strike (Recharge 6). The myrmidon makes one Maul attack. On a hit, the target takes an extra 22 (4d10) thunder damage, and the target must succeed on a DC 14 Strength saving throw or be knocked prone.

FILIP BURBURAN

FIRE ELEMENTAL MYRMIDON
Medium Elemental, Typically Neutral

Armor Class 18 (plate)
Hit Points 123 (19d8 + 38)
Speed 40 ft.

STR	DEX	CON	INT	WIS	CHA
13 (+1)	18 (+4)	15 (+2)	9 (−1)	10 (+0)	10 (+0)

Damage Resistances bludgeoning, piercing, and slashing from nonmagical attacks
Damage Immunities fire, poison
Condition Immunities paralyzed, petrified, poisoned, prone
Senses darkvision 60 ft., passive Perception 10
Languages Ignan, one language of its creator's choice
Challenge 7 (2,900 XP)   **Proficiency Bonus** +3

Illumination. The myrmidon sheds bright light in a 20-foot radius and dim light in a 40-foot radius.

Water Susceptibility. For every 5 feet the myrmidon moves in 1 foot or more of water, it takes 2 (1d4) cold damage.

ACTIONS

Multiattack. The myrmidon makes three Scimitar attacks.

Scimitar. Melee Weapon Attack: +7 to hit, reach 5 ft., one target. *Hit:* 7 (1d6 + 4) force damage.

Fiery Strikes (Recharge 6). The myrmidon uses Multiattack. Each attack that hits deals an extra 7 (2d6) fire damage.

WATER ELEMENTAL MYRMIDON
Medium Elemental, Typically Neutral

Armor Class 18 (plate)
Hit Points 127 (17d8 + 51)
Speed 40 ft., swim 40 ft.

STR	DEX	CON	INT	WIS	CHA
18 (+4)	14 (+2)	15 (+3)	8 (−1)	10 (+0)	10 (+0)

Damage Resistances acid; bludgeoning, piercing, and slashing from nonmagical attacks
Damage Immunities poison
Condition Immunities paralyzed, petrified, poisoned, prone
Senses darkvision 60 ft., passive Perception 10
Languages Aquan, one language of its creator's choice
Challenge 7 (2,900 XP)   **Proficiency Bonus** +3

ACTIONS

Multiattack. The myrmidon makes three Trident attacks.

Trident. Melee or Ranged Weapon Attack: +7 to hit, reach 5 ft. or range 20/60 ft., one target. *Hit:* 7 (1d6 + 4) force damage, or 8 (1d8 + 4) force damage if used with two hands to make a melee attack.

Freezing Strikes (Recharge 6). The myrmidon uses Multiattack. Each attack that hits deals an extra 5 (1d10) cold damage. A target that is hit by one or more of these attacks has its speed reduced by 10 feet until the end of the myrmidon's next turn.

> When I first saw a fire giant dreadnought, I doubted the giant could even move. I quickly learned my error.
>
> —Mordenkainen

FIRE GIANT DREADNOUGHT
Huge Giant, Typically Lawful Evil

Armor Class 21 (plate, Dual Shields)
Hit Points 187 (15d12 + 90)
Speed 30 ft.

STR	DEX	CON	INT	WIS	CHA
27 (+8)	9 (−1)	23 (+6)	8 (−1)	10 (+0)	11 (+0)

Saving Throws Dex +4, Con +11, Cha +5
Skills Athletics +13, Perception +5
Damage Immunities fire
Senses passive Perception 15
Languages Giant
Challenge 14 (11,500 XP)   **Proficiency Bonus** +5

Dual Shields. The giant carries two shields, which together give the giant +3 to its AC (accounted for above).

ACTIONS

Multiattack. The giant makes two Fireshield or Rock attacks.

Fireshield. *Melee Weapon Attack:* +13 to hit, reach 5 ft., one target. *Hit:* 22 (4d6 + 8) bludgeoning damage plus 7 (2d6) fire damage plus 7 (2d6) piercing damage.

Rock. *Ranged Weapon Attack:* +13 to hit, range 60/240 ft., one target. *Hit:* 30 (4d10 + 8) bludgeoning damage.

Shield Charge (Recharge 5–6). The giant moves up to 30 feet in a straight line and can move through the space of any creature smaller than Huge. The first time it enters a creature's space during this move, that creature must succeed on a DC 21 Strength saving throw or take 36 (8d6 + 8) bludgeoning damage plus 14 (4d6) fire damage and be pushed up to 30 feet and knocked prone.

FIRE GIANT DREADNOUGHT

Most fire giants value not just strength but also skill at forgecraft. The foundry is the heart of any fire giant community. It is a temple, school, proving ground, and political hub rolled into one.

Those whose primary virtue is brawn are usually consigned to the lowliest of tasks, such as working forge bellows or moving coal. However, the strongest among these can excel at and gain rank through a specialized role: the dreadnought.

Dreadnoughts are massively powerful fire giants who wield two huge shields like plow blades. These shields bear spikes on their exterior and have hollow interiors into which the dreadnought pours hot coals at the first sign of danger. Armed with these two shields, the dreadnought can present a fiery wall to any attacker. When the dreadnought has finished, often all that is left of a foe is a smoking smear on the floor.

When not called on to fight, dreadnoughts maintain their strength by using their shields to shove huge quantities of coal, stone, or ore about the foundry. Occasionally, dreadnoughts are called on by their superiors to accompany a war or diplomatic delegation and use their fierce and intimidating demeanor to strengthen the delegation's position.

FIRENEWTS

Originally from the Elemental Plane of Fire, fire-newts can be found on the Material Plane near hot springs and volcanoes. These amphibians need hot water to live, becoming sluggish after spending a week away from a source of moist heat. Firenewts therefore delve for sources of heat in the earth, and a firenewt lair features a network of channels and sluices to circulate hot liquid through the area.

FIRENEWT WARLOCK OF IMIX

Firenewts who serve Imix, Prince of Evil Fire, live in militaristic theocracies that revere elemental fire in its most destructive incarnation and promote aggression and cruelty. Firenewt warlocks of Imix lead these theocracies or serve as advisors to a high priest.

FIRENEWT WARRIOR

A firenewt warrior can spew fire. Many of these warriors have a close relationship with giant striders (in this book). They provide shelter, food, and breeding grounds in their lairs for giant striders, which then voluntarily serve them as mounts.

FIRENEWT WARLOCK OF IMIX
Medium Elemental, Typically Neutral Evil

Armor Class 10 (13 with mage armor)
Hit Points 33 (6d8 + 6)
Speed 30 ft.

STR	DEX	CON	INT	WIS	CHA
13 (+1)	11 (+0)	12 (+1)	9 (−1)	11 (+0)	14 (+2)

Damage Immunities fire
Senses darkvision 120 ft., passive Perception 10
Languages Draconic, Ignan
Challenge 1 (200 XP)   **Proficiency Bonus** +2

Amphibious. The firenewt can breathe air and water.

Devil's Sight. Magical darkness doesn't impede the firenewt's darkvision.

Imix's Blessing. When the firenewt reduces an enemy to 0 hit points, the firenewt gains 5 temporary hit points.

ACTIONS

Multiattack. The firenewt makes three Morningstar or Fire Ray attacks.

Morningstar. *Melee Weapon Attack:* +3 to hit, reach 5 ft., one target. *Hit:* 5 (1d8 + 1) piercing damage.

Fire Ray. *Ranged Spell Attack:* +4 to hit, range 120 ft., one target. *Hit:* 5 (1d6 + 2) fire damage.

Spellcasting. The firenewt casts one of the following spells, using Charisma as the spellcasting ability (spell save DC 12):

At will: *guidance, light, mage armor, mage hand, prestidigitation*

FIRENEWT WARRIOR
Medium Elemental, Typically Neutral

Armor Class 13 (shield)
Hit Points 27 (5d8 + 5)
Speed 30 ft.

STR	DEX	CON	INT	WIS	CHA
10 (+0)	13 (+1)	12 (+1)	7 (−2)	11 (+0)	8 (−1)

Damage Immunities fire
Senses passive Perception 10
Languages Draconic, Ignan
Challenge 1/2 (100 XP)   **Proficiency Bonus** +2

Amphibious. The firenewt can breathe air and water.

ACTIONS

Multiattack. The firenewt makes two Scimitar attacks.

Scimitar. *Melee Weapon Attack:* +3 to hit, reach 5 ft., one target. *Hit:* 4 (1d6 + 1) slashing damage.

Spit Fire (Recharges after a Short or Long Rest). The firenewt spits fire at a creature within 10 feet of it. The creature must make a DC 11 Dexterity saving throw, taking 9 (2d8) fire damage on a failed save, or half as much damage on a successful one.

FLAIL SNAIL

A flail snail is a creature of elemental earth that is prized for its multihued shell. It may seem harmless, but if a creature big enough to be a threat approaches too close, the snail flashes a scintillating light and attacks with its mace-like tentacles.

Left undisturbed, a flail snail moves slowly along the ground. It consumes everything on the surface, including rocks, sand, and soil, and it stops periodically to relish crystal growths and other large mineral deposits. It leaves behind a shimmering trail that quickly solidifies into a thin and nearly transparent layer. This glassy residue can be harvested and cut to form window panes. It can also be heated and spun into other glass objects. Some folk make a living from trailing flail snails to collect this glass.

USING THE SHELL OF A FLAIL SNAIL

A flail snail shell weighs about 250 pounds and has numerous uses. An intact shell can sell for 5,000 gp.

Many hunters seek the shell for its antimagic properties. A skilled armorer can make three shields from one shell. For 1 month, each shield gives its wielder the snail's Antimagic Shell trait. When the shield's magic fades, it becomes an exotic shield that is the perfect item from which to make a *spellguard shield*.

A flail snail shell can also be used to make a *robe of scintillating colors*. The shell is ground and added to the dye applied to the fabric. The powder is also a material component of the ritual that enchants the robe.

FLAIL SNAIL
Large Elemental, Unaligned

Armor Class 16 (natural armor)
Hit Points 52 (5d10 + 25)
Speed 10 ft.

STR	DEX	CON	INT	WIS	CHA
17 (+3)	5 (−3)	20 (+5)	3 (−4)	10 (+0)	5 (−3)

Damage Immunities fire, poison
Condition Immunities poisoned
Senses darkvision 60 ft., tremorsense 60 ft., passive Perception 10
Languages —
Challenge 3 (700 XP)   **Proficiency Bonus** +2

Antimagic Shell. The snail has advantage on saving throws against spells, and any creature making a spell attack against the snail has disadvantage on the attack roll.

If the snail succeeds on its saving throw against a spell or a spell's attack roll misses it, the snail's shell converts some of the spell's energy into a burst of destructive force if the spell is of 1st level or higher; each creature within 30 feet of the snail must make a DC 15 Constitution saving throw, taking 3 (1d6) force damage per level of the spell on a failed save, or half as much damage on a successful one.

ACTIONS

Multiattack. The snail makes five Flail Tentacle attacks.

Flail Tentacle. *Melee Weapon Attack:* +5 to hit, reach 10 ft., one target. *Hit:* 5 (1d4 + 3) bludgeoning damage.

Scintillating Shell (Recharges after a Short or Long Rest). The snail's shell emits dazzling, colored light until the end of the snail's next turn. During this time, the shell sheds bright light in a 30-foot radius and dim light for an additional 30 feet, and creatures that can see the snail have disadvantage on attack rolls against it. In addition, any creature within the bright light and able to see the snail when this power is activated must succeed on a DC 15 Wisdom saving throw or be stunned until the light ends.

Shell Defense. The flail snail withdraws into its shell. Until it emerges, it gains a +4 bonus to its AC and is restrained. It can emerge from its shell as a bonus action on its turn.

CORY TREGO-ERDNER

FLIND

When the demon lord Yeenoghu (appears in this book) wants to create a particularly fearsome war band leader, he transforms an exceptionally strong and vicious gnoll into a demonic warrior known as a flind.

A war band of demon-worshiping gnolls typically contains only one flind, and that creature sets the war band's path. Because of its special connection to Yeenoghu, a flind uses demonic insight to guide the gnolls toward weak prey ripe for slaughter.

Unlike other leaders who might skulk behind their minions, a flind leads the charge in battle. Its flail causes wracking pain, paralysis, and disorientation in those it strikes.

FLIND

Medium Fiend (Gnoll), Typically Chaotic Evil

Armor Class 16 (breastplate)
Hit Points 127 (15d8 + 60)
Speed 30 ft.

STR	DEX	CON	INT	WIS	CHA
20 (+5)	14 (+2)	19 (+4)	11 (+0)	13 (+1)	12 (+1)

Saving Throws Con +8, Wis +5
Skills Intimidate +5, Perception +5
Senses darkvision 60 ft., passive Perception 15
Languages Gnoll, Abyssal
Challenge 9 (5,000 XP)   **Proficiency Bonus** +4

Aura of Bloodthirst. If the flind isn't incapacitated, any creature that has Rampage can make a Bite attack as a bonus action while within 10 feet of the flind.

ACTIONS

Multiattack. The flind makes one Flail of Chaos attack, one Flail of Pain attack, and one Flail of Paralysis attack, or it makes three Longbow attacks.

Flail of Chaos. *Melee Weapon Attack:* +9 to hit, reach 10 ft., one target. *Hit:* 10 (1d10 + 5) bludgeoning damage, and the target must make a DC 16 Wisdom saving throw. On a failed save, the target must use its reaction, if available, to make one melee attack against a random creature, other than the flind, within its reach. If there's no creature within reach, the target instead moves half its speed in a random direction.

Flail of Pain. *Melee Weapon Attack:* +9 to hit, reach 10 ft., one target. *Hit:* 10 (1d10 + 5) bludgeoning damage plus 16 (3d10) psychic damage.

Flail of Paralysis. *Melee Weapon Attack:* +9 to hit, reach 10 ft., one target. *Hit:* 10 (1d10 + 5) bludgeoning damage, and the target must succeed on a DC 16 Constitution saving throw or be paralyzed until the end of its next turn.

Longbow. *Ranged Weapon Attack:* +6 to hit, range 150/600 ft., one target. *Hit:* 6 (1d8 + 2) piercing damage.

Fraz-Urb'luu

Fraz-Urb'luu is the Prince of Deception and Demon Lord of Illusions. He uses every trick, every ounce of demonic cunning, to manipulate his enemies—mortal and Fiend alike—to do his will. Fraz-Urb'luu can create dreamlands and mind-bending fantasies able to deceive the most discerning foes.

Once imprisoned for centuries below Castle Greyhawk on the world of Oerth, Fraz-Urb'luu has slowly rebuilt his power in the Abyss. He seeks the pieces of the legendary *staff of power* taken from him by those who imprisoned him and commands his servants to do likewise.

The Prince of Deception's true form is like that of a great gargoyle, some 12 feet tall, with an extended, muscular neck; a smiling face framed by long, pointed ears and lank, dark hair; and bat-like wings are furled against his powerful shoulders. He can assume other forms, however, from the hideous to the beautiful.

Many of the cultists of Fraz-Urb'luu aren't even aware they serve the Prince of Deception, believing their master is a beneficent being and granter of wishes, some lost god or Celestial, or even another Fiend. Fraz-Urb'luu wears all these masks and more. He particularly delights in aiding demon-hunters against his demonic adversaries, driving the hunters to greater and greater atrocities in the name of their cause, only to eventually reveal his true nature and claim their souls as his own.

Fraz-Urb'luu's Lair

Fraz-Urb'luu's lair lies within the abyssal realm of Hollow's Heart, a plain of white dust with few structures on it. The lair itself is the city of Zoragmelok, a circular fortress surrounded by adamantine walls topped with razors and hooks. Corkscrew towers loom above twisted domes and vast amphitheaters, forming a surreal and disorienting cityscape.

The challenge rating of Fraz-Urb'luu is 24 (62,000 XP) when he's encountered in his lair.

Lair Actions

On initiative count 20 (losing initiative ties), Fraz-Urb'luu can take one of the following lair actions when in his lair; he can't take the same lair action two rounds in a row:

Conjure Walls and Doors. Fraz-Urb'luu causes up to five doors within the lair to become walls and an equal number of doors to appear on walls where there previously were none.

Psychic Anguish. Fraz-Urb'luu creates a wave of anguish. Each creature he can see within the lair must succeed on a DC 23 Wisdom saving throw or take 33 (6d10) psychic damage.

Simulacrum. Fraz-Urb'luu chooses one Humanoid within the lair and instantly creates a simulacrum of that creature (as if created with the *simulacrum* spell). This simulacrum obeys Fraz-Urb'luu's commands and is destroyed on the next initiative count 20.

Regional Effects

The region containing Fraz-Urb'luu's lair is warped by his magic, creating one or more of the following effects:

Beguiling Realm. Within 6 miles of the lair, all Charisma (Persuasion) and Wisdom (Insight) checks have disadvantage, and all Charisma (Deception) and Charisma (Performance) checks have advantage.

Nostalgic Pangs. Sapient creatures within 1 mile of the lair frequently see hallucinations of long-dead friends and comrades that vanish after only a brief glimpse.

Twisted Paths. Roads and paths within 6 miles of the lair twist and turn back on themselves, making navigation in the area exceedingly difficult.

If Fraz-Urb'luu dies, these effects fade over the course of 1d10 days.

Cultists of Fraz-Urb'luu

Fraz-Urb'luu grants his cultists the Liar's Eye trait.

Liar's Eye. This creature has advantage on Wisdom (Insight or Perception) checks.

As a bonus action, the creature detects the location of all illusions and hidden creatures within 15 feet of it.

Fraz-Urb'luu

Large Fiend (Demon), Chaotic Evil

Armor Class 18 (natural armor)
Hit Points 337 (27d10 + 189)
Speed 40 ft., fly 40 ft.

STR	DEX	CON	INT	WIS	CHA
29 (+9)	12 (+1)	25 (+7)	26 (+8)	24 (+7)	26 (+8)

Saving Throws Dex +8, Con +14, Int +15, Wis +14
Skills Deception +15, Perception +14, Stealth +8
Damage Resistances cold, fire, lightning
Damage Immunities poison; bludgeoning, piercing, and slashing that is nonmagical
Condition Immunities charmed, exhaustion, frightened, poisoned
Senses truesight 120 ft., passive Perception 24
Languages all, telepathy 120 ft.
Challenge 23 (50,000 XP)   **Proficiency Bonus** +7

Legendary Resistance (3/Day). If Fraz-Urb'luu fails a saving throw, he can choose to succeed instead.

Magic Resistance. Fraz-Urb'luu has advantage on saving throws against spells and other magical effects.

Undetectable. Fraz-Urb'luu can't be targeted by divination magic, perceived through magical scrying sensors, or detected by abilities that sense demons or Fiends.

Actions

Multiattack. Fraz-Urb'luu makes one Bite attack and two Fist attacks, and he uses Phantasmal Terror.

Bite. *Melee Weapon Attack:* +16 to hit, reach 10 ft., one target. *Hit:* 19 (3d6 + 9) force damage.

Fist. *Melee Weapon Attack:* +16 to hit, reach 10 ft., one target. *Hit:* 22 (3d8 + 9) force damage.

Phantasmal Terror. Fraz-Urb'luu targets one creature he can see within 120 feet of him. The target must succeed on a DC 23 Wisdom saving throw, or it takes 16 (3d10) psychic damage and is frightened of Fraz-Urb'luu until the end of its next turn.

Spellcasting. Fraz-Urb'luu casts one of the following spells, requiring no material components and using Charisma as the spellcasting ability (spell save DC 23):

At will: *alter self* (can become Medium when changing his appearance), *detect magic*, *dispel magic*, *phantasmal force*
3/day each: *mislead*, *programmed illusion*, *seeming*
1/day each: *modify memory*, *project image*

Legendary Actions

Fraz-Urb'luu can take 3 legendary actions, choosing from the options below. Only one legendary action option can be used at a time and only at the end of another creature's turn. Fraz-Urb'luu regains spent legendary actions at the start of his turn.

Tail. *Melee Weapon Attack:* +16 to hit, reach 15 ft., one target. *Hit:* 20 (2d10 + 9) force damage. If the target is a Large or smaller creature, it is also grappled (escape DC 24), and it is restrained until the grapple ends. Fraz-Urb'luu can grapple only one creature with his tail at a time.

Terror (Costs 2 Actions). Fraz-Urb'luu uses Phantasmal Terror.

FROGHEMOTH

Huge Monstrosity, Unaligned

Armor Class 14 (natural armor)
Hit Points 161 (14d12 + 70)
Speed 30 ft., swim 30 ft.

STR	DEX	CON	INT	WIS	CHA
23 (+6)	13 (+1)	20 (+5)	2 (−4)	12 (+1)	5 (−3)

Saving Throws Con +9, Wis +5
Skills Perception +9, Stealth +5
Damage Resistances fire, lightning
Senses darkvision 60 ft., passive Perception 19
Languages —
Challenge 10 (5,900 XP)   **Proficiency Bonus** +4

Amphibious. The froghemoth can breathe air and water.

Shock Susceptibility. If the froghemoth takes lightning damage, it suffers two effects until the end of its next turn: its speed is halved, and it has disadvantage on Dexterity saving throws.

ACTIONS

Multiattack. The froghemoth makes one Bite attack and two Tentacle attacks, and it can use Tongue.

Bite. *Melee Weapon Attack:* +10 to hit, reach 5 ft., one target. *Hit:* 22 (3d10 + 6) piercing damage, and the target is swallowed if it is a Medium or smaller creature. A swallowed creature is blinded and restrained, has total cover against attacks and other effects outside the froghemoth, and takes 10 (3d6) acid damage at the start of each of the froghemoth's turns.

The froghemoth's gullet can hold up to two creatures at a time. If the froghemoth takes 20 damage or more on a single turn from a creature inside it, the froghemoth must succeed on a DC 20 Constitution saving throw at the end of that turn or regurgitate all swallowed creatures, each of which falls prone in a space within 10 feet of the froghemoth. If the froghemoth dies, any swallowed creature is no longer restrained by it and can escape from the corpse using 10 feet of movement, exiting prone.

Tentacle. *Melee Weapon Attack:* +10 to hit, reach 20 ft., one target. *Hit:* 19 (3d8 + 6) bludgeoning damage, and the target is grappled (escape DC 16) if it is a Huge or smaller creature. Until the grapple ends, the froghemoth can't use this tentacle on another target. The froghemoth has four tentacles.

Tongue. The froghemoth targets one Medium or smaller creature that it can see within 20 feet of it. The target must make a DC 18 Strength saving throw. On a failed save, the target is pulled into an unoccupied space within 5 feet of the froghemoth.

FROGHEMOTH

A froghemoth is an amphibious predator as big as an elephant. It lairs in swamps and has four tentacles, a thick rubbery hide, a fang-filled maw with a prehensile tongue, and an extendable stalk sporting three bulbous eyes that face in different directions.

Froghemoths are creatures not of this world. A journal purportedly written long ago by the wizard Lum describes strange, cylindrical chambers of metal buried in the ground from which froghemoths emerged, but no reliable reports of the location of such places exist.

Every few years, a froghemoth can lay a fertile egg without mating. The froghemoth cares nothing for its egg and might eat the hatchling. A young froghemoth's survival thus depends on its parent leaving it behind in indifference. A newborn froghemoth grows to full size over a period of months by indiscriminately preying on other creatures in its swampy domain. It learns to hide its enormous body in murky pools, keeping only its eyestalk above water to watch for passing creatures. When food comes within reach, the froghemoth erupts from its pool, tentacles and tongue flailing. It can grab several targets at once; it wraps its tongue around one and pulls it in to be devoured while holding the rest at bay.

If bullywugs (see the *Monster Manual*) come across a froghemoth, the bullywugs may treat the froghemoth as a god and do all they can to coax the monster into their den. A froghemoth can be tamed (after a fashion) by offering it food, and bullywugs can communicate with it on a basic level, so the creature might eat only a few bullywugs before following the rest. The bullywugs gather food as tribute for it, provide it with a comfortable lair, protect it from harm, and try to ensure that any of its offspring reach maturity.

giant doesn't give enough honor to Vaprak or fails to heed Vaprak's visions, injuries the frost giant sustains heal wrong, resulting in discolored skin; warty scars; and vestigial body parts, such as extra digits, limbs, and even heads. The touch of Vaprak can no longer be hidden then, and the everlasting one is either killed or exiled by their clan. Sometimes small communities of everlasting ones gather and even reproduce, passing the "blessing" and worship of Vaprak from one generation to the next.

Frost Giant Everlasting One

To hold its place or rise within the ordning, a frost giant must routinely face mighty foes in single combat. Some seek out magic that will aid them, but enchanted objects can be taken or lost. True greatness relies on personal prowess. Faced with this truth, a frost giant might seek a supernatural gift from Vaprak the Destroyer.

Vaprak is a ferocious god of strength and hunger also worshiped by some ogres and trolls. He likes to tempt frost giants with dreams of glory followed by nightmares of bloody cannibalism. Those who don't shrink from such visions or report them to priests of Thrym receive more of the same. If a frost giant comes to relish these dreams and nightmares, as some do, Vaprak sets a troll upon a sacred quest to find the frost giant and meet the giant in secret. The troll offers up its own body to be devoured in Vaprak's name. Only the boldest and most determined frost giants can finish such a gory feast.

After devouring the troll sent by Vaprak, bones and all, a frost giant becomes an everlasting one, gaining tremendous strength, an ill temper, and a troll's regenerative ability. With these gifts, the frost giant can swiftly claim the title of jarl and easily fend off rivals for decades. However, if the frost

FROST GIANT EVERLASTING ONE
Huge Giant, Typically Chaotic Evil

Armor Class 15 (patchwork armor)
Hit Points 189 (14d12 + 98)
Speed 40 ft.

STR	DEX	CON	INT	WIS	CHA
25 (+7)	9 (−1)	24 (+7)	9 (−1)	10 (+0)	12 (+1)

Saving Throws Str +11, Con +11, Wis +4,
Skills Athletics +11, Perception +4
Damage Immunities cold
Senses darkvision 60 ft., passive Perception 14
Languages Giant
Challenge 12 (8,400 XP)　　　　**Proficiency Bonus** +4

Extra Heads. The giant has a 25 percent chance of having more than one head. If it has more than one, it has advantage on Wisdom (Perception) checks and on saving throws against being blinded, charmed, deafened, frightened, stunned, or knocked unconscious.

Regeneration. The giant regains 10 hit points at the start of its turn. If the giant takes acid or fire damage, this trait doesn't function at the start of its next turn. The giant dies only if it starts its turn with 0 hit points and doesn't regenerate.

ACTIONS

Multiattack. The giant makes two Greataxe or Rock attacks.

Greataxe. *Melee Weapon Attack:* +11 to hit, reach 10 ft., one target. *Hit:* 26 (3d12 + 7) slashing damage, or 30 (3d12 + 11) slashing damage while raging.

Rock. *Ranged Weapon Attack:* +11 to hit, range 60/240 ft., one target. *Hit:* 29 (4d10 + 7) bludgeoning damage.

BONUS ACTION

Vaprak's Rage (Recharges after a Short or Long Rest). The giant enters a rage. The rage lasts for 1 minute or until the giant is incapacitated. While raging, the giant gains the following benefits:

- The giant has advantage on Strength checks and Strength saving throws.
- When it makes a melee weapon attack, the giant gains a +4 bonus to the damage roll.
- The giant has resistance to bludgeoning, piercing, and slashing damage.

Frost Salamander

Frost salamanders are natives of the Plane of Ice, also called the Frostfell, which rests between the Plane of Air and the Plane of Water. Frost salamanders especially like to hunt warm-blooded creatures. They sometimes travel to frigid climes on the Material Plane by wandering through planar gates.

Frost salamanders' aggressive appetite for any heat source leads them to attack expeditions and settlements that other predators would avoid, as they often mistake the fire of a forge or a campfire for a large, tasty meal. Azers (see the *Monster Manual*) use this predilection to hunt frost salamanders. Venturing into the Frostfell, they use large fires to lure these creatures into traps, then kill them and collect their hides and fangs for use in crafting weapons and armor.

Although frost salamanders can burrow their way through loose soil, they prefer to dig into ice. They roll around in piles of broken chunks of ice, allowing it to scratch their backs as they grind it down. This habit leads them to create extensive networks of ice caves, which become ever larger as they claw fresh chunks of ice from the walls of their lairs.

A frost salamander that dwells in a lair for a while carves out enough space to allow a small army to camp within. Inexperienced travelers who come across these caves see them as a welcome shelter, though they are anything but. Frost salamanders greedily devour any prey foolhardy enough to try sleeping in their lairs.

On rare occasions, frost giants (see the *Monster Manual*) capture and tame these creatures, using them to burrow into the ice to help create outposts and fortresses.

FROST SALAMANDER
Huge Elemental, Unaligned

Armor Class 17 (natural armor)
Hit Points 168 (16d12 + 64)
Speed 60 ft., burrow 40 ft., climb 40 ft.

STR	DEX	CON	INT	WIS	CHA
20 (+5)	12 (+1)	18 (+4)	7 (−2)	11 (+0)	7 (−2)

Saving Throws Con +8, Wis +4
Skills Perception +4
Damage Vulnerabilities fire
Damage Immunities cold
Senses darkvision 60 ft., tremorsense 60 ft., passive Perception 14
Languages Primordial
Challenge 9 (5,000 XP)   **Proficiency Bonus** +4

Burning Fury. When the salamander takes fire damage, its Freezing Breath automatically recharges.

ACTIONS

Multiattack. The salamander makes one Bite attack and four Claw attacks.

Bite. *Melee Weapon Attack:* +9 to hit, reach 15 ft., one target. *Hit:* 9 (1d8 + 5) piercing damage plus 5 (1d10) cold damage.

Claw. *Melee Weapon Attack:* +9 to hit, reach 10 ft., one target. *Hit:* 8 (1d6 + 5) piercing damage.

Freezing Breath (Recharge 6). The salamander exhales chill wind in a 60-foot cone. Each creature in that area must make a DC 17 Constitution saving throw, taking 44 (8d10) cold damage on a failed save, or half as much damage on a successful one.

GAUTH

Medium Aberration (Beholder), Typically Lawful Evil

Armor Class 15 (natural armor)
Hit Points 52 (7d8 + 21)
Speed 0 ft., fly 20 ft. (hover)

STR	DEX	CON	INT	WIS	CHA
10 (+0)	14 (+2)	16 (+3)	15 (+2)	15 (+2)	13 (+1)

Saving Throws Int +5, Wis +5, Cha +4
Skills Perception +5
Condition Immunities prone
Senses darkvision 120 ft., passive Perception 15
Languages Deep Speech, Undercommon
Challenge 6 (2,300 XP)   **Proficiency Bonus** +3

Stunning Gaze. When a creature that can see the gauth's central eye starts its turn within 30 feet of the gauth, the gauth can force it to make a DC 14 Wisdom saving throw if the gauth isn't incapacitated and can see the creature. A creature that fails the save is stunned until the start of its next turn.

Unless surprised, a creature can avert its eyes at the start of its turn to avoid the saving throw. If the creature does so, it can't see the gauth until the start of its next turn, when it can avert its eyes again. If the creature looks at the gauth in the meantime, it must immediately make the save.

Death Throes. When the gauth dies, the magical energy within it explodes, and each creature within 10 feet of it must make a DC 14 Dexterity saving throw, taking 13 (3d8) force damage on a failed save, or half as much damage on a successful one.

ACTIONS

Bite. *Melee Weapon Attack:* +3 to hit, reach 5 ft., one target. *Hit:* 9 (2d8) piercing damage.

Eye Rays. The gauth shoots three of the following magical eye rays at random (roll three d6s, and reroll duplicates), targeting one to three creatures it can see within 120 feet of it:

1: Devour Magic Ray. The target must succeed on a DC 14 Dexterity saving throw or have one of its magic items lose all magical properties until the start of the gauth's next turn. If the object is a charged item, it also loses 1d4 charges. Determine the affected item randomly, ignoring single-use items such as potions and scrolls.

2: Enervation Ray. The target must make a DC 14 Constitution saving throw, taking 18 (4d8) necrotic damage on a failed save, or half as much damage on a successful one.

3: Fire Ray. The target must succeed on a DC 14 Dexterity saving throw or take 22 (4d10) fire damage.

4: Paralyzing Ray. The target must succeed on a DC 14 Constitution saving throw or be paralyzed for 1 minute. The target can repeat the saving throw at the end of each of its turns, ending the effect on itself on a success.

5: Pushing Ray. The target must succeed on a DC 14 Strength saving throw or be pushed up to 15 feet away from the gauth and have its speed halved until the start of the gauth's next turn.

6: Sleep Ray. The target must succeed on a DC 14 Wisdom saving throw or fall asleep and remain unconscious for 1 minute. The target awakens if it takes damage or another creature takes an action to wake it. This ray has no effect on Constructs and Undead.

GAUTH

A gauth is a hungry, tyrannical creature similar to a beholder that eats magic and tries to exact tribute from anything weaker than itself. Its body is about 4 feet in diameter, with six eyestalks, a central eye (sometimes surrounded by multiple smaller eyes), and four small grasping tentacles near its mouth. It has color and texture variations similar to a true beholder.

A gauth can survive on meat but prefers to sustain itself with power drained from magic objects. If starved of magic for several weeks, it is forced back to its home plane, so it constantly seeks new items to drain. A gauth might employ creatures to bring it items that can provide it with sustenance.

When the ritual to summon a spectator goes wrong, a gauth might push itself through the flawed connection, arriving immediately or several minutes later. It might present itself as a beholder to ignorant creatures in an attempt to intimidate them, or as a spectator to its summoner in order to drain magic items it is expected to guard.

A beholder (see the *Monster Manual*) usually drives away or kills any gauths that enter its territory, but it might choose to force them to serve it as lieutenants. Gauths are less xenophobic than beholders, so they might form small clusters and work together, though they're just as likely to ignore each other entirely.

SCOTT MURPHY

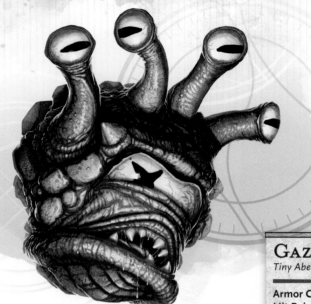

Gazer

A gazer is a tiny manifestation of the dreams of a beholder. It resembles the beholder who dreamed it into existence, but its body is only 8 inches wide and it has only four eyestalks. It follows its creator like a devoted, aggressive puppy, and sometimes small packs of these creatures patrol their master's lair for vermin to kill and lone creatures to harass.

A gazer can't speak any languages but can approximate words and sentences it hears, mimicking them in a high-pitched, mocking manner. Beholders find gazers amusing and tolerate their presence like spoiled pets. Some beholders with wizard minions insist they take a gazer as a familiar because the beholders can see through the eyes of these creatures.

A wild gazer (one living separately from a beholder) is territorial, eats bugs and little animals, and is known for playing with its food. A lone wild gazer avoids picking fights with creatures that are Medium or larger, but a pack of them might take on larger prey. A gazer might follow the folk in its territory, noisily mimicking their speech and generally being a nuisance, until they leave the area, but it flees if confronted by something it can't kill.

Variant: Gazer Familiar

Spellcasters who are interested in unusual familiars find that gazers are eager to serve someone who has magical power. Unless its master is strict, a gazer familiar can be unruly, behaving aggressively toward other Tiny creatures. A gazer serving as a familiar has the following trait:

Familiar. The gazer can serve another creature as a familiar, forming a telepathic bond with its willing master, provided that the master is at least a 3rd-level spellcaster. While the two are bonded, the master can sense what the gazer senses as long as they are within 1 mile of each other. If its master causes it physical harm, the gazer will end its service as a familiar, breaking the telepathic bond.

Gazer
Tiny Aberration (Beholder), Typically Neutral Evil

Armor Class 13
Hit Points 13 (3d4 + 6)
Speed 0 ft., fly 30 ft. (hover)

STR	DEX	CON	INT	WIS	CHA
3 (−4)	17 (+3)	14 (+2)	3 (−4)	10 (+0)	7 (−2)

Saving Throws Wis +2
Skills Perception +4, Stealth +5
Condition Immunities prone
Senses darkvision 60 ft., passive Perception 14
Languages —
Challenge 1/2 (100 XP)   **Proficiency Bonus** +2

Mimicry. The gazer can mimic simple sounds of speech it has heard, in any language. A creature that hears the sounds can tell they are imitations with a successful DC 10 Wisdom (Insight) check.

Actions

Bite. *Melee Weapon Attack:* +5 to hit, reach 5 ft., one target. *Hit:* 1 piercing damage.

Eye Rays. The gazer shoots two of the following magical eye rays at random (roll two d4s, and reroll duplicates), choosing one or two targets it can see within 60 feet of it:

1: **Dazing Ray.** The targeted creature must succeed on a DC 12 Wisdom saving throw or be charmed until the start of the gazer's next turn. While the target is charmed in this way, its speed is halved, and it has disadvantage on attack rolls.
2: **Fear Ray.** The targeted creature must succeed on a DC 12 Wisdom saving throw or be frightened until the start of the gazer's next turn.
3: **Frost Ray.** The target must succeed on a DC 12 Dexterity saving throw or take 10 (3d6) cold damage.
4: **Telekinetic Ray.** If the target is a creature that is Medium or smaller, it must succeed on a DC 12 Strength saving throw or be moved up to 30 feet directly away from the gazer. If the target is a Tiny object that isn't being worn or carried, the gazer moves it up to 30 feet in any direction. The gazer can also exert fine control on objects with this ray, such as manipulating a simple tool or opening a container.

Bonus Actions

Aggressive. The gazer moves up to its speed toward a hostile creature that it can see.

Geryon

Geryon is locked in an endless struggle with Levistus for control of Stygia. The two have fought for centuries, each displacing the other innumerable times. Currently, Levistus claims lordship over Stygia, but he has been trapped in an enormous block of ice at the command of Asmodeus. In response, Geryon is marshaling his followers, hoping to use this opportunity to replace his hated rival.

Among the archdevils, Geryon is known for his martial prowess. He is a ferocious hunter and a relentless tracker. He often joins his troops in battle; he loves to feel flesh and steel sundered beneath his claws and to taste his foes' blood. Yet Geryon's ferocity has also limited his ability to collect souls and forge an effective hierarchy. Sages who study the Nine Hells believe the battle for control of Stygia is a test staged by Asmodeus in hopes of purging the worst impulses from both Geryon and Levistus—or discovering a competent replacement for both.

Geryon's Lair

Geryon has recently reclaimed his ancient fortress, Coldsteel, a sprawling complex that rises from the icy center of Stygia. He roams the passages, spitting oaths of vengeance against Asmodeus and hatching schemes to reclaim his standing from Levistus.

The challenge rating of Geryon is 23 (50,000 XP) when he's encountered in his lair.

Lair Actions

On initiative count 20 (losing initiative ties), Geryon can take one of the following lair actions; he can't take the same lair action two rounds in a row:

Banish. Geryon casts the *banishment* spell.

Chill Blast. Geryon causes a blast of cold to burst from the ground at a point he can see within 120 feet of him. The cold fills a cube, 10 feet on each side, centered on that point. Each creature in that area must succeed on a DC 21 Constitution saving throw or take 28 (8d6) cold damage.

Hateful Restraints. Geryon targets one creature he can see within 60 feet of him. The target must succeed on a DC 21 Wisdom saving throw or become restrained for 1 minute. The target can end the effect on itself if it deals any damage to one or more of its allies.

Regional Effects

The region containing Geryon's lair is warped by his magic, creating one or more of the following effects:

Chilling Wind. Freezing strong winds howl around the area within 1 mile of the lair.

Enervating Screams. Howls and screams fill the air within 1 mile of the lair. Any creature that finishes a short or long rest in this area must succeed on a DC 21 Wisdom saving throw or derive no benefit from the rest.

Hellish Doorways. Sapient creatures within 1 mile of the lair frequently see shimmering portals leading to places they consider safe. Passing through a portal always deposits a traveler somewhere in Stygia.

If Geryon dies, these effects fade over the course of 1d10 days.

Cultists of Geryon

Geryon grants his cultists special abilities. Members of his cult can gain the Crushing Blow trait. Cult leaders can also gain the Indomitable Strength trait.

Crushing Blow (Recharges after a Short or Long Rest). As a bonus action, the creature gains a bonus to the damage roll of its next melee weapon attack roll that hits within the next minute. The bonus equals its Strength modifier (minimum of +1).

Indomitable Strength (Recharge 5–6). As a reaction when this creature takes damage, it can roll a d10 and subtract the number rolled from the damage.

Variant: Sound the Horn

Geryon can have an action that allows him to summon minotaurs.

Sound the Horn (1/Day). Geryon blows his horn, which causes 5d4 **minotaurs** (see the *Monster Manual*) to appear in unoccupied spaces of his choice within 600 feet of him. The minotaurs roll initiative when they appear, and they obey his commands. They remain until they die or Geryon uses an action to dismiss any or all of them.

Geryon
Huge Fiend (Devil), Lawful Evil

Armor Class 19 (natural armor)
Hit Points 300 (24d12 + 144)
Speed 30 ft., fly 50 ft.

STR	DEX	CON	INT	WIS	CHA
29 (+9)	17 (+3)	22 (+6)	19 (+4)	16 (+3)	23 (+6)

Saving Throws Dex +10, Con +13, Wis +10, Cha +13
Skills Deception +13, Intimidation +13, Perception +10
Damage Resistances bludgeoning, piercing, and slashing from nonmagical attacks that aren't silvered
Damage Immunities cold, fire, poison
Condition Immunities charmed, exhaustion, frightened, poisoned
Senses truesight 120 ft., passive Perception 20
Languages all, telepathy 120 ft.
Challenge 22 (41,000 XP)   **Proficiency Bonus** +7

Legendary Resistance (3/Day). If Geryon fails a saving throw, he can choose to succeed instead.

Magic Resistance. Geryon has advantage on saving throws against spells and other magical effects.

Regeneration. Geryon regains 20 hit points at the start of his turn. If he takes radiant damage, this trait doesn't function at the start of his next turn. Geryon dies only if he starts his turn with 0 hit points and doesn't regenerate.

Actions

Multiattack. Geryon makes one Claw attack and one Stinger attack.

Claw. *Melee Weapon Attack:* +16 to hit, reach 15 ft., one target. *Hit:* 23 (4d6 + 9) cold damage. If the target is Large or smaller, it is grappled (DC 24), and it is restrained until the grapple ends. Geryon can grapple one creature at a time. If the target is already grappled by Geryon, the target takes an extra 27 (6d8) cold damage.

Stinger. *Melee Weapon Attack:* +16 to hit, reach 20 ft., one creature. *Hit:* 14 (2d4 + 9) force damage, and the target must succeed on a DC 21 Constitution saving throw or take 13 (2d12) poison damage and become poisoned until it finishes a short or long rest. The target's hit point maximum is reduced by an amount equal to half the poison damage taken. This reduction lasts until the poisoned condition is removed. The target dies if its hit point maximum is reduced to 0.

Spellcasting. Geryon casts one of the following spells, requiring no material components and using Charisma as the spellcasting ability (spell save DC 21):

At will: *alter self* (can become Medium when changing his appearance), *detect magic*, *ice storm*, *invisibility* (self only), *locate object*, *suggestion*, *wall of ice*
1/day: *banishment*

Teleport. Geryon teleports, along with any equipment he is wearing and carrying, up to 120 feet to an unoccupied space he can see.

Legendary Actions

Geryon can take 3 legendary actions, choosing from the options below. Only one legendary action option can be used at a time and only at the end of another creature's turn. Geryon regains spent legendary actions at the start of his turn.

Infernal Glare. Geryon targets one creature he can see within 60 feet of him. The target must succeed on a DC 23 Wisdom saving throw or become frightened of Geryon until the end of its next turn.
Teleport. Geryon uses Teleport.
Swift Sting (Costs 2 Actions). Geryon makes one Stinger attack.

Out of curiosity, I once tamed a giant strider. Several potions of fire resistance later, the creature was purring in my lap, and I didn't feel a thing.

—Mordenkainen

We might have discovered the key to unlock Mordenkainen's frigid heart: magical pets!
TASHA

Giant Strider

Large Elemental, Unaligned

Armor Class 14 (natural armor)
Hit Points 22 (3d10 + 6)
Speed 50 ft.

STR	DEX	CON	INT	WIS	CHA
18 (+4)	13 (+1)	14 (+2)	4 (−3)	12 (+1)	6 (−2)

Damage Immunities fire
Senses passive Perception 11
Languages —
Challenge 1 (200 XP) **Proficiency Bonus** +2

Fire Absorption. Whenever the giant strider is subjected to fire damage, it takes no damage and regains a number of hit points equal to half the fire damage dealt.

Actions

Bite. *Melee Weapon Attack:* +6 to hit, reach 5 ft., one target. *Hit:* 8 (1d8 + 4) piercing damage.

Fire Burst (Recharge 5–6). The giant strider hurls a gout of flame at a point it can see within 60 feet of it. Each creature in a 10-foot-radius sphere centered on that point must make a DC 12 Dexterity saving throw, taking 14 (4d6) fire damage on a failed save, or half as much damage on a successful one. The fire spreads around corners, and it ignites flammable objects in that area that aren't being worn or carried.

Giant Strider

These fierce and majestic monsters exhibit attributes of both birds and reptiles, but are truly neither. Giant striders have a supernatural affinity to fire and can spit gouts of flame at distant enemies. They are most often found in tropical, volcanically active areas or regions that similarly provide sources of both water and extreme heat.

Firenewts prize giant striders and seek to adopt them whenever possible. They provide for stables of these creatures in their lairs, and in return, the giant striders voluntarily serve as mounts for firenewt warriors (in this book).

RICHARD WHITTERS

My travels in Wildspace are always brightened by my giff associates. Their use of gunpowder reminds me of my own explosive wizardry. Spectacular!

—Mordenkainen

GIFF

It's easy to spot giff in a room: these burly folk are 7-foot-tall, hippopotamus-headed people. In Wildspace and the associated ports, giff are most often encountered as spacefaring mercenaries. These troops are renowned for their martial training and love of explosives and are typically armed with gleaming pistols and muskets. The stat block here represents one of those mercenaries.

Every aspect of these spacefaring giff's society is organized along military lines. From birth until death, each has a military rank. Promotions don't depend on age but are granted by a superior as a reward for valor.

Muskets and grenades are the specialties of many giff regiments. The bigger the boom, the brighter the flash, and the thicker the smoke it produces, the greater the glory for the one wielding the weapon. Giff mercenaries have been known to accept payment in kegs of gunpowder in preference to gold, gems, or other currency.

GUNPOWDER BY THE KEG

In addition to their personal gunpowder weapons, giff ships and mercenary companies carry spare gunpowder in kegs. In an emergency, or if a large explosion is needed, a whole keg can be detonated. A giff lights the fuse on the keg and can then throw the keg up to 15 feet as part of the same action. The keg explodes at the start of the giff's next turn. Each creature within 20 feet of the exploding keg must make a DC 12 Dexterity saving throw. On a failed save, a creature takes 24 (7d6) fire damage and is knocked prone. On a successful save, a creature takes half as much damage and isn't knocked prone.

Every other keg of gunpowder within 20 feet of an exploding keg has a 50 percent chance of also exploding. Check each keg only once per turn, no matter how many other kegs explode around it.

GIFF
Medium Humanoid, Any Alignment

Armor Class 16 (breastplate)
Hit Points 60 (8d8 + 24)
Speed 30 ft.

STR	DEX	CON	INT	WIS	CHA
18 (+4)	14 (+2)	17 (+3)	11 (+0)	12 (+1)	12 (+1)

Senses passive Perception 11
Languages Common
Challenge 3 (700 XP)   **Proficiency Bonus** +2

Firearms Knowledge. The giff's mastery of its weapons enables it to ignore the loading property of muskets and pistols.

Headfirst Charge. The giff can try to knock a creature over; if the giff moves at least 20 feet in a straight line and ends within 5 feet of a Large or smaller creature, that creature must succeed on a DC 14 Strength saving throw or take 7 (2d6) bludgeoning damage and be knocked prone.

ACTIONS

Multiattack. The giff makes two Longsword, Musket, or Pistol attacks.

Longsword. Melee Weapon Attack: +6 to hit, reach 5 ft., one target. Hit: 8 (1d8 + 4) slashing damage, or 9 (1d10 + 4) slashing damage if used with two hands.

Musket. Ranged Weapon Attack: +4 to hit, range 40/120 ft., one target. Hit: 8 (1d12 + 2) piercing damage.

Pistol. Ranged Weapon Attack: +4 to hit, range 30/90 ft., one target. Hit: 7 (1d10 + 2) piercing damage.

Fragmentation Grenade (1/Day). The giff throws a grenade up to 60 feet, and the grenade explodes in a 20-foot-radius sphere. Each creature in that area must make a DC 15 Dexterity saving throw, taking 17 (5d6) piercing damage on a failed save, or half as much damage on a successful one.

Girallon

A girallon looks like an oversized, four-armed ape with grayish-tan skin and white fur. Its vicious fangs and claws reveal it to be a monstrous predator.

Girallons are most common in temperate or warm forest environments abundant with life. They share apes' adeptness at climbing, although few trees can support the weight of these half-ton creatures. The ruins of cities, especially those found in deep forests and jungles, seem to attract girallons. They see a city's buildings as a superior sort of forest whose uppermost "branches" can safely support them. The creatures can easily scale walls and battlements, and they perch on tower tops and other high vantages to keep an eye on the surrounding area.

When girallons can't climb, they stalk the forest floor, lurk in narrow ravines or shallow caves, or hide in ruined sites while waiting for prey to come near. A girallon is surprisingly stealthy, considering its size and its lack of camouflage.

Girallons form loose bands of several individuals and their offspring, usually led by a dominant adult that also tends to be the oldest member of the group. When on the hunt away from their lair, girallons use roars and body language to communicate with one another over distance. Each individual typically hunts alone and widely separated from the others to ensure that everyone gets adequate fodder. The leader might organize members to work together to make a big kill, however. If they succeed, everyone in the group shares the spoils, with the best parts going to those caring for their young.

Girallons' strange appearance and attraction to ruins lead sages to believe they were created through magic to serve as guardians for some lost empire. When that empire fell ages ago, girallons turned feral and spread out across the world.

Numerous creatures have tried to tame, subjugate, or cooperate with the monsters. For instance, some forest-dwelling peoples capture girallons and train them to serve as sentinels. Recognizing that girallons are peaceful among their own kind, other folk have learned how to approach a group's leader, offering food and other gifts in hopes of establishing an alliance with the creatures.

Girallons that are well treated might be willing to serve as guards, though they lack the intelligence to take on tasks more complicated than attacking strangers who enter their domain. A girallon that's captured when young and carefully trained could end up in a seemingly unlikely place, such as guarding the entrance to a city's thieves' guild. Those who would keep a girallon must always be wary, however, because the creature could revert to its predatory nature at any time.

Girallon
Large Monstrosity, Unaligned

Armor Class 13
Hit Points 59 (7d10 + 21)
Speed 40 ft., climb 40 ft.

STR	DEX	CON	INT	WIS	CHA
18 (+4)	16 (+3)	16 (+3)	5 (−3)	12 (+1)	7 (−2)

Skills Perception +5, Stealth +5
Senses darkvision 60 ft., passive Perception 15
Languages —
Challenge 4 (1,100 XP)   **Proficiency Bonus** +2

Actions

Multiattack. The girallon makes one Bite attack and four Claw attacks.

Bite. *Melee Weapon Attack:* +6 to hit, reach 5 ft., one creature. *Hit:* 7 (1d6 + 4) piercing damage.

Claw. *Melee Weapon Attack:* +6 to hit, reach 10 ft., one target. *Hit:* 7 (1d6 + 4) slashing damage.

Bonus Actions

Aggressive. The girallon moves up to its speed toward a hostile creature that it can see.

Githyanki

Githyanki descend from an ancient people who were also the progenitors of githzerai (also in this book). These tall, gaunt folk have potent psionic powers and dwell, for the most part, on the Astral Plane. Among the best-known githyanki are the bellicose followers of the Lich Queen Vlaakith. They terrorize the Astral Plane, raiding into other planes to plunder the multiverse of its magic and riches.

Githyanki Gish

Gish blend their magical abilities with swordplay to become dangerous foes in battle. Their specialized capabilities make them well suited for assassination, raiding, and espionage.

Githyanki Gish
Medium Humanoid (Gith, Wizard), Any Alignment

Armor Class 17 (half plate)
Hit Points 130 (20d8 + 40)
Speed 30 ft.

STR	DEX	CON	INT	WIS	CHA
17 (+3)	15 (+2)	14 (+2)	16 (+3)	15 (+2)	16 (+3)

Saving Throws Con +6, Int +7, Wis +6
Skills Insight +6, Perception +6, Stealth +6
Senses passive Perception 16
Languages Gith
Challenge 10 (5,900 XP)   **Proficiency Bonus** +4

Actions

Multiattack. The githyanki makes three Longsword or Telekinetic Bolt attacks, or it makes one of those attacks and uses Spellcasting.

Longsword. *Melee Weapon Attack:* +7 to hit, reach 5 ft., one target. *Hit:* 7 (1d8 + 3) slashing damage, or 8 (1d10 + 3) slashing damage if used with two hands, plus 22 (5d8) psychic damage.

Telekinetic Bolt. *Ranged Spell Attack:* +7 to hit, range 120 ft., one target. *Hit:* 28 (8d6) force damage.

Spellcasting (Psionics). The githyanki casts one of the following spells, requiring no spell components and using Intelligence as the spellcasting ability (spell save DC 15):

At will: *light, mage hand* (the hand is invisible), *message*
3/day each: *fireball, invisibility, nondetection* (self only)
1/day each: *dimension door, plane shift, telekinesis*

Bonus Actions

Astral Step (Recharge 4–6). The githyanki teleports, along with any equipment it is wearing or carrying, up to 30 feet to an unoccupied space it can see.

Githyanki Kith'rak

Militarized githyanki cultures assign ranks and responsibilities to citizens. Groups of ten warriors follow the commands of sarths (githyanki warriors; see the *Monster Manual*), while ten sarths obey the commands of a mighty kith'rak. These champions undergo torturous training and psionic testing until they can command the respect of their underlings.

Githyanki Supreme Commander

Supreme commanders lead armies, each one commanding ten kith'raks, who in turn lead the rest of their forces. Most supreme commanders ride red dragons (see the *Monster Manual*) into battle.

Githyanki Kith'rak
Medium Humanoid (Gith), Any Alignment

Armor Class 18 (plate)
Hit Points 180 (24d8 + 72)
Speed 30 ft.

STR	DEX	CON	INT	WIS	CHA
18 (+4)	16 (+3)	17 (+3)	16 (+3)	15 (+2)	17 (+3)

Saving Throws Con +7, Int +7, Wis +6
Skills Intimidation +7, Perception +6
Senses passive Perception 16
Languages Gith
Challenge 12 (8,400 XP)   **Proficiency Bonus** +4

Actions

Multiattack. The githyanki makes three Greatsword attacks.

Greatsword. *Melee Weapon Attack:* +8 to hit, reach 5 ft., one target. *Hit:* 11 (2d6 + 4) slashing damage plus 17 (5d6) psychic damage.

Spellcasting (Psionics). The githyanki casts one of the following spells, requiring no spell components and using Intelligence as the spellcasting ability (spell save DC 15):

At will: *mage hand* (the hand is invisible)
3/day each: *blur, nondetection* (self only)
1/day each: *plane shift, telekinesis*

Bonus Actions

Astral Step (Recharge 4–6). The githyanki teleports, along with any equipment it is wearing or carrying, up to 30 feet to an unoccupied space it can see.

Rally the Troops. The githyanki magically ends the charmed and frightened conditions on itself and each creature of its choice that it can see within 30 feet of it.

Reactions

Parry. The githyanki adds 4 to its AC against one melee attack that would hit it. To do so, the githyanki must see the attacker and be wielding a melee weapon.

GITHYANKI
SUPREME COMMANDER

GITHYANKI KITH'RAK

GITHYANKI GISH

GITHYANKI SUPREME COMMANDER

Medium Humanoid (Gith), Any Alignment

Armor Class 18 (plate)
Hit Points 187 (22d8 + 88)
Speed 30 ft.

STR	DEX	CON	INT	WIS	CHA
19 (+4)	17 (+3)	18 (+4)	16 (+3)	16 (+3)	18 (+4)

Saving Throws Con +9, Int +8, Wis +8
Skills Insight +8, Intimidation +9, Perception +8
Senses passive Perception 18
Languages Gith
Challenge 14 (11,500 XP)   **Proficiency Bonus** +5

Legendary Resistance (3/Day). If the githyanki fails a saving throw, it can choose to succeed instead.

ACTIONS

Multiattack. The githyanki makes two Silver Greatsword attacks.

Silver Greatsword. *Melee Weapon Attack:* +12 to hit, reach 5 ft., one target. *Hit:* 14 (2d6 + 7) slashing damage plus 17 (5d6) psychic damage. On a critical hit against a target in an astral body (as with the *astral projection* spell), the githyanki can cut the silvery cord that tethers the target to its material body, instead of dealing damage.

Spellcasting (Psionics). The githyanki casts one of the following spells, requiring no spell components and using Intelligence as the spellcasting ability (spell save DC 16):

At will: *mage hand* (the hand is invisible)
3/day each: *levitate* (self only), *nondetection* (self only)
1/day each: *Bigby's hand*, *mass suggestion*, *plane shift*, *telekinesis*

BONUS ACTIONS

Astral Step. The githyanki teleports, along with any equipment it is wearing or carrying, up to 30 feet to an unoccupied space it can see.

REACTIONS

Parry. The githyanki adds 5 to its AC against one melee attack that would hit it. To do so, the githyanki must see the attacker and be wielding a melee weapon.

LEGENDARY ACTIONS

The githyanki can take 3 legendary actions, choosing from the options below. Only one legendary action option can be used at a time and only at the end of another creature's turn. The githyanki regains spent legendary actions at the start of its turn.

Command Ally. The githyanki targets one ally it can see within 30 feet of it. If the target can see or hear the githyanki, the target can make one melee weapon attack using its reaction, if available, and has advantage on the attack roll.
Attack (2 Actions). The githyanki makes one Silver Greatsword attack.

G

Githzerai

Githzerai are otherworldly folk with psionic powers who share an ancestral link to githyanki (also in this book). The githzerai followers of the great leader Zaerith Menyar-Ag-Gith are an ascetic people who live apart from the rest of the cosmos, within the confines of fortresses floating through the chaos of Limbo. Instead of imposing their will on other peoples, they focus on controlling and manipulating their endlessly malleable home.

Githzerai Anarch

Anarchs are githzerai sages and mystics who lead communities and maintain the adamantine citadels that serve as strong points in Limbo and on other planes. They have formidable psionic capabilities and are able to manipulate the unformed substance of their adopted plane with a thought.

An Anarch's Lair

In Limbo, githzerai anarchs create islands of tranquility in this turbulent plane. An anarch can use its psionic power to give form to formless substance, creating mountains, lakes, and structures to serve as a foundation for a githzerai community.

The anarch's challenge rating is 17 (18,000 XP) when it's encountered in its lair.

Lair Actions. On initiative count 20 (losing initiative ties), the anarch can take one of the following lair actions; the anarch can't take the same lair action two rounds in a row:

Create Object. The anarch casts the *creation* spell (as a 9th-level spell) using the unformed substance of Limbo instead of shadow material. If used in Limbo, the object remains until the anarch's concentration is broken, regardless of its composition. If the anarch moves more than 120 feet from the object, the anarch's concentration breaks.

Move Object. The anarch can magically move an object it can see within 150 feet of it by making a Wisdom check with advantage. The DC depends on the object's size: DC 5 for Tiny, DC 10 for Small, DC 15 for Medium, DC 20 for Large, and DC 25 for Huge or larger.

Psionic Bolt. The anarch casts the *lightning bolt* spell (at 5th level), but the anarch can change the damage type from lightning to cold, fire, psychic, radiant, or thunder. If the spell deals damage other than fire or lightning, it doesn't ignite flammable objects.

Regional Effects. The region containing an anarch's lair is warped by its presence, which creates one or more of the following effects:

Form Substance. In Limbo, the anarch can spend 10 minutes stabilizing a 5-mile area centered on it, causing the unformed substance to take whatever inanimate form the anarch chooses. During that process, the anarch determines the shape and composition of the forms created.

Stabilize Object. The anarch stabilizes any object created in Limbo and brought to the Material Plane for as long as the anarch remains within 1 mile of it (no action required).

If the anarch dies, these effects end after 1d6 rounds. All formed substance becomes a chaotic churn of energy and matter, unraveling into unformed substance that dissipates 1d6 rounds later.

Githzerai Anarch
Medium Humanoid (Gith), Any Alignment

Armor Class 20 (Psychic Defense)
Hit Points 144 (17d8 + 68)
Speed 30 ft., fly 40 ft. (hover)

STR	DEX	CON	INT	WIS	CHA
16 (+3)	21 (+5)	18 (+4)	18 (+4)	20 (+5)	14 (+2)

Saving Throws Str +8, Dex +10, Int +9, Wis +10
Skills Arcana +9, Insight +10, Perception +10
Senses passive Perception 20
Languages Gith
Challenge 16 (15,000 XP)   **Proficiency Bonus** +5

Legendary Resistance (3/Day). If the githzerai fails a saving throw, it can choose to succeed instead.

Psychic Defense. While the githzerai is wearing no armor and wielding no shield, its AC includes its Wisdom modifier.

Actions

Multiattack. The githzerai makes three Unarmed Strike attacks.

Unarmed Strike. *Melee Weapon Attack:* +10 to hit, reach 5 ft., one target. *Hit:* 9 (1d8 + 5) bludgeoning damage plus 18 (4d8) psychic damage.

Spellcasting (Psionics). The githzerai casts one of the following spells, requiring no spell components and using Wisdom as the spellcasting ability (spell save DC 18):

At will: *mage hand* (the hand is invisible)
3/day each: *see invisibility*, *telekinesis*
1/day each: *globe of invulnerability*, *plane shift*, *wall of force*

Legendary Actions

The githzerai can take 3 legendary actions, choosing from the options below. Only one legendary action option can be used at a time and only at the end of another creature's turn. The githzerai regains spent legendary actions at the start of its turn.

Strike. The githzerai makes one Unarmed Strike attack.
Teleport. The githzerai teleports, along with any equipment it is wearing or carrying, to an unoccupied space it can see within 30 feet of it.
Change Gravity (Costs 3 Actions). The githzerai casts the *reverse gravity* spell, using Wisdom as the spellcasting ability. The spell has the normal effect, except that the githzerai can orient the area in any direction and creatures and objects fall toward the end of the area.

Githzerai Anarch
(center) with Two
Githzerai Enlightened

Githzerai Enlightened

Some spiritual githzerai spend long hours in meditation to transcend the limits of their forms and to apprehend the nature of reality. Zerths who complete the next tier of their training become known as the enlightened.

Githzerai Enlightened

Medium Humanoid (Gith), Any Alignment

Armor Class 18 (Psychic Defense)
Hit Points 112 (15d8 + 45)
Speed 40 ft.

STR	DEX	CON	INT	WIS	CHA
14 (+2)	19 (+4)	16 (+3)	17 (+3)	19 (+4)	13 (+1)

Saving Throws Str +6, Dex +8, Int +7, Wis +8
Skills Arcana +7, Insight +8, Perception +8
Senses passive Perception 18
Languages Gith
Challenge 10 (5,900 XP)   **Proficiency Bonus** +4

Psychic Defense. While the githzerai is wearing no armor and wielding no shield, its AC includes its Wisdom modifier.

Actions

Multiattack. The githzerai makes three Unarmed Strike attacks.

Unarmed Strike. *Melee Weapon Attack:* +8 to hit, reach 5 ft., one target. *Hit:* 13 (2d8 + 4) bludgeoning damage plus 18 (4d8) psychic damage.

Spellcasting (Psionics). The githzerai casts one of the following spells, requiring no spell components and using Wisdom as the spellcasting ability (spell save DC 16):

At will: *mage hand* (the hand is invisible)
3/day: *see invisibility*
1/day each: *plane shift*, *teleport*

Temporal Strike (Recharge 6). *Melee Weapon Attack:* +8 to hit, reach 5 ft., one creature. *Hit:* 13 (2d8 + 4) bludgeoning damage plus 52 (8d12) psychic damage. The target must succeed on a DC 16 Wisdom saving throw or move 1 round forward in time. A target moved forward in time vanishes for the duration. When the effect ends, the target reappears in the space it left or in an unoccupied space nearest to that space if it's occupied.

Reactions

Slow Fall. When the githzerai falls, it reduces any falling damage it takes by 50.

Gnolls

The first gnolls were hyenas transformed by magic. Many of them were then corrupted by the demon lord Yeenoghu. Whether in service to Yeenoghu or dedicated to the survival of their kin, gnoll war bands seek to soften up foes with surprise attacks and to leave no survivors alive.

Gnoll Flesh Gnawer

These gnolls eschew the use of ranged weapons in favor of short blades that they wield with great speed and efficiency. In the thick of a fight, they dash across the battlefield, slashing and snarling as they run down stragglers and finish off wounded foes.

Gnoll Hunter

Hunters are the stealthiest gnolls in a war band. In the vanguard, they creep around, picking off isolated opposition while clearing the way for the rest of the force to advance.

Hunters are particularly skilled with the longbow, and they fire arrows with viciously barbed heads. Even when a hunter doesn't kill their target with their first shot, the arrow strike brings so much pain that the victim is hobbled in its attempt to run away.

Gnoll Flesh Gnawer
Medium Monstrosity, Typically Chaotic Evil

Armor Class 14 (studded leather)
Hit Points 22 (4d8 + 4)
Speed 30 ft.

STR	DEX	CON	INT	WIS	CHA
12 (+1)	14 (+2)	12 (+1)	8 (−1)	10 (+0)	8 (−1)

Saving Throws Dex +4
Senses darkvision 60 ft., passive Perception 10
Languages Gnoll
Challenge 1 (200 XP)   **Proficiency Bonus** +2

Actions

Multiattack. The gnoll makes one Bite attack and two Shortsword attacks.

Bite. *Melee Weapon Attack:* +4 to hit, reach 5 ft., one target. *Hit:* 4 (1d4 + 2) piercing damage.

Shortsword. *Melee Weapon Attack:* +4 to hit, reach 5 ft., one target. *Hit:* 5 (1d6 + 2) piercing damage.

Sudden Rush. Until the end of the turn, the gnoll's speed increases by 60 feet and it doesn't provoke opportunity attacks.

Bonus Actions

Rampage. After the gnoll reduces a creature to 0 hit points with a melee attack on its turn, the gnoll moves up to half its speed and makes a Bite attack.

Gnoll Hunter
Medium Monstrosity, Typically Chaotic Evil

Armor Class 13 (leather armor)
Hit Points 22 (4d8 + 4)
Speed 30 ft.

STR	DEX	CON	INT	WIS	CHA
14 (+2)	14 (+2)	12 (+1)	8 (−1)	12 (+1)	8 (−1

Skills Perception +3, Stealth +4
Senses darkvision 60 ft., passive Perception 13
Languages Gnoll
Challenge 1/2 (100 XP)   **Proficiency Bonus** +2

Actions

Multiattack. The gnoll makes two Bite, Spear, or Longbow attacks.

Bite. *Melee Weapon Attack:* +4 to hit, reach 5 ft., one target. *Hit:* 4 (1d4 + 2) piercing damage.

Spear. *Melee or Ranged Weapon Attack:* +4 to hit, reach 5 ft. or range 20/60 ft., one target. *Hit:* 5 (1d6 + 2) piercing damage, or 6 (1d8 + 2) piercing damage when used with two hands to make a melee attack.

Longbow. *Ranged Weapon Attack:* +4 to hit, range 150/600 ft., one target. *Hit:* 6 (1d8 + 2) piercing damage, and the target's speed is reduced by 10 feet until the end of its next turn.

Bonus Actions

Rampage. After the gnoll reduces a creature to 0 hit points with a melee attack on its turn, the gnoll moves up to half its speed and makes a Bite attack.

The life cycle of Yeenoghu's gnolls begins and ends with eating. They eat their enemies, they eat one another, and they're freed from their hunger only in death.

—Mordenkainen

GNOLL WITHERLING
Medium Undead, Typically Chaotic Evil

Armor Class 12 (natural armor)
Hit Points 11 (2d8 + 2)
Speed 30 ft.

STR	DEX	CON	INT	WIS	CHA
14 (+2)	8 (−1)	12 (+1)	5 (−3)	5 (−3)	5 (−3)

Damage Immunities poison
Condition Immunities exhaustion, poisoned
Senses darkvision 60 ft., passive Perception 7
Languages understands Gnoll but can't speak
Challenge 1/4 (50 XP)   **Proficiency Bonus** +2

Unusual Nature. The witherling doesn't require air, food, drink, or sleep.

ACTIONS

Multiattack. The witherling makes two Bite or Spiked Club attacks.

Bite. *Melee Weapon Attack:* +4 to hit, reach 5 ft., one target. *Hit:* 4 (1d4 + 2) necrotic damage.

Spiked Club. *Melee Weapon Attack:* +4 to hit, reach 5 ft., one target. *Hit:* 4 (1d4 + 2) piercing damage.

BONUS ACTIONS

Rampage. After the witherling reduces a creature to 0 hit points with a melee attack on its turn, the gnoll moves up to half its speed and makes one Bite attack.

REACTIONS

Vengeful Strike. In response to a gnoll being reduced to 0 hit points within 30 feet of the witherling, the witherling makes one Bite or Spiked Club attack.

GNOLL WITHERLING

Sometimes the gnolls of Yeenoghu turn against each other, perhaps to determine who rules a war band or because of extreme starvation. Even under ordinary circumstances, gnolls that are deprived of victims for too long struggle to control their hunger and violent urges. Eventually, they fight among themselves.

The survivors devour the flesh of their slain comrades but preserve the bones. Then, by invoking rituals to Yeenoghu (appears in this book) they bring the remains back to a semblance of life in the form of a gnoll witherling.

Witherlings travel with their comrades and try to kill anything in their path. They don't eat and aren't motivated by hunger, leaving more flesh for the rest of the war band.

GRAY RENDER

A curious impulse drives the gray render. Despite its hulking form and terrible appetite, it wants most of all to bond with an intelligent creature and, once bonded, to give its life to protect that creature. Great strength and a ferocious nature make gray renders fierce guardians, but they lack a shred of cunning.

Gray renders reproduce by forming nodules on their bodies that, on reaching maturity, break off to begin life as young gray renders. They feel no obligation to their young and have no inclination to gather with others of their kind. Instead, each has an overpowering need to bond with an intelligent creature. When one encounters a suitable master, it sings to that creature—a weird, warbling cry accompanied by scratching at the earth and a show of deference. Once it forms a bond, a gray render serves its master devotedly.

A gray render might be a strong ally, but it's always an unpredictable one. In combat, a gray render fights viciously and never willingly harms its master, but outside battle, it might cause considerable difficulties. It might follow its master despite being told to stay put, destroy its master's house, burrow holes through a ship's hull, attack out of jealousy, or worse.

The Gray Render Quirks table presents possible quirks for gray renders that can be generated randomly or selected as desired.

GRAY RENDER QUIRKS

d12	Quirk
1	Hates horses and other mounts
2	Roars loudly when its bonded creature is touched by another creature
3	Likes to snuggle
4	Uproots and chews on trees
5	Has terrific and eye-watering flatulence
6	Brings offerings of meat to its bonded creature
7	Compulsively digs up the ground
8	Attacks carts and wagons as if they were terrible monsters
9	Howls when it rains
10	Whines piteously in the dark
11	Buries treasure it finds
12	Chases birds, leaping into the air to catch them, heedless of the destruction it causes

GRAY RENDER
Large Monstrosity, Typically Chaotic Neutral

Armor Class 19 (natural armor)
Hit Points 189 (18d10 + 90)
Speed 30 ft.

STR	DEX	CON	INT	WIS	CHA
19 (+4)	13 (+1)	20 (+5)	3 (−4)	6 (−2)	8 (−1)

Saving Throws Str +8, Con +9
Skills Perception +2
Senses darkvision 60 ft., passive Perception 12
Languages —
Challenge 12 (8,400 XP)   **Proficiency Bonus** +4

ACTIONS

Multiattack. The gray render makes one Bite attack and two Claw attacks.

Bite. *Melee Weapon Attack:* +8 to hit, reach 5 ft., one target. *Hit:* 17 (2d12 + 4) piercing damage. If the target is Medium or smaller, the target must succeed on a DC 16 Strength saving throw or be knocked prone.

Claw. *Melee Weapon Attack:* +8 to hit, reach 10 ft., one target. *Hit:* 13 (2d8 + 4) slashing damage, plus 10 (3d6) bludgeoning damage if the target is prone.

REACTIONS

Bloody Rampage. When the gray render takes damage, it makes one Claw attack against a random creature within its reach, other than its master.

GRAZ'ZT

The appearance of this demon lord is a warning that not all that is beautiful is good. Every plane and curve of his nine-foot-tall body, every glance of his burning eyes, promises a mixture of pleasure and pain. Graz'zt can transform himself at will, appearing in any humanlike form that pleases him or his onlookers, all equally tempting in their own ways. In every form, though, a subtle wrongness pervades his beauty, from the cruel cast of his features to the six fingers on each hand and six toes on each foot.

Graz'zt surrounds himself with the finest of things and the most attractive of servants, and he adorns himself in silks and leathers both striking and disturbing in their workmanship. His lair and those of his cultists are pleasure palaces where nothing is forbidden save moderation and kindness.

Cults devoted to him are secret societies of indulgence, often using their debauchery to subjugate others through blackmail, addiction, and manipulation. They wear alabaster masks with ecstatic expressions and ostentatious dress and body ornamentation to their secret assignations.

Although he prefers charm and subtle manipulation, Graz'zt is capable of terrible violence when provoked. He wields the greatsword Angdrelve, also called Wave of Sorrow, whose wavy, razor-edged blade drips acid at his command.

GRAZ'ZT'S LAIR

Graz'zt's principal lair is his Argent Palace, a grandiose structure in the city of Zelatar, found within his abyssal domain of Azzagrat. Graz'zt's demonic influence radiates outward in a tangible ripple, warping reality around him. Given enough time in a single location, Graz'zt can twist it with his power.

Graz'zt's lair is a den of ostentation and hedonism. It is adorned with finery and decorations so decadent that even the wealthiest of mortals would blush at the excess. Within Graz'zt's lairs, devotees and subjects alike are forced to slake Graz'zt's thirst for pageantry.

LAIR ACTIONS

On initiative count 20 (losing initiative ties), Graz'zt can take one of the following lair actions; he can't take the same lair action two rounds in a row:

Command. Graz'zt casts the *command* spell on every creature of his choice in the lair. He needn't see each one, but he must be aware that an individual is in the lair to target that creature. He issues the same command to all the targets.

RICHARD WHITTERS

Conjure Mirrors. Smooth surfaces within the lair become as reflective as a polished mirror. Until a different lair action is used, creatures within the lair have disadvantage on Dexterity (Stealth) checks made to hide.

REGIONAL EFFECTS

The region containing Graz'zt's lair is warped by his magic, creating one or more of the following effects:

Agitated Beasts. Wild beasts within 6 miles of the lair break into frequent conflicts and coupling, mirroring the behavior that occurs during their mating seasons.

Beguiling Realm. Within 6 miles of the lair, all Wisdom (Insight) checks have disadvantage, and all Charisma (Deception) and Charisma (Persuasion) checks have advantage.

Mirrors Everywhere. Flat surfaces within 1 mile of the lair that are made of stone or metal become highly reflective, as though polished to a shine. These surfaces become supernaturally mirrorlike.

If Graz'zt dies, these effects fade over the course of 1d10 days.

CULTISTS OF GRAZ'ZT

Graz'zt grants his cultists special abilities. His cultists can gain the Joy from Pain trait, while his cult leaders can gain the Master of Pleasures trait.

Joy from Pain. Whenever this creature suffers a critical hit, it can make one melee weapon attack as a reaction.

Master of Pleasures. As a reaction when this creature takes damage, it can magically grant 5 temporary hit points to itself and up to three allies within 30 feet of it.

GRAZ'ZT

Large Fiend (Demon), Chaotic Evil

Armor Class 20 (natural armor)
Hit Points 346 (33d10 + 165)
Speed 40 ft.

STR	DEX	CON	INT	WIS	CHA
22 (+6)	15 (+2)	21 (+5)	23 (+6)	21 (+5)	26 (+8)

Saving Throws Dex +9, Con +12, Wis +12
Skills Deception +15, Insight +12, Perception +12, Persuasion +15
Damage Resistances cold, fire, lightning
Damage Immunities poison; bludgeoning, piercing, and slashing that is nonmagical
Condition Immunities charmed, exhaustion, frightened, poisoned
Senses truesight 120 ft., passive Perception 22
Languages all, telepathy 120 ft.
Challenge 24 (62,000 XP)   **Proficiency Bonus** +7

Legendary Resistance (3/Day). If Graz'zt fails a saving throw, he can choose to succeed instead.

Magic Resistance. Graz'zt has advantage on saving throws against spells and other magical effects.

ACTIONS

Multiattack. Graz'zt makes two Wave of Sorrow attacks. He can replace one attack with a use of Spellcasting.

Wave of Sorrow (Greatsword). *Melee Weapon Attack:* +13 to hit, reach 10 ft., one target. *Hit:* 20 (4d6 + 6) force damage plus 14 (4d6) acid damage.

Spellcasting. Graz'zt casts one of the following spells, requiring no material components and using Charisma as the spellcasting ability (spell save DC 23):

At will: *charm person, detect magic, dispel magic*
3/day each: *darkness, dominate person, telekinesis, teleport*
1/day each: *dominate monster, greater invisibility*

Teleport. Graz'zt teleports, along with any equipment he is wearing or carrying, up to 120 feet to an unoccupied space he can see.

BONUS ACTIONS

Change Shape. Graz'zt transforms into a form that resembles a Medium Humanoid or back into his true form. Aside from his size, his statistics are the same in each form. Any equipment he is wearing or carrying isn't transformed.

REACTIONS

Negate Spell (Recharge 5–6). Graz'zt tries to interrupt a spell he sees a creature casting within 60 feet of him. If the spell is 3rd level or lower, the spell fails and has no effect. If the spell is 4th level or higher, Graz'zt makes a Charisma check against a DC of 10 + the spell's level. On a success, the spell fails and has no effect.

LEGENDARY ACTIONS

Graz'zt can take 3 legendary actions, choosing from the options below. Only one legendary action option can be used at a time and only at the end of another creature's turn. Graz'zt regains spent legendary actions at the start of his turn.

Abyssal Magic. Graz'zt uses Spellcasting or Teleport.
Attack. Graz'zt makes one Wave of Sorrow attack.
Dance, My Puppet! One creature charmed by Graz'zt that Graz'zt can see must use its reaction to move up to its speed as Graz'zt directs.

Grungs

Grungs are frog-like folk found in rain forests and tropical jungles. These amphibians prefer shade and live in trees, but they maintain hatcheries for their offspring in well-guarded ground-level pools. About three months after hatching, a grung tadpole takes on the shape of an adult, and after another six months, the grung reaches maturity.

Born in a wide range of colors, grungs most often appear in shades of green, blue, purple, red, orange, and gold. All grungs secrete a substance that is harmless to them but poisonous to other creatures, and sometimes that substance has a special effect based on the grung's color (see "Variant: Grung Poison"). They also use this venom to poison their weapons.

Grung

The grung stat block represents a typical grung warrior or hunter, met either in a grung community or traveling elsewhere as a mercenary, game warden, guard, or bandit.

Grung Elite Warrior

A grung elite warrior typically leads a group of grung and other warriors into battle and is often accompanied by a grung wildling.

Grung Wildling

Gifted with druidic magic, a grung wildling typically serves as an advisor, a healer, and a nurturer of crops.

Grung
Small Humanoid, Any Alignment

Armor Class 12
Hit Points 11 (2d6 + 4)
Speed 25 ft., climb 25 ft.

STR	DEX	CON	INT	WIS	CHA
7 (−2)	14 (+2)	15 (+2)	10 (+0)	11 (+0)	10 (+0)

Saving Throws Dex +4
Skills Athletics +2, Perception +2, Stealth +4, Survival +2
Damage Immunities poison
Condition Immunities poisoned
Senses passive Perception 12
Languages Grung
Challenge 1/4 (50 XP) **Proficiency Bonus** +2

Amphibious. The grung can breathe air and water.

Poisonous Skin. Any creature that grapples the grung or otherwise comes into direct contact with the grung's skin must succeed on a DC 12 Constitution saving throw or become poisoned for 1 minute. A poisoned creature no longer in direct contact with the grung can repeat the saving throw at the end of each of its turns, ending the effect on itself on a success.

Standing Leap. The grung's long jump is up to 25 feet and its high jump is up to 15 feet, with or without a running start.

Water Dependency. If the grung isn't immersed in water for at least 1 hour during a day, it suffers 1 level of exhaustion at the end of that day. The grung can recover from this exhaustion only through magic or by immersing itself in water for at least 1 hour.

Actions

Dagger. *Melee or Ranged Weapon Attack:* +4 to hit, reach 5 ft. or range 20/60 ft., one target. *Hit:* 4 (1d4 + 2) piercing damage plus 5 (2d4) poison damage.

Variant: Grung Poison

A creature poisoned by a grung can suffer an additional effect that depends on the grung's color, as described below. This effect lasts until the creature is no longer poisoned by the grung.

Blue Grung. The poisoned creature must make a loud noise at the start and end of its turn.

Gold Grung. The creature is charmed by the grung and can speak Grung.

Green Grung. The poisoned creature can't move except to climb or make standing jumps. If the creature is flying, it can't take any actions or reactions unless it lands.

Orange Grung. The poisoned creature is frightened of its allies.

Purple Grung. The poisoned creature feels a desperate need to soak itself in liquid or mud. It can't take actions or move except to do so or to reach a body of liquid or mud.

Red Grung. The poisoned creature must use its action to eat if food is within reach.

Grung Elite Warrior

Small Humanoid, Any Alignment

Armor Class 13
Hit Points 49 (9d6 + 18)
Speed 25 ft., climb 25 ft.

STR	DEX	CON	INT	WIS	CHA
7 (−2)	16 (+3)	15 (+2)	10 (+0)	11 (+0)	12 (+1)

Saving Throws Dex +5
Skills Athletics +2, Perception +2, Stealth +5, Survival +2
Damage Immunities poison
Condition Immunities poisoned
Senses passive Perception 12
Languages Grung
Challenge 2 (450 XP)   **Proficiency Bonus** +2

Amphibious. The grung can breathe air and water.

Poisonous Skin. Any creature that grapples the grung or otherwise comes into direct contact with the grung's skin must succeed on a DC 12 Constitution saving throw or become poisoned for 1 minute. A poisoned creature no longer in direct contact with the grung can repeat the saving throw at the end of each of its turns, ending the effect on itself on a success.

Standing Leap. The grung's long jump is up to 25 feet and its high jump is up to 15 feet, with or without a running start.

Water Dependency. If the grung isn't immersed in water for at least 1 hour during a day, it suffers 1 level of exhaustion at the end of that day. The grung can recover from this exhaustion only through magic or by immersing itself in water for at least 1 hour.

Actions

Dagger. *Melee or Ranged Weapon Attack:* +5 to hit, reach 5 ft. or range 20/60 ft., one target. *Hit:* 5 (1d4 + 3) piercing damage plus 5 (2d4) poison damage.

Shortbow. *Ranged Weapon Attack:* +5 to hit, range 80/320 ft., one target. *Hit:* 6 (1d6 + 3) piercing damage plus 5 (2d4) poison damage.

Mesmerizing Chirr (Recharge 6). The grung makes a chirring noise to which grungs are immune. Each Humanoid or Beast that is within 15 feet of the grung and able to hear it must succeed on a DC 12 Wisdom saving throw or be stunned until the end of the grung's next turn.

Grung Wildling

Small Humanoid, Any Alignment

Armor Class 16 (natural armor)
Hit Points 27 (5d6 + 10)
Speed 25 ft., climb 25 ft.

STR	DEX	CON	INT	WIS	CHA
7 (−2)	16 (+3)	15 (+2)	10 (+0)	15 (+2)	11 (+0)

Saving Throws Dex +5
Skills Athletics +2, Perception +4, Stealth +5, Survival +4
Damage Immunities poison
Condition Immunities poisoned
Senses passive Perception 14
Languages Grung
Challenge 1 (200 XP)   **Proficiency Bonus** +2

Amphibious. The grung can breathe air and water.

Poisonous Skin. Any creature that grapples the grung or otherwise comes into direct contact with the grung's skin must succeed on a DC 12 Constitution saving throw or become poisoned for 1 minute. A poisoned creature no longer in direct contact with the grung can repeat the saving throw at the end of each of its turns, ending the effect on itself on a success.

Standing Leap. The grung's long jump is up to 25 feet and its high jump is up to 15 feet, with or without a running start.

Water Dependency. If the grung isn't immersed in water for at least 1 hour during a day, it suffers 1 level of exhaustion at the end of that day. The grung can recover from this exhaustion only through magic or by immersing itself in water for at least 1 hour.

Actions

Dagger. *Melee or Ranged Weapon Attack:* +5 to hit, reach 5 ft. or range 20/60 ft., one target. *Hit:* 5 (1d4 + 3) piercing damage plus 5 (2d4) poison damage.

Shortbow. *Ranged Weapon Attack:* +5 to hit, range 80/320 ft., one target. *Hit:* 6 (1d6 + 3) piercing damage plus 5 (2d4) poison damage.

Spellcasting. The grung casts one of the following spells, using Wisdom as the spellcasting ability (spell save DC 12):

At will: *druidcraft*
3/day each: *cure wounds*, *spike growth*
2/day: *plant growth*

Guard Drake

A guard drake is a reptilian creature created out of dragon scales by means of a bizarre and grisly ritual. When trained properly, a drake is obedient and territorial, which makes it an excellent watch beast that can follow simple commands.

Tiamat's cult practices the ritual to create guard drakes, as do other groups that are skilled in arcana and associated with Dragons. The ritual requires a chromatic dragon's aid; the dragon typically helps to reward its allies or worshipers with a valuable servant.

The ritual, which takes several days, requires 10 pounds of fresh dragon scales (donated by the dragon allied with the group), a large amount of fresh meat, and an iron cauldron. When the process is complete, a Small egg emerges from the cauldron and hatches within a few hours.

A newly hatched guard drake imprints upon the first creature that feeds it (usually the one planning to train it), establishing an aggressive but trusting bond with that individual. A guard drake is fully grown within two to three weeks and can be trained in the same length of time. It is the equivalent of a guard dog in terms of what it can be trained to do.

A guard drake resembles the type of dragon it was created from, but with a wingless, squat, muscular build. A drake can't reproduce, nor can its scales be used to make other guard drakes.

Variant: Chromatic Drakes

Each type of chromatic dragon's scales creates a guard drake that resembles a wingless, stunted version of that type of dragon, with unique abilities related to that type. Each has the special features described below.

Black Guard Drake. The drake can breathe air and water, has a swimming speed of 30 feet, and has resistance to acid damage.

Blue Guard Drake. The drake has a burrowing speed of 20 feet and resistance to lightning damage.

Green Guard Drake. The drake can breathe air and water, has a swimming speed of 30 feet, and has resistance to poison damage.

Red Guard Drake. The drake has climbing speed of 30 feet and resistance to fire damage.

White Guard Drake. The drake has a burrowing speed of 20 feet, a climbing speed of 30 feet, and resistance to cold damage.

Guard Drake
Medium Dragon, Unaligned

Armor Class 14 (natural armor)
Hit Points 52 (7d8 + 21)
Speed 30 ft.

STR	DEX	CON	INT	WIS	CHA
16 (+3)	11 (+0)	16 (+3)	4 (−3)	10 (+0)	7 (−2)

Skills Perception +2
Senses darkvision 60 ft., passive Perception 12
Languages understands Draconic but can't speak
Challenge 2 (450 XP)   **Proficiency Bonus** +2

Actions

Multiattack. The guard drake makes one Bite attack and one Tail attack.

Bite. *Melee Weapon Attack:* +5 to hit, reach 5 ft., one target. *Hit:* 7 (1d8 + 3) piercing damage.

Tail. *Melee Weapon Attack:* +5 to hit, reach 5 ft., one target. *Hit:* 6 (1d6 + 3) bludgeoning damage.

HELLFIRE ENGINE

Hellfire engines are semiautonomous bringers of destruction. Amnizus (in this book) and other devilish generals hold them in reserve until they are needed to repel an incursion by demons or crusading mortals, but occasionally one of these magical-mechanical hybrids gets loose, driven berserk by its need to destroy.

Hellfire engines take many forms, but all of them have one purpose: to mow down foes in waves. They are incapable of subtlety or trickery, but their destructive capability is immense.

Mortal creatures slain by hellfire engines are doomed to join the infernal legions in mere hours unless powerful magic-wielders intervene on their behalf. The archdukes of the Nine Hells would like nothing better than to modify this magic so it works against demons, too, but that discovery has eluded them so far.

HELLFIRE ENGINE
Huge Construct, Typically Lawful Evil

Armor Class 18 (natural armor)
Hit Points 216 (16d12 + 112)
Speed 40 ft.

STR	DEX	CON	INT	WIS	CHA
20 (+5)	16 (+3)	24 (+7)	2 (−4)	10 (+0)	1 (−5)

Saving Throws Dex +8, Wis +5, Cha +0
Damage Resistances cold, psychic; bludgeoning, piercing, and slashing from nonmagical attacks that aren't silvered
Damage Immunities fire, poison
Condition Immunities charmed, deafened, exhaustion, frightened, paralyzed, poisoned, unconscious
Senses darkvision 120 ft., passive Perception 10
Languages understands Infernal but can't speak
Challenge 16 (15,000 XP)   **Proficiency Bonus** +5

Immutable Form. The hellfire engine is immune to any spell or effect that would alter its form.

Magic Resistance. The hellfire engine has advantage on saving throws against spells and other magical effects.

Unusual Nature. The hellfire engine doesn't require air, food, drink, or sleep.

ACTIONS

Flesh-Crushing Stride. The hellfire engine moves up to its speed in a straight line. During this move, it can enter Large or smaller creatures' spaces. A creature whose space the hellfire engine enters must make a DC 18 Dexterity saving throw. On a successful save, the creature is pushed to the nearest space out of the hellfire engine's path. On a failed save, the creature falls prone and takes 28 (8d6) bludgeoning damage.

If the hellfire engine remains in the prone creature's space, the creature is also restrained until it's no longer in the same space as the hellfire engine. While restrained in this way, the creature, or another creature within 5 feet of it, can make a DC 18 Strength check. On a success, the creature is shunted to an unoccupied space of its choice within 5 feet of the hellfire engine and is no longer restrained.

Hellfire Weapons. The hellfire engine uses one of the following options (choose one or roll a d6):

1–2: Bonemelt Sprayer. The hellfire engine spews acidic flame in a 60-foot cone. Each creature in the cone must make a DC 20 Dexterity saving throw, taking 11 (2d10) fire damage plus 18 (4d8) acid damage on a failed save, or half as much damage on a successful one. Creatures that fail the saving throw are drenched in burning acid and take 5 (1d10) fire damage plus 9 (2d8) acid damage at the end of their turns. An affected creature or another creature within 5 feet of it can take an action to scrape off the burning fuel.

3–4: Lightning Flail. *Melee Weapon Attack:* +10 to hit, reach 15 ft., one creature. *Hit:* 18 (3d8 + 5) bludgeoning damage plus 22 (5d8) lightning damage. Up to three other creatures of the hellfire engine's choice that it can see within 30 feet of the target must each make a DC 20 Dexterity saving throw, taking 22 (5d8) lightning damage on a failed save, or half as much damage on a successful one.

5–6: Thunder Cannon. The hellfire engine targets a point within 120 feet of it that it can see. Each creature within 30 feet of that point must make a DC 20 Dexterity saving throw, taking 27 (5d10) bludgeoning damage plus 19 (3d12) thunder damage on a failed save, or half as much damage on a successful one.

If the chosen option kills a creature, the creature's soul rises from the River Styx as a lemure in Avernus in 1d4 hours. If the creature isn't revived before then, only a *wish* spell or killing the lemure and casting *true resurrection* on the creature's original body can restore it to life. Constructs and devils are immune to this effect.

Hobgoblin Devastator

Hobgoblins with a prodigious talent for magic sometimes undergo grueling training to become hobgoblin devastators. Devastators are spellcasters who call down fireballs and other destructive magic in the defense of the court they serve, whether that court is in the Feywild or the Material Plane. A hobgoblin devastator on the battlefield is a boon to their allies and a threat to every foe around them.

Far from being cloistered academics, hobgoblin devastators are masters of the battlefield. In addition to tactical applications of the magical arts, they learn the basics of weapon use, and they measure their deeds by the enemies defeated though their magic. They have the respect of other members of the host and receive obedience and deference from many quarters.

In the Feywild, many archfey seek to bolster their armies' might with the services of hobgoblin devastators.

GOBLINOIDS OF THE FEYWILD

The goblinoid peoples—goblins, hobgoblins, and bugbears—first appeared in the Feywild millennia ago, and they resided there until the god Maglubiyet conquered them. They then spread throughout the multiverse, with many of them ending up on the worlds of the Material Plane. Most goblinoids encountered on those worlds are members of families that have been away from the Feywild for centuries, and over time, those lineages have become Humanoid. Fey goblinoids, who still bear the magic of the Feywild, are rare on the Material Plane but not unheard of. Hobgoblin devastators are examples of such Fey folk, as are hobgoblin iron shadows and nilbogs (also in this book).

HOBGOBLIN DEVASTATOR
Medium Fey (Goblinoid), Typically Lawful Neutral

Armor Class 13 (studded leather)
Hit Points 45 (7d8 + 14)
Speed 30 ft.

STR	DEX	CON	INT	WIS	CHA
13 (+1)	12 (+1)	14 (+2)	16 (+3)	13 (+1)	11 (+0)

Skills Arcana +5
Senses darkvision 60 ft., passive Perception 11
Languages Common, Goblin
Challenge 4 (1,100 XP) **Proficiency Bonus** +2

Army Arcana. When the hobgoblin casts a spell that causes damage or that forces other creatures to make a saving throw, it can choose itself and any number of allies to be immune to the damage caused by the spell and to succeed on the required saving throw.

ACTIONS

Multiattack. The hobgoblin makes two Quarterstaff or Devastating Bolt attacks.

Quarterstaff. *Melee Weapon Attack:* +3 to hit, reach 5 ft., one target. *Hit:* 4 (1d6 + 1) bludgeoning damage, or 5 (1d8 + 1) bludgeoning damage if used with two hands, plus 13 (3d8) force damage.

Devastating Bolt. *Ranged Spell Attack:* +5 to hit, range 60 ft., one target. *Hit:* 21 (4d8 + 3) force damage, and the target is knocked prone.

Spellcasting. The hobgoblin casts one of the following spells, using Intelligence as the spellcasting ability (spell save DC 13):

At will: *mage hand, prestidigitation*
2/day each: *fireball, fly, fog cloud, gust of wind, lightning bolt*

ERIC BELISLE

HOBGOBLIN IRON SHADOW

Iron shadows are hobgoblin martial artists who serve fey and mortal courts as secret police, scouts, and assassins. They spy to ferret out treachery, rebellion, and betrayal and deal with it ruthlessly. Iron shadows possess agility and stamina matched only by their ironclad commitment to the will of their masters. They wield a deadly combination of unarmed fighting techniques and shadow magic to deceive and defeat their foes. While on secret missions, they wear masks crafted to resemble monsters, both to conceal their identities and to strike fear into their foes.

An iron shadow is usually recruited from the ranks of the Feywild's hobgoblin armies or from among the hobgoblins who have resided in the Material Plane for centuries. A candidate for admission undergoes a series of tests designed to reveal any potential for treachery. Those who fail are slain, while those who pass receive secret training in the arts of magic and stealth. This indoctrination is a slow and arduous process; many aspirants don't finish it, and years might go by during which the iron shadows welcome no new members into their ranks. When a recruit's training is complete, they are tasked with conducting assassinations and spy missions.

HOBGOBLIN IRON SHADOW
Medium Fey (Goblinoid), Typically Lawful Neutral

Armor Class 15 (Unarmored Defense)
Hit Points 32 (5d8 + 10)
Speed 40 ft.

STR	DEX	CON	INT	WIS	CHA
14 (+2)	16 (+3)	15 (+2)	14 (+2)	15 (+2)	11 (+0)

Skills Acrobatics +5, Athletics +4, Stealth +5
Senses darkvision 60 ft., passive Perception 12
Languages Common, Goblin
Challenge 2 (450 XP)   **Proficiency Bonus** +2

Unarmored Defense. While the hobgoblin is wearing no armor and wielding no shield, its AC includes its Wisdom modifier.

ACTIONS

Multiattack. The hobgoblin makes four attacks, each of which can be an Unarmed Strike or a Dart attack. It can also use Shadow Jaunt once, either before or after one of the attacks.

Unarmed Strike. *Melee Weapon Attack:* +5 to hit, reach 5 ft., one target. *Hit:* 5 (1d4 + 3) bludgeoning damage.

Dart. *Ranged Weapon Attack.* +5 to hit, range 20/60 ft., one target. *Hit:* 5 (1d4 + 3) piercing damage.

Shadow Jaunt. The hobgoblin teleports, along with any equipment it is wearing or carrying, up to 30 feet to an unoccupied space it can see. Both the space it leaves and its destination must be in dim light or darkness.

Spellcasting. The hobgoblin casts one of the following spells, using Intelligence as the spellcasting ability (spell save DC 12):

At will: *minor illusion, prestidigitation*
1/day each: *charm person, disguise self, silent image*

Why does the howler sing? Doing so causes its prey to flee, and surely stealth would make for better hunting in howling Pandemonium. There is only one answer: the creature can taste fear.

—Mordenkainen

HOWLER

A far-off wail precedes the sight of a howler. Even at a distance, listeners' minds cringe at the sound and fill with horror at the realization that the noise is drawing closer. When howlers go on the prowl, courage isn't enough to stand up against them.

These nightmare creatures are native to Pandemonium, but they can be found on most of the Lower Planes, where they are trained as war hounds. Howlers can be domesticated, after a fashion, but they respond only to brutal training in which they are forced to recognize the trainer as the pack's undisputed leader. A trained pack then follows its leader without hesitation. Howler packs course over the battlefields of the Blood War and also serve evil mortals powerful and vicious enough to command their loyalty.

Howlers rely on speed, numbers, and their mind-numbing howling to corner prey before they tear it apart. Their howls flood the minds of their victims, making complex thought impossible. Listeners can do little more than stare in horror and stumble around the battlefield in a search for safety. Fiends especially prize howlers for this reason, because for a few crucial moments in a battle, their howls can neutralize an enemy.

HOWLER
Large Fiend, Typically Chaotic Evil

Armor Class 16 (natural armor)
Hit Points 90 (12d10 + 24)
Speed 40 ft.

STR	DEX	CON	INT	WIS	CHA
17 (+3)	16 (+3)	15 (+2)	5 (−3)	14 (+2)	6 (−2)

Skills Perception +5
Damage Resistances cold, fire, lightning; bludgeoning, piercing, and slashing from nonmagical attacks
Condition Immunities frightened
Senses darkvision 60 ft., passive Perception 15
Languages understands Abyssal but can't speak
Challenge 8 (3,900 XP)   **Proficiency Bonus** +3

Pack Tactics. A howler has advantage on attack rolls against a creature if at least one of the howler's allies is within 5 feet of the creature and the ally isn't incapacitated.

ACTIONS

Multiattack. The howler makes two Rending Bite attacks.

Rending Bite. *Melee Weapon Attack:* +6 to hit, reach 5 ft., one target. *Hit:* 10 (2d6 + 3) piercing damage, plus 22 (4d10) psychic damage if the target is frightened. This attack ignores damage resistance.

Mind-Breaking Howl (Recharge 4–6). The howler emits a keening howl in a 60-foot cone. Each creature in that area must succeed on a DC 13 Wisdom saving throw or take 16 (3d10) psychic damage and be frightened until the end of the howler's next turn. While a creature is frightened in this way, its speed is halved, and it is incapacitated. A target that successfully saves is immune to the Mind-Breaking Howl of all howlers for the next 24 hours.

BRYNN METHENEY

H

Hutijin

Politics in the Nine Hells are anything but predictable. Alliances form all the time, but most wind up unraveling due to treachery. Nevertheless, for all their backbiting and betrayal, devils do occasionally display loyalty, offering unwavering service to their masters. One such example is Hutijin, a duke of Cania and loyal servant of Mephistopheles.

Across the Hells, Hutijin's name fills lesser devils with fear and loathing, for this duke commands two companies of pit fiends (see the *Monster Manual*). With such soldiers under his command, Hutijin can easily crush any rival who gets in his way while also defending Mephistopheles against armies seeking to contest his dominion. Hutijin has amassed enough power to challenge the lord of Cania, but he has never wavered in his support for his master—suggesting, perhaps, that Mephistopheles has some hold over him.

Outside the Nine Hells, Hutijin is a relatively obscure figure, known only to the most learned infernal scholars. He has no cults of his own, and his servants are few in number. The reason is simple: Hutijin hates mortals. When summoned from the Hells, he repays the instigator with a long and agonizing death.

Mephistopheles forbids Hutijin from making too many forays into the Material Plane, since the duke's absence leaves him vulnerable to his rivals. Other archdevils know how much Hutijin despises mortals and have secretly disseminated the means to call him from the Nine Hells in the hope of distracting the archdevil long enough for them to assail Mephistopheles. Hutijin sends devils into the Material Plane to eradicate mention of his name and destroy those who have learned of him, but the summonings still occur. When called from his post, he negotiates as quickly as he can, usually closing a deal with little cost to the summoner. However, once the deal has been fulfilled, Hutijin repays the interruption with death.

HUTIJIN

Large Fiend (Devil), Lawful Evil

Armor Class 19 (natural armor)
Hit Points 200 (16d10 + 112)
Speed 30 ft., fly 60 ft.

STR	DEX	CON	INT	WIS	CHA
27 (+8)	15 (+2)	25 (+7)	23 (+6)	19 (+4)	25 (+7)

Saving Throws Dex +9, Con +14, Wis +11
Skills Intimidation +14, Perception +11
Damage Resistances cold; bludgeoning, piercing, and slashing from nonmagical attacks that aren't silvered
Damage Immunities fire, poison
Condition Immunities charmed, exhaustion, frightened, poisoned
Senses truesight 120 ft., passive Perception 21
Languages all, telepathy 120 ft.
Challenge 21 (33,000 XP)   **Proficiency Bonus** +7

Infernal Despair. Each creature within 30 feet of Hutijin that isn't a devil makes saving throws with disadvantage.

Legendary Resistance (3/Day). If Hutijin fails a saving throw, he can choose to succeed instead.

Magic Resistance. Hutijin has advantage on saving throws against spells and other magical effects.

Regeneration. Hutijin regains 20 hit points at the start of his turn. If he takes radiant damage, this trait doesn't function at the start of his next turn. Hutijin dies only if he starts his turn with 0 hit points and doesn't regenerate.

ACTIONS

Multiattack. Hutijin makes one Bite attack, one Claw attack, one Mace attack, and one Tail attack.

Bite. *Melee Weapon Attack:* +15 to hit, reach 5 ft., one target. *Hit:* 15 (2d6 + 8) fire damage. The target must succeed on a DC 22 Constitution saving throw or become poisoned. While poisoned in this way, the target can't regain hit points, and it takes 10 (3d6) poison damage at the start of each of its turns. The poisoned target can repeat the saving throw at the end of each of its turns, ending the effect on itself on a success.

Claw. *Melee Weapon Attack:* +15 to hit, reach 10 ft., one target. *Hit:* 17 (2d8 + 8) cold damage.

Mace. *Melee Weapon Attack:* +15 to hit, reach 5 ft., one target. *Hit:* 15 (2d6 + 8) force damage.

Tail. *Melee Weapon Attack:* +15 to hit, reach 10 ft., one target. *Hit:* 19 (2d10 + 8) thunder damage.

Spellcasting. Hutijin casts one of the following spells, requiring no material components and using Charisma as the spellcasting ability (spell save DC 22):

At will: *alter self* (can become Medium when changing his appearance), *detect magic*, *hold monster*, *invisibility* (self only), *lightning bolt*, *suggestion*, *wall of fire*
3/day: *dispel magic*

Teleport. Hutijin teleports, along with any equipment he is wearing and carrying, up to 120 feet to an unoccupied space he can see.

REACTIONS

Fearful Voice (Recharge 5–6). In response to taking damage, Hutijin utters a dreadful word of power. Each creature within 30 feet of him that isn't a devil must succeed on a DC 22 Wisdom saving throw or become frightened of him for 1 minute. A creature can repeat the saving throw at the end of each of its turns, ending the effect on itself on a success. A creature that saves against this effect is immune to his Fearful Voice for 24 hours.

LEGENDARY ACTIONS

Hutijin can take 3 legendary actions, choosing from the options below. Only one legendary action option can be used at a time and only at the end of another creature's turn. Hutijin regains spent legendary actions at the start of his turn.

Attack. Hutijin makes one Claw, Mace, or Tail attack.
Teleport. Hutijin uses Teleport.
Lightning Storm (Costs 2 Actions). Hutijin releases lightning in a 30-foot radius, blocked only by total cover. All other creatures in that area must each make a DC 22 Dexterity saving throw, taking 18 (4d8) lightning damage on a failed save, or half as much damage on a successful one.

Hydroloth

Like the thought-stealing waters of the River Styx they inhabit, hydroloths filch the memories of creatures they attack, stealing away thoughts for delivery to whatever master they happen to serve. Hydroloths also savor finding lost things, especially those that have been swallowed up in the deeps.

For amphibious assaults or underwater conflicts, hydroloths have no equal among yugoloths. They sometimes hire themselves out to attack and scuttle ships and raid coastal settlements.

Hydroloth

Medium Fiend (Yugoloth), Typically Neutral Evil

Armor Class 15
Hit Points 135 (18d8 + 54)
Speed 20 ft., swim 40 ft.

STR	DEX	CON	INT	WIS	CHA
12 (+1)	21 (+5)	16 (+3)	19 (+4)	10 (+0)	14 (+2)

Skills Insight +4, Perception +4
Damage Vulnerabilities fire
Damage Resistances cold, lightning; bludgeoning, piercing, and slashing from nonmagical attacks
Damage Immunities acid, poison
Condition Immunities poisoned
Senses blindsight 60 ft., darkvision 60 ft., passive Perception 14
Languages Abyssal, Infernal, telepathy 60 ft.
Challenge 9 (5,000 XP)   **Proficiency Bonus** +4

Amphibious. The hydroloth can breathe air and water.

Magic Resistance. The hydroloth has advantage on saving throws against spells and other magical effects.

Secure Memory. The hydroloth is immune to the waters of the River Styx, as well as any effect that would steal or modify its memories or detect or read its thoughts.

Watery Advantage. While submerged in liquid, the hydroloth has advantage on attack rolls.

Actions

Multiattack. The hydroloth makes two Bite or Claw attacks. It can replace one attack with a use of Spellcasting.

Bite. *Melee Weapon Attack:* +9 to hit, reach 5 ft., one target. *Hit:* 16 (2d10 + 5) force damage plus 9 (2d10) psychic damage.

Claw. *Melee Weapon Attack:* +9 to hit, reach 5 ft., one target. *Hit:* 14 (2d8 + 5) force damage plus 9 (2d10) psychic damage.

Spellcasting. The hydroloth casts one of the following spells, requiring no material components and using Intelligence as the spellcasting ability (spell save DC 16):

At will: *darkness, detect magic, dispel magic, invisibility* (self only)
3/day each: *control water, crown of madness, fear, suggestion*

Steal Memory (1/Day). The hydroloth targets one creature it can see within 60 feet of it. The target takes 14 (4d6) psychic damage, and it must make a DC 16 Intelligence saving throw. On a successful save, the target becomes immune to this hydroloth's Steal Memory for 24 hours. On a failed save, the target loses all proficiencies; it can't cast spells; it can't understand language; and if its Intelligence and Charisma scores are higher than 5, they become 5. Each time the target finishes a long rest, it can repeat the saving throw, ending the effect on itself on a success. A *greater restoration* or *remove curse* spell cast on the target ends this effect early.

Teleport. The hydroloth teleports, along with any equipment it is wearing or carrying, up to 60 feet to an unoccupied space it can see.

JUIBLEX

Called the Faceless Lord and the Oozing Hunger
in ancient grimoires, Juiblex is demon lord of slime
and ooze, a noxious creature that doesn't care about
the plots and schemes of others of its kind. It exists
only to consume, digesting and transforming living
matter into more of itself.

A true horror, Juiblex is a mass of bubbling slime,
swirling black and green, with glaring red eyes
floating and shifting within it. It can rise up like a
20-foot hill, lashing out with dripping pseudopods
to drag victims into its bulk. Those consumed by
Juiblex are obliterated.

JUIBLEX'S LAIR

Juiblex's principal lair is known as the Slime Pits, a
realm that Juiblex shares with Zuggtmoy (who also
appears in this book). This layer of the Abyss, which
is also known as Shedaklah, is a bubbling morass
of fetid sludge. The landscape is covered in vast ex-
panses of caustic slimes, and strange organic forms
rise from the oceans of ooze at Juiblex's command.

Juiblex's challenge rating is 24 (62,000 XP) when
encountered in its lair.

LAIR ACTIONS

On initiative count 20 (losing initiative ties), Juiblex
can take one of the following lair actions; it can't
take the same lair action two rounds in a row:

Green Slime. A green slime (see the *Dungeon Master's Guide*) appears on a spot on the ceiling that
Juiblex chooses within the lair. The slime disinte-
grates after 1 hour.

Slippery Slime. Juiblex slimes a square area of
ground it can see within the lair. The area can be
up to 10 feet on a side. When the slime appears,
each creature on it must succeed on a DC 21
Dexterity saving throw or fall prone and slide 10
feet in a random direction determined by a d8 roll.
When a creature enters the area for the first time
on a turn or ends its turn there, that creature must
make the same save.

The slime lasts for 1 hour or until it is burned
away with fire. If the slime is set on fire, it burns
away after 1 round. Any creature that starts
its turn in the burning slime takes 22 (4d10)
fire damage.

Sticky Slime. Juiblex slimes a square area of
ground it can see within the lair. The area can be
up to 10 feet on a side. When the slime appears,
each creature in that area must succeed on a DC
21 Strength saving throw or become restrained.
When a creature enters the area for the first time
on a turn or ends its turn there, that creature must
make the same save.

A restrained creature is stuck as long as it remains in the slimy area or until it breaks free. The restrained creature, or another creature that can reach it, can use its action to try to break free and must succeed on a DC 21 Strength check.

The slime lasts for 1 hour or until it is burned away with fire. If the slime is set on fire, it burns away after 1 round. Any creature that starts its turn in the burning slime takes 22 (4d10) fire damage.

REGIONAL EFFECTS

The region containing Juiblex's lair is warped by its magic, creating one or more of the following effects:

Acidic Water. Small bodies of water, such as ponds or wells, within 1 mile of the lair turn highly acidic, corroding any object that touches them.

Corrupted Nature. Within 6 miles of the lair, all Wisdom (Medicine) and Wisdom (Survival) checks have disadvantage.

Slime. Surfaces within 6 miles of the lair are frequently covered by a thin film of slime, which is slick and sticks to anything that touches it.

If Juiblex dies, these effects fade over the course of 1d10 days.

CULTISTS OF JUIBLEX

The Faceless Lord grants its cultists special abilities. Lesser followers can gain the Liquid Movement trait. The most dedicated devotees of ooze can also gain the Slimy Organs trait.

Liquid Movement. As an action, this creature can move up to 20 feet through spaces no more than an inch in diameter. It must end this movement in a space that can accommodate its full size. Otherwise, it takes 5 force damage and returns to the space where it began this movement.

Slimy Organs. This creature has resistance to bludgeoning, piercing, and slashing damage from nonmagical attacks.

Whenever this creature suffers a critical hit or is reduced to 0 hit points, it sprays acid; each creature within 5 feet of it takes acid damage equal to its number of Hit Dice.

JUIBLEX
Huge Fiend (Demon), Chaotic Evil

Armor Class 18 (natural armor)
Hit Points 350 (28d12 + 168)
Speed 30 ft., climb 30 ft.

STR	DEX	CON	INT	WIS	CHA
24 (+7)	10 (+0)	23 (+6)	20 (+5)	20 (+5)	16 (+3)

Saving Throws Dex +7, Con +13, Wis +12
Skills Perception +12
Damage Resistances cold, fire, lightning
Damage Immunities acid, poison; bludgeoning, piercing, and slashing that is nonmagical
Condition Immunities blinded, charmed, deafened, exhaustion, frightened, grappled, paralyzed, petrified, poisoned, prone, restrained, stunned, unconscious
Senses truesight 120 ft., passive Perception 22
Languages all, telepathy 120 ft.
Challenge 23 (50,000 XP)   **Proficiency Bonus** +7

Foul. Any creature other than an Ooze that starts its turn within 10 feet of Juiblex must succeed on a DC 21 Constitution saving throw or be poisoned until the start of the creature's next turn.

Legendary Resistance (3/Day). If Juiblex fails a saving throw, it can choose to succeed instead.

Magic Resistance. Juiblex has advantage on saving throws against spells and other magical effects.

Regeneration. Juiblex regains 20 hit points at the start of its turn. If it takes fire or radiant damage, this trait doesn't function at the start of its next turn. Juiblex dies only if it starts its turn with 0 hit points and doesn't regenerate.

Spider Climb. Juiblex can climb difficult surfaces, including upside down on ceilings, without needing to make an ability check.

ACTIONS

Multiattack. Juiblex makes three Acid Lash attacks.

Acid Lash. *Melee or Ranged Weapon Attack:* +14 to hit, reach 10 ft. or range 60/120 ft., one target. *Hit:* 21 (4d6 + 7) acid damage. Any creature killed by this attack is drawn into Juiblex's body, where the corpse is dissolved after 1 minute.

Eject Slime (Recharge 5–6). Juiblex spews out a corrosive slime, targeting one creature that it can see within 60 feet of it. The target must succeed on a DC 21 Dexterity saving throw or take 55 (10d10) acid damage. Unless the target avoids taking all of this damage, any metal armor worn by the target takes a permanent –1 penalty to the AC it offers, and any metal weapon the target is carrying or wearing takes a permanent –1 penalty to damage rolls. The penalty worsens each time a target is subjected to this effect. If the penalty on an object drops to –5, the object is destroyed. The penalty on an object can be removed by the *mending* spell.

Spellcasting. Juiblex casts one of the following spells, requiring no material components and using Wisdom as the spellcasting ability (spell save DC 20):

At will: *detect magic*
3/day each: *contagion, gaseous form*

LEGENDARY ACTIONS

Juiblex can take 3 legendary actions, choosing from the options below. Only one legendary action option can be used at a time and only at the end of another creature's turn. Juiblex regains spent legendary actions at the start of its turn.

Attack. Juiblex makes one Acid Lash attack.

Corrupting Touch (Costs 2 Actions). *Melee Weapon Attack:* +14 to hit, reach 10 ft., one creature. *Hit:* 21 (4d6 + 7) poison damage, and the target is slimed. Until the slime is scraped off with an action, the target is poisoned, and any creature, other than an Ooze, is poisoned while within 10 feet of the target.

Ki-rin

Ki-rins are noble, celestial creatures. In the Outer Planes, ki-rins in service to benevolent deities take a direct role in the eternal struggle between good and evil. In the mortal world, ki-rins are celebrated far and wide as harbingers of destiny, guardians of the sacred, and counterbalances to the forces of evil.

Ki-rins are an embodiment of good, and simply beholding one can evoke fear or awe in an observer. A typical ki-rin looks like a muscular stag, covered in golden scales lined in some places with golden fur. It has a long mane and tail, coppery cloven hooves, and a spiral-shaped coppery horn just above and between its luminous violet eyes. In a breeze or when aloft, the creature's scales and hair appear to blaze with a holy, golden fire.

Beyond their coloration, ki-rins vary in appearance based on the deity each one reveres and the function each typically performs in service to that god. Some resemble gigantic unicorns; these are often used as guardians. Others have draconic features and tend to be aggressive foes of evil. Having one horn is most common, but a particularly fierce ki-rin might have two horns or a set of antlers like those of a great stag.

In many lands, common folk view ki-rins as heralds of good fortune. They consider seeing a ki-rin fly overhead a blessing and events that happen on such a day especially auspicious. If a ki-rin alights during a ceremony such as a birth announcement or a coronation, everyone present understands that the creature is telling them the person so honored could become a great force for good. Ki-rins have also been known to appear at the sites of great battles to inspire and strengthen the side of good or to rescue heroes from certain death.

Ki-rins are attracted to the worship of deities of courage, loyalty, selflessness, and truth, as well as to the advancement of just societies. For instance, in the Forgotten Realms, ki-rins rally mostly to Torm, although they also serve his allies Tyr and Ilmater. Ki-rins that serve good deities go wherever they are commanded; a ki-rin from an Upper Plane might venture to the Material Plane on a mission, usually as a scout, a messenger, or a spy. A ki-rin living on the Material Plane claims a territory to watch over, and one ki-rin might safeguard an area that encompasses several nations.

Lair of Luxury

On the celestial planes, ki-rins reside in lofty, elegant aeries filled with luxurious objects. On the Material Plane, a ki-rin chooses a similar location for its lair, such as atop a tall pinnacle or within a cloud solidified by the ki-rin's magic. The chosen location

is almost always hard to reach, and only those mortals who have the tenacity to complete the daunting journey to a ki-rin's lair can prove themselves worthy of speaking with its occupant. Many of those who do end up pledging service to the creature. They study under its tutelage in its lair and serve as its agents in the world. These followers might travel incognito across the land, seeking news of growing evil and working behind the scenes, or they might be champions of their master's cause, out to defeat villainy wherever it is found.

When viewed from the outside, a ki-rin's lair is indistinguishable from a natural site, and the entrance is difficult for visitors to find and reach. Inside, the lair is a serene and comfortable place, its ambiance a mix between palace and temple. If the ki-rin has taken creatures into its service, its lair doubles as a sacred site wherein the ki-rin not only rests but also teaches of holy mysteries.

Lair Actions

On initiative count 20 (losing initiative ties), a ki-rin can take one of the following lair actions, and it must finish a long rest before taking the chosen lair action again:

Create Comforts. The ki-rin conjures up one or more permanent objects made of soft, plant-based material—including manufactured objects like pillows, rope, blankets, and clothing—that can collectively fill no more than a 20-foot cube. The objects materialize 1 minute later in unoccupied spaces of the ki-rin's choice on the floor of the lair.

Create Stone and Metal. The ki-rin conjures up one or more temporary objects made of stone or metal that can collectively fill no more than a 2-foot cube. The objects materialize 1 minute later in unoccupied spaces of the ki-rin's choice on the floor of the lair, and the objects vanish after 1 hour.

Create Wood. The ki-rin conjures up one or more permanent objects made of wood, or similarly hard plant-based material, that can collectively fill no more than a 10-foot cube. The objects materialize 1 minute later in unoccupied spaces of the ki-rin's choice on the floor of the lair.

Regional Effects

A ki-rin's Celestial nature transforms the region around its lair. Any of the following magical effects is possible for travelers to encounter in the vicinity:

Blessed Nature. Beasts, Plants, and Celestials within 3 miles of the ki-rin's lair grow more vigorous as they evolve toward an idealized form. Such creatures are rarely aggressive toward others that aren't normally prey.

Controlled Weather. A ki-rin can cast *control weather* while it is within 3 miles of its lair. The spell's point of origin is always the point outdoors closest to the center of its lair. The ki-rin doesn't need to maintain a clear path to the sky or to concentrate for the change in weather to persist.

Pure Waters. Water flows pure within 3 miles of a ki-rin's lair. Any purposeful corruption of the water lasts for no longer than 3 minutes.

Realm of Respite. Curses, diseases, and poisons on creatures are suppressed when those creatures are within 3 miles of the lair, unless the creatures are Aberrations, Fiends, or Undead.

Safe Descents. Within 3 miles of the lair, winds buoy creatures that fall due to no act of the ki-rin or its allies. Such creatures descend at a rate of 60 feet per round and take no falling damage. Aberrations, Fiends, and Undead don't gain this benefit, falling as normal.

When the ki-rin dies, all these effects disappear immediately, although the invigorating effect on flora and fauna remains for 3 years.

Ki-rin

Large Celestial, Typically Lawful Good

Armor Class 20 (natural armor)
Hit Points 153 (18d10 + 54)
Speed 60 ft., fly 120 ft. (hover)

STR	DEX	CON	INT	WIS	CHA
21 (+5)	16 (+3)	16 (+3)	19 (+4)	20 (+5)	20 (+5)

Skills Perception +9, Insight +9, Religion +8
Damage Immunities poison
Condition Immunities poisoned
Senses darkvision 120 ft., truesight 30 ft., passive Perception 19
Languages all, telepathy 120 ft.
Challenge 12 (8,400 XP)   **Proficiency Bonus** +4

Legendary Resistance (3/Day). If the ki-rin fails a saving throw, it can choose to succeed instead.

Magic Resistance. The ki-rin has advantage on saving throws against spells and other magical effects.

Actions

Multiattack. The ki-rin makes two Hoof attacks and one Horn attack, or it makes two Sacred Fire attacks.

Hoof. *Melee Weapon Attack:* +9 to hit, reach 15 ft., one target. *Hit:* 10 (2d4 + 5) force damage.

Horn. *Melee Weapon Attack:* +9 to hit, reach 5 ft., one target. *Hit:* 14 (2d8 + 5) radiant damage.

Sacred Fire. *Ranged Spell Attack:* +9 to hit, range 120 ft., one target. *Hit:* 18 (3d8 + 5) radiant damage.

Spellcasting. The ki-rin casts one of the following spells, requiring no material components and using Wisdom as the spellcasting ability (spell save DC 17):

At will: *light, major image* (6th-level version), *thaumaturgy*
3/day each: *cure wounds, dispel magic, lesser restoration, sending*
1/day each: *banishment, calm emotions, create food and water, greater restoration, plane shift, protection from evil and good, revivify, wind walk*

Legendary Actions

The ki-rin can take 3 legendary actions, choosing from the options below. Only one legendary action option can be used at a time and only at the end of another creature's turn. The ki-rin regains spent legendary actions at the start of its turn.

Move. The ki-rin moves up to half its speed without provoking opportunity attacks.

Smite. The ki-rin makes one Hoof, Horn, or Sacred Fire attack.

Believe it or not, I like kobolds. I find their oscillation between bravery and cowardice endlessly entertaining. In fact, I'd say kobolds are proof of the universe's most fundamental lesson: there is always something bigger than you.

—Mordenkainen

KOBOLD DRAGONSHIELD

Kobold dragonshields are champions of their people. Almost all dragonshields begin life as normal kobolds, then are chosen by a dragon and invested with power for the purpose of protecting the dragon's eggs, but once every few years a kobold hatches with an innate version of the dragonshield's abilities. In either case, a dragonshield is skilled at hand-to-hand combat and bears a shield made of dragon scales, as well as scars from desperate fights.

Dragonshields know they have a place of honor among those who venerate dragons, but—being kobolds at heart—most of them feel unworthy of their status and are desperate to prove themselves deserving of it. But they also have the ability to rally in the face of certain death, inspiring others to follow them into battle.

KOBOLD DRAGONSHIELD

Small Dragon, Any Alignment

Armor Class 15 (leather, shield)
Hit Points 44 (8d6 + 16)
Speed 20 ft.

STR	DEX	CON	INT	WIS	CHA
12 (+1)	15 (+2)	14 (+2)	8 (−1)	9 (−1)	10 (+0)

Skills Perception +1
Damage Resistances see Dragon's Resistance below
Senses darkvision 60 ft., passive Perception 11
Languages Common, Draconic
Challenge 1 (200 XP)   **Proficiency Bonus** +2

Dragon's Resistance. The kobold has resistance to a type of damage based on the color of dragon that invested it with power (choose or roll a d10): 1–2, acid (black or copper); 3–4, cold (silver or white); 5–6, fire (brass, gold, or red); 7–8, lightning (blue or bronze); 9–10, poison (green).

Heart of the Dragon. If the kobold is frightened or paralyzed by an effect that allows a saving throw, it can repeat the save at the start of its turn to end the effect on itself and all kobolds within 30 feet of it. Any kobold that benefits from this trait (including the dragonshield) has advantage on its next attack roll.

Pack Tactics. The kobold has advantage on an attack roll against a creature if at least one of the kobold's allies is within 5 feet of the creature and the ally isn't incapacitated.

Sunlight Sensitivity. While in sunlight, the kobold has disadvantage on attack rolls, as well as on Wisdom (Perception) checks that rely on sight.

ACTIONS

Multiattack. The kobold makes two Spear attacks.

Spear. *Melee or Ranged Weapon Attack:* +3 to hit, reach 5 ft. or range 20/60 ft., one target. *Hit:* 4 (1d6 + 1) piercing damage, or 5 (1d8 + 1) piercing damage if used with two hands to make a melee attack.

KOBOLD INVENTOR

A kobold inventor builds improvised weapons to gain an advantage in combat. These weapons last for only one or two attacks before they break and typically work only for the inventor, but they might be surprisingly effective in the meantime. The weapons don't have to be lethal—often one serves its purpose if it distracts, scares, or confuses a creature long enough for the inventor to kill that foe.

KOBOLD INVENTOR
Small Humanoid, Any Alignment

Armor Class 12
Hit Points 13 (3d6 + 3)
Speed 30 ft.

STR	DEX	CON	INT	WIS	CHA
7 (−2)	15 (+2)	12 (+1)	14 (+2)	10 (+0)	8 (−1)

Senses darkvision 60 ft., passive Perception 10
Languages Common, Draconic
Challenge 1/4 (50 XP)   **Proficiency Bonus** +2

Pack Tactics. The kobold has advantage on an attack roll against a creature if at least one of the kobold's allies is within 5 feet of the creature and the ally isn't incapacitated.

Sunlight Sensitivity. While in sunlight, the kobold has disadvantage on attack rolls, as well as on Wisdom (Perception) checks that rely on sight.

ACTIONS

Dagger. *Melee or Ranged Weapon Attack:* +4 to hit, reach 5 ft. or range 20/60 ft., one target. *Hit:* 4 (1d4 + 2) piercing damage.

Sling. *Ranged Weapon Attack:* +4 to hit, range 30/120 ft., one target. *Hit:* 4 (1d4 + 2) bludgeoning damage.

Weapon Invention. The kobold uses one of the following options (choose one or roll a d8); the kobold can use each one no more than once per day:

1: Acid. The kobold hurls a flask of acid. *Ranged Weapon Attack:* +4 to hit, range 5/20 ft., one target. *Hit:* 7 (2d6) acid damage.

2: Alchemist's Fire. The kobold throws a flask of alchemist's fire. *Ranged Weapon Attack:* +4 to hit, range 5/20 ft., one target. *Hit:* 2 (1d4) fire damage at the start of each of the target's turns. The target can end this damage by using its action to make a DC 10 Dexterity check to extinguish the flames.

3: Basket of Centipedes. The kobold throws a small basket into a 5-foot-square space within 20 feet of it. A **swarm of insects** (centipedes; see the *Monster Manual*) with 11 hit points emerges from the basket and rolls initiative. At the end of each of the swarm's turns, there's a 50 percent chance that the swarm disperses.

4: Green Slime Pot. The kobold throws a clay pot full of green slime at the target, and it breaks open on impact. *Ranged Weapon Attack:* +4 to hit, range 5/20 ft., one target. *Hit:* 5 (1d10) acid damage, and the target is covered in slime until a creature uses its action to scrape or wash the slime off. A target covered in the slime takes 5 (1d10) acid damage at the start of each of its turns.

5: Rot Grub Pot. The kobold throws a clay pot into a 5-foot-square space within 20 feet of it, and it breaks open on impact. A **swarm of rot grubs** (in this book) emerges from the shattered pot and remains a hazard in that square.

6: Scorpion on a Stick. The kobold makes a melee attack with a **scorpion** (see the *Monster Manual*) tied to the end of a 5-foot-long pole. *Melee Weapon Attack:* +4 to hit, reach 5 ft., one target. *Hit:* 1 piercing damage, and the target must make a DC 9 Constitution saving throw, taking 4 (1d8) poison damage on a failed save, or half as much damage on a successful one.

7: Skunk in a Cage. The kobold releases a skunk into an unoccupied space within 5 feet of it. The skunk has a walking speed of 20 feet, AC 10, 1 hit point, and no effective attacks. It rolls initiative and, on its turn, uses its action to spray musk at a random creature within 5 feet of it. The target must succeed on a DC 9 Constitution saving throw, or it retches and is incapacitated for 1 minute. The target can repeat the saving throw at the end of each of its turns, ending the effect on itself on a success. A creature that doesn't need to breathe or is immune to poison automatically succeeds on the saving throw. Once the skunk has sprayed its musk, it can't do so again until it finishes a short or long rest.

8: Wasp Nest in a Bag. The kobold throws a small bag into a 5-foot-square space within 20 feet of it. A **swarm of insects** (wasps; see the *Monster Manual*) with 11 hit points emerges from the bag and rolls initiative. At the end of each of the swarm's turns, there's a 50 percent chance that the swarm disperses.

CHRIS SEAMAN

KOBOLD SCALE SORCERER

Kobold scale sorcerers have an innate talent for arcane magic, making them highly valuable members of their communities. These sorcerers typically fill the role of advisor, and when threatened, a scale sorcerer lashes out with coloful magic.

A scale sorcerer who resides in or near a dragon's lair may serve as that dragon's diplomat and mouthpiece—anticipating the dragon's needs, issuing commands to others on the dragon's behalf, and reporting information back to the dragon. Such scale sorcerers often wear artificial wings, which are a sign of their draconic office. Scale sorcerers are just as awed by and respectful of dragons as others who venerate these mighty creatures, but they know that duty requires them not to fawn over their master at all times. They also understand that their frequent proximity to their dragon master means they would probably be the first to die if their master became angry or displeased, so they frantically maintain a balance between adoration and terror in their behavior toward their master.

KOBOLD SCALE SORCERER
Small Humanoid, Any Alignment

Armor Class 15 (natural armor)
Hit Points 27 (5d6 + 10)
Speed 30 ft.

STR	DEX	CON	INT	WIS	CHA
7 (−2)	15 (+2)	14 (+2)	10 (+0)	9 (−1)	14 (+2)

Skills Arcana +2, Medicine +1
Senses darkvision 60 ft., passive Perception 9
Languages Common, Draconic
Challenge 1 (200 XP)   **Proficiency Bonus** +2

Pack Tactics. The kobold has advantage on an attack roll against a creature if at least one of the kobold's allies is within 5 feet of the creature and the ally isn't incapacitated.

Sunlight Sensitivity. While in sunlight, the kobold has disadvantage on attack rolls, as well as on Wisdom (Perception) checks that rely on sight.

ACTIONS

Multiattack. The kobold makes two Dagger or Chromatic Bolt attacks. It can replace one attack with a use of Spellcasting.

Dagger. *Melee or Ranged Weapon Attack:* +4 to hit, reach 5 ft. or range 20/60 ft., one target. *Hit:* 4 (1d4 + 2) piercing damage.

Chromatic Bolt. *Ranged Spell Attack:* +4 to hit, range 60 feet, one target. *Hit:* 9 (2d6 + 2) of a type of the kobold's choice: acid, cold, fire, lightning, poison, or thunder.

Spellcasting. The kobold casts one of the following spells, requiring no material components and using Charisma as the spellcasting ability (spell save DC 12):

At will: *mage hand, prestidigitation*
2/day each: *charm person, fog cloud, levitate*

Korred

Korreds are unpredictable, secretive Fey with strong ties to earth and stone. Because of their magical hair and mystical understanding of minerals, they are sought after by treasure-hunting dwarves and others who desire wealth beneath the earth.

Korreds prefer to keep their own company but occasionally consort with creatures of elemental earth such as galeb duhr (see the *Monster Manual*). They often gather with other korreds to perform ceremonial dances, beating out rhythms on stone with their hooves and clubs. In the depths of the Material Plane, korreds typically flee from other creatures, but they become aggressive when they feel insulted or are annoyed by the sounds of mining.

Korreds can hurl boulders far larger than it seems they should be able to, shape stone as though it were clay, and swim through rock. They also gain supernatural strength just from standing on the ground.

Magical Hair

Korreds have hair all over their bodies, but the hair that grows from their heads is magical. When cut, it transforms into whatever material was used to cut it. Korreds use iron shears to cut lengths of this magical hair, then twist the strands together to create iron ropes that they can manipulate, animating them to bind or snake around creatures and objects. Korreds take great pride in their hair and equally great offense at anyone who attempts to cut it without permission.

KORRED

Small Fey, Typically Chaotic Neutral

Armor Class 17 (natural armor)
Hit Points 93 (11d6 + 55)
Speed 30 ft., burrow 30 ft.

STR	DEX	CON	INT	WIS	CHA
23 (+6)	14 (+2)	20 (+5)	10 (+0)	15 (+2)	9 (−1)

Skills Athletics +9, Perception +5, Stealth +5
Damage Resistances bludgeoning, piercing, and slashing from nonmagical attacks
Senses darkvision 120 ft., tremorsense 120 ft., passive Perception 15
Languages Dwarvish, Gnomish, Sylvan, Terran, Undercommon
Challenge 7 (2,900 XP)   **Proficiency Bonus** +3

Stone Camouflage. The korred has advantage on Dexterity (Stealth) checks made to hide in rocky terrain.

ACTIONS

Multiattack. The korred makes two Greatclub or Rock attacks.

Greatclub. *Melee Weapon Attack:* +9 to hit, reach 5 ft., one target. *Hit:* 10 (1d8 + 6) bludgeoning damage, or 19 (3d8 + 6) bludgeoning damage if the korred is on the ground.

Rock. *Ranged Weapon Attack:* +9 to hit, range 60/120 ft., one target. *Hit:* 10 (1d8 + 6) bludgeoning damage, or 19 (3d8 + 6) bludgeoning damage if the korred is on the ground.

Spellcasting. The korred casts one of the following spells, requiring no spell components and using Wisdom as the spellcasting ability (spell save DC 13):

At will: *commune with nature* (as an action), *meld into stone, stone shape*
1/day: *Otto's irresistible dance*

BONUS ACTIONS

Command Hair. The korred has at least one 50-foot-long rope woven out of its hair. The korred commands one such rope within 30 feet of it to move up to 20 feet and entangle a Large or smaller creature that the korred can see. The target must succeed on a DC 13 Dexterity saving throw or become grappled by the rope (escape DC 13). Until this grapple ends, the target is restrained. The korred can use a bonus action to release the target, which is also freed if the korred dies or becomes incapacitated.

A rope of korred hair has AC 20 and 20 hit points. It regains 1 hit point at the start of each of the korred's turns while the rope has at least 1 hit point and the korred is alive. If the rope drops to 0 hit points, it is destroyed.

KRAKEN PRIEST

A kraken can seem godlike to folk who have faced its fury. Those who mistake its might for divine power and those who seek to appease the monster through veneration are sometimes rewarded with power, to serve thereafter as kraken priests.

Every kraken priest undergoes a change in appearance that reflects the kraken's influence, although each one differs in how their reverence is displayed. One kraken priest might have ink-black eyes and a suckered tentacle for a tongue, while another has a featureless face and a body covered in eyes and mouths that dribble seawater. These horrific manifestations intensify when the kraken possesses its minion to utter dire pronouncements.

KRAKEN PRIEST
Medium Monstrosity, Typically Chaotic Evil

Armor Class 15 (natural armor)
Hit Points 75 (10d8 + 30)
Speed 30 ft., swim 30 ft.

STR	DEX	CON	INT	WIS	CHA
12 (+1)	10 (+0)	16 (+3)	10 (+0)	15 (+2)	14 (+2)

Skills Perception +5
Senses passive Perception 15
Languages any two languages
Challenge 5 (1,800 XP)   **Proficiency Bonus** +3

Amphibious. The priest can breathe air and water.

ACTIONS

Multiattack. The priest makes two Thunderous Touch or Thunderbolt attacks.

Thunderous Touch. *Melee Spell Attack:* +5 to hit, reach 5 ft., one target. *Hit:* 27 (5d10) thunder damage.

Thunderbolt. *Ranged Spell Attack:* +5 to hit, range 60 ft., one target. *Hit:* 11 (2d10) lightning damage plus 11 (2d10) thunder damage, and the target is knocked prone.

Spellcasting. The priest casts one of the following spells, requiring no material components and using Wisdom as the spellcasting ability (spell save DC 13):

At will: *command, create or destroy water*
3/day each: *control water, darkness, water breathing, water walk*
1/day: *Evard's black tentacles*

Voice of the Kraken (Recharges after a Short or Long Rest). A kraken speaks through the priest with a thunderous voice audible within 300 feet. Creatures of the priest's choice that can hear the kraken's words (which are spoken in Abyssal, Infernal, or Primordial) must succeed on a DC 14 Wisdom saving throw or be frightened of the priest for 1 minute. A frightened target can repeat the saving throw at the end of each of its turns, ending the effect on itself on a success.

Imagine a hive of ants the size of horses, but the ants are wearing armor.

—Mordenkainen

KRUTHIKS

Kruthiks are chitin-covered reptiles that hunt in packs and nest in sprawling subterranean warrens. They are attracted to sources of heat, such as dwarven forges and pools of molten lava, and carve out lairs as close to such locations as possible. As they burrow through the earth, they leave behind tunnels—evidence that is often the first clue to the nearby presence of a kruthik hive. Kruthiks also make use of preexisting underground chambers, incorporating them into their lairs when they can.

Kruthiks communicate with one another through a series of hisses and chittering noises. These sounds can often be heard in advance of a kruthik attack. Whenever their lair is invaded, kruthik guards send out an alarm by rapidly tapping the stone floor with their sharp legs.

In addition to having an acute sense of smell, kruthiks can see in the dark and can detect vibrations in the earth around them. They take the scent of their own dead as a warning and avoid areas where many other kruthiks have died. Slaying a sufficient number of kruthiks in one area might cause the remaining hive members to move elsewhere.

Although they can feed on carrion, kruthiks prefer live prey. They kill enemies by impaling them on their spiked limbs, then grind up the flesh and bones with mandibles strong enough to chew rock. When several kruthiks gang up on a single foe, they become frenzied and even more lethal.

Kruthiks abide the presence of Constructs, Elementals, Oozes, and Undead, and they use such creatures to help guard their hive. They are smart enough to barricade some tunnels and dig new ones that keep their neighbors away from their eggs.

YOUNG KRUTHIK

Kruthiks hatch from eggs laid by female adults. Each egg is about the size of an adult human's head and hatches within a month. Tiny kruthik hatchlings are harmless and rarely stray far from the nest. They feed primarily on offal and one another. Within a month, the survivors become young kruthiks large enough to hunt and defend themselves.

ZACK STELLA

YOUNG KRUTHIK
Small Monstrosity, Unaligned

Armor Class 16 (natural armor)
Hit Points 9 (2d6 + 2)
Speed 30 ft., burrow 10 ft., climb 30 ft.

STR	DEX	CON	INT	WIS	CHA
13 (+1)	16 (+3)	13 (+1)	4 (−3)	10 (+0)	6 (−2)

Skills Perception +4
Senses darkvision 30 ft., tremorsense 60 ft., passive Perception 14
Languages Kruthik
Challenge 1/8 (25 XP)   **Proficiency Bonus** +2

Pack Tactics. The kruthik has advantage on an attack roll against a creature if at least one of the kruthik's allies is within 5 feet of the creature and the ally isn't incapacitated.

Tunneler. The kruthik can burrow through solid rock at half its burrowing speed and leaves a 2½-foot-diameter tunnel in its wake.

ACTIONS

Stab. *Melee Weapon Attack:* +5 to hit, reach 5 ft., one target. *Hit:* 5 (1d4 + 3) piercing damage.

K

Other creatures that abide in hives serve a purpose in the natural world. Bees pollinate flowers. Termites make earth out of wood. Kruthiks, by contrast, slay societies.

—Mordenkainen

Adult Kruthik

It takes six months of steady eating for a young kruthik to reach adult size. The natural life span of an adult kruthik is roughly seven years.

Adult kruthiks grow spiky protrusions on their legs and can fling these dagger-sized spikes at enemies beyond the reach of their claws.

Kruthik Hive Lord

A hive lord rules each kruthik hive. When the hive lord dies, the surviving members of the hive abandon their lair and search for a new one. When a suitable location is found, the largest kruthik in the hive undergoes a metamorphosis, forming a cocoon around itself and emerging several weeks later as a hive lord—a bigger and smarter kruthik with the ability to spray digestive acid from its maw. The hive lord claims the largest chamber of the lair and keeps several adult kruthiks nearby as bodyguards.

Kruthik Hive Lord

Large Monstrosity, Unaligned

Armor Class 20 (natural armor)
Hit Points 102 (12d10 + 36)
Speed 40 ft., burrow 20 ft., climb 40 ft.

STR	DEX	CON	INT	WIS	CHA
19 (+4)	16 (+3)	17 (+3)	10 (+0)	14 (+2)	10 (+0)

Skills Perception +8
Senses darkvision 60 ft., tremorsense 60 ft., passive Perception 18
Languages Kruthik
Challenge 5 (1,800 XP)   **Proficiency Bonus** +3

Pack Tactics. The kruthik has advantage on an attack roll against a creature if at least one of the kruthik's allies is within 5 feet of the creature and the ally isn't incapacitated.

Tunneler. The kruthik can burrow through solid rock at half its burrowing speed and leaves a 10-foot-diameter tunnel in its wake.

Actions

Multiattack. The kruthik makes two Stab or Spike attacks.

Stab. *Melee Weapon Attack:* +7 to hit, reach 10 ft., one target. *Hit:* 9 (1d10 + 4) piercing damage.

Spike. *Ranged Weapon Attack:* +6 to hit, range 30/120 ft., one target. *Hit:* 7 (1d6 + 4) piercing damage.

Acid Spray (Recharge 5–6). The kruthik sprays acid in a 15-foot cone. Each creature in that area must make a DC 14 Dexterity saving throw, taking 22 (4d10) acid damage on a failed save, or half as much damage on a successful one.

Adult Kruthik

Medium Monstrosity, Unaligned

Armor Class 18 (natural armor)
Hit Points 39 (6d8 + 12)
Speed 40 ft., burrow 20 ft., climb 40 ft.

STR	DEX	CON	INT	WIS	CHA
15 (+2)	16 (+3)	15 (+2)	7 (–2)	12 (+1)	8 (–1)

Skills Perception +5
Senses darkvision 60 ft., tremorsense 60 ft., passive Perception 15
Languages Kruthik
Challenge 2 (450 XP)   **Proficiency Bonus** +2

Pack Tactics. The kruthik has advantage on an attack roll against a creature if at least one of the kruthik's allies is within 5 feet of the creature and the ally isn't incapacitated.

Tunneler. The kruthik can burrow through solid rock at half its burrowing speed and leaves a 5-foot-diameter tunnel in its wake.

Actions

Multiattack. The kruthik makes two Stab or Spike attacks.

Stab. *Melee Weapon Attack:* +5 to hit, reach 5 ft., one target. *Hit:* 6 (1d6 + 3) piercing damage.

Spike. *Ranged Weapon Attack:* +5 to hit, range 20/60 ft., one target. *Hit:* 5 (1d4 + 3) piercing damage.

LEUCROTTA

A leucrotta is what you would get if you took the head of a giant badger, the legs of a deer, and the body of a large hyena, then put them together and reanimated them with demon ichor without bothering to cover up the stink of death.

The first leucrottas came into being alongside some gnolls during the rampages of Yeenoghu (appears in this book) on the Material Plane. While many of the hyenas that ate Yeenoghu's kills transformed into gnolls, others underwent more bizarre changes; leucrottas were the most numerous of these.

As clever as it is cruel, a leucrotta loves to deceive, torture, and kill. Creatures who venerate Yeenoghu—particularly his gnoll followers—view leucrottas with great respect. Although a leucrotta is unlikely to lead a gnoll war band, it can influence the leader and might agree to carry the leader into battle and offer advice during the fight. Followers of Yeenoghu also see leucrottas as a form of entertainment. They enjoy watching a leucrotta work almost as much as they like doing their own killing, since leucrottas are meticulous in their cruelty and able to draw out kills for better and longer sport. And when there are no victims to be had, a leucrotta can mimic the delightful squeals of a suffering victim.

A leucrotta is so loathsome that few outside of its own kind can stand to be around one for long. Its horrific, hodgepodge body oozes a foul stench. This reek is outdone only by the creature's breath, which issues from a maw that drips fluid corrupted with rot and digestive juices. In place of fangs, a leucrotta has bony ridges as hard as steel that can crush bones and lacerate flesh. These plates are so tough that a leucrotta can use them to peel plate armor away from the body of a slain knight.

A leucrotta's stench would normally warn away prey long before the creature could attack. It has two natural capabilities, however, that give it an advantage. First, a leucrotta's tracks are nearly impossible to distinguish from those of common deer. Second, it can duplicate the call or the vocal expressions of just about any creature it has heard. The monster uses its mimicry to lure in potential victims, then attacks while they are confused or unaware of the actual threat.

LEUCROTTA
Large Monstrosity, Typically Chaotic Evil

Armor Class 14 (natural armor)
Hit Points 67 (9d10 + 18)
Speed 50 ft.

STR	DEX	CON	INT	WIS	CHA
18 (+4)	14 (+2)	15 (+2)	9 (−1)	12 (+1)	6 (−2)

Skills Deception +2, Perception +5
Senses darkvision 60 ft., passive Perception 15
Languages Abyssal, Gnoll
Challenge 3 (700 XP) **Proficiency Bonus** +2

Mimicry. The leucrotta can mimic Beast sounds and Humanoid voices. A creature that hears the sounds can tell they are imitations only with a successful DC 14 Wisdom (Insight) check.

Stench. Any creature other than a leucrotta or gnoll that starts its turn within 5 feet of the leucrotta must succeed on a DC 12 Constitution saving throw or be poisoned until the start of the creature's next turn. On a successful saving throw, the creature is immune to the Stench of all leucrottas for 1 hour.

ACTIONS

Multiattack. The leucrotta makes one Bite attack and one Hooves attack.

Bite. *Melee Weapon Attack:* +6 to hit, reach 5 ft., one target. *Hit:* 8 (1d8 + 4) piercing damage. If the leucrotta scores a critical hit, it rolls the damage dice three times, instead of twice.

Hooves. *Melee Weapon Attack:* +6 to hit, reach 5 ft., one target. *Hit:* 11 (2d6 + 4) bludgeoning damage.

BONUS ACTIONS

Kicking Retreat. Immediately after the leucrotta makes a Hooves attack, it takes the Disengage action.

BRYNN METHENEY

LEVIATHAN

A leviathan is an immense creature that acts as a force of nature, dragging ships down to the ocean's depths and washing away coastal settlements. When called forth, a leviathan arises from a large body of water and takes on the form of a gigantic serpent.

Usually found only on the Elemental Plane of Water, a leviathan sometimes swims through a portal to another world, where tritons, sea elves, and other aquatic folk attempt to contain it. Nihilistic cults have also been known to perform arduous rituals to summon a leviathan to a world, with the aim of using the creature to destroy coastal communities. Those cultists often consider it a blessing to drown themselves in the elemental's waters.

LEVIATHAN

Gargantuan Elemental, Typically Neutral

Armor Class 17
Hit Points 328 (16d20 + 160)
Speed 40 ft., swim 120 ft.

STR	DEX	CON	INT	WIS	CHA
27 (+8)	24 (+7)	30 (+10)	2 (−4)	18 (+4)	17 (+3)

Saving Throws Wis +10, Cha +9
Damage Resistances bludgeoning, piercing, and slashing from nonmagical attacks
Damage Immunities acid, poison
Condition Immunities exhaustion, grappled, paralyzed, petrified, poisoned, prone, restrained, stunned
Senses darkvision 60 ft., passive Perception 14
Languages —
Challenge 20 (25,000 XP)   **Proficiency Bonus** +6

Legendary Resistance (3/Day). If the leviathan fails a saving throw, it can choose to succeed instead.

Partial Freeze. If the leviathan takes 50 cold damage or more during a single turn, the leviathan partially freezes; until the end of its next turn, its speeds are reduced to 20 feet, and it makes attack rolls with disadvantage.

Siege Monster. The leviathan deals double damage to objects and structures.

Water Form. The leviathan can enter a hostile creature's space and stop there. It can move through a space as narrow as 1 inch wide without squeezing.

ACTIONS

Multiattack. The leviathan makes one Slam attack and one Tail attack.

Slam. *Melee Weapon Attack:* +14 to hit, reach 20 ft., one target. *Hit:* 21 (2d12 + 8) bludgeoning damage plus 13 (2d12) acid damage.

Tail. *Melee Weapon Attack:* +14 to hit, reach 20 ft., one target. *Hit:* 19 (2d10 + 8) bludgeoning damage plus 10 (3d6) acid damage.

Tidal Wave (Recharge 6). The leviathan magically creates a wave of water that extends from a point it can see within 120 feet of itself. The wave is up to 250 feet long, up to 250 feet tall, and up to 50 feet wide. Each creature in the wave must make a DC 24 Strength saving throw. On a failed save, a creature takes 45 (7d12) bludgeoning damage and is knocked prone. On a successful save, a creature takes half as much damage and isn't knocked prone. The water spreads out across the ground in all directions, extinguishing unprotected flames in its area and within 250 feet of it, and then it vanishes.

LEGENDARY ACTIONS

The leviathan can take 3 legendary actions, choosing from the options below. Only one legendary action option can be used at a time and only at the end of another creature's turn. The leviathan regains spent legendary actions at the start of its turn.

Move. The leviathan moves up to its speed.
Slam (Costs 2 Actions). The leviathan makes one Slam attack.

LARS GRANT-WEST

MARTIAL ARTS ADEPT
Medium Humanoid, Any Alignment

Armor Class 16 (Unarmored Defense)
Hit Points 60 (11d8 + 11)
Speed 40 ft.

STR	DEX	CON	INT	WIS	CHA
11 (+0)	17 (+3)	13 (+1)	11 (+0)	16 (+3)	10 (+0)

Skills Acrobatics +5, Insight +5, Stealth +5
Senses passive Perception 13
Languages any one language (usually Common)
Challenge 3 (700 XP)   **Proficiency Bonus** +2

Unarmored Defense. While the adept is wearing no armor and wielding no shield, its AC includes its Wisdom modifier.

ACTIONS

Multiattack. The adept makes three Unarmed Strike attacks or five Dart attacks.

Unarmed Strike. *Melee Weapon Attack:* +5 to hit, reach 5 ft., one target. *Hit:* 7 (1d8 + 3) bludgeoning damage. Once per turn, the adept can cause one of the following additional effects (choose one or roll a d4):

1–2: Knock Down. The target must succeed on a DC 13 Dexterity saving throw or be knocked prone.
3–4: Push. The target must succeed on a DC 13 Strength saving throw or be pushed up to 10 feet directly away from the adept.

Dart. *Ranged Weapon Attack:* +5 to hit, range 20/60 ft., one target. *Hit:* 5 (1d4 + 3) piercing damage.

REACTIONS

Deflect Missile. In response to being hit by a ranged weapon attack, the adept deflects the missile. The damage it takes from the attack is reduced by 1d10 + 3. If the damage is reduced to 0, the adept catches the missile if it's small enough to hold in one hand and the adept has a hand free.

MARTIAL ARTS ADEPT

Martial arts adepts are disciplined monks with extensive training in hand-to-hand combat. Some protect monasteries; others travel the world seeking enlightenment or new forms of combat to master. A few become bodyguards, trading their combat prowess and loyalty for food and lodging.

Some martial artists adorn themselves with tattoos to honor inspirations or instructors, or to memorialize profound lessons, triumphs, or defeats. You may roll on the Martial Arts Adept Tattoos table to determine what sort of tattoo an adept bears.

MARTIAL ARTS ADEPT TATTOOS

d8	Tattoo
1	Patterning on the arms that make them look as though they were made of marble or granite
2	Colorful dragon scales
3	Collage of playful Elemental or Fey creatures
4	Constellations on the palm of each hand
5	Passage from a fighting manual
6	Beautiful but poisonous flowers
7	Two couatls swirling around each other, rendered in metallic ink
8	Detailed landscape depicting natural beauty

BRYAN SOLA

MARUT

Large Construct (Inevitable), Typically Lawful Neutral

Armor Class 22 (natural armor)
Hit Points 432 (32d10 + 256)
Speed 40 ft., fly 30 ft. (hover)

STR	DEX	CON	INT	WIS	CHA
28 (+9)	12 (+1)	26 (+8)	19 (+4)	15 (+2)	18 (+4)

Saving Throws Int +12, Wis +10, Cha +12
Skills Insight +10, Intimidation +12, Perception +10
Damage Resistances thunder; bludgeoning, piercing, and
slashing from nonmagical attacks
Damage Immunities poison
Condition Immunities charmed, frightened, paralyzed,
poisoned, unconscious
Senses darkvision 60 ft., passive Perception 20
Languages all but rarely speaks
Challenge 25 (75,000 XP) **Proficiency Bonus** +8

Immutable Form. The marut is immune to any spell or effect
that would alter its form.

Legendary Resistance (3/Day). If the marut fails a saving throw,
it can choose to succeed instead.

Magic Resistance. The marut has advantage on saving throws
against spells and other magical effects.

Unusual Nature. The marut doesn't require air, food,
drink, or sleep.

ACTIONS

Multiattack. The marut makes two Unerring Slam attacks.

Unerring Slam. *Melee Weapon Attack:* automatic hit, reach 5 ft.,
one target. *Hit:* 60 force damage, and the target is pushed up
to 5 feet away from the marut if it is Huge or smaller.

Blazing Edict (Recharge 5–6). Arcane energy emanates from
the marut's chest in a 60-foot cube. Every creature in that area
takes 45 radiant damage. Each creature that takes any of this
damage must succeed on a DC 20 Wisdom saving throw or be
stunned until the end of the marut's next turn.

Plane Shift (3/Day). The marut casts *plane shift*, requiring no
material components and using Intelligence as the spellcasting
ability. The marut can cast the spell normally, or it can cast the
spell on an unwilling creature it can see within 60 feet of it. If it
uses the latter option, the targeted creature must succeed on a
DC 20 Charisma saving throw or be banished to a teleportation
circle in the Hall of Concordance in Sigil.

MARUT

The nigh-unstoppable inevitables serve a singular
purpose: they enforce contracts forged in the Hall
of Concordance in the city of Sigil. Primus, the
leader of the modrons, created maruts and other inevitables to bring order to dealings between planar
folk. A wide array of disparate creatures, including
yugoloths, will enter into a contract with inevitables if asked.

The Hall of Concordance is an embassy of pure
law in Sigil, the City of Doors. In the hall, parties
who agree to mutual terms—and who pay the requi-
site gold to the Kolyarut, a mechanical engine of ab-
solute jurisprudence—can have their contract chis-
eled onto a sheet of gold that is placed in the chest of
a marut. From that moment until the contract is fulfilled, the marut is bound to enforce its terms and to
punish any party who breaks them. A marut resorts
to lethal force only if a contract calls for it, if the contract is fully broken, or if the marut is attacked.

Inevitables care nothing for the spirit of an
agreement, only the letter. A marut enforces what
is written, not what was meant by or supposed to
be understood from the writing. The Kolyarut re-
jects contracts that contain vague, contradictory,
or unenforceable terms. Beyond that, it doesn't
care whether both parties understand what they're
agreeing to.

CORY TREGO-ERDNER

Master Thief

Medium Humanoid, Any Alignment

Armor Class 16 (studded leather)
Hit Points 84 (13d8 + 26)
Speed 30 ft.

STR	DEX	CON	INT	WIS	CHA
11 (+0)	18 (+4)	14 (+2)	11 (+0)	11 (+0)	12 (+1)

Saving Throws Dex +7, Int +3
Skills Acrobatics +7, Athletics +3, Perception +3, Sleight of Hand +7, Stealth +7
Senses passive Perception 13
Languages any one language (usually Common) plus thieves' cant
Challenge 5 (1,800 XP)   **Proficiency Bonus** +3

Evasion. If the thief is subjected to an effect that allows it to make a Dexterity saving throw to take only half damage, the thief instead takes no damage if it succeeds on the saving throw and only half damage if it fails, provided the thief isn't incapacitated.

Actions

Multiattack. The thief makes three Shortsword or Short-bow attacks.

Shortsword. *Melee Weapon Attack:* +7 to hit, reach 5 ft., one target. *Hit:* 7 (1d6 + 4) piercing damage plus 3 (1d6) poison damage.

Shortbow. *Ranged Weapon Attack:* +7 to hit, range 80/320 ft., one target. *Hit:* 7 (1d6 + 4) piercing damage plus 3 (1d6) poison damage.

Bonus Actions

Cunning Action. The thief takes the Dash, Disengage, or Hide action.

Reactions

Uncanny Dodge. The thief halves the damage that it takes from an attack that hits it. The thief must be able to see the attacker.

Master Thief

Master thieves are known for perpetrating daring heists. They tend to develop a romanticized reputation. A master thief might "retire" from hands-on work to run a thieves' guild, spearhead some covert enterprise, or enjoy a quiet life of luxury.

When a master thief completes a challenging heist, they often leave behind a calling card to taunt their victims. You may roll on the Master Thief Calling Cards table to determine what a master thief leaves behind.

Master Thief Calling Cards

d10	Calling Card
1	Tiny, folded paper cat
2	Red bird feather
3	Rose petal
4	Figurine made from twigs and twine
5	Small note with the words "It's been fun!" written on it in an ornate script
6	Glass bead that looks like an eye
7	Pistachio shells
8	Two playing cards balanced against each other, resembling a tent
9	Worthless coin with a bite mark in it
10	Chalk or charcoal sketch of a domino mask

Maurezhi

Medium Fiend (Demon), Typically Chaotic Evil

Armor Class 15 (natural armor)
Hit Points 88 (16d8 + 16)
Speed 30 ft.

STR	DEX	CON	INT	WIS	CHA
14 (+2)	17 (+3)	12 (+1)	11 (+0)	12 (+1)	15 (+2)

Skills Deception +5
Damage Resistances cold, fire, lightning, necrotic; bludgeoning, piercing, and slashing from nonmagical attacks
Damage Immunities poison
Condition Immunities charmed, exhaustion, poisoned
Senses darkvision 120 ft., passive Perception 11
Languages Abyssal, Elvish, telepathy 120 ft.
Challenge 7 (2,900 XP)   **Proficiency Bonus** +3

Assume Form. The maurezhi can assume the appearance of any Medium Humanoid it eats. It remains in this form for 1d6 days, during which time the form gradually decays until, when the effect ends, the form sloughs from the demon's body.

Magic Resistance. The maurezhi has advantage on saving throws against spells and other magical effects.

Actions

Multiattack. The maurezhi makes one Bite attack and one Claw attack.

Bite. *Melee Weapon Attack:* +6 to hit, reach 5 ft., one target. *Hit:* 14 (2d10 + 3) piercing damage. If the target is a Humanoid, its Charisma score is reduced by 1d4. This reduction lasts until the target finishes a short or long rest. The target dies if this reduces its Charisma to 0. It rises 24 hours later as a **ghoul** (see the *Monster Manual*), unless it has been revived or its corpse has been destroyed.

Claw. *Melee Weapon Attack:* +6 to hit, reach 5 ft., one target. *Hit:* 12 (2d8 + 3) slashing damage. If the target is a creature other than an Undead, it must succeed on a DC 12 Constitution saving throw or be paralyzed for 1 minute. The target can repeat the saving throw at the end of each of its turns, ending the effect on itself on a success.

Raise Ghoul (Recharge 5–6). The maurezhi targets one dead **ghoul** or **ghast** (see the *Monster Manual*) it can see within 30 feet of it. The target is revived with all its hit points.

Maurezhi

When Doresain, the King of Ghouls, corrupted a society of elves, he created a new sort of demon—the maurezhi—to lead packs of ghouls and ghasts (both appear in the *Monster Manual*) on the Material Plane.

When a maurezhi consumes the corpse of a Humanoid it has slain—a process that takes about 10 minutes—it instantly assumes the creature's appearance as it was in life. The new appearance begins to rot away over the next few days, eventually revealing the demon's original form.

A maurezhi is contagion incarnate. Its bite can drain a victim's sense of self. If this affliction is allowed to go far enough, the victim is infected with an unholy hunger for flesh that overpowers their personality and transforms them into a ghoul.

> I once pulled a whole bottle of fine strawberry liquor from the belly of a maw demon. No clue where it might've devoured such a find, but I'm not complaining.
>
> TASHA

MAW DEMON

Maw demons share the ceaseless hunger for carnage and mortal flesh of their master, Yeenoghu, who appears in this book. After a maw demon rests for 8 hours, anything devoured by it is transported directly into the Lord of Savagery's gullet.

Maw demons appear among gnoll war bands that worship Yeenoghu, usually summoned as part of ritual offerings of freshly slain Humanoids made to him. The gnolls don't command the demons, which simply accompany the war band and attack whatever creatures the gnolls fall upon.

Because maw demons are indiscriminate in their hunger, their stomachs contain all manner of oddities in addition to the remains of their recent prey. You may choose one or more items appropriate for your campaign for a maw demon to contain, or roll on the Maw Demon's Stomach Contents table.

MAW DEMON'S STOMACH CONTENTS

d8	Stomach Contents
1	Intact wine skin with wine still in it
2	Iron skillet
3	Remnants of silk banner embroidered with a moon-and-stars motif
4	Corroded gauntlet with skeletal hand in it
5	Assorted keys
6	Old leather boot
7	Beehive
8	Humanoid teeth

MAW DEMON

Medium Fiend (Demon), Typically Chaotic Evil

Armor Class 13 (natural armor)
Hit Points 33 (6d8 + 6)
Speed 30 ft.

STR	DEX	CON	INT	WIS	CHA
14 (+2)	8 (−1)	13 (+1)	5 (−3)	8 (−1)	5 (−3)

Damage Resistances cold, fire, lightning
Damage Immunities poison
Condition Immunities charmed, frightened, poisoned
Senses darkvision 60 ft., passive Perception 9
Languages understands Abyssal but can't speak
Challenge 1 (200 XP)   **Proficiency Bonus** +2

ACTIONS

Bite. *Melee Weapon Attack:* +4 to hit, reach 5 ft., one target. *Hit:* 11 (2d8 + 2) piercing damage.

Disgorge (Recharge 6). The demon vomits in a 15-foot cube. Each creature in that area must succeed on a DC 11 Dexterity saving throw or take 11 (2d10) acid damage and fall prone in the spew.

Meazel

Meazels are malicious hermits who fled to the Shadowfell to escape their mortal existence and contemplate their misery. There the shadows transformed them, and their bitterness made them twisted and cruel. Now hate burns in their hearts, and they resent any intrusion into their suffering, waylaying travelers who venture too close to their lairs.

The evil that corrupted meazels also imbued them with magical powers that allow them to move through shadows with ease. They can step from one pool of darkness into another one, using this talent to ambush prey. Sometimes they snatch victims around the throat with their strangling cords and then step away; other times they ferry their victims to isolated spots and then leave the hapless souls to the designs of whatever horrors lurk there.

Any creatures meazels draw through the shadows are cursed by the meazels' baleful magic. The curse acts as a beacon; sorrowsworn (which appear in this book), Undead, and other terrors sense where they are located and descend on the stranded victims to tear them apart.

Meazel
Medium Monstrosity, Typically Neutral Evil

Armor Class 13
Hit Points 35 (10d8 – 10)
Speed 30 ft.

STR	DEX	CON	INT	WIS	CHA
8 (–1)	17 (+3)	9 (–1)	14 (+2)	13 (+1)	10 (+0)

Skills Perception +3, Stealth +5
Senses darkvision 120 ft., passive Perception 13
Languages Common
Challenge 1 (200 XP)   **Proficiency Bonus** +2

Actions

Garrote. *Melee Weapon Attack:* +5 to hit, reach 5 ft., one target of the meazel's size or smaller. *Hit:* 6 (1d6 + 3) bludgeoning damage, and the target is grappled (escape DC 13 with disadvantage). Until the grapple ends, the target takes 10 (2d6 + 3) bludgeoning damage at the start of each of the meazel's turns. The meazel can't make weapon attacks while grappling a creature in this way.

Shortsword. *Melee Weapon Attack:* +5 to hit, reach 5 ft., one target. *Hit:* 6 (1d6 + 3) piercing damage plus 3 (1d6) necrotic damage.

Shadow Teleport (Recharge 5–6). The meazel, any equipment it is wearing or carrying, and any creature it is grappling teleport to an unoccupied space within 500 feet of it, provided that the starting space and the destination are in dim light or darkness. The destination must be a place the meazel has seen before, but it need not be within line of sight. If the destination space is occupied, the teleportation leads to the nearest unoccupied space.

Any other creature the meazel teleports becomes cursed for 1 hour or until the curse is ended by *remove curse* or *greater restoration*. Until this curse ends, every Undead and every creature native to the Shadowfell within 300 feet of the cursed creature can sense it, which prevents that creature from hiding from them.

Bonus Actions

Shadow Stealth. While in dim light or darkness, the meazel takes the Hide action.

SCOTT MURPHY

MEENLOCK

Meenlocks are Fey that invoke terror and seek to destroy all that is good, innocent, and beautiful. These bipeds have the heads and claws of crustaceans, and they primarily live in forests, although they adapt well to urban and subterranean settings.

Meenlocks are spawned by fear. When terror overwhelms a creature in the Feywild or another location where the Feywild's influence is strong, one or more meenlocks might spontaneously arise in the shadows or darkness nearby. If more than one meenlock is born, a lair also magically forms. The earth creaks and moans as narrow, twisting tunnels open up within it. One of these passageways serves as the lair's only entrance, and a large central chamber serves as the meenlocks' den. Inside the warren, black moss covers every surface, muffling sound.

A meenlock can supernaturally sense areas of darkness and shadow in its vicinity and can teleport from one darkened space to another—enabling it to sneak up on its prey or run away when outmatched. Meenlocks also project a supernatural aura that instills terror in those nearby.

TELEPATHIC TORMENT

Up to four meenlocks can telepathically torment one incapacitated creature, filling its mind with disturbing sounds and dreadful imagery. Participating meenlocks can't use their telepathy for any other purpose during this time, though they can move about and take actions and reactions as normal. This torment has no effect on a creature that is immune to the frightened condition. If the creature is susceptible and remains incapacitated for 1 hour, the creature must make a Wisdom saving throw, taking 10 (3d6) psychic damage on a failed save, or half as much damage on a successful one. The save DC is 10 + the number of meenlocks participating in the torment, considering only those that remain within sight of the victim for the entire hour and aren't incapacitated during it. The process can be repeated. A Humanoid that drops to 0 hit points as a result of this damage instantly transforms into a meenlock at full health and under the DM's control. Only a *wish* spell or divine intervention can restore a transformed creature to its former state.

MEENLOCK
Small Fey, Typically Neutral Evil

Armor Class 15 (natural armor)
Hit Points 31 (7d6 + 7)
Speed 30 ft.

STR	DEX	CON	INT	WIS	CHA
7 (−2)	15 (+2)	12 (+1)	11 (+0)	10 (+0)	8 (−1)

Skills Perception +4, Stealth +6, Survival +2
Condition Immunities frightened
Senses darkvision 120 ft., passive Perception 14
Languages telepathy 120 ft.
Challenge 2 (450 XP)   **Proficiency Bonus** +2

Fear Aura. Any Beast or Humanoid that starts its turn within 10 feet of the meenlock must succeed on a DC 11 Wisdom saving throw or be frightened until the start of the creature's next turn.

Light Sensitivity. While in bright light, the meenlock has disadvantage on attack rolls, as well as on Wisdom (Perception) checks that rely on sight.

ACTIONS

Claw. *Melee Weapon Attack:* +4 to hit, reach 5 ft., one target. *Hit:* 7 (2d4 + 2) slashing damage, and the target must succeed on a DC 11 Constitution saving throw or be paralyzed for 1 minute. The target can repeat the saving throw at the end of each of its turns, ending the effect on itself on a success.

BONUS ACTIONS

Shadow Teleport (Recharge 5–6). The meenlock teleports to an unoccupied space within 30 feet of it, provided that both the space it's teleporting from and its destination are in dim light or darkness. The destination need not be within line of sight.

MARK BEHM, MIN YUM

MERREGON

The souls of fallen soldiers, mercenaries, and body-guards who served evil without reservation often find everlasting servitude in the Nine Hells as merregons. These faceless foot soldiers are the Hells' legionnaires, tasked with protecting their infernal plane and its rulers against intruders.

Merregons have no individuality and hence no need for faces. Every merregon legionnaire has a metal mask bolted to its head. Markings on the mask indicate the only elements of the wearer's identity that matter: the commander it serves and the layer of the Nine Hells it protects.

Because of their unshakable loyalty, merregons form the backbone of many devils' protective retinues. They shrink from no task, no matter how dangerous. Unless ordered to fall back, they never retreat from a fight.

MERREGON
Medium Fiend (Devil), Typically Lawful Evil

Armor Class 16 (natural armor)
Hit Points 45 (6d8 + 18)
Speed 30 ft.

STR	DEX	CON	INT	WIS	CHA
18 (+4)	14 (+2)	17 (+3)	6 (−2)	12 (+1)	8 (−1)

Damage Resistances cold; bludgeoning, piercing, and slashing from nonmagical attacks that aren't silvered
Damage Immunities fire, poison
Condition Immunities frightened, poisoned
Senses darkvision 60 ft., passive Perception 11
Languages understands Infernal but can't speak, telepathy 120 ft.
Challenge 4 (1,100 XP)   **Proficiency Bonus** +2

Devil's Sight. Magical darkness doesn't impede the merregon's darkvision.

Magic Resistance. The merregon has advantage on saving throws against spells and other magical effects.

ACTIONS

Multiattack. The merregon makes three Halberd attacks.

Halberd. *Melee Weapon Attack:* +6 to hit, reach 10 ft., one target. *Hit:* 9 (1d10 + 4) slashing damage.

Heavy Crossbow. *Ranged Weapon Attack:* +4 to hit, range 100/400 ft., one target. *Hit:* 7 (1d10 + 2) piercing damage.

REACTIONS

Loyal Bodyguard. When another Fiend within 5 feet of the merregon is hit by an attack roll, the merregon causes itself to be hit instead.

Merrenoloth

The grim captains of the ferries on the River Styx, merrenoloths can navigate safely through the worst storms and always stay on course. Wielding fiery oars, merrenoloths strike fear into anyone who forcefully boards their vessels.

Lair Actions

On initiative count 20 (losing initiative ties) while captaining a vessel, the merrenoloth can take one of the following lair actions; it can't take the same lair action two rounds in a row:

Gale. The air within 60 feet of the vessel is filled with wind. Until initiative count 20 on the next round, that area is difficult terrain, and when a Medium or smaller creature flies into that area or starts its turn flying there, it must succeed on a DC 13 Strength saving throw or be knocked prone.

Propel. A strong wind propels the vessel, increasing its speed by 30 feet until initiative count 20 on the next round.

Repair. The vessel regains 22 (4d10) hit points.

Regional Effects

A merrenoloth imbues its vessel with magic that creates one or more of the following effects:

Unerring. The vessel always stays on course to the destination the merrenoloth names.

Unsinkable. The vessel doesn't sink even if its hull is breached.

If the merrenoloth dies, these effects fade over the course of 1d6 hours.

Merrenoloth

Medium Fiend (Yugoloth), Typically Neutral Evil

Armor Class 13
Hit Points 40 (9d8)
Speed 30 ft., swim 40 ft.

STR	DEX	CON	INT	WIS	CHA
8 (−1)	17 (+3)	10 (+0)	17 (+3)	14 (+2)	11 (+0)

Saving Throws Dex +5, Int +5
Skills History +5, Nature +5, Perception +4, Survival +4
Damage Resistances cold, fire, lightning; bludgeoning, piercing, and slashing from nonmagical attacks
Damage Immunities acid, poison
Condition Immunities poisoned
Senses blindsight 60 ft., darkvision 60 ft., passive Perception 14
Languages Abyssal, Infernal, telepathy 60 ft.
Challenge 3 (700 XP)   **Proficiency Bonus** +2

Magic Resistance. The merrenoloth has advantage on saving throws against spells and other magical effects.

Actions

Multiattack. The merrenoloth makes one Oar attack and uses Fear Gaze.

Oar. *Melee Weapon Attack:* +5 to hit, reach 5 ft., one target. *Hit:* 8 (2d4 + 3) fire damage.

Fear Gaze. The merrenoloth targets one creature it can see within 60 feet of it. The target must succeed on a DC 13 Wisdom saving throw or become frightened of the merrenoloth for 1 minute. The frightened target can repeat the saving throw at the end of each of its turns, ending the effect on itself on a success.

Spellcasting. The merrenoloth casts one of the following spells, requiring no material components and using Intelligence as the spellcasting ability (spell save DC 13):

At will: *charm person, darkness, detect magic, dispel magic, gust of wind*
3/day: *control water*

Bonus Actions

Teleport. The merrenoloth teleports, along with any equipment it is wearing or carrying, up to 60 feet to an unoccupied space it can see.

MINDWITNESS

If a beholder is stunned and brought to the brine pool of an elder brain (appears in this book), the beholder can be converted into a mindwitness. This alters some of its eye rays and transforms four of its eyestalks into tentacles similar to a mind flayer's. The mindwitness is psychically imprinted with devotion to the elder brain and submission to illithid commands.

A mindwitness's primary function is to improve telepathic communication in a mind flayer colony. A creature in telepathic communication with a mindwitness can converse through it to as many as seven other creatures the mindwitness can see, rapidly disseminating commands and other information.

If separated from its illithid masters, a mindwitness seeks out other telepathic creatures to tell it what to do. Mindwitnesses have been known to ally with flumphs (see the *Monster Manual*) and planar beings such as demons, shifting their worldview and alignment to match those of their new masters.

MINDWITNESS
Large Aberration, Typically Lawful Neutral

Armor Class 15 (natural armor)
Hit Points 75 (10d10 + 20)
Speed 0 ft., fly 20 ft. (hover)

STR	DEX	CON	INT	WIS	CHA
10 (+0)	14 (+2)	14 (+2)	15 (+2)	15 (+2)	10 (+0)

Saving Throws Int +5, Wis +5
Skills Perception +8
Condition Immunities prone
Senses darkvision 120 ft., passive Perception 18
Languages Deep Speech, Undercommon, telepathy 600 ft.
Challenge 5 (1,800 XP)   **Proficiency Bonus** +3

Telepathic Hub. When the mindwitness receives a telepathic message, it can telepathically share that message with up to seven other creatures within 600 feet of it that it can see.

ACTIONS

Multiattack. The mindwitness makes one Bite attack and one Tentacles attack, or it uses Eye Ray three times.

Bite. *Melee Weapon Attack:* +5 to hit, reach 5 ft., one target. *Hit:* 16 (4d6 + 2) piercing damage.

Tentacles. *Melee Weapon Attack:* +5 to hit, reach 10 ft., one creature. *Hit:* 20 (4d8 + 2) psychic damage. If the target is Large or smaller, it is grappled (escape DC 13), and it must succeed on a DC 13 Intelligence saving throw or be restrained until this grapple ends.

Eye Ray. The mindwitness shoots one magical eye ray at random (roll a d6, and reroll if the ray has already been used this turn), choosing one target it can see within 120 feet of it:

1: Aversion Ray. The targeted creature must make a DC 13 Charisma saving throw. On a failed save, the target has disadvantage on attack rolls for 1 minute. The target can repeat the saving throw at the end of each of its turns, ending the effect on itself on a success.

2: Fear Ray. The targeted creature must succeed on a DC 13 Wisdom saving throw or be frightened for 1 minute. The target can repeat the saving throw at the end of each of its turns, ending the effect on itself on a success.

3: Psychic Ray. The target must succeed on a DC 13 Intelligence saving throw or take 27 (6d8) psychic damage.

4: Slowing Ray. The targeted creature must make a DC 13 Dexterity saving throw. On a failed save, the target's speed is halved for 1 minute. In addition, the creature can't take reactions, and it can take either an action or a bonus action on its turn but not both. The creature can repeat the saving throw at the end of each of its turns, ending the effect on itself on a success.

5: Stunning Ray. The targeted creature must succeed on a DC 13 Constitution saving throw or be stunned for 1 minute. The target can repeat the saving throw at the end of each of its turns, ending the effect on itself on a success.

6: Telekinetic Ray. If the target is a creature, it must make a DC 13 Strength saving throw. On a failed save, the mindwitness moves it up to 30 feet in any direction, and it is restrained by the ray's telekinetic grip until the start of the mindwitness's next turn or until the mindwitness is incapacitated.

If the target is an object weighing 300 pounds or less that isn't being worn or carried, it is telekinetically moved up to 30 feet in any direction. The mindwitness can also exert fine control on objects with this ray, such as manipulating a simple tool or opening a door or a container.

DAVE DORMAN

MOLOCH

Exiled from the Nine Hells, Moloch would do anything to reclaim his position. Long ago, Moloch earned his place among the other archdevils through the glory he won driving demons out of the Nine Hells. Asmodeus rewarded him by elevating him to the rulership of Malbolge.

For eons, Moloch ruled his domain, vying against the other archdevils as he sought still greater power. This animosity worked in Asmodeus's favor, since Asmodeus knew that Moloch's scheming helped keep the other archdevils in check. The arrangement unraveled, however, when Moloch took the night hag named Malagard for his advisor. Her poisonous words gradually convinced him to attempt to topple Asmodeus. The conspiracy nearly succeeded, but was ultimately thwarted. Moloch was stripped of his station and sentenced to death—only the timely use of a planar portal allowed him to escape.

Moloch wasted no time in preparing for his return. He amassed an army of devils and monsters and left them to make final preparations for invading the Nine Hells, while he ventured to the Material Plane in search of an artifact that would ensure his success. But while there, he became trapped, leaving his armies at the mercy of his enemies. They were destroyed in short order.

Moloch was rendered nearly powerless by this failure. He schemes of ways to reclaim his former status, but every time he enters the Nine Hells, he is demoted to an imp (see the *Monster Manual*) and can't regain his normal powers until he leaves. Thus, he lives a split existence, sometimes plotting in Malbolge or other layers of the Hells and at other times wandering the planes in search of magical might or secrets that might help him win back his title.

Rumors suggest that he can often be found in Sigil, where he bargains with yugoloths to build yet another army with which he might invade Malbolge and wrest the throne from Glasya. Bereft as he is, he has little to offer in exchange, so he might bargain with mortals to gain their aid in acquiring coin, jewels, and other riches in return for knowledge about the Nine Hells and the other planes.

Most of Moloch's cultists have switched allegiance to one of the other archdevils, but idols constructed to honor him still stand in deep dungeons, their jeweled eyes and the remnants of power they hold drawing monstrous worshipers and unwise adventurers into places where his foul influence remains.

MOLOCH

Large Fiend (Devil), Lawful Evil

Armor Class 19 (natural armor)
Hit Points 253 (22d10 + 132)
Speed 30 ft.

STR	DEX	CON	INT	WIS	CHA
26 (+8)	19 (+4)	22 (+6)	21 (+5)	18 (+4)	23 (+6)

Saving Throws Dex +11, Con +13, Wis +11, Cha +13
Skills Deception +13, Intimidation +13, Perception +11
Damage Resistances cold; bludgeoning, piercing, and slashing from nonmagical attacks that aren't silvered
Damage Immunities fire, poison
Condition Immunities charmed, exhaustion, frightened, poisoned
Senses darkvision 120 ft., passive Perception 21
Languages all, telepathy 120 ft.
Challenge 21 (33,000 XP)   **Proficiency Bonus** +7

Legendary Resistance (3/Day). If Moloch fails a saving throw, he can choose to succeed instead.

Magic Resistance. Moloch has advantage on saving throws against spells and other magical effects.

Regeneration. Moloch regains 20 hit points at the start of his turn. If he takes radiant damage, this trait doesn't function at the start of his next turn. Moloch dies only if he starts his turn with 0 hit points and doesn't regenerate.

ACTIONS

Multiattack. Moloch makes one Bite attack, one Claw attack, and one Many-Tailed Whip attack.

Bite. *Melee Weapon Attack:* +15 to hit, reach 5 ft., one target. *Hit:* 26 (4d8 + 8) fire damage.

Claw. *Melee Weapon Attack:* +15 to hit, reach 10 ft., one target. *Hit:* 17 (2d8 + 8) force damage.

Many-Tailed Whip. *Melee Weapon Attack:* +15 to hit, reach 30 ft., one target. *Hit:* 13 (2d4 + 8) lightning damage plus 11 (2d10) thunder damage. If the target is a creature, it must succeed on a DC 24 Strength saving throw or be pulled up to 30 feet in a straight line toward Moloch.

Breath of Despair (Recharge 5–6). Moloch exhales in a 30-foot cube. Each creature in that area must succeed on a DC 21 Wisdom saving throw or take 27 (5d10) psychic damage, drop whatever it is holding, and become frightened of Moloch for 1 minute. While frightened in this way, a creature must take the Dash action and move away from Moloch by the safest available route on each of its turns, unless there is nowhere to move, in which case it needn't take the Dash action. If the creature ends its turn in a location where it doesn't have line of sight to Moloch, the creature can repeat the saving throw, ending the effect on itself on a success.

Spellcasting. Moloch casts one of the following spells, requiring no material components and using Charisma as the spellcasting ability (spell save DC 21):

At will: *alter self* (can become Medium when changing his appearance), *confusion*, *detect magic*, *fly*, *major image*, *stinking cloud*, *suggestion*, *wall of fire*

Teleport. Moloch teleports, along with any equipment he is wearing or carrying, up to 120 feet to an unoccupied space he can see.

LEGENDARY ACTIONS

Moloch can take 3 legendary actions, choosing from the options below. Only one legendary action option can be used at a time and only at the end of another creature's turn. Moloch regains spent legendary actions at the start of his turn.

Attack. Moloch makes one Bite, Claw, or Many-Tailed Whip attack.
Teleport. Moloch uses Teleport.
Cast a Spell (Costs 2 Actions). Moloch uses Spellcasting.

Moloch obsesses over the power he lost, rather than thinking of the power he could gain elsewhere in the planes. What a pity he so wastes his potential.

—Mordenkainen

Molydeus

The fearsome molydeus speaks for the demon lord it serves and enforces its master's will. This demon is 12 feet tall, and its bipedal body has a slavering wolf's head and a fanged serpent's head. Its demon lord can speak and see through the serpent head; this master also uses the molydeus to guard treasures, slay foes, and terrify troops into obedience.

A molydeus's demon lord bestows on it a powerful weapon that dissolves if the molydeus dies. The weapon's form varies depending on the creator, but that doesn't affect the weapon's capabilities.

Variant: Demon Summoning

You can give a molydeus the ability to summon other demons.

Summon Demon (1/Day). As an action, the molydeus has a 50 percent chance of summoning its choice of 1d6 **babaus** (also in this book), 1d4 **chasmes**, or one **marilith** (the chasme and marilith appear in the *Monster Manual*) A summoned demon appears in an unoccupied space within 60 feet of the molydeus, acts as an ally of the molydeus, and can't summon other demons. It remains for 1 minute, until it or the molydeus dies, or until the molydeus dismisses it as an action.

Molydeus

Huge Fiend (Demon), Typically Chaotic Evil

Armor Class 19 (natural armor)
Hit Points 216 (16d12 + 112)
Speed 40 ft.

STR	DEX	CON	INT	WIS	CHA
28 (+9)	22 (+6)	25 (+7)	21 (+5)	24 (+7)	24 (+7)

Saving Throws Str +16, Con +14, Wis +14, Cha +14
Skills Perception +21
Damage Resistances cold, fire, lightning; bludgeoning, piercing, and slashing from nonmagical attacks
Damage Immunities poison
Condition Immunities blinded, charmed, deafened, frightened, poisoned, stunned
Senses truesight 120 ft., passive Perception 31
Languages Abyssal, telepathy 120 ft.
Challenge 21 (33,000 XP)   **Proficiency Bonus** +7

Legendary Resistance (3/Day). If the molydeus fails a saving throw, it can choose to succeed instead.

Magic Resistance. The molydeus has advantage on saving throws against spells and other magical effects.

Actions

Multiattack. The molydeus makes one Demonic Weapon attack, one Snakebite attack, and one Wolf Bite attack.

Demonic Weapon. *Melee Weapon Attack:* +16 to hit, reach 15 ft., one target. *Hit:* 35 (4d12 + 9) force damage. If the target has at least one head and the molydeus rolled a 20 on the attack roll, the target is decapitated and dies if it can't survive without that head. A target is immune to this effect if it takes none of the damage, has legendary actions, or is Huge or larger. Such a creature takes an extra 27 (6d8) force damage from the hit.

Snakebite. *Melee Weapon Attack:* +16 to hit, reach 15 ft., one creature. *Hit:* 16 (2d6 + 9) poison damage. The target must succeed on a DC 22 Constitution saving throw, or its hit point maximum is reduced by an amount equal to the damage taken. This reduction lasts until the target finishes a long rest. The target transforms into a **manes** (see the *Monster Manual*) if this reduces its hit point maximum to 0. This transformation can be ended only by a *wish* spell.

Wolf Bite. *Melee Weapon Attack:* +16 to hit, reach 10 ft., one target. *Hit:* 25 (3d10 + 9) necrotic damage.

Spellcasting. The molydeus casts one of the following spells, requiring no material components and using Charisma as the spellcasting ability (spell save DC 22):

At will: *dispel magic, polymorph, telekinesis, teleport*
3/day: *lightning bolt*

Legendary Actions

The molydeus can take 3 legendary actions, choosing from the options below. Only one legendary action option can be used at a time and only at the end of another creature's turn. The molydeus regains spent legendary actions at the start of its turn.

Attack. The molydeus makes one Demonic Weapon or Snakebite attack.
Move. The molydeus moves without provoking opportunity attacks.
Cast a Spell (Costs 2 Actions). The molydeus uses Spellcasting.

CHRISTOPHER BURDETT

MORKOTH

Ancient and devious, morkoths are voracious collectors. Each one floats through the planes on a strange, mobile island, amassing the valuables, oddities, and castoffs of the multiverse in a massive, ever-growing collection.

The first morkoths arose in the Astral Plane when the petrified body of a deity of greed and strife collided with a remnant of celestial matter imbued with life-giving magic. The collision released a storm of chaotic energy and sent countless islands spinning away into the void. Within some of them, bits of the god's petrified flesh came back to life as morkoths: tentacled monstrosities brimming with malice and greed.

Morkoths are driven by greed and selfishness mixed with a yearning for conflict. They hoard vast stores of treasure, knowledge, and captives on their islands. Some of these prisoners are the descendants of people captured generations before; they might know of no other world outside their island.

A morkoth may allow a visitor to bargain for something or someone it has claimed if that visitor offers the morkoth something it desires more. It shows no mercy, however, to those who break a deal or try to steal from it. A morkoth knows every person and object in its collection.

A morkoth's island has the qualities of a dreamscape. It holds a jumble of objects and creatures the morkoth has collected, some of which date from forgotten times. An island might have natural-looking illumination, but most are shrouded in twilight, and on any of them, mists and shadows can appear without notice. The environment is warm and wet, a subtropical or tropical climate that keeps the morkoth and its "guests" comfortable.

Each island glides on planar currents and is safe from most harmful external effects—one could float in the skies of Avernus in the Nine Hells without harm to it or its residents. A morkoth's island might be found anywhere from the bottom of the ocean to the void of the Astral Plane. Anything on or within a certain distance of a morkoth's isle is drawn with it in its journey through the planes. Thus, people from lost civilizations and creatures or objects from bygone ages might be found within a morkoth's dominion.

Some islands travel a specific route, arriving at the same destinations regularly over a cycle of years. Others are tied to a particular place or group of locales, and still others move erratically through the cosmos. Occasionally, a morkoth learns to direct its island's movement.

A MORKOTH'S LAIR

A morkoth claims dominion over an entire island, and it also maintains a central sanctum on that isle. This lair is most often a twisted network of narrow tunnels that connect several underground chambers, although other structural forms might be incorporated. The morkoth dwells among the creatures and objects it prizes most in a spacious vault at the center of the warren, where the celestial fragments that make up the island's core are also located. Sections of the lair and its center might be kept dry to better protect and preserve collected objects and creatures, but most of the lair is underwater.

A morkoth encountered in its lair has a challenge rating of 12 (8,400 XP).

LAIR ACTIONS

On initiative count 20 (losing initiative ties), the morkoth can take one of the following lair actions:

Cast a Spell. The morkoth casts *darkness*, *dispel magic*, or *misty step*, using Intelligence as its spellcasting ability and without expending a spell slot.

Hypnotize. The morkoth uses its Hypnosis action, originating at a point within 120 feet of itself. It doesn't need to see the effect's point of origin.

REGIONAL EFFECTS

The island surrounding a morkoth's lair is warped by the creature's presence, creating the following effects:

Alter Water. With a thought (no action required), the morkoth can initiate a change in the water within its lair that takes effect 1 minute later. The water can be as breathable and clear as air, or it can be normal water (ranging in clarity from murky to clear).

Locate Creatures and Objects. The morkoth is aware of any new arrival, whether an object or a creature, on its island or in its sanctum. As an action, the morkoth can locate any one creature or object on the island. Visitors to the island feel as though they are being watched, even when they aren't.

Lost Possessions. Each time a creature that has been on the island for less than a year finishes a short or long rest, it must make a DC 10 Intelligence saving throw. On a failure, the creature has misplaced one possession (chosen by the player, if the creature is that player's character). The possession remains nearby but concealed for a short time, so it can be recovered with a successful DC 15 Wisdom (Perception) check. An object that is misplaced but not recovered ends up in the morkoth's lair 1 hour later. If the creature later goes to the morkoth's lair, its lost possessions stand out in its perception and are easily recovered.

Supernatural Lure. Entrances to the morkoth's lair have an enchantment that the morkoth can activate or suppress at any time while it's in its lair and not incapacitated. Any creature within 30 feet of such an entrance and able to see it must make a DC 15 Wisdom saving throw. On a failed save, the creature feels an intense urge to use its movement on each of its turns to enter the lair and to move toward the morkoth's location (the target doesn't realize it's heading toward a creature). The target moves toward the morkoth by the most direct route. As soon as it can see the morkoth, the target can repeat the saving throw, ending the effect on itself on a success. It can also repeat the saving throw at the end of each of its turns and every time it takes damage.

If the morkoth dies, these regional effects end immediately.

MORKOTH

Large Aberration, Typically Chaotic Evil

Armor Class 17 (natural armor)
Hit Points 165 (22d10 + 44)
Speed 25 ft., swim 50 ft.

STR	DEX	CON	INT	WIS	CHA
14 (+2)	14 (+2)	14 (+2)	20 (+5)	15 (+2)	13 (+1)

Saving Throws Dex +6, Int +9, Wis +6
Skills Arcana +9, History +9, Perception +10, Stealth +6
Senses blindsight 30 ft., darkvision 120 ft., passive Perception 20
Languages telepathy 120 ft.
Challenge 11 (7,200 XP)   **Proficiency Bonus** +4

Amphibious. The morkoth can breathe air and water.

ACTIONS

Multiattack. The morkoth makes either two Bite attacks and one Tentacles attack or three Bite attacks.

Bite. *Melee Weapon Attack:* +6 to hit, reach 5 ft., one target. *Hit:* 9 (2d6 + 2) slashing damage plus 10 (3d6) psychic damage.

Tentacles. *Melee Weapon Attack:* +6 to hit, reach 15 ft., one target. *Hit:* 15 (3d8 + 2) bludgeoning damage, and the target is grappled (escape DC 14) if it is a Large or smaller creature. Until this grapple ends, the target is restrained and takes 15 (3d8 + 2) bludgeoning damage at the start of each of its turns, and the morkoth can't use its tentacles on another target.

Hypnosis. The morkoth projects a 30-foot cone of magical energy. Each creature in that area must make a DC 17 Wisdom saving throw. On a failed save, the creature is charmed by the morkoth for 1 minute. While charmed in this way, the target tries to get as close to the morkoth as possible, using its actions to Dash until it is within 5 feet of the morkoth. A charmed target can repeat the saving throw at the end of each of its turns and whenever it takes damage, ending the effect on itself on a success. If a creature's saving throw is successful or the effect ends for it, the creature has advantage on saving throws against the morkoth's Hypnosis for 24 hours.

Spellcasting. The morkoth casts one of the following spells, requiring no material components and using Intelligence as the spellcasting ability (spell save DC 17):

At will: *detect magic, mage hand*
3/day each: *darkness, dimension door, dispel magic, lightning bolt, sending*

REACTIONS

Spell Reflection. If the morkoth makes a successful saving throw against a spell or a spell attack misses it, the morkoth can choose another creature (including the spellcaster) it can see within 120 feet of it. The spell targets the chosen creature instead of the morkoth. If the spell forced a saving throw, the chosen creature makes its own save. If the spell was an attack, the attack roll is rerolled against the chosen creature.

MOUTH OF GROLANTOR

Hill giants consume spoiled food and diseased carcasses with as much enthusiasm as children eating dessert and rarely suffer for such eating habits. When one of their kind becomes incapable of keeping down food, that giant is seen, among hill giant worshipers of the god Grolantor, as the vessel of a message from the deity.

The sickened giant's compatriots separate the giant from the rest of the community, often trapping them in a cage or tying them to a post. A priest of Grolantor visits the famished giant daily, trying to read portents in the puddles of bile the hill giant retches up. If the sickness soon passes, they allow the hill giant to rejoin society. If not, the hill giant is instead starved to the point of desperation so Grolantor's hunger can be given a mouth in the world.

A mouth of Grolantor is revered as a holy embodiment of Grolantor's aching hunger. Unlike a typical sluggish hill giant, a mouth of Grolantor is thin as a whippet, alert like a bird, and constantly twitchy. Mouths are kept perpetually imprisoned or shackled; if they break free, they're sure to kill anyone nearby before they're brought down or escape on a killing spree. The only time mouths of Grolantor are set loose is during a war, during a raid against an enemy settlement, or in a last-ditch defense of Grolantor's faithful. When a mouth of Grolantor has slaughtered and eaten their fill of enemies, they pass out amid the gory remains of their victims, making them easy to recapture.

MOUTH OF GROLANTOR

Huge Giant (Hill Giant), Typically Chaotic Evil

Armor Class 14 (natural armor)
Hit Points 105 (10d12 + 40)
Speed 50 ft.

STR	DEX	CON	INT	WIS	CHA
21 (+5)	10 (+0)	18 (+4)	5 (−3)	7 (−2)	5 (−3)

Skills Perception +1
Condition Immunities frightened
Senses passive Perception 11
Languages Giant
Challenge 6 (2,300 XP)   **Proficiency Bonus** +3

Mouth of Chaos. The giant is immune to the *confusion* spell.

On each of its turns, the giant uses all its movement to move toward the nearest creature or whatever else it might perceive as food. Roll a d10 at the start of each of the giant's turns to determine its action for that turn:

1–3: The giant makes three Fist attacks against one random creature within reach. If no creatures are within reach, the giant flies into a rage and gains advantage on all attack rolls until the end of its next turn.

4–5: The giant makes one Fist attack against each creature within reach. If no creatures are within reach, the giant makes one Fist attack against itself.

6–7: The giant makes one Bite attack against one random creature within reach. If no other creatures are within reach, its eyes glaze over and it is stunned until the start of its next turn.

8–10: The giant makes one Bite attack and two Fist attacks against one random creature within reach. If no creatures are within reach, the giant flies into a rage and gains advantage on all attack rolls until the end of its next turn.

ACTIONS

Bite. *Melee Weapon Attack:* +8 to hit, reach 5 ft., one creature. *Hit:* 15 (3d6 + 5) piercing damage, and the giant magically regains hit points equal to the damage dealt.

Fist. *Melee Weapon Attack:* +8 to hit, reach 10 ft., one target. *Hit:* 18 (3d8 + 5) bludgeoning damage.

Nabassu

The insatiable nabassus prowl the multiverse in search of souls to devour. If they think they can kill a creature and consume its soul, they attack—even if that other creature is a demon, including another nabassu.

Most other demons shun nabassus and force them to live on the fringes of the Abyss. There, nabassus pick off weaker demons or, if the situation warrants, gather in packs to take down larger prey. Some especially powerful nabassus even search for demon lords' amulets.

Whenever magic pulls demons from the Abyss to the Material Plane, nabassus try to get summoned so that they can embark on a feast of souls there. A summoned nabassu seeks to break free so that it can devour the soul of its summoner and then feed on the souls of whatever other creatures it can catch. One way a summoner can avoid this fate is by providing a steady supply of souls to the nabassu, which might persuade the demon to be cooperative—as long as the supply lasts.

Nabassu

Medium Fiend (Demon), Typically Chaotic Evil

Armor Class 18 (natural armor)
Hit Points 190 (20d8 + 100)
Speed 40 ft., fly 60 ft.

STR	DEX	CON	INT	WIS	CHA
22 (+6)	14 (+2)	21 (+5)	14 (+2)	15 (+2)	17 (+3)

Saving Throws Str +11, Dex +7
Skills Perception +7
Damage Resistances cold, fire, lightning; bludgeoning, piercing, and slashing from nonmagical attacks
Damage Immunities poison
Condition Immunities poisoned
Senses darkvision 60 ft., passive Perception 17
Languages Abyssal, telepathy 120 ft.
Challenge 15 (13,000 XP)   **Proficiency Bonus** +5

Demonic Shadows. The nabassu darkens the area around its body in a 10-foot radius. Nonmagical light can't illuminate this area of dim light.

Devour Soul. A nabassu can eat the soul of a creature it has killed within the last hour, provided that creature is neither a Construct nor an Undead. The devouring requires the nabassu to be within 5 feet of the corpse for at least 10 minutes, after which it gains a number of Hit Dice (d8s) equal to half the creature's number of Hit Dice. Roll those dice, and increase the nabassu's hit points by the numbers rolled. For every 4 Hit Dice the nabassu gains in this way, its attacks deal an extra 3 (1d6) damage on a hit. The nabassu retains these benefits for 6 days. A creature devoured by a nabassu can be restored to life only by a *wish* spell.

Magic Resistance. The nabassu has advantage on saving throws against spells and other magical effects.

Actions

Multiattack. The nabassu makes one Bite attack and one Claw attack, and it uses Soul-Stealing Gaze.

Bite. *Melee Weapon Attack:* +11 to hit, reach 5 ft., one target. *Hit:* 38 (5d12 + 6) necrotic damage.

Claw. *Melee Weapon Attack:* +11 to hit, reach 5 ft., one target. *Hit:* 28 (4d10 + 6) force damage.

Soul-Stealing Gaze. The nabassu targets one creature it can see within 30 feet of it. If the target isn't a Construct or an Undead, it must succeed on a DC 16 Charisma saving throw or take 13 (2d12) necrotic damage. The target's hit point maximum is reduced by an amount equal to the necrotic damage dealt, and the nabassu regains hit points equal to half that amount. This reduction lasts until the target finishes a short or long rest. The target dies if its hit point maximum is reduced to 0, and if the target is a Humanoid, it immediately rises as a **ghoul** (see the *Monster Manual*) under the nabassu's control.

CLAUDIO POZAS

NAGPA

Medium Monstrosity (Wizard), Typically Neutral Evil

Armor Class 19 (natural armor)
Hit Points 203 (37d8 + 37)
Speed 30 ft.

STR	DEX	CON	INT	WIS	CHA
9 (−1)	15 (+2)	12 (+1)	23 (+6)	18 (+4)	21 (+5)

Saving Throws Int +12, Wis +10, Cha +11
Skills Arcana +12, Deception +11, History +12, Insight +10, Perception +10
Senses truesight 120 ft., passive Perception 20
Languages Common plus up to five other languages
Challenge 17 (18,000 XP)   **Proficiency Bonus** +6

ACTIONS

Multiattack. The nagpa makes three Staff or Deathly Ray attacks. It can replace one attack with a use of Spellcasting.

Staff. *Melee Weapon Attack:* +8 to hit, reach 5 ft., one target. *Hit:* 9 (2d6 + 2) bludgeoning damage plus 24 (7d6) necrotic damage.

Deathly Ray. *Ranged Spell Attack:* +12 to hit, range 120 ft., one target. *Hit:* 30 (7d6 + 6) necrotic damage.

Spellcasting. The nagpa casts one of the following spells, using Intelligence as the spellcasting ability (spell save DC 20):

At will: *detect magic, mage hand, message, minor illusion*
2/day each: *fireball, fly, hold person, suggestion, wall of fire*
1/day each: *dominate person, etherealness, feeblemind*

BONUS ACTIONS

Corruption. The nagpa targets one creature it can see within 90 feet of it. The target must make a DC 20 Charisma saving throw. An evil creature makes the save with disadvantage. On a failed save, the target is charmed by the nagpa until the start of the nagpa's next turn. On a successful save, the target becomes immune to the nagpa's Corruption for the next 24 hours.

Paralysis (Recharge 6). The nagpa forces each creature within 30 feet of it to make a DC 20 Wisdom saving throw, excluding Undead and Constructs. On a failed save, a target is paralyzed for 1 minute. A paralyzed target can repeat the saving throw at the end of each of its turns, ending the effect on itself on a success.

NAGPA

Long ago, the Raven Queen cursed a cabal of powerful wizards for meddling in a ritual that would have helped avert a war between the gods. She transformed them into the scabrous, birdlike creatures known as nagpas and rendered them able to acquire new lore and magical power only from the ruins of fallen civilizations and great calamities.

Nagpas still fear the Raven Queen and do their best to avoid her and her agents. When it's impossible to do so, they become cringing, fawning things, eager to please and thereby escape further attention from her cold gaze. All the original thirteen remain alive, thanks to their cunning and their willingness to do whatever is necessary to survive.

Hungry to claim more power despite the Raven Queen's curse, nagpas strive to bring about world-shaking destruction. From the shadows, they manipulate events to bring about ruin. They can bring to bear an array of spells to turn other creatures into their agents, influencing their decisions in subtle ways and making them unwitting accomplices in their own destruction. Nagpas are extraordinarily patient and pursue several schemes simultaneously, so if one plan goes awry, they can shift their focus to another. Typically, nagpas emerge from the shadows only when they can deliver a finishing blow. They then revel in the grand devastation their plotting brought about—looting libraries, plundering vaults, and prying secrets of arcane lore and power from the wreckage.

Narzugon

Paladins who make deals with devils and carry their twisted sense of honor into the afterlife are especially valuable to the archdukes of the Nine Hells. These narzugons act as horrific perversions of knights errant, carrying out their masters' will.

Narzugons wield hell-forged lances that shunt the souls of any they killed to the River Styx for rebirth as lemures (see the *Monster Manual*). Every lance bears the marks of both a narzugon and its master.

Narzugon

Medium Fiend (Devil), Typically Lawful Evil

Armor Class 20 (plate armor, shield)
Hit Points 112 (15d8 + 45)
Speed 30 ft.

STR	DEX	CON	INT	WIS	CHA
20 (+5)	10 (+0)	17 (+3)	16 (+3)	14 (+2)	19 (+4)

Saving Throws Dex +5, Con +8, Cha +9
Skills Perception +12
Damage Resistances acid, cold; bludgeoning, piercing, and slashing from nonmagical attacks that aren't silvered
Damage Immunities fire, poison
Condition Immunities charmed, frightened, poisoned
Senses darkvision 120 ft., passive Perception 22
Languages Common, Infernal, telepathy 120 ft.
Challenge 13 (10,000 XP)   **Proficiency Bonus** +5

Infernal Tack. The narzugon wears spurs that are part of *infernal tack*, which allow it to summon its nightmare companion as an action.

Magic Resistance. The narzugon has advantage on saving throws against spells and other magical effects.

Actions

Multiattack. The narzugon makes three Hellfire Lance attacks. It also uses Infernal Command or Terrifying Command.

Hellfire Lance. *Melee Weapon Attack:* +10 to hit, reach 10 ft., one target. *Hit:* 11 (1d12 + 5) piercing damage plus 16 (3d10) fire damage. If this damage kills a creature with a soul, the soul rises from the River Styx as a **lemure** (see the *Monster Manual*) in Avernus in 1d4 hours. If the creature isn't revived before then, only a *wish* spell or killing the lemure and casting *true resurrection* on the creature's original body can restore it to life. Constructs and devils are immune to this effect.

Infernal Command. Each ally of the narzugon within 60 feet of it can't be charmed or frightened until the end of the narzugon's next turn.

Terrifying Command. Each creature within 60 feet of the narzugon that isn't a Fiend must succeed on a DC 17 Charisma saving throw or become frightened of the narzugon for 1 minute. A creature can repeat the saving throw at the end of each of its turns, ending the effect on itself on a success. A creature that makes a successful saving throw is immune to this narzugon's Terrifying Command for 24 hours.

Healing (1/Day). The narzugon, or one creature it touches, regains 100 hit points.

Each narzugon claims a nightmare (see the *Monster Manual*) as its mount. These steeds are bound by *infernal tack* (see below) and must respond to the summons and commands of the spurs' wearer.

Magic Item: Infernal Tack

Wondrous Item, Legendary (Requires Attunement by a Creature of Evil Alignment)

A rider binds a nightmare to its service with *infernal tack*, which consists of a bridle, bit, reins, saddle, and stirrups, along with spurs that are worn by the rider. A nightmare equipped with *infernal tack* must serve whoever wears the spurs until the wearer dies or the tack is removed.

You can use an action to call a nightmare equipped with *infernal tack* by clashing the spurs together or scraping them through blood. The nightmare appears at the start of your next turn, within 20 feet of you. It acts as your ally and takes its turn on your initiative count. It remains for 1 day, until you or it dies, or until you dismiss it as an action. If the nightmare dies, it reforms in the Nine Hells within 24 hours, after which you can summon it again.

The tack doesn't conjure a nightmare; one must first be subdued so the tack can be placed on it. No nightmare accepts this forced servitude willingly, but some eventually form strong loyalties to their masters and become true partners in evil.

ILYA SHKIPIN

Neogi

A neogi looks like an outsize spider with an eel's neck and head. It can poison the body and the mind of its targets and can subjugate even beings that are physically superior.

Neogi usually dwell in far-flung locations on the Material Plane, as well as in the Astral Plane and the Ethereal Plane. They left their home world long ago to conquer and devour creatures in other realms. During this era, they dominated umber hulks and used them to build sleek, spidery ships capable of traversing the multiverse.

Neogi Hatchling

A neogi lives about a century. When an individual is rendered weak by advanced age, the other neogi in the group overpower it and inject it with a special poison. The toxin transforms the old neogi into a bloated mass of flesh. Younger neogi lay their eggs atop it, and when the hatchlings emerge, they devour the old neogi and one another until only a few of the strongest newborns are left. The surviving neogi hatchlings begin their lives under the control of adult neogi. They must learn about their society and earn a place in it, and each one starts its training by gaining mastery over an umber hulk.

Neogi (Adult)

The mentality of neogi is alien to many other peoples. Because adult neogi have the power to control minds, they consider doing so to be entirely appropriate. Their society makes no distinction between individuals, aside from the ability that a given creature has to control others, and they don't comprehend the emotional aspects of existence that humans and similar beings experience. To a neogi, hatred is as foreign a sensation as love, and showing loyalty in the absence of authority is foolishness.

Neogi mark themselves and those they capture through the use of dyes, transformational magic, and other markings intended to signify rank, achievements, and the identity of the individual's leader. By these signs, neogi can identify each others' place in the hierarchy—and they must defer to those of higher station or risk harsh punishment.

Neogi Master

Neogi masters use magic, as a result of a pact between neogi and aberrant entities they met during their journey from their home world. These entities—known by such names as Acamar, Caiphon, Gibbeth, and Hadar—resemble stars and embody the essence of evil.

Neogi Hatchling
Tiny Aberration, Typically Lawful Evil

Armor Class 11
Hit Points 7 (3d4)
Speed 20 ft., climb 20 ft.

STR	DEX	CON	INT	WIS	CHA
3 (−4)	13 (+1)	10 (+0)	6 (−2)	10 (+0)	9 (−1)

Senses darkvision 60 ft., passive Perception 10
Languages —
Challenge 1/8 (25 XP)   **Proficiency Bonus** +2

Mental Fortitude. The neogi has advantage on saving throws against being charmed or frightened, and magic can't put the neogi to sleep.

Spider Climb. The neogi can climb difficult surfaces, including upside down on ceilings, without needing to make an ability check.

Actions

Bite. *Melee Weapon Attack:* +3 to hit, reach 5 ft., one target. *Hit:* 3 (1d4 + 1) piercing damage plus 3 (1d6) poison damage, and the target must succeed on a DC 10 Constitution saving throw or become poisoned for 1 minute. A target can repeat the saving throw at the end of each of its turns, ending the effect on itself on a success.

> *Only the malevolent or the desperate do business with neogi. I generally advise against working with beings who view you as property or prey.*
>
> *—Mordenkainen*

NEOGI

Small Aberration, Typically Lawful Evil

Armor Class 15 (natural armor)
Hit Points 33 (6d6 + 12)
Speed 30 ft., climb 30 ft.

STR	DEX	CON	INT	WIS	CHA
6 (−2)	16 (+3)	14 (+2)	13 (+1)	12 (+1)	15 (+2)

Skills Intimidation +4, Perception +3
Senses darkvision 60 ft., passive Perception 13
Languages Common, Deep Speech, Undercommon
Challenge 3 (700 XP)   **Proficiency Bonus** +2

Mental Fortitude. The neogi has advantage on saving throws against being charmed or frightened, and magic can't put the neogi to sleep.

Spider Climb. The neogi can climb difficult surfaces, including upside down on ceilings, without needing to make an ability check.

ACTIONS

Multiattack. The neogi makes one Bite attack and two Claw attacks.

Bite. *Melee Weapon Attack:* +5 to hit, reach 5 ft., one target. *Hit:* 6 (1d6 + 3) piercing damage plus 14 (4d6) poison damage, and the target must succeed on a DC 12 Constitution saving throw or become poisoned for 1 minute. A target can repeat the saving throw at the end of each of its turns, ending the effect on itself on a success.

Claw. *Melee Weapon Attack:* +5 to hit, reach 5 ft., one target. *Hit:* 8 (2d4 + 3) slashing damage.

BONUS ACTIONS

Enslave (Recharges after a Short or Long Rest). The neogi targets one creature it can see within 30 feet of it. The target must succeed on a DC 14 Wisdom saving throw or be magically charmed by the neogi for 1 day, or until the neogi dies or is more than 1 mile from the target. The charmed target obeys the neogi's commands and can't take reactions, and the neogi and the target can communicate telepathically with each other at a distance of up to 1 mile. Whenever the charmed target takes damage, it can repeat the saving throw, ending the effect on itself on a success.

NEOGI MASTER

Medium Aberration (Warlock), Typically Lawful Evil

Armor Class 15 (natural armor)
Hit Points 71 (11d8 + 22)
Speed 30 ft., climb 30 ft.

STR	DEX	CON	INT	WIS	CHA
6 (−2)	16 (+3)	14 (+2)	16 (+3)	12 (+1)	18 (+4)

Saving Throws Wis +3
Skills Arcana +5, Deception +6, Intimidation +6, Perception +3, Persuasion +6
Senses darkvision 120 ft., passive Perception 13
Languages Common, Deep Speech, Undercommon, telepathy 30 ft.
Challenge 4 (1,100 XP)   **Proficiency Bonus** +2

Devil's Sight. Magical darkness doesn't impede the neogi's darkvision.

Mental Fortitude. The neogi has advantage on saving throws against being charmed or frightened, and magic can't put the neogi to sleep.

Spider Climb. The neogi can climb difficult surfaces, including upside down on ceilings, without needing to make an ability check.

ACTIONS

Multiattack. The neogi makes one Bite attack and one Claw attack, or it makes two Tentacle of Hadar attacks.

Bite. *Melee Weapon Attack:* +5 to hit, reach 5 ft., one target. *Hit:* 6 (1d6 + 3) piercing damage plus 14 (4d6) poison damage, and the target must succeed on a DC 12 Constitution saving throw or become poisoned for 1 minute. A target can repeat the saving throw at the end of each of its turns, ending the effect on itself on a success.

Claw. *Melee Weapon Attack:* +5 to hit, reach 5 ft., one target. *Hit:* 8 (2d4 + 3) piercing damage.

Tentacle of Hadar. *Ranged Spell Attack:* +6 to hit, range 120 ft., one target. *Hit:* 14 (3d6 + 4) necrotic damage, and the target can't take reactions until the end of the neogi's next turn, as a spectral tentacle clings to the target.

Spellcasting. The neogi casts one of the following spells, using Charisma as the spellcasting ability (spell save DC 14):

At will: *guidance, mage hand, minor illusion, prestidigitation*
1/day each: *dimension door, hold person, hunger of Hadar*

BONUS ACTIONS

Enslave (Recharges after a Short or Long Rest). The neogi targets one creature it can see within 30 feet of it. The target must succeed on a DC 14 Wisdom saving throw or be magically charmed by the neogi for 1 day, or until the neogi dies or is more than 1 mile from the target. The charmed target obeys the neogi's commands and can't take reactions, and the neogi and the target can communicate telepathically with each other at a distance of up to 1 mile. Whenever the charmed target takes damage, it can repeat the saving throw, ending the effect on itself on a success.

NEOTHELID

Gargantuan Aberration, Typically Chaotic Evil

Armor Class 16 (natural armor)
Hit Points 232 (15d20 + 75)
Speed 30 ft.

STR	DEX	CON	INT	WIS	CHA
27 (+8)	7 (–2)	21 (+5)	3 (–4)	16 (+3)	12 (+1)

Saving Throws Int +1, Wis +8, Cha +6
Senses blindsight 120 ft. (blind beyond this radius), passive Perception 13
Languages —
Challenge 13 (10,000 XP)　　　　　**Proficiency Bonus** +5

Creature Sense. The neothelid is aware of the presence of creatures within 1 mile of it that have an Intelligence score of 4 or higher. It knows the distance and direction to each creature, as well as each creature's Intelligence score, but can't sense anything else about it. A creature protected by a *mind blank* spell, a *nondetection* spell, or similar magic can't be perceived in this manner.

Magic Resistance. The neothelid has advantage on saving throws against spells and other magical effects.

ACTIONS

Tentacles. *Melee Weapon Attack:* +13 to hit, reach 15 ft., one target. *Hit:* 21 (3d8 + 8) bludgeoning damage plus 11 (2d10) psychic damage. If the target is a Large or smaller creature, it must succeed on a DC 18 Strength saving throw or be swallowed by the neothelid. A swallowed creature is blinded and restrained, it has total cover against attacks and other effects outside the neothelid, and it takes 21 (6d6) acid damage at the start of each of the neothelid's turns.

If the neothelid takes 30 damage or more on a single turn from a creature inside it, the neothelid must succeed on a DC 18 Constitution saving throw at the end of that turn or regurgitate all swallowed creatures, which fall prone in a space within 10 feet of the neothelid. If the neothelid dies, a swallowed creature is no longer restrained by it and can escape from the corpse by using 20 feet of movement, exiting prone.

Acid Breath (Recharge 5–6). The neothelid exhales acid in a 60-foot cone. Each creature in that area must make a DC 18 Dexterity saving throw, taking 35 (10d6) acid damage on a failed save, or half as much damage on a successful one.

Spellcasting (Psionics). The neothelid casts one of the following spells, requiring no spell components and using Wisdom as the spellcasting ability (spell save DC 16):

At will: *levitate*
1/day each: *confusion*, *feeblemind*, *telekinesis*

NEOTHELID

A slime-covered worm of immense size, a neothelid is the result of the mind flayer reproductive cycle gone horribly wrong. When an illithid colony collapses, typically after an external assault, and the elder brain (appears in this book) is killed, the colony's tadpoles are suddenly freed from their fate. They no longer serve as food—and are no longer fed by their caretakers. Driven by hunger, they turn to devouring one another. Only one tadpole survives out of the thousands in the colony's pool, and it emerges as a neothelid.

Neothelids know nothing beyond their predatory existence. They prowl subterranean passages, using their rudimentary psionic abilities to search out and incapacitate brains to sate their constant hunger, growing ever more vicious. These creatures can spray tissue-dissolving enzymes from their tentacle ducts, reducing victims to puddles of slime and leaving only the pulsing brains unharmed. They have no knowledge of their link to illithids, so they're just as likely to prey on mind flayers as on anything else.

Mind flayers consider neothelids dangerous abominations—normally they eat or destroy any tadpoles that grow larger than a few inches in length without being implanted in a brain so they can't become such threats. Neothelids are not intelligent enough for elder brains to detect, so mind flayers are always alert for signs of their presence and organize hunting parties to exterminate any of these murderous worms they learn of.

NIGHTWALKER

The Negative Plane is a place of death, anathema to all living things. Yet there are some who would tap into its fell power and use its energy for sinister ends. Most individuals prove unequal to the task. Those not destroyed outright are sometimes drawn inside the plane and replaced by nightwalkers—terrifying Undead creatures that devour all life they encounter.

One can reach the Negative Plane from the Shadowfell in places where the barrier between the planes is thin. Stepping onto the Negative Plane is almost always fatal since the plane sucks the life and soul from creatures, annihilating most at once. The few who survive by sheer luck or by harnessing some rare form of protective magic soon discover that they can't leave as easily as they arrived.

Worse, for each creature that enters the plane, a nightwalker is released to take its place. In order for a trapped creature to escape, the released nightwalker must be lured back to the Negative Plane by offerings of life for it to devour. If the nightwalker is destroyed, the trapped creature has no hope of escape.

Generally, a nightwalker on the Material Plane is attracted to elements of the world associated with the creature responsible for its creation, which can provide clues as to who the trapped creature is. This attraction doesn't indicate a willingness to engage with the world, though; nightwalkers exist to make life extinct, and they prioritize anything associated with the trapped creature for destruction.

NIGHTWALKER
Huge Undead, Typically Chaotic Evil

Armor Class 14
Hit Points 337 (25d12 + 175)
Speed 40 ft., fly 40 ft.

STR	DEX	CON	INT	WIS	CHA
22 (+6)	19 (+4)	24 (+7)	6 (−2)	9 (−1)	8 (−1)

Saving Throws Con +13
Damage Resistances acid, cold, fire, lightning, thunder; bludgeoning, piercing, and slashing from nonmagical attacks
Damage Immunities necrotic, poison
Condition Immunities exhaustion, frightened, grappled, paralyzed, petrified, poisoned, prone, restrained
Senses darkvision 120 ft., passive Perception 9
Languages —
Challenge 20 (25,000 XP)   **Proficiency Bonus** +6

Annihilating Aura. Any creature that starts its turn within 30 feet of the nightwalker must succeed on a DC 21 Constitution saving throw or take 21 (6d6) necrotic damage. Undead are immune to this aura.

Life Eater. A creature dies if reduced to 0 hit points by the nightwalker and can't be revived except by a *wish* spell.

Unusual Nature. The nightwalker doesn't require air, food, drink, or sleep.

ACTIONS

Multiattack. The nightwalker makes two Enervating Focus attacks, one of which can be replaced by Finger of Doom, if available.

Enervating Focus. *Melee Weapon Attack:* +12 to hit, reach 15 ft., one target. *Hit:* 28 (5d8 + 6) necrotic damage. The target must succeed on a DC 21 Constitution saving throw or its hit point maximum is reduced by an amount equal to the necrotic damage taken. This reduction lasts until the target finishes a long rest. The target dies if its hit point maximum is reduced to 0.

Finger of Doom (Recharge 6). The nightwalker points at one creature it can see within 300 feet of it. The target must succeed on a DC 21 Wisdom saving throw or take 39 (6d12) necrotic damage and become frightened until the end of the nightwalker's next turn. While frightened in this way, the creature is also paralyzed. If a target's saving throw is successful, the target is immune to the nightwalker's Finger of Doom for the next 24 hours.

NILBOG

Small Fey (Goblinoid), Typically Chaotic Neutral

Armor Class 13 (leather armor)
Hit Points 7 (2d6)
Speed 30 ft.

STR	DEX	CON	INT	WIS	CHA
8 (−1)	14 (+2)	10 (+0)	10 (+0)	8 (−1)	15 (+2)

Skills Stealth +6
Senses darkvision 60 ft., passive Perception 9
Languages Common, Goblin
Challenge 1 (200 XP)   **Proficiency Bonus** +2

Nilbogism. Any creature that attempts to damage the nilbog must first succeed on a DC 12 Charisma saving throw or be charmed until the end of the creature's next turn. A creature charmed in this way must use its action praising the nilbog.

The nilbog can't regain hit points, including through magical healing, except through its Reversal of Fortune reaction.

ACTIONS

Fool's Scepter. *Melee Weapon Attack:* +4 to hit, reach 5 ft., one target. *Hit:* 5 (1d6 + 2) bludgeoning damage.

Mocking Word. The nilbog targets one creature it can see within 60 feet of it. The target must succeed on a DC 12 Wisdom saving throw or take 5 (2d4) psychic damage and have disadvantage on its next attack roll before the end of its next turn.

Spellcasting. The nilbog casts one of the following spells, using Charisma as the spellcasting ability (spell save DC 12):

At will: *mage hand, Tasha's hideous laughter*

BONUS ACTIONS

Nimble Escape. The nilbog takes the Disengage or Hide action.

REACTIONS

Reversal of Fortune. In response to another creature dealing damage to the nilbog, the nilbog reduces the damage to 0 and regains 3 (1d6) hit points.

NILBOG

When Maglubiyet conquered the goblin gods, a trickster deity was determined to get the last laugh. Although Maglubiyet shattered its essence, this trickster god survives in a splintered form as possessing spirits that cause disorder unless they are appeased. Goblins have no name for this deity and dare not give it one, lest Maglubiyet use its name to ensnare and crush it as he did their other deities. They call the possessing spirit, as well as the goblin possessed by it, a nilbog ("goblin" spelled backward), and they revel in the chaos a nilbog sows.

Whenever goblinoids form a host, there is a chance that a goblin will become possessed by a nilbog, particularly if the goblins have been mistreated by their betters. The possessed goblin turns into a wisecracking, impish creature fearless of reprisal. This nilbog also gains strange powers that drive others to do the opposite of what they desire. Attacking the possessed goblin is foolhardy, and killing them just prompts the spirit to possess another goblin. The only way to keep a nilbog from wreaking havoc is to treat it well and give it respect and praise.

Among fey courts, the risk of attracting a nilbog has given rise to the practice of always including at least one goblin jester. This jester is allowed to go anywhere and do whatever they please, hopefully preventing a nilbog from manifesting. The position of jester is much sought-after among the courts' goblins, because even if the jester is obviously not a nilbog, the court must indulge their chaotic behavior.

NILBOGISM

A nilbog is an invisible spirit that possesses only goblins. When bereft of a host, the spirit has a flying speed of 30 feet, it can't be attacked, and it is immune to all damage and conditions. Acting on initiative count 20 (losing initiative ties), the only action it can take is to attempt to possess a goblin within 5 feet of it.

A goblin targeted by the spirit must succeed on a DC 15 Charisma saving throw or become possessed. While possessed, the goblin uses the nilbog stat block. If the save succeeds, the spirit can't possess that goblin for 24 hours.

If its host is killed or the possession is ended by a spell such as *hallow*, *magic circle*, or *protection from evil and good*, the spirit searches for another goblin to possess. The spirit can leave its host at any time, but it won't do so willingly unless it knows there's another potential host nearby. A goblin stripped of their nilbog spirit reverts to their normal statistics and loses the traits they gained while possessed.

A lemure emerges from the Styx wiped of memory, yet the patterns of evil it performed in life remain indelibly inscribed upon its soul ...

But those who lacked ambition cannot climb the hierarchical ladder of the Hells.

They instead step down, becoming nupperibos.

—Mordenkainen

Nupperibo

No soul is turned away from the Nine Hells, but the truly worthless—those whose evil acts in life arose from carelessness and inaction more than anything else—are suitable only to become nupperibos. These pitiful creatures shuffle across the landscape, driven to purposeful action only when the clouds of swarming vermin that surround them find them prey to destroy or when a greater fiendish power commands it.

Individually, nupperibos are weak, but they're rarely alone and can be dangerous when gathered into packs. Clouds of stinging insects, stirges (see the *Monster Manual*), and other vermin surround them in a terrifying, reeking sheath that torments any non-devil that draws near.

A nupperibo knows nothing but the desire to destroy non-Fiends. Once a nupperibo's vermin cloud senses a potential meal, any nearby nupperibos pursue that prey tirelessly until it or the nupperibos are slain, or some other potential victim crosses the devils' path and distracts them.

Nupperibos unthinkingly obey any command they receive telepathically from another devil. This blind loyalty makes them the easiest of infernal troops to lead into battle, but their presence in a legion does nothing to elevate its general's status.

Nupperibo
Medium Fiend (Devil), Typically Lawful Evil

Armor Class 13 (natural armor)
Hit Points 11 (2d8 + 2)
Speed 20 ft.

STR	DEX	CON	INT	WIS	CHA
16 (+3)	11 (+0)	13 (+1)	3 (−4)	8 (−1)	1 (−5)

Skills Perception +1
Damage Resistances acid, cold
Damage Immunities fire, poison
Condition Immunities blinded, charmed, frightened, poisoned
Senses blindsight 20 ft. (blind beyond this radius), passive Perception 11
Languages understands Infernal but can't speak
Challenge 1/2 (100 XP)   **Proficiency Bonus** +2

Cloud of Vermin. Any creature, other than a devil, that starts its turn within 20 feet of one or more nupperibos must succeed on a DC 11 Constitution saving throw or take 5 (2d4) acid damage. A creature within the areas of two or more nupperibos makes the saving throw with disadvantage.

Driven Tracker. In the Nine Hells, the nupperibo can flawlessly track any creature that has taken damage from any nupperibo's Cloud of Vermin within the previous 24 hours.

Actions

Bite. Melee Weapon Attack: +5 to hit, reach 5 ft., one target. Hit: 6 (1d6 + 3) piercing damage.

RALPH HORSLEY

> *Mind flayers unleash all manner of foul experiments upon the planes with little thought for the consequences. Here, though, I suspect another influence: Juiblex.*
>
> —Mordenkainen

OBLEXES

By experimenting on the slimes, jellies, and puddings that infest the depths of the Underdark, mind flayers created a special breed of Ooze, the oblex—a slime capable of assaulting the minds of other creatures. These pools of jelly are cunning hunters that feed on thoughts and memories. The sharper the mind, the better the meal, so oblexes hunt targets more likely to be intelligent, such as wizards and other spellcasters. When suitable fare comes within reach, an oblex draws its body up to engulf its victim. As it withdraws, it plunders the creature's mind, leaving its prey befuddled and confused—or dead.

When oblexes feed on thoughts, they can form weird copies of their prey to use as lures, which helps them harvest even more victims for their mind flayer masters.

OBLEX SPAWN

An oblex devours memories not only to sustain its existence, but also to spawn new oblexes. Each time it fully drains the memories of a victim, it gains the creature's personality—now twisted by the oblex's foul nature. The more memories an oblex steals, the larger it becomes, until it must shed a personality it has absorbed or else become uncontrolled and erratic. This act spawns a new oblex.

Newly formed oblexes lack the capabilities of their older kin. They seek only to feed on memories and grow until they can impersonate their victims.

ADULT AND ELDER OBLEXES

Older oblexes, called adults and elders, have eaten so many memories that they can form duplicates of the creatures they have devoured from the substance of their bodies, sending these copies off to lure prey into their clutches while remaining tethered to the slime by long tendrils of goo. These duplicated creatures are indistinguishable from their victims except for a faint sulfurous smell. Oblexes use these duplicates to lead prey into danger or to infiltrate settlements so they can feed on superior victims.

OBLEX SPAWN

Tiny Ooze, Typically Lawful Evil

Armor Class 13
Hit Points 18 (4d4 + 8)
Speed 20 ft.

STR	DEX	CON	INT	WIS	CHA
8 (−1)	16 (+3)	15 (+2)	14 (+2)	11 (+0)	10 (+0)

Saving Throws Int +4, Cha +2
Condition Immunities blinded, charmed, deafened, exhaustion, prone
Senses blindsight 60 ft. (blind beyond this radius), passive Perception 12
Languages —
Challenge 1/4 (50 XP)   **Proficiency Bonus** +2

Amorphous. The oblex can move through a space as narrow as 1 inch wide without squeezing.

Aversion to Fire. If the oblex takes fire damage, it has disadvantage on attack rolls and ability checks until the end of its next turn.

Unusual Nature. The oblex doesn't require sleep.

ACTIONS

Pseudopod. *Melee Weapon Attack:* +5 to hit, reach 5 ft., one target. *Hit:* 5 (1d4 + 3) bludgeoning damage plus 2 (1d4) psychic damage.

An oblex wants memories, but not to serve any end of its own making. Oblexes are hungry for memories and personalities because they are empty without such nourishment.

In this way they serve their creators, illithids. An oblex in the range of an elder brain's powers provides everything necessary for the mind flayers to find choice victims.

—Mordenkainen

ADULT OBLEX
Medium Ooze, Typically Lawful Evil

Armor Class 14
Hit Points 75 (10d8 + 30)
Speed 20 ft.

STR	DEX	CON	INT	WIS	CHA
8 (−1)	19 (+4)	16 (+3)	19 (+4)	12 (+1)	15 (+2)

Saving Throws Int +7, Cha +5
Skills Deception +5, Perception +4, plus one of the following: Arcana +7, History +7, Nature +7, or Religion +7
Condition Immunities blinded, charmed, deafened, exhaustion, prone
Senses blindsight 60 ft. (blind beyond this radius), passive Perception 14
Languages Common plus two more languages
Challenge 5 (1,800 XP)　　　　**Proficiency Bonus** +3

Amorphous. The oblex can move through a space as narrow as 1 inch wide without squeezing.

Aversion to Fire. If the oblex takes fire damage, it has disadvantage on attack rolls and ability checks until the end of its next turn.

Unusual Nature. The oblex doesn't require sleep.

ACTIONS

Multiattack. The oblex makes two Pseudopod attacks, and it uses Eat Memories.

Pseudopod. *Melee Weapon Attack:* +7 to hit, reach 5 ft., one target. *Hit:* 11 (2d6 + 4) bludgeoning damage plus 7 (2d6) psychic damage.

Eat Memories. The oblex targets one creature it can see within 5 feet of it. The target must succeed on a DC 15 Wisdom saving throw or take 18 (4d8) psychic damage and become memory drained until it finishes a short or long rest or until it benefits from the *greater restoration* or *heal* spell. Constructs, Oozes, Plants, and Undead succeed on the save automatically.

While memory drained, the target must roll a d4 and subtract the number rolled from its ability checks and attack rolls. Each time the target is memory drained beyond the first, the die size increases by one: the d4 becomes a d6, the d6 becomes a d8, and so on until the die becomes a d20, at which point the target becomes unconscious for 1 hour. The effect then ends.

The oblex learns all the languages a memory-drained target knows and gains all its skill proficiencies.

Spellcasting (Psionics). The oblex casts one of the following spells, requiring no spell components and using Intelligence as the spellcasting ability (spell save DC 15):

3/day each: *charm person* (as 5th-level spell), *detect thoughts*, *hypnotic pattern*

BONUS ACTIONS

Sulfurous Impersonation. The oblex extrudes a piece of itself that assumes the appearance of one Medium or smaller creature whose memories it has stolen. This simulacrum appears, feels, and sounds exactly like the creature it impersonates, though it smells faintly of sulfur. The oblex can impersonate 1d4 + 1 different creatures, each one tethered to its body by a strand of slime that can extend up to 120 feet away. The simulacrum is an extension of the oblex, meaning that the oblex occupies its space and the simulacrum's space simultaneously. The tether is immune to damage, but it is severed if there is no opening at least 1 inch wide between the oblex and the simulacrum. The simulacrum disappears if the tether is severed.

ELDER OBLEX

Huge Ooze, Typically Lawful Evil

Armor Class 16 (natural armor)
Hit Points 115 (10d12 + 50)
Speed 20 ft.

STR	DEX	CON	INT	WIS	CHA
15 (+2)	16 (+3)	21 (+5)	22 (+6)	13 (+1)	18 (+4)

Saving Throws Int +10, Cha +8
Skills Arcana +10, Deception +8, History +10, Nature +10, Perception +5, Religion +10
Condition Immunities blinded, charmed, deafened, exhaustion, prone
Senses blindsight 60 ft. (blind beyond this radius), passive Perception 15
Languages Common plus six more languages
Challenge 10 (5,900 XP)   **Proficiency Bonus** +4

Amorphous. The oblex can move through a space as narrow as 1 inch wide without squeezing.

Aversion to Fire. If the oblex takes fire damage, it has disadvantage on attack rolls and ability checks until the end of its next turn.

Unusual Nature. The oblex doesn't require sleep.

ACTIONS

Multiattack. The elder oblex makes two Pseudopod attacks, and it uses Eat Memories.

Pseudopod. *Melee Weapon Attack:* +7 to hit, reach 10 ft., one target. *Hit:* 17 (4d6 + 3) bludgeoning damage plus 14 (4d6) psychic damage.

Eat Memories. The oblex targets one creature it can see within 5 feet of it. The target must succeed on a DC 18 Wisdom saving throw or take 44 (8d10) psychic damage and become memory drained until it finishes a short or long rest or until it benefits from the *greater restoration* or *heal* spell. Constructs, Oozes, Plants, and Undead succeed on the save automatically.

While memory drained, the target must roll a d4 and subtract the number rolled from its ability checks and attack rolls. Each time the target is memory drained beyond the first, the die size increases by one: the d4 becomes a d6, the d6 becomes a d8, and so on until the die becomes a d20, at which point the target becomes unconscious for 1 hour. The effect then ends.

The oblex learns all the languages a memory-drained target knows and gains all its skill proficiencies.

Spellcasting (Psionics). The oblex casts one of the following spells, requiring no spell components and using Intelligence as the spellcasting ability (spell save DC 18):

At will: *charm person* (as 5th-level spell), *detect thoughts*
3/day each: *dimension door*, *dominate person*, *hypnotic pattern*, *telekinesis*

BONUS ACTIONS

Sulfurous Impersonation. The oblex extrudes a piece of itself that assumes the appearance of one Medium or smaller creature whose memories it has stolen. This simulacrum appears, feels, and sounds exactly like the creature it impersonates, though it smells faintly of sulfur. The oblex can impersonate 2d6 + 1 different creatures, each one tethered to its body by a strand of slime that can extend up to 120 feet away. The simulacrum is an extension of the oblex, meaning that the oblex occupies its space and the simulacrum's space simultaneously. The tether is immune to damage, but it is severed if there is no opening at least 1 inch wide between the oblex and the simulacrum. The simulacrum disappears if the tether is severed.

ERIC BELISLE

Ogre Battering Ram

Large Giant, Typically Chaotic Evil

Armor Class 11 (hide armor)
Hit Points 76 (9d10 + 27)
Speed 40 ft.

STR	DEX	CON	INT	WIS	CHA
19 (+4)	8 (−1)	16 (+3)	5 (−3)	7 (−2)	7 (−2)

Senses darkvision 60 ft., passive Perception 8
Languages Common, Giant
Challenge 4 (1,100 XP) **Proficiency Bonus** +2

Siege Monster. The ogre deals double damage to objects and structures.

Actions

Multiattack. The ogre makes two Bash attacks.

Bash. *Melee Weapon Attack:* +6 to hit, reach 5 ft., one target. *Hit:* 15 (2d10 + 4) bludgeoning damage, and the ogre can push the target 5 feet away if the target is a Huge or smaller creature.

Reactions

Block the Path. When a creature enters a space within 5 feet of the ogre, the ogre makes a Bash attack against that creature. If the attack hits, the target's speed is reduced to 0 until the start of the ogre's next turn.

Ogre Bolt Launcher

Large Giant, Typically Chaotic Evil

Armor Class 13 (hide armor)
Hit Points 59 (7d10 + 21)
Speed 40 ft.

STR	DEX	CON	INT	WIS	CHA
19 (+4)	12 (+1)	16 (+3)	5 (−3)	7 (−2)	7 (−2)

Senses darkvision 60 ft., passive Perception 8
Languages Common, Giant
Challenge 2 (450 XP) **Proficiency Bonus** +2

Actions

Fist. *Melee Weapon Attack:* +6 to hit, reach 5 ft., one target. *Hit:* 9 (2d4 + 4) bludgeoning damage.

Bolt Launcher. *Ranged Weapon Attack:* +3 to hit, range 120/480 ft., one target. *Hit:* 17 (3d10 + 1) piercing damage.

Ogres of War

Ogres love to rush headlong into battle, but with enough time and patience, some of them learn to carry out specialized missions. The names they are given—the battering ram, the bolt launcher, the chain brute, and the howdah—reflect their particular functions. These jobs are tailored to take advantage of an ogre's strengths.

Ogre Battering Ram

An ogre battering ram carries an enormous club that's primarily used for bashing doors into kindling but also works well for smashing foes. These ogres are drilled in two simple tasks: rushing forward to shatter enemy fortifications and using their weapons to force an advancing enemy to halt.

Ogre Bolt Launcher

A bolt launcher carries a gigantic crossbow—a weapon so large it's essentially an ogre-held ballista. An ogre bolt launcher can load this immense weapon and loose its deadly missile as quickly as a dwarf handles a crossbow. The bolts are so large that few ogres can carry more than a half dozen at a time, but bolt launchers have been known to uproot small trees or tear beams out of buildings and launch those when their ammunition runs low.

Ogre Chain Brute

An ogre chain brute wields a great spiked chain, swinging it with both hands in a wide circle to knock foes off their feet. Alternatively, the ogre can swing the chain in a crushing overhead smash.

Ogre Howdah

The most unusual of the specialized ogres, the howdah carries a palisaded wooden fort on its back. The fort serves as a fighting platform for up to four Small people. Ogre howdahs are most often seen bearing bow- and spear-wielding goblins into battle, or perhaps kobolds or deep gnomes (all three appear in the *Monster Manual*), but they might also transport other Small folk.

Ogre Chain Brute
Large Giant, Typically Chaotic Evil

Armor Class 11 (hide armor)
Hit Points 59 (7d10 + 21)
Speed 40 ft.

STR	DEX	CON	INT	WIS	CHA
19 (+4)	8 (−1)	16 (+3)	5 (−3)	7 (−2)	7 (−2)

Senses darkvision 60 ft., passive Perception 8
Languages Common, Giant
Challenge 3 (700 XP) **Proficiency Bonus** +2

Actions

Fist. *Melee Weapon Attack:* +6 to hit, reach 5 ft., one target. *Hit:* 9 (2d4 + 4) bludgeoning damage.

Chain Smash (Recharge 6). *Melee Weapon Attack:* +6 to hit, reach 10 ft., one target. *Hit:* 13 (2d8 + 4) bludgeoning damage, and the target must succeed on a DC 14 Constitution saving throw or be stunned for 1 minute. The target repeats the saving throw if it takes damage and at the end of each of its turns, ending the effect on itself on a success.

Chain Sweep. The ogre swings its chain, and each creature within 10 feet of it must make a DC 14 Dexterity saving throw. On a failed saving throw, a creature takes 8 (1d8 + 4) bludgeoning damage and is knocked prone. On a successful save, the creature takes half as much damage and isn't knocked prone.

Ogre Howdah
Large Giant, Typically Chaotic Evil

Armor Class 15 (breastplate, shield)
Hit Points 59 (7d10 + 21)
Speed 40 ft.

STR	DEX	CON	INT	WIS	CHA
19 (+4)	8 (−1)	16 (+3)	5 (−3)	7 (−2)	7 (−2)

Senses darkvision 60 ft., passive Perception 8
Languages Common, Giant
Challenge 2 (450 XP) **Proficiency Bonus** +2

Howdah. The ogre carries a compact fort on its back. Up to four Small creatures can ride in the fort without squeezing. To make a melee attack against a target within 5 feet of the ogre, they must use spears or weapons with reach. Creatures in the fort have three-quarters cover against attacks and effects from outside it. If the ogre dies, creatures in the fort are placed in unoccupied spaces within 5 feet of the ogre.

Actions

Fist. *Melee Weapon Attack:* +6 to hit, reach 5 ft., one target. *Hit:* 11 (2d6 + 4) bludgeoning damage.

CHRIS SEAMAN

OINOLOTH

Grim specters of death, oinoloths bring pestilence wherever they go. When armies recognize their awful forms, their mere appearance causes soldiers to break ranks and flee, lest they succumb to one of the awful plagues that oinoloths let loose.

Oinoloths solve thorny problems by killing everyone involved. They are typically hired as a last resort when a siege has gone on too long or an army has proven too strong to overcome. Once summoned, oinoloths stalk the killing field, poisoning the ground and sickening creatures they encounter. Sometimes they might be hired to lift the very plagues they spread, but the price for such work is high, and the effort turns the creatures they save into debilitated wrecks.

OINOLOTH

Medium Fiend (Yugoloth), Typically Neutral Evil

Armor Class 17 (natural armor)
Hit Points 119 (14d8 + 56)
Speed 40 ft.

STR	DEX	CON	INT	WIS	CHA
19 (+4)	17 (+3)	18 (+4)	17 (+3)	16 (+3)	19 (+4)

Saving Throws Con +8, Wis +7
Skills Deception +8, Intimidation +8, Perception +7
Damage Resistances cold, fire, lightning; bludgeoning, piercing, and slashing from nonmagical attacks
Damage Immunities acid, poison
Condition Immunities poisoned
Senses blindsight 60 ft., darkvision 60 ft., passive Perception 17
Languages Abyssal, Infernal, telepathy 60 ft.
Challenge 12 (8,400 XP)   **Proficiency Bonus** +4

Magic Resistance. The oinoloth has advantage on saving throws against spells and other magical effects.

ACTIONS

Multiattack. The oinoloth makes two Claw attacks, and it uses Spellcasting or Teleport.

Claw. *Melee Weapon Attack:* +8 to hit, reach 5 ft., one target. *Hit:* 14 (3d6 + 4) slashing damage plus 22 (4d10) necrotic damage.

Corrupted Healing (Recharge 6). The oinoloth touches one willing creature within 5 feet of it. The target regains all its hit points. In addition, the oinoloth can end one disease on the target or remove one of the following conditions from it: blinded, deafened, paralyzed, or poisoned. The target then gains 1 level of exhaustion, and its hit point maximum is reduced by 7 (2d6). This reduction can be removed only by a *wish* spell or by casting *greater restoration* on the target three times within the same hour. The target dies if its hit point maximum is reduced to 0.

Spellcasting. The oinoloth casts one of the following spells, requiring no material components and using Charisma as the spellcasting ability (spell save DC 16):

At will: *darkness*, *detect magic*, *dispel magic*, *hold monster*, *invisibility* (self only)
1/day each: *feeblemind*, *globe of invulnerability*

Teleport. The oinoloth teleports, along with any equipment it is wearing or carrying, up to 60 feet to an unoccupied space it can see.

BONUS ACTIONS

Bringer of Plagues (Recharge 5–6). The oinoloth blights the area in a 30-foot-radius sphere centered on itself. The blight lasts for 24 hours. While the area is blighted, all normal plants there wither and die.

Furthermore, when a creature moves into the blighted area or starts its turn there, that creature must make a DC 16 Constitution saving throw. On a failed save, the creature takes 14 (4d6) poison damage and is poisoned. On a successful save, the creature is immune to the oinoloth's Bringer of Plagues for the next 24 hours.

The poisoned creature can't regain hit points. After every 24 hours that elapse, the poisoned creature can repeat the saving throw. On a failed save, the creature's hit point maximum is reduced by 5 (1d10). This reduction lasts until the poison ends, and the target dies if its hit point maximum is reduced to 0. The poison ends after the creature successfully saves against it three times.

MICHAEL BERUBE

ORCUS

Orcus is the Demon Prince of Undeath, also known as the Blood Lord. While he takes pleasure in the sufferings of the living, he far prefers the company and service of Undead. His desire is to see all life quenched and the multiverse transformed into a vast necropolis populated solely by Undead creatures under his command.

Orcus rewards those who spread death in his name by granting them a small portion of his power. The least of these become ghouls and zombies (both appear in the *Monster Manual*) that serve in his legions, while his favored servants are the cultists and necromancers who murder the living and then manipulate the dead, emulating their dread master.

Orcus is a bestial creature of corruption with a diseased, decaying look. He has the lower body of a goat and a humanlike upper body with a belly swollen with rot. Great bat wings sprout from his shoulders, and his head is like the skull of a goat, the flesh nearly rotted from it. In one hand, he wields the legendary *Wand of Orcus*, which is described in the *Dungeon Master's Guide*.

ORCUS'S LAIR

Orcus makes his lair in the fortress city of Naratyr, which is on Thanatos, the layer of the Abyss that he rules. Surrounded by a moat fed by the River Styx, Naratyr is an eerily quiet and cold city, its streets empty for hours at a time. The central castle of bone has interior walls of flesh and carpets made of woven hair. The city contains wandering Undead, many of which are engaged in continuous battles with one another.

LAIR ACTIONS

On initiative count 20 (losing initiative ties), Orcus can take one of the following lair actions; he can't take the same lair action two rounds in a row:

Deadly Utterance. Orcus's voice booms throughout the lair. His utterance causes one creature of his choice to be subjected to *power word kill*. Orcus needn't see the creature, but he must be aware that the individual is in the lair.

Grasp of the Dead. Orcus causes skeletal arms to rise from an area on the ground in a 20-foot square that he can see. They last until the next

RICHARD WHITTERS

initiative count 20. Each creature in that area when the arms appear must succeed on a DC 23 Strength saving throw or be restrained until the arms disappear or until Orcus releases them (no action required).

Undead Servants. Orcus causes up to six corpses within the lair to rise as **skeletons**, **zombies**, or **ghouls** (all appear in the *Monster Manual*). These Undead obey his telepathic commands, which can reach anywhere in the lair.

REGIONAL EFFECTS

The region containing Orcus's lair is warped by his magic, creating one or more of the following effects:

Charnel Realm. The air is filled with the stench of rotting flesh, and buzzing flies grow thick within the region.

Undead Beasts. Dead Beasts periodically animate as Undead mockeries of their former selves. Skeletal and zombie versions of local wildlife are commonly seen in the area.

If Orcus dies, these effects fade over the course of 1d10 days.

CULTISTS OF ORCUS

Orcus grants his rank-and-file cultists the Undying Soul trait, and his cult leaders can gain the Aura of Death trait.

Undying Soul (Recharges after a Short or Long Rest). If this creature is reduced to 0 hit points, it immediately makes a DC 10 Constitution saving throw. If it succeeds, it is instead reduced to 1 hit point.

Aura of Death. This creature emanates a deathly aura that extends 30 feet in every direction from its space while it isn't incapacitated. The aura is blocked by total cover. While in the aura, the creature and any friendly Undead are immune to the frightened condition and have resistance to radiant damage. Enemies have disadvantage on death saving throws while in the aura.

ORCUS
Huge Fiend (Demon), Chaotic Evil

Armor Class 17 (natural armor), 20 with the *Wand of Orcus*
Hit Points 405 (30d12 + 210)
Speed 40 ft., fly 40 ft.

STR	DEX	CON	INT	WIS	CHA
27 (+8)	14 (+2)	25 (+7)	20 (+5)	20 (+5)	25 (+7)

Saving Throws Dex +10, Con +15, Wis +13
Skills Arcana +12, Perception +12
Damage Resistances cold, fire, lightning
Damage Immunities necrotic, poison; bludgeoning, piercing, and slashing that is nonmagical
Condition Immunities charmed, exhaustion, frightened, poisoned
Senses truesight 120 ft., passive Perception 22
Languages all, telepathy 120 ft.
Challenge 26 (90,000 XP)   **Proficiency Bonus** +8

Legendary Resistance (3/Day). If Orcus fails a saving throw, he can choose to succeed instead.

Magic Resistance. Orcus has advantage on saving throws against spells and other magical effects.

Master of Undeath. Orcus can cast *animate dead* (at will) and *create undead* (3/day). He chooses the level at which the spells are cast, and the creatures created by them remain under his control indefinitely. Additionally, he can cast *create undead* even when it isn't night.

Special Equipment. Orcus wields the *Wand of Orcus*.

ACTIONS

Multiattack. Orcus makes three *Wand of Orcus*, Tail, or Necrotic Bolt attacks.

Wand of Orcus. *Melee Weapon Attack:* +19 to hit, reach 10 ft., one target. *Hit:* 24 (3d8 + 11) bludgeoning damage plus 13 (2d12) necrotic damage.

Tail. *Melee Weapon Attack:* +16 to hit, reach 10 ft., one target. *Hit:* 21 (3d8 + 8) force damage plus 9 (2d8) poison damage.

Necrotic Bolt. *Ranged Spell Attack:* +15 to hit, range 120 ft., one target. *Hit:* 29 (5d8 + 7) necrotic damage.

Conjure Undead (1/Day). While holding the *Wand of Orcus*, Orcus conjures Undead creatures whose combined average hit points don't exceed 500. These creatures magically rise up from the ground or otherwise form in unoccupied spaces within 300 feet of Orcus and obey his commands until they are destroyed or until he dismisses them as an action.

Spellcasting. Orcus casts one of the following spells, requiring no material components and using Charisma as the spellcasting ability (spell save DC 23):

At will: *detect magic*
3/day: *dispel magic*
1/day: *time stop*

Wand Spellcasting. While holding the *Wand of Orcus*, Orcus casts one of the following spells (spell save DC 18), some of which require charges; the wand has 7 charges to fuel these spells, and it regains 1d4 + 3 charges daily at dawn:

At will: *animate dead* (as an action), *blight*, *speak with dead*
1 charge each: *circle of death*, *finger of death*
2 charges: *power word kill*

LEGENDARY ACTIONS

Orcus can take 3 legendary actions, choosing from the options below. Only one legendary action option can be used at a time and only at the end of another creature's turn. Orcus regains spent legendary actions at the start of his turn.

Attack. Orcus makes one Tail or Necrotic Bolt attack.
Creeping Death (Costs 2 Actions). Orcus chooses a point on the ground that he can see within 100 feet of him. A cylinder of swirling necrotic energy 60 feet tall and with a 10-foot radius rises from that point and lasts until the end of Orcus's next turn. Creatures in that area have vulnerability to necrotic damage.

Orthon

When an archduke of the Nine Hells needs a creature tracked, found, and either done away with or captured, the task usually falls to an orthon. These devils are infernal bounty hunters, tireless in their pursuit of their quarry across the multiverse.

Orthons are infamous for their sharp senses. Because an orthon can become invisible at will, its quarry is often unaware of being hunted until the orthon strikes. This invisibility can be disrupted when the devil is attacked, however, so a strong counterattack is often the best defense against it.

Orthons value the challenge of the chase and the thrill of one-on-one combat above all else. An orthon's first loyalty is to its archduke, but one with no immediate assignment might work for anyone who promises it a worthy struggle against a lethal foe. Because they travel widely, orthons are unequaled as guides through the layers of the Nine Hells.

ORTHON
Large Fiend (Devil), Typically Lawful Evil

Armor Class 17 (half plate)
Hit Points 105 (10d10 + 50)
Speed 30 ft., climb 30 ft.

STR	DEX	CON	INT	WIS	CHA
22 (+6)	16 (+3)	21 (+5)	15 (+2)	15 (+2)	16 (+3)

Saving Throws Dex +7, Con +9, Wis +6
Skills Perception +10, Stealth +11, Survival +10
Damage Resistances cold; bludgeoning, piercing, and slashing from nonmagical attacks that aren't silvered
Damage Immunities fire, poison
Condition Immunities charmed, exhaustion, poisoned
Senses darkvision 120 ft., truesight 30 ft., passive Perception 20
Languages Common, Infernal, telepathy 120 ft.
Challenge 10 (5,900 XP)   **Proficiency Bonus** +4

Magic Resistance. The orthon has advantage on saving throws against spells and other magical effects.

Actions

Infernal Dagger. *Melee Weapon Attack:* +10 to hit, reach 5 ft., one target. *Hit:* 11 (2d4 + 6) force damage, and the target must make a DC 17 Constitution saving throw, taking 22 (4d10) poison damage on a failed save, or half as much damage on a successful one. On a failure, the target is also poisoned for 1 minute. The poisoned target can repeat the saving throw at the end of each of its turns, ending the effect on itself on a success.

Brass Crossbow. *Ranged Weapon Attack:* +7 to hit, range 100/400 ft., one target. *Hit:* 14 (2d10 + 3) force damage. The target also suffers one of the following effects of the orthon's choice; the orthon can't use the same effect two rounds in a row:

Acid. The target must make a DC 17 Constitution saving throw, taking 17 (5d6) acid damage on a failed save, or half as much damage on a successful one.

Blindness. The target takes 5 (1d10) radiant damage. In addition, the target and each creature within 20 feet of it must succeed on a DC 17 Dexterity saving throw or be blinded until the end of the orthon's next turn.

Concussion. The target and each creature within 20 feet of it must make a DC 17 Constitution saving throw, taking 13 (2d12) thunder damage on a failed save, or half as much damage on a successful one.

Entanglement. The target must succeed on a DC 17 Dexterity saving throw or be restrained for 1 hour by strands of sticky webbing. The target can escape by taking an action to make a DC 17 Strength or Dexterity check and succeeding.

Paralysis. The target takes 22 (4d10) lightning damage and must succeed on a DC 17 Constitution saving throw or be paralyzed for 1 minute. The paralyzed target can repeat the saving throw at the end of each of its turns, ending the effect on itself on a success.

Tracking. For the next 24 hours, the orthon knows the direction and distance to the target, as long as it's on the same plane of existence. If the target is on a different plane, the orthon knows which one, but not the exact location there.

Bonus Actions

Invisibility Field (Recharge 4–6). The orthon becomes invisible. Any equipment it wears or carries is also invisible as long as the equipment is on its person. This invisibility ends immediately after it makes an attack roll or is hit by an attack roll.

Reactions

Explosive Retribution. In response to dropping to 15 hit points or fewer, the orthon explodes. All other creatures within 30 feet of it must each make a DC 17 Dexterity saving throw, taking 9 (2d8) fire damage plus 9 (2d8) thunder damage on a failed save, or half as much damage on a successful one. The orthon, its infernal dagger, and its brass crossbow are destroyed.

ILYA SHKIPIN

To rise like a phoenix from the ashes—so many use that quaint colloquialism. Little do they know about the true horror of such a rebirth.

—Mordenkainen

PHOENIX

Releasing a phoenix from the Inner Planes creates an explosion of fire that spreads across the sky. An enormous fiery bird forms in the center of the flames and smoke—an elder Elemental possessed by a need to burn everything to ash. The phoenix rarely stays in one place for long as it strives to transform the world into an inferno.

PHOENIX

Gargantuan Elemental, Typically Neutral

Armor Class 18
Hit Points 175 (10d20 + 70)
Speed 20 ft., fly 120 ft.

STR	DEX	CON	INT	WIS	CHA
19 (+4)	26 (+8)	25 (+7)	2 (−4)	21 (+5)	18 (+4)

Saving Throws Wis +10, Cha +9
Damage Resistances bludgeoning, piercing, and slashing from nonmagical attacks
Damage Immunities fire, poison
Condition Immunities exhaustion, grappled, paralyzed, petrified, poisoned, prone, restrained, stunned
Senses darkvision 60 ft., passive Perception 15
Languages —
Challenge 16 (15,000 XP)   **Proficiency Bonus** +5

Fiery Death and Rebirth. If the phoenix dies, it explodes. Each creature in 60-foot-radius sphere centered on the phoenix must make a DC 20 Dexterity saving throw, taking 22 (4d10) fire damage on a failed save, or half as much damage on a successful one. The fire ignites flammable objects in the area that aren't being worn or carried.

The explosion destroys the phoenix's body and leaves behind an egg-shaped cinder, which weighs 5 pounds. The cinder deals 21 (6d6) fire damage to any creature that touches it, though no more than once per round. The cinder is immune to all damage, and after 1d6 days, it hatches a new phoenix.

Fire Form. The phoenix can move through a space as narrow as 1 inch wide without squeezing.

Any creature that touches the phoenix or hits it with a melee attack while within 5 feet of it takes 5 (1d10) fire damage. In addition, the phoenix can enter a hostile creature's space and stop there. The first time it enters a creature's space on a turn, that creature takes 5 (1d10) fire damage.

With a touch, the phoenix can also ignite flammable objects that aren't being worn or carried (no action required).

Flyby. The phoenix doesn't provoke opportunity attacks when it flies out of an enemy's reach.

Illumination. The phoenix sheds bright light in a 60-foot radius and dim light for an additional 60 feet.

Legendary Resistance (3/Day). If the phoenix fails a saving throw, it can choose to succeed instead.

Siege Monster. The phoenix deals double damage to objects and structures.

ACTIONS

Multiattack. The phoenix makes one Beak attack and one Fiery Talons attack.

Beak. *Melee Weapon Attack:* +13 to hit, reach 15 ft., one target. *Hit:* 15 (2d6 + 8) fire damage.

Fiery Talons. *Melee Weapon Attack:* +13 to hit, reach 15 ft., one target. *Hit:* 17 (2d8 + 8) fire damage.

LEGENDARY ACTIONS

The phoenix can take 3 legendary actions, choosing from the options below. Only one legendary action option can be used at a time and only at the end of another creature's turn. The phoenix regains spent legendary actions at the start of its turn.

Move. The phoenix moves up to its speed.
Peck. The phoenix makes one Beak attack.
Swoop (Costs 2 Actions). The phoenix moves up to its speed and makes one Fiery Talons attack.

QUICKLING

Quicklings rocket through twisted forests where the unseelie fey hold sway, both in the Feywild and in the world. These slender Fey resemble miniature elves with feral features and cold eyes that gleam like jewels. Racing faster than the eye can track, they appear as little more than blurry waverings in the air.

Quicklings owe their existence—and their plight—to the Queen of Air and Darkness, the dread ruler of the Gloaming Court. Once a species of lazy and egotistical Fey, quicklings' predecessors were late in answering the queen's summons one time too many. To hasten their pace and teach them to mind her will, the queen sped up their internal clocks and shrank them. Her curse gave quicklings amazing speed but also accelerated their passage through life—no quickling lives longer than fifteen years.

The mortal realm is a ponderous place to a quickling's eye: a hurricane creeps gradually across the sky, a torrent of rain drifts earthward like lazy snowflakes, lightning crawls in a meandering path from cloud to cloud. The slow and boring world seems to be populated by torpid creatures whose deep, mooing speech lacks meaning.

To other creatures, quicklings seem blindingly fast, vanishing into an indistinct blur as they move. Their cruel laughter is a burst of rapid staccato sounds, their speech a shrill squeal. Only when quicklings deliberately slow down, which they prefer not to do, can other beings properly see, hear, and comprehend them. Never truly at rest, "stationary" quicklings constantly pace and shift in place, as though they can't wait to be off again.

Quicklings have a capricious nature that goes well with their energy level: they think as fast as they run, and they are always up to something. They spend most of their time perpetrating acts of mischief on slower creatures. One rarely passes up an opportunity to tie a person's bootlaces together, move the stool a creature is about to sit on, or unbuckle a saddle while no one's looking.

Tricks of that sort are hardly the limit of quicklings' artful malice, however. They don't commit outright murder, but they can ruin lives in plenty of other ways: stealing an important letter, swiping coins collected for the poor, planting a stolen item in someone's bag. Quicklings enjoy causing suffering that transcends mere mischief, especially when the blame for their actions falls on others and creates discord.

QUICKLING
Tiny Fey, Typically Chaotic Evil

Armor Class 16
Hit Points 10 (3d4 + 3)
Speed 120 ft.

STR	DEX	CON	INT	WIS	CHA
4 (−3)	23 (+6)	13 (+1)	10 (+0)	12 (+1)	7 (−2)

Skills Acrobatics +8, Sleight of Hand +8, Stealth +8, Perception +5
Senses darkvision 60 ft., passive Perception 15
Languages Common, Sylvan
Challenge 1 (200 XP)   **Proficiency Bonus** +2

Blurred Movement. Attack rolls against the quickling have disadvantage unless it is incapacitated or its speed is 0.

Evasion. If the quickling is subjected to an effect that allows it to make a Dexterity saving throw to take only half damage, it instead takes no damage if it succeeds on the saving throw and only half damage if it fails, provided it isn't incapacitated.

ACTIONS

Multiattack. The quickling makes three Dagger attacks.

Dagger. *Melee or Ranged Weapon Attack:* +8 to hit, reach 5 ft. or range 20/60 ft., one target. *Hit:* 8 (1d4 + 6) piercing damage.

REDCAP

A redcap is a homicidal Fey creature born of blood lust. Redcaps, although small, have formidable strength, which they use to hunt and kill without hesitation or regret.

In the Feywild, or where that plane touches the material world at a fey crossing, if a sentient creature acts on an intense desire for bloodshed, one or more redcaps might appear where the blood of a slain person soaks the ground. At first, new redcaps look like tiny bloodstained mushrooms just pushing their caps out of the soil. When moonlight shines on one of these caps, a creature that resembles a wizened and undersized gnome with a hunched back and a sinewy frame springs from the earth. The creature has a pointed leather cap, clothing of similar material, heavy iron boots, and a heavy bladed weapon. From the moment redcaps awaken, they desire only murder and carnage, and they constantly seek to satisfy these cravings.

Redcaps lack subtlety. They live for direct confrontation and the mayhem of mortal combat. Even if a redcap wanted to be stealthy, the creature's iron boots force them to take ponderous, thunderous steps. When a redcap is near potential prey, though, they can close the distance quickly and get in a vicious swing of their weapon before the target can react.

Redcaps' desire to slay is rooted in their will to survive. To sustain their unnatural existence, they must soak their hats in the fresh blood of their victims. When redcaps are born, their hats are coated with wet blood, and they know that if the blood isn't replenished at least once every three days, they will vanish as if they had never been.

Some redcaps can sense the being whose murderous acts led to their birth. They typically use this innate connection to find their creator and make that creature their first victim, though they might instead seek out their maker to enjoy proximity to a kindred spirit. Although redcaps don't usually operate in groups, an individual responsible for the creation of multiple redcaps at the same site could attract the entire group to serve as cohorts, emulating that individual's murderous handiwork. Some hags and wicked mages know methods to call redcaps out of the Feywild and might likewise put teams of them to work as grisly servants.

In any case, if a redcap works with another being, the redcap demands to be paid in victims. A patron who tries to stifle a redcap's natural and necessary urge for blood risks becoming the redcap's next target.

REDCAP
Small Fey, Typically Chaotic Evil

Armor Class 14 (natural armor)
Hit Points 45 (6d6 + 24)
Speed 25 ft.

STR	DEX	CON	INT	WIS	CHA
18 (+4)	13 (+1)	18 (+4)	10 (+0)	12 (+1)	9 (−1)

Skills Athletics +6, Perception +3
Senses darkvision 60 ft., passive Perception 13
Languages Common, Sylvan
Challenge 3 (700 XP)   **Proficiency Bonus** +2

Iron Boots. The redcap has disadvantage on Dexterity (Stealth) checks.

Outsize Strength. While grappling, the redcap is considered to be Medium. Also, wielding a heavy weapon doesn't impose disadvantage on its attack rolls.

ACTIONS

Multiattack. The redcap makes three Wicked Sickle attacks.

Wicked Sickle. *Melee Weapon Attack:* +6 to hit, reach 5 ft., one target. *Hit:* 9 (2d4 + 4) slashing damage.

Ironbound Pursuit. The redcap moves up to its speed to a creature it can see and kicks with its iron boots. The target must succeed on a DC 14 Dexterity saving throw or take 20 (3d10 + 4) bludgeoning damage and be knocked prone.

RETRIEVER

The retriever is a potent, spider-like Construct conceived and built by Underdark followers of Lolth for one original purpose—to prowl the Abyss and capture demons for these cultists to enslave or use in their rituals. The automatons proved so effective and so fearsome that they now perform many different missions.

Though retrievers were created to operate only in the Abyss, they are sometimes dispatched when a powerful devotee of Lolth needs some creature or object captured and brought back alive and intact. Only under the rarest of circumstances is a retriever handed over or sold to others, since Lolth's cultists don't want to take the chance that their creations will be turned against them.

RETRIEVER
Large Construct, Typically Lawful Evil

Armor Class 19 (natural armor)
Hit Points 210 (20d10 + 100)
Speed 40 ft., climb 40 ft.

STR	DEX	CON	INT	WIS	CHA
22 (+6)	16 (+3)	20 (+5)	3 (–4)	11 (+0)	4 (–3)

Saving Throws Dex +8, Con +10, Wis +5
Skills Perception +5, Stealth +8
Damage Immunities necrotic, poison, psychic; bludgeoning, piercing, and slashing from nonmagical attacks that aren't adamantine
Condition Immunities charmed, exhaustion, frightened, paralyzed, poisoned
Senses blindsight 30 ft., darkvision 60 ft., passive Perception 15
Languages understands Abyssal, Elvish, and Undercommon but can't speak
Challenge 14 (11,500 XP)   **Proficiency Bonus** +5

Faultless Tracker. The retriever is given a quarry by its master. The quarry can be a specific creature or object the master is personally acquainted with, or it can be a general type of creature or object the master has seen before. The retriever knows the direction and distance to its quarry as long as the two of them are on the same plane of existence. The retriever can have only one such quarry at a time. The retriever also always knows the location of its master.

ACTIONS

Multiattack. The retriever makes two Foreleg attacks, and it uses Force Beam or Paralyzing Beam, if available.

Foreleg. *Melee Weapon Attack:* +11 to hit, reach 10 ft., one target. *Hit:* 15 (2d8 + 6) slashing damage.

Force Beam. The retriever targets one creature it can see within 60 feet of it. The target must make a DC 16 Dexterity saving throw, taking 27 (5d10) force damage on a failed save, or half as much damage on a successful one.

Paralyzing Beam (Recharge 5–6). The retriever targets one creature it can see within 60 feet of it. The target must succeed on a DC 18 Constitution saving throw or be paralyzed for 1 minute. The paralyzed target can repeat the saving throw at the end of each of its turns, ending the effect on itself on a success.

If the paralyzed creature is Medium or smaller, the retriever can pick it up as part of the retriever's move and walk or climb with it at full speed.

Spellcasting. The retriever casts one of the following spells, requiring no material components and using Wisdom as the spellcasting ability (spell save DC 13):

3/day each: *plane shift* (only self and up to one incapacitated creature, which is considered willing for the spell), *web*

RUTTERKIN

Rutterkins are warped demons that roam the Abyss in mobs, constantly searching for intruders to surround and devour. These Fiends protect the Abyss from non-demons. When they spot any interlopers, they gather in a crowd and surge forward, emitting a wave of fear in advance of their attacks that leaves their victims terrified and rooted in place.

Creatures bitten by rutterkins are exposed to a terrible disease that infects them with the corrupting influence of the Abyss. Victims afflicted with the disease experience tremendous pain as their bodies become disfigured, flesh twisting around the bones, until they transform to join the mass of manes demons (see the *Monster Manual*) that follow in the wake of the rutterkin mob that laid them low.

> Eugh, rutterkins. You've heard of stinking cloud—now get ready for its sequel, rancid crowd.

> (Mordenkainen, my dear, I know you just died inside when you read that. Kisses!)
> TASHA

RUTTERKIN

Medium Fiend (Demon), Typically Chaotic Evil

Armor Class 12
Hit Points 37 (5d8 + 15)
Speed 20 ft.

STR	DEX	CON	INT	WIS	CHA
14 (+2)	15 (+2)	17 (+3)	5 (−3)	12 (+1)	6 (−2)

Damage Resistances cold, fire, lightning
Damage Immunities poison
Condition Immunities charmed, frightened, poisoned
Senses darkvision 120 ft., passive Perception 11
Languages understands Abyssal but can't speak
Challenge 2 (450 XP)   **Proficiency Bonus** +2

Immobilizing Fear. When a creature that isn't a demon starts its turn within 30 feet of one or more rutterkins, that creature must make a DC 11 Wisdom saving throw. The creature has disadvantage on the save if it's within 30 feet of six or more rutterkins. On a failed save, the creature becomes frightened of the rutterkins for 1 minute. While frightened in this way, the creature is restrained. At the end of each of the frightened creature's turns, it can repeat the saving throw, ending the effect on itself on a success. On a successful save, the creature is immune to the Immobilizing Fear of all rutterkins for 24 hours.

ACTIONS

Bite. *Melee Weapon Attack:* +4 to hit, reach 5 ft., one target. *Hit:* 12 (3d6 + 2) piercing damage. If the target is a creature, it must succeed on a DC 13 Constitution saving throw against disease or become poisoned. At the end of each long rest, the poisoned target can repeat the saving throw, ending the effect on itself on a success. If the target is reduced to 0 hit points while poisoned in this way, it dies and instantly transforms into a living **manes** (see the *Monster Manual*). The transformation can be undone only by a *wish* spell.

SHAWN WOOD

R

Sea Spawn

Many of the stories sung as sea chanteys and re-counted in dockside taverns tell of people lost to the sea—but not merely drowned and gone. Some unfortunates taken by the ocean live on as sea spawn, haunting the waves like tortured reflections of their former selves. Coral encrusts them. Barnacles cling to their cold skin. Lungs that once filled with air can now breathe in water as well.

Tales provide myriad reasons for these strange transformations. Folklore warns against falling in love with a sea elf or merfolk, braving storms in hopes of a bounteous catch, and promising your heart to a sea god. Such cautionary tales disguise the deeper truth: things lurking beneath the waves strive to claim the hearts and minds of land dwellers.

Krakens, morkoths, sea hags, marids, storm giants, dragon turtles (morkoths appear in this book; the others appear in the *Monster Manual*)—all of these and more can mark mortals as their own and claim them as minions. Unlucky folk might become beholden to such a master through a bleak bargain, or they might find themselves cursed by one. Once warped into a fishlike form, a sea spawn can't leave the water for long without courting death.

Sea spawn come in a wide variety of forms. An individual might have a tentacle for an arm, the jaws of a shark, a sea urchin's spines, a whale's fin, octopus eyes, seaweed hair, or any combination of such qualities. Some of these piscine body parts provide them with special abilities.

The Sea Spawn of Purple Rocks

Visitors to a string of islands called the Purple Rocks (in the Forgotten Realms setting) might notice one curious fact about the islands' human inhabitants: no infants or elderly are among them. This is because babies born to the Rocklanders are claimed by a kraken (see the *Monster Manual*) named Slarkrethel. The experience transforms the children into fanatics dedicated to the kraken. They return from the sea as humans, but when they reach old age, they transform into sea spawn and rejoin their master in the depths. Some children return having suffered partial transformations and must conceal themselves from strangers until their full transformation in order to keep the secret of the Purple Rocks.

Kraken priests (in this book) tend to the kraken's flock. Most of the priests are island natives, but some are other sorts of creatures that live in the water around the Purple Rocks, such as merfolk or merrow (both of which appear in the *Monster Manual*), or even sea elves.

ERIC BELISLE

Sea Spawn
Medium Monstrosity, Typically Neutral Evil

Armor Class 11 (natural armor)
Hit Points 32 (5d8 + 10)
Speed 20 ft., swim 30 ft.

STR	DEX	CON	INT	WIS	CHA
15 (+2)	8 (−1)	15 (+2)	6 (−2)	10 (+0)	8 (−1)

Senses darkvision 120 ft., passive Perception 10
Languages understands Aquan and Common but can't speak
Challenge 1 (200 XP)   **Proficiency Bonus** +2

Limited Amphibiousness. The sea spawn can breathe air and water, but it needs to be submerged in the sea at least once a day for 1 minute to avoid suffocating.

Actions

Multiattack. The sea spawn makes two Unarmed Strike attacks and one Piscine Anatomy attack.

Unarmed Strike. *Melee Weapon Attack:* +4 to hit, reach 5 ft., one target. *Hit:* 4 (1d4 + 2) bludgeoning damage.

Piscine Anatomy. The sea spawn uses one of the following options (choose one or roll a d6):

1–2: Bite. *Melee Weapon Attack:* +4 to hit, reach 5 ft., one target. *Hit:* 4 (1d4 + 2) piercing damage.

3–4: Poison Quills. *Melee Weapon Attack:* +4 to hit, reach 5 ft., one creature. *Hit:* 3 (1d6) poison damage, and the target must succeed on a DC 12 Constitution saving throw or be poisoned for 1 minute. The target can repeat the saving throw at the end of each of its turns, ending the effect on itself on a success.

5–6: Tentacle. *Melee Weapon Attack:* +4 to hit, reach 10 ft., one target. *Hit:* 5 (1d6 + 2) bludgeoning damage, and the target is grappled (escape DC 12) if it is a Medium or smaller creature. Until this grapple ends, the sea spawn can't use this tentacle on another target.

SHADOW DANCER

SOUL MONGER

GLOOM WEAVER

SHADAR-KAI

In the gloom of the Shadowfell live shadar-kai, elves whose ancestors served the Raven Queen, a god of death and memory. They were brought to that realm in ages past, so long ago that they're now adapted to its cheerless environment, both physically and mentally.

Eons of exposure to the influence of the Shadowfell has left shadar-kai often joyless and mournful. In that realm, they have pale hair, wrinkled gray skin, and swollen joints that give them a corpselike aspect. They appear more youthful while on other planes, but their skin always retains a deathly ashen hue. When in the Shadowfell, they detest mirrors and avoid keeping things that remind them of their age.

Shadar-kai of the Raven Queen watch over both the Shadowfell and the Material Plane, scouting out choice souls and tragedies that might please their deity. They are rumored to be able to coax worldly events along tragic paths for her amusement. The Raven Queen is famously cryptic even to her most devoted followers, however; their efforts are rewarded only with vague omens they interpret as best they can.

FORTRESS OF MEMORIES

The shadar-kai who are most devoted to the Raven Queen serve her at the Fortress of Memories, her twisted castle in the Shadowfell. The fortress is a mournful place, filled with incessant echoes of the past. Flocks of ravens that act as the Raven Queen's eyes and ears darken the skies around it when they emerge from within, bearing her cryptic messages and omens far and wide across the multiverse.

Within the fortress are items that the Raven Queen finds irresistible: objects invested with deep feelings of sorrow, longing, or remorse. These items are brought to her as gifts from the shadar-kai, and include furniture, clocks, mirrors, jewels, and toys. Ghostly visions of people, places, and pets also appear in the fortress. Any of these things can spontaneously appear about her lair, every object and apparition being a metaphoric representation of some story—great or small—that was saturated with raw emotion.

Shadar-kai encountered outside the Shadowfell are often on quests to find the most sorrow-touched items they can find to bring back to their queen's gloomy castle.

GLOOM WEAVER

Although they're formidable warriors, gloom weavers are often content to hide in the shadows, watching as their very presence affects their victims. Their bleak energy weighs down the heart, causing those nearby to feel the approach of death. If detected, gloom weavers use their shadow magic to reduce enemies to ghastly corpses.

SHADOW DANCER

Those who have fought shadow dancers describe the experience as similar to fighting a living darkness. Every dim alcove and darkened nook is a place the lithe and acrobatic shadow dancers can emerge from to ambush their prey. Using this tactic, they attack their enemies from all angles with a flurry of entangling chains that hold fast and corrupt the flesh. When their quarry is helpless, they dispatch it and then loot the corpse for trinkets, particularly anything colorful and lively to gaze at after they return to the gloom of the Shadowfell.

SOUL MONGER

Wracked with despair over the loss of memories of a brighter time, soul mongers crave the vitality of others. The aching void within a soul monger radiates outward, manifesting as an unbearable weight that drains the vigor of anyone unfortunate enough to be in their presence. Those who have escaped the onslaught of a soul monger can hardly shake the memory of the sound they make—the moan of a tortured soul, lost in a bottomless well of tragedy.

SHADAR-KAI GLOOM WEAVER

Medium Humanoid (Elf), Typically Neutral Evil

Armor Class 14 (17 with *mage armor*)
Hit Points 104 (16d8 + 32)
Speed 30 ft.

STR	DEX	CON	INT	WIS	CHA
11 (+0)	18 (+4)	14 (+2)	15 (+2)	12 (+1)	18 (+4)

Saving Throws Dex +8, Con +6
Damage Immunities necrotic
Condition Immunities charmed, exhaustion
Senses darkvision 60 ft., passive Perception 11
Languages Common, Elvish
Challenge 9 (5,000 XP)   **Proficiency Bonus** +4

Burden of Time. Beasts and Humanoids (except elves) have disadvantage on saving throws while within 10 feet of the shadar-kai.

Fey Ancestry. The shadar-kai has advantage on saving throws against being charmed, and magic can't put it to sleep.

ACTIONS

Multiattack. The shadar-kai makes three Shadow Spear attacks. It can replace one attack with a use of Spellcasting.

Shadow Spear. *Melee or Ranged Weapon Attack:* +8 to hit, reach 5 ft. or range 30/120, one target. *Hit:* 7 (1d6 + 4) piercing damage plus 26 (4d12) necrotic damage. *Hit or Miss:* The spear magically returns to the shadar-kai's hand immediately after a ranged attack.

Spellcasting. The shadar-kai casts one of the following spells, requiring no material components and using Charisma as the spellcasting ability (spell save DC 16):

At will: *arcane eye, mage armor, minor illusion, prestidigitation, speak with dead*
1/day each: *arcane gate, bane, confusion, darkness, fear, major image, true seeing*

REACTIONS

Misty Escape (Recharge 6). When the shadar-kai takes damage, it turns invisible and teleports, along with any equipment it is wearing or carrying, up to 60 feet to an unoccupied space it can see. It remains invisible until the start of its next turn or until it attacks or casts a spell.

SHADAR-KAI SHADOW DANCER

Medium Humanoid (Elf), Any Alignment

Armor Class 15 (studded leather)
Hit Points 71 (13d8 + 13)
Speed 30 ft.

STR	DEX	CON	INT	WIS	CHA
12 (+1)	16 (+3)	13 (+1)	11 (+0)	12 (+1)	12 (+1)

Saving Throws Dex +6, Cha +4
Skills Stealth +6
Damage Resistances necrotic
Condition Immunities charmed, exhaustion
Senses darkvision 60 ft., passive Perception 11
Languages Common, Elvish
Challenge 7 (2,900 XP)   **Proficiency Bonus** +3

Fey Ancestry. The shadar-kai has advantage on saving throws against being charmed, and magic can't put it to sleep.

ACTIONS

Multiattack. The shadar-kai makes three Spiked Chain attacks. It can use Shadow Jump after one of these attacks.

Spiked Chain. *Melee Weapon Attack:* +6 to hit, reach 10 ft., one target. *Hit:* 10 (2d6 + 3) piercing damage. The target must succeed on a DC 14 Dexterity saving throw or suffer one of the following effects (choose one or roll a d6):

1–2: Decay. The target takes 22 (4d10) necrotic damage.
3–4: Grapple. The target is grappled (escape DC 14) if it is a Medium or smaller creature. Until the grapple ends, the target is restrained, and the shadar-kai can't grapple another target.
5–6: Topple. The target is knocked prone.

BONUS ACTIONS

Shadow Jump. The shadar-kai teleports, along with any equipment is it wearing or carrying, up to 30 feet to an unoccupied space it can see. Both the space it teleports from and the space it teleports to must be in dim light or darkness.

Shadar-kai Soul Monger

Medium Humanoid (Elf), Typically Neutral Evil

Armor Class 15 (studded leather)
Hit Points 136 (21d8 + 42)
Speed 30 ft.

STR	DEX	CON	INT	WIS	CHA
8 (−1)	17 (+3)	14 (+2)	19 (+4)	15 (+3)	13 (+1)

Saving Throws Dex +7, Wis +7, Cha +5
Skills Perception +7
Damage Immunities necrotic, psychic
Condition Immunities charmed, exhaustion, frightened
Senses darkvision 60 ft., passive Perception 17
Languages Common, Elvish
Challenge 11 (7,200 XP)   **Proficiency Bonus** +4

Fey Ancestry. The shadar-kai has advantage on saving throws against being charmed, and magic can't put it to sleep.

Magic Resistance. The shadar-kai has advantage on saving throws against spells and other magical effects.

Soul Thirst. When it reduces a creature to 0 hit points, the shadar-kai can gain temporary hit points equal to half the creature's hit point maximum. While the shadar-kai has temporary hit points from this trait, it has advantage on attack rolls.

Weight of Ages. Any Beast or Humanoid (except an elf) that starts its turn within 5 feet of the shadar-kai has its speed reduced by 20 feet until the start of that creature's next turn.

Actions

Multiattack. The shadar-kai makes two Shadow Dagger attacks.

Shadow Dagger. *Melee or Ranged Weapon Attack:* +7 to hit, reach 5 ft. or range 20/60 ft., one target. *Hit:* 13 (4d4 + 3) piercing damage plus 19 (3d12) necrotic damage, and the target has disadvantage on saving throws until the end of the shadar-kai's next turn. *Hit or Miss:* The dagger magically returns to the shadar-kai's hand immediately after a ranged attack.

Spellcasting. The shadar-kai casts one of the following spells, requiring no material components and using Intelligence as the spellcasting ability (spell save DC 16):

1/day each: *bestow curse, finger of death, gaseous form, seeming*

Wave of Weariness (Recharge 4–6). The shadar-kai emits weariness in a 60-foot cube. Each creature in that area must make a DC 16 Constitution saving throw. On a failed save, a creature takes 45 (10d8) psychic damage and suffers 1 level of exhaustion. On a successful save, it takes half as much damage and doesn't gain a level of exhaustion.

ADAM PAQUETTE

Shadow Mastiffs

Shadow mastiffs—hounds of the Shadowfell—move invisibly through the shadows, always on the hunt.

Shadow Mastiff

Shunning sunlight, these hounds are usually met as a pack. Some faiths devoted to deities of gloom and night, such as that of Shar in the Forgotten Realms, perform unholy rites to summon shadow mastiffs to work as temple sentinels and bodyguards.

Shadow Mastiff Alpha

Each pack of shadow mastiffs is led by an alpha, the smartest one of the group. The sound of an alpha's howl strikes terror into those who hear it and is a sure sign that a pack is on the prowl.

Shadow Mastiff Alpha
Medium Monstrosity, Typically Neutral Evil

Armor Class 12
Hit Points 44 (8d8 + 8)
Speed 40 ft.

STR	DEX	CON	INT	WIS	CHA
16 (+3)	14 (+2)	13 (+1)	6 (−2)	12 (+1)	5 (−3)

Skills Perception +5, Stealth +6
Damage Resistances bludgeoning, piercing, and slashing from nonmagical attacks while in dim light or darkness
Senses darkvision 60 ft., passive Perception 15
Languages —
Challenge 3 (700 XP)   **Proficiency Bonus** +2

Ethereal Awareness. The shadow mastiff can see ethereal creatures and objects.

Sunlight Weakness. While in bright light created by sunlight, the shadow mastiff has disadvantage on attack rolls, ability checks, and saving throws.

Actions

Bite. *Melee Weapon Attack:* +5 to hit, reach 5 ft., one target. *Hit:* 10 (2d6 + 3) piercing damage. If the target is a creature, it must succeed on a DC 13 Strength saving throw or be knocked prone.

Terrifying Howl (Recharge 6). The shadow mastiff howls. Any Beast or Humanoid within 300 feet of it must succeed on a DC 11 Wisdom saving throw or be frightened of it for 1 minute. A frightened target can repeat the saving throw at the end of each of its turns, ending the effect on itself on a success. If a target's save is successful or the effect ends for it, the target is immune to any shadow mastiff's Terrifying Howl for the next 24 hours.

Bonus Actions

Shadow Blend. While in dim light or darkness, the shadow mastiff becomes invisible, along with anything it is wearing or carrying. The invisibility lasts until the shadow mastiff uses a bonus action to end it or until the shadow mastiff attacks, is in bright light, or is incapacitated.

Shadow Mastiff
Medium Monstrosity, Typically Neutral Evil

Armor Class 12
Hit Points 33 (6d8 + 6)
Speed 40 ft.

STR	DEX	CON	INT	WIS	CHA
16 (+3)	14 (+2)	13 (+1)	5 (−3)	12 (+1)	5 (−3)

Skills Perception +5, Stealth +6
Damage Resistances bludgeoning, piercing, and slashing from nonmagical attacks while in dim light or darkness
Senses darkvision 60 ft., passive Perception 15
Languages —
Challenge 2 (450 XP)   **Proficiency Bonus** +2

Ethereal Awareness. The shadow mastiff can see ethereal creatures and objects.

Sunlight Weakness. While in bright light created by sunlight, the shadow mastiff has disadvantage on attack rolls, ability checks, and saving throws.

Actions

Bite. *Melee Weapon Attack:* +5 to hit, reach 5 ft., one target. *Hit:* 10 (2d6 + 3) piercing damage. If the target is a creature, it must succeed on a DC 13 Strength saving throw or be knocked prone.

Bonus Actions

Shadow Blend. While in dim light or darkness, the shadow mastiff becomes invisible, along with anything it is wearing or carrying. The invisibility lasts until the shadow mastiff uses a bonus action to end it or until the shadow mastiff attacks, is in bright light, or is incapacitated.

What? Are you expecting me to comment on these creatures? Fine, how's this: a loyal pet deserves a loyal pet.

—Mordenkainen

Trust Mordenkainen to look down on any sort of companionship—even the slavering, venomous, demonic puppy kind.

TASHA

Shoosuva

A shoosuva is a hyena-demon gifted by Yeenoghu (appears in this book) to an especially powerful worshiper (typically a fang of Yeenoghu; see the *Monster Manual*). A shoosuva manifests shortly after a Yeenoghu-worshiping war band achieves a great victory, emerging from a billowing, fetid cloud of smoke as it arrives from the Abyss. In battle, the demon wraps its slavering jaws around one victim while lashing out with the poisonous stinger on its tail to bring down another. A creature immobilized by the poison becomes easy pickings for any nearby members of the war band.

Each shoosuva is bonded to a particular worshiper of Yeenoghu and fights alongside its master. A gnoll that has been gifted with a shoosuva is second only to a flind (appears in this book) in status within a war band dedicated to Yeenoghu.

Shoosuva
Large Fiend (Demon), Typically Chaotic Evil

Armor Class 14 (natural armor)
Hit Points 136 (16d10 + 48)
Speed 40 ft.

STR	DEX	CON	INT	WIS	CHA
18 (+4)	13 (+1)	17 (+3)	7 (−2)	14 (+2)	9 (−1)

Saving Throws Dex +4, Con +6, Wis +5
Damage Resistances cold, fire, lightning
Damage Immunities poison
Condition Immunities charmed, frightened, poisoned
Senses darkvision 60 ft., passive Perception 12
Languages Abyssal, Gnoll, telepathy 120 ft.
Challenge 8 (3,900 XP)   **Proficiency Bonus** +3

Actions

Multiattack. The shoosuva makes one Bite attack and one Tail Stinger attack.

Bite. *Melee Weapon Attack:* +7 to hit, reach 5 ft., one target. *Hit:* 26 (4d10 + 4) piercing damage.

Tail Stinger. *Melee Weapon Attack:* +7 to hit, reach 15 ft., one creature. *Hit:* 13 (2d8 + 4) piercing damage, and the target must succeed on a DC 14 Constitution saving throw or become poisoned. While poisoned in this way, the target is also paralyzed. The target can repeat the saving throw at the end of each of its turns, ending the effect on itself on a success.

Bonus Actions

Rampage. When it reduces a creature to 0 hit points with a melee attack on its turn, the shoosuva can move up to half its speed and make one Bite attack.

Sibriex

Thought to be as old as the Abyss itself, sibriexes haunt remote parts of that plane, where they use their vile abilities to create new horrors and they seek ancient lore. Rivulets of blood and bile cascade from a sibriex's body, polluting the surrounding landscape.

Sibriexes have spent eons amassing knowledge from across the planes, hoarding it for when it

Sibriex

Huge Fiend (Demon), Typically Chaotic Evil

Armor Class 19 (natural armor)
Hit Points 150 (12d12 + 72)
Speed 0 ft., fly 20 ft. (hover)

STR	DEX	CON	INT	WIS	CHA
10 (+0)	3 (−4)	23 (+6)	25 (+7)	24 (+7)	25 (+7)

Saving Throws Int +13, Cha +13
Skills Arcana +13, History +13, Perception +13
Damage Resistances cold, fire, lightning; bludgeoning, piercing, and slashing from nonmagical attacks
Damage Immunities poison
Condition Immunities poisoned
Senses truesight 120 ft., passive Perception 23
Languages all, telepathy 120 ft.
Challenge 18 (20,000 XP)   **Proficiency Bonus** +6

Contamination. The sibriex emits an aura of corruption 30 feet in every direction. Vegetation withers in the aura, and the ground in the aura is difficult terrain for other creatures. Any creature that starts its turn in the aura must succeed on a DC 20 Constitution saving throw or take 14 (4d6) poison damage. A creature that succeeds on the save is immune to this sibriex's Contamination for 24 hours.

Legendary Resistance (3/Day). If the sibriex fails a saving throw, it can choose to succeed instead.

Magic Resistance. The sibriex has advantage on saving throws against spells and other magical effects.

Actions

Multiattack. The sibriex makes three Chain attacks, and it uses Squirt Bile.

Chain. *Melee Weapon Attack:* +13 to hit, reach 15 ft., one target. *Hit:* 20 (2d12 + 7) force damage.

Squirt Bile. The sibriex targets one creature it can see within 120 feet of it. The target must succeed on a DC 20 Dexterity saving throw or take 31 (9d6) acid damage.

Spellcasting. The sibriex casts one of the following spells, requiring no material components and using Charisma as the spellcasting ability (spell save DC 21):

At will: *command, dispel magic, hold monster*
1/day: *feeblemind*

Warp Creature. The sibriex targets up to three creatures it can see within 120 feet of it. Each target must make a DC 20 Constitution saving throw. On a successful save, a creature becomes immune to this sibriex's Warp Creature. On a failed save, the target is poisoned, which causes it to also gain 1 level of exhaustion. While poisoned in this way, the target must repeat the saving throw at the start of each of its turns. Three successful saves against the poison end it, and ending the poison removes any levels of exhaustion caused by it. Each failed save causes the target to gain another level of exhaustion. Once the target reaches 6 levels of exhaustion, it dies and instantly transforms into a living **manes** (see the *Monster Manual*) under the sibriex's control. The transformation of the body can be undone only by a *wish* spell.

Legendary Actions

The sibriex can take 3 legendary actions, choosing from the options below. Only one legendary action option can be used at a time and only at the end of another creature's turn. The sibriex regains spent legendary actions at the start of its turn.

Cast a Spell. The sibriex uses Spellcasting.
Spray Bile. The sibriex uses Squirt Bile.
Warp (Costs 2 Actions). The sibriex uses Warp Creature.

CHRISTOPHER BURDETT

might be useful. Such are their incredible intellects and stores of information that many seek them out, including demon lords. Some sibriexes act as advisors and oracles, manipulating demons into serving their ends, while others parcel out lore only when doing so advances their plans.

Sibriexes can channel the power of the Abyss to create new demons from other creatures. Some demons petition sibriexes for physical gifts, for sibriexes can graft on new body parts to give the demons greater strength, vision, or stamina. Sibriexes never give aid freely, though; they demand a service or a treasure in return for the flesh-shaping they provide.

VARIANT: FLESH WARPING

Creatures that encounter a sibriex can be twisted beyond recognition. Whenever a creature fails a saving throw against the sibriex's Warp Creature effect, you can roll percentile dice and consult the Flesh Warping table to determine an additional effect, which vanishes when Warp Creature ends on the creature. If the creature transforms into a manes, the effect becomes a permanent feature of that body.

A creature can willingly submit to flesh warping, an agonizing process that takes at least 1 hour while the creature stays within 30 feet of the sibriex. At the end of the process, roll once on the table (or choose one effect) to determine how the creature is transformed permanently.

FLESH WARPING

d100	Effect
01–05	The color of the target's hair, eyes, and skin becomes blue, red, yellow, or patterned.
06–10	The target's eyes push out of its head at the end of stalks.
11–15	The target's hands grow claws, which can be used as daggers.
16–20	One of the target's legs grows longer than the other, reducing its walking speed by 10 feet.
21–25	The target's eyes become beacons, filling a 15-foot cone with dim light when they are open.
26–30	A pair of wings, either feathered or leathery, sprout from the target's back, granting it a flying speed of 30 feet.
31–35	The target's ears tear free from its head and scurry away; the target is deafened.
36–40	Two of the target's teeth turn into short tusks.
41–45	The target's skin develops bark-like scales, granting it a +1 bonus to AC but reducing its Charisma score by 2 (to a minimum of 1).
46–50	The target's arms and legs switch places, preventing the target from moving unless it crawls.
51–55	The target's arms become tentacles with fingers on the ends, increasing its reach by 5 feet.
56–60	The target's legs grow incredibly long and springy, increasing its walking speed by 10 feet.
61–65	The target grows a long, thin tail, which it can use as a whip.
66–70	The target's entire eyes turn black, and it gains darkvision out to a range of 120 feet.
71–75	The target swells, tripling its weight.
76–80	The target becomes thin and skeletal, halving its weight.
81–85	The target's head triples in size.
86–90	The target's ears become wings, giving it a flying speed of 5 feet.
91–95	The target's body becomes unusually brittle, causing the target to have vulnerability to bludgeoning, piercing, and slashing damage.
96–00	The target grows another head, causing it to have advantage on saving throws against being charmed, frightened, or stunned.

ALEKSI BRICLOT

Some children have imaginary friends that their parents can't see. Sometimes those invisible friends aren't imaginary.

—Mordenkainen

SKULK

Skulks are the soulless shells of travelers who became lost in the Shadowfell, wandering its gray wastes until they lost all sense of self. They are so devoid of identity that they have become permanently invisible. Only children can see a skulk without the help of a mirror or a special candle. On the rare occasions when a skulk is visible, it appears as a drab, featureless, hairless biped.

A skulk can be summoned from the Shadowfell by performing a ritual, and it is bound to obey the summoner's commands for 30 days. During this time, if the skulk is visible, an astute observer might deduce who summoned it, because the skulk assumes a vague likeness of its master.

Cruel and chaotic, skulks carry out their orders in the most violent manner possible. A summoned skulk can't return to the Shadowfell until it dies, so many throw themselves into creating bloodshed and mayhem with no regard for their own lives.

After killing a person on the Material Plane, some skulks take up a silent imitation of that person's life. In extreme cases, skulks have invaded villages, killed all the occupants, and turned the places into seeming ghost towns where flavorless food is prepared daily, colorless clothes are hung up to dry, and livestock is shifted from pen to pen until it starves.

SKULK
Medium Monstrosity, Typically Chaotic Neutral

Armor Class 14
Hit Points 18 (4d8)
Speed 30 ft.

STR	DEX	CON	INT	WIS	CHA
6 (−2)	19 (+4)	10 (+0)	10 (+0)	7 (−2)	1 (−5)

Saving Throws Con +2
Skills Stealth +8
Condition Immunities blinded
Senses darkvision 120 ft., passive Perception 8
Languages understands Common but can't speak
Challenge 1/2 (100 XP)   **Proficiency Bonus** +2

Fallible Invisibility. The skulk is invisible. This invisibility can be circumvented by three things:

Charnel Candles. The skulk appears as a dim, translucent form in the light of a candle made of fat rendered from a corpse whose identity is unknown.
Children. Humanoid children, aged 10 and under, can see through this invisibility.
Reflective Surfaces. The skulk appears as a drab, smooth-skinned biped if its reflection can be seen in a mirror or on another surface.

Trackless. The skulk leaves no tracks to indicate where it has been or where it's headed.

ACTIONS

Claw. *Melee Weapon Attack:* +6 to hit, reach 5 ft., one target. *Hit:* 6 (1d4 + 4) slashing damage plus 3 (1d6) necrotic damage.

ZACK STELLA

SKULL LORD

Skull lords have claimed vast regions of the Shadowfell as their dominion. From these blighted lands, they wage war against their rivals, commanding hordes of the undying in a bid to establish dominance. Yet skull lords always prove to be their own worst enemies; each is a combined being born from three hateful individuals, and they constantly plot against themselves.

Infighting and treachery brought skull lords into existence. The first of them appeared in the aftermath of Vecna's bid to conquer the world of Greyhawk, after the vampire Kas betrayed Vecna and took his eye and hand. In the confusion resulting from this turn of events, Vecna's warlords turned against each other, and his plans were dashed. In a rage, Vecna gathered up his generals and captains and bound them in groups of three, fusing them into abominations cursed to fight among themselves for all time. Since the first skull lords were exiled into the shadows, others have arisen, typically created from other leaders who betrayed their masters.

SKULL LORD

Medium Undead (Sorcerer), Typically Lawful Evil

Armor Class 18 (plate)
Hit Points 112 (15d8 + 45)
Speed 30 ft.

STR	DEX	CON	INT	WIS	CHA
14 (+2)	16 (+3)	17 (+3)	16 (+3)	15 (+2)	21 (+5)

Skills Athletics +7, History +8, Perception +12, Stealth +8
Damage Resistances cold, necrotic; bludgeoning, piercing, and slashing from nonmagical attacks
Damage Immunities poison
Condition Immunities blinded, charmed, deafened, exhaustion, frightened, poisoned, stunned, unconscious
Senses darkvision 60 ft., passive Perception 22
Languages all the languages it knew in life
Challenge 15 (13,000 XP)   **Proficiency Bonus** +5

Evasion. If the skull lord is subjected to an effect that allows it to make a Dexterity saving throw to take only half the damage, the skull lord instead takes no damage if it succeeds on the saving throw and only half damage if it fails, provided it isn't incapacitated.

Legendary Resistance (3/Day). If the skull lord fails a saving throw, it can choose to succeed instead.

Master of the Grave. While within 30 feet of the skull lord, any Undead ally of the skull lord makes saving throws with advantage, and that ally regains 1d6 hit points whenever it starts its turn there.

Unusual Nature. The skull lord doesn't require air, food, drink, or sleep.

ACTIONS

Multiattack. The skull lord makes three Bone Staff or Deathly Ray attacks.

Bone Staff. *Melee Weapon Attack:* +8 to hit, reach 5 ft., one target. *Hit:* 7 (1d8 + 3) bludgeoning damage plus 21 (6d6) necrotic damage.

Deathly Ray. *Ranged Spell Attack:* +10 to hit, range 60 ft., one target. *Hit:* 27 (5d8 + 5) necrotic damage.

Spellcasting. The skull lord casts one of the following spells, using Charisma as the spellcasting ability (spell save DC 18):

At will: *mage hand, message*
2/day each: *dimension door, fear*
1/day each: *cloudkill, cone of cold*

LEGENDARY ACTIONS

The skull lord can take 3 legendary actions, choosing from the options below. Only one legendary action option can be used at a time and only at the end of another creature's turn. The skull lord regains spent legendary actions at the start of its turn.

Attack. The skull lord makes one Bone Staff or Deathly Ray attack.
Move. The skull lord moves up to its speed without provoking opportunity attacks.
Summon Undead (Costs 2 Actions). The skull lord summons up to five **skeletons** or **zombies** (both appear in the *Monster Manual*) in unoccupied spaces within 30 feet of it. They remain until destroyed. Undead summoned in this way roll initiative, act in the next available turn, and obey the skull lord. The skull lord can have no more than five Undead summoned by this ability at a time.

ILYA SHKIPIN

SLITHERING TRACKER
Medium Ooze, Typically Chaotic Evil

Armor Class 14
Hit Points 39 (6d8 + 12)
Speed 30 ft., climb 30 ft., swim 30 ft.

STR	DEX	CON	INT	WIS	CHA
16 (+3)	19 (+4)	15 (+2)	10 (+0)	14 (+2)	11 (+0)

Skills Stealth +8, Survival +6
Damage Vulnerabilities cold, fire
Damage Resistances bludgeoning, piercing, and slashing from nonmagical attacks
Condition Immunities blinded, deafened, exhaustion, grappled, paralyzed, petrified, prone, restrained, unconscious
Senses blindsight 120 ft., passive Perception 12
Languages understands languages it knew in its previous form but can't speak
Challenge 3 (700 XP)   **Proficiency Bonus** +2

False Appearance. If the slithering tracker is motionless at the start of combat, it has advantage on its initiative roll. Moreover, if a creature hasn't observed the slithering tracker move or act, that creature must succeed on a DC 18 Intelligence (Investigation) check to discern that the slithering tracker isn't a puddle.

Liquid Form. The slithering tracker can enter an enemy's space and stop there. It can also move through a space as narrow as 1 inch wide without squeezing.

Spider Climb. The slithering tracker can climb difficult surfaces, including upside down on ceilings, without needing to make an ability check.

ACTIONS

Slam. *Melee Weapon Attack:* +5 to hit, reach 5 ft., one target. *Hit:* 8 (1d10 + 3) bludgeoning damage.

Life Leech. One Large or smaller creature that the slithering tracker can see within 5 feet of it must succeed on a DC 13 Dexterity saving throw or be grappled (escape DC 13). Until this grapple ends, the target is restrained and unable to breathe unless it can breathe water. In addition, the grappled target takes 16 (3d10) necrotic damage at the start of each of its turns. The slithering tracker can grapple only one target at a time.

While grappling the target, the slithering tracker takes only half any damage dealt to it (rounded down), and the target takes the other half.

BONUS ACTIONS

Watery Stealth. If underwater, the slithering tracker takes the Hide action, and it makes the Dexterity (Stealth) check with advantage.

SLITHERING TRACKER

The quest for revenge sometimes leads those terribly aggrieved to undergo a ritual whereby they transform into bodies of semiliquid sentience known as slithering trackers. Innocuous and insidious at the same time, a slithering tracker flows into places where a normal creature can't go and brings its own brand of watery death down on its quarry.

The ritual for creating a slithering tracker is known to hags, liches, and priests who worship gods of vengeance. It can be performed only on a willing creature that hungers for revenge. The ritual sucks all the moisture from the subject's body, killing it. Yet the subject's mind lives on in the puddle that issues forth from the remains, and so too does its insatiable need for retribution.

A slithering tracker tastes the ground it courses over, seeking any trace of its prey. To kill, a slithering tracker rises up and enshrouds a creature, attempting to drown the creature while also draining it of blood.

Achieving revenge against its target doesn't end a slithering tracker's existence or its hunger for blood. Some slithering trackers remain aware of their purpose and extend their quest for vengeance to others, such as anyone who supported or befriended the original target. Most of the time, though, a tracker's mind can't cope with being trapped in liquid form, unable to communicate, and driven by the desire for blood; after fulfilling its duty, the overwhelmed creature attacks indiscriminately until it is destroyed.

ERIC BELISLE

Sorrowsworn

The Shadowfell's pervasive melancholy sometimes gives rise to strange incarnations of the plane's bleak nature. Sorrowsworn embody the forms of suffering inherent to the shadowy landscape and visit horror on those who stumble into their midst. Each sorrowsworn personifies a different aspect of despair or distress.

Angry Sorrowsworn

Relying on violence to sustain their existence, angry sorrowsworn—sometimes called the Angry—grow more powerful when their foes fight back. If a creature opts not to attack, though, this sorrowsworn becomes confused, and its attacks weaken. It also has two heads, which bicker with each other incessantly.

Hungry Sorrowsworn

Horrible creatures with grasping claws and distended jaws, hungry sorrowsworn—also known as the Hungry—do whatever is necessary to sate their appetites. These greedy devourers stuff their maws with flesh and drink in their victims' screams. When they finish, they lurch away while their bright eyes resume the search for something else to consume.

Lonely Sorrowsworn

The sorrow of isolation afflicts many creatures that lurk in the Shadowfell, but the need for companionship is never manifested more dramatically than in the lonely sorrowsworn—also called the Lonely. When these sorrowsworn spot other creatures, they feel keenly the need for interaction and launch their harpoon-like arms to drag their victims closer.

Lost Sorrowsworn

The Shadowfell turns visitors around until they become marooned in its twisted landscape. Lost sorrowsworn—often referred to as the Lost—are representations of the anxiety and fear people experience when they can't find their way. These sorrowsworn appear desperate and panicked.

Lost sorrowsworn grasp at any creatures they can reach. A victim experiences a flood of fear and panic as its mind buckles under the fury of this assault. The harder a victim's allies fight to break the grasp, the more the victim suffers.

Wretched Sorrowsworn

Horrid little monsters, wretched sorrowsworn—or the Wretched—gather in packs to scour the Shadowfell for prey. These desperate entities subsist on life force; when they find a creature, they surge forward to sink their fangs into their victims and drink deep.

Angry Sorrowsworn
Medium Monstrosity, Typically Neutral Evil

Armor Class 18 (natural armor)
Hit Points 255 (30d8 + 120)
Speed 30 ft.

STR	DEX	CON	INT	WIS	CHA
17 (+3)	10 (+0)	19 (+4)	8 (−1)	13 (+1)	6 (−2)

Skills Perception +11
Damage Resistances bludgeoning, piercing, and slashing while in dim light or darkness
Senses darkvision 60 ft., passive Perception 21
Languages Common
Challenge 13 (10,000 XP)   **Proficiency Bonus** +5

Two Heads. The sorrowsworn has advantage on saving throws against being blinded, charmed, deafened, frightened, stunned, or knocked unconscious.

Rising Anger. If another creature deals damage to the sorrowsworn, the sorrowsworn's attack rolls have advantage until the end of its next turn, and the first time it hits with a Hook attack on its next turn, the attack's target takes an extra 19 (3d12) psychic damage.

On its turn, the sorrowsworn has disadvantage on attack rolls if no other creature has dealt damage to it since the end of its last turn.

Actions

Multiattack. The sorrowsworn makes two Hook attacks.

Hook. *Melee Weapon Attack:* +8 to hit, reach 5 ft., one target. *Hit:* 16 (2d12 + 3) piercing damage.

CORY TREGO-ERDNER

HUNGRY SORROWSWORN
Medium Monstrosity, Typically Neutral Evil

Armor Class 17 (natural armor)
Hit Points 225 (30d8 + 90)
Speed 30 ft.

STR	DEX	CON	INT	WIS	CHA
19 (+4)	10 (+0)	17 (+3)	6 (−2)	11 (+0)	6 (−2)

Damage Resistances bludgeoning, piercing, and slashing while in dim light or darkness
Senses darkvision 60 ft., passive Perception 10
Languages Common
Challenge 11 (7,200 XP)   **Proficiency Bonus** +4

Life Hunger. If a creature within 60 feet of the sorrowsworn regains hit points, the sorrowsworn gains two benefits until the end of its next turn: it has advantage on attack rolls, and its Bite deals an extra 22 (4d10) necrotic damage on a hit.

ACTIONS

Multiattack. The sorrowsworn makes one Bite attack and one Claw attack.

Bite. *Melee Weapon Attack:* +8 to hit, reach 5 ft., one target. *Hit:* 8 (1d8 + 4) piercing damage plus 13 (3d8) necrotic damage.

Claw. *Melee Weapon Attack:* +8 to hit, reach 10 ft., one target. *Hit:* 18 (4d6 + 4) slashing damage. If the target is Medium or smaller, it is grappled (escape DC 16), and it is restrained until the grapple ends. While grappling a creature, the sorrowsworn can't make a Claw attack.

LONELY SORROWSWORN
Medium Monstrosity, Typically Neutral Evil

Armor Class 16 (natural armor)
Hit Points 112 (15d8 + 45)
Speed 30 ft.

STR	DEX	CON	INT	WIS	CHA
16 (+3)	12 (+1)	17 (+3)	6 (−2)	11 (+0)	6 (−2)

Damage Resistances bludgeoning, piercing, and slashing while in dim light or darkness
Senses darkvision 60 ft., passive Perception 10
Languages Common
Challenge 9 (5,000 XP)   **Proficiency Bonus** +4

Psychic Leech. At the start of each of the sorrowsworn's turns, each creature within 5 feet of it must succeed on a DC 15 Wisdom saving throw or take 10 (3d6) psychic damage.

Thrives on Company. The sorrowsworn has advantage on attack rolls while it is within 30 feet of at least two other creatures. It otherwise has disadvantage on attack rolls.

ACTIONS

Multiattack. The sorrowsworn makes one Harpoon Arm attack, and it uses Sorrowful Embrace.

Harpoon Arm. *Melee Weapon Attack:* +7 to hit, reach 60 ft., one target. *Hit:* 21 (4d8 + 3) piercing damage, and the target is grappled (escape DC 15) if it is a Large or smaller creature. The sorrowsworn has two harpoon arms and can grapple up to two creatures at once.

Sorrowful Embrace. Each creature grappled by the sorrowsworn must make a DC 15 Wisdom saving throw, taking 18 (4d8) psychic damage on a failed save, or half as much damage on a successful one. In either case, the sorrowsworn pulls each of those creatures up to 30 feet straight toward it.

Lost Sorrowsworn
Medium Monstrosity, Typically Neutral Evil

Armor Class 15 (natural armor)
Hit Points 78 (12d8 + 24)
Speed 30 ft.

STR	DEX	CON	INT	WIS	CHA
17 (+3)	12 (+1)	15 (+2)	6 (−2)	7 (−2)	5 (−3)

Skills Athletics +6
Damage Resistances bludgeoning, piercing, and slashing while in dim light or darkness
Senses darkvision 60 ft., passive Perception 8
Languages Common
Challenge 7 (2,900 XP)   **Proficiency Bonus** +3

Actions

Multiattack. The sorrowsworn makes two Arm Spike attacks.

Arm Spike. *Melee Weapon Attack:* +6 to hit, reach 10 ft., one target. *Hit:* 14 (2d10 + 3) piercing damage.

Embrace (Recharge 4–6). *Melee Weapon Attack:* +6 to hit, reach 5 ft., one target. *Hit:* 25 (4d10 + 3) piercing damage, and the target is grappled (escape DC 14) if it is a Medium or smaller creature. Until the grapple ends, the target is frightened, and it takes 27 (6d8) psychic damage at the end of each of its turns. The sorrowsworn can grapple only one creature at a time.

Reactions

Tightening Embrace. If the sorrowsworn takes damage, the creature grappled by Embrace takes 18 (4d8) psychic damage.

Wretched Sorrowsworn
Small Monstrosity, Typically Neutral Evil

Armor Class 15 (natural armor)
Hit Points 10 (4d6 − 4)
Speed 40 ft.

STR	DEX	CON	INT	WIS	CHA
7 (−2)	12 (+1)	9 (−1)	5 (−3)	6 (−2)	5 (−3)

Damage Resistances bludgeoning, piercing, and slashing while in dim light or darkness
Senses darkvision 60 ft., passive Perception 8
Languages —
Challenge 1/4 (50 XP)   **Proficiency Bonus** +2

Wretched Pack Tactics. The sorrowsworn has advantage on an attack roll against a creature if at least one of the sorrowsworn's allies is within 5 feet of the creature and the ally isn't incapacitated. The sorrowsworn otherwise has disadvantage on attack rolls.

Actions

Bite. *Melee Weapon Attack:* +3 to hit, reach 5 ft., one target. *Hit:* 6 (1d10 + 1) piercing damage, and the sorrowsworn attaches to the target. While attached, the sorrowsworn can't attack, and at the start of each of the sorrowsworn's turns, the target takes 6 (1d10 + 1) necrotic damage.

The attached sorrowsworn moves with the target whenever the target moves, requiring none of the sorrowsworn's movement. The sorrowsworn can detach itself by spending 5 feet of its movement on its turn. A creature, including the target, can use its action to detach the sorrowsworn.

SPAWN OF KYUSS

Medium Undead, Typically Chaotic Evil

Armor Class 10
Hit Points 76 (9d8 + 36)
Speed 30 ft.

STR	DEX	CON	INT	WIS	CHA
16 (+3)	11 (+0)	18 (+4)	5 (−3)	7 (−2)	3 (−4)

Saving Throws Wis +1
Damage Immunities poison
Condition Immunities exhaustion, poisoned
Senses darkvision 60 ft., passive Perception 8
Languages understands the languages it knew in life but can't speak
Challenge 5 (1,800 XP)   **Proficiency Bonus** +3

Regeneration. The spawn of Kyuss regains 10 hit points at the start of its turn if it has at least 1 hit point and isn't in sunlight or a body of running water. If the spawn takes acid, fire, or radiant damage, this trait doesn't function at the start of the spawn's next turn. The spawn is destroyed only if it starts its turn with 0 hit points and doesn't regenerate.

Worms. If the spawn of Kyuss is targeted by an effect that cures disease or removes a curse, all the worms infesting it wither away, and it loses its Burrowing Worm action.

Unusual Nature. The spawn of Kyuss requires no air, food, drink, or sleep.

ACTIONS

Multiattack. The spawn of Kyuss makes two Claw attacks, and it uses Burrowing Worm.

Claw. *Melee Weapon Attack:* +6 to hit, reach 5 ft., one target. *Hit:* 6 (1d6 + 3) slashing damage plus 7 (2d6) necrotic damage.

Burrowing Worm. A worm launches from the spawn of Kyuss at one Humanoid that the spawn can see within 10 feet of it. The worm latches onto the target's skin unless the target succeeds on a DC 11 Dexterity saving throw. The worm is a Tiny Undead with AC 6, 1 hit point, a 2 (−4) in every ability score, and a speed of 1 foot. While on the target's skin, the worm can be killed by normal means or scraped off using an action (the spawn can use Burrowing Worm to launch a scraped-off worm at a Humanoid it can see within 10 feet of the worm). Otherwise, the worm burrows under the target's skin at the end of the target's next turn, dealing 1 piercing damage to it. At the end of each of its turns thereafter, the target takes 7 (2d6) necrotic damage per worm infesting it (maximum of 10d6), and if it drops to 0 hit points, it dies and then rises 10 minutes later as a spawn of Kyuss. If a worm-infested target is targeted by an effect that cures disease or removes a curse, all the worms infesting it wither away.

SPAWN OF KYUSS

Kyuss was a high priest of Orcus (appears in this book) who plundered corpses from necropolises to create the first spawn of Kyuss. Even centuries after Kyuss's death, his malign disciples continue performing the horrific rites he perfected.

From a distance or in poor light, a spawn of Kyuss looks like an ordinary zombie. As it comes into clearer view, however, the scores of little green worms crawling in and out of it become visible. These worms jump onto nearby Humanoids and burrow into their flesh. A worm that penetrates a Humanoid body makes its way to the creature's brain. Once inside the brain, the worm kills its host and animates the corpse, transforming it into a spawn of Kyuss, which breeds more worms.

Spawn of Kyuss are expressions of Orcus's intent to replace all life with undeath. Left to its own devices, a solitary spawn of Kyuss travels aimlessly. If it stumbles across a living creature, the spawn attacks with the sole intent of creating more spawn. Whether spawn are dispersed or clustered, they reproduce exponentially if nothing stops them.

Stars don't spawn these creatures.

Such beautiful lights shouldn't be blamed for such balefulness.

—*Mordenkainen*

STAR SPAWN

The Material Plane represents only one small part of the multiverse. Beyond the best-known planes of existence lie realms alien to mortal life. Some are so hostile that even a moment's contact is enough to break a mortal's mind. Yet beings do exist that are native to these realms: entities that are ever hungering, searching, warring, and sometimes dreaming. These Elder Evils are far older than most of the mortal peoples and always inimical to such creatures' minds.

However much they might desire to enter and dominate the Material Plane, the Elder Evils are unable or unwilling to leave their realms. Some are imprisoned in their dimensions by external forces, some are inextricably bound to their home realities, and others simply can't find any way out.

The creatures known as star spawn are the heralds, servants, and soldiers of the Elder Evils, capable of taking on forms that can journey to the Material Plane. They arrive most often in the wake of a comet—or perhaps this phenomenon merely signals that star spawn are in the vicinity and available for communication. When the signs are right, cultists gather together, read aloud their blasphemous texts, and conduct the mind-searing rituals that guide star spawn into the world.

ELDER EVIL BLESSINGS

Disciples of certain Elder Evils can bestow supernatural gifts on those who serve that cult, including star spawn. The following powers are unique to specific cults; typically a creature has only one.

CULT OF ATROPUS, THE WORLD BORN DEAD

Gaze of Corruption (Recharge 6). The cultist targets one creature it can see within 30 feet of it. The target must succeed on a DC 15 Constitution saving throw or take 16 (3d10) necrotic damage and be poisoned for 1 minute. The poisoned target can repeat the saving throw at the end of each of its turns, ending the effect on itself on a success.

CULT OF BOREM OF THE LAKE OF BOILING MUD

Borem's Embrace (1/Day). The cultist touches one creature within 5 feet of it. The target must succeed on a DC 15 Dexterity saving throw or be coated in sticky, steaming mud. While it is coated in this way, the target's speed is halved, it can't use reactions, and it takes 10 (3d6) fire damage at the start of each of its turns. The effect lasts for 1 minute, until the cultist is incapacitated or dies, or until the target is immersed in water.

CULT OF HAASK, THE VOICE OF HARGUT

Haask's Presence (1/Day). The cultist transforms into a Tiny, slug-like being and teleports onto the shoulder of a Humanoid that it can see within 30 feet of it. The targeted Humanoid must succeed on a DC 15 Charisma saving throw or be charmed by the cultist. While the target is charmed, the cultist has control of it on the target's next turn. At the end of that turn, the cultist teleports to an unoccupied space it can see within 30 feet of it and returns to its normal form. The cultist can't be targeted directly by any attack or other effect while it's in the slug-like form, but it is subject to areas of effect as normal.

CULT OF THARIZDUN, THE CHAINED GOD

Tharizdun's Spark (Recharge 6). As a bonus action, the cultist touches a simple or martial weapon or a natural weapon, if it has one. The next creature hit by the touched weapon must succeed on a DC 15 Wisdom saving throw or have disadvantage on all ability checks. The affected creature can repeat the saving throw at the end of each minute, ending the effect on itself on a success.

CULT OF TYRANTHRAXUS, THE FLAMED ONE

Radiant Flames (1/Day). Multihued flame surrounds the cultist for 1 minute, until the cultist is incapacitated or dies, or until the cultist extinguishes the flame (no action required). While inflamed, the cultist has telepathy with a range of 30 feet, and it can teleport as a bonus action up to 30 feet to an unoccupied space it can see. In addition, every creature that starts its turn within 5 feet of the cultist must make a DC 15 Dexterity saving throw, taking 16 (3d10) radiant damage on a failed save, or half as much damage on a successful one.

STAR SPAWN GRUE

Fanged and lipless, the ever-grinning, eerily staring grue lopes about on spindly legs and long arms. Bristles and spines project from odd patches of its grayish skin, and its long fingers end in broken and dirty nails. Grues are the weakest of the star spawn. A host of writhing, scrambling grues typically accompanies more powerful star spawn. Their constant chittering and shrieking produce discordant psychic energy that disrupts thought patterns in other creatures, which experience flashing colors, hallucinations, disorientation, and waves of hopelessness.

STAR SPAWN HULK

The hulk is one of the largest of the known star spawn, with glistening, translucent skin. Pale and seemingly lidless eyes glare balefully from a face distorted by too many teeth and too little nose.

Hulks are seldom encountered without a commanding star spawn seer (also in this book) nearby. A hulk appears to have little will of its own and is driven to protect its master.

Star Spawn Hulk

Large Aberration, Typically Chaotic Evil

Armor Class 16 (natural armor)
Hit Points 136 (13d10 + 65)
Speed 30 ft.

STR	DEX	CON	INT	WIS	CHA
20 (+5)	8 (−1)	21 (+5)	7 (−2)	12 (+1)	9 (−1)

Saving Throws Dex +3, Wis +5
Skills Perception +5
Damage Resistances bludgeoning, piercing, and slashing from nonmagical attacks
Condition Immunities charmed, frightened
Senses darkvision 60 ft., passive Perception 15
Languages Deep Speech
Challenge 10 (5,900 XP)   **Proficiency Bonus** +4

Psychic Mirror. If the hulk takes psychic damage, each creature within 10 feet of the hulk takes that damage instead; the hulk takes none of the damage. In addition, the hulk's thoughts and location can't be discerned by magic.

Actions

Multiattack. The hulk makes two Slam attacks. If both attacks hit the same target, the target also takes 9 (2d8) psychic damage and must succeed on a DC 17 Constitution saving throw or be stunned until the end of the target's next turn.

Slam. *Melee Weapon Attack:* +9 to hit, reach 10 ft., one target. *Hit:* 14 (2d8 + 5) bludgeoning damage.

Reaping Arms (Recharge 5–6). The hulk makes a separate Slam attack against each creature within 10 feet of it. Each creature that is hit must also succeed on a DC 17 Dexterity saving throw or be knocked prone.

Star Spawn Grue

Small Aberration, Typically Neutral Evil

Armor Class 11
Hit Points 17 (5d6)
Speed 30 ft.

STR	DEX	CON	INT	WIS	CHA
6 (−2)	13 (+1)	10 (+0)	9 (−1)	11 (+0)	6 (−2)

Damage Immunities psychic
Senses darkvision 60 ft., passive Perception 10
Languages Deep Speech
Challenge 1/4 (50 XP)   **Proficiency Bonus** +2

Aura of Shrieks. Creatures within 20 feet of the grue that aren't Aberrations have disadvantage on saving throws, as well as on attack rolls against creatures other than a star spawn grue.

Actions

Confounding Bite. *Melee Weapon Attack:* +3 to hit, reach 5 ft., one target. *Hit:* 6 (2d4 + 1) piercing damage, and the target must succeed on a DC 10 Wisdom saving throw or attack rolls against it have advantage until the start of the grue's next turn.

BRYNN METHENEY

STAR SPAWN LARVA MAGE

A larva mage is a nightmarish combination of a mortal body and otherworldly substance. When a powerful cultist of a wormlike entity such as Kyuss or Kezef—usually a warlock or other spellcaster—contacts the comet-borne emissary of an Elder Evil, the emissary can merge with a mortal consciousness to create a larva mage. None of the original cultist's personality survives the transformation; what emerges is wholly alien.

STAR SPAWN LARVA MAGE
Medium Aberration, Typically Chaotic Evil

Armor Class 16 (natural armor)
Hit Points 168 (16d8 + 96)
Speed 30 ft.

STR	DEX	CON	INT	WIS	CHA
17 (+3)	12 (+1)	23 (+6)	18 (+4)	12 (+1)	16 (+3)

Saving Throws Dex +6, Wis +6, Cha +8
Skills Perception +6
Damage Resistances cold; bludgeoning, piercing, and slashing from nonmagical attacks
Damage Immunities psychic
Condition Immunities charmed, frightened, paralyzed, petrified, poisoned, restrained
Senses darkvision 60 ft., passive Perception 16
Languages Deep Speech
Challenge 16 (15,000 XP)   **Proficiency Bonus** +5

Return to Worms. When the mage is reduced to 0 hit points, it breaks apart into a **swarm of insects** (see the *Monster Manual*) in the same space. Unless the swarm is destroyed, the mage reforms from it 24 hours later.

ACTIONS

Multiattack. The mage makes three Slam or Eldritch Bolt attacks.

Slam. *Melee Weapon Attack:* +8 to hit, reach 10 ft., one target. *Hit:* 7 (1d8 + 3) bludgeoning damage, and the target must succeed on a DC 19 Constitution saving throw or be poisoned until the end of its next turn.

Eldritch Bolt. *Ranged Spell Attack:* +8 to hit, range 60 ft., one target. *Hit:* 19 (3d10 + 3) force damage.

Plague of Worms (Recharge 6). Each creature other than a star spawn within 10 feet of the mage must succeed on a DC 19 Dexterity saving throw or take 22 (5d8) necrotic damage and be blinded and restrained by masses of swarming worms. The affected creature takes 22 (5d8) necrotic damage at the start of each of the mage's turns. The creature can repeat the saving throw at the end of each of its turns, ending the effect on itself on a success.

Spellcasting. The mage casts one of the following spells, requiring no material components and using Charisma as the spellcasting ability (spell save DC 16):

At will: *mage hand, message, minor illusion*
1/day: *dominate monster*

REACTIONS

Feed on Weakness. When a creature within 20 feet of the mage fails a saving throw, the mage gains 10 temporary hit points.

LEGENDARY ACTIONS

The mage can take 3 legendary actions, choosing from the options below. Only one legendary action option can be used at a time and only at the end of another creature's turn. The mage regains spent legendary actions at the start of its turn.

Slam. The mage makes one Slam attack.
Eldritch Bolt (Costs 2 Actions). The mage makes one Eldritch Bolt attack.
Feed (Costs 3 Actions). Each creature restrained by the mage's Plague of Worms takes 13 (3d8) necrotic damage, and the mage gains 6 temporary hit points.

BEN WOOTTEN

The cultists who blaspheme reality by calling out to Elder Evils often speak of a Far Realm from which these entities hail.

In truth, there is no one place or space from which they come. There is the multiverse of things that are, and there is the multiverse of things that shouldn't be.

—Mordenkainen

STAR SPAWN MANGLER

Medium Aberration, Typically Chaotic Evil

Armor Class 14
Hit Points 71 (13d8 + 13)
Speed 40 ft., climb 40 ft.

STR	DEX	CON	INT	WIS	CHA
8 (−1)	18 (+4)	12 (+1)	11 (+0)	12 (+1)	7 (−2)

Saving Throws Dex +7, Con +4
Skills Stealth +7
Damage Resistances cold
Damage Immunities psychic
Condition Immunities charmed, frightened, prone
Senses darkvision 60 ft., passive Perception 11
Languages Deep Speech
Challenge 5 (1,800 XP)   **Proficiency Bonus** +3

Ambusher. The mangler has advantage on initiative rolls.

ACTIONS

Multiattack. The mangler makes two Claw attacks.

Claw. *Melee Weapon Attack:* +7 to hit, reach 5 ft., one target. *Hit:* 8 (1d8 + 4) slashing damage. If the attack roll has advantage, the target also takes 7 (2d6) psychic damage.

Flurry of Claws (Recharge 5–6). The mangler makes six Claw attacks. Either before or after these attacks, it can move up to its speed without provoking opportunity attacks.

BONUS ACTIONS

Shadow Stealth. While in dim light or darkness, the mangler takes the Hide action.

STAR SPAWN MANGLER

A mangler is a low-slung, creeping horror with multiple gangly arms—it most often has six arms but can have any number from four to eight. Manglers creep along the ground or the walls, sticking to shadows and hiding in spots that seem too shallow or well-lit to conceal anything. They appear smaller than their true size, thanks to their hunched posture and emaciated frames. Cultists summon these creatures to serve as guards and assassins, two roles at which they excel.

A star spawn seer is almost always accompanied by one or more star spawn hulks (also in this book). Not only is a hulk a powerful combatant, but when a seer deals psychic damage to a hulk, the hulk isn't hurt, and the effect ricochets off and expands to assault other creatures.

STAR SPAWN SEER

Medium Aberration, Typically Neutral Evil

Armor Class 17 (natural armor)
Hit Points 153 (18d8 + 72)
Speed 30 ft.

STR	DEX	CON	INT	WIS	CHA
14 (+2)	12 (+1)	18 (+4)	22 (+6)	19 (+4)	16 (+3)

Saving Throws Dex +6, Int +11, Wis +9, Cha +8
Skills Perception +9
Damage Resistances cold; bludgeoning, piercing, and slashing from nonmagical attacks
Damage Immunities psychic
Condition Immunities charmed, frightened
Senses darkvision 60 ft., passive Perception 19
Languages Common, Deep Speech, Undercommon
Challenge 13 (10,000 XP)   **Proficiency Bonus** +5

Out-of-Phase Movement. The seer can move through other creatures and objects as if they were difficult terrain, and its movement doesn't provoke opportunity attacks.

Each creature it moves through takes 5 (1d10) psychic damage; no creature can take this damage more than once per turn. The seer takes 5 (1d10) force damage if it ends its turn inside an object.

ACTIONS

Multiattack. The seer makes two Comet Staff or Psychic Orb attacks.

Comet Staff. *Melee Weapon Attack:* +11 to hit, reach 5 ft., one target. *Hit:* 10 (1d8 + 6) bludgeoning damage plus 18 (4d8) psychic damage, and if the target is a creature, it must succeed on a DC 19 Constitution saving throw or be incapacitated until the end of its next turn.

Psychic Orb. *Ranged Spell Attack:* +11 to hit, range 120 feet, one creature. *Hit:* 27 (5d10) psychic damage.

Collapse Distance (Recharge 6). The seer warps space around one creature it can see within 30 feet of it. That creature must make a DC 19 Wisdom saving throw. On a failed save, the target, along with any equipment it is wearing or carrying, is teleported up to 60 feet to an unoccupied space the seer can see, and then each creature within 10 feet of the target's original space takes 39 (6d12) psychic damage. On a successful save, the target takes 19 (3d12) psychic damage and isn't teleported.

REACTIONS

Bend Space. When the seer would be hit by an attack roll, it teleports, along with any equipment it is wearing or carrying, exchanging positions with another star spawn it can see within 60 feet of it. The other star spawn is hit by the attack instead.

STAR SPAWN SEER

A star spawn seer is most often encountered as the leader of a cult dedicated to one or more Elder Evils. Usually, the seer is the only cult member that grasps the full extent of the horror the cult is venerating. The seer's goal is to tap into vast energy sources and perform the dire rites that will extend a bridge between the Material Plane and the squirming chaos of an Elder Evil's realm.

An entity that appears as a star spawn seer in the Material Plane usually arrives disembodied. When a warlock or other spellcaster establishes communication with it, the seer-entity takes control of the mortal, transforming it into a star spawn seer. Whoever the mortal once was largely vanishes beneath the mass of tumorous skin than builds up in strange whorls all over the seer's body. The mortal's hands become bulky, flipper-like appendages able to grasp the seer's strange staff formed of a blend of flesh, bone, and star stuff.

CHRISTOPHER BURDETT

STEEDERS

Giant hunting spiders, steeders prowl the depths of the Underdark. Female steeders grow larger and stronger than males, and the female often devours the male after breeding. Numerous Underdark folk domesticate steeders, particularly duergar (also in this book). Typically the females serve as steeds in battle, while the males are used as draft animals.

Steeders attempt to tear apart perceived threats—and consider even other steeders enemies. When they're put to work, their handlers must stable them separately from one another and place blinders on them to keep them from attacking each other.

Steeders are intelligent enough to learn simple hand signals and vocal commands, but even a domesticated steeder might turn against its handler. Training a steeder requires a rider to bond with it, a process that begins shortly after the steeder hatches. As it grows, its rider works with it to direct its predatory instincts.

Rather than spinning webs, steeders excrete a viscous substance from their legs. This goo allows them to creep along walls and ceilings and to grapple prey.

Steeders resemble spiders as much as worgs resemble wolves. The creatures may appear similar, but steeders are more than mere vermin.

—Mordenkainen

FEMALE STEEDER
Large Monstrosity, Unaligned

Armor Class 14 (natural armor)
Hit Points 30 (4d10 + 8)
Speed 30 ft., climb 30 ft.

STR	DEX	CON	INT	WIS	CHA
15 (+2)	16 (+3)	14 (+2)	2 (–4)	10 (+0)	3 (–4)

Skills Perception +4, Stealth +7
Senses darkvision 120 ft., passive Perception 14
Languages —
Challenge 1 (200 XP) **Proficiency Bonus** +2

Extraordinary Leap. The distance of the steeder's long jumps is tripled; every foot of its walking speed that it spends on the jump allows it to move 3 feet.

Spider Climb. The steeder can climb difficult surfaces, including upside down on ceilings, without needing to make an ability check.

ACTIONS

Bite. *Melee Weapon Attack:* +5 to hit, reach 5 ft., one target. *Hit:* 7 (1d8 + 3) piercing damage plus 9 (2d8) poison damage.

Sticky Leg. *Melee Weapon Attack:* +5 to hit, reach 5 ft., one Medium or smaller creature. *Hit:* The target is stuck to the steeder's leg and grappled (escape DC 12). The steeder can have only one creature grappled at a time.

MALE STEEDER
Medium Monstrosity, Unaligned

Armor Class 12 (natural armor)
Hit Points 13 (2d8 + 4)
Speed 30 ft., climb 30 ft.

STR	DEX	CON	INT	WIS	CHA
15 (+2)	12 (+1)	14 (+2)	2 (–4)	10 (+0)	3 (–4)

Skills Perception +4, Stealth +5
Senses darkvision 120 ft., passive Perception 14
Languages —
Challenge 1/4 (50 XP) **Proficiency Bonus** +2

Extraordinary Leap. The distance of the steeder's long jumps is tripled; every foot of its walking speed that it spends on the jump allows it to jump 3 feet.

Spider Climb. The steeder can climb difficult surfaces, including upside down on ceilings, without needing to make an ability check.

ACTIONS

Bite. *Melee Weapon Attack:* +4 to hit, reach 5 ft., one target. *Hit:* 6 (1d8 + 2) piercing damage plus 4 (1d8) poison damage.

Sticky Leg. *Melee Weapon Attack:* +4 to hit, reach 5 ft., one Small or Tiny creature. *Hit:* The target is stuck to the steeder's leg and grappled (escape DC 12). The steeder can have only one creature grappled at a time.

STEEL PREDATOR

A steel predator is a merciless machine with one purpose: to locate and kill its target regardless of distance and obstacles.

Steel predators are created by a unique modron, using a machine located in the city of Sigil. It wasn't always headquartered in the City of Doors, however. On its original home, the plane of Mechanus, the ingenious modron was lauded for its invention—until it turned these creations against its superiors. Steel predators wreaked havoc against the modron hierarchy until the rogue modron was trapped and exiled. Now it operates a shop in Sigil where, for a steep price, anyone can commission the manufacture of a steel predator.

To create a steel predator, the modron's machine must be fed something that identifies the predator's target, such as a lock of hair, a well-worn glove, or a much-used weapon. The moment the newly manufactured steel predator emerges, it bounds away in search of its prey. It senses the location of its target across planar boundaries, but such detection is accurate only to within a thousand yards; to close the remaining distance, the steel predator locates its prey by sight and smell.

Once battle is joined, the predator ignores every other threat to attack its target, unless other creatures prevent it from reaching the target. In that case, it does what it must to fulfill its mission.

If all goes according to plan, a steel predator slays its target and then voluntarily returns to Sigil, where it's broken down into parts that can be used in another steel predator. Battle damage can cause this instinct to fail, however, in which case the steel predator lingers in the area, hunting and killing other creatures that resemble its target or that simply live nearby. Such rogue predators are dangerous to anyone in the vicinity.

STEEL PREDATOR
Large Construct, Typically Lawful Neutral

Armor Class 20 (natural armor)
Hit Points 207 (18d10 + 108)
Speed 40 ft.

STR	DEX	CON	INT	WIS	CHA
24 (+7)	17 (+3)	22 (+6)	4 (–3)	14 (+2)	6 (–2)

Skills Perception +7, Stealth +8, Survival +7
Damage Resistances cold, lightning, necrotic, thunder
Damage Immunities poison, psychic; bludgeoning, piercing, and slashing from nonmagical attacks
Condition Immunities charmed, exhaustion, frightened, paralyzed, petrified, poisoned, stunned
Senses blindsight 30 ft., darkvision 60 ft., passive Perception 17
Languages understands Modron and the language of its owner but can't speak
Challenge 16 (15,000 XP)   **Proficiency Bonus** +5

Magic Resistance. The steel predator has advantage on saving throws against spells and other magical effects.

Unusual Nature. The steel predator doesn't require air, food, drink, or sleep.

ACTIONS

Multiattack. The steel predator makes one Bite attack and two Claw attacks.

Bite. *Melee Weapon Attack:* +12 to hit, reach 5 ft., one target. *Hit:* 18 (2d10 + 7) lightning damage.

Claw. *Melee Weapon Attack:* +12 to hit, reach 5 ft., one target. *Hit:* 16 (2d8 + 7) force damage.

Spellcasting. The steel predator casts one of the following spells, requiring no spell components and using Wisdom as the spellcasting ability:

3/day each: *dimension door* (self only), *plane shift* (self only)

Stunning Roar (Recharge 5–6). The steel predator emits a roar in a 60-foot cone. Each creature in that area must make a DC 19 Constitution saving throw. On a failed save, a creature takes 33 (6d10) thunder damage, drops everything it's holding, and is stunned for 1 minute. The stunned creature can repeat the saving throw at the end of each of its turns, ending the effect on itself on a success. On a successful save, a creature takes half as much damage and isn't stunned.

Stone Cursed

Medium Construct, Typically Lawful Evil

Armor Class 17 (natural armor)
Hit Points 19 (3d8 + 6)
Speed 10 ft.

STR	DEX	CON	INT	WIS	CHA
16 (+3)	5 (−3)	14 (+2)	5 (−3)	8 (−1)	7 (−2)

Damage Vulnerabilities bludgeoning
Damage Immunities poison
Condition Immunities charmed, exhaustion, frightened, petrified, poisoned
Senses passive Perception 9
Languages the languages it knew in life
Challenge 1 (200 XP) **Proficiency Bonus** +2

Cunning Opportunist. The stone cursed has advantage on the attack rolls of opportunity attacks.

False Appearance. If the stone cursed is motionless at the start of combat, it has advantage on its initiative roll. Moreover, if a creature hasn't observed the stone cursed move or act, that creature must succeed on a DC 18 Intelligence (Investigation) check to discern that the stone cursed isn't a statue.

Unusual Nature. The stone cursed doesn't require air, food, drink, or sleep.

Actions

Petrifying Claws. *Melee Weapon Attack:* +5 to hit, reach 5 ft., one target. *Hit:* 12 (2d8 + 3) slashing damage. If the target is a creature, it must succeed on a DC 12 Constitution saving throw, or it begins to turn to stone and is restrained until the end of its next turn, when it must repeat the saving throw. The effect ends if the second save is successful; otherwise the target is petrified for 24 hours.

Stone Cursed

Stone cursed are spawned through a foul alchemical ritual performed on a Humanoid that has been turned to stone. The ritual, which requires a mixture of basilisk blood and the ashes from the burned feathers of a cockatrice, awakens a dim echo of the petrified victim's spirit, animating the statue and turning it into a useful guardian.

Stone cursed possess a malevolent drive to slay the living, yet they are utterly loyal to whoever performed the ritual to animate them, and they obey that being's orders to the best of their ability.

In combat, stony claws that drip with thick, gray sludge emerge from a stone cursed's fingers. This alchemical sludge transforms those slashed by the claws into statues.

As part of the ritual used to create a stone cursed, a fist-sized obsidian skull forms within the creature's torso. The skull isn't visible while the stone cursed is active, but when it is slain, the statue shatters and the skull clatters to the ground. Because it is the nexus for the alchemy used to create these horrors, a faint echo of the original victim's memories resonates within the skull. A skilled magic-wielder can attempt to extract memories from it to gain insight into the victim's past or find lore that otherwise would be lost.

Cryptic Whispers

Even though a creature transformed into a stone cursed is long dead, a vague whisper of their memories lives on in the obsidian skull embedded within the stone cursed's body. At the end of a short rest, a character can make a DC 20 Intelligence (Arcana) check to attempt to extract a memory from the skull that is a response to a verbal question posed to the skull by the character. Once this check is made, whether it succeeds or fails, the skull can't be used in this manner again.

Dreamwalkers become divorced from reality by isolation, shame, and their unendingly alien surroundings, and this delirium leaches out into the world around them, affecting other creatures that get too close. Believing that they're living in a dream and that their actions have no real consequences, dreamwalkers act as they please, becoming forces of chaos. As they travel the world, they collect objects and creatures that seem especially significant to them. Over time, the collected things accrete to their bodies, becoming encased in stone.

STONE GIANT DREAMWALKER

Huge Giant, Typically Chaotic Neutral

Armor Class 18 (natural armor)
Hit Points 161 (14d12 + 70)
Speed 40 ft.

STR	DEX	CON	INT	WIS	CHA
23 (+6)	14 (+2)	21 (+5)	10 (+0)	8 (−1)	12 (+1)

Saving Throws Dex +6, Con +9, Wis +3
Skills Athletics +14, Perception +3
Condition Immunities charmed, frightened
Senses darkvision 60 ft., passive Perception 13
Languages Common, Giant
Challenge 10 (5,900 XP)   **Proficiency Bonus** +4

Dreamwalker's Charm. An enemy that starts its turn within 30 feet of the giant must make a DC 13 Charisma saving throw, provided that the giant isn't incapacitated. On a failed save, the creature is charmed by the giant. A creature charmed in this way can repeat the saving throw at the end of each of its turns, ending the effect on itself on a success. Once it succeeds on the saving throw, the creature is immune to this giant's Dreamwalker's Charm for 24 hours.

ACTIONS

Multiattack. The giant makes two Greatclub or Rock attacks.

Greatclub. *Melee Weapon Attack:* +10 to hit, reach 15 ft., one target. *Hit:* 24 (4d8 + 6) bludgeoning damage.

Rock. *Ranged Weapon Attack:* +10 to hit, range 60/240 ft., one target. *Hit:* 22 (3d10 + 6) bludgeoning damage. If the target is a creature, it must succeed on a DC 17 Strength saving throw or be knocked prone.

Petrifying Touch. The giant touches one Medium or smaller creature within 10 feet of it that is charmed by it. The target must make a DC 17 Constitution saving throw. On a failed save, the target becomes petrified, and the giant can adhere the target to its stony body. *Greater restoration* spells and other magic that can undo petrification have no effect on a petrified creature adhered to the giant unless the giant is dead, in which case the magic works normally, freeing the petrified creature as well as ending the petrified condition on it.

STONE GIANT DREAMWALKER

The surface of the world is an alien realm to stone giants: fluctuating, temporary, exposed to gusting wind and sudden rain. It is as wildly changeable as a dream, and that's how they regard it—as a dream. Nothing there is permanent, so nothing there is real. What happens on the surface doesn't matter. Promises and bargains made there needn't be honored. Life and even art hold less value there.

Stone giants sometimes go on dream quests in the surface world, seeking inspiration for their art, a break from decades-long ennui, or satisfaction of simple curiosity. Some who go on these quests let themselves become lost in the dream. Other stone giants are banished to the surface as punishment. Regardless of the reason they ended up on the surface, if they don't take shelter under stone, such stone giants can become dreamwalkers.

Dreamwalkers occupy an odd place of respect outside the stone giant ordning. They are considered outcasts, but their familiarity with the surface world makes them valuable guides, and their insights can help other stone giants grasp the dangers of living in a dream.

Storm Giant Quintessent

Huge Giant, Typically Chaotic Good

Armor Class 12
Hit Points 230 (20d12 + 100)
Speed 50 ft., fly 50 ft. (hover), swim 50 ft.

STR	DEX	CON	INT	WIS	CHA
29 (+9)	14 (+2)	20 (+5)	17 (+3)	20 (+5)	19 (+4)

Saving Throws Str +14, Con +10, Wis +10, Cha +9
Skills Arcana +8, History +8, Perception +10
Damage Resistances cold; bludgeoning, piercing, and slashing from nonmagical attacks
Damage Immunities lightning, thunder
Senses truesight 60 ft., passive Perception 20
Languages Common, Giant
Challenge 16 (15,000 XP)   **Proficiency Bonus** +5

Amphibious. The giant can breathe air and water.

Legendary Resistance (1/Day). If the giant fails a saving throw, it can choose to succeed instead.

Actions

Multiattack. The giant makes two Lightning Sword attacks, or it uses Wind Javelin twice.

Lightning Sword. *Melee Weapon Attack:* +14 to hit, reach 15 ft., one target. *Hit:* 40 (9d6 + 9) lightning damage.

Wind Javelin. The giant coalesces wind into a javelin-like form and hurls it at a creature it can see within 600 feet of it. The javelin deals 19 (3d6 + 9) force damage to the target, striking unerringly. The javelin disappears after it hits.

Legendary Actions

The giant can take 3 legendary actions, choosing from the options below. Only one legendary action option can be used at a time and only at the end of another creature's turn. The giant regains spent legendary actions at the start of its turn.

Gust. The giant targets a creature it can see within 60 feet of it and creates a magical gust of wind around the target, who must succeed on a DC 18 Strength saving throw or be moved up to 20 feet in any horizontal direction the giant chooses.

Thunderbolt (Costs 2 Actions). The giant hurls a thunderbolt at a creature it can see within 600 feet of it. The target must make a DC 18 Dexterity saving throw, taking 22 (4d10) thunder damage on a failed save, or half as much damage on a successful one.

One with the Storm (Costs 3 Actions). The giant vanishes, dispersing itself into the storm surrounding its lair. The giant can end this effect at the start of any of its turns, becoming a giant once more and appearing in any location it chooses within its lair. While dispersed, the giant can't take any actions other than lair actions, and it can't be targeted by attacks, spells, or other effects. The giant can't use this ability outside its lair, nor can it use this ability if another creature is using a *control weather* spell or similar magic to quell the storm.

Storm Giant Quintessent

To forestall the inevitable, some storm giants approaching the end of their natural life spans seek an escape from death. They plumb the depths of their powerful connection to the elements and disperse themselves into nature, transforming into semiconscious storms. The blizzard that rages unendingly around a mountain peak, the vortex that swirls around a remote island, or the thunderstorm that howls ceaselessly up and down a rugged coastline could, in fact, be the undying form of a storm giant clinging to existence.

A storm giant quintessent sheds their armor and weapons but gains the power to form makeshift weapons out of thin air. When the giant has no further use of these elemental weapons, or when the giant dies, the weapons disappear.

A storm giant quintessent can revert to their true giant form temporarily and can maintain that form long enough for the giant to communicate with a mortal, carry out a short task, or defend their home against aggressors.

A Quintessent's Lair

A storm giant quintessent has no need for castles or dungeon lairs. Their lair is usually a secluded region or prominent geographic feature, such as a mountain peak, a great waterfall, a remote island, a fog-shrouded loch, a beautiful coral reef, or a wind-swept desert bluff. The storm in which the giant lives could be a blizzard, a typhoon, a thunderstorm, or a sandstorm, as befits the environment.

Lair Actions

A storm giant quintessent can use lair actions in giant form and while transformed into a storm. On initiative count 20 (losing initiative ties), the giant can take one of the following lair actions; the giant can't take the same lair action two rounds in a row:

Deafening Boom. The giant creates a thunderclap centered on a point anywhere in their lair. Each creature within 20 feet of that point must succeed on a DC 18 Constitution saving throw or be deafened until the end of its next turn.

Fog. The giant creates a 20-foot-radius sphere of fog (or murky water if within water) centered on a point anywhere in its lair. The sphere spreads around corners, and its area is heavily obscured. The fog lasts until the giant disperses it (no action required), and it can't be dispersed by wind.

Gale. The giant creates a 60-foot-long, 10-foot-wide line of strong wind (or strong current within water) originating from a point anywhere in its lair. Each creature in that line must succeed on a DC 18 Strength saving throw or be pushed 15 feet in the direction the wind is blowing. The gust disperses gas or vapor, and it extinguishes candles, torches, and similar unprotected flames in its area. Protected flames, such as those of lanterns, have a 50 percent chance of being extinguished.

Regional Effects

The region containing a storm giant quintessent's lair is warped by the giant's presence, which creates one or more of the following effects:

Downpour. Rain, snow, or blowing dust or sand (whichever is most appropriate) is constant within 1 mile of the lair. Rain causes rivers and streams to fill or overflow their banks; snow, dust, or sand forms deep drifts or dunes.

Lightning. Flashes of lightning and peals of thunder are continual, day and night, within 5 miles of the lair.

Winds. High wind blows within 1 mile of the lair, making it impossible to light a fire unless the location where the fire is lit is protected from the wind.

If the giant dies, the lightning, thunder, and high wind regional effects end immediately. Rain, snow, and blowing dust abate gradually within 1d8 days.

Swarm of Rot Grubs

Rot grubs are finger-sized maggots that eat living and dead creatures, although they can survive on vegetation. They infest corpses and piles of decaying matter and attack anyone that disturbs them. After burrowing into a creature, rot grubs instinctively chew their way toward vital parts.

Rot grubs recoil from flames, and fire is the main weapon against rot grubs once they're inside a body. Magic that neutralizes poison can also stop them before they kill their host.

Single Rot Grub

Rot grubs pose a threat both singly and as a swarm. See the stat block for the mechanics of a swarm of rot grubs. A single rot grub has no stat block.

Any creature that comes into contact with a single rot grub must succeed on a DC 10 Constitution saving throw or be poisoned, as the rot grub burrows into the creature. The poisoned creature takes 3 (1d6) poison damage at the end of each of its turns. Whenever the poisoned creature takes fire damage, the creature can repeat the saving throw, ending the effect on itself on a success. If the poisoned creature ends its turn with 0 hit points, it dies, as the rot grub kills it.

Swarm of Rot Grubs

Medium Swarm of Tiny Beasts, Unaligned

Armor Class 8
Hit Points 22 (5d8)
Speed 5 ft., climb 5 ft.

STR	DEX	CON	INT	WIS	CHA
2 (−4)	7 (−2)	10 (+0)	1 (−5)	2 (−4)	1 (−5)

Damage Vulnerabilities fire
Damage Resistances piercing, slashing
Condition Immunities charmed, frightened, grappled, paralyzed, petrified, prone, restrained
Senses blindsight 10 ft., passive Perception 6
Languages —
Challenge 1/2 (100 XP)   **Proficiency Bonus** +2

Swarm. The swarm can occupy another creature's space and vice versa, and the swarm can move through any opening large enough for a Tiny maggot. The swarm can't regain hit points or gain temporary hit points.

Actions

Bites. *Melee Weapon Attack:* +0 to hit, reach 0 ft., one creature in the swarm's space. *Hit:* 7 (2d6) piercing damage, and the target must succeed on a DC 10 Constitution saving throw or be poisoned. At the end of each of the poisoned target's turns, the target takes 3 (1d6) poison damage. Whenever the poisoned target takes fire damage, the target can repeat the saving throw, ending the effect on itself on a success. If the poisoned target ends its turn with 0 hit points, it dies.

Swashbuckler

Medium Humanoid, Any Alignment

Armor Class 17 (leather armor, Suave Defense)
Hit Points 66 (12d8 + 12)
Speed 30 ft.

STR	DEX	CON	INT	WIS	CHA
12 (+1)	18 (+4)	12 (+1)	14 (+2)	11 (+0)	15 (+2)

Skills Acrobatics +8, Athletics +5, Persuasion +6
Senses passive Perception 10
Languages any one language (usually Common)
Challenge 3 (700 XP)   **Proficiency Bonus** +2

Suave Defense. While the swashbuckler is wearing light or no armor and wielding no shield, its AC includes its Charisma modifier.

Actions

Multiattack. The swashbuckler makes one Dagger attack and two Rapier attacks.

Dagger. *Melee or Ranged Weapon Attack:* +6 to hit, reach 5 ft. or range 20/60 ft., one target. *Hit:* 6 (1d4 + 4) piercing damage.

Rapier. *Melee Weapon Attack:* +6 to hit, reach 5 ft., one target. *Hit:* 8 (1d8 + 4) piercing damage.

Bonus Actions

Lightfooted. The swashbuckler takes the Dash or Disengage action.

Swashbuckler

Swashbucklers are charming ne'er-do-wells who live by their own codes of honor. They crave notoriety, often indulge in romantic trysts, and eke out livings as pirates and corsairs, rarely staying in one place for too long.

Many swashbucklers have a signature flourish with which they embellish their actions to make themselves more memorable. You can roll on the Swashbuckler Flourishes table or choose one of the options to find a suitably dramatic flourish for a swashbuckler.

Swashbuckler Flourishes

d8	Flourish
1	Winks and flashes a charming grin
2	Bows theatrically
3	Constantly flips their dagger
4	Punctuates sentences with a boisterous "Ha-HA!"
5	Sings catchy sea chanteys
6	Dexterously manipulates a silver coin through their fingers
7	Hurls colorful insults
8	Adds showy embellishments to rapier strokes

SWORD WRAITHS

When glory-obsessed warriors die in battle without honor, they might haunt the site as sword wraiths.

SWORD WRAITH COMMANDER

Sword wraith commanders haunt battlefields, attacking anyone who questions their valor but looking kindly on those who sing their praises.

SWORD WRAITH WARRIOR

Sword wraith warriors are most often found on ancient battlefields where soldiers were hemmed in and slaughtered without quarter.

SWORD WRAITH COMMANDER
Medium Undead, Typically Lawful Evil

Armor Class 18 (breastplate, shield)
Hit Points 127 (15d8 + 60)
Speed 30 ft.

STR	DEX	CON	INT	WIS	CHA
18 (+4)	14 (+2)	18 (+4)	11 (+0)	12 (+1)	14 (+2)

Skills Perception +4
Damage Resistances necrotic; bludgeoning, piercing, and slashing from nonmagical attacks
Damage Immunities poison
Condition Immunities exhaustion, frightened, poisoned, unconscious
Senses darkvision 60 ft., passive Perception 14
Languages the languages it knew in life
Challenge 8 (3,900 XP)   **Proficiency Bonus** +3

Turning Defiance. The commander and any other sword wraiths within 30 feet of it have advantage on saving throws against effects that turn Undead.

Unusual Nature. The commander doesn't require air, food, drink, or sleep.

ACTIONS

Multiattack. The commander makes two Longsword or Longbow attacks.

Longsword. *Melee Weapon Attack:* +7 to hit, reach 5 ft., one target. *Hit:* 8 (1d8 + 4) slashing damage, or 9 (1d10 + 4) slashing damage if used with two hands.

Longbow. *Ranged Weapon Attack:* +5 to hit, range 150/600 ft., one target. *Hit:* 6 (1d8 + 2) piercing damage.

Call to Honor (1/Day). If the commander has taken damage during this combat, it gives itself advantage on attack rolls until the end of its next turn, and 1d4 + 1 **sword wraith warriors** appear in unoccupied spaces within 30 feet of it. The warriors last until they drop to 0 hit points, and they take their turns immediately after the commander's turn on the same initiative count.

BONUS ACTIONS

Martial Fury. The commander makes one Longsword or Longbow attack, which deals an extra 9 (2d8) necrotic damage on a hit, and attack rolls against it have advantage until the start of its next turn.

SWORD WRAITH WARRIOR
Medium Undead, Typically Lawful Evil

Armor Class 16 (chain shirt, shield)
Hit Points 45 (6d8 + 18)
Speed 30 ft.

STR	DEX	CON	INT	WIS	CHA
18 (+4)	12 (+1)	17 (+3)	6 (−2)	9 (−1)	10 (+0)

Damage Resistances necrotic; bludgeoning, piercing, and slashing from nonmagical attacks
Damage Immunities poison
Condition Immunities exhaustion, frightened, poisoned, unconscious
Senses darkvision 60 ft., passive Perception 9
Languages the languages it knew in life
Challenge 3 (700 XP)   **Proficiency Bonus** +2

Unusual Nature. The warrior doesn't require air, food, drink, or sleep.

ACTIONS

Battleaxe. *Melee Weapon Attack:* +6 to hit, reach 5 ft., one target. *Hit:* 8 (1d8 + 4) slashing damage, or 9 (1d10 + 4) slashing damage if used with two hands.

Longbow. *Ranged Weapon Attack:* +3 to hit, range 150/600 ft., one target. *Hit:* 5 (1d8 + 1) piercing damage.

BONUS ACTIONS

Martial Fury. The warrior makes one Battleaxe or Longbow attack, and attack rolls against it have advantage until the start of its next turn.

> I believe spite can be an excellent motivator. But unchecked fury? That rarely leads to anything more than a big mess.
>
> TASHA

Tanarukk

Medium Fiend (Demon), Typically Chaotic Evil

Armor Class 14 (natural armor)
Hit Points 95 (10d8 + 50)
Speed 30 ft.

STR	DEX	CON	INT	WIS	CHA
18 (+4)	13 (+1)	20 (+5)	9 (−1)	9 (−1)	9 (−1)

Skills Intimidation +2, Perception +2
Damage Resistances fire, poison
Senses darkvision 60 ft., passive Perception 12
Languages Abyssal, Common, plus any one language
Challenge 5 (1,800 XP)   **Proficiency Bonus** +3

Magic Resistance. The tanarukk has advantage on saving throws against spells and other magical effects.

Actions

Multiattack. The tanarukk makes one Bite attack and one Greatsword attack.

Bite. *Melee Weapon Attack:* +7 to hit, reach 5 ft., one target. *Hit:* 8 (1d8 + 4) piercing damage.

Greatsword. *Melee Weapon Attack:* +7 to hit, reach 5 ft., one target. *Hit:* 11 (2d6 + 4) slashing damage.

Bonus Actions

Aggressive. The tanarukk moves up to its speed toward an enemy that it can see.

Reactions

Unbridled Fury. In response to being hit by a melee attack, the tanarukk can make one Bite or Greatsword attack with advantage against the attacker.

TANARUKK

When demonic influence corrupts the leadership of a people or an organization, the leaders might embrace abyssal magic to make tanarukks, using these ferocious warriors to bolster their followers' strength.

The demon lord Baphomet (appears in this book) gladly shares the secret of creating tanarukks with those who entreat him for power; the cult of Gruumsh has also mastered a ritual for this purpose, and bestows it on those deemed worthy. Whatever process is used corrupts the subject, transforming them into a vicious Fiend.

Although tanarukks are valued as fearsome fighters, they are a threat to their allies off the battlefield. When not in combat, a tanarukk is destructive and volatile and is usually kept imprisoned by its allies. If unrestrained, a free tanarukk embarks on a rampage, attempting to take over by force. Most such coups fail but are costly nonetheless. If a tanarukk does seize the leadership of a group, reckless raiding or even war is the course they inevitably choose.

TITIVILUS

Dispater, the gloomy Lord of Dis, rules from his iron palace, seeming to hide behind its labyrinthine corridors, iron walls, diabolical traps, and monstrous servants. Knowing he has enemies on all sides and fearing he'll be displaced like Moloch, Geryon, and so many others, he almost never travels farther than the sprawling city that lies outside his palace.

Dispater is correct to fear, but the true threat comes not from without. The lord's great error was allowing himself to be seduced by Titivilus, who beguiled his way into being the primary advisor in Dispater's household.

Although Titivilus is inferior in physical strength and power when compared to other archdevils, he compensates with cunning. A shrewd politician, he has clawed his way up through the ranks to become the second-most powerful devil in Dis, entirely by saying the right thing at the right time to get what he wanted. Charming and pleasant, he is a master at negotiation, able to twist words so as to leave his victims confused and believing he's on their side. Through these skills, Titivilus has manipulated everyone along his path to power, either to win them over to his cause or to remove them as a threat.

Since gaining his position, Titivilus has convinced Dispater that countless plots are being hatched against him and that Asmodeus himself seeks to remove Dispater from power. In response, Dispater has withdrawn to his palace and left day-to-day decisions to Titivilus, even authorizing him to answer and negotiate bargains with mortals who attempt to summon Dispater. Titivilus now represents his master and speaks with his voice, a turn of events that leads some to whisper that either Titivilus is Dispater in disguise or Titivilus has removed the archduke and replaced him altogether.

Titivilus recognizes the precariousness of his position. After all, Dispater's acceptance of his plans and his advice can last only so long before some other plotter steps in and reveals the truth. For insurance, Titivilus has begun recruiting outsiders to deal with problem devils, to insulate him against criticism, and, above all, to create complications that he can solve so as to reinforce his value in the eyes of his master. Titivilus finds adventurers well suited to the tasks he needs performed and recruits them directly or through intermediaries, expending them later as his plans require.

TITIVILUS
Medium Fiend (Devil), Lawful Evil

Armor Class 20 (natural armor)
Hit Points 150 (20d8 + 60)
Speed 40 ft., fly 60 ft.

STR	DEX	CON	INT	WIS	CHA
19 (+4)	22 (+6)	17 (+3)	24 (+7)	22 (+6)	26 (+8)

Saving Throws Dex +11, Con +8, Wis +11, Cha +13
Skills Deception +13, Insight +11, Intimidation +13, Persuasion +13
Damage Resistances cold; bludgeoning, piercing, and slashing from nonmagical attacks that aren't silvered
Damage Immunities fire, poison
Condition Immunities charmed, exhaustion, frightened, poisoned
Senses darkvision 120 ft., passive Perception 16
Languages all, telepathy 120 ft.
Challenge 16 (15,000 XP)   **Proficiency Bonus** +5

Legendary Resistance (3/Day). If Titivilus fails a saving throw, he can choose to succeed instead.

Magic Resistance. Titivilus has advantage on saving throws against spells and other magical effects.

Regeneration. Titivilus regains 10 hit points at the start of his turn. If he takes cold or radiant damage, this trait doesn't function at the start of his next turn. Titivilus dies only if he starts his turn with 0 hit points and doesn't regenerate.

Ventriloquism. Whenever Titivilus speaks, he can choose a point within 60 feet of him; his voice emanates from that point.

ACTIONS

Multiattack. Titivilus makes one Silver Sword attack, and he uses Frightful Word.

Silver Sword. *Melee Weapon Attack:* +9 to hit, reach 5 ft., one target. *Hit:* 8 (1d8 + 4) force damage, or 9 (1d10 + 4) force damage if used with two hands, plus 16 (3d10) necrotic damage. If the target is a creature, its hit point maximum is reduced by an amount equal to half the necrotic damage taken.

Frightful Word. Titivilus targets one creature he can see within 10 feet of him. The target must succeed on a DC 21 Wisdom saving throw or become frightened of him for 1 minute. While frightened in this way, the target must take the Dash action and move away from Titivilus by the safest available route on each of its turns, unless there is nowhere to move, in which case it needn't take the Dash action. The target can repeat the saving throw at the end of each of its turns, ending the effect on itself on a success.

Spellcasting. Titivilus casts one of the following spells, requiring no material components and using Charisma as the spellcasting ability (spell save DC 21):

At will: *alter self, major image, nondetection, sending, suggestion*
3/day each: *mislead, modify memory*

Teleport. Titivilus teleports, along with any equipment he is wearing or carrying, up to 120 feet to an unoccupied space he can see.

Twisting Words. Titivilus targets one creature he can see within 60 feet of him. The target must succeed on a DC 21 Charisma saving throw or become charmed by Titivilus for 1 minute. The charmed target can repeat the saving throw if Titivilus deals any damage to it. A creature that succeeds on the saving throw is immune to Titivilus's Twisting Words for 24 hours.

LEGENDARY ACTIONS

Titivilus can take 3 legendary actions, choosing from the options below. Only one legendary action option can be used at a time and only at the end of another creature's turn. Titivilus regains spent legendary actions at the start of his turn.

Corrupting Guidance. Titivilus uses Twisting Words. Alternatively, he targets one creature charmed by him that is within 60 feet of him; that charmed target must succeed on a DC 21 Charisma saving throw, or Titivilus decides how the target acts during its next turn.

Teleport. Titivilus uses Teleport.

Assault (Costs 2 Actions). Titivilus makes one Silver Sword attack, or he uses Frightful Word.

WARREN MAHY

TLINCALLI

Tlincallis, also called scorpion folk, are chitin-covered creatures with a humanlike upper body and the lower body of an enormous scorpion, complete with a stinger at the end of a long tail. These desert creatures range across arid lands, hunting at dawn and dusk. In the hours between, they wait out the day's heat or the night's cold by burying themselves in loose sand or earth or, if the terrain proves too inflexible, lurking in ruins or shallow caves.

Tlincallis stay in one place for only as long as the hunting is good in the immediate area, though they might visit the same way stations over and over during their wanderings. They also settle down temporarily whenever it's time to lay eggs and hatch a new brood of young.

These scorpion folk deposit their eggs in warm places out of direct sunlight, often amid a stand of cacti near their present encampment. The eggs are protected by hard shells coated in paralytic poison similar to that produced by their stingers. This poison leaves most would-be predators that dare to break an egg defenseless when the tlincalli parents come to investigate.

Tlincallis eat what they kill, whether their hunt nets desert animals or a caravan, but when they have new mouths to feed, they are careful to take some of their prey alive. After using their stingers to paralyze victims and their spiked chains to bind them, tlincallis take these captives back to their encampment and tie them to cacti or rock formations. When the sun sets, the newly hatched young emerge from the lair to eat the captives alive.

These predators see themselves as great hunters, and respect others with such skills. If a tlincalli encounters a more powerful hunter, such as a blue dragon, they carefully weigh whether to serve the superior hunter, move on, or fight to the death to remove it as competition.

Tlincallis rarely build cities, make clothing, or mine metals. Instead, they scavenge much of what they need or want. They do, however, melt down scavenged metal to forge crude weapons, armor, and tools.

TLINCALLI

Large Monstrosity, Typically Neutral

Armor Class 15 (natural armor)
Hit Points 85 (10d10 + 30)
Speed 40 ft.

STR	DEX	CON	INT	WIS	CHA
16 (+3)	13 (+1)	16 (+3)	8 (−1)	12 (+1)	8 (−1)

Skills Perception +4, Stealth +4, Survival +4
Senses darkvision 60 ft., passive Perception 14
Languages Tlincalli
Challenge 5 (1,800 XP)   **Proficiency Bonus** +3

ACTIONS

Multiattack. The tlincalli makes one Longsword or Spiked Chain attack and one Sting attack.

Longsword. *Melee Weapon Attack:* +6 to hit, reach 5 ft., one target. *Hit:* 7 (1d8 + 3) slashing damage, or 8 (1d10 + 3) slashing damage if used with two hands.

Spiked Chain. *Melee Weapon Attack:* +6 to hit, reach 10 ft., one target. *Hit:* 6 (1d6 + 3) piercing damage, and the target is grappled (escape DC 11) if it is a Large or smaller creature. Until this grapple ends, the target is restrained, and the tlincalli can't use the spiked chain against another target.

Sting. *Melee Weapon Attack:* +6 to hit, reach 5 ft., one creature. *Hit:* 6 (1d6 + 3) piercing damage plus 14 (4d6) poison damage, and the target must succeed on a DC 14 Constitution saving throw or be poisoned for 1 minute. If it fails the saving throw by 5 or more, the target is also paralyzed while poisoned. The target can repeat the saving throw at the end of each of its turns, ending the effect on itself on a success.

Tortles

Tortles are omnivorous, turtle-like bipeds with shells that cover most of their bodies. Because they carry their homes on their backs, tortles feel little need to stay put for long.

Most tortles like to see how other folk live. A tortle can spend decades away from their native land without feeling homesick, often viewing their current companions as their family.

Tortle

The generic tortle stat block here represents a warrior, especially the sort who travels far and wide.

Tortle Druid

Many tortles view the world as a place of wonder. They live for the chance to hear a soft wind blowing through trees, to watch a frog croaking on a lily pad, or to stand in a crowded marketplace. A tortle druid savors such things more than most, channeling the natural magic of the world around them.

Tortle

Tortle

Medium Humanoid, Any Alignment

Armor Class 17 (natural)
Hit Points 22 (4d8 + 4)
Speed 30 ft.

STR	DEX	CON	INT	WIS	CHA
15 (+2)	10 (+0)	12 (+1)	11 (+0)	13 (+1)	12 (+1)

Skills Athletics +4, Survival +3
Senses passive Perception 11
Languages Aquan, Common
Challenge 1/4 (50 XP)   **Proficiency Bonus** +2

Hold Breath. The tortle can hold its breath for 1 hour.

Actions

Claw. *Melee Weapon Attack:* +4 to hit, reach 5 ft., one target. *Hit:* 4 (1d4 + 2) slashing damage.

Spear. *Melee or Ranged Weapon Attack:* +4 to hit, reach 5 ft. or range 20/60 ft., one target. *Hit:* 5 (1d6 + 2) piercing damage, or 6 (1d8 + 2) piercing damage if used with two hands in melee.

Light Crossbow. *Ranged Weapon Attack:* +2 to hit, range 80/320 ft., one target. *Hit:* 4 (1d8) piercing damage.

Shell Defense. The tortle withdraws into its shell. Until it emerges, it gains a +4 bonus to AC and has advantage on Strength and Constitution saving throws. While in its shell, the tortle is prone, its speed is 0 and can't increase, it has disadvantage on Dexterity saving throws, it can't take reactions, and the only action it can take is a bonus action to emerge.

Tortle Druid

Medium Humanoid, Any Alignment

Armor Class 17 (natural)
Hit Points 33 (6d8 + 6)
Speed 30 ft.

STR	DEX	CON	INT	WIS	CHA
14 (+2)	10 (+0)	12 (+1)	11 (+0)	15 (+2)	12 (+1)

Skills Animal Handling +4, Nature +2, Survival +4
Senses passive Perception 12
Languages Aquan, Common
Challenge 2 (450 XP)   **Proficiency Bonus** +2

Hold Breath. The tortle can hold its breath for 1 hour.

Actions

Multiattack. The tortle makes four Claw attacks or two Nature's Wrath attacks.

Claw. *Melee Weapon Attack:* +4 to hit, reach 5 ft., one target. *Hit:* 4 (1d4 + 2) slashing damage.

Nature's Wrath. *Ranged Spell Attack:* +4 to hit, range 90 ft., one target. *Hit:* 9 (2d6 + 2) damage of a type chosen by the tortle: cold, fire, lightning, or thunder.

Shell Defense. The tortle withdraws into its shell. Until it emerges, it gains a +4 bonus to AC and has advantage on Strength and Constitution saving throws. While in its shell, the tortle is prone, its speed is 0 and can't increase, it has disadvantage on Dexterity saving throws, it can't take reactions, and the only action it can take is a bonus action to emerge.

Spellcasting. The tortle casts one of the following spells, using Wisdom as the spellcasting ability (spell save DC 12):

At will: *druidcraft, guidance*
2/day each: *cure wounds, hold person, speak with animals, thunderwave*

Trapper

A trapper is a manta-like creature that usually lurks in subterranean environments. It can change the color and texture of its tough, outward-facing side to help it blend in with its surroundings, while its soft, inward-facing side clings to the floor, wall, or ceiling in its hunting territory. It remains motionless as it waits for prey to come close. When a target is within its reach, it peels itself away from the surface and wraps around its prey, crushing, smothering, and then digesting it. Only a scattering of bones, metal, treasure, and other indigestible bits is left behind.

A trapper's ability to alter the color and texture of its outer side enables it to blend in with any surface made of stone, earth, or wood, masking its presence to any but the most rigorous scrutiny. It can't change its texture to that of a grassy or snow-covered surface, but it is just cunning enough to change its color to match and then conceal itself under a thin layer of vegetation or actual snow.

A trapper that lurks on the floor of its hunting grounds can cover any remains there with its body, making them look like irregularities in the surface. The creature might instead attach itself to a nearby wall or a ceiling, using the remnants as bait; any creature that stops to investigate the bones for valuables becomes the trapper's next meal.

A trapper needs to eat a halfling-sized meal once per week to remain sated. Given a steady supply of food, trappers are content to stay in one place, making them a threat along well-traveled dungeon corridor and on routes through the wilderness that see a lot of traffic. When prey is scarce, a trapper enters a state of hibernation that can last for months, though it is still aware when prey comes near. A trapper on the verge of starvation might defy its instincts and abandon its old territory in search of better hunting.

Trapper
Large Monstrosity, Unaligned

Armor Class 13 (natural armor)
Hit Points 68 (8d10 + 24)
Speed 20 ft., climb 20 ft.

STR	DEX	CON	INT	WIS	CHA
17 (+3)	10 (+0)	17 (+3)	2 (−4)	13 (+1)	4 (−3)

Skills Stealth +2
Senses blindsight 30 ft., darkvision 60 ft., passive Perception 11
Languages —
Challenge 3 (700 XP)   **Proficiency Bonus** +2

False Appearance. If the trapper is motionless on a floor, wall, or ceiling at the start of combat, it has advantage on its initiative roll. Moreover, if a creature hasn't observed the trapper move or act, that creature must succeed on a DC 18 Intelligence (Investigation) check to discern that the trapper isn't part of the floor, wall, or ceiling.

Spider Climb. The trapper can climb difficult surfaces, including upside down on ceilings, without needing to make an ability check.

Actions

Smother. One Large or smaller creature within 10 feet of the trapper must succeed on a DC 13 Dexterity saving throw or be grappled (escape DC 13). Until the grapple ends, the target takes 13 (3d6 + 3) bludgeoning damage plus 3 (1d6) acid damage at the start of each of its turns. While grappled in this way, the target is restrained, blinded, and deprived of air. The trapper can smother only one creature at a time.

TROLLS

Trolls that are nearly obliterated but survive and regenerate from mere scraps of flesh can display bizarre features. Radically transformed trolls like the rot trolls, spirit trolls, and venom trolls that follow are especially likely to arise when trolls regenerate in the presence of magical emanations, planar energy, disease, or death on a vast scale, or if their bodies were damaged by elemental forces. These unusual forms can also be produced and shaped by the ritual magic of evil spellcasters or by trolls' own practices, as is the case for dire trolls.

DIRE TROLL
Huge Giant, Typically Chaotic Evil

Armor Class 15 (natural armor)
Hit Points 172 (15d12 + 75)
Speed 40 ft.

STR	DEX	CON	INT	WIS	CHA
22 (+6)	15 (+2)	21 (+5)	9 (−1)	11 (+0)	5 (−3)

Saving Throws Wis +5, Cha +2
Skills Perception +10
Damage Resistances bludgeoning, piercing, and slashing from nonmagical attacks
Condition Immunities frightened, poisoned
Senses darkvision 60 ft., passive Perception 20
Languages Giant
Challenge 13 (10,000 XP)   **Proficiency Bonus** +5

Regeneration. The troll regains 10 hit points at the start of its turn. If the troll takes acid or fire damage, it regains only 5 hit points at the start of its next turn. The troll dies only if it is hit by an attack that deals 10 or more acid or fire damage while the troll has 0 hit points.

ACTIONS

Multiattack. The troll makes one Bite attack and four Claw attacks.

Bite. *Melee Weapon Attack:* +11 to hit, reach 10 ft., one target. *Hit:* 10 (1d8 + 6) piercing damage plus 5 (1d10) poison damage.

Claw. *Melee Weapon Attack:* +11 to hit, reach 10 ft., one target. *Hit:* 16 (3d6 + 6) slashing damage.

Whirlwind of Claws (Recharge 5–6). Each creature within 10 feet of the troll must make a DC 19 Dexterity saving throw, taking 44 (8d10) slashing damage on a failed save, or half as much damage on a successful one.

DIRE
TROLL

VAPRAK THE DESTROYER

Although trolls are rarely devout and seldom ponder spiritual questions, some fear and venerate the entity known as Vaprak the Destroyer. Vaprak's true nature is something of a mystery, but Vaprak is always portrayed as a horrid, misshapen, greenish creature strongly resembling a troll. Vaprak is given to fits of mindless destruction and uncontrollably fears the plots and ambitions of other deities.

Vaprak's troll worshipers believe this god devours the souls of those who have been cooked or digested (slain by fire or acid). Otherwise, the god spits the soul back into the world to regenerate a new body.

DIRE TROLL

Trolls kill and eat almost anything—including, in rare cases, other trolls. This cannibalism has the effect of causing a troll to grow to an unusually large size. The resulting dire trolls crave more and more troll flesh to fuel their continued growth.

Dire trolls also increase their size by grafting flesh onto themselves. When a slab of quivering troll flesh is bound against a fresh wound on a dire troll, the dire troll's regenerative capacity incorporates the new mass into the troll's own musculature. Even more horrifying are the multiple arms, eyes, claws, and organs that dire trolls tear from their victims and graft onto themselves in this manner.

RALPH HORSLEY

ROT
TROLL

ROT TROLL

A troll infused with waves of necrotic energy as it regenerates can develop a symbiotic relationship with that deathly power. The troll's body withers, and the flesh falls away from the body as quickly as it forms. Eventually a rot troll becomes unable to regenerate, though the troll still heals normally. The creature courses with necrotic energy; simply standing near a rot troll exposes other creatures to lethal emanations.

SPIRIT TROLL

A troll blasted with psychic energy can take a non-physical form upon regenerating. The troll's psyche survives, but the body is as insubstantial as shadow. The troll might be unaware of the transition—the creature still moves and attacks with teeth and claws as ever—but now the troll strikes at victims' minds.

ROT TROLL
Large Giant, Typically Chaotic Evil

Armor Class 16 (natural armor)
Hit Points 138 (12d10 + 72)
Speed 30 ft.

STR	DEX	CON	INT	WIS	CHA
18 (+4)	13 (+1)	22 (+6)	5 (−3)	8 (−1)	4 (−3)

Skills Perception +3
Damage Immunities necrotic
Senses darkvision 60 ft., passive Perception 13
Languages Giant
Challenge 9 (5,000 XP)   **Proficiency Bonus** +4

Rancid Degeneration. At the end of each of the troll's turns, each creature within 5 feet of it takes 11 (2d10) necrotic damage, unless the troll has taken acid or fire damage since the end of its last turn.

ACTIONS

Multiattack. The troll makes one Bite attack and two Claw attacks.

Bite. *Melee Weapon Attack:* +8 to hit, reach 5 ft., one target. *Hit:* 9 (1d10 + 4) piercing damage plus 16 (3d10) necrotic damage.

Claw. *Melee Weapon Attack:* +8 to hit, reach 5 ft., one target. *Hit:* 11 (2d6 + 4) slashing damage plus 7 (2d6) necrotic damage.

SPIRIT TROLL
Large Giant, Typically Chaotic Evil

Armor Class 17 (natural armor)
Hit Points 130 (20d10 + 20)
Speed 30 ft.

STR	DEX	CON	INT	WIS	CHA
1 (−5)	17 (+3)	13 (+1)	8 (−1)	9 (−1)	16 (+3)

Skills Perception +3
Damage Resistances acid, cold, fire; bludgeoning, piercing, and slashing from nonmagical attacks
Condition Immunities exhaustion, grappled, paralyzed, petrified, prone, restrained, unconscious
Senses darkvision 60 ft., passive Perception 13
Languages Giant
Challenge 11 (7,200 XP)   **Proficiency Bonus** +4

Incorporeal Movement. The troll can move through other creatures and objects as if they were difficult terrain. It takes 5 (1d10) force damage if it ends its turn inside an object.

Regeneration. The troll regains 10 hit points at the start of its turn. If the troll takes psychic or force damage, this trait doesn't function at the start of the troll's next turn. The troll dies only if it starts its turn with 0 hit points and doesn't regenerate.

ACTIONS

Multiattack. The troll makes one Bite attack and two Claw attacks.

Bite. *Melee Weapon Attack:* +7 to hit, reach 5 ft., one creature. *Hit:* 19 (3d10 + 3) psychic damage, and the target must succeed on a DC 15 Wisdom saving throw or be stunned for 1 minute. The stunned target can repeat the saving throw at the end of each of its turns, ending the effect on itself on a success.

Claw. *Melee Weapon Attack:* +7 to hit, reach 5 ft., one creature. *Hit:* 19 (3d10 + 3) psychic damage.

RALPH HORSLEY

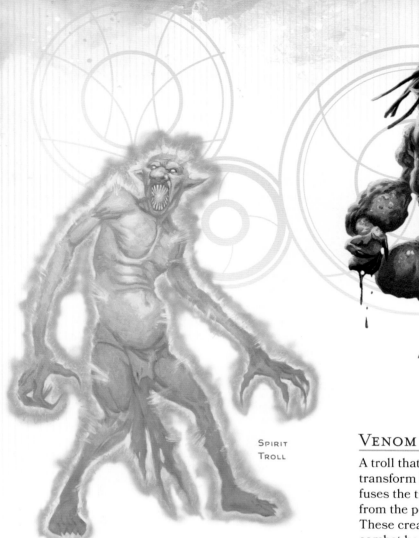

Spirit
Troll

Venom
Troll

Venom Troll

A troll that survives massive doses of poison might transform into a venom troll. Lingering poison infuses the troll's blood and tissue, and poison leaks from the pores to coat the troll's fangs and claws. These creatures are especially dangerous in close combat because poison drips off their flesh and sprays out from every wound they receive.

Venom Troll
Large Giant, Typically Chaotic Evil

Armor Class 15 (natural armor)
Hit Points 94 (9d10 + 45)
Speed 30 ft.

STR	DEX	CON	INT	WIS	CHA
18 (+4)	13 (+1)	20 (+5)	7 (–2)	9 (–1)	7 (–2)

Skills Perception +5
Damage Immunities poison
Condition Immunities poisoned
Senses darkvision 60 ft., passive Perception 15
Languages Giant
Challenge 7 (2,900 XP)   **Proficiency Bonus** +3

Poison Splash. When the troll takes damage of any type but psychic, each creature within 5 feet of the troll takes 9 (2d8) poison damage.

Regeneration. The troll regains 10 hit points at the start of its turn. If the troll takes acid or fire damage, this trait doesn't function at the start of the troll's next turn. The troll dies only if it starts its turn with 0 hit points and doesn't regenerate.

Actions

Multiattack. The troll makes one Bite attack and two Claw attacks.

Bite. *Melee Weapon Attack:* +7 to hit, reach 5 ft., one creature. *Hit:* 7 (1d6 + 4) piercing damage plus 4 (1d8) poison damage, and the target is poisoned until the start of the troll's next turn.

Claw. *Melee Weapon Attack:* +7 to hit, reach 5 ft., one target. *Hit:* 11 (2d6 + 4) slashing damage plus 4 (1d8) poison damage.

Venom Spray (Recharge 6). The troll slices itself with a claw, releasing a spray of poison in a 15-foot cube. The troll takes 7 (2d6) slashing damage, which can't be reduced in any way. Each creature in the area must make a DC 16 Constitution saving throw. On a failed save, a creature takes 18 (4d8) poison damage and is poisoned for 1 minute. On a successful save, the creature takes half as much damage and isn't poisoned. A poisoned creature can repeat the saving throw at the end of each of its turns, ending the effect on itself on a success.

RALPH HORSLEY

ULITHARID

Very rarely, when a tadpole from the brine pool of an elder brain (appears in this book) is implanted into a creature, that creature transforms into an ulitharid: a larger and more potent mind flayer with six tentacles. Illithids innately recognize that an ulitharid's survival is more important than their own. An elder brain's reaction to the rise of an ulitharid varies. In most colonies, the ulitharid becomes an elder brain's most favored servant, invested with power and authority. In others, the elder brain perceives an ulitharid as a potential rival and manipulates or quashes the ulitharid's ambitions accordingly.

When an ulitharid finds sharing leadership with an elder brain insufferable, it breaks off from the colony, taking a group of mind flayers with it, and moves to another location to form a new colony. After the death of the ulitharid's body, a special process transforms its brain into a new elder brain for the colony.

This process doesn't work on the brain of an ulitharid that dies a natural death, as such brains are too decrepit to be used. Instead, each ulitharid carries a psionically enhanced staff; when the ulitharid is ready to give up its life, it attaches the staff to the back of its head, and the staff cracks open its skull, enabling its brain to be extracted. The brain and the staff are then planted in the ulitharid's corpse, causing it to dissolve into ichor. This psionically potent slime helps to fuel the transformation of the area into a brine pool for the embryonic elder brain.

ULITHARID

Large Aberration (Mind Flayer), Typically Lawful Evil

Armor Class 15 (breastplate)
Hit Points 127 (17d10 + 34)
Speed 30 ft.

STR	DEX	CON	INT	WIS	CHA
15 (+2)	12 (+1)	15 (+2)	21 (+5)	19 (+4)	21 (+5)

Saving Throws Int +9, Wis +8, Cha +9
Skills Arcana +9, Insight +8, Perception +8, Stealth +5
Senses darkvision 120 ft., passive Perception 18
Languages Deep Speech, Undercommon, telepathy 2 miles
Challenge 9 (5,000 XP)　　　　**Proficiency Bonus** +4

Creature Sense. The ulitharid is aware of the presence of creatures within 2 miles of it that have an Intelligence score of 4 or higher. It knows the distance and direction to each creature, as well as each creature's Intelligence score, but can't sense anything else about it. A creature protected by a *mind blank* spell, a *nondetection* spell, or similar magic can't be perceived in this manner.

Magic Resistance. The ulitharid has advantage on saving throws against spells and other magical effects.

Psionic Hub. If an elder brain establishes a psychic link with the ulitharid, the elder brain can form a psychic link with any other creature the ulitharid can detect using its Creature Sense. Any such link ends if the creature falls outside the telepathy ranges of both the ulitharid and the elder brain. The ulitharid can maintain its psychic link with the elder brain regardless of the distance between them, so long as they are both on the same plane of existence. If the ulitharid is more than 5 miles away from the elder brain, it can end the psychic link at any time (no action required).

ACTIONS

Tentacles. *Melee Weapon Attack:* +9 to hit, reach 10 ft., one creature. *Hit:* 27 (4d10 + 5) psychic damage. If the target is Large or smaller, it is grappled (escape DC 14) and must succeed on a DC 17 Intelligence saving throw or be stunned until this grapple ends.

Extract Brain. *Melee Weapon Attack:* +9 to hit, reach 5 ft., one incapacitated Humanoid grappled by the ulitharid. *Hit:* 55 (10d10) piercing damage. If this damage reduces the target to 0 hit points, the ulitharid kills the target by extracting and devouring its brain.

Mind Blast (Recharge 5–6). The ulitharid magically emits psychic energy in a 60-foot cone. Each creature in that area must succeed on a DC 17 Intelligence saving throw or take 31 (4d12 + 5) psychic damage and be stunned for 1 minute. A target can repeat the saving throw at the end of each of its turns, ending the effect on itself on a success.

Spellcasting (Psionics). The ulitharid casts one of the following spells, requiring no spell components and using Intelligence as the spellcasting ability (spell save DC 17):

At will: *detect thoughts, levitate*
1/day each: *dominate monster, feeblemind, mass suggestion, plane shift* (self only), *project image, scrying, telekinesis*

Vampiric Mist

In billowing clouds of fog lurk vampiric mists, the wretched remnants of vampires that were prevented from finding rest. Indistinguishable from the mists they lurk within, they strike unseen and undetected to bleed their victims dry.

Vampiric mists, sometimes called crimson mists, are all that remain of vampires who couldn't return to their burial places after being defeated or suffering some mishap. Denied the restorative power of these places, the vampires' bodies dissolve into mist. The transformation strips the intelligence and personality from them until only an unholy, insatiable thirst for blood remains.

Indistinguishable from fog aside from the charnel reek it exudes, a vampiric mist descends on a creature and causes the blood in the creature's body to ooze through its pores or spill out from its eyes, nose, and mouth. This blood wafts out from the victim like crimson smoke, which the mist then consumes. The feeding causes no pain or discomfort to the victim, so vampiric mists can feed on sleepers without waking them. The more a mist feeds, the redder it gets, such that it turns pink, then red, and finally a deep scarlet hue; when sated, it rains blood droplets wherever it goes.

Like sharks in water, vampiric mists can scent blood from up to a mile away. Any injury, no matter how small, might catch their attention and draw them toward their victims. In battle, a mist focuses its attacks on injured targets, since open wounds are a more ready source of blood.

Vampiric Mist
Medium Undead, Typically Chaotic Evil

Armor Class 13
Hit Points 30 (4d8 + 12)
Speed 0 ft., fly 30 ft. (hover)

STR	DEX	CON	INT	WIS	CHA
6 (−2)	16 (+3)	16 (+3)	6 (−2)	12 (+1)	7 (−2)

Saving Throws Wis +3
Damage Resistances acid, cold, lightning, necrotic, thunder; bludgeoning, piercing, and slashing from nonmagical attacks
Damage Immunities poison
Condition Immunities charmed, exhaustion, grappled, paralyzed, petrified, poisoned, prone, restrained
Senses darkvision 60 ft., passive Perception 11
Languages —
Challenge 3 (700 XP)   **Proficiency Bonus** +2

Life Sense. The mist can sense the location of any creature within 60 feet of it, unless that creature's type is Construct or Undead.

Forbiddance. The mist can't enter a residence without an invitation from one of the occupants.

Misty Form. The mist can occupy another creature's space and vice versa. In addition, if air can pass through a space, the mist can pass through it without squeezing. Each foot of movement in water costs it 2 extra feet, rather than 1 extra foot. The mist can't manipulate objects in any way that requires fingers or manual dexterity.

Sunlight Hypersensitivity. The mist takes 10 radiant damage whenever it starts its turn in sunlight. While in sunlight, the mist has disadvantage on attack rolls and ability checks.

Unusual Nature. The mist doesn't require air or sleep.

Actions

Life Drain. The mist touches one creature in its space. The target must succeed on a DC 13 Constitution saving throw (Undead and Constructs automatically succeed), or it takes 10 (2d6 + 3) necrotic damage, the mist regains 10 hit points, and the target's hit point maximum is reduced by an amount equal to the necrotic damage taken. This reduction lasts until the target finishes a long rest. The target dies if its hit point maximum is reduced to 0.

JON HODGSON

Vargouille

Shrieking, flapping, and hideous to behold—with a body like a severed head and wings in place of ears—vargouilles boil out of the Abyss to infest other planes of existence, such as Carceri, where they are a menace. Each vargouille carries a disease that creates more of its kind; a flock of vargouilles on the wing is a plague of chaos and evil.

Swarms of vargouilles flap through the caverns and skies of the Abyss. They are given little regard by powerful and intelligent demons since vargouilles can do them no harm. Even the weakest demon, such as a manes or a dretch, fears vargouilles only if they appear in great numbers. In the Lower Planes, vargouilles rarely get the chance to eat live prey other than vermin. More often, they lap up the ichor left behind when one Fiend kills another.

Because of their hunger for living prey, vargouilles are eager to escape the Lower Planes. On rare occasions, summoning a demon to another plane can bring a vargouille along for the ride, attached like a tick. The precautions a mortal takes to control a summoned demon rarely account for a stowaway, enabling the vargouille to escape into the world.

Vargouilles that roam free on the Material Plane are a dire threat to all creatures. Their awful shrieking can paralyze other creatures with fear, which also makes the creatures susceptible to the vargouille's curse. If the curse is allowed to run its course, an abyssal spirit invades the person's body, causing a gruesome transformation. Over a period of hours, the victim's head takes on fiendish aspects, such as fangs, tentacles, and horns. At the same time, the person's ears grow larger, expanding into wing-like appendages. In the final moments, the victim's head tears away from the body in a fountain of blood, becoming another vargouille, which often then eagerly laps up the blood spilling from its former body. Sunlight or the brilliant illumination of a *daylight* spell can delay this transformation; otherwise, only magic can overcome the curse.

Vargouille
Tiny Fiend, Typically Chaotic Evil

Armor Class 12
Hit Points 18 (4d4 + 8)
Speed 5 ft., fly 40 ft.

STR	DEX	CON	INT	WIS	CHA
6 (−2)	14 (+2)	14 (+2)	4 (−3)	7 (−2)	2 (−4)

Damage Resistances cold, fire, lightning
Damage Immunities poison
Condition Immunities poisoned
Senses darkvision 60 ft., passive Perception 8
Languages understands Abyssal, Infernal, and any languages it knew before becoming a vargouille but can't speak
Challenge 1 (200 XP)　　　　**Proficiency Bonus** +2

Actions

Bite. *Melee Weapon Attack:* +4 to hit, reach 5 ft., one target. *Hit:* 5 (1d6 + 2) piercing damage plus 10 (3d6) poison damage.

Abyssal Curse. The vargouille targets one incapacitated Humanoid within 5 feet of it. The target must succeed on a DC 12 Charisma saving throw or become cursed. The cursed target loses 1 point of Charisma after each hour, as its head takes on fiendish aspects. The curse doesn't advance while the target is in sunlight or the area of a *daylight* spell; don't count that time. When the cursed target's Charisma becomes 2, it dies, and its head tears from its body and becomes a new vargouille. Casting *remove curse*, *greater restoration*, or a similar spell on the target before the transformation is complete can end the curse. Doing so undoes the changes made to the target by the curse.

Stunning Shriek (Recharge 5–6). The vargouille shrieks. Each Humanoid and Beast within 30 feet of the vargouille and able to hear it must succeed on a DC 12 Wisdom saving throw or be frightened of the vargouille until the end of the vargouille's next turn. While frightened in this way, a target is stunned. If a target's saving throw is successful or the effect ends for it, the target is immune to the Stunning Shriek of all vargouilles for 1 hour.

Vegepygmies

Vegepygmies are fungus creatures that live in simple bands, hunting for sustenance and spreading the spores by which they reproduce. Also called mold folk or moldies, vegepygmies inhabit dark, moist areas, so they're most commonly found underground or in forests where little sunlight penetrates. A vegepygmy feels kinship with other plant and fungus creatures, and thus vegepygmy bands coexist well with creatures such as myconid adults, shriekers, and violet fungi (all appear in the *Monster Manual*).

Although they prefer to eat fresh meat, bone, and blood, vegepygmies can absorb nutrients from soil and many sorts of organic matter, so they rarely go hungry. A vegepygmy can hiss and make other noises by forcing air through its mouth, but it can't speak in a conventional sense. Among themselves, vegepygmies communicate by hissing, gestures, and tapping. Vegepygmies build and craft little; any gear they have is acquired from other creatures or built by copying simple construction they have witnessed.

Vegepygmy

Typical vegepygmies originate from the remains left behind when a Humanoid or a Giant is killed by russet mold (see "Russet Mold" below). One or more vegepygmies emerge from the corpse a day later.

Vegepygmy Chief

As a vegepygmy ages, it grows tougher and develops spore clusters on its body. Other vegepygmies defer to these so-called chiefs. A chief can expel its spores in a burst, infecting nearby creatures. If a creature dies while infected, its corpse produces vegepygmies the same way russet mold does.

Thorny Vegepygmy

If a Beast such as a dog or a bear dies from russet mold, the result is a bestial moldy called a thorny, instead of a bipedal vegepygmy. Thornies are less intelligent than other vegepygmies, but they are larger and more ferocious and have thorn-covered bodies.

Russet Mold

Few know for sure where russet mold came from. One historical account tells of adventurers in a mountain range discovering russet mold and vegepygmies in a peculiar metal dungeon full of strange life. Another story says that explorers found russet mold in a crater left by a falling star, with vegepygmies infesting the forest nearby.

The mold is found only in places that are dark, warm, and wet. Russet mold that spreads out across a metal object can be mistaken for rust, and a successful DC 15 Intelligence (Nature) or Wisdom (Survival) check is required to identify it.

Effects of the Mold

Any creature that comes within 5 feet of russet mold must make a DC 13 Constitution saving throw as the mold emits a puff of spores. On a failed save, the creature is poisoned. While poisoned in this way, the creature takes 7 (2d6) poison damage at the start of each of its turns. The creature can repeat the saving throw at the end of each of its turns, ending the effect on itself on a success. Any magic that neutralizes poison or cures disease kills the infestation. A creature reduced to 0 hit points by the mold dies. If the dead creature is a Beast, a Giant, or a Humanoid, one or more vegepygmies emerge from its body 24 hours later: one from a Small corpse, two from a Medium corpse, four from a Large corpse, eight from a Huge corpse, or sixteen from a Gargantuan corpse.

Destroying the Mold

Russet mold can be hard to kill, since weapons and most types of damage do it no harm. Effects that deal acid, necrotic, or radiant damage kill 1 square foot of russet mold per 1 damage dealt. A pound of salt, a gallon of alcohol, or magic that cures disease kills russet mold in a square area that is 10 feet on a side. Sunlight kills any russet mold in the light's area.

Vegepygmy
Small Plant, Typically Neutral

Armor Class 13 (natural armor)
Hit Points 13 (3d6 + 3)
Speed 30 ft.

STR	DEX	CON	INT	WIS	CHA
7 (−2)	14 (+2)	13 (+1)	6 (−2)	11 (+0)	7 (−2)

Skills Perception +2, Stealth +4
Damage Resistances lightning, piercing
Senses darkvision 60 ft., passive Perception 12
Languages Vegepygmy
Challenge 1/4 (50 XP)   **Proficiency Bonus** +2

Plant Camouflage. The vegepygmy has advantage on Dexterity (Stealth) checks it makes in any terrain with ample obscuring vegetation.

Regeneration. The vegepygmy regains 3 hit points at the start of its turn. If it takes cold, fire, or necrotic damage, this trait doesn't function at the start of the vegepygmy's next turn. The vegepygmy dies only if it starts its turn with 0 hit points and doesn't regenerate.

Actions

Claw. Melee Weapon Attack: +4 to hit, reach 5 ft., one target. Hit: 5 (1d6 + 2) slashing damage.

Sling. Ranged Weapon Attack: +4 to hit, range 30/120 ft., one target. Hit: 4 (1d4 + 2) bludgeoning damage.

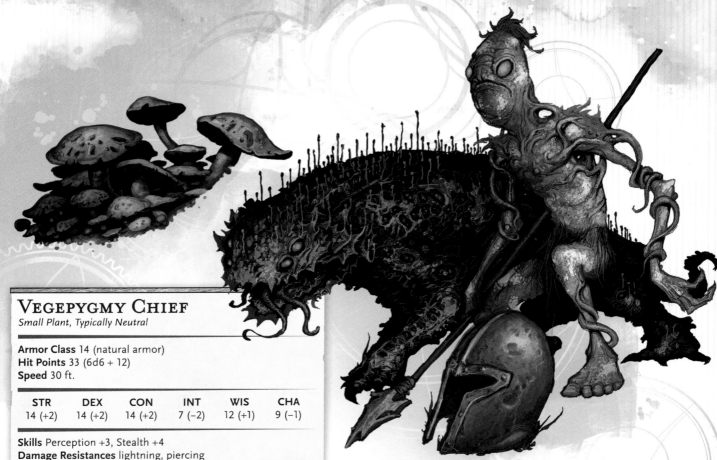

VEGEPYGMY CHIEF

Small Plant, Typically Neutral

Armor Class 14 (natural armor)
Hit Points 33 (6d6 + 12)
Speed 30 ft.

STR	DEX	CON	INT	WIS	CHA
14 (+2)	14 (+2)	14 (+2)	7 (−2)	12 (+1)	9 (−1)

Skills Perception +3, Stealth +4
Damage Resistances lightning, piercing
Senses darkvision 60 ft., passive Perception 13
Languages Vegepygmy
Challenge 2 (450 XP)   **Proficiency Bonus** +2

Plant Camouflage. The vegepygmy has advantage on Dexterity (Stealth) checks it makes in any terrain with ample obscuring vegetation.

Regeneration. The vegepygmy regains 5 hit points at the start of its turn. If it takes cold, fire, or necrotic damage, this trait doesn't function at the start of the vegepygmy's next turn. The vegepygmy dies only if it starts its turn with 0 hit points and doesn't regenerate.

ACTIONS

Multiattack. The vegepygmy makes two Claw attacks or two melee Spear attacks.

Claw. *Melee Weapon Attack:* +4 to hit, reach 5 ft., one target. *Hit:* 5 (1d6 + 2) slashing damage.

Spear. *Melee or Ranged Weapon Attack:* +4 to hit, reach 5 ft. or range 20/60 ft., one target. *Hit:* 5 (1d6 + 2) piercing damage, or 6 (1d8 + 2) piercing damage if used with two hands to make a melee attack.

Spores (1/Day). A 15-foot-radius cloud of toxic spores extends out from the vegepygmy. The spores spread around corners. Each creature in that area that isn't a Plant must succeed on a DC 12 Constitution saving throw or be poisoned. While poisoned in this way, a target takes 9 (2d8) poison damage at the start of each of its turns. A target can repeat the saving throw at the end of each of its turns, ending the effect on itself on a success.

THORNY VEGEPYGMY

Medium Plant, Typically Neutral

Armor Class 14 (natural armor)
Hit Points 27 (5d8 + 5)
Speed 30 ft.

STR	DEX	CON	INT	WIS	CHA
13 (+1)	12 (+1)	13 (+1)	2 (−4)	10 (+0)	6 (−2)

Skills Perception +4, Stealth +3
Damage Resistances lightning, piercing
Senses darkvision 60 ft., passive Perception 14
Languages —
Challenge 1 (200 XP)   **Proficiency Bonus** +2

Plant Camouflage. The thorny has advantage on Dexterity (Stealth) checks it makes in any terrain with ample obscuring vegetation.

Regeneration. The thorny regains 5 hit points at the start of its turn. If it takes cold, fire, or necrotic damage, this trait doesn't function at the start of the thorny's next turn. The thorny dies only if it starts its turn with 0 hit points and doesn't regenerate.

Thorny Body. At the start of its turn, the thorny deals 2 (1d4) piercing damage to any creature grappling it.

ACTIONS

Bite. *Melee Weapon Attack:* +3 to hit, reach 5 ft., one target. *Hit:* 10 (2d8 + 1) piercing damage.

WAR PRIEST

Medium Humanoid (Cleric), Any Alignment

Armor Class 18 (plate)
Hit Points 117 (18d8 + 36)
Speed 30 ft.

STR	DEX	CON	INT	WIS	CHA
16 (+3)	10 (+0)	14 (+2)	11 (+0)	17 (+3)	13 (+1)

Saving Throws Con +6, Wis +7
Skills Intimidation +5, Religion +4
Senses passive Perception 13
Languages any two languages
Challenge 9 (5,000 XP)   **Proficiency Bonus** +4

ACTIONS

Multiattack. The war priest makes two Maul attacks, and it uses Holy Fire.

Maul. *Melee Weapon Attack:* +7 to hit, reach 5 ft., one target. *Hit:* 10 (2d6 + 3) bludgeoning damage plus 10 (3d6) radiant damage.

Holy Fire. The war priest targets one creature it can see within 60 feet of it. The target must make a DC 15 Wisdom saving throw. On a failed save, the target takes 12 (2d8 + 3) radiant damage, and it is blinded until the start of the war priest's next turn. On a successful save, the target takes half as much damage and isn't blinded.

Spellcasting. The war priest casts one of the following spells, using Wisdom as the spellcasting ability (spell save DC 15):

At will: *light, spare the dying, thaumaturgy*
1/day each: *banishment, command, dispel magic, flame strike, guardian of faith, hold person, lesser restoration, revivify*

BONUS ACTIONS

Healing Light (2/Day). The war priest or one creature of its choice within 60 feet of it regains 12 (2d8 + 3) hit points.

WAR PRIEST

War priests worship deities of war, protection, and strategy. They plan tactics, lead soldiers into battle, confront enemy spellcasters, and tend to casualties. A war priest might command an army or serve as the right hand of a warlord (appears in this book) on the battlefield.

War priests typically adorn themselves with a symbol of their faith. You can roll on the War Priest Holy Symbols table below, or choose one that fits your campaign.

WAR PRIEST HOLY SYMBOLS

d8	Holy Symbol
1	Vial of iridescent liquid
2	Hilt of a broken sword
3	Piece of stained glass from a shrine
4	Clay figurine of a ki-rin or another Celestial
5	Torch carved so that a hand appears to be holding the flame
6	Circlet of woven reeds
7	Scrimshawed bone
8	Vessel such as a cup, a jug, an urn, or an amphora

MARTA NAEL

WARLOCKS

Warlocks gain arcane might through magical pacts with mysterious entities. While some use their abilities to serve the sources of their power, others use them to undermine or even destroy these entities.

WARLOCK OF THE ARCHFEY

Warlocks of the Archfey gain their powers through magical pacts forged with lords of the Feywild. These warlocks commonly associate with lesser Fey creatures such as boggles, quicklings, and redcaps (all appear in this book) or even satyrs and sprites (both appear in the *Monster Manual*).

WARLOCK OF THE ARCHFEY
Medium Humanoid, Any Alignment

Armor Class 13 (16 with *mage armor*)
Hit Points 67 (15d8)
Speed 30 ft.

STR	DEX	CON	INT	WIS	CHA
9 (−1)	16 (+3)	11 (+0)	11 (+0)	12 (+1)	18 (+4)

Saving Throws Wis +3, Cha +6
Skills Arcana +2, Deception +6, Nature +2, Persuasion +6
Condition Immunities charmed
Senses passive Perception 11
Languages any two languages (usually Sylvan)
Challenge 4 (1,100 XP)   **Proficiency Bonus** +2

ACTIONS

Multiattack. The warlock makes two Rapier attacks, or it uses Bewildering Word twice.

Rapier. *Melee Weapon Attack:* +5 to hit, reach 5 ft., one target. *Hit:* 7 (1d8 + 3) piercing damage plus 7 (2d6) force damage.

Bewildering Word. The warlock utters a magical bewilderment, targeting one creature it can see within 60 feet of it. The target must succeed on a DC 14 Wisdom saving throw or take 9 (2d8) psychic damage and have disadvantage on attack rolls until the end of the warlock's next turn.

Spellcasting. The warlock casts one of the following spells, using Charisma as the spellcasting ability (spell save DC 14):

At will: *dancing lights, disguise self, mage armor* (self only), *mage hand, minor illusion, prestidigitation, speak with animals*
1/day each: *charm person, dimension door, hold monster*

REACTIONS

Misty Escape (Recharges after a Short or Long Rest). In response to taking damage, the warlock turns invisible and teleports, along with any equipment it is wearing or carrying, up to 60 feet to an unoccupied space it can see. It remains invisible until the start of its next turn or until it attacks, makes a damage roll, or casts a spell.

WARLOCK OF THE FIEND

Warlocks of the Fiend gain their powers through magical pacts forged with archfiends of the Lower Planes. These warlocks often keep imps or quasits (see the *Monster Manual*) as companions, and they tend toward philosophical extremes: consorting with fiendish cults or dedicating their lives to destroying such cults.

WARLOCK OF THE FIEND
Medium Humanoid, Any Alignment

Armor Class 13 (16 with *mage armor*)
Hit Points 78 (12d8 + 24)
Speed 30 ft.

STR	DEX	CON	INT	WIS	CHA
10 (+0)	16 (+3)	15 (+2)	12 (+1)	12 (+1)	18 (+4)

Saving Throws Wis +4, Cha +7
Skills Arcana +4, Deception +7, Persuasion +7, Religion +4
Damage Resistances fire
Senses darkvision 60 ft., passive Perception 11
Languages any two languages (usually Abyssal or Infernal)
Challenge 7 (2,900 XP)   **Proficiency Bonus** +3

Dark One's Own Luck (Recharges after a Short or Long Rest). When the warlock makes an ability check or saving throw, it can add a d10 to the roll. It can do this after the roll is made but before any of the roll's effects occur.

ACTIONS

Multiattack. The warlock makes three Scimitar attacks.

Scimitar. *Melee Weapon Attack:* +6 to hit, reach 5 ft., one target. *Hit:* 6 (1d6 + 3) bludgeoning damage plus 14 (4d6) fire damage.

Hellfire. Green flame explodes in a 10-foot-radius sphere centered on a point within 120 feet of the warlock. Each creature in that area must make a DC 15 Dexterity saving throw, taking 16 (3d10) fire damage and 11 (2d10) necrotic damage on a failed save, or half as much damage on a successful one.

Spellcasting. The warlock casts one of the following spells, using Charisma as the spellcasting ability (spell save DC 15):

At will: *alter self, mage armor* (self only), *mage hand, minor illusion, prestidigitation*
1/day each: *banishment, plane shift, suggestion*

REACTIONS

Fiendish Rebuke (3/Day). In response to being damaged by a visible creature within 60 feet of it, the warlock forces that creature to make a DC 15 Constitution saving throw, taking 22 (4d10) necrotic damage on a failed save, or half as much damage on a successful one.

WARLOCK OF THE GREAT OLD ONE

Warlocks of the Great Old One gain their powers through magical pacts forged with eldritch entities from strange and distant realms of existence. Some of these warlocks associate with cultists devoted to these entities, as well as Aberrations that share their goals, yet other warlocks of the Great Old One are experts at rooting out the chaos and wickedness inspired by bizarre beings from beyond the stars.

WARLOCK OF THE GREAT OLD ONE

Medium Humanoid, Any Alignment

Armor Class 13 (16 with *mage armor*)
Hit Points 91 (14d8 + 28)
Speed 30 ft.

STR	DEX	CON	INT	WIS	CHA
9 (−1)	16 (+3)	15 (+2)	12 (+1)	12 (+1)	18 (+4)

Saving Throws Wis +4, Cha +7
Skills Arcana +4, History +4
Damage Resistances psychic
Senses darkvision 60 ft., passive Perception 11
Languages any two languages, telepathy 30 ft.
Challenge 6 (2,300 XP)   **Proficiency Bonus** +3

Whispering Aura. At the start of each of the warlock's turns, each creature of its choice within 10 feet of it must succeed on a DC 15 Wisdom saving throw or take 10 (3d6) psychic damage, provided the warlock isn't incapacitated.

ACTIONS

Multiattack. The warlock makes two Dagger attacks.

Dagger. *Melee or Ranged Weapon Attack:* +6 to hit, reach 5 ft. or range 20/60 ft., one target. *Hit:* 5 (1d4 + 3) piercing damage plus 10 (3d6) psychic damage.

Howling Void. The warlock opens a momentary extraplanar rift within 60 feet of it. The rift is a scream-filled, 20-foot cube. Each creature in that area must make a DC 15 Wisdom saving throw. On a failed save, a creature takes 9 (2d8) psychic damage and is frightened of the warlock until the start of the warlock's next turn. On a successful save, a creature takes half as much damage and isn't frightened.

Spellcasting. The warlock casts one of the following spells, using Charisma as the spellcasting ability (spell save DC 15):

At will: *detect magic, guidance, levitate, mage armor* (self only), *mage hand, minor illusion, prestidigitation, speak with dead*
1/day each: *arcane gate, detect thoughts, true seeing*

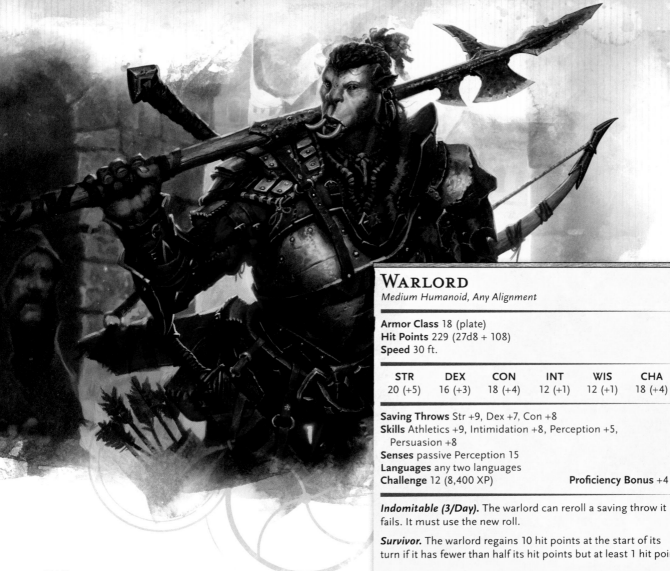

WARLORD

Warlords are legendary battlefield commanders, whose names are spoken with awe. After a string of decisive victories, a warlord could easily take on the role of monarch or general and attract followers willing to die for the warlord's banner.

Warlords urge their troops into the fray with shouted exhortations. You can roll on the Warlord Battle Cries table to select one, or choose a battle cry that fits with your campaign.

WARLORD BATTLE CRIES

d8	Battle Cry
1	"Remember why we fight!"
2	"Victory awaits!"
3	"For the crown!"
4	"Be monstrous to the enemy!"
5	"Fight so they fear us!"
6	"Weapons drawn! Spells at the ready!"
7	"To the Abyss with them!"
8	"You know what to do!"

WARLORD
Medium Humanoid, Any Alignment

Armor Class 18 (plate)
Hit Points 229 (27d8 + 108)
Speed 30 ft.

STR	DEX	CON	INT	WIS	CHA
20 (+5)	16 (+3)	18 (+4)	12 (+1)	12 (+1)	18 (+4)

Saving Throws Str +9, Dex +7, Con +8
Skills Athletics +9, Intimidation +8, Perception +5, Persuasion +8
Senses passive Perception 15
Languages any two languages
Challenge 12 (8,400 XP)   **Proficiency Bonus** +4

Indomitable (3/Day). The warlord can reroll a saving throw it fails. It must use the new roll.

Survivor. The warlord regains 10 hit points at the start of its turn if it has fewer than half its hit points but at least 1 hit point.

ACTIONS

Multiattack. The warlord makes two Greatsword or Shortbow attacks.

Greatsword. *Melee Weapon Attack:* +9 to hit, reach 5 ft., one target. *Hit:* 12 (2d6 + 5) slashing damage.

Shortbow. *Ranged Weapon Attack:* +7 to hit, range 80/320 ft., one target. *Hit:* 6 (1d6 + 3) piercing damage.

LEGENDARY ACTIONS

The warlord can take 3 legendary actions, choosing from the options below. Only one legendary action option can be used at a time and only at the end of another creature's turn. The warlord regains spent legendary actions at the start of its turn.

Command Ally. The warlord targets one ally it can see within 30 feet of it. If the target can see or hear the warlord, the target can make one weapon attack as a reaction and gains advantage on the attack roll.

Weapon Attack. The warlord makes one Greatsword or Shortbow attack.

Frighten Foe (Costs 2 Actions). The warlord targets one creature it can see within 30 feet of it. If the target can see or hear it, the target must succeed on a DC 16 Wisdom saving throw or be frightened of the warlord until the end of warlord's next turn.

CAIO MONTEIRO

WASTRILITH

Found in the waters of the Abyss and other bodies of water contaminated by that plane's fell influence, wastriliths establish themselves as lords of the deep and rule their dominions with cruelty.

A wastrilith pollutes the waters around it. Its noxious presence even affects nearby sources of water when the demon travels on land. The corrupted water, which contains a measure of the demon's essence, responds to the wastrilith's commands—perhaps hardening to prevent foes from escaping or erupting in a surge that drags victims into its reach.

Creatures that ingest water corrupted by a wastrilith risk their very souls. Those who drink the poisonous liquid might wither away until they finally die, or they remain alive only to become thralls of chaos and evil. To represent this defilement, you can use the optional rule on abyssal corruption in chapter 2 of the *Dungeon Master's Guide*, causing the poisoned creature to be corrupted.

WASTRILITH

Large Fiend (Demon), Typically Chaotic Evil

Armor Class 18 (natural armor)
Hit Points 157 (15d10 + 75)
Speed 30 ft., swim 80 ft.

STR	DEX	CON	INT	WIS	CHA
19 (+4)	18 (+4)	21 (+5)	19 (+4)	12 (+1)	14 (+2)

Saving Throws Str +9, Con +10
Damage Resistances cold, fire, lightning; bludgeoning, piercing, and slashing from nonmagical attacks
Damage Immunities poison
Condition Immunities poisoned
Senses darkvision 120 ft., passive Perception 11
Languages Abyssal, telepathy 120 ft.
Challenge 13 (10,000 XP)　　　**Proficiency Bonus** +5

Amphibious. The wastrilith can breathe air and water.

Corrupt Water. At the start of each of the wastrilith's turns, exposed water within 30 feet of it is befouled. Underwater, this effect lightly obscures the area until a current clears it away. Water in containers remains corrupted until it evaporates.

A creature that consumes this foul water or swims in it must make a DC 18 Constitution saving throw. On a successful save, the creature is immune to the foul water for 24 hours. On a failed save, the creature takes 14 (4d6) poison damage and is poisoned for 1 minute. At the end of this time, the poisoned creature must repeat the saving throw. On a failure, the creature takes 18 (4d8) poison damage and is poisoned until it finishes a long rest.

If another demon drinks the foul water as an action, it gains 11 (2d10) temporary hit points.

Magic Resistance. The wastrilith has advantage on saving throws against spells and other magical effects.

ACTIONS

Multiattack. The wastrilith makes one Bite attack and two Claw attacks, and it uses Grasping Spout.

Bite. *Melee Weapon Attack:* +9 to hit, reach 10 ft., one target. *Hit:* 30 (4d12 + 4) piercing damage.

Claw. *Melee Weapon Attack:* +9 to hit, reach 10 ft., one target. *Hit:* 18 (4d6 + 4) slashing damage.

Grasping Spout. The wastrilith magically launches a spout of water at one creature it can see within 60 feet of it. The target must make a DC 17 Strength saving throw, and it has disadvantage if it's underwater. On a failed save, it takes 22 (4d8 + 4) acid damage and is pulled up to 60 feet toward the wastrilith. On a successful save, it takes half as much damage and isn't pulled.

BONUS ACTIONS

Undertow. If the wastrilith is underwater, it causes all water within 60 feet of it to be difficult terrain for other creatures until the start of its next turn.

WIZARDS

Wizards pursue magical power through the study of arcane texts. Some travel the world searching for esoteric tomes, while others train lesser wizards or collaborate with colleagues to create new spells.

APPRENTICE WIZARD

Apprentices are novice arcane spellcasters who serve more experienced wizards or attend school. They perform menial work like cooking or cleaning in exchange for education in the ways of magic.

ABJURER WIZARD

Abjurers specialize in creating protective magical wards. Monarchs, nobles, and other wealthy individuals commonly hire abjurers to provide protection.

CONJURER WIZARD

Conjurers summon creatures from other planes of existence and teleport themselves and others in the blink of an eye.

DIVINER WIZARD

Diviners peer into the future and know that knowledge is power. They might act aloof and mysterious, hinting at omens and secrets, or they might be know-it-alls, spilling insights to advance their own status.

ENCHANTER WIZARD

Enchanters know how to magically influence minds. Benign enchanters use this magic to defuse violence and sow peace, while malevolent enchanters are some of the most evil of all spellcasters.

EVOKER WIZARD

Evokers harness arcane energy to destroy. Many armies employ evokers to rain destruction down on enemy forces.

ILLUSIONIST WIZARD

Illusionists twist light, sound, and even thought to create illusory effects. Some illusionists are delightful entertainers, while others are devilish tricksters.

NECROMANCER WIZARD

Necromancers study the interaction of life, death, and undeath. Some necromancers dig up or purchase corpses to create Undead servitors. A few instead use their powers for good, hunting Undead.

TRANSMUTER WIZARD

Transmuters are masters at transforming physical forms. They typically view magical transmutation as a path to riches, enlightenment, or apotheosis.

APPRENTICE WIZARD
Medium Humanoid, Any Alignment

Armor Class 10 (13 with *mage armor*)
Hit Points 13 (3d8)
Speed 30 ft.

STR	DEX	CON	INT	WIS	CHA
10 (+0)	10 (+0)	10 (+0)	14 (+2)	10 (+0)	11 (+0)

Skills Arcana +4, History +4
Senses passive Perception 10
Languages any one language (usually Common)
Challenge 1/4 (50 XP)   **Proficiency Bonus** +2

ACTIONS

Arcane Burst. *Melee or Ranged Spell Attack:* +4 to hit, reach 5 ft. or range 120 ft., one target. *Hit:* 7 (1d10 + 2) force damage.

Spellcasting. The apprentice casts one of the following spells, using Intelligence as the spellcasting ability (spell save DC 12):

At will: *mage hand, prestidigitation*
1/day each: *burning hands, disguise self, mage armor*

Abjurer Wizard

Medium Humanoid, Any Alignment

Armor Class 12 (15 with *mage armor*)
Hit Points 104 (16d8 + 32)
Speed 30 ft.

STR	DEX	CON	INT	WIS	CHA
9 (−1)	14 (+2)	14 (+2)	18 (+4)	12 (+1)	11 (+0)

Saving Throws Int +8, Wis +5
Skills Arcana +8, History +8
Senses passive Perception 11
Languages any four languages
Challenge 9 (5,000 XP)   **Proficiency Bonus** +4

Actions

Multiattack. The abjurer makes three Arcane Burst attacks.

Arcane Burst. *Melee or Ranged Spell Attack:* +8 to hit, reach 5 ft. or range 120 ft., one target. *Hit:* 20 (3d10 + 4) force damage.

Force Blast. Each creature in a 20-foot cube originating from the abjurer must make a DC 16 Constitution saving throw. On a failed save, a creature takes 36 (8d8) force damage and is pushed up to 10 feet away from the abjurer. On a successful save, a creature takes half as much damage and isn't pushed.

Spellcasting. The abjurer casts one of the following spells, using Intelligence as the spellcasting ability (spell save DC 16):

At will: *dancing lights, mage hand, message, prestidigitation*
2/day each: *dispel magic, lightning bolt, mage armor*
1/day each: *arcane lock, banishment, globe of invulnerability, invisibility, wall of force*

Reactions

Arcane Ward (Recharge 4–6). When the abjurer or a creature it can see within 30 feet of it takes damage, the abjurer magically creates a protective barrier around itself or the other creature. The barrier reduces the damage to the protected creature by 26 (4d10 + 4), to a minimum of 0, and then vanishes.

Conjurer Wizard

Medium Humanoid, Any Alignment

Armor Class 12 (15 with *mage armor*)
Hit Points 58 (13d8)
Speed 30 ft.

STR	DEX	CON	INT	WIS	CHA
9 (−1)	14 (+2)	11 (+0)	17 (+3)	12 (+1)	11 (+0)

Saving Throws Int +6, Wis +4
Skills Arcana +6, History +6
Senses passive Perception 11
Languages any four languages
Challenge 6 (2,300 XP)   **Proficiency Bonus** +3

Actions

Multiattack. The conjurer makes three Arcane Burst attacks.

Arcane Burst. *Melee or Ranged Spell Attack:* +6 to hit, reach 5 ft. or range 120 ft., one target. *Hit:* 19 (3d10 + 3) force damage.

Spellcasting. The conjurer casts one of the following spells, using Intelligence as the spellcasting ability (spell save DC 14):

At will: *dancing lights, mage hand, prestidigitation*
2/day each: *fireball, mage armor, unseen servant*
1/day each: *fly, stinking cloud, web*

Bonus Actions

Benign Transportation (Recharge 4–6). The conjurer teleports, along with any equipment it is wearing or carrying, up to 30 feet to an unoccupied space that it can see. If it instead chooses a space within range that is occupied by a willing Small or Medium creature, they both teleport, swapping places.

Summon Elemental (1/Day). The conjurer magically summons an **air elemental**, an **earth elemental**, a **fire elemental**, or a **water elemental** (all appear in the *Monster Manual*). The elemental appears in an unoccupied space within 60 feet of the conjurer, whom it obeys. It takes its turn immediately after the conjurer. It lasts for 1 hour, until it or the conjurer dies, or until the conjurer dismisses it as a bonus action.

DIVINER WIZARD
Medium Humanoid, Any Alignment

Armor Class 12 (15 with *mage armor*)
Hit Points 90 (20d8)
Speed 30 ft.

STR	DEX	CON	INT	WIS	CHA
9 (−1)	14 (+2)	11 (+0)	18 (+4)	12 (+1)	11 (+0)

Saving Throws Int +7, Wis +4
Skills Arcana +7, History +7
Senses passive Perception 11
Languages any four languages
Challenge 8 (3,900 XP)   **Proficiency Bonus** +3

ACTIONS

Multiattack. The diviner makes three Arcane Burst attacks.

Arcane Burst. *Melee or Ranged Spell Attack:* +7 to hit, reach 5 ft. or range 120 ft., one target. *Hit:* 20 (3d10 + 4) radiant damage.

Overwhelming Revelation (Recharge 5–6). The diviner magically creates a burst of illumination in a 10-foot-radius sphere centered on a point within 120 feet of it. Each creature in that area must make a DC 15 Wisdom saving throw. On a failed save, a creature takes 45 (10d8) psychic damage and is stunned until the end of the diviner's next turn. On a successful save, the creature takes half as much damage and isn't stunned.

Spellcasting. The diviner casts one of the following spells, using Intelligence as the spellcasting ability (spell save DC 15):

At will: *light, mage hand, message, prestidigitation*
2/day each: *arcane eye, detect magic, detect thoughts, fly, lightning bolt, locate object, mage armor, Rary's telepathic bond*
1/day: *true seeing*

REACTIONS

Portent (3/Day). When the diviner or a creature it can see makes an attack roll, a saving throw, or an ability check, the diviner rolls a d20 and chooses whether to use that roll in place of the d20 rolled for the attack roll, saving throw, or ability check.

ENCHANTER WIZARD
Medium Humanoid, Any Alignment

Armor Class 12 (15 with *mage armor*)
Hit Points 49 (11d8)
Speed 30 ft.

STR	DEX	CON	INT	WIS	CHA
9 (−1)	14 (+2)	11 (+0)	17 (+3)	12 (+1)	11 (+0)

Saving Throws Int +6, Wis +4
Skills Arcana +6, History +6
Senses passive Perception 11
Languages any four languages
Challenge 5 (1,800 XP)   **Proficiency Bonus** +3

ACTIONS

Multiattack. The enchanter makes three Arcane Burst attacks.

Arcane Burst. *Melee or Ranged Spell Attack:* +6 to hit, reach 5 ft. or range 120 ft., one target. *Hit:* 19 (3d10 + 3) psychic damage.

Spellcasting. The enchanter casts one of the following spells, using Intelligence as the spellcasting ability (spell save DC 14):

At will: *friends, mage hand, message*
2/day each: *charm person, mage armor, hold person, invisibility, suggestion, tongues*

REACTIONS

Instinctive Charm (Recharge 4–6). When a visible creature within 30 feet of the enchanter makes an attack roll against it, the enchanter forces the attacker to make a DC 14 Wisdom saving throw. On a failed save, the attacker redirects the attack roll to the creature closest to it, other than the enchanter or itself. If multiple eligible creatures are closest, the attacker chooses which one to target.

Evoker Wizard
Medium Humanoid, Any Alignment

Armor Class 12 (15 with *mage armor*)
Hit Points 121 (22d8 + 22)
Speed 30 ft.

STR	DEX	CON	INT	WIS	CHA
9 (−1)	14 (+2)	12 (+1)	17 (+3)	12 (+1)	11 (+0)

Saving Throws Int +7, Wis +5
Skills Arcana +7, History +7
Senses passive Perception 11
Languages any four languages
Challenge 9 (5,000 XP)   **Proficiency Bonus** +4

Actions

Multiattack. The evoker makes three Arcane Burst attacks.

Arcane Burst. *Melee or Ranged Spell Attack:* +7 to hit, reach 5 ft. or range 120 ft., one target. *Hit:* 25 (4d10 + 3) force damage.

Sculpted Explosion (Recharge 4–6). The evoker unleashes a magical explosion of a particular damage type: cold, fire, lightning, or thunder. The magic erupts in a 20-foot-radius sphere centered on a point within 150 feet of the evoker. Each creature in that area must make a DC 15 Dexterity saving throw. The evoker can select up to three creatures it can see in the area to ignore the explosion, as the evoker sculpts the energy around them. On a failed save, a creature takes 40 (9d8) damage of the chosen type and is knocked prone. On a successful save, a creature takes half as much damage and isn't knocked prone.

Spellcasting. The evoker casts one of the following spells, using Intelligence as the spellcasting ability (spell save DC 15):

At will: *light, mage hand, message, prestidigitation*
2/day each: *ice storm, lightning bolt, mage armor*
1/day: *wall of ice*

ZACK STELLA

ILLUSIONIST WIZARD

Medium Humanoid, Any Alignment

Armor Class 12 (15 with *mage armor*)
Hit Points 44 (8d8 + 8)
Speed 30 ft.

STR	DEX	CON	INT	WIS	CHA
9 (−1)	14 (+2)	13 (+1)	16 (+3)	11 (+0)	12 (+1)

Saving Throws Int +5, Wis +2
Skills Arcana +5, History +5
Senses passive Perception 10
Languages any four languages
Challenge 3 (700 XP)   **Proficiency Bonus** +2

ACTIONS

Multiattack. The illusionist makes two Arcane Burst attacks.

Arcane Burst. *Melee or Ranged Spell Attack:* +5 to hit, reach 5 ft. or range 120 ft., one target. *Hit:* 14 (2d10 + 3) psychic damage.

Spellcasting. The illusionist casts one of the following spells, using Intelligence as the spellcasting ability (spell save DC 13):

At will: *dancing lights, mage hand, minor illusion*
2/day each: *disguise self, invisibility, mage armor, major image, phantasmal force, phantom steed*

BONUS ACTIONS

Displacement (Recharge 5–6). The illusionist projects an illusion that makes the illusionist appear to be standing in a place a few inches from its actual location, causing any creature to have disadvantage on attack rolls against the illusionist. The effect lasts for 1 minute, and it ends early if the illusionist takes damage, if it is incapacitated, or if its speed becomes 0.

Necromancer Wizard

Medium Humanoid, Any Alignment

Armor Class 12 (15 with *mage armor*)
Hit Points 110 (20d8 + 20)
Speed 30 ft.

STR	DEX	CON	INT	WIS	CHA
9 (−1)	14 (+2)	12 (+1)	17 (+3)	12 (+1)	11 (+0)

Saving Throws Int +7, Wis +5
Skills Arcana +7, History +7
Damage Resistances necrotic
Senses passive Perception 11
Languages any four languages
Challenge 9 (5,000 XP)   **Proficiency Bonus** +4

Actions

Multiattack. The necromancer makes three Arcane Burst attacks.

Arcane Burst. *Melee or Ranged Spell Attack:* +7 to hit, reach 5 ft. or range 120 ft., one target. *Hit:* 25 (4d10 + 3) necrotic damage.

Spellcasting. The necromancer casts one of the following spells, using Intelligence as the spellcasting ability (spell save DC 15):

At will: *dancing lights, mage hand, prestidigitation*
2/day each: *bestow curse, dimension door, mage armor, web*
1/day: *circle of death*

Bonus Actions

Summon Undead (1/Day). The necromancer magically summons five **skeletons** or **zombies** (both appear in the *Monster Manual*). The summoned creatures appear in unoccupied spaces within 60 feet of the necromancer, whom they obey. They take their turns immediately after the necromancer. Each lasts for 1 hour, until it or the necromancer dies, or until the necromancer dismisses it as a bonus action.

Reactions

Grim Harvest. When the necromancer kills a creature with necrotic damage, the necromancer regains 9 (2d8) hit points.

RANDY VARGAS

Transmuter Wizard
Medium Humanoid, Any Alignment

Armor Class 12 (15 with *mage armor*)
Hit Points 49 (11d8)
Speed 30 ft.

STR	DEX	CON	INT	WIS	CHA
9 (−1)	14 (+2)	11 (+0)	17 (+3)	12 (+1)	11 (+0)

Saving Throws Int +6, Wis +4
Skills Arcana +6, History +6
Senses passive Perception 11
Languages any four languages
Challenge 5 (1,800 XP)   **Proficiency Bonus** +3

Transmuter's Stone. The transmuter carries a magic stone it crafted. The stone grants it one of the following benefits while bearing the stone; the transmuter chooses the benefit at the end of each long rest:

Darkvision. The transmuter has darkvision out to a range of 60 feet.

Resilience. The transmuter has proficiency in Constitution saving throws.

Resistance. The transmuter has resistance to acid, cold, fire, lightning, or thunder damage (transmuter's choice whenever choosing this benefit).

Speed. The transmuter's walking speed is increased by 10 feet.

Actions

Multiattack. The transmuter makes three Arcane Burst attacks.

Arcane Burst. *Melee or Ranged Spell Attack:* +6 to hit, reach 5 ft. or range 120 ft., one target. *Hit:* 19 (3d10 + 3) acid damage.

Spellcasting. The transmuter casts one of the following spells, using Intelligence as the spellcasting ability (spell save DC 14):

At will: *light, message, prestidigitation*
2/day each: *fireball, hold person, knock, mage armor, polymorph, slow*
1/day: *telekinesis*

Bonus Actions

Transmute (Recharge 4–6). The transmuter casts *alter self* or changes the benefit of Transmuter's Stone if bearing the stone.

WOOD WOAD

A wood woad is a powerful bipedal Plant invested with the soul of someone who gave up life to become an everlasting guardian.

The ritual to create a wood woad is a primeval secret passed down through generations of forest-dwelling societies and druid circles. Performing the ritual isn't necessarily an evil act if the victim-to-be is a willing sacrifice.

In the ritual, a living person's chest is pierced and the heart removed. A seed is pushed into the heart, which is then placed in a tree. Any hollow or crook will do, but often a special cavity is carved out of the trunk. The tree is bathed and watered with the blood of the sacrificed victim, and the body is buried among the tree's roots. After three days, a sprout emerges from the ground at the base of the tree and swiftly grows into a bipedal form.

This new body, armored in tough bark and bearing a gnarled club and shield, is at once ready to perform its duty. The one who performed the ritual sets the wood woad to its task, and the creature follows those orders unceasingly.

A wood woad has a hole where its heart would be, just as does the body of its former self, buried in the earth. Those who become wood woads trade their free will and all sense of sentiment for supernatural strength and a deathless duty. They exist only to protect woodlands and the people who tend them. A wood woad's face is void and expressionless, except for the motes of light that swim about in its eye sockets. Wood woads speak little, and when not called on to take action, they root themselves in the earth and silently take sustenance from it.

Like trees, wood woads need only sunlight, air, and nutrients from the earth to go on living. Because they are undying, some wood woads outlive their original purpose. The site a wood woad guards might lose its power or significance over time, or those whom it was assigned to guard might die. If it is freed from its specific duties, a wood woad might roam to find another place of natural beauty or fey influence to watch over.

Wood woads are drawn to creatures that have close ties to nature and that protect and respect the land, such as druids and treants (both appear in the *Monster Manual*). Some treants have wood woad servants by virtue of age-old pacts with druids or Fey that performed the rituals, while others acquire the services of freed wood woads that find renewed purpose in serving a kindred guardian.

WOOD WOAD
Medium Plant, Typically Lawful Neutral

Armor Class 18 (natural armor, shield)
Hit Points 75 (10d8 + 30)
Speed 30 ft., climb 30 ft.

STR	DEX	CON	INT	WIS	CHA
18 (+4)	12 (+1)	16 (+3)	10 (+0)	13 (+1)	8 (−1)

Skills Athletics +7, Perception +4, Stealth +4
Damage Vulnerabilities fire
Damage Resistances bludgeoning, piercing
Condition Immunities charmed, frightened
Senses darkvision 60 ft., passive Perception 14
Languages Sylvan
Challenge 5 (1,800 XP)   **Proficiency Bonus** +3

Plant Camouflage. The wood woad has advantage on Dexterity (Stealth) checks it makes in any terrain with ample obscuring vegetation.

Regeneration. The wood woad regains 10 hit points at the start of its turn if it is in contact with the ground. If the wood woad takes fire damage, this trait doesn't function at the start of the wood woad's next turn. The wood woad dies only if it starts its turn with 0 hit points and doesn't regenerate.

Tree Stride. Once on each of its turns, the wood woad can use 10 feet of its movement to step magically into one living tree within 5 feet of it and emerge from a second living tree within 60 feet of it that it can see, appearing in an unoccupied space within 5 feet of the second tree. Both trees must be Large or bigger.

ACTIONS

Multiattack. The wood woad makes two Club attacks.

Club. Melee Weapon Attack: +7 to hit, reach 5 ft., one target. Hit: 14 (4d4 + 4) force damage.

Xvarts

Xvarts are cowardly, greedy creatures spawned by a renegade demigod, Raxivort. They have blue skin, orange eyes, and receding hairlines, mirroring their creator's appearance. They stand about 3 feet tall.

Raxivort spent centuries watching over the treasury of Graz'zt (appears in this book), and in time, Raxivort plundered his lord's vault. One of the treasures he stole was the *Infinity Spindle*, a crystalline shard that could transform even a creature as lowly as Raxivort into a demigod. After his apotheosis, Raxivort forged the Black Sewers, a realm within Pandemonium that he filled with his beloved creatures, rats and bats, which xvarts befriend to this day. He enjoyed his reign only briefly before Graz'zt unleashed his vengeance. The demon prince urged villains far and wide to pursue the *Infinity Spindle* for themselves and destroy Raxivort.

Xvart

Fleeing his pursuers, Raxivort wandered across the multiverse and spawned xvarts, who not only look like him but also cause any magic that could reveal his location to point to the nearest xvart instead.

Xvart Warlock of Raxivort

Some xvarts are spawned with a trace of Raxivort's divine energy. These xvarts usually form a pact with him and wield magic in his service as warlocks.

Xvart
Small Monstrosity, Typically Chaotic Evil

Armor Class 13 (leather armor)
Hit Points 7 (2d6)
Speed 30 ft.

STR	DEX	CON	INT	WIS	CHA
8 (−1)	14 (+2)	10 (+0)	8 (−1)	7 (−2)	7 (−2)

Skills Stealth +4
Senses darkvision 30 ft., passive Perception 8
Languages Abyssal
Challenge 1/8 (25 XP)   **Proficiency Bonus** +2

Raxivort's Tongue. The xvart can communicate with ordinary bats and rats, as well as giant bats and giant rats.

Actions

Shortsword. *Melee Weapon Attack:* +4 to hit, reach 5 ft., one target. *Hit:* 5 (1d6 + 2) piercing damage. If at least one of the xvart's allies is within 5 feet of the target, the xvart can push the target 5 feet if the target is a Medium or smaller creature.

Sling. *Ranged Weapon Attack:* +4 to hit, range 30/120 ft., one target. *Hit:* 4 (1d4 + 2) bludgeoning damage.

Bonus Actions

Low Cunning. The xvart takes the Disengage action.

Xvart Warlock of Raxivort
Small Monstrosity, Typically Chaotic Evil

Armor Class 12 (15 with *mage armor*)
Hit Points 22 (5d6 + 5)
Speed 30 ft.

STR	DEX	CON	INT	WIS	CHA
8 (−1)	14 (+2)	12 (+1)	8 (−1)	11 (+0)	12 (+1)

Skills Stealth +3
Senses darkvision 30 ft., passive Perception 10
Languages Abyssal
Challenge 1 (200 XP)   **Proficiency Bonus** +2

Raxivort's Blessing. When the xvart reduces an enemy to 0 hit points, the xvart gains 4 temporary hit points.

Raxivort's Tongue. The xvart can communicate with ordinary bats and rats, as well as giant bats and giant rats.

Actions

Multiattack. The xvart makes two Scimitar or Raxivort's Bite attacks.

Scimitar. *Melee Weapon Attack:* +4 to hit, reach 5 ft., one target. *Hit:* 5 (1d6 + 2) slashing damage.

Raxivort's Bite. *Ranged Spell Attack:* +3 to hit, range 30 ft., one creature. *Hit:* 7 (1d10 + 2) poison damage.

Spellcasting. The xvart casts one of the following spells, requiring no material components and using Charisma as the spellcasting ability (spell save DC 11):

At will: *detect magic, mage armor* (self only), *mage hand, minor illusion, prestidigitation*
1/day each: *burning hands, invisibility*

Bonus Actions

Low Cunning. The xvart takes the Disengage action.

Yagnoloth

Anyone who would contract yugoloths for a task usually ends up dealing with a yagnoloth. Cunning negotiators, these strange Fiends handle the writing of contracts for their fellow yugoloths. Once a yagnoloth is hired, it communicates its employer's desires to the yugoloths it commands.

Although they are entrusted with leading lesser yugoloths, yagnoloths ultimately take their orders from arcanaloths and ultroloths. Aside from their superiors, yagnoloths have full authority over and expect obedience from the yugoloths under their command. Yagnoloths follow the dictates of the contracts they negotiate but always include a loophole to escape their obligations if the situation warrants.

A yagnoloth has one arm of human size and one giant-sized arm. During negotiations, the yagnoloth uses its human-sized arm to draft and sign contracts. When a show of force is necessary or when combat is joined, it attacks with its brutally powerful giant arm.

Yagnoloth

Large Fiend (Yugoloth), Typically Neutral Evil

Armor Class 17 (natural armor)
Hit Points 147 (14d10 + 70)
Speed 40 ft.

STR	DEX	CON	INT	WIS	CHA
19 (+4)	14 (+2)	21 (+5)	16 (+3)	15 (+2)	18 (+4)

Saving Throws Dex +6, Int +7, Wis +6, Cha +8
Skills Deception +8, Insight +6, Perception +6, Persuasion +8
Damage Resistances cold, fire, lightning; bludgeoning, piercing, and slashing from nonmagical attacks
Damage Immunities acid, poison
Condition Immunities poisoned
Senses blindsight 60 ft., darkvision 60 ft., passive Perception 16
Languages Abyssal, Infernal, telepathy 60 ft.
Challenge 11 (7,200 XP)   **Proficiency Bonus** +4

Magic Resistance. The yagnoloth has advantage on saving throws against spells and other magical effects.

Actions

Multiattack. The yagnoloth makes one Electrified Touch attack and one Massive Arm attack, or it makes one Massive Arm attack and uses Battlefield Cunning, if available, or Teleport.

Electrified Touch. *Melee Weapon Attack:* +8 to hit, reach 5 ft., one target. *Hit:* 27 (6d8) lightning damage.

Massive Arm. *Melee Weapon Attack:* +8 to hit, reach 15 ft., one target. *Hit:* 23 (3d12 + 4) force damage. If the target is a creature, it must succeed on a DC 16 Constitution saving throw or become stunned until the end of the yagnoloth's next turn.

Battlefield Cunning (Recharge 4–6). Up to two allied yugoloths within 60 feet of the yagnoloth that can hear it can use their reactions to make one melee attack each.

Life Leech. The yagnoloth touches one incapacitated creature within 15 feet of it. The target takes 36 (7d8 + 4) necrotic damage, and the yagnoloth gains temporary hit points equal to half the damage dealt. The target must succeed on a DC 16 Constitution saving throw, or its hit point maximum is reduced by an amount equal to half the necrotic damage taken. This reduction lasts until the target finishes a long rest, and the target dies if its hit point maximum is reduced to 0.

Spellcasting. The yagnoloth casts one of the following spells, requiring no material components and using Charisma as the spellcasting ability (spell save DC 16):

At will: *darkness, detect magic, dispel magic, invisibility (self only), suggestion*
3/day: *lightning bolt*

Teleport. The yagnoloth teleports, along with any equipment it is wearing or carrying, up to 60 feet to an unoccupied space it can see.

YEENOGHU

The Beast of Butchery appears as a great scarred gnoll, towering 14 feet tall. Yeenoghu is the Gnoll Lord, and his creations are made in his twisted image. When the demon lord hunted across the Material Plane, packs of hyenas followed in his wake, and those that ate of great Yeenoghu's kills became gnolls. Few others worship the Beast of Butchery, but those who do tend to take on a gnoll-like aspect, hunching over and filing their teeth down to points.

Yeenoghu wants nothing more than slaughter and senseless destruction. Gnolls are his favorite instruments, and he drives his gnoll followers to ever-greater atrocities in his name, even imbuing some of their commanders with his powers, which transforms them into flinds (in this book). Yeenoghu takes pleasure in causing fear before death, and he sows sorrow and despair through destroying beloved things. He doesn't parlay; to meet him is to do battle with him—unless he becomes bored and wanders away. The Beast of Butchery has a long rivalry with Baphomet, the Horned King (appears in this book), and the two demon lords and their followers attack one another on sight.

The Gnoll Lord is covered in matted fur and leathery hide, and his face resembles a grinning predator's skull. He wields a triple-headed flail called the Butcher, which he can summon into his hand at will, although he is as likely to tear his prey apart with his teeth.

YEENOGHU'S LAIR

Yeenoghu's lair in the Abyss is called the Death Dells. Its barren hills and ravines serve as a hunting ground, where he pursues captured mortals in a cruel game. Yeenoghu's lair is a place of blood and death, populated by gnolls, hyenas, and ghouls (see the *Monster Manual*), and there are few structures or signs of civilization on his layer of the Abyss.

The challenge rating of Yeenoghu is 25 (75,000 XP) when he's encountered in his lair.

LAIR ACTIONS

On initiative count 20 (losing initiative ties), Yeenoghu can take one of the following lair actions; he can't take the same lair action two rounds in a row:

Incite the Pack. Until the next initiative count 20, all gnolls and hyenas within the lair are enraged, causing them to have advantage on melee weapon attack rolls and causing attack rolls to have advantage against them.

Iron Spike. Yeenoghu causes an iron spike—5 feet tall and 1 inch in diameter—to burst from the ground at a point he can see within 100 feet of him. Any creature in the space where the spike emerges must make a DC 24 Dexterity saving throw. On a failed save, the creature takes 27 (6d8) piercing damage and is restrained by being impaled on the spike. A creature can use an action to remove itself (or a creature it can reach) from the spike, ending the restrained condition.

Pack Rush. Each gnoll or hyena that Yeenoghu can see can use its reaction to move up to its speed.

REGIONAL EFFECTS

The region containing Yeenoghu's lair is warped by his magic, creating one or more of the following effects:

Savage Predators. Predatory beasts within 6 miles of the lair become unusually savage, killing far more than what they need for food. Carcasses of prey are left to rot in an unnatural display of wasteful slaughter.

Spiky Terrain. Within 1 mile of the lair, large iron spikes grow out of the ground and stone surfaces. Yeenoghu impales the bodies of the slain on these spikes.

If Yeenoghu dies, these effects fade over the course of 1d10 days.

CULTISTS OF YEENOGHU

Yeenoghu grants special abilities to his cultists. His most devoted followers gain the Gnashing Jaws action and the Rampage bonus action, while cult leaders gain the Aura of Bloodthirst trait.

Gnashing Jaws. *Melee Weapon Attack:* bonus to hit equal to this creature's proficiency bonus plus its Strength modifier, reach 5 ft., one target. *Hit:* 1d4 + this creature's Strength modifier piercing damage.

Rampage. When this creature reduces a creature to 0 hit points with a melee attack on its turn, it can take a bonus action to move up to half its speed and make one Gnashing Jaws attack.

Aura of Bloodthirst. If this creature isn't incapacitated, any creature that has Rampage can make its Gnashing Jaws attack as a bonus action while within 10 feet of this creature.

YEENOGHU

Huge Fiend (Demon), Chaotic Evil

Armor Class 20 (natural armor)
Hit Points 333 (23d12 + 184)
Speed 50 ft.

STR	DEX	CON	INT	WIS	CHA
29 (+9)	16 (+3)	23 (+8)	15 (+3)	24 (+7)	15 (+2)

Saving Throws Dex +10, Con +15, Wis +14
Skills Intimidation +9, Perception +14
Damage Resistances cold, fire, lightning
Damage Immunities poison; bludgeoning, piercing, and slashing that is nonmagical
Condition Immunities charmed, exhaustion, frightened, poisoned
Senses truesight 120 ft., passive Perception 24
Languages all, telepathy 120 ft.
Challenge 24 (62,000 XP) **Proficiency Bonus** +7

Legendary Resistance (3/Day). If Yeenoghu fails a saving throw, he can choose to succeed instead.

Magic Resistance. Yeenoghu has advantage on saving throws against spells and other magical effects.

ACTIONS

Multiattack. Yeenoghu makes three Flail attacks.

Flail. *Melee Weapon Attack:* +16 to hit, reach 15 ft., one target. *Hit:* 22 (2d12 + 9) force damage. If it's his turn, Yeenoghu can cause the target to suffer one of the following additional effects, each of which he can apply only once per turn:

Confusion. The target must succeed on a DC 17 Wisdom saving throw or be affected by the *confusion* spell until the start of Yeenoghu's next turn.

Force. The target takes an extra 13 (2d12) force damage.

Paralysis. The target must succeed on a DC 17 Constitution saving throw or be paralyzed until the start of Yeenoghu's next turn.

Bite. *Melee Weapon Attack:* +16 to hit, reach 10 ft., one target. *Hit:* 20 (2d10 + 9) acid damage.

Spellcasting. Yeenoghu casts one of the following spells, requiring no material components and using Charisma as the spellcasting ability (spell save DC 17):

At will: *detect magic*
3/day each: *dispel magic, fear, invisibility*
1/day: *teleport*

BONUS ACTIONS

Rampage. When Yeenoghu reduces a creature to 0 hit points with a melee attack, he moves up to half his speed and makes one Bite attack.

LEGENDARY ACTIONS

Yeenoghu can take 3 legendary actions, choosing from the options below. Only one legendary action option can be used at a time and only at the end of another creature's turn. Yeenoghu regains spent legendary actions at the start of his turn.

Charge. Yeenoghu moves up to his speed.

Swat Away. Yeenoghu makes one Flail attack. If the attack hits, the target must succeed on a DC 24 Strength saving throw or be pushed up to 15 feet in a straight line away from Yeenoghu. If the saving throw fails by 5 or more, the target is also knocked prone.

Savage (Costs 2 Actions). Yeenoghu makes a separate Bite attack against each creature within 10 feet of him.

Yeth Hound

Large Fey, Typically Neutral Evil

Armor Class 14 (natural armor)
Hit Points 51 (6d10 + 18)
Speed 40 ft., fly 40 ft. (hover)

STR	DEX	CON	INT	WIS	CHA
18 (+4)	17 (+3)	16 (+3)	5 (−3)	12 (+1)	7 (−2)

Skills Perception +5
Damage Immunities bludgeoning, piercing, and slashing from nonmagical attacks not made with silvered weapons
Condition Immunities charmed, exhaustion, frightened
Senses darkvision 60 ft., passive Perception 15
Languages understands Common, Elvish, and Sylvan but can't speak
Challenge 4 (1,100 XP)   **Proficiency Bonus** +2

Sunlight Banishment. If the yeth hound starts its turn in sunlight, it is transported to the Ethereal Plane. While sunlight shines on the spot from which it vanished, the hound must remain in the Deep Ethereal. After sunset, it returns to the Border Ethereal at the same spot, whereupon it typically sets out to find its pack or its master. The hound is visible on the Material Plane while it is in the Border Ethereal, and vice versa, but it can't affect or be affected by anything on the other plane. Once it is adjacent to its master or a pack mate that is on the Material Plane, a yeth hound in the Border Ethereal can return to the Material Plane as an action.

Telepathic Bond. While the yeth hound is on the same plane of existence as its master, it can magically convey what it senses to its master, and the two can communicate telepathically with each other.

Actions

Bite. *Melee Weapon Attack:* +6 to hit, reach 5 ft., one target. *Hit:* 11 (2d6 + 4) piercing damage, plus 14 (4d6) psychic damage if the target is frightened.

Baleful Baying. The yeth hound bays magically. Every enemy within 300 feet of the hound that can hear it must succeed on a DC 13 Wisdom saving throw or be frightened of the hound until the end of the hound's next turn or until the hound is incapacitated. A frightened target that starts its turn within 30 feet of the hound must use all its movement on that turn to get as far from the hound as possible, must finish the move before taking an action, and must take the most direct route, even if hazards lie that way. A target that successfully saves is immune to the baying of all yeth hounds for the next 24 hours.

Yeth Hound

Granted by mighty Fey to individuals who please them, yeth hounds serve their masters like hunting dogs. They race in pursuit of their prey, running it down until it's too exhausted to fight back. Only the threat of dawn drives the pack back into hiding.

A pack of yeth hounds can be created by powerful Fey such as the Queen of Air and Darkness. Each pack's master can telepathically communicate with their yeth hounds to give the pack commands from afar. If a pack's master is killed, the hounds seek out a new master, typically an evil vampire, necromancer, or hag (all appear in the *Monster Manual*).

A yeth hound stands about 5 feet tall at the shoulder and weighs around 400 pounds. Its head has a human-like face and glowing red eyes. The creature gives off a smoky odor.

Yeth hounds make a ghastly baying sound that causes most creatures to flee in terror. They chase those who run and torment them before closing in for the kill. Those that fight back discover that mundane weapons partially pass through yeth hounds as if they were made of fog, but magic weapons and silvered weapons can strike true.

Yeth hounds can't stand sunlight. A pack hunts at night and seeks to return to its dark den before dawn. If a yeth hound is exposed to natural sunlight, it fades away, vanishing into the Ethereal Plane, and its master can retrieve it only after sunset.

YUAN-TI ANATHEMA

As part of their quest for godhood, a yuan-ti abomination might perform a ritual that, if successful, transforms them into an even greater form: a yuan-ti anathema. This ritual demands the sacrifice of hundreds of snakes and requires the abomination to bathe in the blood of their enemies. The transformation is quick but painful.

Anathemas consider themselves demigods on the path to greater divinity. They demand obeisance from weaker creatures and use every resource at their disposal to war against neighbors, seeking the captives, sacrifices, glory, and riches the anathemas believe they need to achieve true divinity.

Anathemas don't age, allowing them to pursue their goals until the end of days. Truly powerful ones might rule multiple yuan-ti cities and bring entire regions under their control.

YUAN-TI ANATHEMA
Huge Monstrosity, Typically Neutral Evil

Armor Class 16 (natural armor)
Hit Points 189 (18d12 + 72)
Speed 40 ft., climb 40 ft., swim 40 ft.

STR	DEX	CON	INT	WIS	CHA
23 (+6)	13 (+1)	19 (+4)	19 (+4)	17 (+3)	20 (+5)

Skills Perception +11, Stealth +5
Damage Resistances acid, fire, lightning
Damage Immunities poison
Condition Immunities poisoned
Senses blindsight 30 ft., darkvision 60 ft., passive Perception 21
Languages Abyssal, Common, Draconic
Challenge 12 (8,400 XP)   **Proficiency Bonus** +4

Magic Resistance. The anathema has advantage on saving throws against spells and other magical effects.

Ophidiophobia Aura. Any creature of the anathema's choice, other than a snake or a yuan-ti, that starts its turn within 30 feet of the anathema must succeed on a DC 17 Wisdom saving throw or become frightened of snakes and yuan-ti. A frightened target can repeat the saving throw at the end of each of its turns, ending the effect on itself on a success. If a target's saving throw is successful or the effect ends for it, the target is immune to this anathama's aura for the next 24 hours.

Six Heads. The anathema has advantage on saves against being blinded, charmed, deafened, frightened, stunned, or knocked unconscious.

ACTIONS

Multiattack (Anathema Form Only). The anathema makes two Claw attacks and one Flurry of Bites attack.

Claw (Anathema Form Only). *Melee Weapon Attack:* +10 to hit, reach 10 ft., one target. *Hit:* 13 (2d6 + 6) slashing damage.

Flurry of Bites (Anathema Form Only). *Melee Weapon Attack:* +10 to hit, reach 10 ft., one creature. *Hit:* 27 (6d6 + 6) piercing damage plus 14 (4d6) poison damage.

Constrict (Snake Form Only). *Melee Weapon Attack:* +10 to hit, reach 15 ft., one Large or smaller creature. *Hit:* 16 (3d6 + 6) bludgeoning damage plus 7 (2d6) acid damage, and the target is grappled (escape DC 16). Until this grapple ends, the target is restrained, and it takes 16 (3d6 + 6) bludgeoning damage plus 7 (2d6) acid damage at the start of each of its turns. The anathema can constrict only one creature at a time.

Spellcasting (Anathema Form Only). The anathema casts one of the following spells, requiring no material components and using Charisma as the spellcasting ability (spell save DC 17):

At will: *animal friendship* (snakes only)
3/day each: *darkness, entangle, fear, polymorph, suggestion*

BONUS ACTIONS

Change Shape. The anathema transforms into a Huge constrictor snake or back into its true form. Its statistics are the same in each form. Any equipment it is wearing or carrying isn't transformed.

Tasha once likened histachii to the bees that tend to larvae in beehives. It is a fanciful view of a horrific process.

—*Mordenkainen*

Yuan-ti Broodguard

Broodguards were once Humanoids, but they have been transformed by yuan-ti into simpleminded, scaly Monstrosities that do their serpentine masters' bidding. The transformation process warps not only a subject's body but also their mind, making them instinctively obey any yuan-ti and filling them with a seething rage at the sight of non-reptilian creatures.

Although broodguards can no longer think as clearly as before their transformation, they are able to perform simple yet important tasks in the community, such as guarding eggs or patrolling for intruders. Yuan-ti refer to broodguards as "histachii," which means "egg-watchers."

Most broodguards are made from human captives forced to consume a magical brew that renders them helpless and unable to fight off the inevitable transformation. A human transformed into a broodguard loses all semblance of who they once were. A broodguard is hairless and emaciated, with scaly skin. They have a forked tongue, and they smell faintly of rotting meat. Broodguards can speak but rarely do so, preferring to communicate via snake-like hisses and guttural noises.

Making a Broodguard

Yuan-ti create broodguards from captured Humanoids. Each subject is fed a special potion that immediately renders it incapacitated and transforms it into a broodguard over the next 1d6 + 6 days. A subject forced to imbibe the brew can make a DC 15 Constitution saving throw; on a success, it takes 14 (4d6) poison damage and is otherwise unaffected.

A spell such as *lesser restoration* or *remove curse* can end the transformation process at any time before it runs its course. After the process is complete, only a *wish* spell can reverse the effect.

Yuan-ti Broodguard
Medium Monstrosity, Typically Neutral Evil

Armor Class 14 (natural armor)
Hit Points 45 (7d8 + 14)
Speed 30 ft.

STR	DEX	CON	INT	WIS	CHA
15 (+2)	14 (+2)	14 (+2)	6 (−2)	11 (+0)	4 (−3)

Saving Throws Str +4, Dex +4, Wis +2
Skills Perception +2
Damage Immunities poison
Condition Immunities charmed, paralyzed, poisoned
Senses darkvision 60 ft., passive Perception 12
Languages Abyssal, Common, Draconic
Challenge 2 (450 XP)　　　　　**Proficiency Bonus** +2

Reckless. At the start of its turn, the broodguard can gain advantage on all melee weapon attack rolls it makes during that turn, but attack rolls against it have advantage until the start of its next turn.

Actions

Multiattack. The broodguard makes one Bite attack and two Claw attacks.

Bite. *Melee Weapon Attack:* +4 to hit, reach 5 ft., one target. *Hit:* 6 (1d8 + 2) piercing damage.

Claw. *Melee Weapon Attack:* +4 to hit, reach 5 ft., one target. *Hit:* 5 (1d6 + 2) slashing damage.

Yuan-ti Mind Whisperer

Mind whisperers are yuan-ti malison spellcasters who enter into a pact with the serpent god Sseth, the Sibilant Death. They use their abilities to convert others to their faith, increase their personal power, and befuddle the minds of their enemies.

Mind whisperers are elusive, manipulative, unpredictable, and willing to cheat or kill comrades and rivals alike if doing so benefits them. The worshipers of Sseth have their hands in many schemes, often plying the middle ground between two factions, and thus spend a lot of energy making sure none of their allies learn of their conflicting connections. Even among Sseth-worshiping communities, mind whisperers are known for being self-important, sneaky, and prone to flee at the first sign of trouble.

YUAN-TI MIND WHISPERER

Medium Monstrosity (Warlock), Typically Neutral Evil

Armor Class 14 (natural armor)
Hit Points 71 (13d8 + 13)
Speed 30 ft.

STR	DEX	CON	INT	WIS	CHA
16 (+3)	14 (+2)	13 (+1)	14 (+2)	14 (+2)	16 (+3)

Saving Throws Wis +4, Cha +5
Skills Deception +5, Stealth +4
Damage Immunities poison
Condition Immunities poisoned
Senses darkvision 120 ft., passive Perception 12
Languages Abyssal, Common, Draconic
Challenge 4 (1,100 XP)　　　　**Proficiency Bonus** +2

Devil's Sight. Magical darkness doesn't impede the yuan-ti's darkvision.

Magic Resistance. The yuan-ti has advantage on saving throws against spells and other magical effects.

Sseth's Blessing. When the yuan-ti reduces an enemy to 0 hit points, the yuan-ti gains 9 temporary hit points.

ACTIONS

Multiattack. The yuan-ti makes two Bite attacks and one Scimitar attack, or it makes two Spectral Fangs attacks.

Bite. *Melee Weapon Attack:* +5 to hit, reach 5 ft., one target. *Hit:* 5 (1d4 + 3) piercing damage plus 7 (2d6) poison damage.

Scimitar (Yuan-ti Form Only). *Melee Weapon Attack:* +5 to hit, reach 5 ft., one target. *Hit:* 6 (1d6 + 3) slashing damage.

Spectral Fangs. *Ranged Spell Attack:* +5 to hit, range 120 ft., one target. *Hit:* 16 (3d8 + 3) psychic damage.

Spellcasting (Yuan-ti Form Only). The yuan-ti casts one of the following spells, requiring no material components and using Charisma as the spellcasting ability (spell save DC 13):

At will: *animal friendship* (snakes only), *message*, *minor illusion*, *prestidigitation*
3/day: *suggestion*
2/day each: *detect thoughts*, *hypnotic pattern*

BONUS ACTIONS

Change Shape. The yuan-ti transforms into a Medium snake or back into its true form. Its statistics are the same in each form. Any equipment it is wearing or carrying isn't transformed. If it dies, it stays in its current form.

DAARKEN

Yuan-ti Nightmare Speaker

Nightmare speakers are yuan-ti malison priests who make a pact with the Dendar the Night Serpent to feed their deity the fears and nightmares of their victims in exchange for power in the mortal world. These priests receive nightmarish visions from Dendar that they interpret as prophecies, and they then use their magic and influence to make these visions come true.

Nightmare speakers revel in torturing others, keeping their victims in a constant state of fear and dread. They prefer to terrify rather than kill their opponents. They manipulate communities for the purpose of acquiring more victims and enjoy the company of Undead.

Yuan-ti Nightmare Speaker

Medium Monstrosity (Warlock), Typically Neutral Evil

Armor Class 14 (natural armor)
Hit Points 71 (13d8 + 13)
Speed 30 ft.

STR	DEX	CON	INT	WIS	CHA
16 (+3)	14 (+2)	13 (+1)	14 (+2)	12 (+1)	16 (+3)

Saving Throws Wis +3, Cha +5
Skills Deception +5, Stealth +4
Damage Immunities poison
Condition Immunities poisoned
Senses darkvision 120 ft., passive Perception 11
Languages Abyssal, Common, Draconic
Challenge 4 (1,100 XP)   **Proficiency Bonus** +2

Devil's Sight. Magical darkness doesn't impede the yuan-ti's darkvision.

Magic Resistance. The yuan-ti has advantage on saving throws against spells and other magical effects.

Actions

Multiattack. The yuan-ti makes one Constrict attack and one Scimitar attack, or it makes two Spectral Fangs attacks.

Constrict. *Melee Weapon Attack:* +5 to hit, reach 10 ft., one target. *Hit:* 10 (2d6 + 3) bludgeoning damage, and the target is grappled (escape DC 14) if it is a Large or smaller creature. Until this grapple ends, the target is restrained. The yuan-ti can constrict only one creature at a time.

Scimitar (Yuan-ti Form Only). *Melee Weapon Attack:* +5 to hit, reach 5 ft., one target. *Hit:* 6 (1d6 + 3) slashing damage.

Spectral Fangs. *Ranged Spell Attack:* +5 to hit, range 120 ft., one target. *Hit:* 16 (3d8 + 3) necrotic damage.

Invoke Nightmare (Recharges after a Short or Long Rest). The yuan-ti taps into the nightmares of one creature it can see within 60 feet of it and creates an illusory, immobile manifestation of the creature's deepest fears, visible only to that creature. The target must make a DC 13 Intelligence saving throw. On a failed save, the target takes 22 (4d10) psychic damage and is frightened of the manifestation, believing it to be real. The yuan-ti must concentrate to maintain the illusion (as if concentrating on a spell), which lasts for up to 1 minute and can't be harmed. The target can repeat the saving throw at the end of each of its turns, ending the illusion on a success or taking 11 (2d10) psychic damage on a failure.

Spellcasting (Yuan-ti Form Only). The yuan-ti casts one of the following spells, requiring no material components and using Charisma as the spellcasting ability (spell save DC 13):

At will: *animal friendship* (snakes only), *mage hand, message, prestidigitation*
3/day: *suggestion*
2/day each: *darkness, fear*

Bonus Actions

Change Shape. The yuan-ti transforms into a Medium snake or back into its true form. Its statistics are the same in each form. Any equipment it is wearing or carrying isn't transformed. If it dies, it stays in its current form.

Yuan-ti Pit Master

With snakes for arms, pit masters are yuan-ti malison priests who have made a pact with the god Merrshaulk and seek to rouse him from his slumber by sacrificing Humanoids to him. They are the most traditionalist yuan-ti and believe that they are best equipped to achieve the goals of their people.

Pit masters are deeply involved in yuan-ti's long-term plan to take over Humanoid governments, as well as in the ongoing effort to protect their cities from discovery or attacks by hostiles. They oppose reckless behavior and argue for a slow, cautious approach in all matters.

Yuan-ti Pit Master

Medium Monstrosity (Warlock), Typically Neutral Evil

Armor Class 14 (natural armor)
Hit Points 88 (16d8 + 16)
Speed 30 ft.

STR	DEX	CON	INT	WIS	CHA
16 (+3)	14 (+2)	13 (+1)	14 (+2)	12 (+1)	16 (+3)

Saving Throws Wis +4, Cha +6
Skills Deception +6, Stealth +5
Damage Immunities poison
Condition Immunities poisoned
Senses darkvision 120 ft., passive Perception 11
Languages Abyssal, Common, Draconic
Challenge 5 (1,800 XP) **Proficiency Bonus** +3

Devil's Sight. Magical darkness doesn't impede the yuan-ti's darkvision.

Magic Resistance. The yuan-ti has advantage on saving throws against spells and other magical effects.

Actions

Multiattack. The yuan-ti makes three Bite attacks or two Spectral Fangs attacks.

Bite. *Melee Weapon Attack:* +6 to hit, reach 5 ft., one target. *Hit:* 5 (1d4 + 3) piercing damage plus 7 (2d6) poison damage.

Spectral Fangs. *Ranged Spell Attack:* +6 to hit, range 120 ft., one target. *Hit:* 16 (3d8 + 3) poison damage.

Merrshaulk's Slumber (1/Day). The yuan-ti targets up to five creatures that it can see within 60 feet of it. Each target must succeed on a DC 13 Constitution saving throw or fall into a magical sleep and be unconscious for 10 minutes. A sleeping target awakens if it takes damage or if someone uses an action to shake or slap it awake. This magical sleep has no effect on a creature immune to being charmed.

Spellcasting (Yuan-ti Form Only). The yuan-ti casts one of the following spells, requiring no material components and using Charisma as the spellcasting ability (spell save DC 14):

At will: *animal friendship* (snakes only), *guidance, mage hand, message*
3/day: *suggestion*
2/day each: *hold person, invisibility*

Bonus Actions

Change Shape. The yuan-ti transforms into a Medium snake or back into its true form. Its statistics are the same in each form. Any equipment it is wearing or carrying isn't transformed. If it dies, it stays in its current form.

DAARKEN

YUAN-TI TEMPLE

Level 5: Temple Mount

N

ALTAR

PATIO

Level 3: Abomination level

ABOMINATION QUARTERS

ABOMINATION QUARTERS

GATHERING HALL

ABOMINATION QUARTERS

ABOMINATION QUARTERS

Level 4: Malison level

MALISON QUARTERS

RITUALS

LIBRARY

Level 2: Yuan-ti Faithful Level

HEAT ROOM

HEATED BATH

CAPTIVES

EGG CHAMBER

SHRINE

YUAN-TI CHAMBERS

TORTURE CHAMBER

STOREROOM

OVERSEER

ARMORY AND SMITHY

KITCHEN

SIDE VIEW

LEVEL 5
LEVEL 4
LEVEL 3
LEVEL 2
LEVEL 1

Level 1: Cultist Level

CULTIST QUARTERS

CULTIST QUARTERS

GUARD

KITCHEN

BATH

TEMPLE

SHRINE

GUARD

CULTIST QUARTERS

CULTIST QUARTERS

☐ = 10 FEET

JARED BLANDO

ZARATAN

When a zaratan is summoned from the Elemental Plane of Earth, the ground rises up to take the shape of a hulking, armored reptile. A zaratan's steps trigger shock waves severe enough to level structures. It expresses its rage through trumpeting calls and the occasional boulder or blast of debris it spews from its cavernous maw. If seriously injured, a zaratan retracts its appendages to gain shelter beneath its impervious shell, biding its time until it recovers and can resume its march.

ZARATAN

Gargantuan Elemental, Typically Neutral

Armor Class 21 (natural armor)
Hit Points 307 (15d20 + 150)
Speed 40 ft., swim 40 ft.

STR	DEX	CON	INT	WIS	CHA
30 (+10)	10 (+0)	30 (+10)	2 (–4)	21 (+5)	18 (+4)

Saving Throws Wis +12, Cha +11
Damage Resistances cold, fire, lightning; bludgeoning, piercing, and slashing from nonmagical attacks
Damage Immunities poison
Condition Immunities exhaustion, paralyzed, petrified, poisoned, stunned
Senses darkvision 60 ft., tremorsense 60 ft., passive Perception 15
Languages —
Challenge 22 (41,000 XP)   **Proficiency Bonus** +7

Legendary Resistance (3/Day). If the zaratan fails a saving throw, it can choose to succeed instead.

Siege Monster. The elemental deals double damage to objects and structures (included in Earth-Shaking Movement).

ACTIONS

Multiattack. The zaratan makes one Bite attack and one Stomp attack.

Bite. *Melee Weapon Attack:* +17 to hit, reach 20 ft., one target. *Hit:* 28 (4d8 + 10) force damage.

Stomp. *Melee Weapon Attack:* +17 to hit, reach 20 ft., one target. *Hit:* 26 (3d10 + 10) thunder damage.

Spit Rock. *Ranged Weapon Attack:* +17 to hit, range 120 ft./240 ft., one target. *Hit:* 31 (6d8 + 10) force damage.

Spew Debris (Recharge 5–6). The zaratan exhales rocky debris in a 90-foot cube. Each creature in that area must make a DC 25 Dexterity saving throw. A creature takes 33 (6d10) bludgeoning damage on a failed save, or half as much damage on a successful one. A creature that fails the save by 5 or more is knocked prone.

BONUS ACTIONS

Earth-Shaking Movement. After moving at least 10 feet on the ground, the zaratan sends a shock wave through the ground in a 120-foot-radius circle centered on itself. That area becomes difficult terrain for 1 minute. Each creature on the ground that is concentrating must succeed on a DC 25 Constitution saving throw or the creature's concentration is broken.

The shock wave deals 100 thunder damage to all structures in contact with the ground in the area. If a creature is near a structure that collapses, the creature might be buried; a creature within half the distance of the structure's height must make a DC 25 Dexterity saving throw. On a failed save, the creature takes 17 (5d6) bludgeoning damage, is knocked prone, and is trapped in the rubble. A trapped creature is restrained, requiring a successful DC 20 Strength (Athletics) check as an action to escape. Another creature within 5 feet of the buried creature can use its action to clear rubble and grant advantage on the check. If three creatures use their actions in this way, the check is an automatic success. On a successful save, the creature takes half as much damage and doesn't fall prone or become trapped.

LEGENDARY ACTIONS

The zaratan can take 3 legendary actions, choosing from the options below. Only one legendary action option can be used at a time and only at the end of another creature's turn. The zaratan regains spent legendary actions at the start of its turn.

Stomp. The zaratan makes one Stomp attack.
Move. The zaratan moves up to its speed.
Spit (Costs 2 Actions). The zaratan makes one Spit Rock attack.
Retract (Costs 2 Actions). The zaratan retracts into its shell. Until it takes its Emerge action, it has resistance to all damage, and it is restrained. The next time it takes a legendary action, it must take its Revitalize or Emerge action.
Revitalize (Costs 2 Actions). The zaratan can use this option only if it is retracted in its shell. It regains 52 (5d20) hit points. The next time it takes a legendary action, it must take its Emerge action.
Emerge (Costs 2 Actions). The zaratan emerges from its shell and makes one Spit Rock attack. It can use this option only if it is retracted in its shell.

BRYNN METHENEY

Zariel

Once a mighty angel charged with watching the tides of the Blood War, Zariel succumbed to the corrupting influence of the Nine Hells and fell from grace. Asmodeus admired Zariel's passion for war and offered her rulership of Avernus. She accepted his offer, and he transformed her into an archdevil.

Zariel's rise in status came at the expense of Bel, her pit fiend predecessor. Zariel and Bel hate each other. To keep Bel busy and out of her sight, Zariel tasks him with forging weapons, armor, and gruesome demon-slaying machines.

To replenish her legions, Zariel needs the souls of mortals to create lemures, which she can then promote to higher forms of devils. She is keenly interested in collecting souls from the greatest warriors on the Material Plane. She bargains hard, and there is little hope of wriggling out of a pact. However, she expects the best from her servants, so she allows her mortal followers to live out their lives provided they continue to hone their talents to increase their value. As a result, Zariel's servants are universally effective, disciplined, and dangerous.

Zariel's Lair

Zariel makes her lair in a basalt citadel that rises up in Avernus. From nearly a mile away, one can hear the screams coming from burned victims chained to the stronghold's wall—the dying remains of those who failed to impress the archdevil. The stronghold, covering five square miles, is surrounded by walls reinforced with high turrets. Devils of all kinds crawl over the structure, ensuring that no intruders breach their defenses.

Lair Actions

On initiative count 20 (losing initiative ties), Zariel can take one of the following lair actions; she can't take the same lair action two rounds in a row:

Fireball. Zariel casts the *fireball* spell.

Infernal Illusions. Zariel casts the *major image* spell four times, targeting different areas with it. Zariel prefers to create images of intruders' loved ones being burned alive. Zariel doesn't need to concentrate on the spells, which end on initiative count 20 of the next round. Each creature that can see these illusions must succeed on a DC 26 Wisdom saving throw or become frightened of the illusion for 1 minute. A frightened creature can repeat the saving throw at the end of each of its turns, ending the effect on itself on a success.

Regional Effects

The region containing Zariel's lair is warped by her magic, which creates one or more of the following effects:

Hellscape. The area within 9 miles of the lair is filled with screaming voices and the stench of burning meat.

Pyres. Once every 60 feet within 1 mile of the lair, 10-foot-high gouts of flame rise from the ground. Any creature or object that touches the flame takes 7 (2d6) fire damage, though it can take this damage no more than once per round.

Smoke. The area within 2 miles of the lair, but no closer than 500 feet, is filled with smoke, which causes the area to be heavily obscured. The smoke can't be cleared away.

If Zariel dies, these effects fade over the course of 1d10 days.

> *That which falls from grace may yet rise to regain it. If Zariel were to return to her celestial self, how glorious would be the tales!*
>
> —*Mordenkainen*

Cultists of Zariel

Zariel grants special abilities to her most loyal cultists. They can gain the Ferocious Surge trait, and her cult's leaders can also gain the Infernal Tactics trait.

Ferocious Surge (Recharges after a Short or Long Rest). When this creature hits with an attack roll that isn't a critical hit, it can turn the hit into a critical hit.

Infernal Tactics. Immediately after rolling initiative, this creature can choose itself and up to three allies it can see if it isn't incapacitated. It can swap the initiative results of the chosen creatures among them.

Zariel

Large Fiend (Devil), Lawful Evil

Armor Class 21 (natural armor)
Hit Points 420 (29d10 + 261)
Speed 50 ft., fly 150 ft.

STR	DEX	CON	INT	WIS	CHA
27 (+8)	24 (+7)	28 (+9)	26 (+8)	27 (+8)	30 (+10)

Saving Throws Int +16, Wis +16, Cha +18
Skills Intimidation +18, Perception +16
Damage Resistances cold, fire, radiant; bludgeoning, piercing, and slashing from nonmagical attacks that aren't silvered
Damage Immunities necrotic, poison
Condition Immunities charmed, exhaustion, frightened, poisoned
Senses darkvision 120 ft., passive Perception 26
Languages all, telepathy 120 ft.
Challenge 26 (90,000 XP)   **Proficiency Bonus** +8

Devil's Sight. Magical darkness doesn't impede Zariel's darkvision.

Legendary Resistance (3/Day). If Zariel fails a saving throw, she can choose to succeed instead.

Magic Resistance. Zariel has advantage on saving throws against spells and other magical effects.

Regeneration. Zariel regains 20 hit points at the start of her turn. If she takes radiant damage, this trait doesn't function at the start of her next turn. Zariel dies only if she starts her turn with 0 hit points and doesn't regenerate.

Actions

Multiattack. Zariel makes three Flail or Longsword attacks. She can replace one attack with a use of Horrid Touch, if available.

Flail. *Melee Weapon Attack:* +16 to hit, reach 10 ft., one target. *Hit:* 17 (2d8 + 8) force damage plus 36 (8d8) fire damage.

Longsword. *Melee Weapon Attack:* +16 to hit, reach 10 ft., one target. *Hit:* 17 (2d8 + 8) radiant damage, or 19 (2d10 + 8) radiant damage when used with two hands, plus 36 (8d8) fire damage.

Horrid Touch (Recharge 5–6). Zariel touches one creature within 10 feet of her. The target must succeed on a DC 26 Constitution saving throw or take 44 (8d10) necrotic damage and be poisoned for 1 minute. While poisoned in this way, the target is blinded and deafened. The target can repeat the saving throw at the end of each of its turns, ending the effect on itself on a success.

Spellcasting. Zariel casts one of the following spells, requiring no material components and using Charisma as the spellcasting ability (spell save DC 26):

At will: *alter self* (can become Medium when changing her appearance), *detect evil and good*, *fireball*, *invisibility* (self only), *major image*, *wall of fire*
3/day each: *blade barrier*, *dispel evil and good*, *finger of death*

Teleport. Zariel teleports, along with any equipment she is wearing or carrying, up to 120 feet to an unoccupied space she can see.

Legendary Actions

Zariel can take 3 legendary actions, choosing from the options below. Only one legendary action option can be used at a time and only at the end of another creature's turn. Zariel regains spent legendary actions at the start of her turn.

Teleport. Zariel uses Teleport.
Immolating Gaze (Costs 2 Actions). Zariel turns her magical gaze toward one creature she can see within 120 feet of her and commands it to burn. The target must succeed on a DC 26 Wisdom saving throw or take 22 (4d10) fire damage.

ZUGGTMOY

The Demon Queen of Fungi, Lady of Rot and Decay, Zuggtmoy is an alien creature whose only desire is to infect the living with spores, transforming them into her mindless servants and, eventually, into decomposing hosts for the mushrooms, molds, and other fungi that she spawns.

Zuggtmoy is utterly inhuman, but she can mold her fungoid form into an approximation of a bipedal shape, including the skeletal-thin figure depicted in grimoires and ancient art, draped and veiled in mycelia and lichen. Indeed, much of her appearance and manner, and that of her servants, is a mockery of mortal life and its many facets.

Zuggtmoy's cultists often follow her unwittingly. Most are fungus-infected to some degree, whether through inhaling her mind-controlling spores or being transformed to the point where flesh and fungus become one. Such cultists are fungal extensions of the Demon Queen's will. Their devotion might begin with the seemingly harmless promises offered by exotic spores and mushrooms, but it quickly consumes them, body and soul.

ZUGGTMOY'S LAIR

Zuggtmoy's principal lair is her palace on Shedak-lah. It consists of two dozen immense mushrooms of pale yellow and rancid brown. These massive fungi are some of the largest in existence. They are surrounded by a field of acidic puffballs and poisonous vapors. The mushrooms are interconnected by bridges of shelf fungus, and countless chambers have been hollowed out inside their rubbery stalks.

LAIR ACTIONS

On initiative count 20 (losing initiative ties), Zuggtmoy can take one of the following lair actions; she can't take the same lair action two rounds in a row:

Rally Plants. Up to four Plant creatures that are friendly to Zuggtmoy and that Zuggtmoy can see can use their reactions to move up to their speed and make one weapon attack.

Summon Fungi. Zuggtmoy causes four **gas spores** or **violet fungi** (both appear in the *Monster Manual*) to appear in unoccupied spaces that she chooses within the lair. They vanish after 1 hour.

Unleash Spores. Zuggtmoy uses either her Infestation Spores or her Mind Control Spores, centered on a mushroom or other fungus within her lair, instead of on herself.

REGIONAL EFFECTS

The region containing Zuggtmoy's lair is warped by her magic, creating one or more of the following effects:

Corrupted Nature. Within 6 miles of the lair, all Wisdom (Medicine) and Wisdom (Survival) checks have disadvantage.

Fungal Infestation. Molds and fungi grow on surfaces within 6 miles of the lair, even where they would normally find no purchase.

Mutating Vegetation. Vegetation within 1 mile of the lair becomes infested with parasitic fungi, slowly mutating as it is overwhelmed.

If Zuggtmoy dies, these effects fade over the course of 1d10 days.

CULTISTS OF ZUGGTMOY

Zuggtmoy's cultists are primarily mindless victims of her children's strange spores. The spores burrow into a victim's brain, turning it into a fanatic servitor. Each victim gains the Spore Kissed trait.

Spore Kissed. This creature is immune to the charmed and frightened conditions. In addition, if it is reduced to 0 hit points, each creature within 10 feet of it takes poison damage equal to its number of Hit Dice.

ZUGGTMOY

Large Fiend (Demon), Chaotic Evil

Armor Class 18 (natural armor)
Hit Points 304 (32d10 + 128)
Speed 30 ft.

STR	DEX	CON	INT	WIS	CHA
22 (+6)	15 (+2)	18 (+4)	20 (+5)	19 (+4)	24 (+7)

Saving Throws Dex +9, Con +11, Wis +11
Skills Perception +11
Damage Resistances cold, fire, lightning
Damage Immunities poison; bludgeoning, piercing, and slashing that is nonmagical
Condition Immunities charmed, exhaustion, frightened, poisoned
Senses truesight 120 ft., passive Perception 21
Languages all, telepathy 120 ft.
Challenge 23 (50,000 XP)   **Proficiency Bonus** +7

Legendary Resistance (3/Day). If Zuggtmoy fails a saving throw, she can choose to succeed instead.

Magic Resistance. Zuggtmoy has advantage on saving throws against spells and other magical effects.

ACTIONS

Multiattack. Zuggtmoy makes three Pseudopod attacks.

Pseudopod. *Melee Weapon Attack:* +13 to hit, reach 10 ft., one target. *Hit:* 15 (2d8 + 6) force damage plus 9 (2d8) poison damage.

Spellcasting. Zuggtmoy casts one of the following spells, requiring no material components and using Charisma as the spellcasting ability (spell save DC 22):

At will: *detect magic, locate animals or plants*
3/day each: *dispel magic, entangle, plant growth*
1/day each: *etherealness, teleport*

BONUS ACTIONS

Infestation Spores (3/Day). Zuggtmoy releases spores that burst out in a cloud that fills a 20-foot-radius sphere centered on her, and it lingers for 1 minute. Any creature in the cloud when it appears, or that enters it later, must make a DC 19 Constitution saving throw. On a successful save, the creature can't be infected by these spores for 24 hours. On a failed save, the creature is infected with a disease called the spores of Zuggtmoy, which lasts until the creature is cured of the disease or dies. While infected in this way, the creature can't be reinfected, and it must repeat the saving throw at the end of every 24 hours, ending the infection on a success. On a failure, the infected creature's body is slowly taken over by fungal growth, and after three such failed saves, the creature dies and is reanimated as a spore servant if it's a type of creature that can be (see the "Myconids" section in the *Monster Manual*).

Mind Control Spores (Recharge 5–6). Zuggtmoy releases spores that burst out in a cloud that fills a 20-foot-radius sphere centered on her, and it lingers for 1 minute. Humanoids and Beasts in the cloud when it appears, or that enter it later, must make a DC 19 Wisdom saving throw. On a successful save, a creature can't be infected by these spores for 24 hours. On a failed save, the creature is infected with a disease called the influence of Zuggtmoy for 24 hours. While infected in this way, the creature is charmed by her and can't be reinfected by these spores.

REACTIONS

Protective Thrall. When Zuggtmoy is hit by an attack roll, one creature within 10 feet of her that is charmed by her is hit by the attack instead.

LEGENDARY ACTIONS

Zuggtmoy can take 3 legendary actions, choosing from the options below. Only one legendary action option can be used at a time and only at the end of another creature's turn. Zuggtmoy regains spent legendary actions at the start of her turn.

Attack. Zuggtmoy makes one Pseudopod attack.
Exert Will. One creature charmed by Zuggtmoy that she can see must use its reaction, if available, to move up to its speed as she directs or to make one weapon attack against a target that she designates.

APPENDIX
MONSTER LISTS

STAT BLOCKS BY CREATURE TYPE

ABERRATIONS
Balhannoth, 55
Berbalang, 61
Choker, 76
Cranium rat, 83
Death kiss, 85
Derro, 91
Derro savant, 92
Elder brain, 120
Gauth, 133
Gazer, 134
Mindwitness, 181
Morkoth, 186
Neogi, 192
Neogi hatchling, 191
Neogi master, 192
Neothelid, 193
Star spawn grue, 227
Star spawn hulk, 227
Star spawn larva mage, 228
Star spawn mangler, 229
Star spawn seer, 230
Swarm of cranium rats, 83
Ulitharid, 249

BEASTS
Aurochs, 71
Brontosaurus, 95
Deep rothé, 71
Deinonychus, 95
Dimetrodon, 95
Dolphin, 97
Hadrosaurus, 96
Ox, 72
Quetzalcoatlus, 96
Stegosaurus, 96
Swarm of rot grubs, 237
Velociraptor, 96

CELESTIALS
Ki-rin, 162

CONSTRUCTS
Cadaver collector, 68
Clockwork bronze scout, 79
Clockwork iron cobra, 79
Clockwork oaken bolter, 80
Clockwork stone
    defender, 80
Duergar hammerer, 112

Duergar screamer, 112
Hellfire engine, 152
Marut, 173
Retriever, 209
Steel predator, 232
Stone cursed, 233

DRAGONS
Guard drake, 151
Kobold dragonshield, 163

ELEMENTALS
Air elemental
    myrmidon, 122
Earth elemental
    myrmidon, 122
Elder tempest, 121
Fire elemental
    myrmidon, 123
Firenewt warlock
    of Imix, 125
Firenewt warrior, 125
Flail snail, 126
Frost salamander, 132
Leviathan, 171
Phoenix, 206
Water elemental
    myrmidon, 123
Zaratan, 278

FEY
Annis hag, 47
Autumn eladrin, 115
Bheur hag, 62
Boggle, 65
Darkling, 84
Darkling elder, 84
Dolphin delighter, 97
Hobgoblin devastator, 153
Hobgoblin iron shadow, 154
Korred, 166
Meenlock, 178
Nilbog, 195
Quickling, 207
Redcap, 208
Spring eladrin, 116
Summer eladrin, 116
Winter eladrin, 117
Yeth hound, 271

FIENDS
Alkilith, 44
Amnizu, 46
Armanite, 50
Babau, 52
Bael, 54
Baphomet, 58
Barghest, 60
Black abishai, 38
Blue abishai, 39
Bulezau, 67
Canoloth, 69
Demogorgon, 90
Dhergoloth, 94
Draegloth, 98
Dybbuk, 113
Flind, 127
Fraz-Urb'luu, 129
Geryon, 136
Graz'zt, 148
Green abishai, 40
Howler, 155
Hutijin, 157
Hydroloth, 158
Juiblex, 160
Maurezhi, 175
Maw demon, 176
Merregon, 179
Merrenoloth, 180
Moloch, 183
Molydeus, 184
Nabassu, 188
Narzugon, 190
Nupperibo, 196
Oinoloth, 202
Orcus, 204
Orthon, 205
Red abishai, 40
Rutterkin, 210
Shoosuva, 216
Sibriex, 217
Stench kow, 72
Tanarukk, 240
Titivilus, 242
Vargouille, 251
Wastrilith, 258
White abishai, 41
Yagnoloth, 268
Yeenoghu, 270
Zariel, 280
Zuggtmoy, 282

GIANTS
Cloud giant smiling one, 81
Dire troll, 246
Fire giant dreadnought, 124
Frost giant everlast-
    ing one, 131
Mouth of Grolantor, 187
Ogre battering ram, 200
Ogre bolt launcher, 200
Ogre chain brute, 201
Ogre howdah, 201
Rot troll, 247
Spirit troll, 247
Stone giant dream-
    walker, 234
Storm giant quint-
    essent, 235
Venom troll, 248

HUMANOIDS
Abjurer wizard, 260
Apprentice wizard, 259
Archdruid, 48
Archer, 49
Bard, 59
Blackguard, 63
Champion, 74
Conjurer wizard, 260
Diviner wizard, 261
Drow arachnomancer, 99
Drow favored consort, 100
Drow house captain, 101
Drow inquisitor, 102
Drow matron mother, 104
Drow shadowblade, 105
Duergar despot, 107
Duergar kavalrachni, 107
Duergar mind master, 108
Duergar soulblade, 109
Duergar stone guard, 110
Duergar warlord, 111
Duergar xarrorn, 111
Enchanter wizard, 261
Evoker wizard, 262
Giff, 138
Githyanki gish, 140
Githyanki kith'rak, 140
Githyanki supreme com-
    mander, 141
Githzerai anarch, 142

Stat Blocks by Challenge Rating

Sword wraith warrior, 239
Trapper, 245
Vampiric mist, 250

Challenge 4
Babau, 52
Barghest, 60
Clockwork iron cobra, 79
Clockwork stone
    defender, 80
Deathlock, 86
Dybbuk, 113
Girallon, 139
Hobgoblin devastator, 153
Merregon, 179
Neogi master, 192
Ogre battering ram, 200
Stegosaurus, 96
Warlock of the Archfey, 255
Yeth hound, 271
Yuan-ti mind whisperer, 274
Yuan-ti nightmare
    speaker, 275

Challenge 5
Adult oblex, 198
Allip, 45
Banderhobb, 56
Brontosaurus, 95
Catoblepas, 70
Clockwork oaken bolter, 80
Enchanter wizard, 261
Kraken priest, 167
Kruthik hive lord, 169
Master thief, 174
Mindwitness, 181
Spawn of Kyuss, 225
Star spawn mangler, 229
Swarm of cranium rats, 83
Tanarukk, 240
Tlincalli, 243
Transmuter wizard, 265
Wood woad, 266
Yuan-ti pit master, 276

Challenge 6
Annis hag, 47
Bodak, 64
Conjurer wizard, 260
Duergar warlord, 111
Gauth, 133
Mouth of Grolantor, 187
Warlock of the Great
    Old One, 256
White abishai, 41

Challenge 7
Air elemental
    myrmidon, 122
Armanite, 50
Bheur hag, 62
Black abishai, 38
Dhergoloth, 94
Draegloth, 98
Earth elemental
    myrmidon, 122
Fire elemental
    myrmidon, 123
Korred, 166
Lost sorrowsworn, 224
Maurezhi, 175
Shadar-kai shadow
    dancer, 213
Venom troll, 248
Warlock of the Fiend, 255
Water elemental
    myrmidon, 123

Challenge 8
Blackguard, 63
Canoloth, 69
Corpse flower, 82
Deathlock mastermind, 87
Diviner wizard, 261
Howler, 155
Shoosuva, 216
Sword wraith com-
    mander, 239

Challenge 9
Abjurer wizard, 260
Champion, 74
Drow house captain, 101
Evoker wizard, 262
Flind, 127
Frost salamander, 132
Hydroloth, 158
Lonely sorrowsworn, 223
Necromancer wizard, 264
Rot troll, 247
Shadar-kai gloom
    weaver, 213
Ulitharid, 249
War priest, 254

Challenge 10
Alhoon, 43
Autumn eladrin, 115
Death kiss, 85
Elder oblex, 199
Froghemoth, 130
Githyanki gish, 140

Githzerai enlightened, 143
Orthon, 205
Spring eladrin, 116
Star spawn hulk, 227
Stone giant dream-
    walker, 234
Summer eladrin, 116
Winter eladrin, 117

Challenge 11
Alkilith, 44
Balhannoth, 55
Cloud giant smiling one, 81
Drow shadowblade, 105
Hungry sorrowsworn, 223
Morkoth, 186
Shadar-kai soul monger, 214
Spirit troll, 247
Yagnoloth, 268

Challenge 12
Archdruid, 48
Boneclaw, 66
Duergar despot, 107
Eidolon, 114
Frost giant everlast-
    ing one, 131
Githyanki kith'rak, 140
Gray render, 146
Ki-rin, 162
Oinoloth, 202
Warlord, 257
Yuan-ti anathema, 272

Challenge 13
Angry sorrowsworn, 222
Devourer, 93
Dire troll, 246
Drow arachnomancer, 99
Narzugon, 190
Neothelid, 193
Star spawn seer, 230
Wastrilith, 258

Challenge 14
Cadaver collector, 68
Drow inquisitor, 102
Elder brain, 120
Fire giant dreadnought, 124
Githyanki supreme com-
    mander, 141
Retriever, 209

Challenge 15
Green abishai, 40
Nabassu, 188
Skull lord, 220

Challenge 16
Githzerai anarch, 142
Hellfire engine, 152
Phoenix, 206
Star spawn larva mage, 228
Steel predator, 232
Storm giant quint-
    essent, 235
Titivilus, 242

Challenge 17
Blue abishai, 39
Nagpa, 189

Challenge 18
Amnizu, 46
Drow favored consort, 100
Sibriex, 217

Challenge 19
Bael, 54
Red abishai, 40

Challenge 20
Drow matron mother, 104
Leviathan, 171
Nightwalker, 194

Challenge 21
Astral dreadnought, 51
Hutijin, 157
Moloch, 183
Molydeus, 184

Challenge 22
Geryon, 136
Zaratan, 278

Challenge 23
Baphomet, 58
Elder tempest, 121
Fraz-Urb'luu, 129
Juiblex, 160
Zuggtmoy, 282

Challenge 24
Graz'zt, 148
Yeenoghu, 270

Challenge 25
Marut, 173

Challenge 26
Demogorgon, 90
Orcus, 204
Zariel, 280

STAT BLOCKS BY ENVIRONMENT

ARCTIC CREATURES

CR	Creatures
1/4	Gnoll witherling
1/2	Gnoll hunter
1	Gnoll flesh gnawer
2	Guard drake
3	Vampiric mist
4	Warlock of the Archfey
6	Warlock of the Great Old One
7	Bheur hag, lost sorrowsworn, warlock of the Fiend
9	Frost salamander
10	Winter eladrin
12	Boneclaw
13	Dire troll
20	Nightwalker
23	Elder tempest

COASTAL CREATURES

CR	Creatures
1/8	Dolphin
1/4	Dimetrodon, tortle
1/2	Skulk
1	Sea spawn
2	Quetzalcoatlus, tortle druid
3	Deep scion, dolphin delighter, merrenoloth, swashbuckler, vampiric mist
5	Kraken priest
8	Canoloth, shoosuva
9	Flind, lonely sorrowsworn
10	Stone giant dreamwalker
11	Balhannoth, morkoth, spirit troll
12	Eidolon, frost giant everlasting one, ki-rin
13	Wastrilith
16	Storm giant quintessent
17	Blue abishai, nagpa
20	Leviathan
23	Elder tempest

DESERT CREATURES

CR	Creatures
1/8	Young kruthik
1/2	Firenewt warrior
1	Meazel, stone cursed, vargouille
2	Adult kruthik, berbalang, guard drake, yuan-ti broodguard
3	Leucrotta
4	Dybbuk, yuan-ti mind whisperer, yuan-ti nightmare speaker

CR	Creatures
5	Kruthik hive lord, spawn of Kyuss, tlincalli, yuan-ti pit master
7	Lost sorrowsworn, warlock of the Fiend
8	Howler
9	Champion, lonely sorrowsworn, necromancer wizard, rot troll, war priest
10	Githyanki gish, githzerai enlightened, orthon, summer eladrin
12	Boneclaw, eidolon, githyanki kith'rak, ki-rin, oinoloth, yuan-ti anathema
14	Githyanki supreme commander, retriever
15	Skull lord
16	Phoenix, storm giant quintessent
17	Nagpa
20	Nightwalker
22	Zaratan

FOREST CREATURES

CR	Creatures
1/8	Boggle
1/4	Gnoll witherling, grung, kobold inventor, vegepygmy, velociraptor
1/2	Darkling, gnoll hunter, skulk
1	Choker, clockwork bronze scout, deinonychus, gnoll flesh gnawer, grung wildling, kobold dragonshield, kobold scale sorcerer, meazel, nilbog, quickling, thorny vegepygmy
2	Darkling elder, grung elite warrior, guard drake, hobgoblin iron shadow, meenlock, shadow mastiff, vegepygmy chief, yuan-ti broodguard
3	Archer, flail snail, redcap, shadow mastiff alpha, vampiric mist
4	Barghest, clockwork iron cobra, clockwork stone defender, girallon, hobgoblin devastator, stegosaurus, warlock of the Archfey, yeth hound, yuan-ti mind whisperer, yuan-ti nightmare speaker
5	Brontosaurus, clockwork oaken bolter, wood woad, yuan-ti pit master
7	Korred, lost sorrowsworn, shadar-kai shadow dancer, venom troll
8	Corpse flower, shoosuva
9	Flind, rot troll
10	Autumn eladrin, spring eladrin, summer eladrin, winter eladrin
11	Hungry sorrowsworn, spirit troll
12	Archdruid, eidolon, gray render, yuan-ti anathema
13	Dire troll
14	Retriever
17	Nagpa
22	Zaratan

Grassland Creatures

CR	Creatures
1/4	Gnoll witherling, hadrosaurus, ox, velociraptor
1/2	Gnoll hunter, stench kow
1	Clockwork bronze scout, deinonychus, gnoll flesh gnawer, meazel
2	Aurochs, hobgoblin iron shadow, ogre bolt launcher, ogre howdah
3	Leucrotta, ogre chain brute, sword wraith warrior, vampiric mist
4	Barghest, clockwork iron cobra, clockwork stone defender, hobgoblin devastator, ogre battering ram, stegosaurus, yeth hound
5	Brontosaurus, clockwork oaken bolter
6	Mouth of Grolantor
8	Howler, shoosuva, sword wraith commander
9	Flind
10	Spring eladrin
12	Eidolon, ki-rin
14	Cadaver collector
22	Zaratan
23	Elder tempest

Hill Creatures

CR	Creatures
1/8	Boggle, neogi hatchling, xvart
1/4	Gnoll witherling, kobold inventor
1/2	Firenewt warrior, gnoll hunter
1	Clockwork bronze scout, deinonychus, firenewt warlock of Imix, giant strider, gnoll flesh gnawer, kobold dragonshield, kobold scale sorcerer, meazel, nilbog, xvart warlock of Raxivort
2	Aurochs, hobgoblin Iron Shadow, ogre bolt launcher, ogre howdah, quetzalcoatlus, shadow mastiff
3	Neogi, ogre chain brute, redcap, shadow mastiff alpha
4	Barghest, clockwork iron cobra, clockwork stone defender, hobgoblin devastator, neogi master, ogre battering ram, yeth hound
5	Clockwork oaken bolter, tanarukk
6	Annis hag, mouth of Grolantor, warlock of the Great Old One
8	Howler, shoosuva
9	Flind
10	Stone giant dreamwalker
12	Gray render
13	Dire troll
22	Zaratan
23	Elder tempest

Mountain Creatures

CR	Creatures
1/8	Young kruthik
1/4	Derro, kobold inventor, star spawn grue
1/2	Firenewt warrior
1	Clockwork bronze scout, choker, duergar soulblade, firenewt warlock of Imix, giant strider, kobold dragonshield, kobold scale sorcerer, meazel, stone cursed
2	Adult kruthik, aurochs, duergar hammerer, duergar kavalrachni, duergar mind master, duergar stone guard, duergar xarrorn, guard drake, ogre bolt launcher, ogre howdah, quetzalcoatlus
3	Duergar screamer, ogre chain brute, vampiric mist
4	Barghest, clockwork iron cobra, clockwork stone defender, ogre battering ram, warlock of the Archfey
5	Clockwork oaken bolter, kruthik hive lord, tanarukk
6	Annis hag, duergar warlord, warlock of the Great Old One
7	Lost sorrowsworn
9	Lonely sorrowsworn
10	Githyanki gish, githzerai enlightened, stone giant dreamwalker
11	Balhannoth, cloud giant smiling one
12	Archdruid, duergar despot, eidolon, githyanki kith'rak, ki-rin
13	Dire troll, star spawn seer
14	Fire giant dreadnought, githyanki supreme commander
16	Phoenix, star spawn larva mage, storm giant quintessent
19	Red abishai
22	Zaratan
23	Elder tempest

Swamp Creatures

CR	Creatures
1/4	Dimetrodon, hadrosaurus, oblex spawn, star spawn grue, vegepygmy, wretched sorrowsworn
1/2	Darkling, skulk, swarm of rot grubs
1	Meazel, vargouille, thorny vegepygmy
2	Darkling elder, guard drake, meenlock, shadow mastiff, vegepygmy chief
3	Flail snail, redcap, shadow mastiff alpha, sword wraith warrior, vampiric mist
4	Warlock of the Archfey
5	Adult oblex, allip, catoblepas
6	Bodak
7	Lost sorrowsworn, maurezhi, venom troll
8	Corpse flower

CR	Creatures
9	Rot troll
10	Elder oblex, froghemoth, sword wraith commander
11	Spirit troll
12	Archdruid
13	Star spawn seer, wastrilith
15	Nabassu, skull lord
17	Nagpa
20	Nightwalker

UNDERDARK CREATURES

CR	Creatures
0	Cranium rat
1/8	Boggle, neogi hatchling, xvart, young kruthik
1/4	Deep rothé, derro, kobold inventor, male steeder, oblex spawn, wretched sorrowsworn
1/2	Chitine, darkling, firenewt warrior, gazer, skulk, swarm of rot grubs
1	Choker, duergar soulblade, female steeder, firenewt warlock of Imix, giant strider, kobold dragonshield, kobold scale sorcerer, maw demon, meazel, nilbog, vargouille, xvart warlock of Raxivort
2	Adult kruthik, darkling elder, duergar hammerer, duergar kavalrachni, duergar mind master, duergar stone guard, duergar xarrorn, guard drake, yuan-ti broodguard
3	Cave fisher, choldrith, derro savant, duergar screamer, flail snail, neogi, slithering tracker, trapper, vampiric mist
4	Babau, barghest, neogi master, yuan-ti mind whisperer, yuan-ti nightmare speaker
5	Adult oblex, kruthik hive lord, mindwitness, spawn of Kyuss, swarm of cranium rats, tanarukk, yuan-ti pit master
6	Bodak, duergar warlord, gauth, warlock of the Great Old One
7	Armanite, dhergoloth, draegloth, lost sorrowsworn, shadar-kai shadow dancer, venom troll, warlock of the Fiend
8	Blackguard, canoloth, howler
9	Drow house captain, shadar-kai gloom weaver, lonely sorrowsworn, rot troll, ulitharid
10	Alhoon, death kiss, elder oblex, froghemoth, orthon
11	Alkilith, balhannoth, drow shadowblade, hungry sorrowsworn, shadar-kai soul monger, spirit troll
12	Duergar despot, oinoloth, yuan-ti anathema
13	Angry sorrowsworn, devourer, dire troll, drow arachnomancer, neothelid, wastrilith
14	Drow inquisitor, elder brain, fire giant dreadnought, retriever

CR	Creatures
15	Nabassu, skull lord
17	Nagpa
18	Drow favored consort, sibriex
20	Drow matron mother, nightwalker
22	Zaratan

UNDERWATER CREATURES

CR	Creatures
1/8	Dolphin
1	Sea spawn
3	Deep scion, dolphin delighter
5	Kraken priest
11	Morkoth
12	Archdruid
13	Wastrilith
16	Storm giant quintessent
20	Leviathan

URBAN CREATURES

CR	Creatures
0	Cranium rat
1/8	Boggle
1/4	Apprentice wizard, kobold inventor, oblex spawn, ox, wretched sorrowsworn
1/2	Darkling, skulk, stench kow
1	Kobold scale sorcerer, meazel, stone cursed
2	Bard, darkling elder, guard drake, meenlock
3	Archer, giff, illusionist wizard, martial arts adept, slithering tracker, swashbuckler, vampiric mist
4	Babau, deathlock, dybbuk, warlock of the Archfey
5	Adult oblex, allip, banderhobb, enchanter wizard, master thief, swarm of cranium rats, transmuter wizard
6	Bodak, conjurer wizard, warlock of the Great Old One, white abishai
7	Black abishai, lost sorrowsworn, maurezhi, shadar-kai shadow dancer, warlock of the Fiend
8	Blackguard, canoloth, corpse flower, deathlock mastermind, diviner wizard
9	Abjurer wizard, champion, evoker wizard, lonely sorrowsworn, necromancer wizard, shadar-kai gloom weaver, war priest
10	Elder oblex, githyanki gish, githzerai enlightened, orthon
11	Alkilith, hungry sorrowsworn, shadar-kai soul monger, yagnoloth
12	Boneclaw, eidolon, githyanki kith'rak, warlord
13	Angry sorrowsworn, star spawn seer
14	Githyanki supreme commander
15	Green abishai, nabassu
16	Steel predator
17	Blue abishai, nagpa
19	Red abishai